# The Steel Queen

KIRALYNN EPICS

**Forthcoming books by Karen L Azinger**

*The Silk & Steel Saga*

Book One: *The Steel Queen*

Book Two: *The Flame Priest*

Book Three: *The Skeleton King*

Book Four: *The Poison Priestess*

Book Five: *The Battle Immortal*

# THE STEEL QUEEN

### BOOK ONE OF

## THE SILK & STEEL SAGA

## Karen L. Azinger

KIRALYNN EPICS

Published by Kiralynn Epics L.P. 2011

Copyright © Karen L. Azinger 2011

First published in the United States of America by Kiralynn Epics 2011

Front Cover Artwork Copyright Greg Bridges © 2010

Celtic Lettering used with permission of Alfred M Graphics Art Studio

The Author asserts the moral right to be identified as the author of this work

ISBN 978-0-9835160-0-2

Library of Congress Control Number: 2011906065

# ACKNOWEDGEMENTS

It takes a lot of people to make the dream of a book come true. First and foremost, to my husband Rick, who is always keen for the next adventure and always believes no matter the odds. To my best friend, first reader and sword sister, Danae Powers, who listened from the very first chapter. To my writer friend, Peggy Lowe, a critique circle of one. To my first editor, Bill Johnson, a story really is a promise. To my alpha readers, Mike, Nick, Diane, Mary, John, Stuart, Tanya, Chris, Cheryl, Bob, and Gina, your enthusiasm kept me going through all the bleak times. To my beta readers, Christine, Ruthie, Lydia, and Mallory, for that very important final read. To Greg Bridges for the totally awesome front cover and the book spine. To Peggy Lowe, graphic artist extraordinaire, for the back cover, the map and the logo, well done! To Pat for the much needed help with formatting. To Violet Lowe for my author photo. To my Facebook friends for being so keen to read the book. And to my mom, for everything, I so hope you know.

# Prologue

J amis stood at attention before the Door. He hated this posting. None passed through the Door save the screaming and the damned...and those that dragged them to their fate. Casting a sideways glance at the rune-covered copper, turned green with age, he shuddered. All manner of beasts and humans had been dragged through that portal...but it was the things that crept back out that haunted his dreams. In truth, he did not know what lay beyond the Door, he never wanted to know. He would have prayed to all the gods to remain ignorant, but down here, who listened to prayers except the Dark Lord? Clutching his spear, Jamis fixed his gaze on the stairs and kept his prayers to himself. Time crawled. His back ached and he longed to lean against the cold stone wall, but he dared not. Just a fortnight ago, he'd watched Emmet flayed alive for sleeping at his post, a bloody reminder to stay vigilant.

He touched the gorget at his throat, once a talisman of pride, now the collar that chained him to this subterranean post. Clad in silver and covered in runes, the gorget marked him as a guard of the Door. Six year ago, he'd endured a trial of questions from the priests and then watched as a temple seer cast his fortune on rune-carved bones. Most of the questions were lost to memory but the bones had declared him favored by the Dark. Having gained the silver gorget, he received better quarters in a higher tier, and more pay, but now it seemed a beggar's bargain. So deep underground, in this god-forsaken place, Jamis felt watched...watched by something that bore him nothing but malice.

Footsteps clattered down the stairs and Jamis lowered his spear to bar the Door.

A young hatchet-faced man in black-and-gold armor appeared. Jamis smothered his surprise. He'd expected one of the guard captains, or a dark-robed priest, but not the general, not down here.

General Haith barked an order over his left shoulder. "Hurry."

Behind him, two soldiers struggled down the stairs carrying a massive block of dark-stained wood between them. A barrel-chested man lumbered behind, his face masked in black, the head of his great silver axe gleaming in the torchlight. *Another execution,* Jamis wondered if the axe would claim a criminal, a sinner, or another sacrifice.

The general halted in front of the Door. *"Sion rasmathus."*

The Door trembled and then swung open.

Tendrils of icy air laden with the stench of rot eddied around Jamis's boots. Sweat trickled down his back like frosty fingers. The general and his party passed through, but Jamis did not look. Curiosity killed down here and Jamis refused to be tempted. Alone in the antechamber, he distracted himself with thoughts of Marisa, and his two little ones, Janelle and Kayla, waiting for him in the city above. He couldn't wait for his shift to end, to feel the warmth of their embrace, but time seemed to have frozen, shackling him to his duty.

The two soldiers burst through the Door and ran for the stairs. Taking the stairs two at a time, they trailed a sour reek of fear.

Unnerved, Jamis locked his gaze on the opposite stairway, but the rest of his senses remained fixed on the Door. His neck hairs bristled, a soldier's sixth sense warning that danger lurked behind, yet there was nothing to fight but shadows. He gripped his spear, needing to feel the certainty of steel, knowing he dared not let rumors banished reason.

An odd, slithering sound came from the stairs. A tall skeleton of a man leaning on an iron staff shuffled into view, his dark robes dragging behind. The cowl of his robe slipped back to reveal a shock of long white hair framing a ravaged face. Broken veins spider-webbed his ruined skin and his cheeks hung hollow like empty sacks, yet the dark eyes glared cold and keen.

It was the Mordant, the lord of the citadel.

Jamis fell prostrate, his face pressed to the floor, praying to avoid the chilling stare. Iron clicked on stone, drawing near, the staff stopping beside his face. "Rise." The sibilant rasp froze the air. "Rise and follow."

The imperious voice jerked Jamis like a chain. Drenched in a sudden sweat, he staggered to his feet and bowed to the Mordant, before turning to face the Door. A veteran of a dozen battles, he told himself there was nothing to fear...but the lie coiled cold in his stomach. A rotten stench clogged the Doorway, making him gag as he followed the Mordant across the rune-carved threshold.

Jamis stifled a gasp, his gaze skittering around a vast cavern carved from nightmares. Red stalactites hung from a vault of rough rock, as if the earth had wept blood that slowly petrified. Beneath the vault of weeping stone, a great golden pentacle stretched across a black marble floor like an altar awaiting an offering. Flaming braziers stood at the five points, filling the cavern with a flickering light. The light did little to dispel the menace. Power pulsed in the shadows, waiting to be summoned.

The Darkness was *alive*.

*Mortals did not belong here*, Jamis wanted to run. Needing a bulwark against his fears, he fixed his gaze on the two men standing beneath the pulsing shadows. General Haith stood at one of the braziers while the executioner cradled his axe above the dark-stained block of wood.

The block stood empty, waiting for a sacrifice. Jamis wondered if it waited for him, but then a worse fear twisted his guts, remembering those things that had crawled from the Door. Death at the block would be a far cleaner fate. Struggling to keep his dignity, Jamis shambled forward till he reached the edge of the golden pentacle. His footsteps slowed, somehow knowing if he crossed the Dark Lord's symbol he'd be lost.

"Stop." the Mordant rasped.

Jamis froze, clutching his spear, shocked by the reprieve.

The Mordant began to circle the pentacle, his black robes fluttered behind like a windblown wraith...yet there was no wind. Muttering chants in a strange tongue, the Mordant woke the chamber. Flames roared from the braziers, licking the vaulted ceiling, releasing plumes of red sparks that fell like scorching cinders. The air crackled with power, the breath of a thunderstorm eager to strike. Shadows coalesced overhead, taking the form of gibbering demons. And then the braziers dimmed.

Darkness pressed down, forcing Jamis to his knees. Crouching low, he held his breath lest the Darkness enter him.

The Mordant handed his iron staff to the general and made his way to the center of the pentacle. Casting a shadow larger than legend, he stood before the executioner's block. Throwing his head back, the Mordant thrust his hands up toward the red stalactites. His face flushed with ecstasy, he cried, "One lifetime is not enough! Let the bond between us be renewed. May the Dark Lord reign over all of Erdhe!"

The wizard shrugged the robe from his bony shoulders. Bile rose in Jamis's throat at the sight of the sagging, ruined flesh, the dark runes burned into the old man's shriveled skin, but then the Mordant knelt. Understanding struck like a knife. Jamis realized he was not the one slated for sacrifice, but then why was he here?

The Mordant set his head on the block. Jamis stared in shock, unable to believe the lord of the citadel would sacrifice his own life...unable to imagine what such a sacrifice would invoke. He longed to look away, but felt compelled to watch. The executioner swung the half-moon blade in a mighty arc. The silver axe flashed down. Blood spurted and the Mordant's head toppled to the floor with a gruesome thud. The general strode forward, lifting the severed head by its long white hair; a trophy, a triumph, an offering.

The dead eyes flew open.

Two crimson beams of light speared from the Mordant's eyes piercing Jamis. The severed head began to laugh, a terrible, mocking sound that thundered through the cavern. Jamis screamed, his soul seared by the red light. The sudden stink of urine flooded his nose.

The red light slowly faded like two spent embers. The braziers dulled as if snuffed out by a giant hand. Absolute darkness prevailed.

Something stirred overhead, a brooding menace unleashed by the sacrifice. Huddled on the floor, Jamis sought to hide within the darkness, but something found him. Pain pierced him, like a hundred frozen daggers stabbing at his heart, inserting slivers of darkness beneath his skin. He writhed across the cold marble floor, screaming in agony, but then it stopped. Gasping for breath, he waited.

The braziers re-ignited.

Squinting against the light, Jamis checked his body, but there was no blood and no gaping wounds. His stare raced around the cavern, seeking his attacker, but he found only shadows. Shuddering, he reclaimed his spear, and struggled to stand, wondering what fate awaited him.

General Haith remained in the center of the pentacle, but the severed head he held aloft had changed. Withered and shrunken, the head had aged a century, as if death revealed the true age of the Mordant. The general stared at Jamis. "Bare your chest."

Afraid to obey, but too fearful to resist, Jamis dropped his spear and clawed his way out of his armor. Ripping his tunic in haste, he stared at his chest. A dark mark slowly appeared above his heart, like a rune tattooed from beneath his skin. *"No!"*

The general laughed. "You have been marked by the Dark Lord. Remember what you have seen here this day. Now go!"

Jamis fled.

He didn't remember running out of the chamber or climbing the long spiral of stairs to the surface. Bursting free of the subterranean staircase, he collapsed in the courtyard, gasping for breath. Crisp, clean night air flooded his lungs, but he couldn't purge the taint he felt inside himself. He clawed at his chest, contorting to peer down at his bared flesh, but the rune remained, like a curse beneath his skin. Convulsing on the cold stones, he emptied his stomach, but he could not empty his mind. Twisting his head away from the sour stench, Jamis sought the light of the stars in the night sky. The stars were still there, but his world was forever changed. He'd learned a truth he never wanted to know. The Darkness was real and all the light in the world could not banish the nightmare from his soul.

# Thirty years later...

## 1

# Katherine

Kath took the steps two at a time, racing the light from the rising sun to the battlement at the top of Castlegard's tallest tower. If she hurried she'd have time enough to work out the riddle. The question had been nagging her since dinner last night, but she needed the view to be sure. Rounding the last spiral, she stepped out onto the windswept battlement. A single knight stood watch alongside the brooding gargoyles, his maroon cloak billowing over a silver surcoat. Too old for the field of battle, Sir Bredon's eyes were still keen enough for the lookout towers. Without turning he said, "Hello, Imp."

Kath smiled. To the knights and the candidates she was the "Imp"; to the ruined veterans she was "Little Sister". No one saw her for what she really was. In some ways being invisible gave her an advantage; age was a trap for a girl and a curse for a woman. At fifteen, she wanted to avoid the trap for as long as possible. Crossing the battlement to stand next to the knight, she leaned on the wall, the crisp wind tugging at her unruly blonde hair. "Anything out there?" Sir Bredon pointed to the northern horizon. "A patrol returning from the north but otherwise it's quiet."

Kath spotted the dust cloud on the valley floor. She held her breath; half hoping an enemy pursued the patrol. Peace was boring.

"No cause for alarm." Sir Bredon walked a lazy circuit around the parapet, keeping his gaze on the countryside below. "Aren't you supposed to be somewhere?"

Kath scowled. "It's too early to be at the healery. And besides, I have a riddle to solve."

"A riddle?"

"Last night at dinner, Father said that Castlegard could almost defend itself, that any attacking force would have to overcome eleven defenses created by the ancient builders." The riddle challenged Kath, giving her the chance to prove she knew the castle better than anyone. "I think I've worked them out, but I need the view to be sure."

The tower gave her a perfect eagle-eye view of the great concentric castle and the broad saddle-shaped valley below. The valley breached the east-west range of mountains that separated the southern kingdoms from the lands of the Mordant. The castle guarded the valley, holding the Mordant's hordes in check. It made sense, but Kath thought the explanation was too simple for a castle raised by the ancient mages. In many ways, Castlegard was itself a riddle; the construction of the inner walls so seamless they looked as if they'd been molded from molten granite.

Running her hand along the impossibly smooth mage-stone, Kath could easily believe the ballads the bards sang about the making of the castle in the days of high magic. The mage-stone walls showed no sign of wear despite more than thirty generations of use. Magic used to raise such a castle was long since gone from the land, destroyed during the War of Wizards, but Castlegard remained as a marvel of older times. Whatever the truth behind the castle's origins, legends agreed that Castlegard was invincible and no army had so far proved the claim false.

"Eleven you said?"

"Some of them are easy." Buffeted by the chilly wind, Kath tucked her hair behind her ears and wished that she'd worn a cloak. "The greensward makes approaching enemies vulnerable to arrows, and the moat looks peaceful enough but I know it's deep." Last summer, she'd probed the murky depths with a broken lance, never finding the bottom. "Three has to be the drawbridges and four the gatehouses protecting the bridge mechanisms. Then there's the iron gate and the first curtain wall but they probably count as one. It gets tricky inside the first wall." The eight-sided castle was a series of fortified walls, separated by traps and tricks. The outer walls, raised by the sweat of ordinary stonemasons, were challenging, but the soaring inner castle, raised by the magic of ancient wizards, was surely impregnable. "I've heard the knight marshal say there's nothing but traps between the two walls."

Sir Bredon nodded. "Mage-stone's not the only reason the castle's never fallen."

Mentally mapping a pathway through the gauntlet of defenses, Kath had to agree. "Between the two walls, I count two portcullises, a gated pass-through, an archery cross-fire yard, and a dead-end corridor." She frowned. "But that only makes nine."

"Don't forget the murder holes over the pass-through."

"Ah yes!" She'd heard tales about the murder holes which allowed defenders to rain boiling pitch on invaders trapped within the walls. "That makes ten, but we're still short by one." She leaned farther out. It was probably something sneaky, crafted into the pass-through or one of the gates. Her gaze roamed the castle walls, but the last defense remained a mystery. "Do you know what we've missed?"

"No, but if the king says there's eleven then there has to be one more."

"Perhaps the last defense can't be seen from above, like a trapdoor or a pit of spikes."

The knight shrugged, "Makes sense."

Kath resolved to explore the walls and ferret out the answer. Setting aside the riddle, her mind turned to a deeper problem. Perhaps Sir Bredon could help since he served on the Council of Candidates. Reaching into the pocket of her squire's tunic, she closed her hand around her good luck charm and tried to make her voice sound casual. "Sir Bredon, do you know the knight-candidate, Blaine?"

When he replied, his voice was laden with disapproval. "Knight-candidates have no time for skinny girls, especially not the king's daughter." Wrapping his maroon cloak around his shoulders, he turned his back on her and strode away.

Kath scrambled to keep pace, "It's not what you think," but he didn't reply. Walking in the knight's chilly shadow, she considered ways to break his silence, perhaps a bargain of sorts. "Sir Thorlin is slated to spar with Sir Brent on the morrow, a great sword against a battle axe," she offered. "They say the odds are three to one in favor of Thorlin."

Sir Bredon threw her a hard look. "Wagering on sparring rounds is forbidden."

"The odds are wrong."

He raised a bushy eyebrow, his voice gruff. "What does a girl know of odds?"

"My mornings are spent in the healery."

He stopped in mid-stride and turned to stare down at her, a glint of avarice in his dark eyes. "And?"

"And I want to know about Blaine."

He gave her a slow nod.

"Sir Thorlin has a bad left shoulder, an old war wound from patrolling the steppes. Damp weather makes it ache. He's been to the healer for a poultice. I know because I ground the mustard seed myself. Sir Thorlin will fight tomorrow, but his left shoulder will not be at full strength. So you see, the odds are wrong, Sir Brent will win the bout."

Sir Bredon grunted, "Good to know," and resumed walking.

"And Blaine?"

"Tall, lanky, blonde, comes from the farms of Tubor." He stopped to gaze down at the sleepy village nestled in the valley below. "Blaine came to the castle as part of the peasants' levy. He's the son of a pig farmer, but he's taken well to training. Some of the veterans speak highly of him." He cast a sideways glance in her direction. "The young buck will have his chance to earn a knight's maroon cloak. Why?"

Kath chewed her lip, trying to frame the question. "If Blaine succeeds in the trials, do you think he'll follow the old ways?"

"A strange question, Imp." He turned to walk the battlements and Kath fell into step beside him. They completed a circuit before he spoke again. "The king would say the Octagon is built on honor, and so it is, but some of the younger knights stray from the old ways. The maroon is not what it once was. Combat exposes a man's true mettle. Blaine's test will come in the trials. From what I've seen of him, he'll make a good addition to the maroon."

Relief washed through her. Blaine was different from the others, fighting with his mind instead of just the strength of his arm. For her dream to have a chance, he had to be a man of honor. She stared down into the great yard, surprised to find sunlight dancing across the curtain wall. The morning was slipping away, and by order of her lord father, Kath was supposed to be at the healery gaining a "lady's education". The thought was enough to sour her stomach. She longed to practice swords with the squires, but that would never be allowed.

Bidding Sir Bredon a good day, she raced down the tower stairs taking them two at a time. Rounding the last spiral, she found a maroon-cloaked knight blocking her way. Kath glared at Sir Raymond, a sour-faced nobleman from a minor barony in Radagar, one of the few knights she went out of her way to avoid. She tried ducking around him but a mailed arm snaked out to block her way.

"Can't keep away from me, aye, *princess*?"

He was always taunting her with rude remarks, but so far it was only words, and only when he caught her alone. Kath recoiled against the wall, watching for an opportunity to run past.

He leered at her. "You're a skinny, wild thing, but a man could do worse than wed a princess. You hide under that baggy squire's tunic, but I've has noticed those young tits of yours shaping the gray wool." His leer deepened. "Your father thinks you're a child, but we know better, don't we *princess*? Maybe this will be the year I ask for your hand. You could do worse than a baron's son and a knight of the Octagon. What do you say to that, *princess*?" His right hand reached out to touch her face.

It was all the opportunity she needed. She spit in his face, aiming for his eyes, and dodged around his outstretched hand. He roared in anger but Kath was already well past. She sprinted for the tower doorway, dashing out into the safety of the open courtyard. He wouldn't bother her if there were witnesses around.

Her father would banish Sir Raymond if he knew about the knight's behavior, but Kath's greater fear was having her father realize she was old enough for marriage. Better to keep her silence and stay in Castlegard. Time was her enemy. Shaking off the rude encounter, she detoured through the great kitchen, comforted by the smells of fresh-baked bread and the warm greetings of the kitchen folk. She filched a quarter loaf of bread for breakfast, and a handful of leftover meat scraps to feed to the healer's giant frost owl. It seemed to Kath that if you could win over the pet, the master was sure to follow.

She took a short cut through the great yard, waving to the crippled veterans. She loved arguing with them about the relative sword skills of the squires and knight-candidates. Without realizing it the veterans were giving her a practical education in the principles of arms practice. Kath absorbed every detail, but there was no time for talk this morning, she was already late.

A cavalcade of knights thundered through the ironbound gate, shattering the peace of the morning. The returning patrol rode in disciplined ranks, a proud flourish of maroon capes and burnished helmets. Sunlight glinted off arms and armor, making a grand sight. Kath paused in mid-stride, swelling with pride, but then she noticed that the horses appeared lathered and blowing hard. They'd been overridden; something was wrong. A shiver of apprehension feathered down her spine.

The captain reined in his stallion and dismounted, his voice a beacon of command. "Wounded man here! Get the healer and the knight marshal!"

Weapons jangled as the knights dismounted. Warhorses stamped and churned, fighting their bridles and whinnying for attention. The yard became a whirlpool of snorting horses and armored men, a chaotic swirl of sweat, leather, and steel. Ignored by the knights, Kath waded amongst them, just a piece of flotsam caught on the tide of curiosity. Making her way toward the central knot of maroon-cloaked knights, Kath caught a glimpse of a man in bloodstained leathers slipping from the back of a warhorse. A flash of bead-embroidery marked him as a stranger, the patrol must have found him on their rounds. She crept closer, angling for a better view. Two knights lowered the stranger to the ground, laying him on his side. A pair of arrows protruded from his back, two circular stains of blood leached into the cream-colored leather. Kath stifled a gasp; the arrows were fletched in gold and black, the colors of the Mordant.

"Where's the healer?" The urgent shout echoed through the yard.

The knights shifted, obscuring Kath's view. Crouching, she peered between their legs, and found herself staring straight into the stranger's face. Shock rippled through her. Whirls of tattooed blue covered the man's skin, turning his face into the snarling mask of a mountain lion. "*A Painted Warrior!*" She'd heard tales of the renegade fighters of the far north but she'd never seen one in Castlegard. She studied his face, finding the blue tattoos oddly compelling; a fitting mask for war. But beneath the whirls of blue, his flesh was ghost-pale, his breath a ragged rattle from between parched lips.

Her healer's training took over. Kath scrambled to the side of a warhorse and untied a water skin, then pushed her way back to the Painted Warrior.

A voice of command split the air. "I need a report." The stern-faced knight marshal stepped into the central clearing, his one-eyed gaze staring down at the wounded man. "Where was he found?"

The patrol captain answered. "At the extreme northern end of our ranging, left for dead in the grasslands. We held the horses to a gallop, hoping to get him to the healer in time."

The marshal's one-eyed stare found Kath, pinning her to the ground, a mouse caught by an eagle. Trying to justify her presence, she lifted the water skin. "He needs water." The marshal gave her a skeptical scowl, but gestured for her to proceed.

She knelt by the man, gently pouring water over his face and across his cracked lips. The blue tattoos were even more striking up close. The snarling mountain lion seemed more than mortal, like something out of myth, man and animal melded together. And his clothing was almost as exotic, supple cream-white leathers embroidered with glass beads, the pattern showing a pale blue flower on a field of white. Kath wondered at the story behind the mountain lion, behind the delicate blue flowers. The Painted Warrior gasped like a man desperate for life. Startled, Kath nearly dropped the water skin. His eyes still closed, he turned his head toward the cool wet flow, his mouth open for more. She tilted the spout against his lips. Water trickled down the side of his face, but he swallowed more than he lost.

Overhead, the marshal growled, "Did he say anything on the ride south?"

A knight answered, "Nothing of note."

"Get the healer, I want this man saved."

The Painted Warrior's eyes flew open, wild and urgent. Kath shrank back but her movement drew the man's attention. Sky-blue eyes stared up at her and Kath thought she saw recognition in his face, but that was impossible. His gaze drilled into her, latching onto something deep inside, something that she didn't have a name for. Struggling for breath, his words barely audible, he rasped, *"The Mordant seeks to be reborn!"*

His words shivered through Kath, lodging in her soul.

The knight marshal crouched beside her, demanding answers. "Tell us about the Mordant's forces. Why were you so far south?"

A tattooed hand shot out, grasping the front of Kath's tunic with surprising strength.

The Painted Warrior pulled her close, his breath sour against her face. *"Claim the war helm! Yours...to...use."* His words beat against her with the strength of destiny.

Then his eyes widened and his back arched in pain. His fist released her, the arm falling limp, the eyes glazing. A death rattle gurgled from his lips, a trickle of blood escaping his mouth and he slumped backward the spark of life gone.

Kath rocked back on her heels, struck by loss and confusion. She wanted to send a prayer to Valin, but she didn't even know the man's name.

The marshal sighed, "The arrow fletchings reveal more than the ravings of a dead man."

Commands were issued and men snapped to obey but Kath sat in a fog. Mailed arms reached past her, lifting the Painted Warrior from the ground. The soldiers wrapped the body in a cloak and carried it away. The patrol of knights followed the marshal to the King's Tower, a jangle of armor and weapons. Stable boys took command of the warhorses, ushering the great beasts out of the yard and sweeping up the dung. Even the old veterans found a reason to leave. A shroud of stillness settled across the yard as if the gods stood watch.

Numb, Kath sat forgotten on the hard-packed earth. The dying words of the Painted Warrior shivered through her mind, *"Claim the war helm."* She shuddered; bound by death to a man she did not even know. She reached for the empty water skin, replacing the stopper and only then noticed the bloody handprint staining her tunic like a blazon. Death had left its mark.

# 2

# Katherine

Kath crept up the tower stairs, careful not to make a sound. She'd left the great hall while the others still lingered over supper, certain she would not be missed. After retrieving a cloak, she used the castle's secret ways to slip past a handful of guards. Quiet as a ghost, she made her way up the tower, her doe-skin boots nothing but a whisper on the mage-stone stairs. In all of Castlegard only the Octagon Tower was forbidden to her, but Kath knew the way. She'd dared it once before, drawn by the challenge as much as a burning curiosity, but never during a trial and never when it mattered so much.

Shadows darkened the staircase, an orange sun setting beyond the arrow-slit windows. Kath trailed a hand along the inner wall, counting the turns of the spiral. A cold wind gusted from above, warning her that she neared the top. Kath slunk low, peering through the open doorway, relieved to find the battlement empty. To be safe, she circled at a crouch till she reached the far side. Of the many towers of Castlegard, the Octagon was unique. Crowned by crenellated battlements, the eight-sided tower was hollow, protecting an octagonal courtyard of mage-stone open to the night sky above. Hiding behind a merlon, she peered into the tower's hollow heart.

Torchlight blazed below, awaiting the start of the trials. Her breath caught, knowing she spied on hallowed ground. An iron throne sat against the south wall while an altar to Valin dominated the north. Between the king and the warrior god, a great maroon octagon stretched across the center, a battlefield of blood-red marble inset in the floor. Kath stared at the blood-stained marble, wondering how many dreams had died there, wondering if her own would survive the night.

Footsteps echoed from below. Kath ducked behind the merlon. She'd come for the gods-eye view but she dared not be found. Her heart hammering, she waited till curiosity got the better of her. Daring a glance over the merlon, she was surprised to find the knight marshal below. Second only to the king, the one-eyed marshal placed an array of weapons upon the altar to Valin. So these were the weapons of the trial. Keen-edged, they gleamed in the torchlight as if blessed by the god. Kath gave them a hungry stare, knowing which one she'd choose. It was always the sword for her, the weapon of heroes, the very symbol of the warrior god, but for her dreams to come true, Blaine would need to win his trial. Gripping her good luck charm, she sent a silent prayer to Valin.

Knowing the trial was still hours away, Kath set her back to the merlon, sitting cross-legged on the cold stone floor. Huddled beneath her wool cloak, she tried to keep warm, watching as the sunset faded to dusk and the first stars appeared in the night sky. Dragon, Knight and Swan, she studied the star patterns, counting three shooting stars before the Great Ladle rose in the east.

Horns echoed from below. Startled, Kath peered over the edge, watching as the king and his officers entered the hollow tower. Bowing to Valin's altar, the king took a seat upon the iron throne, setting his great blue sword across his knees. From this angle, Kath could not see her father's expression but she could well imagine his stern gaze set in a sun-weathered face. Honor and discipline meant everything to the king and he would expect to see both in the trials. The horns blared again and the champions entered the tower. Eight knights in elaborate armor claimed their stations at the corners of the marble octagon. Kath studied the knights, guessing their names by their size and their weapons. One towered over the others, *Trask,* a vile-tempered knight with the strength of an ogre and the brutal fighting style of a berserker. Kath shuddered, making the hand sign against evil. Rumors said the champions were chosen by lots, but judging by the eight waiting below, Blaine's luck had turned dark. His trial would be difficult if not deadly.

The king gestured and the marshal climbed the steps to settle a maroon cloak across the altar. A commotion at the doorway caught Kath's stare. Blaine appeared at the entrance. Dressed in simple armor, devoid of any weapons, he stood straight and tall, waiting to be summoned, but this time there would be no trumpet blare, no fanfare, just a lowly knight-candidate called to the octagon to prove his worth. She studied his face, finding a strange mixture of anxiety and elation. Kath could well relate, for the same feelings raged within her. Driven by dreams, she'd come to witness the trial, knowing the outcome would determine two destinies not one.

# 3

# Blaine

The candidate strode through the door into the Octagon Tower, the
crucible where knights were made or broken. Mage-stone walls
soared to crenellated battlements open to the night sky, as if the
ancient builders wanted the heavens to stand in judgment of his trial.
Taking a deep breath, he nodded toward the jeweled stars, acknowledging
the gods and praying for victory. The night carried a chill, the last vestige
of winter, but if the stars held any reply he could not tell. Eager to prove
his worth, he turned his gaze toward the king.

King Ursus of Castlegard sat upon an iron throne, his face chiseled
with the stern lines of duty, a hero's great sword across his knees. Age was
clearly upon him, yet he wore only steel and leather as befitted a warrior-
king who counted his wealth in loyal swords. The silver-haired king
leaned forward, pinning the candidate with an unyielding stare. "What
name will you be known by?"

Pride swelled within him. "Blaine, sire."

"And what lineage do you offer to the Octagon?"

Thinking of the poverty of his father's farm, Blaine struggled to keep
the shame from his voice. "None save what I earn here this night."

The king nodded. "The brotherhood of the maroon accepts all those
found to be worthy. We few are the sword and shield of the southern
kingdoms, standing against the Mordant's hordes. Are you ready for your
trial?"

"Yes, sire."

Raising his voice, the king cried out the words of ritual. "Let the
swords decide the candidate's worth!"

A thrill shivered through Blaine the chance to change his fate was at
hand. He turned to face the center of the hollow tower. A blood-red

marble octagon stretched across the heart of the floor, defining his crucible. Eight knights stood stationed at the corners, their helms closed, their weapons drawn, torchlight reflecting off bright steel. Daunting in their maroon armor and elaborate helmets, the knights seemed more than mortal.

Blaine studied his opponents, guessing their names by their size and chosen weapon. One towered above the others, a brooding hulk holding a moon-shaped battleaxe. *Trask.* So the nobleman dared bring his grudge to the octagon. Anger threaded through Blaine; there was more on trial here than his dreams.

Undaunted, he bowed to the eight champions. By tradition, candidates showed their faces in the octagon. Blaine wore a simple half-helm and plain gray armor devoid of any emblem or device save the heart-rune. All candidates came to the trial stripped of their name, lineage, and past deeds, but the trappings of noblemen meant nothing to Blaine. His dreams and his future depended on the trial.

"Choose your weapon!" The one-eyed knight marshal unveiled the weapons arrayed on the altar stone. Flickering torchlight illumed the marshal's empty eye socket and scar-crossed face, making him appear a demon, or a harbinger of doom, but Blaine refused to flinch from the wages of war. Answering the call, he climbed the stairs to the rough-hewn block of red granite, a fitting altar for the warrior god. A knight stood on either side; one held an ornate sand glass and the other a battle horn, the timekeepers for the trial. Blaine studied the weapons while the knight marshal whispered a warning, "Think first and choose well, for each warrior may bear but a single weapon within the octagon. May Valin, the god of warriors, guide your hand."

Weapons gleamed in the torchlight, death crafted into steel. A flanged mace, the spiked ball and chain of a morningstar, the half-moon blade of a war axe, a heavy cavalry saber, a hand-and-a-half claymore, and a two-handed great sword, he'd trained with them all, but his gaze was drawn to the great sword, the weapon of heroes. He reached for the five-foot great sword with its double-edged blade and sturdy cross-hilt. It felt good in his hands. Well balanced and honed to a fine, silk-cutting edge; the blade was as beautiful as it was deadly. For the fight of his life he could choose no other weapon.

Under the gaze of the king and the night stars, he entered the octagon. Bowing to each knight, he used the time to assess his opponents. Trask would be his toughest fight but none would be easy. Taking a deep breath, he tightened his grip on the great sword and nodded to the knight marshal, prepared to claim his destiny.

"The candidate has entered the octagon." The voice of the one-eyed marshal rang with authority. "Let no man interfere."

A knight turned the sand glass and a trumpeter sounded the battle horn. The first maroon knight surged into the octagon, a blur of armor and sharpened steel. Blaine whirled to meet the attacker and the two great swords met with a fearsome clash. The first blow shuddered down Blaine's arms, a warning of things to come. Disengaging, he counterattacked, searching for an opening to the knight's heart-rune. Stroke, parry, and evade, he plunged into the fight, hammering his opponent with a whirlwind of blows. *I must finish him quickly; with eight against one time is my greatest enemy.* A sword flashed toward his face but he parried the blow. Dancing away, he felt sweat drip down his back, a warning that the bout was taking too long. *Remember, balance is the key!* He feinted toward his opponent's knees. The knight bought the feint, lowering his guard for the parry. Blaine's great sword slipped into the opening to tag the maroon heart-rune. His sword struck true. Victory's thrill rushed through him but the trial had just begun. He gulped air but he had no time to recover. As the defeated knight stepped out of the octagon, a second leapt to take his place.

The trial became a blur of sweat and steel. Each round lasted only a few minutes, but to Blaine those minutes stretched to an eternity. With no time to recover, he faced a different challenge in every round: the brute strength of the mace, the sly finesse of the morningstar, the madness of the berserker's battleaxe, the slashing quickness of the saber, and the disciplined strength of the great sword. After five grueling rounds, Blaine still held the octagon but the fight had taken its toll. His arms ached with strain and his breath turned ragged. Cuts on his forehead and sword arm wept blood. Sweat stung his eyes.

A fresh knight wielding a great sword rushed in to take up the fight. *Great sword against great sword, the weapons are equal, but he is fresh. Time to overplay fatigue.* Blaine slipped sideways, letting his footwork drag. Slowing the speed of his sword till his parries were just in time, he let the point of his sword dip, as if the weight of it was too heavy. The maroon knight took the bait, pressing in with an overextended lunge. Blaine beat the great sword away and counterattacked. Swift as a snake, his sword tagged the maroon heart-rune.

*Six down, two to go*, his heart pounded like thunder, his tunic drenched in sweat under his armor. Blaine moved to the center of the octagon. A cold finger of warning shivered down his spine. *Footsteps rushed from behind.* Raising his sword, he whirled. The gleam of a battleaxe sped toward his face. He jerked backwards but the axe followed, catching him just below the eyes. His nose-guard collapsed with a sickening crunch. Pain exploded across his face. He staggered backwards, reaching up to feel the wound. Blood gushed from his broken nose and a deep cut under his left eye...but he still had a face.

The maroon knight towered over him. "Taste my axe, *farmer-boy!*"

"*Trask!*" Blaine spat the name like a curse.

Passing the battleaxe back and forth between massive hands, the huge knight growled a taunt. "You're not worthy."

"You're wrong." Blaine tore the ruined half-helm from his head and hurled it aside. Wiping the blood from his face, he retreated to the far side of the octagon, buying time to gather his strength, but the ploy failed. With a roar, Trask crossed the arena with surprising speed. Blaine raised his sword just in time. Struggling for breath, he retreated under the onslaught, but the half-moon blade pursued with a vengeance, a wicked blur in the torchlight. *Clang!* His sword parried a ferocious blow. The force nearly drove Blaine to his knees. Twisting away, he disengaged and dodged a second blow. But the silver axe gave chase, always aiming for his head or neck, persistent as an executioner's blade. An icy fear ripped through Blaine; *Trask seeks my life instead of the heart-rune!* He flicked a desperate glance toward the iron throne but the king sat stern and impassive.

Steel whistled toward Blaine's face. He jerked backwards, avoiding the killing blow. Desperate to end the bout, he feinted to the left and then risked falling to his knees. Ducking under the head-high swing of the axe, he gained an opening. When the axe whispered overhead, Blaine thrust his sword up inside Trask's guard. His sword tagged the heart-rune. Relief flooded through him. Breathing hard, he sagged back on his heels, flushed with victory.

Above him, Trask snarled, converting the horizontal axe swing into a downward slash. Time slowed to a heartbeat. The silver axe loomed overhead. Blaine froze, shocked by the dishonor of the blow. He dodged at the last moment...but not quick enough. Steel struck steel and the armor on his left shoulder crumpled under the blow. Blaine slammed to the floor, pain surging through him. Out of the corner of his eye he saw the silver axe raised for the killing stroke. He tried to lift his sword but his left hand wouldn't obey. Gripping the hilt with his right, he rolled away.

The axe struck stone, scarring the octagon. Blaine staggered to his feet. Blood flowed from his broken nose, his left arm hung useless, and his shoulder throbbed. One-handed, he struggled to raise the point of the great sword, but the tip wavered like a rum-soaked drunk.

Trask flicked up the visor of his helmet and Blaine met the cold stare of the maroon knight. Death was coming. Even so, he held his ground; dreams did not die easily.

"Run, peasant. Show yourself a craven." Trask raised the battleaxe in a two-handed executioner's grip. Torchlight glittered on the half-moon blade.

Blaine refused to move, bracing himself for the blow.

The call of a battle horn split the night, signaling that the sands of the glass had run out. Trask hesitated, held frozen by the sound of the horn. Then bound by ritual if not by honor, he snarled a string of curses and stalked away. Blaine sagged with relief; death had passed. He sent a fervent prayer to Valin, the god of warriors, and stumbled to the center of the octagon. Needles danced up and down his useless left arm. Grinding his teeth against the pain, he sought to find the strength for one more round.

The final knight entered the arena. The spiked ball of the morningstar whirled through the air, carving a circle of destruction. Blaine lurched away, bitterly regretting his choice of weapon. Unable to lift the great sword, he wondered if pride would be his downfall, but then the knight of the morningstar did something unexpected. He lowered his weapon and raised the visor of his helm, revealing a sun-creased face and an auburn mustache. Sir Bearhart nodded to Blaine, then turned his gaze to the king, his voice ringing against the mage-stone walls. "For the honor of the Octagon." Saluting the king, the veteran knight remained statue-still.

Half in a daze, Blaine gasped for breath. Pride swelled within him: honor still lived in the brotherhood of the maroon.

The horn sounded a triumphant blare, announcing the final turn of the sand glass. With his heart-rune untouched, Blaine had survived the trial.

Sir Bearhart bowed and retreated to his original station. Blaine leaned on his sword, staring up at the king. Silence descended like a fog, wrapping him in a cocoon of stillness. Bone-weary, he swayed, dizzy on his feet, afraid to believe it was over. The warrior-king pounded his mailed fist against the arm of the iron throne, shattering the silence. "Let the candidate approach!"

Bloody and battered, Blaine dropped to one knee, waiting to hear the words he'd yearned for all his life.

"A new candidate has passed the trial of combat and proven himself worthy. As king of Castlegard, I welcome you to the knights of the Octagon!" King Ursus smiled, his voice a mixture of pride and compassion. "Arise, Sir Blaine, and greet your brothers in arms!"

Joy and pride rushed through Blaine; the son of a farmer had gained the title of knight.

# 4

# Katherine

Kath watched from the tower top as the king embraced Blaine. *He'd done it!* Blaine's trial had been difficult, nigh on deadly, but he'd done it, he'd gained his maroon cloak. Elation thrummed through Kath, knowing her dream was one step closer to reality.

Ducking low, she hid behind the battlement, lest she be seen. Sitting beneath the stars, her back pressed to the cold mage-stone of the forbidden tower, her dreams ran rampant. She longed to hold a sword in her hands, but more than that, she felt the call to lead. Her older brothers all had their places in the octagon. One of them would eventually earn the right to rule, but never a daughter, never a girl. The octagon trial offered her best chance to change her fate.

But everything would be for naught if she was caught. She dared not think what would happen if the knights caught her defiling their secret trials.

As the sounds of celebration faded and the knights made their way from the tower, Kath forced herself to wait, counting to one hundred, and then to two hundred. Finally satisfied it was safe, she crept to the well of stairs that honeycombed the outer wall of the tower. The staircase gaped open, dark and empty.

Kath slipped down the stairs two at a time, one hand trailing along the inner wall. At the bottom of the fifth spiral, darkness gave way to torchlight. Muffled voices brought her to an abrupt halt. Keeping to the shadows, she peered around the curved inner wall, shocked to find a pair of maroon cloaks blocking the stairwell. Her breath caught. Except for the tower guards, all the knights should be celebrating in the great hall.

The two men stood abnormally close, furtive whispers swirling between them. Kath thought she head Trask's name mentioned among the whispers. Blaine's fight with the battleaxe had been fearsome to behold. Kath was still shocked by the dishonor of Trask's blow...and the king had said nothing; that shocked her almost as much. Something foul festered in the maroon, something brought to light by the trial. Kath crept towards the two knights, tempted to eavesdrop, but time was against her. With the trial over, the guards would soon resume their rounds; she had to find her way out. Crouched in the shadows, Kath studied the two knights as if they were enemies. She'd often heard the knight marshal say that the key to an enemy's weakness lay in his motives. The two knights acted as if they did not want to be overheard. Perhaps they'd move if they thought someone was coming. Kath ransacked her pockets for an agate-colored pebble she'd found earlier that morning. Leaning into the torchlight, she flicked her wrist, aiming low. The pebble skittered into the far hallway, a clatter of stone on stone.

Startled, the two knights stilled. Kath held her breath and at last they moved off down the hallway, but she forced herself to wait. When the retreating footsteps fell silent, she bolted, her soft doeskin boots whispering down the stairs. Her heart hammering, she peered into the torch-lit hallway, relieved to find it empty. Dashing to the opposite wall, she counted three torches to the left and then pressed the raised octagon on the bottom of the metal bracket. A low rumble came from behind the stone wall. A hidden door clicked open, releasing a breath of stale air. Anxious to be gone, she plunged into the narrow opening. Ignoring the spiders and the strands of broken webs, she reached for another raised octagon and pressed it. The door closed behind her, cloaking her in darkness.

Silence surrounded her, but to Kath it seemed welcoming. The musty stillness of the lower tunnels beckoned. The underground passageways provided a sanctuary, her secret retreat. Fumbling in the dark, she found her flint waiting on the top step and struck a flame to a candle stub. Pale light illuminated the ancient walls. Here within these forgotten halls she could be herself, practicing with rusty swords and ferreting out the secrets of the past. But soon she'd have the chance to do more. Running her hand along the impossibly smooth mage-stone walls, she descended the stairs to the underground passage, dreaming of a future full of swords.

# 5

# The Knight Marshal

The knight marshal swung his one-eyed gaze across the faces of the nine captains, finally settling on the king. "We dare not drop our guard."

On the far side of the council table, Sir Rannock argued. "But there's been no sign of the enemy. The north is quiet despite the Painted Warrior's warning."

The marshal parried the argument. "Peace is often a delusion, a way for the Mordant to lull his enemies into the trap of complacency. Battle-readiness must be the standing order for each keep, wall, and outpost within the domain of Castlegard." He watched their faces, seeing more than one nod of agreement, but the decision rested with the king.

King Ursus tugged on his silver beard, his face thoughtful. "We've had no reports of movement in the steppes, yet the marshal has the truth of it. The Mordant is a clever opponent, full of deceit. The Octagon must remain vigilant. Let the order stand."

The marshal eased back in his chair and watched as the knight-captains made their reports. King Ursus took and gave counsel, but when it came to the review of the ledgers by the quartermaster, the king cut the meeting short. The warrior-king had little patience for the coin-counters endless litany of silvers owed, golds spent, and coppers collected. Trusting the quartermaster to see to it that the ledgers balanced, the king dismissed them all with a wave of his hand.

The marshal stood to leave, but the king's voice pulled him back. "Not you, Osbourne."

Changing directions, the marshal moved to stand with his back to the roaring fireplace. Heat beat against him, easing the ache of old war wounds. Overhead, faded battle banners hung from the rafters, a proud testament to the long history of the Octagon Knights. So much history, so much blood shed, the marshal tallied the cost of battles won and lost.

The door closed and he was alone with his king.

King Ursus contemplated a goblet of wine, the maps, messages, and ledgers strewn across the table seemingly forgotten. Age was clearly upon the king, yet he still cut an imposing figure with the broad shoulders and thick arms of a seasoned warrior. Even at council, the king dressed in battle-scarred fighting leathers, his great blue sword, Honor's Edge, never far from his hand.

The king sent a baleful glare toward his marshal. "You saw did you not? You saw, you were the judge of the trials, and yet you said nothing."

Osbourne considered his words. The marshal only had one eye left to him, yet it was his king who had a blind spot for honor. "Yes, sire, I saw. Blaine struck a clean blow to the heart rune yet Trask ignored it. Not honorable combat for the octagon, but not without precedent either."

"Sir Bearhart preserved the honor of the Octagon, while you did nothing."

"But sire, it *is* a trial by combat."

"There are rules," the king's voice held a dangerous edge.

Osbourne decided, no matter the cost, to say what he thought. "Sire, there are some who say we place too much emphasis on honor. They argue that our enemies, nay even our allies, will not fight with honor. That honor is nothing more than a shroud for dead heroes." He took a deep breath and forced the words out. "What Trask did in the Octagon was dishonorable yet it represents the truth of battle, especially against the Mordant."

"*Truth! I'll give you truth!*" The king roared in anger, his metal goblet smashing against the stone fireplace, narrowly missing the marshal's head. Red wine dripped down the stone like an open wound. "Take a good look at this room, Osbourne. The Octagon is built on honor!"

The marshal endured the king's wrath, knowing that reason always supplanted anger.

A sullen silence settled between them. The king reached for a fresh goblet, filling it to the brim. Taking a long swallow, he wiped his mouth with the back of his hand and growled, "How deep is the rot?"

"A minority of knights, but one that is not silent. Noblemen all, the faction seems to be gaining strength. Trask is one of the leaders. To these men, a candidate like Blaine, a commoner, is a weak link. They'd rather see him die in the trials than have a peasant take the maroon."

"And you, Osbourne? Does your silence at the trial indicate you side with this faction?"

The marshal shook his head. "Blaine will make a fine addition."

"Then why did you not interfere?"

The truth tasted sour in his mouth. "There is little honor outside of these walls. What Trask did in the trial is a lesson worth teaching. We can expect no honor from our enemies."

"And thus you said nothing."

Osbourne felt the king's stare boring into him, and he knew what the king saw. A map of honorable scars crisscrossed his face and his left eye socket gaped empty. He knew the empty socket was ugly, even shocking, but he deliberately left it uncovered so the knight-candidates could see the cost of war. Loyalty was writ large across his face; old wounds gained fighting at the king's side.

The king sighed. "Bitter as it is, we will let the lesson stand...but we will *not* allow the rot to fester."

Osbourne nodded, quick to note the rare use of the royal "we", a sure indicator his king was not pleased.

"The Octagon has always been outnumbered by the forces of the Mordant. We must keep to the old ways if we are to succeed against the dark hordes. Honor gives men courage and purpose. Honor enables ordinary men to do extraordinary deeds. If just one man dares to reach high in times of need, then others will follow. A single act can turn the tide of battle." He stared pointedly at his marshal. "You know what I mean."

He'd fought at his king's side all his life. "As you say, sire."

"When the knight-candidates debate the treachery at Dymtower remind them of Raven Pass. See to it that you teach them the lessons of honor." The king slammed his fist onto the table, quaking the maps and goblets. "By Valin, I will not have honor fade from the ranks of the maroon! Not while I hold this throne!"

Silence fell between them. The knight marshal waited for orders.

"Trask should be stripped of his maroon cloak." The king's voice held a deadly edge.

"Our ranks are too thin." When the king did not respond to this, the marshal added, "Sire, I loathe the man as much as you do, but he *is* good with a battleaxe. When the Mordant breaks the peace, we will need every blade."

"And so you would forge a long chain built with weak links rather than a short one of unquestionable strength."

"We do not have the luxury of choice!"

"There is always a choice...and always consequences. Necessity be damned to the nine hells." The king spread a scrolled map across the table and with a calloused finger traced the line of mountains dividing the far north from the kingdoms of Erdhe. "See to it that Trask is given duty at Cragnoth Keep. Perhaps a tour of duty at the frozen keep will teach the arrogant wretch a lesson. If nothing else, it will put some distance between *Sir* Trask and the knight-candidates."

The marshal did not agree, preferring to keep trouble close at hand, but he knew better than to press the argument. Bowing, he acknowledged the king's command.

"And," the king continued, "I'll have the names of this minority of knights who side with Trask. I want them dispersed through the ranks, with none of them given guard duty in the king's tower or at the gates of Castlegard. Perhaps dispersed the poison will dissipate. So let it be done." He waved his hand in weary dismissal.

As Osbourne reached for the door, the king added, "And see to it that this new knight is given a blade of blue steel."

The marshal blinked his one good eye in surprise. In a quiet voice he said, "There are knights more deserving. Blue steel blades are meant for heroes. They should be reserved for the very best of the Octagon."

"No Osbourne, a blue blade given to Sir Blaine will remind the rest of the knights of the importance of honor...a lesson that is sorely needed. Honor fought in the octagon last night. I'll see it rewarded. When stories circulate of a newly-made knight with a blue steel blade, the young men will flock to our banner. With enough recruits, we'll no longer need brutes like Trask. And since the miners have finally struck a new vein of blue ore, Castlegard can afford it, despite the quartermaster's dreary ledgers." He paused, "Besides, I liked what I saw in the trials. Sir Blaine fights with his mind not just with his muscles. Reminds me of a younger you. That feint of fatigue was very well done. Give Blaine a blade of blue steel and we will see what he can do with it. Allow an old man to bet on a better future."

"Sire, I would never presume to bet against you." The knight marshal bowed and left to attend to the king's orders. He would have to do some serious thinking about where to post Trask's compatriots in order to neutralize the faction. That problem would take time to work out. On the other hand...a weapon of blue steel...he was looking forward to issuing the orders. If the decision were his to make, blue steel weapons would be exclusive to the best knights of the Octagon instead of being sold for gold to the highest bidders among Castlegard's allies. The problem with selling arms to allies was that you never knew when you were really selling to an enemy. He'd often had this argument with the king. It was the only argument the knight marshal always lost. As Castlegard's best source of income, the sale of the rare blue steel weapons would continue.

At least this time, one of the fabled blades would remain in Castlegard. He wondered how many weapons they'd get out of this latest vein. Castlegard's mine was rich in conventional iron ore, but the veins of blue were sporadic and short-lived. The marshal had been a young man, just a squire, the last time the miners had struck a blue vein. That thin seam yielded only enough ore for three weapons of blue steel. Three blades that were forever sharp and capable of cleaving armor...blades meant to be wielded by heroes. The marshal was not a superstitious man, but he couldn't help wondering if the reappearance of the blue ore was a sign from the gods, a sign that heroes were once again needed in the lands of Erdhe.

# 6

# Steffan

The dank gray sky pissed rain. Steffan hunched in the saddle, under his oilskin, but it was no use, he was soaked to the bone. He cursed the sky but kept the horse moving deeper into the woods. The crone's cave had to be nearby.

Sick of the rain and the endless forest, he forced the gelding to a faster pace. Wyeth was such a godforsaken land, nothing but old-growth forest and the occasional small village full of superstitious peasants. As the third son of a baron of Wyeth, the back woods should be familiar, but Steffan was merely passing through on his way to something better. He used his father's title with those who were ignorant, but it was a hollow joke. Steffan's family was so poor that his signet ring was made of tin and his lord father's was merely silver. He shook his head. Only *his* family would stoop to using signet rings of tin.

Disgusted with an empty title cloaked in poverty, he'd left his father's keep years ago to make his own fortune, shaking the dung from his boots as he walked out of the door. Relying on his dark good looks, his quick wit, and skills at dice, he'd traveled the southern kingdoms of Erdhe. He'd dallied with a rich widow in Coronth, run a con in Radagar, and diced with the wealthy of Lanverness. He'd done all right for himself, acquiring a taste for the finer things in life. Gold filled his saddlebags and he rode a good horse with solid bloodlines, but Steffan wanted more, much more. He'd heard rumors in the backrooms of alehouses about a quick way to power, a way to a better life. The rumors had cropped up often enough that he'd decided to take a chance tracking down the truth. The old crone, Helsbeth, was the next link in the chain of dark whispers.

The gelding plodded through the mud. The sky brightened and then dimmed again but the rain never let up. He was beginning to think that he'd drown in the saddle when he found the cave. A bear skull hung with beads and red feathers stood impaled on a pole, marking the entrance. Steffan reminded himself that the hedge witch had a reputation for potions laced with curses from the Dark side. He'd be sure to avoid anything she offered to drink or eat.

Tying the gelding to the pole, he ducked under the low entrance to the cave. A wall of smoke stung his eyes and he coughed on the harsh tang. As his eyes adjusted to the gloom, he glimpsed a figure huddled beneath blankets feeding herbs to a small fire.

"Saw you coming, we did, come in, come in."

Steffan let his sodden oilskin drop to the cave floor and walked forward to take a seat in front of the fire. Warmth from the fire was worth the bite of the strange blue smoke.

The snaggletoothed crone leaned forward, peering at him through the flames. The crusty blanket slipped back to reveal a shock of white hair and pale skin stretched thin across a hawk-nose and a pointed chin. The face was ancient but the eyes were filled with cunning. She studied him and laughed. "A young lordling no less, come to Helsbeth for something from the Dark side, but we wonder if he'll pay the price? We wonder if he even *knows* the price?" Her head bobbed like a chicken pecking at each word. "Tell Helsbeth what you came for, lordling, and together we'll find the price."

"I'm chasing dark whispers about a way to power, power that comes from the Dark Lord. I've been told you know the way."

The crone cackled. "The Dark Lord is it? The lordling reaches high."

Soaked from the long wet ride, Steffan had little patience for the crone's prattle. "Do you know the way or not, old woman?"

"Only a hedge witch am I, brushing crumbs of power from the hem of the Dark Lord's cloak, but I know what you seek. The dedicates, the ones with the gift." She leaned toward the fire. "Only a hedge witch, but we know more than you lordling, oh yes we do, for the bones tell me, they tell me true."

"I've coin in my purse, so stop babbling and name your price."

The crone rocked from side to side. "So the lordling learns quickly does he, for there is always a price, *always*, especially with the Dark Lord." She extracted a small soiled pouch from beneath her blankets, and from it spilled a collection of bleached bones onto the rough rock floor. Peering at the pattern, her nose almost touching the bones, she muttered, "The bones name the price, the bones name the price. Flames burn with Darkness, a raven flies to Coronth. Life and death intertwined, blurred into one. Aha!" The crone leered through the flames. "Something from the past, something from the present, and something from the future, the bones name the price for your questions. Three answers, three payments, so shall it be."

Steffan's head felt cloudy: it must have been the blue smoke. Reaching into his pocket, he removed a handful of gold coins. "I'll pay for information, not riddles. Speak plainly, old woman, and tell me what you know."

Bobbing like a chicken, the crone cackled, "The gold will pay for now, yes, yes. So we will tell you a secret, the Dark Lord is *real*. He is not like the other gods who only watch from above. The Dark Lord's dedicates can feel his touch, know his will. He gives those who serve him great gifts, power, beauty, and wealth...but the greatest gift of all is *eternal* life!"

The words sparked a flame within Steffan, confirming what his soul had always known. He whispered, *"One lifetime is not enough."*

The crone cackled, "Yes, now the lordling knows! Pay us for the now, pay us the price for the secret!"

Steffan tossed the handful of coins across the cave. The gold fell among the bones, coins clattering against stone. The crone plucked the gold from the floor, the coins disappearing into the folds of her blanket.

Eager to hear more, Steffan leaned forward. "Where do I find these dedicates?"

"First the rest of the price, lordling. You know in the dark of your heart that Helsbeth speaks the truth. Pay the price of the bones and we will tell you more. Pay us with the past and we will point you toward the future."

He shook his head to clear it of the smoke. "What do you mean, old woman, how can I pay you with the past?"

Her eyes glittered in the firelight and a bony finger pointed toward his right hand. "Give me the shiny ring, the token of your past and we will speak of the future."

He looked down at his tin signet ring and laughed. "You drive a shrewd bargain, old woman, but so be it." He wrestled the ring off his finger and tossed it to the crone, happy to be rid of it.

She caught it neatly and stared at it like a precious treasure.

"Tell me about the dedicates."

"Yes, yes, we hold the past, so we point to the future. The dedicates assemble in old forgotten places, places rich with ancient power where it is easy for the god to reach through. The oldest of these places is the Dark Oracle: you seek the Eye of the Dark Lord."

He'd heard rumors of a Dark Oracle, but he never heard enough to seek it out. "And where do I find this Dark Oracle?"

The old woman's cackle echoed around the small cave. "Knew it we did! The bones told us true! Told us you'd be hasty and ask the wrong question! But ask you did. And the Dark Lord wants you, oh yes he does, the bones tell me so. Pay the price, lordling, and we'll tell you what we know."

For a moment the crone's face seemed transformed into a death mask, red eyes peering at him from the gaping sockets of a skull. Steffan gasped, shaking his head to banish the illusion. It had to be the smoke. "You have my gold, you have my ring, so what is your price now, old woman?"

"The bones need to be fed. Magic feeds off life and death. A man's seed is ripe with life, full of the future. Pay the bones with your future. Let me milk your seed, spilling it out onto the bones, and we'll tell you what we know!"

His manhood shriveled beneath his codpiece. He had no intention of letting the old witch touch his rod. He'd end up shriveled for life! But he wanted the information. "I'll feed your bones, old woman, but first the information."

The old witch rocked back and forth humming a strange tune. "You seek to trick us, oh yes you do. Swear on your soul, lordling, swear on your very soul to feed the bones."

Steffan placed his right hand over his heart. "I swear on my soul to feed the bones."

The old witch cackled, "You're sworn, lordling, you're sworn. Seek the Oracle in the south of Radagar, in a wet, dank place. It's all we know, but we'll tell you one thing more, be prepared to give the Dark Lord his due!" The old woman cackled madly. "Three questions we answered; now pay the final price, lordling. Feed the bones! Feed the bones!"

Steffan rose to his feet, and stood there for a moment, swaying from the smoke. He took a moment to clear his head and then walked around the fire toward the crone. Her head bobbed in front of his crotch, a thread of drool dangling from the side of her mouth. Disgusted, Steffan reached down with his left hand to undo the laces of his codpiece. His right hand reached for the dirk tucked in the belt behind his back. The witch leaned forward, her gaze focused on his crotch. The hand with the dirk snaked out, burying six inches of steel in the crone's chest. "I'll feed the bones, old woman!"

He pulled the dirk free with a wet, sucking sound. Keeping his word, he held the witch over the bones, letting her blood spatter a red pattern across the ivory-colored bones. The old woman's hands scrabbled against her chest, trying to hold back the tide of blood.

Steffan whispered, "It won't be long now, old woman. Take a last look at your precious bones. Do you see your own death written among them?"

The crone wheezed, struggling to speak. "Asked the wrong question, lordling, yes you did. *You never asked the price!*"

A shiver ran through Steffan. He shook the witch, trying force more answers out of her, but the body was lifeless. The corpse slumped forward, covering the bones. He cleaned his dirk on her soiled blanket and picked up his oilskin on the way out.

The rain felt good against his face, clean and cold, clearing his head of the smoke. Shaking off his premonition of dread, he focused instead on what he'd learned. The prize was even greater than he'd ever imagined. Vaulting into the saddle, Steffan spurred the gelding toward the south. One lifetime was not enough!

# 7

# Blaine

Expectations of war filled the great castle. Rumors about the Painted Warrior rippled through the barracks, stirring fears and hopes, giving renewed purpose the knights. Sword strokes in the training yard held a new rhythm, a fierce beat revealing an undercurrent of urgency. Squires and knight-candidates honed their skills, hoping to be worthy. Sworn knights kept their blades sharp and their armor close at hand. Even the maimed veterans felt the thrill of war, retelling tales of daring to any who would listen, stories that roused the heart to honor and courage. Blaine drank it all in, eager for a chance at glory. As the son of a peasant farmer, he had more to prove than most. Blaine sought the marshal, asking for patrol duty, hoping to wet his sword against the enemy, but his request was denied. His left shoulder still hadn't healed and his fight with Trask had left his face a mass of purple bruises. Disappointed, he consoled himself with the ceremony to come. In another fortnight he'd swear his life to the Octagon, but before he took his vows, he must choose his First Weapon.

Legend said that the candidate's choice of First Weapon defined his knighthood. Blaine knew his choice should be based purely on his abilities, his strength, and his reach, but he longed to be worthy of his childhood heroes...and all of his heroes carried swords, two-handed great swords.

Castlegard's forge throbbed with heat and soot and the smell of hot metal, but the fall of hammers was strangely silent, replaced by a storm of whispers. Blaine found the masters, smiths, and apprentices gathered in the back, all clustered around a small wooden crate. He angled his way into the crowd, using his height to peer over the shoulders of two young apprentices. His breath caught in his throat. *"Blue ore."* The words whispered out of Blaine without thought, "Can I touch it?"

A collective gasp filled the forge, the others pulling away from Blaine as if he had the plague. Finding himself suddenly alone in an island of space, Blaine searched their faces trying to understand his offense. A rumble of laughter broke the tension. Otto, the master swordsmith, said, "He's too young to know better. Only a raw knight-candidate could ask such a question."

Blaine felt his face flush red. "I meant no offense."

Burly and bald with eyebrows that looked like thick slashes of soot, the master smith had a rumbling voice that matched his size. "Of course you didn't. But by the king's orders, no one but the master of the forge so much as touches blue ore." Ignoring the armed guard that stood at the side of the crate, the master reached down and removed a fist-sized lump of sapphire-blue ore, holding it aloft so that it winked in the firelight. "A king's ransom and a smith's dream forged together to make a knight's soul." Staring at Blaine with a penetrating gaze, the master said, "What form will your soul take, I wonder?"

Blaine could only stare, confused by the strange question.

"What's your name, candidate?"

"Blaine. The knight marshal ordered me here for my First Weapon."

"So you're the one!"

Blaine was sinking in a sea of confusion but no one seemed to notice.

The master settled the ore back in the crate and clapped his meaty hands, breaking the spell. "Back to work, people! We've weapons to forge and armor to repair and it won't get done if you stand around gawking."

Smiths and apprentices scurried back to hammers, bellows, and tongs. The throbbing heartbeat of the forge returned. The master turned to Blaine. "Come with me."

Blaine followed the master to a small courtyard behind the forge. A strange assortment of half-formed weapons adorned the four walls. All the leather-wrapped hilts were finished, but unworked bars of steel took the place of true blades. The master gestured to the implements. "This is where we measure successful knight-candidates for their First Weapon. We take pride in crafting a weapon designed to suit the reach, strength, and fighting style of each knight." The master gestured to a wall filled with implements shaped like battleaxes. "Two-handed battleaxes crafted for the wild style of berserkers, or maces for knights who bull their way through battles with pure brute strength. Then there is the morningstar, a rare combination of brute force and finesse...but I don't think any of these are right for you, are they?" He looked Blaine up and down. "The weapon is the very soul of the knight. Which will you choose?"

The words came of their own will. "A sword."

"The weapon of pride and honor. But what type of sword?"

"In the trial, I chose the great sword, but the weight was almost my undoing. The four-foot claymore has almost as much reach but also offers the flexibility of being wielded with a strong hand. So I thought to choose a claymore."

"Honor and flexibility, a difficult alloy." The master selected three implements, each with the hilt of a two-handed great sword. Handing the longest to Blaine, he said, "Swing this one."

"But I asked for a claymore."

A broad smile stretched across the master's face. "No, what you really asked for is a great sword you can wield with one hand."

"But that's not possible."

"It's entirely possible...if the great sword is made of blue steel!"

Blaine could barely believe his ears, yet his heart raced with excitement. Blue steel weapons were for heroes, not fresh-made knights.

The big smith clapped Blaine on the back hard enough to make his teeth rattle. "I like you, Sir Knight! Your face tells me that you're honest enough to know you haven't yet earned a hero's blade. I'll enjoy crafting this sword for you."

"For Valin's sake, how is this possible?"

The master grinned, "By order of the king, signed and sealed. But whatever the king's reasons, the blade is mine to craft and yours to wield. And now we have work to do. Show me your swing. The design of the blade must be worthy of the metal."

Blaine wrapped his hands around the hilt of the five-foot weapon and began executing the classical forms. Elated by the thought of the blue steel blade, he celebrated by plunging into the patterned dance of the sword, each swing of the blade dispatching an imaginary foe. In his mind, he cleaved a path through the Mordant's hordes, all the way to the very gates of the Dark Citadel. Tightening his grip on the hilt, Blaine danced the steel, imagining deeds worthy of the ancient heroes, deeds worthy of a blue steel blade.

# 8

# Katherine

**M**oonlight streamed through the narrow windows of colored glass, filling Valin's chapel with a sense of peace. Others might be surprised to find peace in the warrior god's chapel but Kath knew peace could exist only in the shadow of a strong sword and a stout shield. Bowing before the iron sculpture of a mailed fist thrusting a great sword up to the heavens, she paid homage to the warrior god, asking for his help in achieving her dreams. After lighting a candle at the altar, she retreated to an oak pew in the back of the chapel and curled into her hiding place beneath the bench.

A moment later the double doors flew open, admitting a maroon-cloaked honor guard.

Kath held her breath, thankful when their footsteps passed her by. Peering around the side of the pew, she watched as the guards escorted the three knight-candidates to the central altar of rough stone. In the flickering candlelight, they presented their arms to Valin, laying their First Weapons atop identical shields, their silver fields emblazoned with the maroon octagon. When men joined the Octagon, they left the heraldry of their past behind, but while the shields all bore the same emblem, the weapons were as different as the men. Kath knew each one. She'd practically lived in the forge over the last fortnight watching the smiths pound raw steel into gleaming blades. John's weapon suited his fighting style, a wicked double-headed battleaxe. Kirk's choice was a hand-and-a-half claymore. And then there was Blaine's blade, a hero's great sword forged of rare blue steel.

Bowing low, the candidates stepped back from their arms. Sir Clement, the-sergeant-of-arms, broke the silence. "By ancient tradition the candidates stand vigil with their arms on the eve before knighthood.

It's tradition but it is not mandatory. Will you stand vigil, or will you go, returning at sunrise for the oath taking?"

Kath reached into the pocket of her tunic to grasp her good luck charm. Holding it tight, she prayed to Valin for Blaine to remain.

John spoke first, his voice too loud for the small chapel. "I know a far better tradition of hosting the honor guard to ales at the Iron Tankard. Drinks are on us!"

The sergeant did not reply, but several of the guards clapped John on the back. "Kirk, what about you?"

"I'm with John."

The sergeant nodded. "It's your choice. And you Blaine?"

Blaine shook his head. "The king has honored me with a blue blade. I'll stay the night and stand vigil."

John hissed, "A night on your knees won't make you worthy of that blue blade, pig farmer."

The sergeant intervened. "You've each made your choice." He dismissed the guards and the other two candidates, and then turned to Blaine and saluted, fist against his chest. "May you find the strength of Valin in your vigil." Then he strode down the narrow aisle, the doors of the chapel closing behind him with a dull thud.

Kath watched as Blaine knelt in front of the altar. In the light of the votive candles, his silver surcoat shimmered like a drawn sword against the dull gray stones of the chapel.

Kneeling in the back, Kath kept her own vigil. She yearned for a chance to matter, worse than a tree yearns for sunlight, but being born a girl she was always overshadowed. Staring at the altar, she prayed for her boon to be answered, but if the gods heard, she could not tell. Cold from the stone floor seeped through her hose and into her knees. An owl returned from the night hunt to hoot in the rafters, its eerie call echoing through the chapel. The night seemed to last forever. Kath's gaze wandered to the statues crowding the stone archways, deities known as the Lords of Light, waiting for the prayers of men. All the gods were welcome in Castlegard, except for the Dark Lord of hell, or the strange Flame God of Coronth, but Kath's prayers were solely for Valin, the god of warriors, whose ways were as honest and as straightforward as a steel sword.

Unbidden, a tattooed face filled her mind. The Painted Warrior remained a riddle. After his death, the castle had stood at alert for more than a fortnight, but the threat of the Mordant's hordes never came. Most shrugged off the warning as the ravings of a man at death's door, but Kath took his message to heart, wondering at the meaning behind the words. Candles guttered, sending shadows dancing across the stone floor. Blaine remained erect in his vigil, but Kath's knees hurt. Sleep stalked her. She slumped down on the hard stone floor, resting her aching back against the oak pew, struggling to stay awake till dawn.

She dreamt of holding a sword aloft in victory, defeating the Mordant at the gates of the Dark Citadel, an army of Octagon knights at her back.

Her head banged against the pew and she woke with a start. She glanced up at the stain glass windows, relieved to find them dark. The moon had set but she hadn't missed the dawn.

Soft footsteps moved down the aisle. "Imp! What are you doing under there? It's almost dawn: you should be in bed!"

Startled to find Blaine staring at her, Kath stalled for time. "Have you named your sword yet?"

He looked at her as if she'd lost her mind. "You know the stories as well as I do. It takes time for the name of a blue sword to become known." Scowling, he added, "You shouldn't be here. Get back to bed before someone finds you gone."

The first rays of morning light struck the east windows, illuminating the stained glass with a brilliant blaze. A smile of triumph spread across her face. Turning her gaze back to Blaine, she said in a clear voice, "Sir Knight, on this thy day of knighthood, I would be the first to beg a boon of thee. By thy honor and thy sword, will thou grant my request?"

His mouth dropped open in shock. "You what?"

She flinched, wondering if she'd gotten it wrong. "I would be the first to beg a boon of thee, will thou grant me my request...those are the right words, aren't they?"

"No one *begs boons* anymore! Boons are something from out of childhood stories. Now be gone before you get us both into trouble."

Kath stood her ground. "The master healer said that the granting of boons on the day of knighthood was an ancient and noble tradition. I thought that a knight with a blue blade might be the type of man who would honor such a tradition. Where is your honor now, *Sir Knight*, or was your vigil just a sham?"

He glared for a moment but then he dropped to one knee. "My lady, I would hear your boon, but by *tradition*, your request must be something that is within my power to grant. What would you have of me?"

He was mocking her but Kath refused to be baited. "I want you to teach me to wield a sword."

"But you're a girl! Why do *you* want to wield a sword? Your lord father would have my head!"

Disgust warred with anger and words that were long buried came to the surface. "In this world, you are nobody unless you can wield a sword, and I will not be nobody! My life will count for something!" She took a deep breath. "I have watched you in the practice yard and even in the octagon. You are slender compared to most of the other knights. You fight with your mind as much as with the strength of your arm. I know that I will never have the strength of a knight, but if I learned your style of fighting I could hold my own. I *will* learn to wield a sword and I know you are the one to teach me. Will you grant my boon or will you dishonor yourself on your first day of knighthood?"

"You're only a girl. You don't have what it takes to wield a sword."

"So you won't grant my boon?"

"Swords are dangerous. We all have scars from the practice yard and worse from battle. For Valin's sake, just look at the knight marshal's ruined face and that gaping eye socket of his!"

"My mother died birthing me. I'll take my chances with the sword."

"You're impossible!"

She stared at him, waiting.

"Choose a different boon, something sensible."

Crossing her arms, she refused to retreat.

"It takes strength and reach to wield a sword. You don't have either and you never will."

"I'm only asking for a chance to learn."

Blaine strode to the altar. Grasping Kirk's claymore, he drew the sword, letting the empty sheath clatter to the floor. Naked steel glittered in the candlelight, a promise and a threat. "Come here."

Kath stared at the claymore and then back at him. When boys came to Castlegard for training, they were tested with a two-foot infantry sword...not a four-foot claymore. She considered the challenge, feeling the weight of Blaine's stare, knowing he wanted her to recant...but her dreams would not be denied. "I'll take the test but it won't change anything."

He handed her the sword, hilt first. "You can use two hands with the claymore. As always, the test is to sixty, the same as for the boys."

Standing barely a head taller than the weapon, Kath accepted the sword. Bracing her legs in a wide stance for strength, she lifted the claymore and extended her arms, holding the sword straight before her. Strain rippled through her arms, back, and chest, but she held it steady.

Once the blade was horizontal, Blaine began counting aloud, using the slow, rhythmic cadence of a weapons master.

Kath tried to ignore the count, focusing on the blade, trying to hold it steady. By the count of twenty, her arms ached; by thirty, the tip began to dip and waiver. Biting her lip, she steadied the sword. At forty-five, sweat dripped from her brow and her arms shook with fatigue, but the blade remained horizontal. At fifty-five, her back was bowed and her strength was gone, but she refused to give up. Tightening her grip on the sword, she made it to the full count, but even then she did not drop the blade. Fighting through the pain, she found the will to hold the sword until the count reached sixty-seven, at which point her arms gave out and the point of the claymore clanged to the stone floor. Quivering from exertion, she waited for Blaine's decision.

"There's more to you than meets the eye." A note of unwilling respect filled his voice as he took the sword, sheathing the claymore and replacing it atop Kirk's shield. When he turned back to her, his face was thoughtful. "Valin only knows what good it will do, or for that matter what trouble it will cause, but I'll grant your boon, on one condition. The lessons will be done in secret. If word gets out, your father will have our hides. Agreed?"

Kath nodded solemnly, then flashed him a radiant smile. "Thank you." Turning, she ran for the chapel doors.

Halfway down the aisle, she saw the brass handles turn and the double doors begin to open. She dove to the floor between two pews.

The stern voice of the sergeant-at-arms rang through the chapel. "The knight-candidates are called to the great hall to swear their lives to the king and the Octagon. Gather up your arms and follow me."

From her hiding place, Kath watched as John and Kirk strode to the altar to recover their weapons, looking bleary-eyed and disheveled. In the candlelight of the chapel, the son of a farmer looked more like a knight than either of them.

As the three knight-candidates filed out of the chapel, Kath thought of her boon, a chance to learn the sword. She hoped the Painted Warrior's shade would be satisfied. Perhaps the gods listened to prayers after all.

# 9

# Liandra

Beauty to beguile, spies to ensnare, and gold, always gold, to tempt, to trap, to control. Liandra, the Queen of Lanverness used weapons more subtle than swords to preserve her crown and kingdom. Erdhe was crowded with kings, but Liandra was the only sovereign queen on the board. Peace reigned in Erdhe and Lanverness was by far the wealthiest of the kingdoms, but the queen was not seduced by success. Ever vigilant, Liandra spread her web of spies to guard her throne.

Her shadowmen had just returned with a harvest of new secrets. Liandra sifted through their reports, searching for advantages. A vein of blue ore had been discovered in Castlegard, a threat in the wrong hands but a possible opportunity for Lanverness...and perhaps a chance to further unsettle the ambitious men of her court. Something to consider. A second source warned of the growing cult of the Flame God in Coronth, a threat on her northern border. Religions could be dangerous; she would have to keep a close eye on Coronth. But the message that most concerned her was the news that a Painted Warrior had been found, felled by arrows fletched with the Mordant's colors. Castlegard readied for war. Liandra hoped the Octagon Knights could hold the threat in check. Perhaps she could find a way to bolster the knights, not with men but with golds.

A timid knock interrupted her thoughts. "Come."

The door eased open. A tow-headed lad in the emerald livery of a royal page bowed low. "Majesty, your council awaits."

"The lords can wait." She gave the boy a gracious smile. "Waiting is good for noblemen. It reminds them that they serve."

The lad's blue eyes went round as an owl's. He retreated, shutting the door behind him.

The boy would learn, but sometimes she wondered about her loyal lords. Liandra knew what her lords thought of her. A prize to be wooed, a wealthy widow ripe for the plucking, but more than a few had discovered sharp thorns hidden among the roses. Her shrewder courtiers called her the Spider Queen behind her back, wary of her silken webs...but how else was a woman to rule? Sighing, she gathered up the coded dispatches and consigned them to the fire, watching till the scraps of parchment blackened to ash. Information was a form of wealth, and the queen never squandered a penny.

Arranging the pleats of her silken gown, her dagged sleeves nearly touching the floor, she left the haven of her solar and swept through the gilded halls of Castle Tandroth. A herald banged his iron-shod staff against the marble floor, announcing her arrival at the council chambers. "The Lords of Light save her majesty, the Queen of Lanverness!"

Petite in size yet great in presence, the raven-haired queen captured the attention of every man in the room. Ten powerful lords leapt from their seats and bowed low, eager to gain her royal favor. Liandra greeted each of them with a nod or a name as she took her seat at the head of the table. Even in the privacy of the council chambers, she made use of a raised dais bearing a carved wooden throne to remind her lords that she was above them.

She studied her royal council, a talented group of men drawn from across the kingdom. Liandra prized intellect over ambition, but all too often she had to settle for the grasping and the greedy. Men flocked to her court in droves, drawn by the opulence and power of the Rose Throne. Choosing the best among them, she used competition to harness their energies to the needs of the kingdom. Liandra made good use of her lords, but she never gave them her trust.

The lords gave their reports, covering everything from farm yields to taxes collected. No detail was too small. The queen grilled her counselors, dissecting each report. Satisfied, she focused her gaze on the Master Archivist, a tall scarecrow of a man draped in somber robes of black. He was the one man in the court the queen considered her intellectual equal, and as such, he served as her spymaster. "Lord Highgate, what news from your shadowmen?"

The other lords leaned forward, an eager flock of vultures. As rehearsed, the queen's spymaster played his part well. "Our sources tell us that Castlegard has struck another vein of blue ore. We await the formal announcement to start the bidding for blue steel weapons."

"That *is* good news." The queen fingered the strand of pearls at her neck. "Decades have passed since the last auction of blue steel weapons.

We will not let this opportunity pass us by. Lanverness must have its heroes. We order the royal treasury to purchase *three* blue steel blades."

The lord treasurer, a short, rotund man with retreating gray hair, let out a strangled gasp, "B-but your majesty, the price will be staggering! Surely *one* would be enough. After all, it is a time of peace!"

The queen studied her treasurer with narrowed eyes. "Blue steel weapons are held in awe by the people. They say that blue steel is the weapon of heroes. We, of course, do not succumb to this myth, but we see no harm if the people apply this legend to our royal sons."

"But..."

The queen lifted her bejeweled hand. "We consider it a small price to pay for the love of the people."

The treasurer wilted under her stare, bowing his head in capitulation. "Yes, majesty."

"Besides," continued the queen, "we cannot think of a better place to spend Lanverness gold than Castlegard. King Ursus and his Octagon Knights are the first and best defense against the forces of the Mordant. The purchase of these swords will be a long-term investment in the defense of Lanverness. Prepare a scroll for our royal signature. Bidding wars are never to the buyer's advantage."

Nods of assent rippled around the table, all except for Lord Turner. Tall and blond and strikingly handsome, Lord Turner's stare bordered on insolence. "Why *three* blue blades when you have but *two* sons?"

The queen hid a smile. Lord Turner was one of the overly ambitious ones, always making overtures that were carefully deflected. Free of the yoke of a wedding ring, Liandra intended to avoid a second entanglement, but by design she let her councilors hope. "A good question, Lord Turner. Two swords for our two royal sons and one for the queen's protector."

"And who better to wield the third blade than the commander of your royal guard?"

She gave him a coy smile. "Perhaps, Lord Turner, perhaps."

He smoldered under her gaze, and she let him stew. She turned toward a wiry lord with a flamboyant shock of red hair. "Lord sheriff, we have heard troublesome news about our neighbors to the north. It seems the kingdom of Coronth has fallen under the thrall of a new god. This rabid fever for the so-called "Flame God" has the potential to spill across our borders and infect our people. This cannot be allowed. We expect your office to be vigilant on this matter."

"Yes, your majesty," replied the lord sheriff. "May I ask if you want the army involved or just the constable force?"

Liandra liked to keep a deliberate tension between the army and the law-keeping sheriffs. "Just use the constable force. We prefer to keep this matter as low key as possible. History tells us that religions flourish when their adherents are persecuted. There will be no persecutions in Lanverness, merely an assisted exodus. Do you understand?"

"Perfectly, your majesty. Perhaps the Rose Court should send inquiries to the kingdoms of Radagar and Navarre since they also share borders with Coronth."

"An interesting suggestion." The queen turned to the Master Archivist. "Lord Highgate, we would have your opinion on this matter."

His answer came sharp as a dagger. "The kingdom of Radagar exports only treachery in the form of sellswords and poisons. Tension between the southern kingdoms is a business opportunity for Radagar. Better to let the jackals slumber in ignorance. But Navarre is a different matter. The seaside kingdom shares our passion for peace and prosperity."

The queen inclined her head toward her spymaster. "We will take the lord sheriff's advice and send a scroll to Navarre enquiring about their experience with this Flame God. Prepare a letter for our signature."

The master bowed, "As you wish."

"And now we have other duties to attend to." The queen rose and extended her hand. The lords scrambled to their feet, vying to be first to kiss the great emerald ring. One at a time, they took their leave, but Lord Turner lingered the longest. "I'll have that third sword."

Her only answer was a suggestive smile.

Sweeping out of the council chamber, she found a crowd of courtiers lurking in the hallway, waiting to pounce. They followed her through the castle hallways, providing a constant chatter of suggestions, petitions, and advice. She gave them smiles, seldom replying, listening instead for subtle nuances hidden beneath the chatter. Undeterred by her silence, her entourage kept pace, following her to the very doors of her private quarters, where a pair of guards with crossed spears kept them at bay.

Shorn of her courtiers, the queen swept into the small dining room, but even here she was not alone. Servants scurried about, lighting candles and making final adjustments to the crystal goblets and silver service that graced the central table. Tempting smells of oven-roasted river trout and fresh baked bread swirled through the chamber.

The queen took her place at the round table and with a wave gave permission for her sons to be admitted. Two strapping young men in the green and white livery of House Tandroth joined her at the table. Crown Prince Stewart was nineteen and Prince Danly seventeen. They both had dark hair and chiseled features reminiscent of their father's dashing good looks.

The queen settled into her chair, resigned to a conversation limited to sword tourneys, the latest stallion standing stud, and the most recent hunt. Quite proficient in these topics, she never let her sons suspect she was bored; instead she watched and listened, judging them as a queen rather than as a mother. They both had the impressive physique of their father, but unfortunately they also had his brains, or lack thereof. It was past time to select their brides. She would have to take a close look at the daughters of the other royal houses of Erdhe. Intelligence, beauty, cunning, and a gift for multiplying golds were the attributes needed for a daughter-in-law. Her lifetime of work must not be wasted. One of her sons would one day wear the king's crown, but it would be a queen of Liandra's choosing who would continue her rule.

# 10

# Sam

The ordeal started in the small hours of the morning. A fierce banging on his shop door pulled Sam Springwater from a dreamless sleep. Before he could untangle himself from his wife and the bed sheets, soldiers of the Flame were pounding up the stairs to his bedroom. Bursting through the door, they grabbed him by the arms and dragged him down the stairs. His scream echoed through the house. "*I'm innocent! Let me go!*"

The soldiers ignored his plea. Outside, they forced him into a set of wooden stocks mounted on the open bed of a wagon. Cold iron shackles snapped tight around his wrists and neck, bitter proof that the nightmare was real. Quaking with fear, he searched the soldiers' faces for a shred of mercy. Recognizing one pockmarked face, a seed of hope bloomed. "You're Sergeant Villars, aren't you? A friend of my son, Samson! You know I'm no heretic!"

The sergeant leaned close, garlic on his breath. "The Flames need a sinner and you've been chosen." A wicked light flickered in his eyes. "But I'll give you a choice, sinner, I'll take you or the old woman. You decide."

Sam felt the blood drain from his face. "Not my wife!"

The sergeant laughed and clicked the last lock closed. The soldiers unhitched the draft horses from the wagon and then marched off, leaving Sam chained to the stocks, screaming at the top of his lungs. He knew the waiting was a kind of torture, a lesson to his neighbors, but Sam could not keep silent. His dignity fled in the face of panic. Screams howled out of him, beating against the stone-faced houses.

None of his neighbors came to help. None of them even looked out their windows to see what was going on. They just slammed their wooden shutters closed to keep out his screams. His wife, pale-faced and shaking, peered out of their shop door. Seeing the soldiers gone, she pulled herself up onto the wagon and tried to free him. Her fingernails tore, clawing at the iron shackles till her hands dripped blood. Defeated by the heavy locks, she dropped to her knees, sobbing. Sam begged her to run and find their son, a sergeant in the city garrison. Surely his son could right this wrong. He watched as his wife ran toward the garrison, her white nightshirt flapping like a specter in the empty street. When she disappeared from sight, he slumped against his chains, left alone in a world gone mad. Everything was turned upside down, the innocent taking the place of the sinner, yet he prayed to all the gods that his son would return before the soldiers and set things right.

They came back for him at dawn, a dozen soldiers in the red livery of the Flame. They brought a team of horses and hitched them to the wagon. Two soldiers drove the wagon while the rest marched alongside. He begged them to tell him his crime. He asked if they knew his son, but the one thing he didn't ask was about the fate that awaited him. As a member of the temple he'd avoided the ritual "Test of Faith", but he'd heard enough about it from his neighbors. Sam paid his tithe and went to worship; there was no reason for him to be treated as a heretic. Struggling against the shackles, he yelled, but no one listened.

People emerged from their homes and shops. Lining the streets, they watched the procession pass. Some tossed rotten fruit. One leaned out of a second story window and emptied a chamber pot over his head. Others jeered at him, their faces contorted in hate. He knew most of them, either by face or by name. "I am Sam Springwater, the baker! You know my shop! I've been a loyal citizen of Coronth for more than sixty years! You've bought my bread! You know me. I'm your neighbor! You know I'm a humble servant of the Flame! This is wrong! Help me!"

His words fell on deaf ears. The mob celebrated, drunk with thoughts of the coming spectacle. Numb with shock, Sam lost his voice as the wagon lurched into the center of the city, into the great square just below the Temple of the Flame. Packed with screaming citizens come for the weekly spectacle, the noise was deafening. The wagon forged a path through the faithful, lurching to a halt next to the charcoal pit. Soldiers released him from the stocks. His legs gave out, as if his bones had turned to water. Soldiers grabbed his arms. Chaining his hands in front of him, they stood him on his feet.

Great drums of the temple began their rhythmic pounding. The crowd quieted in anticipation, hypnotically swaying to the rhythm.

Through tear-filled eyes, Sam scanned the crowd, desperate for a savior. The massive brass doors of the temple opened, disgorging a procession of red-robed priests. At the rear of the procession, the burly

Keeper of the Flame bore a great golden torch lit with holy fire, a beacon to the faithful.

The crowd screamed in adulation. The Keeper reached the heart of the square and lowered the torch to the pit. Flames whooshed to life, roaring to three times the height of a tall man. Fierce heat forced the crowd back, opening an island of space around the flaming pit. Sam flinched away, but the soldiers held him tight. One whispered in his ear, "It won't be long now, sinner." The drums stilled and the crowd turned to stare at the temple. A glittering figure emerged to stand on the temple steps. A hush swept through the crowd. Tall and stately, dressed in cloth of gold, the Pontifax descended the steps, making his way toward the sacred flames. His great ruby amulet flashed in the sunlight, a symbol of his holy office. Adoring followers reached out to touch the hem of his robe as he passed. Mothers held their children out hoping for a blessing. Moving with stately grace, the Pontifax made his way through the crowd. Mounting the raised dais above the flaming pit, he lifted his arms to the heavens, his voice filling the square. "My people! Hear me and know that the Flame God loves you. Walk his Fires and be freed of your sins!" The crowd roared, but the Pontifax stilled them with a single gesture. "A sinner stands before us." He pointed an accusing finger at Sam. "This brother has fallen from grace. He worships false idols. Even here, in the city of the Flame God, he maintains a carving to the winged one, Marut, on the lintel of the door to his shop. But the Flame God loves him and will give him a chance to redeem his sins. Shall we give him his chance?"

The crowd roared their reply. "Yes!"

Hearing the accusation, Sam tried to shout over the crowd. "But that old carving has been there since before I bought the shop! It has nothing to do with me! Let me go! I'll carve out the lintel myself. I'll donate all my earnings to the temple! Please let me go!" But the crowd roared, drowning his words.

The Pontifax held up a hand. "We will not ask something of our followers that we will not do ourselves. Therefore, I will take the Test of Faith. Let my sins be cleansed. Let me demonstrate my love for the Flame."

A hush fell over the crowd. Even Sam fell silent, enthralled by the promise of a miracle. The Pontifax knelt in prayer before the flaming pit while an acolyte reverently removed the sandals from his feet. Barefoot, he grasped his ruby amulet with both hands, and strode into the towering flames. Fire crackled around the Pontifax, fierce with heat, but the flames could not touch the holy man. Minutes seemed like an eternity. The crowd stared transfixed. Even Sam could not look away, caught up in the wonder, desperate to believe.

The bonfire snapped and crackled as the Pontifax strode through the flames. His face serene, the holy man emerged on the far side without even a smudge on his golden robe or a singe to his long gray hair. Women rushed forward, swooning at his feet. The crowd screamed with religious ecstasy, celebrating the miracle. Sam slumped in his chains, slick with sweat, overcome by a desperate mixture of hope and fear.

The Pontifax climbed the steps to the dais and gazed down at Sam, his face full of benevolence. "Now my brother, repent your sins. The faithful have no fear of the Sacred Flames. A true heart will pass through untouched. A false heart will be cleansed of sin, consumed by the Holy Fire. Now walk the Test of Faith!"

Quaking with fear, Sam appealed to the Pontifax, "Spare me! I'm innocent!" but the soldiers drove him forward, their swords poking into his back. Heat beat against him. He teetered on the edge of the pit, flames singing his hair. Sam clawed at the iron shackles and tried to back away but the swords were relentless. Desperate, Sam searched for the courage to believe. The Pontifax had proven the miracle of the Flames; perhaps if Sam believed he could survive the fire. He stared into the Holy Fire, seeking salvation, seeking the face of god, but all he saw were the roaring flames of hell. Surely this was the work of the Dark Lord, not a benevolent, loving god. A sword jabbed in him in the back, thrusting Sam into the flames. Understanding came too late. He screamed as Darkness reached for him in the form of fire.

#

Oily black smoke belched to the heavens, another sinner taken by the Flame God. The Pontifax leaned toward the Keeper of the Flame and asked, "Who was that peasant anyway?"

"Just a baker. A citizen who paid his tithes but tried to ignore our temple rallies. His death should put the fear of god in those who avoid the Test of Faith. Beside, his business wasn't all that good so the temple won't miss the tithe."

The Pontifax nodded. "Excellent. Thorough as always." They walked back toward the temple in companionable silence. Watching the crowd, the Pontifax added, "Have the acolytes invite some of the prostrating women from the ceremony to the Residence tonight. There are other ways they can worship."

Smiling, the Keeper replied, "It shall be done."

The Pontifax clapped his brother priest on the back. "And we'll need a fresh sinner for next week's ceremony."

"Don't worry, Enlightened One, there are plenty of sinners in Coronth, plenty of fodder for the Flames."

# 11

# Blaine

Blaine forced the battleaxe away from his face and retreated two steps trying to catch his breath. His armor baked him like an oven-roasted partridge. Sweat dripped into his eyes and his ragged breathing echoed in the confines of his helmet. Seven sparring rounds in one afternoon and still they taunted him. Caged by his own pride, Blaine refused to give up. Lifting the heavy training sword, he settled into a fighting stance, wondering how many more days of sparring he'd have to endure. He'd asked to be assigned to patrol the steppes but so far his requests were all denied.

A mace swung towards his face. Ignoring his screaming muscles, Blaine raised his sword for the parry. Steel clanged against steel. The ferocity of the blow staggered him. The second blow dented the crown of his helmet and sent him sprawling.

From the sidelines, someone sneered, "That's it, pig farmer, wallow in the dirt. You're not worthy of a maroon cloak, let alone a blue blade."

The jeer cut Blaine to the core. Struggling to his knees, he levered himself upright. Swaying, he lifted the blade. "Who's next?"

Ringing laughter met his challenge. "You're not worthy, pig farmer. Try us tomorrow, or better yet, give up the cloak and save yourself the beating."

Blaine tightened his grip on the sword, trying to ignore their barbs. He'd learned the hard way that it was better not to respond.

The knights hurled a final insult and headed toward the armory. Blaine dropped his guard. He'd survived another day. Prying the dented helmet off, he wiped the grime from his face. His brother knights made him pay a steep price for his sword. He never thought owning a blue steel weapon would be so painful.

Blaine felt a hard stare crawl up his back. Pivoting, he looked for a new threat, but only found the knight marshal watching from the edge of the yard. He speared Blaine with his one-eyed gaze and then nodded before walking off.

The marshal often watched the afternoon sparring rounds, but he never said anything and he never interfered. Abandoned by both the marshal and the king, Blaine resented their silence. Why give him a blade of blue steel and then leave him to molder in the sparring yards? He would never earn the respect of his fellow knights while safe in Castlegard, but the choice was not his, forced to wait for the orders that would let him earn the sword. In the meantime, he'd do his best to win the battle of the sparring yard, although some days just staying on his feet seemed a challenge.

Tired and sore, he limped to the benches to retrieve his blue sword. The great blade was too deadly for practice, yet it was never far from his hand. He slung the harness across his back so that the sapphire-blue hilt projected over his right shoulder. Whole again, he walked toward the armory at the far end of the yard.

Blaine trudged through the double doors, into a cavernous room lined with weapons, shields, and helms. The other knights made a point of turning their backs. The young squire, Devlan, was the only one to acknowledge him. The boy gave him a shy smile, scrambling to help.

"Hello Dev, the armor is a bit mangled and dented again, not to mention the state of the body inside. You'll have to give me a hand getting it off."

The squire reverently set Blaine's blue blade on a bench before helping with his armor. Afflicted with a bad case of hero worship, the boy hardly ever spoke a word, but he never failed to leap to Blaine's assistance.

Freed of the dented armor, Blaine selected a half-helm from some shelves and then headed for the stables. He was tired but he had a promise to keep. He'd been skeptical about training the Imp. When they'd first started, some six full moons ago, he'd argued that the girl should take up a distance weapon, distance being her best defense, but the girl stood her ground, insisting on the sword. So they compromised and did both. He'd teach the girl the sword, but she'd also learn to wield throwing axes, an obscure weapon that could fell a knight in plate armor at a distance of twenty feet. Used by peasants, throwing axes were spurned by knights, so Blaine approached Otto, the master swordsmith and delicately raised the possibility of having an apprentice forge a pair of axes. A fortnight later, the master smith produced a pair of perfectly balanced throwing axes made to just the right scale for the Imp. Both weapons bore the maker's mark of an anvil in an octagon, the mark of the master smith. But the most surprising aspect was their handles. Carved into the image of a hawk with folded wings, the handles bore the ancient heraldic symbol of Castlegard; the blazon the Kings of Castlegard gave up when they swore allegiance to the Octagon. Seeing the carved handles, Blaine had gasped. Either he'd drunk too much ale in town that night or the master smith was a very shrewd man. When Blaine tried to thank the master, the big smith forestalled him saying, "She has the heart of an untamed hawk and I am honored to forge weapons worthy of her."

Humbled by the master's generosity and insights, Blaine asked the smith to hold the weapons until the Imp could claim them for herself. Blaine would never forget the way the Imp's face lit up when the master presented her with her First Weapons. From her reaction, Blaine would have sworn that someone had just given her the world. Both men were astonished when the girl stood on tiptoes to give the big smith a kiss on his rough cheek. Embarrassed, Blaine had turned away. In the heat of the forge it was obvious that the master smith's heart had melted.

They spent a part of every day practicing in an abandoned cellar. The Imp drew a chalk outline of Blaine on the door for a target, dubbing the outline 'the Empty Knight'. The girl took to the lessons like a duck to water, proving an apt pupil with the axes as well as a with a short sword, almost as if she was graced by the touch of Valin. After six turns of the moon, the Imp grew proficient with her throwing axes, but to reach the next level of swordsmanship she needed to train on open ground instead of the smooth mage-stone floors of the castle. Balance was the key to swordsmanship and the Imp needed uneven ground to understand the true importance of the lesson.

Blaine held his horse to a canter, the spare helm tucked in his saddlebag. He found the Imp waiting in the small clearing in the heart of the old oak forest, sunlight streaming through the autumn trees. Dressed, as usual, in a rumpled gray squire's tunic, she stood beneath the lattice of branches, a wooden training sword in her hand. It must have been a trick of the afternoon light but for a moment the sword looked as if it belonged there.

Shaking his head to clear the illusion, Blaine secured his horse in the dappled shade of a massive live oak and hung the harness with his great blue sword from a gnarled branch. Tossing the Imp the half-helm he'd borrowed from the armory, he hefted a wooden training sword. "Come on, Imp, show me what you can do with that blade."

She tucked her tangled blond hair up under the helm and then advanced across the clearing, sword at the ready. Flashing him a disarming smile, she sprang forward with a low lunge aimed at his belly.

The wooden swords met with a clatter. "Good try, Imp, but you'll have to do better than that."

Her second thrust snaked toward him, twice as quick as the first. Blaine parried and they settled into a dance of swords, their steps matching the rhythmic clacking of wooden blades as they fought beneath the trees. He let the Imp set the tempo, content to observe his pupil. She tried every trick he'd shown her and one or two he hadn't. There was no doubt she had spirit as well as skill, but then again they were only using wooden swords.

She pressed the attack and Blaine retreated, leading her deeper into the forest, choosing a direction strewn with a jumble of exposed roots. Quick to see the new twist, the Imp did a good job of keeping her sword up while maintaining her balance. Impressed, Blaine went on the attack, forcing her toward a tumble of boulders.

Intent on their swordplay, he didn't hear the drumming of hoof-beats until the two knights cantered into the clearing. Too late to hide, he hissed, "Pull your helm lower. Keep your eyes down, and your mouth shut. With Valin's luck you'll pass as a squire."

From the edge of the clearing the first knight bellowed, "What's going on here? Sword practice for squires is forbidden outside of the sparring yard!"

Blaine grimaced, recognizing the knights. Mounted on chargers, their maroon capes streaming behind them, the knights projected the perfect image of nobility...but he knew better. These two were nothing but trouble. Edging away from the Imp, he yelled, "What are you two doing here? Have you abandoned your post in the mountains, or been kicked out in disgrace?"

The knights rode straight for Blaine, stopping a sword's length in front of him. Sir Lewis's chestnut stallion pawed the earth, throwing up clods of dirt. Respectful of the warhorse, Blaine edged backward.

Leering down, Sir Lewis sneered, "Well if it isn't the good Sir Blaine." Staring pointedly at the wooden training sword in Blaine's hand, the knight added, "I see you finally found a sword worthy of your deeds."

The second knight, Sir Raymond, urged his horse forward, crowding Blaine back toward the trees. "If it's extra practice you want, pig farmer, we'll give it to you, although from what we've heard, you're getting more than enough bruises in the sparring yard." Both knights laughed, an ugly sound. Sir Raymond dismounted. Sir Lewis joined him, sword in hand.

Blaine scrambled backward. He'd succeeded in distracting them, but naked steel was more than he'd bargained for. He threw a shout to the girl. "Ride for the castle, *squire!*"

Sir Lewis advanced. "That's right, boy, ride away and leave the pig farmer to his betters."

Unsheathing their swords, the two knights closed on Blaine, chainmail and light helms against his leather jerkin and a wooden practice sword. Blaine backed away, shocked by the threat. "Knights don't draw steel on an unarmed man. Especially not a sworn brother!"

Sir Lewis barked a twisted laugh. "You're such a naïve bastard, pig farmer. A peasant's son has no right to wear the maroon."

A vicious sword cut swept toward Blaine's head. Ducking the blow at the last instant, he dodged behind an oak tree. The two knights split, coming at him from opposite sides. "Come on *Sir* Blaine, show us what you can do with that great wooden sword of yours."

Blaine backed away, forced to retreat in the opposite direction of his blue sword. Sir Raymond aimed a wicked slash at Blaine's knees. Dodging the saber, Blaine found himself facing Sir Lewis's blade. He heard the whisper of steel as it sped towards his face. Without thinking, he parried the second saber with the wooden training sword. The wooden blade shattered on impact but the parry deflected the steel.

The two knights stalked him, two cats chasing a defenseless mouse. Angry and frustrated, Blaine backed away, deflecting their swords with nothing but a wooden hilt.

Behind him he heard a horse approaching at a gallop. Blaine prayed to Valin that it wasn't another of Sir Lewis's cronies.

Sir Raymond's saber paused in mid-stroke. He stared over Blaine's shoulder, his eyes growing wide in disbelief, his voice a harsh hiss. "What the devil is *she* doing here?"

Blaine dared a backwards glance, shocked at the sight. The Imp flew toward him at a reckless gallop, brandishing his sheathed sword aloft, her blond hair streaming behind like a battle banner. Drawing near, she yelled, "Catch!" and hurled the great sword toward him as she sped past.

Catching the sword, Blaine unsheathed the blue blade and whirled to face the two base knights. Justice lent fury to his sword. In three strides he was on them, his sword descending in a great blue arc. A saber met the great sword in a mighty clang, but the blue blade never slowed. Cleaving the saber in half, it struck Sir Lewis in the shoulder; slicing clean through chainmail as if it was leather, laying him open to the bone. Screaming in agony, the wounded knight crumpled to the ground.

Shocked by the power of blue steel, Blaine wrenched his blade free with a fountain of blood, and turned to face the second knight. "Would you like a taste of blue steel?"

Whey-faced, Sir Raymond backed away.

Mollified, Blaine lowered his sword. "Take this screaming disgrace of a knight back to the castle with you. Neither of you are worthy to wear the maroon."

Blaine strode past the two cravens. Vaulting into the saddle, he urged his horse to a gallop, intent on catching the Imp. He exited the forest in time to see the girl reach the safety of the castle gates. Blaine slowed his mount to a walk, needing time to recover. The power of blue steel awed him; he hadn't meant to deal such a terrible wound to a brother knight. Doubt gnawed at him, shocked to be attacked by two knights of the Octagon. Wiping the blood from his sword, his hands shook as he sheathed his blade. His first battle with his blue steel sword and he'd drawn blood from a fellow knight. He shivered at the ill-omen. And then there was the Imp. The girl had sacrificed her secret to bring him his sword. Dazed from the battle, Blaine let his horse meander back to the castle. He caught up to the Imp at the stables. She stood at the entrance, concern writ across her face. Before she could speak, he motioned her to silence and handed his horse over to the care of a squire.

Mired in worry, they walked from the stable to the inner yard of the castle. Questions boiled across the Imp's face but she had the discipline to hold her tongue.

When they reached the Knights' Tower, he turned and stared at her, his voice solemn. "Thank you for my sword, my Lady." Watching the blush spread across her face, he knew she understood. He lowered his voice to a whisper. "Raymond recognized you."

A touch of fear filled her eyes, followed by a grim acceptance of the truth. "It's not fair."

He couldn't agree more. "Sir Lewis was badly injured in the fight. I don't know how those two cravens will report the incident, but I suggest you hide your axes in a safe place, a place you can always reach, no matter how your father reacts."

Her eyes widened. She clenched her fists, as if readying for a storm, but her voice was formal. "Thank you, Sir Blaine, for honorably fulfilling my boon. I could not have wished for a better weapons teacher. I will always be in your debt." She bowed and then left him standing in the courtyard.

Watching her walk away, Blaine thought that the master swordsmith had the truth of it, she truly was an untamed hawk...pity she'd been born a girl.

# 12

# Duncan

Duncan raised his longbow. Planting his feet wide, he summoned the strength of his entire body. Pulling from his legs through his chest and into his arms, he curved the massive bow, savoring its savage power as he fixed his will upon the distant target. At the herald's signal, he released. A black-fletched arrow thrummed skyward. Without thought, he reached for another. Draw and loose, he fell into a deadly rhythm, his world narrowing to the straining power of the bent yew and the swift release of his will-threaded arrows. A horn sounded just as his last arrow struck the target's heart. The crowd roared its approval of their one-eyed champion. Duncan lowered his bow and the world intruded. He was surprised to discover that he'd loosed twenty-six arrows in the allotted minute, all but one finding its mark. Scanning the other targets, only one other contestant, the yeoman from Wyeth, had equaled his feat. Duncan nodded to him, acknowledging his skill, and then waved to the crowd for their support. Unstringing his longbow, he wiped the yew down while waiting for the judges' decision. From his view of the targets it would be a tough call, but he hoped to claim the golden arrow for Navarre.

Ten judges huddled around the targets.

A fresh sea breeze blew across the tournament field. The banner of Navarre, a white osprey eagle soaring on a field of red and blue checks, snapped overhead. Duncan leaned on his bow, savoring the sights. The sun-drenched greensward was a riot of colors and sounds. Spectators filled the benches along the seaward side, while bright silk pavilions for the royals and the competitors ran along the city side. The view from the tourney ground was magnificent. The sparkling white limestone walls of the capital city rose to the east, while Castle Seamount, perched on a rocky outcrop surrounded by a turquoise ocean, lay to the west. It was a beautiful setting for his last tournament.

A horn sounded and the herald stepped up to the raised dais, his voice sweeping across the field. "There is a tie of twenty-five arrows for both Duncan Treloch of Navarre and Jon Tanner of Wyeth." The crowd roared its approval, but the herald raised his hand for silence. "Based on the points scored for accuracy, with a total count of one hundred and fifty-two, a new record in the history of the Royal Tournament, the winner of the longbow competition is Jon Tanner of Wyeth!"

A thin cheer rose from the crowd; those spectators wearing the red and blue of Navarre far outnumbered the visitors from Wyeth.

Duncan bowed, hiding his disappointment, and went to congratulate the winner. "I shot my best yet was bested. A well-deserved victory, Jon." The two men clasped hands with the mutual respect of friends who were also fierce competitors. In a rueful voice, Duncan added, "A shame as this may be my last chance to compete for a while."

The yeoman gave him a wry smile. "It's past time I won, you mangy scoundrel. If memory serves, you've beaten me the last four times, so you've no reason to complain." Untying the leather brace from his left forearm, he added, "And what do you mean you won't be competing? Don't let *my* victory scare you away from the tournament grounds."

Duncan flagged down a boy struggling to carry several large flagons of ale for the tournament feast. Lightening the boy's load by one, he motioned Jon toward a bench. "I've stayed in one place too long, almost long enough to set down roots. It's time I took to the road."

Jon gave him a questioning look. "So where are you bound?"

"This tournament honors the eighteenth naming day of the Royal Js. It's a long-standing tradition for the royal heirs of Navarre to begin their Wayfaring shortly after they turn eighteen. I've pledged to be a companion for this Wayfaring." Duncan took a long pull from the flagon, enjoying the woody flavor of the summer ale.

"What's a Wayfaring and why should it stop you from competing?"

Duncan handed him the flagon. "The Royal Js are septuplets, each with an equal chance to gain the throne of Navarre. To prepare for the throne, the heirs embark on a Wayfaring, striving to become excellent at a skill, or a trade, so they can bring this knowledge back to Navarre and better serve the kingdom. Each of the Royal Js must petition the king and council with proposals for their Wayfaring. Once a proposal is accepted, the council works to set up fosterings or apprenticeships within the other kingdoms of Erdhe. A companion accompanies each heir for the first year of the Wayfaring. I've offered to serve as a companion." Duncan reclaimed the ale. "So I predict a lot more prize golds in your purse, my friend."

"You Navarrens are a strange people." Jon shook his head, disbelief on his face. "No other kingdom would willingly scatter their heirs across all of Erdhe. So where will this mad goose-chase take you?"

"Juliana loves the sea and will prentice with the merchant fleet. The sea and I do not mix so that is not for me. James will go to Tubor to study wine-making. I could have been a great help with the wine tasting, but unfortunately he already has a companion. The little beauty, Jemma, will go to Lanverness to study commerce at the queen's court, but I cannot think of anything duller than counting coppers. Jayson, the scrollish one, will go to the Delta to study some strange new waterwheel. So that leaves Justin, Jordan, and Jared." Pausing for a sip of ale, he continued, "Justin will train to be a bard and will start under Master Haldor in Wyeth. Jared will go to Castlegard to train with the knights of the Octagon. Jordan wanted Castlegard as well, but the maroon knights would never train a woman, so Jordan will go to the Kiralynn monks to study the art of war. King Ivor has asked me to watch over Jordan, so I'm off to the Southern Mountains for a year or two."

"I thought the monks were a myth?"

"Apparently not."

"So you're banished to the ends of Erdhe to serve as wet nurse to a girl?"

Duncan scowled. "You men of Wyeth are too bloody narrow-minded when it comes to your women."

"Speaking of women," the archer leaned close, a gleam in his eye. "I've noticed how the lovelies fall for that rogue image you feign with your black leathers and pirate eye patch." His voice dropped to a whisper. "I'm sure you have more than your fair share of beauties tucked away in Seaside. Why not introduce me to a few?"

Disliking the leer on the archer's face, Duncan avoided the question by hailing a servant carrying a platter piled high with roasted quail. Leaving the archer with a full plate and a fresh flagon, Duncan went in search of better company. While the two men had talked, the tourney feast had been laid out around them. Savory smells of roast boar and fresh-baked apples tantalized the senses. Brightly clad jugglers roamed the grounds, a gaggle of laughing children trailing in their wake. At the heart of the field, the royals sat upon a raised dais, where King Ivor, Queen Megan, and their family were already being served. Duncan wove a path through the crowded trestle tables. Serving girls and silk-clad noblewomen flashed suggestive smiles his way. Some brushed close, rubbing their silks against his black leathers like cats claiming a prize. Duncan greeted most of them by name, offering a wink and a smile, but he made no promises. Friends hailed him and he took a seat at their table just below the royal dais. Accepting a trencher of roast venison and grilled onions, he settled down to enjoy the feast.

The sun set in a blaze of gold. Charcoal braziers scattered throughout the tournament grounds flared to life, adding light, heat, and charm to the evening's festivities. Trumpets blared and a herald claimed the center of the royal dais, his voice booming across the field. "My lords and my ladies, we end this sumptuous feast by announcing the winners of the tournament. The silver arrow, awarded to the winner of the fifteen to twenty year olds, is bestowed upon Prince Jared of Navarre!"

The crowd stood, roaring its approval. Prince Jared rose from the bench at the royals' table and approached the king. Duncan noted the look of pride on the king's face as he embraced his dark-haired son and handed him the silver arrow. The prince acknowledged the crowd, holding his prize aloft. Duncan raised a tankard in salute; at least the silver arrow would remain in Navarre if not the golden.

A flaming arrow arched across the darkening sky.

Duncan shot up from his bench to shout a warning. "*Look out!*"

Prince Jared shoved the king to the left and dove to the right. The arrow thunked into the wooden dais between them. More arrows arched across the twilight sky, blazing a trail of fire. Screams split the air, the crowd overturning benches, frantic to flee the field.

Duncan's first instinct was to rush for the attacker, but the rioting crowd blocked his path. Grabbing his longbow and quiver, he vaulted onto the dais and then onto the tabletop. Hoping no one noticed, he lifted the black leather patch from his left eye and scanned the edge of the crowd. The grounds roiled with confusion, people pushing in all directions, cries and screams cutting the night. Another arrow scored the sky and Duncan traced the line of fire to the far side of the field. The enemy archer stood alone, his bow already bent for the next strike. Stringing his longbow, Duncan took aim with his left eye, loosing three black-fletched arrows in quick succession.

The assault of flaming arrows stopped.

Duncan flipped the black patch over his eye and jumped from the table to help the royals. Guards swarmed around three wounded figures. Commander Isador, the king's brother, bellowed orders. Clusters of people helped the victims while others fought to put out the fires. The royal guard encircled the dais, facing outward with swords drawn.

Duncan forced his way through the press of people. Seeing him, Commander Isador snapped, "Did you get the attackers?"

"A single archer from the edge of the field. I managed to put an arrow or two in him. The guards should have him by now. Is the king all right?"

"He's taken an arrow in the chest. We need to get him to Master Simmons. A young page took an arrow while protecting the king. The lad is dead, a hero's death. A third arrow grazed Prince Jared's arm, but the wound isn't serious. I want you to take responsibility for the king while I deal with the attacker."

Duncan said, "I suggest you send heralds through the city with word we've taken the assassin. Panic could spread if the people think the city is under attack."

Isador nodded and turned to call for a herald.

An empty wagon, driven by Princess Jordan, thundered up to the dais and the guards scrambled to get out of the way. Duncan joined the knot of people gently lifting the king onto the wagon bed. Once the king was secure, Duncan settled the queen and the wounded prince in the back and ordered the guards to follow. Climbing onto the front seat, he took the reins and lashed the horses to a gallop. He hoped the rogue archer survived to answer for his crimes. Whatever the reason for the ambush, the attack proved the peace of Erdhe was more fragile than anyone suspected.

# 13

# Katherine

Kath ran through the passageways of the inner castle, desperately searching for a weapon. Glancing back, she struggled to keep a small lead on the attackers. Wearing the black and gold of the Mordant and wielding massive war clubs studded with steel spikes, the misshapen attackers looked more like ogres than men. Kath didn't know how the castle's defenses had been breached, but she was certain if the attackers caught her, she'd be killed.

She kept running, her footsteps beating a desperate rhythm through the empty passageways. All the hallways were made of mage-stone, the same as the inner parts of Castlegard, yet nothing looked familiar. Confused and lost, Kath chose a door at random and burst into a small windowless chamber. It was a dead end, a trap. Kath scrambled back out onto the landing just as the ogres crashed into the room below. Out of choices, she retreated into the chamber and shut the door, thankful that it had a sturdy bolt. Praying to all the Lords of Light that the enemy would pass her by, she pressed her ear to the door and strained to hear over the thundering of her heart. Heavy footsteps pounded up the stairs, sealing the trap.

Kath backed against the far wall, her gaze locked on the door.

War clubs thundered against the oak door, a drumbeat of death. The door gave way, splintering into a thousand shards. The first hairy monster lumbered into the room, his war club raised to strike. Kath stood frozen, staring up at certain death. But as the club began its descent, she suddenly found herself falling back *through* the stone wall!

Gasping for breath, Kath sat up, surprised to find herself safe in her own bed. "Not again." Drenched in sweat, she shivered beneath her blankets. She'd had this same nightmare five times in the last fortnight.

Kath wondered if her dreams had anything to do with the Painted Warrior. She couldn't help remembering the bloody handprint he'd left on the front of her tunic, as if she'd been marked for death. Perhaps the dreams were some kind of omen or a harbinger of doom. She shuddered at the thought of Castlegard falling to the Mordant. If her dreams were portents of the future, then she needed to find a way to change the outcome. But to protect Castlegard she'd have to tell someone, someone who would take her warnings to heart. Her father was not the sort of man to pay heed to the nightmares of a girl. Besides, after today's incident in the woods, Kath didn't want to see the king. Neither Sir Lewis nor Sir Raymond had returned to the castle. She'd hung around the great yard listening to rumors and watching the outer gate, but there was no sign of the knights and no mention of a fight in the woods. Evening fell and she worried her way through dinner, waiting for an angry summons, but none came. Kath couldn't guess what tale the two rogue knights would weave, but she could easily imagine her father's wrath. Her worst fear was to be forced into a marriage with some faceless noble to form an alliance. She shook her head, banishing the thought. Her personal problems were nothing compared to her nightmares; she couldn't let Castlegard fall. She needed to confide in someone who would take her seriously. The master healer was the most learned person Kath knew, and he had a reputation for reading dreams and portents. In the morning she would try to get him alone. She just hoped he would take her seriously.

Having made the decision, she burrowed back under the covers, but something hard jabbed her ribs. Fishing through the bedding, she found her good luck charm, a small mage-stone gargoyle, just large enough to fit in the palm of her hand. It must have fallen from her bedside table, but instead of putting it back she clutched it tight, needing a talisman against her dreams. *"Castlegard must not fall."*

# 14

# Steffan

A trail of dark rumors drew him south. Steffan followed the whispers across the kingdoms of Erdhe, collecting clues to the location of the Dark Lord's Oracle. His quest took him to alchemists, fortunetellers, hedge witches, priests, and bards, anyone likely to have such arcane information. He paid for the information with gold, with flagons of wine, and with sexual favors. Sometimes he paid for the information with blood...always their blood. Steffan found a way to meet every price.

At last he knew enough to seek out the Oracle in the black heart of the great southern swamps of Radagar. Beneath a waning moon, he rode a black gelding down a dirt road that was barely more than a goat track. The swamp was thick with the smell of death and decay, the air thrummed with life that thrived on both. Pulling his wool cloak tight around his neck, Steffan tried to hide from the biters and the bloodsuckers, but it was no use. The creatures of the swamp found a way to extract their blood-price from man and beast. The gelding shied, annoyed by the bites. Steffan kept the reins taut, holding his mount to a slow trot, not wanting to miss the tree. When he finally found it, he realized the massive oak couldn't be missed. The hangman's tree stood alone on an earthen mound lapped by the dark waters of the swamp. One rotten corpse and several empty ropes dangled from the claw-like limbs. The stench of the dead blended with the fetid air of the swamp.

Steffan tied the gelding to the nearby hitching post and took from his saddlebags a greasy chicken wrapped in cloth, a flagon of cheap wine, a hooded lantern, and a flint. Climbing the small hill, he sat with his back to the tree facing out over the swamp. Lighting the lantern, he arranged the hood so that the light shone away from the tree and across the swamp and then he sat back to eat his dinner, wondering if anyone would answer the summons. He gnawed on a chicken leg, tossing the bone out into the swamp. A sudden thrashing of the waters sent waves rippling to the base of the tree. He kept the rest of the bones by his side.

The moon was halfway across the midnight sky when Steffan spied a flat-bottomed skiff gliding through the swirling mists. Poled by a man in dark robes, it drew close to shore, touching solid ground with a wet sucking sound. Leaving his lantern, Steffan stepped aboard, holding out a single gold piece for the fee. The ferryman's face was hidden in the deep folds of a hooded robe. He took the gold and pointed to the rear of the skiff, silent as death. Steffan lurched toward the seat as the ferryman poled back out into the murky waters.

"Tell me about the Oracle." The swamp swallowed his question, the sound of water rippling along the side of the skiff his only reply. Steffan wasn't surprised. He'd found the Dark Lord's servants to be secretive. It was even possible that the man no longer had a tongue.

Steffan settled back on the seat, peering into the night. His eyes adjusted to the darkness of the swamp only to find faint points of light winking from the marsh grass. The lights seemed to follow the skiff, as if they were strange glowing eyes watching from the dark. Moving deeper into the swamp, the night sounds became muted and then strangely silent, as if the creatures of the swamp feared to disturb the Dark Lord's domain. The skiff glided through a labyrinth of drowned trees. Twisted branches twined overhead, cloaked in long shrouds of ghostly moss. Steffan hunched beneath his cloak to avoid the living lace.

A dark figure holding a burning staff appeared before them, seeming to walk on the very waters of the swamp. The ferryman steered toward the apparition. The flat-bottomed boat shuddered to a stop, water lapping at its sides. The ferryman held the skiff in place, silently pointing inland.

"What, here?" but he got no answer. Steffan stepped onto uncertain ground, his boots sinking deep into muck. He watched as the ferryman poled the skiff back out into the murky waters, abandoning Steffan to his fate.

The apparition approached at a stately pace, his blazing staff a lone gleam in the night. Steffan collected himself, waiting. The dark figure stopped a sword's length away, his face well-hidden within the hood of his robe. "Your name?"

"Steffan Cantor, third son of Baron Cantor of Wyeth."

"What do you seek?"

"I seek the Dark Oracle. To the Dark Lord's gatekeeper I bring this small offering." Reaching into his tunic, Steffan extracted a purse brimming with gold pieces. "Show me the way."

Slender white fingers plucked the purse from his hand. "Your offering is accepted. Follow me and find the Dark Lord." The gatekeeper turned and strode into the gloom, his flaming staff serving as a beacon.

Wary of the treacherous footing, Steffan kept close to his guide. A turn of an hourglass passed before he spied a curtain wall looming over the gnarled trees, a solid haven in a sea of muck and mire. Towering over thirty feet high and made of black basalt, the wall was pierced by a single iron-studded gate. As they drew closer, the great gate swung silently open, like a mouth hungry for a meal. Unchallenged by any guards, the gatekeeper entered the fortress. Steffan hesitated and then followed. The walls of the basalt fortress hid a surprise. A beautiful villa, built entirely of black marble, rested upon a small hill. Climbing the hill, they passed between elegant marble colonnades and entered an atrium lined with burning sconces. A dozen guards in black armor stood at rigid attention between the columns but Steffan's gaze was drawn to a raised dais at the far end of the atrium. A dark-haired woman sat alone upon a jet-black throne. The gatekeeper approached and bowed low. "Priestess, I bring you Steffan Cantor, third son of Baron Cantor of Wyeth. He has entered the domain of the Dark Lord of his own free will." Bowing for a second time, the gatekeeper withdrew.

Steffan's breath caught in his throat, the priestess was stunning. She had an aquiline face and white porcelain skin crowned by an elaborate arrangement of raven-black hair. Her low-cut black velvet gown invited closer inspection. The woman was clearly an accomplished predator. Focusing on her eyes, he realized she was enjoying the visual review. Taking a risk, he bowed again, this time in an elaborate, courtly fashion. Gazing back into her face, he thought she looked like a cat that had just tasted cream. The gamble had paid off.

"What do you seek, Steffan of Wyeth?" Her voice was velvet laced with steel.

"I seek the Oracle so that I may take service with the Dark Lord."

"What do you hope to gain from the Dark Lord?"

The words whispered from his soul. "*One lifetime is not enough...*"

Her dark eyebrows arched, a sly smile playing across her perfect lips. "So, the ultimate prize. The Dark Lord gives his dedicates many gifts, but each additional lifetime must be earned. Only a rare few ever win the ultimate prize." Her velvet voice husked, "Are you one of those few?"

"*Yes!*"

"Arrogant as well as handsome." Her voice became a velvet whip. "And do you know the price for the Dark Lord's favor?"

He'd bought the answer with the skill of his dagger, killing a priest to win the knowledge. "I offer the Dark Lord my soul."

"Do you, Steffan of Wyeth, make this bargain of your own free will?"

"I do."

"And do you understand that once given, your soul will *never* be returned to you?"

"Yes, I understand."

The Priestess gave a throaty laugh. "I doubt that you do. Few understand the nature of the Dark Lord's price...until it is too late."

Steffan shivered, reminded of the crone's dying words.

The Priestess eased back on her throne, watching him with hooded eyes. Her long black gown shifted to reveal a shapely thigh, a deliberate temptation. In a low sultry voice, she said, "And what will you pay the Dark Lord's Priestess for granting you access to the Oracle?"

The question caught him off guard. "My lady, I did not know that the Priestess of the Oracle required payment."

"You obviously do not understand the nature of the god you seek to serve. Let me enlighten you. The Dark Lord *feeds* off both the pleasures and the pains that his dedicates harvest from the people of Erdhe. I *worship* him by taking my own pleasure. So I will ask you again, Steffan of Wyeth, what will you *pay* to the Priestess of the Oracle?"

Steffan let the question hang in the air. His eyes raked across her perfect body; so statuesque, she could have been carved out of cold, white marble. He wondered how long it would take him to heat the marble to a red-hot glow. "My lady, I doubt the meager golds in my purse would please you...but perhaps I can pleasure you in other ways?"

With a sultry smile the Priestess purred, "It is something to consider." She rose from her throne and prowled down the steps of the dais, the long slit in her gown revealing a flash of shapely white thigh. Steffan let his eyes linger on all that was revealed.

Drawing close, the Priestess reached out with a languid hand. Steffan's heart raced as her fingers stroked the contours of his face and ran down the front of his jerkin. With a wicked smile she plunged her hand into his breeches to take his measure. Instead of diminishing him, it only made him harder. "Your offer is accepted," she purred. "Pleasure me for the span of a day and tomorrow night you will face the Dark Lord's Oracle."

Releasing him, she turned and walked from the atrium.

He followed through black marble hallways to a luxurious suite dominated by a large bed on a raised dais. As night blurred into day she pressed him to the limits of his skill and his stamina, and then took him beyond, using him in ways he'd never imagined. Her body was both insatiable and addictive. At some point the next day he passed out in a haze of exhaustion and woke alone to find the purple glow of twilight framed by the black columns. Naked and sticky from sex, every part of his body ached, but it was a sweet ache. Rising, he found a copper tub steaming with hot water and fragrant spices. A platter of sweet cakes and a flagon of red wine waited on a side table. He took the luxuries as a sign that he'd pleased the Priestess. After his bath, he recovered his clothes from the tangled bed sheets and dressed. Everything was there, including the dagger in his boot and the dirk sheathed in the back of his belt.

A slight breeze stirred, bringing him the hint of her scent. Crushed violets mixed with a touch of musky sandalwood and something else, something mysterious, something he couldn't put a name to. He breathed deep, drinking in her fragrance...and found himself stiff with wanting.

The Priestess glided into the room. Her dark eyes raked across him, lingering at the telltale bulge. He watched her face, hoping she'd accept his ardent invitation. He thought he caught a glint of amusement in her eyes, and something else, something predatory or perhaps...proprietary. A warning sounded in his mind but Steffan quelled the thought, hoping for a repeat of the night.

Stiff and formal, her words poured cold water on his hopes. "Steffan of Wyeth, it is time for you to meet the Dark Lord."

Bowing low, he said, "I am ready and willing."

She gave him an enigmatic smile, a silky challenge in her voice, "Follow me." She led him outside to a copse of twisted hawthorns. In the center of the trees was a raised well contained by a ring of black basalt. The place felt heavy with the age of centuries. An involuntary shiver ran down Steffan's spine. The Priestess gestured toward the raised well. "This is the Oracle of the Dark Lord. Look deep into the waters to see his wisdom, to learn his will. Look deep and surrender your soul to him. May the Dark Lord's pleasure reign." Bowing, she turned and left Steffan to his fate.

Now that the moment was upon him, he hesitated, not really sure what it meant to surrender one's soul. He wasn't sure if he *had* a soul. He'd always believed that souls were nothing more then the invention of priests, created to crush ordinary men beneath the burden of guilt. Steffan rarely felt remorse. If remorse was the stuff of souls, then who needed it? Why should he hesitate to give the Dark Lord something that had no apparent value? Unbidden, a fragment of a forgotten childhood rhyme drifted into his mind, *"The soul is the key to immortality."* Superstitious prattle! He banished the meaningless cradle rhyme, remembering instead his time with the Priestess. If last night was any measure of what it meant to serve the Dark Lord then he was eager for more.

Kneeling at the edge of the well, he gazed down into the waters of the Oracle. Jet black and shiny as a mirror; he saw his reflection in the unbroken water. He saw the stars in the night sky above. Just as boredom began to beckon, an unseen force jerked him toward the dark waters, sucking the very essence out of his body. Disembodied, he floated in a vast Darkness. He was nothing in the face of infinity. Steffan fought to maintain a sense of self, knowing he was a mere mote in the eye of the Dark Lord. Images pulsed against him. In the Dark God's eye he saw places that he had never been, people that he had never met. He understood dark designs that he could never have imagined and learned the skills he would need to succeed. With a roaring sound he was plucked from the eye and thrust back into the frail body of a mortal, left sagging on the basalt stones to gasp for breath. Eventually he saw through his own eyes again. His reflection stared back at him. He looked exactly same except for a lock of snow-white hair at his temple. Relief washed through him. He'd lost nothing and gained much.

Pushing away from the well, he gathered himself and left the hawthorn grove. Returning to the villa, he found the Priestess seated on her throne in the atrium. She smiled, "I see the Dark Lord has accepted your offering."

Steffan bowed low. "I must be on my way. The Dark Lord has need of me."

She gave him a penetrating look. "It is forbidden to talk of anything beyond the meeting of the gatekeeper."

Steffan nodded.

"Every experience at the Oracle will be unique, both in terms of the price and the visions. See that you remember this when you come again. Now go and may the Dark Lord's pleasure reign."

He turned to find the gatekeeper waiting. The dark-robed keeper led him back to the ferry. Impatience gnawed at Steffan like a hungry beast. He was needed in Coronth. He had much to do in the service of the Dark Lord.

# 15

# Katherine

Kath knocked on the door to the healery, then entered without waiting for a reply. She found the master sitting with his back to the door, concocting a potion at his workbench.

"For once you're early." Without turning, Master Quintus continued pouring a yellow liquid into a boiling flask. "What mischief brings you here before the first patient?" The bitter smell of alum wafted from the flask.

Kath thrust her hands into her pockets and stared at the master's broad back. Now that she was here, she really didn't know how to start.

The healer took the flask from the brazier and turned to stare at her. "You're early, you're tongue-tied, and you didn't even bring meat scraps for Snowman." At the sound of his name, the giant frost owl gave a low hoot.

Kath tightened her grip on her gargoyle, resolved to see this through. "I need to talk to someone who'll believe me...it's important."

The master gave her a piercing stare and then banked the fire in the brazier. Rising from his bench, he locked the outer door and took a seat behind his cluttered desk. "Tell me what's bothering you."

"I've been having dreams...nightmares. They're so real that when I wake up in the middle of them, as I always do, it takes me a while to work out it was just a dream. But what *really* scares me is that I've had the same nightmare over and over again." Before she lost her nerve, she rushed on. "I'm worried it's a portent of the future and if I don't somehow heed the warning then Castlegard will fall to the forces of the Mordant." She ran out of words and sat still, staring at him.

"So you've come for a matter of dreams," the master said in the scholarly voice she knew so well, "a difficult subject. Great masters have spent their entire lives studying them and yet the questions remain unanswered." He bent down, reaching for a scroll from his cabinet. "Some think dreams are the voice of the gods speaking directly to man, although the message can be somewhat garbled. So it's possible your dreams are a warning of a dark future, just as you suggested. Of course, the other prevalent theory is that dreams are a special way our minds have of telling us something we already know but refuse to acknowledge. Whatever the interpretation, a frequently repeated dream usually contains an important message, a message that should not be ignored."

"So, what do you believe? Do dreams come from our minds or from the gods?"

"There are good arguments for both theories. In my opinion, the question is not so much *where* the dream comes from, but *what* is the message behind it? The trouble with dreams is that they are often confusing and indirect, a sort of riddle, so the most obvious message is usually not the true meaning." Picking up a quill and a clean sheet of parchment, he mused, "The key to working out the message of a repeating dream is to examine the details that remain the same. So think carefully about the dream that you had last night and tell me what elements always appear in your other nightmares."

Passing her good luck charm from hand to hand, Kath replayed her dreams in her mind. "I am always being chased by powerful enemies who want to kill me. Sometimes they're men, and sometimes they're ogres, but they're always soldiers of the Mordant. I am always running through Castlegard but I'm lost in a part of the castle that I've never seen before. This part of the dream never makes any sense because I don't think that there *is* a part of the castle where I haven't been. Anyway, I always end up trapped in a dead end, with nowhere to hide, no weapons to fight with, and no way to escape. Then, when I am about to be killed, somehow I fall *through* a solid stone wall into the safety of another room. Then I wake up, surprised to be alive."

The master's quill scratched across the scroll. Then, chewing the feathered end, he sat back to study his notes. "Well, the most unusual element of the dream is the part about being magically saved from death, so I assume the message has something to do with the *fact* that you're saved, or else it has to do with the *manner* in which you are saved." He paused, "In your dreams, are you always 'saved' the same way, by falling *through* a solid stone wall?"

Kath nodded, wondering where this was going.

"Falling through a solid stone wall is a very imaginative way to be saved, don't you think?" The master began to rummage through the scrolls in his cabinet. "You know, Kath, your dreams might not come from the gods, or from your mind. In fact, I think they may come from a third source. Have you ever heard of a focus?"

"No."

"Focuses are the last magic left in the lands of Erdhe."

*"Magic?"* Kath made the hand sign against evil but the master didn't seem to notice. "Ah here it is," he triumphantly plucked a scroll tied with a purple ribbon from the bottom of the cabinet. Unrolling it, he began to read, "focuses are imbued with the only magic known to have survived the War of Wizards. In the days of high magic, apprentice wizards selected a "focus" to help them meditate, to focus their thoughts and hone the skills of their magic. The "focus" was a small object that the apprentice mage could hold in his or her hand, a crystal, a stone, a gem, a piece of jewelry, a carving. By focusing on the object, the apprentice cleared her mind of all other distractions, enabling the invocation of magic. With constant use, the focus absorbed some of the magic of their mages. Most focuses were destroyed in the War of Wizards, but those that survived are most often found in and around ruins from that era. People with latent magical talents have an uncanny ability to find the lost artifacts. For example, if asked to select one object from ten different items, a person with latent magical abilities will be drawn to select the single focus among the ordinary items. Over time, the focus will induce dreams of magic. These dreams are the key to understanding the magic locked within. But the magic can only be wielded if the person is touching the focus. If the focus is lost, then the person will 'lose' the ability to do magic. Focuses are only capable of invoking minor magics of limited range and scope, as the higher magics died out with the great mages during the War of Wizards."

Kath sat spellbound but also appalled. Magic was not a part of her world.

The master gave her a thoughtful look. "Legends say that Castlegard was created near the end of the Age of Magic. Is it possible that you have found a focus?"

Kath unclenched her fist, wondering if she held the answer. "I found this in an unused part of the castle." She set her good luck charm on the corner of the desk. "I've had it for about a year now. It's my good luck charm, you see, so I carry it with me everywhere."

The master studied the small stone gargoyle. He looked but he did not touch it. "Tell me, do you keep this with you when you sleep at night?"

"On the table next to my bed."

"Then I think that we have solved at least part of the riddle. I believe your 'good luck charm' is a focus and it is using your dreams to teach you the lost magic of its original master." His voice deepened. "You are very lucky, Kath, focuses are rare and very valuable, even more valuable than Sir Blaine's blue steel blade."

She stared at the gargoyle as if it was a poisonous viper. "But everyone knows magic is evil. The War of Wizards nearly destroyed the world."

"Nothing but superstitions and fear bred of ignorance. It's just magic, Kath. Of itself it is neither 'good' nor 'evil'; it all depends on how you use it. Think of it like a sword. A sword can be used for good or evil depending on the hand that wields it. But people fear magic because it is much more powerful than a single sword."

"But what should I do with it?"

"Keep it with you always. Keep it hidden and safe. From what you've told me, it's possible this little statue may save your life some day." The master healer leaned back in his chair, a thoughtful look on his face. "I need to ask your permission to write to a trusted colleague about your focus. This colleague is an expert and may be know more about your little gargoyle. Do I have your permission?"

Kath nodded, still stunned from the idea of magic

"Thank you for trusting me. You can come to me any time." Getting up from his desk, he added, "Now my usual remedy for nightmares is always a good dose of sunshine, so off you go." He stood and ushered her out the door.

#

Late that night, a giant frost owl rose up out of Castlegard's inner yard and flew south on silent wings, a sealed message tied to its talons.

# 16

# Blaine

Ugly rumors swirled around Castlegard. A knight of the maroon was dead and the rumors named it murder. Instead of taking Sir Lewis to the castle, Sir Raymond had bundled the wounded knight on his charger and retreated back to the mining garrison in the mountains, spinning a tale of ambush by bandits seeking blue ore. A courier was sent to Castlegard with a report of the ambush and a squad of knights was dispatched to pick up the trail of the bandits, only to find that there was no trail. The knight marshal arrived at the garrison in time to question Sir Lewis on his deathbed. Returning to Castlegard, he questioned Blaine, listening without comment, reserving judgment for the king.

All of Castlegard held its breath waiting for the punishment to fall. Blaine's imagination ran wild with possibilities, all of them terrible, but first he had to attend the formal sentencing of the rogue knight.

In the outer yard, a giant octagon had been inscribed in the hard-packed dirt. The king, the knight marshal, and the other veterans stood at the start of the long maroon chain while Blaine took his place among the other fresh-made knights. Six hundred and eighty-two knights stood with their shields facing inwards, forming a living octagon.

A lone soldier waited in the octagon's center, standing beside a burning brazier. Chosen by lots, he wore a black hood. The knight marshal signaled and a horn sounded, echoing off the mage-stone walls. Guards forcibly marched the prisoner to the heart of the octagon.

Blaine studied Sir Raymond's face. Captivity had transformed his arrogance into cringing fear. Blaine wondered how he'd ever earned a maroon cloak.

The marshal snapped open a scroll and read the charges. "Raymond of Radagar, you are accused of defiling your oath to the Octagon, first by attacking an unarmed brother, second by contributing to the death of Sir Lewis, and finally by lying to your officers. Proof of your thrice-fold guilt was confirmed by the deathbed confession of Sir Lewis. By the king's judgment, you are condemned on all counts. With the murder of Sir Lewis you have earned a death sentence, but King Ursus has chosen to be merciful. By order of the king, you will be stripped of all rights and symbols of knighthood. Branded as a false knight, you will be driven from the castle, and given five days to flee the lands of Castlegard. Your execution will be immediate if you ever return. The knights of the Octagon, once your brothers-in-arms, bear witness to your shame. Let the sentence be carried out."

The knights drew their weapons and began beating their shields in a slow rhythm. Guards forced the prisoner to his knees. Something snapped in Raymond. Struggling against the guards, his face contorted in hate. "I curse you all! I spit on your hollow honor! May the Dark Lord take the Octagon!"

A soldier backhanded the prisoner. King Ursus unsheathed a dagger and stepped up to the false knight. With two quick slashes, he sliced Raymond's maroon cloak free, letting the wind snatch it away. More cuts and the surcoat hung in tatters. The king stepped back, his words a low growl. "Finish it."

Two guards tightened their hold on the condemned man while a third grabbed Raymond's hair from behind. The soldier hooded in black removed a glowing red brand from the brazier. The unmade knight gibbered in fear and squirmed at the sight. A scream split the courtyard as a broken octagon was branded into Raymond's right cheek, his face forever scared with shame. The sickening smell of burnt flesh filled the yard as the second brand was applied. Dowsing the craven with water, the guards brought the screams to a sputtering end.

A sack of rations and a flask of water were hung around the neck of the unmade knight. Guards marched him at sword point to the gates of Castlegard, expelling him from the castle. The iron-studded gates closed with a loud clang, signally the end of the ritual. The king dismissed the knights, leaving the yard with the marshal.

Shaken, Blaine returned to his quarters in the Knights' Tower, wondering if he'd glimpsed his own fate. Avoiding the stares of his fellow knights, he stowed his shield and then retreated to the solitude atop Needle Tower.

Sitting on the parapet with only the stone gargoyles for company, he wondered at his fate. For the tenth time that day, he lovingly polished his blue steel sword. Gleaming with deadly beauty, the sword symbolized his hopes and his dreams. By tradition, the design of the hilt reflected the heraldry or deeds of the original knight, but in Blaine's case, both were blank. After much thought, he'd chosen an octagon for the pommel and wings for the cross-guard. He'd dedicated his great sword to Valin, the Octagon, and the winged goddess of Justice, but the only blood the sword had shed was that of a fellow knight. Blaine shuddered at the irony. He wouldn't be surprised if the king gave the blue sword to another knight, one capable of a hero's deeds. His stomach churned, knowing all of his dreams were at risk.

As a bloody sun sank toward the horizon, Blaine hurried to the King's Tower to learn his fate. Guards admitted him to the chamber outside the king's solar. He took a seat on one of two hard wooden benches. Tattered battle banners hung from the ceiling and dented armor covered the walls, symbols of ancient glory. Blaine studied them, trying to calm his fears. A guard opened the outer door admitting a young lass in a blue frock. Blaine flicked a glance her way and then returned his gaze to the corbelled ceiling, mired in his own problems.

"Hello, Sir Blaine."

The girl's voice ambushed him. Demure in her blue frock, the Imp sat small and slight beneath the battle banners. Blaine gaped in shock, but then understanding dawned. Surrounded by the trappings of war, any girl would be out of place in Castlegard.

The knight marshal opened the inner door. "You can both come in now."

"Both?"

The marshal gave Blaine a curt nod that brooked no arguments. Inside the solar, the king sat on a wooden throne, a scroll in his lap, his face stern. Blaine bowed low, his mouth dry. Pine logs crackled in the blazing fireplace, providing the only sound. The king eventually broke the silence. "You have both disappointed me. My daughter does not know her sex, and you, Sir Blaine, do not know your place. Your combined follies might have been overlooked but one knight is dead and another is unmade. Changes are required."

The Imp spoke first. "Father, it is not that I do not know my sex, it is just that I wish to wield a sword. I do not understand why I cannot *be* the one and *do* the other."

"*Silence!*" The king roared, glaring at his only daughter. "It is most unnatural." He tugged on his beard, his voice gruff. "It is not entirely your fault. When your mother died giving you life, I was left alone to raise a daughter when I only knew how to raise sons. Castlegard has never been a place for daughters, or even wives. Perhaps I should have fostered you out at birth instead of letting you run wild, but the past is gone; we are here to speak of the future." He lifted the scroll. "Queen Liandra of Lanverness has offered to purchase three weapons of blue steel. After much consideration, I have decided to accept the queen's offer, but only on the condition that she agrees to foster you. If Queen Liandra cannot turn you into a lady then no one can."

"But I don't want to go!"

The king's stare was implacable. The Imp fell to her knees. "*Please* father, do not make me leave! I belong here! Castlegard is my home!"

"It has been decided." The king tugged on his silver beard, his gaze softening. "Your mother was a fine woman. Her last thought was for her newborn daughter. In a birthing room crowded with death, I swore to see you settled in a good marriage. It is past time I kept that oath."

"But my brothers all have places in the Octagon! Why can't I..."

"Your brothers serve, just as you will serve, bringing an alliance through your marriage bed."

A strangled cry escaped her, "*No!*"

"Honor and duty, daughter, honor and duty!"

"But I want to make a difference..."

The king stilled her with a piercing stare. "You've run wild for too long, daughter. You will go to Lanverness and conduct yourself as befits a princess of Castlegard. You will learn to be a lady and prepare yourself for the duties of marriage. You leave in six days. Make sure you are ready. You are dismissed."

The king's dismissal fell like an executioner's blade, cold and final. Blaine watched as the girl rose from her knees, stiff and formal, her green eyes frozen hard like winter lakes, her mouth set in a defiant slash. She bowed to the king, as a vassal to a lord, and left the solar, her back as straight as a sword. As the heavy wooden door shuddered closed, Blaine wondered if the king would get what he wanted from his daughter simply by issuing an order.

"Sir Blaine, you pose a different problem."

Blaine's attention snapped back to his king. A bead of sweat trickled down his back.

"I cannot fault you for defending yourself against the attack by those two cravens. Sir Lewis would have lived if Raymond had brought him straight to Castlegard instead of dragging him up into the mountains. Raymond's actions were equivalent to murder; he has paid for his deeds. As to my daughter, Katherine has explained how she tricked you into giving her weapons practice. It was wrong of her to ask it, but you, at least, were honorable in meeting the boon." The king paused. "Many knights are envious of your blue blade and many more will be angry with the death of Sir Lewis and the unmaking of Raymond. It is time for you to serve away from Castlegard."

Blaine's heart leaped at the thought of proving himself in battle.

"I am assigning you to guard my daughter, Princess Katherine, during her term of fostering. Be prepared to leave with her party in six days time." The king gave him a wave of dismissal.

Blaine stood frozen. "Surely there are better ways my sword can serve the Octagon? Sire, send me to the border to serve."

The knight marshal glared at him. "Enough! You have your orders. Honor your oath and obey your king."

Chagrined, Blaine dropped to one knee and bowed his head. "Yours to command."

The king's voice was stern, "Indeed. See that you remember. You are dismissed."

Swallowing his frustration, Blaine rose and turned to leave. As he reached for the door, the king said, "Tell me one thing, does my daughter have any skill with weapons?"

"She is a natural, sire, blessed by Valin."

The crack of the fire was the only reply.

Blaine left the king's solar. Avoiding the other knights, he hastened to his post on the barbican over the south gate. Given the events of the day, he welcomed the solitude of guard duty. Stars crowded the night sky but he did not notice them. He walked the length of the barbican, his mind raging with questions. Blue steel was forged for war not peace. Why waste a blue steel blade to guard a princess in Lanverness? His gaze was caught by the faint glow of candlelight from the town nestled in the valley below. The light seemed to mock him, a sign of peace in the dark landscape.

"Nice night."

The knight marshal stood atop the steps. Blaine relaxed his stance but not his attention. "All quiet, sir."

The marshal nodded.

Blaine continued his patrol, his gaze jumping between the surrounding countryside and the one-eyed commander. But the marshal remained statue-still, wrapped in a maroon cloak, staring out over the wall. On his fourth tour, Blaine's frustration boiled over. "Sir, may I ask a question?"

"You're going to ask me why the king gave you a blue blade."

Blaine could only nod.

"Do you think you deserve a blue steel blade?"

"No, sir."

"Do you want to be worthy of your blue blade?"

"Yes, sir!"

"Those are two of the many reasons why the king gave you a hero's sword. A blue steel blade marks a man. To some it is a mark of prowess, to others a mark of rank, of wealth, or of privilege, but I see a blue blade as a mark of responsibility, a responsibility to make a difference. Sometimes the man shapes the task and other times the task shapes the man. Carrying the blue blade has already begun to shape you."

"But why not transfer me to one of the border keeps? Let me use the blue blade against the soldiers of the Mordant instead of sending me to Lanverness?"

"Do you fight the same with a battle axe as with a great sword?"

"No, of course not." Baffled, Blaine added, "They're totally different weapons, each suited to their own styles of fighting."

"Exactly, a good general does not deploy a knight with a blue blade in the same way he deploys the rest. You should have known that for yourself. Now let me give you a piece of advice. That night in the Octagon, when you earned the maroon, what weapon enabled you to succeed at the trial by combat?"

"I chose the great sword."

"Wrong. You chose the great sword but the weapon that gave you your greatest advantage was your mind. Never underestimate the advantage of out-thinking your adversary, with or without a sword in your hand." The marshal nodded. "Time for you to return to your watch."

Blaine had only taken a few steps when he heard the marshal say, "And Blaine, the king was pleased with the design of your sword hilt. Justice is a cause worthy of a blue blade. Use the sword well."

Blaine pivoted, only to find that he was once more alone on the battlements.

# 17

# Samson

Samson didn't know it at the time, but his journey started when a crazed old woman ambushed him at his guard post beside the city gates. Barefoot and dressed in a nightshirt that did little to hide her sagging breasts, the old woman appeared out of nowhere, screaming like a banshee. Digging her claws into his arm, she tried to drag him back through the city gates. He pushed the hag away and she stumbled backwards, tripped and fell. With the wind knocked out of her, the screaming came to an abrupt stop. She pushed the mop of wild tangled hair out of her face. *"Samson, help me!"*

Shocked, Samson recognized his mother. Throwing his cloak around her, he bundled her into the guardroom, thankful it was empty, and sat her in a chair. Pouring a cup of steaming tea, he pressed the cup into her shaking hands and tried to get her to drink. He drank a cup himself, hoping to wake from the nightmare. The simple act of drinking tea brought a small spark of sanity back to her eyes. In a quavering voice, his mother told him how guards had burst into their bedroom and taken his father away in chains. "You must save him!" she begged.

A chill claimed him. With the sun almost directly overhead, the rituals in the temple square would be long over, but Samson had to see for himself. Knowing his mother was not fit to walk the streets alone, he took her to a cheap hostel and left her in the safety of a private room and then sprinted for the temple square. The closer he got to the square the more people jammed the streets. Breaking through a final logjam of celebrants, Samson entered the square. Suddenly reluctant, he edged towards the smoldering pit, his stomach roiling at the smell of burnt flesh. A greasy charcoal lump lay in sprawled in the pit, the sole remains of this morning's heretic. He stared at the lump, refusing to believe it was his father. With no way to identify the victim, Samson decided to check the bakery; perhaps it was all a mistake.

As he neared the street he heard the mob. A frenzied mob ransacked his parents' bakery and their home above the shop. One neighbor leaned out of the upper window and tossed clothing to the waiting arms of his wife. Strangers poured out of the bakery brandishing rolling pins and baking tins. Spilled flour whitened the street, guilty footprints leading in all directions. Samson ducked into a side alley and heaved his breakfast onto the cobblestones. The nightmare was true. But his father was only a baker: how could they do this to an innocent man?

And then another thought struck him. As the son of a proven heretic, he might well join his father in the flaming pit. He needed to get himself and his mother out of Coronth, beyond the reach of the priests. Pulling his half helm down over his face, Samson pushed his way into the shop and up the stairs to his parents' bedroom. The closet and drawers stood empty, but the looters had missed the wood planks that hid the attic space over the bed. Moving the planks aside, he found the basket where his mother stored their winter clothes. The basket was too much to carry. Grabbing a sheet, he filled it with the most useful clothes and flung it, sack-like, over his back. A stranger and a neighbor fought over the things he left behind. Samson was sorely tempted to unsheathe his sword and give the looters what they truly deserved, but he fought to contain his rage and fled the house.

Racing through the city streets, he returned to the hostel where he'd left his mother. He found her curled up on the bed asleep, her long hair disheveled, tears crusting her cheeks. So old and frail, Samson knew they'd need plenty of coin to escape the priests. Draping the salvaged clothes over the chair so she'd see them when she woke, he left the hostel and made his way back to his barracks.

Soldiers passed him in the streets, their red tabards suddenly sinister. Samson hesitated at the fortress gates, his stomach knotted with dread, but he knew time was his enemy. Saluting the guards, he strode into the garrison like a sergeant with orders. He went straight to the supply room and was relieved to find the quartermaster absent. There he grabbed three leather rucksacks and scanned the shelves for useful supplies. Rolls of blue cloth crammed into the far corner caught his eye; everything else was red and gold for the Flame God of Coronth. He quickly filled two of the rucksacks with blankets, flints, cloaks, and water flasks. On impulse, he took one of the rolls of blue cloth, shoving it into the bottom of a rucksack. Slipping out of the supply room, he headed for his barracks. The central hall was deserted except for three soldiers dicing at the far end. Trying to walk calmly, Samson made his way to the small chamber he shared with another sergeant. Sergeant Elder was the ambitious type, always volunteering for guard duty at the temple rituals. Elder was the last person Samson wanted to run into but he needed to get the coins from his chest.

Luck was with him; the chamber was empty. He rummaged through the chest till he found the small leather pouch that held his savings. Mostly silvers with too few golds but it was all the coin he had. The wages of a city guard were nothing to brag about. As he tucked the pouch and a few items of clothing into the last rucksack, he heard the door creak open. Samson palmed the padlock from the chest and turned.

The short burly sergeant entered the chamber. "Springwater, what are you doing here? I thought that you had guard duty at the north gate?"

"I finished the morning watch and now I'm on break. How about you?"

"I had duty in the temple square. We baked a baker this morning! Funny thing was that when he baked he didn't smell like bread or pie or cake...he smelled like roast pork!" Elder slapped his thigh and repeated the punch line. "*Baked* a baker and he smelled like roast *pork*!" Suddenly he stopped laughing and looked pointedly at Samson. "What's the matter? You're not laughing at my joke." His eyes lit up. "I remember now, you're the son of a baker. I'm willing to bet that you're the son of a *baked* baker." He noticed the rucksacks, "and you're planning to *run!* Seems I've caught myself a heretic's boy!"

"Can't you forget you saw me?"

"Afraid I can't do that, heretic boy. Turning you in might just be what I need to get that next promotion."

As the sergeant reached the door, Samson sprang to his feet. Using all of his pent-up rage, he hit Elder in the back of the head with the heavy padlock. The sergeant's skull dented with a wet crunch and the man slumped to the floor. Samson opened the door a crack and peered out, but the hallway was empty. Closing the door, he tried to stop shaking, sweat dripping from his brow. At the start of the day, he'd been a proud sergeant in the city guard. Now he was the son of a heretic, a deserter, and a murderer. He had to get out of this insane city before worse happened.

He wrestled the burly sergeant onto his bunk and covered him with a blanket. Slinging the three rucksacks over his shoulder, Samson stepped out into the hallway. He wanted to run but he forced himself to walk. By the time he reached the streets, he was drenched in sweat.

Samson returned to the hostel, thankful to find his mother awake and dressed, but when he looked in her eyes he realized something had broken in her mind. She called him 'Sam' instead of 'Samson', mistaking him for his father. The loss stabbed at his heart. With a cry of despair he wrapped her in his arms and wept into her snow-white hair.

Then, empty of tears, he struggled to collect himself. He changed into a brown homespun tunic and a leather jerkin recovered from his chest in the barracks, stuffing the now-hated uniform back into the bottom of the rucksack. Strapping on his short sword, he hid the blade beneath a green wool cloak. Wearing the sword was a risk. In Balor, only members of the guards wore swords, but Samson felt naked without it. After draping a wool cloak around his mother's shoulders, he gathered up the rucksacks and shepherded her out of the hostel.

His mother posed a problem of another sort. A short frail woman in her late fifties, she would not be able to walk far. The only thing he could think of was to catch a ride with one of the farm wagons returning to the countryside after a day at the market. He steered his mother through the maze of streets to the vegetable market on the south side of the city.

The square was crowded with farmers hawking their produce from the back of their wagons, creating a noisy din. Women wandered between the wagons, baskets on their arms. Taking his mother firmly by the elbow, Samson steered her through the rows of wagons, looking for a sympathetic face. He stopped at a wagon full of cabbages. Pretending to study the vegetables he tried to get up the courage to talk to the farmer. Before he could say a word the farmer leaned over and whispered, "Looking for a ride out of town?"

Startled, Samson nodded.

The man winked at him. "Men your age don't usually shop for vegetables and you're toting *three* rucksacks. You might as well carry a false idol on a staff for the priests to see."

Under the cover of his cloak, Samson put his hand on his sword hilt.

"Oh, don't worry, I won't turn you in, but you won't be leaving the city in my wagon. If you've the golds, go see old Chammers, three wagons down, the one selling turnips. He's the one to ask. Now buy one of me cabbages for helping you out; it will look better if you have a bit of green in your hand. That'll be ten coppers for a cabbage."

The price was outrageous but Samson didn't argue. Three wagons down, they came to the turnip farmer. He was short and fat, with shifty eyes and Samson didn't like the look of him, but before he could say anything, the farmer leaned down and whispered, "It's late in the day, boyo, and you're lucky I haven't sold my seats in the wagon. Thirty golds will get you and the old lady a ride to the other side of Hillsbrook, but I'll see the golds first."

Samson stared slack-jawed. The farmer was asking for more than half the golds in his purse for a ride that would only take them as far as the first village south of Balor.

"Close your mouth, boyo, you won't catch any flies that way," the farmer said in a snide voice. "I'm the only farmer who's still giving rides to heretics, so pay the gold or go somewhere else...unless of course you want to buy my turnips?"

Samson was desperate. "Fine, but half the golds now and the other half when we get to the village."

"Fair enough, laddiebuck, now bury those rucksacks under my turnips before you attract any more attention and get the old lady up on the front seat while I hitch my team."

He handed the farmer the golds. Once he got his mother settled, he spied a farmer selling apples and realized he hadn't eaten since early that morning. His stomach rumbling with hunger, he decided to buy a few before they left. While he was choosing a dozen, the apple-seller leaned over and whispered, "Saw you talking to Chammers, the turnip farmer. You can trust him to get you as far as Hillsbrook but if you sleep in his barn you'll wake to find swords in your face. Pay him for the night in the barn or he'll be suspicious; just make sure you're long gone before sunrise."

Samson stared at the man.

"Lots of people fleeing Balor these days," the apple farmer went on. "Most farmers used to help till the guards made an example of the ones that did. Farmers aren't immune to the Flames, you know. Chammers is the only one who still runs heretics." He lowered his voice to a whisper. "He's cut a deal with one of the guard captains. The guards let him through the city gates and then the good captain is proclaimed a hero when he captures the runaways in his barn the next morning. Chammers and the captain split your golds. A lot more golds in running heretics than there is in turnip farming." He handed Samson a twelfth apple with a knowing look and then got back atop his wagon, hawking his apples in a loud voice.

Samson walked back to the turnip farmer's wagon in a daze. He climbed up onto the seat and handed his mother an apple. He took another for himself and just held it in his hand, amazed that the simple whim to buy an apple could turn out to make all the difference between life and death.

As they approached the city gates, Samson sat hunched down in his seat but it didn't seem to matter, for none of the guards challenged the wagon.

On the ride south, Chammers regaled them with stories of all the people he'd saved from the Flame. Samson listened in silence, clutching the golden apple tight in his hand. A short time later, the wagon exited the village of Hillsbrook and turned onto the farmer's land. As they pulled up to the barn, Chammers said, "Got you here safe just as I promised. I'll take my other fifteen golds now."

Samson helped his mother down from the wagon, retrieved his rucksacks and then paid the man his money. Chammers smiled, pocketing the gold. "You and the old lady have had a long day. Why don't you spend the night in my barn? Sweet-smelling hay to sleep on and a barrel of water to wash with. Only cost you a gold apiece for the night."

For that price, Samson could spend a fortnight in a good inn with a hot dinner served in his room every night. Instead of arguing, he fished out two golds.

Laughing, Chammers bid them a good night. Samson closed the barn door and then settled his mother in the hay. While she slept, he kept watch, waiting for the depths of night. By the light of the crescent moon, he and his mother slipped out of the barn and began their long walk south. They walked at night and hid by day. With his mother on his arm, their progress slowed to a hobbled walk, but they did the best they could.

The long march south took its toll. When the apples ran out Samson used his money to buy food but the prices were outrageous and his coin did not last long. When the money ran out, he bartered away two of the rucksacks. After that, he was forced to beg for food, for a ride in a wagon, or for shelter. A few people helped, but most turned him away with stony faces, or worse, threw rocks to drive him off.

He saw other refugees on the road or in the woods, but they were afraid of strangers and always kept their distance. All the refugees had the same haunted look in their eyes.

It seemed to Samson that there was no charity, no heart, left in the people of Coronth, one more thing burned to ashes by the Flame God. Too numb to think, he kept putting one foot in front of the other, walking an endless road south, desperate to escape the reach of the priests.

# 18

# Katherine

The bodice of the gown threatened to suffocate Kath. She plucked at the bindings, needing to breathe. Oblivious to her discomfort, the two seamstresses fluttered around like butterflies, making final adjustments and babbling about the proper way to walk and the correct way to curtsey. Kath escaped at the first opportunity, changing into her squire's garb and disappearing to a remote part of the castle.

Leaving was hard. She didn't want to forget anything. She ran to the deserted basement of Needle Tower where she'd learned to throw her axes. Lighting a torch, she closed the great wooden doors and gave the Empty Knight a last inspection. The chalk outline was almost invisible but the many axe cuts had carved a crude head and torso into the door. Running her hand across the rough carving, Kath smiled knowing her first sparring partner was now a permanent part of Castlegard. Saluting the Empty Knight, she ran for the master healer's quarters.

She entered the healery without knocking and found the inner doors closed; Master Quintus must be with a patient. Settling into the master's stuffed armchair, Kath waited, studying the clutter on the master's desk.

At last the door opened and the healer shepherded out a knight with a bandaged arm. "Come back tomorrow. You'll be fine as long as the wound doesn't fester." The master closed the outer door and turned to face Kath. "So you're to be fostered in Lanverness."

Kath scowled. "I came to ask if you've learned anything more about my gargoyle?" She set the small figurine on the corner of his desk.

"I wrote to my friend but I've yet to get a reply. Your little gargoyle may have been lost since the War of Wizards." The master began to rummage through the drawers of his desk, eventually producing a long thin strip of leather cord. "It might be better if you wore the gargoyle around your neck as opposed to putting it in your pocket. Pockets are easily picked, especially on the road." With Kath's assent, the master deftly wrapped the leather cord around the neck of the small statue and then made a larger loop, tying it fast with a healer's knot. He gently settled the loop around her neck. "Remember, there are those who would kill to obtain your little gargoyle, so keep it hidden. Someday it might save your life."

Nodding, she tucked the small figurine inside her squire's tunic, the stone cold against her skin. "But how will I learn what it does?"

"The key is in your dreams. Understanding will eventually come. Magic is very powerful, especially in a world where it is almost forgotten."

She bit her lip. "Thank you for your help."

"There will be others to help you."

"Who?"

"It's not for me to say. They will find you in their own time."

"But how will I know them?"

"Use your own judgment. Trust only those who give you the freedom to choose your own path. Make your own destiny, Kath. Don't wait for others to define your life."

A shiver ran down her back.

The master looked away. "Now you best be off. I'm sure you have many things to do before your departure tomorrow."

Kath went to leave but then turned back, ambushing the healer with a quick hug, and then sprinted for the door, wiping her sleeve across her eyes. Blurry-eyed, she sprinted through the great yard and headed for the forge.

The sound of hammers hitting anvils cheered her mood. Always a hive of activity, Castlegard's forge never slept and she always felt comfortable among the weapon smiths. Slipping inside, Kath stood in the corner, out of the way. Basking in the heat, she breathed in the familiar scents of hot metal, burning charcoal, and sweat. She imagined the forge smelled like the breath of dragons and that every weapon made was meant for the hand of a hero. Cloaked in shadows, she watched as her friends worked red-hot steel into new blades. She scanned the forge searching for Master Otto, wanting to thank him again for her throwing axes, but things did not go as planned. A bellows boy noticed her standing in the corner and let out a cry of, "The princess!"

The ring of the hammers stopped and everyone turned to look. The master swordsmith stepped from the backroom, a broad smile on his soot-stained face. "We hoped you'd come by today. We're all going to miss you." One of the bellows boys emerged from the back of the forge and rushed to hand Otto a bundle of rags. The master extended the bundle to Kath. "These are for you, so you won't forget your friends in the forge."

Surprised and touched, Kath accepted the bundle. Unwrapping the rags, she found a slender dagger in a supple doeskin sheath with leather ties at the top and bottom. She drew the dagger, examining the blade. Six inches of fine Castlegard steel with the mark of the octagon on the small cross hilt, a dagger worthy of a knight.

Teeg, the head apprentice, said, "It's from the apprentice smiths. We drew lots to see which of us would forge it." His face reddened. "And the doeskin sheath is specially made. Strap it to your leg where no one will see it."

Kath grinned and removed her boot. She handed Teeg the sheathed dagger. Kneeling, the apprentice blushed as he strapped the dirk to the outside of her calf. She pulled her boot back on, hiding the dagger. Teeg stepped back and said, "Now you'll always have good Castlegard steel for protection."

Kath was afraid she might cry, but the master swordsmith came to her rescue. "There's something else in the bundle."

Inside the rags, she uncovered a beautiful piece of tooled leather. A great red hawk was embossed across the back, its wings spread wide and talons extended for the kill. It seemed a type of harness, with hawk wings spread from shoulder to shoulder. She gave the master swordsmith a puzzled look.

"Try it on; it's for your throwing axes!" She shrugged into it and he showed her how to fit two axe heads into pockets sewn under the hawk's talons. The pockets were angled so the axe handles followed the line of the hawk's wings, projecting out over each shoulder. Kath reached back for an imaginary axe and realized the handles were perfectly position for throwing. With practice, she should be able to grab an axe from the harness and throw it all in one smooth, efficient motion. She gave the master swordsmith a heartfelt smile. "Thank you."

An apprentice smith began to belt out a story of how Kath, a princess of Castlegard, single-handedly slew an ogre with her throwing axes and everyone joined in with embellishments. A competition erupted for the most outrageous story, with Kath the heroine of every tale. She listened with wide eyes, drinking in the stories, wishing even the smallest of tales could be true. As the stories grew more preposterous, the forge rocked with merriment. Kath marveled at her friends. Truly shared laughter was the best way to say farewell.

# 19

# Duncan

Castle Seamount had deep dungeons but no torturer. Captured by the royal guards, the rogue archer was cast in chains and locked in the dungeons that tunneled beneath the sea. Carved from black basalt, the dark, dank cells had a subtle way of influencing the minds of prisoners; it was only a matter of time till he talked. Duncan watched from the shadows, sensing the prisoner held a key to a riddle, a riddle that threatened the peace of the southern kingdoms.

Master Simmons changed the prisoner's bandages every morning, checking for signs of fever or infection, while softly prodding the boy with questions and subtle suggestions. The healer gave the boy an audience that tried to listen more than it spoke. Commander Isador had the boy at night. A tall imposing figure dressed in the surcoat of the royal guards, he probed the boy about assassination plots and co-conspirators, about links to the Mordant and possible ties to the rulers of Coronth. Short of violence, the commander did his best to become the boy's worst nightmare.

Hidden in the background, Duncan witnessed the boy's early mornings with the healer and late nights with the commander. He scanned the boy for signs of fear or remorse, for evidence of truth or lies. After three days, Duncan was prepared to share his findings with the king.

Troubled by his thoughts, he climbed from darkness back into light. At the top of the king's tower, arrow-slit windows brought a breath of sea air. Duncan breathed deep, the salty tang replacing the molder of the dungeons. A pair of guards admitted him to the king's antechamber. Commander Isador and Counselor Igraine waited inside. Both were the king's siblings though they looked nothing alike. The commander was an imposing man, over six feet tall with jet black hair, dark eyes and a lightening temper. In stark contrast, the counselor was a small mousy woman with drab brown hair, sharp features, and ocean blue eyes that never missed a thing. Dressed in plum-colored robes, the counselor turned from the fireplace to address Duncan. "Master Simmons is with the king. When the healer is finished, the king will hear your report."

Worried for his friend, Duncan asked, "How is he?"

"The arrow passed clean through his chest. He's lost a fair amount of blood and has burns across his chest, but the worst fear is the danger to his lung. With bed rest and good care, he may recover."

Relief washed through him.

Master Simmons opened the door from the king's sleeping chamber. "The king will see you now. Take care that you do not over tax him. Call me if you need me." The master gestured for the three of them to enter the king's bedchamber.

King Ivor sat in the middle of a giant four-post bed, propped up by a mound of pillows against a carved wooden headboard. He greeted his advisors with a wry smile. "A bit different than our normal council chambers but we'll just have to make do. Pull up some chairs and explain to me the riddle posed by this boy from Coronth."

The three advisors moved armchairs into a crescent on the right side of the bed. Once seated, Duncan began his report. "The attacker is a seventeen-year-old named Leonard Farmer from the capital city of Balor in Coronth. On the surface, the attack seems to be a twisted form of revenge over the boy's perceived loss of the tournament, the primary target being Prince Jared, not your majesty. The boy claims there are no co-conspirators or assassination plots and I believe him. The assault at the tourney was essentially unplanned, yet danger lurks beneath the surface of his actions." Duncan paused. "The boy shows no remorse for the attack. In fact, he believes it was justified 'in the eyes of his god'. Consumed by this religion of the Flame, he believes that anyone who does not conform to the teachings of the Flame God is an 'unbeliever' or an 'infidel'. In the eyes of this new religion, there is no value to the life of an unbeliever."

A sharp gasp came from the counselor. "So this religion can then be used as an excuse to commit any crime against any infidel?"

"Just so."

"Religion used as a tool to divide."

Duncan nodded, his face grim. "To divide and conquer."

A deadly stillness settled over the chamber.

Duncan stared at the king. "We're lucky the boy survived my arrows, or we would have missed the warning."

King Ivor sighed. "There was another warning but it was too vague. The Queen of Lanverness sent a courier with concerns about the growing cult of the Flame." His hand brushed against the bandage across his chest. "And now this religion strikes at the heart of Navarre."

Commander Isador leaned forward, his face stern. "Sire, this new religion poses a serious threat. We must bolster the western border."

The king paled. "How do we fight a religion?"

Duncan knew there was no good answer to the king's question. The counselor broke the silence. "In terms of how we *fight* a religion, I suppose the best we can do is to try to contain it within Coronth. We can only hope this new religion will burn itself out with time... no pun intended."

Commander Isador said, "Shall I call up the guards and double the patrols on our western border?"

"Yes Isador, make it so."

"And what about the fate of the attacker?" The commander pressed, "I say we arrange a public execution and give him the justice he deserves. His death should serve as a deterrent to other fanatics."

The king shook his head. "No, Isador, the problem with lopping off heads is that we can't change our minds and put them back on later. And as to setting an example, I doubt the fanatics of Coronth are really watching. No, the boy will stay in the dungeons. Justice can wait." King Ivor turned to look at his sister. "Igraine, I'd like you to work with Master Simmons to see if you can free the boy of his possession by this Flame religion. If we can release him then we may gain a weapon to use against other fanatics. And, Igraine, I want you to work with Duncan to craft a statement for the people of Seaside. They'll be expecting an explanation for the attack. I want them warned of the possible dangers of this new religion, but it must be done in a way that does not lead to fear or violence."

Duncan said, "I suggest we enlist Justin to help with this task. The prince more than proved his worth on the night of the attack. With his music and his presence, he found a way to ease the peoples' fears. On the night of the tournament, the people of Seaside entered the taverns with fear but they left with a renewed belief in themselves and in the royal family."

Pride stole across the king's face. "So there *are* advantages to having a bard in the family! I thought so, despite the grumblings of the council. So much for claiming there is no 'value' in music. Yes, by all means, get Justin involved."

The talk of Justin had brought some welcome color to the king's face. Given the severity of his wound, Duncan thought it best to give the grim problem of Coronth a rest. "Speaking of the Wayfaring, with the recent turn of events, should we keep the Royal Js in Navarre?"

The king shook his head. "The Wayfaring is too important, although the travel plans will have to be modified to avoid Coronth. And I want extra guards assigned to each of my children. They'll not leave Navarre without protection."

Commander Isador said, "I'll see that it is done."

"For added safety, Jemma, Justin, and Jordan should journey together." He turned his gaze to Duncan. "You and Justin will need to stay in Navarre for at least a fortnight to prepare the message for the people. Once you reach Lanverness, I want you to meet with Queen Liandra and apprise her of the risk of this new religion. You are to remain at the Rose Court for at least three turns of the moon, serving as Navarre's ambassador to the queen's court."

"What about the Royal Js, sire?"

"I'm sure Justin will enjoy spending time at the Rose Court and I will give Jordan orders to assess the battle readiness of the army of Lanverness before she travels to her Wayfaring with the Kiralynn monks."

Considering the tasks that lay ahead, Duncan asked, "Sire, it might be helpful if I knew the terms of agreement for the fosterings."

With a wave of his hand, the king deferred the question to his sister. Igraine explained, "Justin's training will be the most expensive. Master Haldor demanded one thousand golds for a three-year apprenticeship and any golds that Justin brings in through his performances for the first two years are to go to the master to pay for the boy's room and board. An outrageous sum but then Master Haldor is the best bard in all of Erdhe. As to the fostering of Jemma, Queen Liandra has not asked for anything in return. This simply means we do not yet know what the price will be. The Spider Queen does nothing for free."

The commander interjected, "Rumor has it the queen is spinning a web to catch wives for her two sons."

The king smiled. "The queen may spin her webs but it will be up to our Jemma to decide if she wants to be caught. She has a mind of her own and a stubborn streak as well. Liandra will find our Jemma is not so easy to manipulate." The king turned to Duncan. "Take Jemma with you when you brief the queen. Once you leave Lanverness, I'll expect her to continue discussions with the queen regarding Coronth."

"As you wish, majesty. And what is the fostering arrangement for Princess Jordan?"

Igraine answered, "The arrangement with the monks is most unusual. A year ago, we received an unsolicited scroll from the Grand Master of the Kiralynn Order inviting one or more of the Royal J's to spend their

Wayfaring at their monastery in the Southern Mountains." Igraine hesitated, her glance seeking the king. "The curious part is, the monks specifically asked for Jordan."

Duncan smothered his surprise. "They asked for Jordan by name?"

Igraine nodded.

"And you're sending her to them?"

The king answered, "There are few places in Erdhe willing to foster a woman wielding a sword." The king met Duncan's stare. "It is one of the many reasons I asked you to join Jordan on her Wayfaring. The monks are too mysterious for most, but Igraine assures me the Kiralynn Order serves the Light. Jordan will go to the monks to learn the art of war and you will discover the truth behind their request."

Duncan nodded. "It seems Erdhe is awash in plots."

The king gave him a weary look. "Navarre is a small kingdom. We must chart the currents of change if we are to navigate them."

Master Simmons poked his head in the room and said, "The king has had enough for the day. You should let him rest."

Before they reached the door, King Ivor added one last order, "I want all of you to think about ways to defeat this new religion. We will hope for peace, but if it comes to war, we may need more than swords to triumph."

Duncan bowed, fearing the truth of the king's words.

# 20

# Blaine

Blaine searched the castle but the Imp was not to be found. Annoyed, he slung his shield across his back and his saddlebag over his shoulder and descended the tower stairs. Reaching the great yard, he was stunned by the crowd. Flour-stained cooks and scruffy stable hands mingled with the folk of the forge. From Master Otto down to the youngest bellows boy, half the castle had turned out for their leave taking. The Imp was a pest, but the girl had a knack for making friends among the castle folk.

Blaine threaded his way through the crowd, hoping the girl waited with her escort. He joined three knights, one smith, and two squires, their horses packed and ready for travel, but the Imp was not among them. Muttering a curse, he greeted his horse with an apple and then strapped his bags to his saddle. His gaze roved the escort. He knew all of them save one. Sir Tyrone stood out with his ebony-colored skin. Tall with a lick of gray in his long curly hair, he carried a great sword strapped to his back. Rumors ran rampant about the black knight, saying that he came from some distant land or that he'd done a great deed to join the Octagon, but rumors had a tendency to exaggerate. Blaine wasn't sure what to believe, but the king must have a reason for assigning him to the escort detail. In addition to Sir Tyrone, he'd be traveling with Captain Tellor, Sir Kirk, and Carl, a big swordsmith from the forge, and two senior squires. It was a small escort for a princess but the kingdoms of Erdhe had long been at peace.

Blaine secured his shield to his saddle and then scanned the crowd for Kath. The journey hadn't started yet he'd already lost the Imp.

The crowd parted like a field of grain before the wind, revealing the king. King Ursus was a force to be reckoned with. His hair showed his age, a regal mane of silver, yet he moved with the grace of a seasoned warrior, the hilt his great blue sword rearing over his left shoulder. His face held a look of mild surprise. Blaine wondered if the king was pleased or annoyed by the revelation of his daughter's popularity.

The king cast a stern gaze across the escort detail. "Captain Tellor, you have your orders. Convey my daughter safely to Lanverness and return with the down-payment for the queen's blue swords. Ride quickly, serve well, and bring honor to the Octagon." He glared at Blaine, "And just where is my daughter?"

As Blaine braced for the king's anger, the crowd parted and the Imp emerged. Clad in her usual squire's garb, she'd tied her unruly long blonde hair with a leather cord, a saddlebag thrown over her shoulder. "I'm here, father." Her voice held a note of defiance but her eyes were wary, a badger baiting a bear.

The king frowned. "Katherine, you're a princess of Castlegard yet you persist in acting like a foundling. I paid the seamstresses good coin for their work. I expected to see you dressed as a lady. Once again you disappoint."

The Imp's mouth tightened to a stubborn slash. "It's a long ride to Lanverness. We'll make better time if I actually *ride* the horse instead of being carried like a sack of grain." She crossed her arms. "And besides, my gowns are all packed."

The king's scowl deepened but the Imp stood firm.

The crowd stirred, like foot soldiers caught in the crossfire.

Perhaps it was the crowd, or the fact that his only daughter was leaving, but for once the king relented. "You leave as a wild thing, but I expect you to return as a lady. Two years in the queen's court should be long enough. Ride well, daughter, and bring honor to Castlegard."

The Imp's voice broke, "Always, father." She bowed and then walked toward the chestnut stallion held by a page. The Master of Horse emerged from the crowd, offering her a leg-up to the sixteen-hand warhorse. Kath vaulted into the saddle, looking as if she belonged on the big chestnut.

Captain Tellor gave the order, and the troop formed up. Blaine rode next to Kath. The girl held her head high, riding out of Castlegard on her own terms, never looking back. Cheers and farewell wishes followed them through the gates, across the drawbridge, and out into the world.

Blaine cast a sour look back at the castle. A knight with a blue blade should be riding north against the Mordant, not traveling south to escort a girl to her fostering. Scowling, he thrummed his horse to a canter.

They took the great road south, settling into an easy routine. Captain Tellor rode at the head of the column, setting the pace and choosing the route. The two squires, Todd and Alain, rode in the swirling dust cloud at the rear, each with a packhorse on a long lead. Sir Kirk took responsibility for the squires while Blaine rode with the Imp in the center of the column, enjoying the company of Carl, the master smith, and the black knight, Sir Tyrone.

The countryside was glorious, bedecked with the brilliant colors of early fall. They rode through farmlands busy with the autumn harvest. Villagers stopped to watch their passing. Small boys raced alongside, their face's aglow with hero worship. The cheers intensified when the villagers spied the sapphire hilt of Blaine's great sword. Swelling with pride, Blaine drank in the admiration, until they stopped at a roadhouse for a meal and a night's rest.

The inn was crowded with travelers, yet the owner escorted the knights to a prime table by the fireside. They supped on roast lamb and potatoes and leeks, enjoying a fine meal until the minstrel stopped strumming and locked his gaze on Blaine. "Sir Knight, I would hear the tales of your blue sword. I swear to fashion your feats of glory into a song worthy of your deeds."

Blaine stared at the minstrel as if he was a three-headed dragon, but the crowd took up the request. *"Tell us a tale! Tell us a tale!"* Blaine slunk into his chair, wishing he could disappear, but the chant only intensified. Voices beat against him like sword blows but he had no tale to tell. He was just a fresh-made knight with a sword he hadn't earned. It was too much to endure. Bursting from his chair, he bolted for the door, escaping into the night.

Bleary-eyed, he met the others in the stables the next morning, eager to put the village behind him. Saddling his horse, he kept to himself, riding at the back of the column, his blue sword strapped to his back; his pride and shame.

The days of traveling dulled to routine. Leagues passed and the sting of the minstrel lessened. Riding in the center of the column, between the smith and the black knight, Blaine listened to tales from their past. The two older men had traveled far and wide before pledging themselves to Castlegard. Carl had worked in Radagar and Wyeth before taking a smith's oath to the Octagon. Sir Tyrone's origins were even farther flung. "My parents were spice traders from Yarran. They crossed the Western Ocean and settled in Seaside. Born and raised there, I pestered my parents for stories of our homeland, hungry to hear of a land where all the faces were ebony like mine. On my fifteenth naming day, my parents took me on the long voyage home. The ocean proved a nightmare of storms. Just when I thought we were food for fishes, the master brought the ship to port, landing at a sprawling city on the edge of a verdant jungle. At first I reveled in the sameness of the people, but after a year I realized I felt more like a stranger in Yarran than in Erdhe. With the blessings of my parents, I returned to Erdhe and eventually made my way to Castlegard to take up a sword with the Octagon Knights."

The Imp pulled her horse even with the black knight. "So even though you look like a man from Yarran, on the inside you feel like a man of Erdhe?"

"Just so."

"Looking so different, how did you get the people of Erdhe to accept you?"

"In the seaside kingdom, my skin color was merely an oddity, but outside Navarre I was treated as something less than a man, my dark skin taken as a sign of the Dark Lord. I honed my fighting skills, fending off insults and attacks, living by the sword. Perhaps that's why I was drawn to Castlegard, where a man is judged by his honor and his skill, not the color of his skin."

"Yet you volunteered to make this trip to Lanverness?"

Sir Tyrone flashed a wry smile. "A maroon cloak and a great sword make all the difference. If the people of Erdhe see a black knight of the Octagon perhaps they'll be more accepting of the next dark-skinned man they meet. Besides, I like to travel. Caught the habit from my parents and I can't seem to give it up."

But the Imp was like a terrier worrying a bone. "If the people of Erdhe can accept a black knight, do you think they might accept a girl with a sword?"

The black knight fell silent, he and Blaine both avoiding the Imp's stare. Eventually, Sir Tyrone braved an answer. "It is hard to be different. Not everyone can walk that path. You must decide if the destination is worth the journey." Giving her a half smile, he added, "But you already have four knights and a master smith accustomed to seeing a girl wearing a pair of throwing axes, so perhaps there's a chance."

Mollified, the Imp flashed them a warm smile.

They rounded a bend in the road and Ferrytown came into view, a cluster of whitewashed clapboard buildings nestled against the mist-shrouded shores of Eye Lake. The town looked small but prosperous. Smoke curled skyward from stone chimneys and the smell of fresh baked bread wafted down the road like a temptation.

They took rooms at 'The Gentle Soul', the inn recommended by the stable master. After stowing their saddlebags, they met in the inn's common room, ordering a supper of fish stew and tankards of cider. Blaine tore off a piece of crusty bread and tucked into the savory stew. When he'd taken the edge off his hunger, he looked across the table at Sir Tyrone. "So tell us about the Isle of Souls."

The black knight was a consummate storyteller. With a smile, he settled into the tale. "The stories are legion. Rumors say the Isle is enchanted. For reasons known only to the gods, the gray veil between the present and the future, between this life and the next, is thin on the Isle. Mystics, mediums, and fortunetellers flock there to ply their trade. Lured by the siren's song of seeing the future, people come from all over Erdhe, drawn like bees seeking honey." The black knight gestured to the collection of travelers in the common room. "Predicting the future is a lucrative trade."

Kath's eyes grew as big as gold pieces, but Blaine asked the first question. "So is the Isle part of the kingdom of Tubor?"

"Ferrytown is in Tubor, but the Isle is a Free City. Owing allegiance to no king, it is run by an elected Council of Merchants and Mystics."

The big smith barked a rude laugh. "More like the council of thieves and quacks! If you ask me, the whole Isle is just one big con job. If you're smart, you'll keep a hand on your purse."

Confused, Blaine asked, "So why are *we* going to this den of thieves?"

Carl answered, "Eye Lake is so big it would take weeks to ride around. We'll save time by crossing to the Isle and then to the other side. Of course, the council knows this, so they only operate the ferries in the mornings, forcing travelers to spend at least one night. It's all part of their clever scam to fleece travelers of as many golds as possible." With a wink and a leer, the smith added, "But cheer up lad, it won't be a total waste. The brothels on the Isle are famed throughout Erdhe!"

Blaine glared at the smith, but the Imp did not seem to notice. Kath's stare was fixed on the black knight. "Can the fortunetellers truly see the future?"

"If the future can be seen by mere mortals, then the Isle is the place for it. Of course, it helps if you have a gifted mystic."

"How can you tell?"

"The Guild of Mystics has a way of testing its members, and those who pass display a white 'spirit' hand on the lintel of the door to their shops."

Carl chortled. "Spirit hands! I'll tell you how the quacks pass the test, by passing enough gold across the palm of the tester!" Gulping down the last of his ale, he waved to a serving girl and ordered another.

The Imp ignored him. "So how do the mystics see the future?"

"I expect you can find readers of palms, tarots, crystals, and auras, even those who claim to commune directly with the spirits of the dead."

"Which method would you choose?"

Choking on his cider, Blaine sputtered, "Don't waste good coin on those charlatans!"

The Imp retorted, "Why not? Don't you want to see the future? Mine has to be more than wearing gowns in the queen's stuffy court!"

Sir Tyrone intervened, "Come on, Blaine, let the girl have some fun. Where's the harm in it? If you like, I'll go with her to the Street of Mystics tomorrow night."

Blaine threw up his hands in surrender. "I want no part of it. She's yours to guard."

The black knight nodded. "It will be my pleasure."

Carl slapped a meaty paw across Blaine's shoulder. "Now you're free to visit the brothels me!" Blaine shied away from the big smith, wondering if the morrow would bring magic or mischief.

# 21

# Steffan

Steffan rode the black gelding to a lather each day, always stopping just short of riding it to death. Not that he cared about killing the horse, but it would have been difficult to find a swifter mount, so he tempered his need for speed with logic. Besides, he had work to do at night. He needed to get to Coronth quickly, but it was just as important to arrive with his saddlebags bulging with gold.

Each night he sought out the dicing games that were common in the taverns of Erdhe. He'd always been good at dicing, but now he couldn't lose. Luck with dice was one of three gifts he'd gained while kneeling at the oracle and Steffan was reveling in the Dark Lord's favor.

He started the evenings in the pubs frequented by the locals. The winnings were lean but they added to his purse. As the night advanced, Steffan moved on to the more expensive taverns, enticing the rich to gamble away their golds. As ale pitchers emptied, the golds flowed more freely and the dice always fell in Steffan's favor. If he concentrated hard enough, he could actually lose a roll. He did this just often enough to sucker the gamblers into even bigger bets. His charm was such that most of the losers never objected to his 'remarkable' run of luck, and if they did complain, Steffan was quick to challenge them with his dirk or his sword. He took their golds either way and then moved on to the next town, never staying longer than one night in any one place. As he rode north, his saddlebags grew heavier with golds, gems, and jewelry. It was truly a pleasure to serve the Dark Lord.

His journey northward led him through Pellanor, the capital of Lanverness. The city sprawled beyond its walls, a tangled crush of people, markets, and opportunities. Steffan held the gelding to a walk, threading his way through the wide cobblestone streets, gauging the worth of the place. Crowds thronged the marketplace, the bright velvets and leather of noblemen mixing easily with the homespun wool of merchants and peasants. The steel armor of soldiers was noticeably absent, but the fabled wealth of the Spider Queen was everywhere, from the tallow lanterns lining the cobblestone streets, to the exotic scents of the spice market, to the easy smiles of the people. Soft and full of indulgences, the city was perfect for his needs. Steffan guided the gelding to the most affluent part of town and took a room at one of the better inns. Signing for his room with a flourish, he used the name of 'the Lord Steffan Raven'.

He rose early the next morning and made his way to the Street of Tailors. Lavish with his golds, Steffan insisted on nothing but the best. Spinning a tale of a distant branch of royal blood, Steffan invented a house emblem consisting of a black raven on a blood red field, ordering a black wardrobe trimmed and piped with crimson. In the afternoons he was fitted for new black riding boots and supple black leather gloves, only the finest leathers would do. In the horse market, Steffan sold the black gelding, purchasing a sorrel-colored eighteen-hand warhorse. Trained to kick, rear, or bite on command, the horse would be a valuable ally in dealing with the street-rabble of Coronth. The red stallion proved a magnificent animal, the perfect compliment for the Lord Raven's new image.

In the backstreets of Pellanor, Steffan sought out a gold jeweler with questionable scruples. The man had a weasel face and limited skills, but he had a large furnace capable of casting gold ingots. Reaching an agreement with him, Steffan emptied his saddlebags on the man's workbench, gold and jewelry spilling out in a glitter of wealth.

Dazzled, the jeweler plunged his hands into the tangled mound, avidly sorting gold from silver and gems from jewelry. With the exception of one ruby ring that Steffan had resized to fit his hand, all his winnings were sold for golds. Once his wealth was converted, Steffan ordered the jeweler to melt down the coins and cast the liquid metal into solid ingots. The jeweler worked through the night, Steffan by his side. By mid-morning, six bars of solid gold, a king's ransom, gleamed on the jeweler's workbench.

The jeweler sat hunched at the bench, mesmerized by the ingots. "I've never cast bars of solid gold. Never had a customer ask for it." The man's voice sank to a whisper, "Such a deep luster, such a warm radiance."

Slipping behind the jeweler, Steffan reached for the dirk sheathed at his back. "Glitter enough to ensnare the soul...and never let go." He thrust six inches of cold steel into the jeweler's back, and the man slumped forward, silenced forever. Steffan cleaned the blade on the dead man's tunic, and then wrapped the gold bars in velvet, the perfect lure for the Pontifax of Coronth.

His work done, Steffan set about enjoying the luxuries of the queen's city. His nights were both entertaining and profitable. Seasoned gamblers were always looking for fresh meat. The Lord Raven flashed his ruby ring the size of a pigeon's egg, looking just the part. The gamblers never suspected they invited a stranger with the luck of the Dark Lord to join their games.

On one rainy night, at one of the more exclusive parties, fate, or perhaps the Dark Lord, intervened, offering Steffan a unique opportunity. The Lord Raven found himself dicing opposite Prince Danly of House Tandroth, the second son of the queen of Lanverness. A strapping young man with dashing good looks, the prince bet golds as if he had no limit. Attracted by the prince's careless wealth, Steffan focused the full force of his charm on the young man while making sure the prince's goblet was kept full. Wine flowed and the golds crossed the table, accumulating in front of the Lord Raven. Steffan gazed at the young lordling. "My prince, you bet with the courage of a lion but Lady Fortune smiles elsewhere."

"I merely spread the wealth, a servant to my people." He barked a laugh. "The queen's coffers are bottomless, it won't be missed."

"Surely not bottomless?"

"They say the Spider Queen spins threads of gold from the very air! Webs of wealth, sticky and binding, no telling who they'll bind or what they'll catch." The prince drained his goblet, wiping his mouth with the back of his velvet sleeve. "Yes, my Royal Mother is quite something...an irritating itch, a witch, a bitch." The prince pushed a pile of gold coins into the center of the table. "The Spare Heir takes great pleasure in spending her gold. So roll the dice, if you dare, and let's see if Luck's fortune still favors the Raven."

The prince clearly nursed a hatred for his mother and perhaps all members of the weaker sex. Steffan sensed an opportunity to garner favor with the Dark Lord. "Why don't we make the wager more interesting? Your golds against an evening of entertainment?"

"Entertainment?"

Steffan gave him a rake's smile. "Something unusual, something befitting the depths of the night."

The prince laughed. "I like you, Lord Raven, you're more interesting than most of the nobles of the Rose Court. I'll take your wager."

Steffan scooped up the dice. A hush settled across the room. Well-dressed gentlemen crowded close to witness the outcome. Steffan rolled the dice, a dramatic toss, spinning them across the table. He watched the tumble of ivory, concentrating hard...making sure to lose.

The prince crowed in delight. "Fortune turns! Describe my prize, and it best be worth the wager!"

Steffan stifled a smile. "Anticipation is part of the pleasure. Meet me tomorrow night at the Inn of Three Roses, one turn of the hourglass past sunset, and I'll pay my debt." The prince agreed and the gaming continued. The luck of the dice returned to the Lord Raven. Steffan finished the night with the prince's confidence, as well as most of his golds.

The next morning, Steffan used his charms to gain access to an exclusive bordello, one restricted to wealthy patrons with unusual tastes. In the company of the madam, he inspected each woman. Since his night with the Priestess, Steffan had developed an obsession for tall statuesque women with black hair. One courtesan was close enough to carry the illusion. She also had the flexibility required for the evening ahead. After choosing the courtesan, he toured the mansion to find the perfect setting for his passion play, eventually settling on a small intimate bedchamber with a fireplace, a large stuffed chair, and a four-post bed. He gave the madam detailed instructions as well a very large purse with the promise of more.

Prince Danly arrived early the next evening, hungry with anticipation. At Steffan's suggestion, they had a few drinks before retiring to the bordello. As he suspected, the young prince was familiar with the establishment and even had his favorites among the women. Madam Stock met them at the door, ushering them past the drawing room where selections were usually made and showing them directly to the intimate bedchamber. The prince was clearly puzzled when Steffan followed him inside.

Closing the door behind them, Steffan invited the prince to sit in the armchair. "As a prince of the realm, I am sure you've had ample opportunity to sample the pleasures of many women, but have you ever had the opportunity to *watch* a master take a woman?"

The prince's eyes widened and his pupils dilated, telling Steffan his guess had hit the mark. Hiding his smile, Steffan said, "Since we met over dice, let me offer a little wager to sweeten the night." He produced a large purse from one pocket and two silken ropes from the other. "I propose to tie your hands to the arms of the chair. If the ropes are still in place by the time I'm finished with the woman, then the purse of golds is yours. If either rope is unraveled, then you'll double my purse. Do you accept?" The gleam in the prince's eye was all the answer Steffan needed. Kneeling, he loosely bound the silken ropes around the young man's wrists. Satisfied, he settled on the plush bearskin rug, enjoying the warmth of the fire.

A knock sounded on the door. A statuesque woman with long raven hair entered carrying a tray laden with heated oils and small bowls of exotic spices. Except for a few strands of beads, the woman was naked. Ignoring the prince, the courtesan knelt and slowly undressed Steffan, anointing him with heated oils. Steffan lay still, letting his arousal build. When the room was thick with tension, he moved like a panther, covering the woman and pushing her down into the plush fur of the rug. Lost in the illusion of the priestess, he strove to recreate his one night on the Isle of the Oracle. The courtesan was no match for the priestess, but the night still held its pleasures. Relentless in his desire, he took the woman past the point of exhaustion. The only sounds in the room besides the crackling of the fireplace were the sighs of the woman and the gasps of the prince. Finally sated, Steffan rolled back onto the bearskin rug.

By the light of the glowing embers, he took stock of the prince. The young man's eyes were glazed, his brow beaded with sweat, three wet stains on the front of his unlaced breeches. One silken rope lay at the foot of the chair. "It seems you've enjoyed the entertainment, my lord. Can I assume that my golds will be waiting for me at the Inn of the Three Roses?"

The prince nodded in a dazed fashion. Steffan collected his clothes and dressed. He helped the prince to his feet and bundled him into a blue cape and then into a closed carriage waiting in the back alley.

Steffan slept late the next morning, ordering a hot bath delivered to his room. When he finally made it down to the common room of the inn, the noon meal was being served and the prince was waiting for him. Steffan hid his smile, knowing the Dark seed had taken quick root. Most souls only needed a small twist to turn toward the Dark, and the young prince was no exception.

Shaping his face to look pleasantly surprised, he took a seat at the prince's table, "My Lord, I hardly expected to see you this morning, or perhaps I should say this afternoon. How can I be of service?"

"I just wanted to thank you for the pleasure of your company and for the quality of your entertainment. I'm quite sure that I have never seen the like." The prince removed a small purse from his pocket. "I've brought your winnings and a little extra." Danly set a square-cut emerald on the table, well worth several times the golds owed. "I was hoping you might organize more nights of entertainment for me."

"I am sorry, my prince. I wish I could, but I leave today on urgent business. Perhaps when my business brings me back this way?"

"Let us hope that you return soon. Meanwhile, please accept this emerald with my thanks."

Steffan pocketed the emerald and then shared a pleasant meal with the prince. Once the meal was finished, he bade farewell to the prince and organized his belongings for the trip to Coronth. Steffan left the capital city mounted on a magnificent red warhorse, his saddlebag bulging with gold, his packhorse burdened with purchases. His stay in Pellanor had proved quite profitable. His chance encounter with the prince was especially satisfying, offering him the chance to plant a Dark seed. He wondered what fruit it would bear...perhaps an unexpected gift for the queen. Surely the Dark Lord would be pleased. Putting spurs to his stallion Steffan asked for a gallop. He looked forward to meeting the Pontifax and to gaining favor in the service of the Dark Lord.

## 22

# Katherine

The first pale light of the early morning struck the windowpane releasing Kath from bed. Eager to reach the Isle, she pulled on her squire's tunic and made a quick toilet. Tossing her nightclothes into her saddlebag, she threw the bag over her shoulder and bounded down the stairs to the common room for breakfast.

The innkeeper was busy with something behind the counter otherwise Kath had the room to herself. She moved to the sideboard, taking several slices of bread and a big piece of spicemelon. From Sir Tyrone's tales, she knew that spicemelon only grew on the Isle of Souls and that it was considered a rare delicacy in the other parts of Erdhe. Licking her fingers clean of the sticky juice, she wondered why a fruit would only grow in one place. Absorbed in her breakfast, she was surprised by the innkeeper's shout.

"Get out of here you mangy mouser! This is an inn not a barn! There's no room for your kind in this establishment!" The innkeeper brandished a wooden club at a slight man dressed in green leathers. The man made a gesture of supplication, but the innkeeper only yelled louder. "Get out of here before I split your worthless skull!"

The innkeeper's anger astonished Kath. The stranger looked clean and well dressed and the inn was only half full. It made no sense to turn away business.

The stranger retreated toward the door, but he must have felt Kath's stare, for he turned and looked directly at her. She gasped in shock. The stranger's eyes were golden yellow orbs with vertical slits for pupils: *the man had the eyes of a cat!* Even in bards' songs, she'd never heard of such a thing. Wondering if the stranger was a servant of the Dark Lord, she hastily sketched the hand sign against evil.

Heavy footsteps cascaded down the stairs. Kath was relieved to see the knights enter the common room. Captain Tellor gave her a pointed stare. "No time to sit and eat, just grab something for later. I want to be first in line to catch the ferry."

Grabbing her saddlebag and another piece of spicemelon, she followed the knights to the stable. They saddled their mounts and loaded the two packhorses with practiced ease, reaching the ferry before anyone else. They watched as the ferry master hitched a team of huge draft horses to the complex rope-and-pulley system used to operate the ferry. While they waited, a long line of people formed behind them. Kath wondered if the other travelers were seeking a shortcut across the lake or if they sought a glimpse of the future.

A bell clanged indicating the ferry was ready. Just large enough to hold ten horses and their riders, the ferry was a square wooden raft strung between guide ropes that linked the Isle to the mainland. Captain Tellor led the troop onto the floating platform. Kath made her way to the front, eager to be the first to see the fabled Isle.

A thick fog rose off the lake, hiding the Isle from curious eyes. The bell clanged a second time and the ropes creaked as the platform lurched into the fog, gliding across mirror-still waters. The world became white. Tendrils of fog crept around them, cold as dead fingers. Kath shivered and pulled her wool cloak close. Remembering Sir Tyrone's words, she imagined the fog was the gray veil, separating the present from the future. Kath leaned against the railing, wondering what the future held. For the longest time, she saw nothing, but then a breath of wind opened a window in the fog. A dark cliff loomed overhead, black basalt columns lining a gaping cave, like teeth in the mouth of a hungry beast. Kath stared into the cavern, wondering if anything lurked in the shadows. The ferry passed just beyond the basalt maw, shuddering to a stop at a second dock. Lantern light pierced the fog. A tall gangly man secured the ferry and opened the railed gate. "Welcome to the Isle of Souls. May you see the future clearly."

Kath bit back a retort, for the fog was so thick it hid the very ground. She led her stallion, Dancer, across the dock to a dirt road. The road quickly turned steep, switch-backing up side of the cliff. Mounting, she took it slow, unable to see more than a horse-length in front of her. The knights followed behind, the clop of hooves eerie in the fog. The switchbacks crisscrossed the cliff. Another stride of her horse and the world changed. Her head pierced the fog, her shoulders following. Sunshine beat against her face, providing a welcoming warmth. Staring back across Eye Lake, Kath was astonished by the view. From the height of the ridge, the scene was otherworldly. A blanket of fog surrounded the cliff, rendering it an island of reality on the shores of an insubstantial sea. Kath felt as if she'd ridden into a dream. Clucking to her horse, she urged him up the last switchback.

The Isle of Souls proved full of surprises. When they reached the top, the cliff turned out to be the rim of a small volcano, with a gentle bowl-shaped valley stretched below. Farms dotted the edge with a large town nestled in the heart of the crater. By mid-day they reached the town and settled their mounts at the first stable, but they had to try five inns before they found one with enough vacant rooms. After dumping her saddlebag in her room, Kath entered the common room, surprised to find Sir Blaine waiting with Sir Tyrone. The blond-haired knight gave her a rueful smile. "The fortunetellers don't ply their trade till the evening, so I thought I'd join the two of you in exploring the town."

Kath gave him a welcoming smile. "So where do we go first?"

A sparkle of mischief danced in the black knight's dark eyes. "I was talking to the innkeeper and it seems we're in luck. Turns out the Guild of Mystics holds a festival every turn of the full moon to test their members' ability to commune with the spirit world. Let's claim a spot in the town square and watch the show."

They headed for the Street of Merchants. Kath had never seen so many people. Merchants hawked their wares from tables lining the street, trying to shout above the noise of the crowd. Even the air smelled crowded, a pungent mix of rich perfumes and exotic spices underlain by the ripe stench of the unwashed. Fascinated by her first city, Kath's stare bounced between the crowd and the merchants, catching glimpses of mysterious alleyways off the main street. Beggars beckoned with outstretched hands from the shadows. Remembering the smith's talk of thieves, Kath moved closer to the two knights, pressing her hand to the gargoyle hidden beneath her tunic.

Sir Tyrone forged a path through the crowd, the people melting away at the sight of his octagon surcoat. The street widened into a cobbled square with a slender bell-tower in the center. They found seats on stone steps in front of a large building. Kath sat between the two knights, mesmerized by the spectacle of jesters and mimes working the crowd, evoking pockets of laughter while holding their caps out for offerings. Kath caught a tantalizing whiff of spiced chicken. She traced the scent, surprised to find that it led to a hawker selling grilled lizards impaled on sticks. The lizards smelled tempting but the sight of their jiggling yellow limbs spoiled her hunger. A blare of horns split the air and a rumble of drums signaled the arrival of a procession. Heralds bearing black standards emblazoned with white spirit hands led a procession of dancers and musicians into the square. Bare-chested men pounded drums and women in long flowing gowns blew odd-shaped horns creating a discordant din. Dancers in bright robes followed the musicians, ringing bells and waving long silk ribbons. The square dissolved into a confusing spectacle of noise and swirling colors. Three people wearing plain white shifts emerged from a side street, walking barefooted into the square, seeming oblivious to the chaos around them. Ten black-robed officials followed them, carrying a small ironbound chest and two wooden poles. The strange procession circled the square and then came to rest at the foot of the slender tower. The dancers increased their frenzied performance. Horns blared and drums thundered, creating a terrible noise.

The spectacle was colorful but crazy. Kath leaned toward the black knight and yelled over the noise, "Do you understand?"

Sir Tyrone tapped the shoulder of a well-dressed man sitting in front of him. "Sir, we're strangers to the Isle. Do you know the meaning behind the ritual?"

The man turned, revealing a moon-shaped face and a jovial smile. His eyes widened at the sight of Sir Tyrone. "Of course! My pleasure, Sir Knight! Merchant Hanley at your service, purveyor of exotic spices and other rare goods. I always come for the Festival of Mystics, wouldn't miss it for a fist full of silver." He flashed a ringed hand toward the square. "Everything has its purpose. The noise and the wild dancing attract the spirits beyond the veil, enticing them to come to the human side. The three people dressed in plain white shifts are the mystics. They walk in a trance communing with their gods." The merchant's voice turned serious. "The mystics must be linked to the spirit world in order to survive the test. The old woman, Tabbetha, is one of the best palm readers on the Isle. I go to her myself. She comes highly recommended. The red-haired man is a crystal ball gazer, but I don't know the other one. Of course, the black-robed men are the masters of the Guild of Mystics. They judge the proceedings. Let's watch and see if the spirits grant the mystics the strength to pass the test."

In the square below, one of the guildmasters used a key to open the chest. Reaching inside, he extracted thirteen long knives. Holding each knife aloft for the crowd's inspection, he then used it to slice a spicemelon in half, proving the sharpness of each blade. Once tested, the knives were fitted between the two poles. Kath gasped in disbelief as understanding struck; the knives were the rungs to a ladder! With thirteen knife-rungs, the ladder stretched to twice the height of a tall man. The guildmaster set the ladder against the slender tower. He split a final spicemelon across a rung, proving that the razor-sharp edges pointed up. A second black-robed master paraded a pristine white cloth around the square, placing it at the foot of the ladder.

Silence struck like a thunderclap. The musicians and dancers crumpled to the cobblestones as if all the energy had been sucked out of them. Then a thin gray-haired woman, the oldest of the mystics, approached the ladder. Kath held her breath, watching. Barefoot, the old woman began to climb, as if the rungs were made of wood instead of sharp steel. Kath expected a gush of blood but the mystic climbed without any sign of pain or injury. Reaching the top, she stepped onto the platform of the tower and pulled a bell rope. A deep sonorous tone filled the square. Then, without hesitation, she climbed back down the knife-ladder, stepping onto the white ground cloth before collapsing into the arms of a guildmaster. Kath craned forward, expecting to see a trail of bloody footprints. Even Sir Blaine let out a gasp of surprise when the cloth remained unsoiled. A guildmaster picked up the unsullied cloth and paraded it around the square like a victory banner. The crowd roared its approval.

The fat merchant turned to give them a smug smile. "I knew Tabbetha would pass! The guildmasters will paint a new spirit hand on the lintel of her shop this evening, certifying her for another year." Giving the black knight a conspiring smile, the merchant said, "It's a pretty convincing test. No charlatan would dare climb the ladder of knives! It's why I travel all the way to the Isle to have my fortune told. I wouldn't trust a fortuneteller not certified by the Guild. If you're smart, you'll look for the spirit hand when you select a mystic. Worth the extra golds to get a true reading."

Sir Tyrone asked, "Has anyone ever failed the test?"

"Oh my word yes! It wouldn't be much of test if no one ever failed. The last time I was here, one man made it half way up the ladder before he lost his link to the spirit world. Blood everywhere! He lost half his foot! Never trust a mystic who's missing a foot!" With a knowing wink, the merchant turned back to watch the rest of the trial.

Kath and the two knights looked at each other, not quite sure what to believe. By unspoken agreement, they stayed to watch the remaining two mystics complete the ritual. Both passed the test without leaving a single bloody print on the white telltale sheet.

With the trials complete, the guildmasters invited the crowd to touch the rungs of the ladder and test the keenness of the blades. Most began to disperse but a few skeptics made their way toward the ladder. Kath and the two knights joined the skeptics. Sir Blaine reached the ladder first, running his finger across one of the blades. A fresh sheen of blood appeared on the knife-edge. Kath stood slack-jawed, staring at the bloody knife-rung.

Sucking his finger, Sir Blaine shook his head in disbelief. "I don't know how they did that. Those knives are keen enough to split a hair."

Hope bloomed in Kath. "Does this mean it's true? Can the mystics really see the future?"

Sir Tyrone answered. "I don't know, Imp. The knife-ladder seems real enough to me. If there was a trick I didn't see it."

Stubborn in his skepticism, Blaine said, "Now that we've seen this mummer's farce, what do we do next?"

"Why not join us for an early dinner?" suggested Sir Tyrone. "Afterwards I can take the Imp to the Street of Mystics to have her fortune told."

Kath and Sir Blaine followed the knight back to the Street of Merchants. The noise and bustle seemed to have increased by ten-fold. Cries of, "Love potions for sale!" and "Amulets of protection!" competed with the conversation of the crowd. Tables jutted out from stores fronts, thrusting displays of wares into the flow. Merchants extolled the virtues of their goods while buyers dickered for better prices. Buffeted by so many colors and sounds, everything vied for Kath's attention. Trailing behind the knights, she stared enthralled. One hawker, an old man dressed in flowing robes, caught her attention. "Magical swords blessed by priests of Valin! Guaranteed to bring you victory!" Kath wormed her way through the crowd trying to get a closer look. Swords gleamed on a velvet-draped table. Elaborate hilts wrought with roaring lions and wingspread dragons proved tempting, but Kath knew the true worth of a sword was in its blade. Curious, she reached for a scabbarded short sword when she heard a strange snuffling sound at her elbow. Thinking it was a dog; Kath looked down and found herself staring into the up-turned face of a weird little man sniffing at her clothes. Cruel eyes and yellow teeth filed to sharp points flashed up at her like an evil goblin. Pawing at her tunic, the goblin-man hissed like a cockroach.

Recoiling, Kath pulled away, but the goblin-man scuttled after her. "No!" She reached for one of her axes while scrambling backwards and then tripped and fell hard on the uneven cobbles.

The two knights charged through the crowd. Sir Blaine unsheathed his great blue sword and cleared a space while Sir Tyrone got Kath to her feet. Rising, she scanned the crowd, searching for the goblin-man but there was no sign of him.

The black knight gripped her arm. "Are you all right?"

Kath nodded, clutching her throwing axe. Sir Blaine sheathed his sword and the crowds surged back around them as if nothing had happened. Sir Tyrone steered Kath toward the nearest tavern, his hand firm on her arm. Entering the tavern, the black knight commandeered a table in a quiet corner and ordered three meals of the standard fare. Once seated, the words rushed out of Kath. "I thought a dog was sniffing at me, but it turned out to be this strange little man, grinning with pointed teeth." Her heart raced, remembering. "I thought he was going to bite me! He looked like a goblin...but goblins are only myths, aren't they?"

Sir Tyrone said, "Goblins are only a myth, but you should never have left our protection. The Isle of Souls is a strange place, attracting all sorts. There's no telling what you saw." Glancing across at Sir Blaine, the black knight said, "We need to stay vigilant until we get off the Isle."

Their conversation stopped as the serving girl brought their meal. The standard fare turned out to be lamb stew with a loaf of crusty bread and a mug of cider. Suddenly ravenous, Kath set to eating. The savory stew dulled her fright. Between bites, Kath said, "I still want to have my fortune told."

"A midget with pointy teeth is chasing you and you still want to have your fortune told?" Sir Blaine shook his head. "I say we go back to the inn and call it a night. I've had enough mumbo jumbo for one day!"

"Surely I'll be safe with two knights of the Octagon?"

Blaine grimaced. "I'll tell your fortune and save you the golds. You're going to Lanverness to foster in the queen's court and then your father will arrange a good marriage. What more is there?"

Kath glared at him. "You don't understand. I have to find a way forward."

Sir Tyrone interceded, "Let her have her fun, Blaine. We'll go to the Street of Mystics and then head straight back to the inn. The night is still young and with two knights for escort I'm sure she'll be safe. What do you say?"

With a shrug, Sir Blaine gave in. They finished their meal and paid the fare, making their way out into the evening crowd. The Street of Mystics had a very different feel to the Street of Merchants. Narrow and crowded with small, intimate shops, it teased the mind instead of bludgeoning the senses. Windblown chimes added melody to the mystery. Lanterns gave off a soft yellow glow. Subtle smells of incense wafted like an enticing hand. The street delighted the senses, offering the promise of mysteries waiting to be revealed. Kath was enthralled. Turning to the black knight, she asked, "So how should I choose a mystic?"

"Be guided by your feelings instead of your mind. When you feel drawn to a place that's where we'll stop."

Kath walked down the street drinking in the sights and sounds, searching for a rightness she couldn't explain. Attracted by the pleasant sound of chimes, she stopped at a set of steps descending to a small shop.

A blue lantern shining from the window cast a welcoming light and the white spirit hand marking the lintel seemed to beckon her. "This one."

"I'll go in with you while Sir Blaine stands guard."

Kath opened the shop door. A bell chimed and the soothing fragrance of burning pine boughs reached out to greet her. Parting a curtain of beads, they entered a small room lit by the glow of many candles. A blonde-haired woman swathed in a colorful robe sat cross-legged at a low square table, patiently shuffling a deck of cards. "Be welcome in my house, may you see the future clearly. Please be seated and tell me how I may serve you."

Intrigued, Kath settled into a mound of colorful pillows. Sir Tyrone stood behind her, a comforting presence at her back.

The woman shuffled a worn deck. Her hands were long and elegant, the rings on her fingers catching the light of the candles. "My name is Samantha. I see the future through the tarot. My cards are keyed to the forces of Light." The woman stared at Kath, her pale hands expertly mixing the cards. "Since you seek the wisdom of the Light, you are welcome in my house. For the price of five golds I can help you see the future in the face of the tarot. Do you wish to continue?"

The price seemed exorbitant but Kath placed the coins on the edge of the table. The mystic smiled. "The cards of the tarot tap into the spirit world, uncovering the meaning and direction of our lives. Ask a question of the cards and it will be answered, but think first and ask wisely, for the cards will only answer one question."

Kath didn't need time to think; she knew what she wanted to ask. The question had always burned inside of her. She nodded, waiting for the woman to give her permission to speak.

As if reading her mind, the mystic said, "If you have a patron god, hold the image of that god in your mind and speak your question out loud."

Thinking of the warrior god, Kath said in a firm voice, "Is it my destiny to wield a sword? Where is the war helm?" Kath stifled a gasp, she'd meant to ask only one question but the second had slipped out.

The woman's eyes narrowed. "You tempt the gods with two questions not one. But the Questioner has spoken." Pushing the deck across the table, she said, "Cut the cards into three stacks, one for things that have already been, one for things that are now, and one for things that are yet to come. May the spirits guide your hand and may the cards fall true."

Kath did as she was told. The fortuneteller drew the top card from the second stack and turned it face up, revealing the *Three of Swords*, a woman in armor clutching a great sword. "This represents the Questioner as she is today. The girl stands alone, clutching a sword with determination. Her expression tells us that she did not acquire the sword easily."

Kath stared wide-eyed, amazed by the truth of the card.

Turning the second card in the stack, she revealed a grotesque winged creature hovering above the tormented souls of the damned. *The Devil* covered the *Three of Swords* like a curse. "The Dark Lord has seen you through the eyes of his servants."

A sudden tapping sound came from the window. Kath jumped, darting a glance toward the glass, but it was only a large moon-moth battering itself against the pane, attracted to the candlelight.

The mystic drew the top card from the stack of the future, displaying a mighty great sword clutched in the hand of a mailed fist. Kath's eyes widen, recognizing Valin's symbol. "The *Ace of Swords* represents a triumphant conquest. Victory by force of arms is the Questioner's potential destiny but first the challenges of the gods must be met."

"Now we look to the past." Turning the top card of the first stack, the mystic revealed an inverted font of water pouring out of an ornate chalice. "The inverted *Ace of Cups* symbolizes the absence of a mother's love. Love pours out of the chalice and is lost to time. This loss will influence you for all the days of your life." Kath stared at the golden chalice, wondering how so much could be revealed by a single card.

Jeweled hands reached for the next card. "This card represents your allies in the struggle to achieve your destiny." The card revealed a winged woman triumphant on a mountaintop. "*Justice*, the winged goddess Marut hovers at your side. A powerful ally, but one that is often slow to take action."

"This next card represents the Questioner's inner most hopes and desires." Kath held her breath, desperate for answers. The card revealed a crowned woman wearing armor and holding a great sword aloft. "Relying on her hidden strengths, the *Queen of Swords* forges her own destiny in a world of adversity, ruling by the might of steel. This card indicates that you will achieve your goals but only after facing great challenges."

The words stirred Kath's soul. Destiny reached for her in the form of a riddle. *A queen of swords, a steel queen,* yet Castlegard was only ever ruled by kings.

"This next card represents the greatest challenge facing the Questioner." Turning the card, the woman revealed a prancing jester. "*The Fool* is always chasing a dream that seems just out of reach. The Questioner must decide if her dream is worth the price. Dreams are seldom achieved by walking the safe road. Remember this when the time of choice is upon you."

The fortuneteller's hand hovered over the cards of the future. "And now we come to the last card of the reading. This card is the essence of everything. It represents the gods' answer to the Questioner."

As the mystic reached for the last card, the candles in the room began to flicker and a frantic tapping came from the window. A winged shadow passed across the mystic's face, distorting her features. Her ringed hands convulsed on the tabletop, scattering the cards in all directions. Jerked suddenly upright, the fortuneteller began to speak, but the voice was not her own. A raspy, masculine voice whispered, *"Remember!"*

The sound of the voice sent shivers down Kath's back.

*"Remember the time between! You are an old soul, a chosen of the Lords of Light. Stand fast and remember your purpose. Never relinquish the gargoyle; it is a gift of the Light. Keep it close always. Seek the fox in the forest and the wolf in the high mists, both will aid you. Answer the call from the mountains, but beware...the Ancient Evil awakes behind the safest walls. Remember!"*

Sir Tyrone reached past Kath to shake the woman.

The raspy voice said, *"The Light sees you Sir Knight. Your destiny lies with the Queen of Swords. Guard her well!"* An unseen hand snuffed out the candles, plunging the small room into near darkness.

The fortuneteller shuddered. "The cards?" Her voice was normal but confused. "Why are the cards strewn everywhere?"

Kath noticed that one card had fallen into her lap. She wondered if this was meant to be the gods' answer to her question. With a tentative hand, she turned it face up on the table. Her heartbeat thundered. She did not need the fortuneteller to recognize the card. A winged grotesque grinned up her. It was *The Devil*, the card of the Dark Lord.

# 23

# Liandra

Image was everything. Her ladies-in-waiting fluttered about, applying face powder, rouge, perfume, and jewels, working to perfect the reflection of their sovereign queen. Liandra scrutinized every detail, quick to point out any aspect that did not meet the royal standards. Few understood that the time spent before the mirror was not so much about appearances as it was about image. In a world dominated by kings and knights, the queen wielded her image like a sword, gaining advantage from every nuance of beauty and power. Finally satisfied, the queen dismissed her ladies and summoned her treasurer.

A tepid little teapot of a man, Lord Wesley was excellent with numbers and exacting in his accounts but he had little or no imagination when it came to finding new ways to grow the royal purse. Liandra would have liked to replace him with someone more skilled at multiplying golds instead of merely adding them but the men who were shrewd at commerce also tended to have sticky fingers. At least she could trust him with the royal treasury. He simply did not have the imagination to be a successful thief.

Her chief counselor, the Master Archivist, accompanied her treasurer. Lord Highgate was a tall, thin scarecrow of a man with an exceedingly keen intellect. Of all of her lords, Liandra most enjoyed the mental challenge of her spymaster, often including him in private meetings just to have access to his thoughts. The queen nodded to her spymaster and then gestured for Lord Wesley to begin.

"Your majesty, I am sorry to burden you with dreadful news, but I have just received an urgent report from the overseer of the Redstone mine. Instead of the prized blood-red rubies, the mine is now yielding only very dark stones. The gem-cutters inform me that they will be worthless on the market, seriously damaging our export revenues." Opening a small leather pouch, he offered the queen a handful of uncut rubies. The stones ranged in color from a dark crimson to nearly black.

The queen considered them. "Apart from the unfortunate color, can these rubies still be cut into gemstones?"

Lord Wesley nervously twisted the empty pouch. "As far as I know, the only change is the color, but it's the rich red hue that makes a ruby valuable."

"Is the Redstone the only mine afflicted with this problem?"

"Yes, but the Redstone is by far the kingdom's most valuable producer."

"How do you suggest we respond to this problem?"

Her treasurer paled. "We should close the mine and save the royal treasury the cost of paying the miners...and the royal budget must be adjusted to account for the loss in revenue."

Turning to the Master Archivist, the queen asked, "Lord Highgate, what say you?"

"I see no other course of action but to close the mine and encourage the miners to find more fertile rock."

The queen contemplated the uncut stones. The ruby mines provided a constant flood of wealth, the bedrock of the royal treasury. Liandra could not allow her best mine to fail. She held a stone aloft. The uncut gem caught and held the light, throwing off a spark of dark color from its crimson heart. "Lord Wesley, the Redstone mine will *not* be closed. Instead, the royal treasury will pay a bonus to the miners for discovering the rarest of all rubies, the Royal Ruby, a gem fit for a queen. Urge the miners to increase production. In the meantime, a royal commission will be given to the gem-cutters and jewelers of Pellanor, tasking them to create a necklace worthy of their sovereign. We will have the necklace completed in time for the Harvest Ball. We expect it to be nothing less than exquisite. The craftsmen are ordered to exceed themselves. Are we understood?"

"B-but your majesty, the dark stones are worthless! T-the master gem cutter has assured me that they will not sell on the open market!"

"The value of the ruby lies in its rarity and in its beauty. If the Redstone mine is the only mine to produce the Royal Ruby, then these dark stones are rare. As to beauty, Lanverness defines fashion for the kingdoms of Erdhe and *the queen* defines the fashion for Lanverness. If the queen finds the Royal Ruby to be exquisitely beautiful, who will disagree?"

The light of understanding bloomed in her treasurer's eyes, "Madam, it is truly an honor to serve you."

"One more thing, Lord Wesley. When the Royal Rubies are brought to market, their price will be set at twice that of a conventional ruby. For many people, *price* is the sole measure of *value*. The Royal Rubies will *not* disappoint. We predict they will be quite the rage at in the coming season." With a wave the queen dismissed her treasurer and turned to the Master Archivist. "Tell us, Lord Highgate, is the royal party from Navarre here?"

"Yes, your majesty. They await your presence."

"Good. Navarre is a small kingdom of only middling wealth, but their army of archers is not to be taken lightly. We wish to deepen the alliance between the Osprey and the Rose. We expect you to assist us with this objective."

"As your majesty commands."

Rising, Liandra gestured for her shadowmaster to escort her through the gilded corridors to the audience chamber. At the door to the chamber, a royal herald announced the queen's presence. "All rise for her royal majesty, the sovereign queen of Lanverness. May all the Lords of Light save her majesty, Queen Liandra."

Courtiers in bright silks bowed low as the queen crossed the checkerboard floor. Mounting the dais, she took a seat on an elegant throne sculpted of golden roses. Her gaze swept the crowd, seeking the royal party from Navarre. One in particular caught her interest, a tall, handsome rogue in black leather with the broad chest of an archer and a black patch covering one eye, a lone wolf among the bright plumage of her court. Intrigued, she made a subtle hand sign to the Master Archivist.

Her spymaster led the Navarren party to the dais. "Your majesty, may I present Lord Duncan Treloch, the ambassador from Navarre."

So the rogue had a title, all the more interesting. Putting one booted foot on the first step of the dais, the leather-clad ambassador offered her a scroll sealed with wax. "Your majesty, please accept this note of introduction from King Ivor."

Liandra gave him her warmest smile. "We welcome you to the Rose Court. We hope you will make yourselves at home during your stay with us."

Offering a courtly bow that belied his rough dress, the ambassador said, "You are most generous. With your permission, I would like to present three of the Royal Js of Navarre." The three young people came forward and bowed. "Princess Jordan, who is on her way to the Southern Mountains to study with the Kiralynn monks, Prince Justin, who is on his way to Wyeth to become a bard, and Princess Jemma who will foster here at Pellanor with your majesty in the Rose Court."

"We are pleased to welcome three of the King Ivor's heirs to our court. We count King Ivor and Navarre as strong allies and we are especially pleased that Princess Jemma chose to foster with us. We hope that the four of you will join us for a private dinner tonight where we will have a better chance to get acquainted."

"We would be honored, your majesty."

The queen signaled to the court historian. Lord Penrod, a portly man with snow-white hair stepped forward. Snapping a scroll open with a flourish, he cleared his throat, and began to recount the lengthy history between Lanverness and Navarre. Deliberately wordy, the reading of the scroll was designed to give the queen time to observe her royal visitors. Her gaze lingered on Lord Duncan. The man had a feral quality about him, a sexual magnetism that even Liandra was not immune to. From a woman's perspective, Duncan Treloch was certainly an eye full, but there must be more to the man for King Ivor to select him as his ambassador. The queen smiled, enjoying the masculine puzzle wrapped in black leathers.

Drawing her gaze away from the ambassador, the queen studied Princess Jemma. A petite beauty with milk-white skin, an aquiline nose, and long black hair brushed to a high luster. Her gown was provincial, but the low-cut neckline and dark blue color accented her best features. Clearly the princess possessed a sense of image. If there was a mind behind that pretty face then she might just be what Liandra was looking for in a daughter-in-law.

Next, she turned her gaze to Princess Jordan. Tall and lanky with short sandy hair, Princess Jordan seemed ill at ease in her court gown, the opposite of her petite sister. Liandra wondered why a princess of Navarre would choose to foster with the mysterious Kiralynn monks, another riddle to unravel.

The last member of the royal party was Prince Justin, the aspiring bard. Of middling height, the prince had drab brown hair and sharp features rescued by bright blue eyes. Noticing the queen's stare, the prince flashed a delightful smile and sketched a courtly bow. Liandra took an instant liking to him, sensing a keen wit and a lively character behind his homely appearance. She suspected the young bard would break more than a few hearts.

The Royal Js were an interesting lot. Based on appearances, one would never guess the three were siblings, yet they all seemed to possess a unique and independent depth of character. Clearly King Ivor had done well with his children. A pity her own two sons did not have the same underlying mettle, but perhaps the deficiencies could be corrected with the proper wives. King Ivor may have done Lanverness a great favor by sending his daughters to Pellanor.

Lord Penrod finished reading the scroll of welcome. In the silence that followed, all eyes turned toward the queen. Rising from the throne, she gave her guests a gracious smile. "Now that the official welcome is over, with the exception of Lord Highgate, my counselors are dismissed with thanks for their time." Smiling at the tall man in black leather, the queen said, "Lord Ambassador, would you escort us to dinner?"

Executing a courtly bow, the ambassador offered his arm. Descending from the dais, the queen let her hand rest upon it, noting the corded muscles beneath the black sleeve. With subtle pressure, she directed him out of the chamber and through the hallways, deliberately taking the long way. "We are pleased with your presence, Lord Duncan, but pray tell us why King Ivor saw the need to send us an ambassador?"

"Your majesty, I am an advisor and friend to King Ivor but I do not hold the title of 'lord', so please call me by my given name, Duncan."

So rare to find a man who declined a lord's title; the conversation was barely started and already the queen's interest was piqued. "You are King Ivor's appointed ambassador. As a sign of respect, you will be given the title of 'lord' while you are in our court." She gave him a smile. "It would please us if you would humor us in this matter."

With a bow of his head, Lord Duncan conceded the point. "As you wish, your majesty. As to your question, I am in Lanverness for two reasons. The first is to escort the Royal Js on their Wayfaring. I will eventually go with Princess Jordan to the Southern Mountains to seek out the Kiralynn monks. But before I leave, the king has charged me to broach his concern with Coronth. I do not know if word has yet reached Lanverness, but at a feast following a royal archery tournament a rogue archer from Coronth attacked the royal party, gravely wounding the king."

Her shadowmen had done well. Liandra framed her face to reflect surprise. "We are shocked. We trust King Ivor will recover?"

The ambassador gave her a keen stare. "The king is expected to make a full recovery."

"We are relieved to hear it, but what prompted this attack?"

"Religious zeal."

His words struck at the heart of her fears but she kept her face composed.

"We learned much from the attacker. This new Flame God is jealous. Those who do not worship him are considered infidels. We fear this religion of the Flame can be used to justify any crime against any so-called infidel. King Ivor asked me to seek your counsel."

"There is nothing so dangerous as a religious zealot. Let us hope that Coronth is not breeding them." She nodded gravely at the ambassador. "We thank you for your insights. King Ivor did well to send you. Let us meet tomorrow afternoon to discuss Coronth, but now it is time for dinner and conversation that is more pleasing to the appetite."

Servants bowed as they entered a small, intimate dinning chamber. A round table, set with silver place settings for six, glittered like a jewel in the candle light. As they took their seats a bevy of servants approached, pouring fine wines and presenting platters of poached salmon, spiced lamb, and roasted duckling. The Rose Court was renowned for the delicacies of its kitchen, another carefully cultivated aspect of image.

Between courses, the queen probed the two princesses with conversation. Turning to Princess Jordan, she asked, "Pray tell us why you selected the Kiralynn monks for your Wayfaring?"

"It was not my *choice* but my father's *order*. My choice was to go to Castlegard to train with the knights of the Octagon but my father and his council rejected my proposal claiming the knights would never train a woman." The princess shrugged, a masculine gesture that was at odds with her silk gown. "So instead of going to Castlegard, I am sent to the monks to learn the art of war."

The queen raised her eyebrows. "Common wisdom says the fair sex was not meant to wield a sword. Would the army of Navarre accept the leadership of a woman?"

A twinkle of amusement lit the blue eyes of the princess. "Many would say that a woman is not fit to rule a kingdom alone, and they would be wrong, especially if they said it in Lanverness. Besides, a woman once led the army of Navarre in repulsing an attack of the Mordant's hordes, the renowned General Diana. So I will train with the monks in the event that history repeats itself."

The queen frowned. "War is a wanton waste of men and money, something to be avoided at all costs."

"Tell that to the Mordant. The southern kingdoms cannot afford to be complacent."

The girl had a quick wit and a bold character, but it was unnatural for any woman to take up the sword, especially a princess. Liandra appreciated the girl's forthright spirit but could not condone her misguided choice. "We wish you luck in your training." Turning to Princess Jemma, she said, "We are pleased you chose to foster in our court. Pray tell us what you hope to learn?"

"In the kingdoms of Erdhe, there are many woman married to kings but there is only one queen who rules. I am here, your majesty, to learn how a woman can rule a powerful kingdom. And I wish to learn your secret of prosperity. I would see Navarre grow in wealth and stature among the kingdoms of Erdhe."

Liandra kept her face neutral, but inwardly she was delighted. "So you do not share your sister's desire to wield a sword?"

"Men rule with swords, women rule in other, more subtle ways." Bowing her head, the princess said, "I have come to apprentice with the master."

It seemed Liandra had found the perfect candidate for her future daughter-in-law.

# 24

# Blaine

The Isle of Souls was a day and a half behind them and good riddance to it. Blaine wasn't sure what happened on their only night in the city, but whatever it was, it had scared the Imp. She'd been closed-mouthed ever since, always keeping Sir Tyrone by her side. He glanced back at the two of them, riding close, their heads bent in conversation and resentment flared through him. He'd given up a lot for this girl, the least she could do was talk to him.

Reining his charger in, he dropped back to ride next to her. Their conversation came to a sudden halt. Frustrated, he could not help blurting out, "Can't you tell me what happened on the Isle? Surely the future can't be that bad?"

Kath frowned at him. "I thought you didn't believe in fortunetellers."

"After watching the mystics climb the knife-ladder I'm not sure what I believe."

The Imp gave him a searching look. Blaine could tell she was judging him, trying to see if he was making fun of her. He'd been around the Imp long enough to know that the one thing the girl couldn't stand was to not be taken seriously. "Come on, Imp, you trusted me to train you with the sword. Trust me now and tell me what happened."

She looked skeptical, but relented. "It's hard to explain." Steering her horse closer to him, she kept her voice low. "The fortuneteller said things she couldn't possibly have known. She knew my mother died giving birth to me. She knew my father forbade me to train with weapons. How could she have known these things if she wasn't tied to the spirit world?"

"Did she really say those things or are you reading more into her words than was actually there?"

Sir Tyrone said, "Sir Blaine has a point. Messages from the gods tend to be cryptic. Getting a single word wrong can distort the entire message."

A look of frustration claimed the Imp's face. "But it doesn't make sense. Why don't the gods use the common tongue like everyone else? Why don't they just say what they mean, instead of speaking in riddles?" In a stubborn mutter she added, "I bet the Dark Lord isn't cryptic when he deals with his minions."

The black knight roared with laughter, startling his horse. "Only you would think that way!" He settled his horse and gave her a wry smile. "I'm only a simple knight, so I can't begin to explain the gods, but I think if you asked a priest or a philosopher they'd say that the Lords of Light believe in the free will of mankind. By giving cryptic messages, the gods allow man to choose his own interpretation and thereby choose his own destiny. In contrast, the Dark Lord is only interested in servants and slaves, so he has no problem issuing direct commands." He shrugged. "As mere mortals, we'll just have to do the best we can with the cryptic messages and thank the gods for any help they see fit to give us."

Confused by all the talk of gods, Blaine said, "What are you two taking about? It was just a tarot reading."

Kath and the black knight exchanged stares, then the girl said, "The fortuneteller said the Dark Lord's minions are watching me. And," she dropped her voice to a whisper, "I think it has something to do with the goblin-man." She gave him a troubled glance. "Something strange happened at the end of the reading. The fortuneteller's voice changed and some god or spirit spoke through her. It was scary."

Blaine looked at the black knight. Sir Tyrone met his gaze and nodded. Astonished, Blaine asked, "So what did the god say?"

"It didn't make a lot of sense. The voice said that I was an old soul; dedicated to serving the Lords of Light, and that I should stand fast. Then the voice said something about finding a fox in the forest, a wolf in the mists, and a summons from the mountains. Does that mean anything to you?"

"No." He paused. "So do you even know which god spoke through the mystic?"

"The voice that took over the mystic was raspy and masculine, so I assumed it was Valin."

Blaine gaped, thunderstruck.

"I heard the voice as well." Sir Tyrone said. "The god claimed to speak for the Lords of Light."

Blaine struggled to understand. If the god of warriors was taking a direct interest in the Imp, then he had seriously underestimated her. He stared at Kath, seeing her in a new light. She was a princess of Castlegard, with a preternatural skill for weapons. Looking back on how quickly she'd taken to the sword, he wondered if she really did hold the favor of the warrior god. Meeting her stare, he said in a solemnly voice, "I believe you. After all, you're a princess of Castlegard, a child of the Octagon. What place in all of Erdhe honors Valin more than Castlegard?"

She smiled, a glow of gratitude in her eyes. Blaine had to look away; struck to the heart. "So what do the gods want?" he said after a moment.

"That's the problem; the message doesn't really make sense. I'm meant to wield a sword in the service of the Lords of Light, but apart from that, I don't really understand what the gods want."

Sir Tyrone said, "I am sure the message will become clear with time."

Kath looked at the dark knight. "Yes, but how much time do we have?"

"That I do not know, my lady."

The three companions rode together in silence. Dark forests pressed close to the narrow road, the scent of pine thick in the air. Looking over at Kath, Blaine said, "If Valin has a task for you, then you best be prepared for it. I think we should resume your weapons training."

His suggestion brought an eager light to the girl's eyes. "I agree."

"You're good with your throwing axes but you could be better with the sword. When we stop tonight, I'll borrow two short swords from the squires and give you a lesson with real steel. We dare not waste the warning of the gods."

As the sun dipped toward the horizon, they started to look for a place to spend the night. This part of Wyeth proved to be a wild, untamed land, full of dark forests and rocky outcrops with only a few farms and holdfasts clawed out between the old growth trees. Eventually they found a solitary roadhouse with a sagging roof overgrown with moss and the sign so faded the few remaining letters made no sense. The ramshackle inn offered little hope of comfort, but they would make do.

The innkeeper turned out to be as decrepit as the inn. Hunched with age, the old man gave the knights a thin welcome and showed them to rooms flush with cobwebs and the musty scent of mildew. After dumping their gear, Blaine, Kath, and Sir Tyrone met behind the roadhouse for sword training. Under a twilight sky, Blaine sparred with the girl while Sir Tyrone barked a running commentary. Kath showed no fear of real steel, opening with a flurry of attacks and Blaine pressed her hard. They fought till the last light faded. When Blaine finally called a halt, Kath was swaying from exhaustion and drenched with sweat. He stared at her with renewed respect. Despite her handicap of size and strength, she'd put up a good fight. He saluted her with his sword, winning a weary smile. They sheathed their blades and retreated to the common room, hungry for dinner.

As Blaine scraped the last of the venison stew from his bowl, he was surprised to hear a soft snore to his left. Kath sat slumped over her stew, sound asleep. Chuckling, he prodded her awake and walked her to her room, then returned to the common room to share a pitcher of ale with Tyrone.

Pouring himself a tankard, Blaine said, "So what do you make of this talk of gods?"

"If I hadn't been there myself, I wouldn't believe it. The god named her the *Queen of Swords*."

"But she's only a *girl!*"

Sir Tyrone gave him a piercing stare. "You know better than that."

Blaine's heart hammered in his chest, recognizing the truth. "But what do the gods want?"

"I wish I knew. Valin spoke to me as well. He said my destiny was tied to hers, that I shouldn't leave her side." His face grew solemn. "When we reach Lanverness, I will stay on with her. I don't know what the gods want of her, but she'll have my sword to guard her back."

Blaine sat dumbstruck. Why had the gods spoken to the girl and the black knight, yet said nothing to him? He was the one carrying a hero's blue sword, yet the gods ignored him. If Kath was destined for high adventure, then Blaine refused to be left out. Raising his tankard, he said, "She'll have two swords to guard her back, brother, not one."

# 25

# Katherine

Kath struggled for breath. What little air she managed to get reeked of rotten meat. Clawing her way out of a bad dream, she opened her eyes and stared into the hideous face of an ogre. She gasped in disbelief, but the meaty hand smothering her face and the hairy arm pinning her to the bed were both real. She screamed but only a muffled croak escaped.

The ogre flashed a crooked grin full of sharp teeth and then scooped Kath up against his barrel chest, keeping one hand over her mouth. She kicked against him, but he ignored her blows. She tried to scream but could barely get enough air to breathe. Squirming, she struggled for freedom but the ogre just tightened his bone-crushing grip. Someone opened the door to her room and the giant carried her down the hallway, through the common room, and out into the cool night air.

She caught a glimpse of a crescent moon hanging high in the night sky and knew the knights must still be sleeping. Listening for voices, she heard only the thundering of her own heart. The ogre carried her across the road, plunging into the undergrowth of the forest. Panic bit deep, giving her a surge of wild strength, but her struggles were in vain.

Leaves and branches slapped against her, bending but not breaking. The ogre walked with a ground eating pace. Dark and forbidding, the midnight forest swallowed Kath and her abductors. Deep into the forest, the ogre came to an abrupt stop, dumping Kath onto a bed of leaves. She landed hard, the breath rushing out of her. Before she could make a move to escape, the ogre pinned to the ground. Ropes looped around her ankles, arms, and hands, proving the ogre had an accomplice. Bound and trussed like a pig for the market, Kath glared at her captors.

Out of the dark, an oily voice said, "Well done, Tiny." A man's face loomed down at her. Dark eyes set over a hawk nose. "No use struggling, girlie, the prize needs to behave itself if it doesn't want to be hurt. Do you understand, girlie? Blink if you do."

Kath didn't understand anything but not having any choice in the matter she blinked.

"I'm going to tell Tiny to remove his hand and we are going to put this nice leather gag in your mouth. The prize will be quiet and take the gag or I'll let Tiny play with her. We're too far away for those shiny knights to hear your screams, so you best cooperate."

The ogre removed his hand and the oily man forced a leather gag into her mouth. It all happened so quickly Kath hardly had time to take a deep breath. The gag tasted foul but at least she could breathe. She flexed her back, testing the ropes. There was no play in the knots; she was bound tight.

The man said, "Bolo, come over here and make sure the prize is intact."

A dwarf bent over her, his nose hovering inches from her waist, making a snuffling sound like a hound after a scent. He lifted his head, meeting her gaze. There was no mistaking the cruel eyes and the yellow teeth filed to sharp points. Recognizing the goblin-man from the Isle of Souls, Kath let out a muffled scream.

The goblin-man cackled at her distress then reached beneath her tunic, withdrawing the little gargoyle tied by a leather thong around her neck. In a deep voice that didn't fit with his stunted body, he said, "The prize is here, captain."

The man with the oily voice leaned over, peering at the gargoyle. Kath expected him to take it, but instead he tucked it back inside her tunic. "Bring her."

The ogre scooped her up and threw her face down across the back of a horse like a sack of goods, tying her to the saddle. Looking at the world upside-down, Kath tried to take stock of the situation. There seemed to be four of them: the man with the oily voice, the ogre, the goblin-man, and a second man who carried a bow. The goblin-man rode a pony and the ogre rode a huge draft horse. The knights would have no problem catching up to the pony and the draft horse, provided they knew the direction to ride. Finding the trail was the part that worried her. The knights were peerless fighters but they weren't known for their skills of woodcraft. Kath knew she should leave some sort of trail, but with her hands bound tight there wasn't anything she could do.

The group set off at a gallop, moving deeper into the heart of the forest. Flopping against the side of the horse, the blood rushed to Kath's head. She tried to take note of any landmarks, but she soon passed out. When she came to, she was propped against a tree, still bound and gagged, her body bruised and sore. Desperately thirsty and needing to relieve herself, she tried to scream through the gag. The muffled noise got the attention of the oily man who seemed to be in charge of the marauders.

"So the prize finally wakes!" He squatted next to her, peering at her face. "We're deep in the forest, girlie, where your shiny knights will never find us. Screaming will not bring your friends, but it will annoy me. If I remove the gag, will the prize behave and be quiet? Blink if you agree."

Kath decided being able to talk would be a good start toward getting free. Meeting the oily man's stare, she blinked and then the man reached over and removed the gag.

Working some saliva back into her mouth, Kath croaked, "Water?"

Holding a flagon of water to her lips, he let her drink her fill. Then she said, "What do you want with me?"

The captain patted her chest. It seemed to Kath that he was making sure the gargoyle was still in place. "The prize will be well treated if she behaves. If she gives us any trouble then there will be pain. Does the prize understand?"

"Yes, I will behave, but what do you want with me?"

"We serve a master who collects magic. Bolo found you on the Isle of Souls. Those shiny knights think they're invincible, but they weren't watching, were they? They weren't protecting the prize." The man leaned close, his fetid breath hot on her face. "The prize is destined for the master." Getting to his feet, he added, "We'll rest for a while and I'll leave the gag out of your mouth if you behave. Does the prize agree?"

"I'll behave, but I need to relieve myself. Please?"

The man gave her a calculating look. "It is useless to think of escape. Bolo is a hound of the Dark Lord and he has your scent now, the scent of your magic. You cannot hide from him. If I loose your bonds, you will relieve yourself and then meekly submit to the ropes again. Does the prize agree?"

Trying to look meek, Kath nodded. "I agree."

The man went to his horse and returned with a thick leather collar and a leash. He fixed the collar around Kath's neck and gave the leash a vicious yank. The collar constricted, cutting off her air. She struggled for breath, pain radiating from her neck. When he worked the collar loose, Kath gasped like a fish out of water, pretending to more distress than she actually felt, buying time to think. The leash made her feel like a dog, but the humiliation would be worth it if she could get her hands free.

"You see what the leash does. The prize will obey." The captain kept a tight rein on the leash, as he untied the knots that bound her and then jerked the leash, bringing Kath to her feet. She swayed, struggling to stand, her legs and feet full of jabbing needles. He tugged on the leash and Kath tottered after him. He led her behind a screen of bushes and turned to stare at her. "Do it here."

She glared at him, but his leering smile only widened. Anger burned within her. Asking for privacy would only give him pleasure. She looked away from him and pulled down her leggings to squat, trying to pretend she was alone in the woods. Finished, she rose and stared meekly at the ground, hiding her fury. The man was watching her too closely. Now was not the time to try to escape.

With a jerk of the leash, he led her back to the clearing. He pushed her down to the ground, putting her back against a tree and tying her hands tight. Before he could tie her feet, Kath said, "If you leave my feet free, I can ride the horse and you'll make better time." Casting her eyes to the ground, she made herself meek and small. "Please? I won't give you any trouble."

The man rocked back on his heels, studying her. "The prize has been good so far. I'll leave your feet untied, but see to it that you do not disappoint me." With the extra length of rope, the man lashed her to the tree. After double-checking the knots, he removed the leash from around her neck. Taking the leather gag out of his pocket, the man said, "The prize will open her mouth to take the gag."

Having no choice, Kath submitted.

The man felt under her tunic to make sure the gargoyle was in place and then left to join his companions on the far side of the clearing.

Kath strained to eavesdrop but she couldn't hear anything useful. She flexed her arms and tried to move her hands, but the ropes were too secure. At least her legs were untied, one step closer to freedom. She thanked the gods that she'd been so tired after sword practice that she'd fallen into bed fully dressed, not even bothering to take her boots off. Six inches of good Castlegard steel was strapped inside her right boot. The dagger gave her courage, but she'd have to wait till the time was right. She knew she'd only get one chance.

# 26

# Danly

I mages of his one night with the Lord Raven pulsed in Danly's mind. The courtesan had been nimble and the man relentless. Danly's blood burned with need. He whipped the black stallion into a faster gallop, racing across the autumn countryside, leaving his guard and the capital city far behind.

Cresting a hill crowned with oak trees, the small village came into sight. Danly slowed the lathered stallion to a walk. Approaching the outskirts, he straightened his green velvet jacket and tossed his emerald cape over his shoulder, knowing his good looks and princely attire would attract the stares of the village lasses.

Tinkers' wagons painted in a riot of bright colors crowded the heart of the village. Women carrying baskets circled the wagons like bees to flowers. Danly smiled at the familiar chaos. He made it a habit to visit the outlying villages on their market days, the perfect opportunity to see what treasures the villagers had to offer. Keeping his stallion on a tight rein, he meandered through the wagons and stalls, looking for sellers of ribbons and buttons. Village girls always gravitated to the bright fabrics and shiny trinkets.

Nothing caught his fancy till he came to a stall selling velvet ribbons. A golden beauty bent over the table intently studying the wares. Young and ripe, the lass was just what Danly needed. Dismounting, he led his stallion toward the stall. As if she felt his stare, the girl turned her head slightly. Her face was young and fresh, the crisp autumn air painting a rosy glow on her dimpled cheeks. Making his decision, the prince closed the distance. Leaning beside her, he selected a ribbon of green velvet and held it up to the girl's tawny hair. "This color becomes you, my lady. Allow me to buy it for you as it was obviously meant for you alone."

The girl's brown eyes warily assessed his expensive clothes and fine physique. A blush crept across her face. "Please do not trouble yourself on my account, my lord."

The prince handed a gold coin to the eager merchant. "See, it is already done. The ribbon is yours." Pressing it into her hand, he added, "You must accept it or I will feel your village has no hospitality."

The lass took it, bobbing a curtsey. "Thank you, my lord."

The merchant entered the game, a gleam of avarice in his eyes. "The ribbon only costs two silvers, sir. Would you have your change or would the lady care to select something else?"

Turning to the girl, the prince said in mock distress, "The merchant holds my gold! My lady, you must help me choose something else. Perhaps buttons to go with your ribbon and something for your mother? Surely you will help me spend my gold?"

Delighted by his mock plea, the girl turned to examine the other ribbons. Danly took his time musing over the merchant's wares. Each ribbon had to be held to the girl's hair to find just the right match, their hands casually touching as more time went on. The merchant played along, searching through his wares for the most expensive ribbons. When the purchases were finally selected and wrapped, the prince took the girl's elbow and steered her toward the food stalls at the back of the market. "All this shopping has given me a fierce hunger, would you share a bite to eat with me?"

Falling into step with Danly, the girl replied, "You must try our candied apples, lord, they're the best in all of Lanverness."

He followed the girl to the stall, letting his hand rest lightly on the small of her back, eager for his afternoon treat. Glancing around, he spied his two guards following a discreet distance behind. With a subtle wave, he acknowledged their presence. He could trust them to keep their distance as they were both familiar with his habits.

Turning back to the apple vendor, the prince flashed his gold and bought two candied apples. The caramel-covered apple was too sweet for his tastes, but he praised it to please the girl and steered her away from the bustle. Out of sight of the market, he leaned close to her. "You are too beautiful to let caramel blemish your face." Brushing his lips against the girl's soft skin, he gently nibbled caramel from her cheek. The girl trembled under his touch but she did not pull away.

Nearly bursting with need, Danly discarded his apple, letting his arms fall around her slender waist. His hands played up and down her back in a light caress. He watched as her eyes dilated and her lips bloomed red. Brushing his lips against her ear, he whispered, "Spend the afternoon with me, my lady, and I will show you delights more succulent than your apple."

She pressed her hands against his chest, gaining a feeble distance. "My lord, it would not be right!"

He gently tilted her head up. "What if I told you that I am your prince, the son of Queen Liandra, would that make it any more right?"

Unable to reply, the girl gasped and stared up at him.

Seeing the mixture of doubt and wonder in her eyes, Danly held out his ringed hand as proof. "See, here is my signet ring. The crest of House Tandroth is even emblazoned on the gold buttons of my jacket. So will you spend the afternoon with your prince? Or shall I let you go back to the market?"

In a tremulous voice the girl looked down. "But I have never done anything like this before."

A wicked smile of triumph flashed across Danly's face. Hiding his smile in her golden hair, he murmured, "Who better to have for your first time than a prince of the royal blood?" Dropping to his knee, he captured the girl's hand, kissing it tenderly. "Come, my lady, let us find our bower in the woods." Staring up at her, he waited on bent knee for her assent.

Her resistance crumbled in the face of his gallantry. He rose and swept the girl off of her feet, lightly setting her on the saddle of his stallion. Leading the horse toward the woods, he sang a love song popular with minstrels, his ardor hardening with each step. The hunt was always so deliciously easy. Silly country girls dreamt of princes and romantic love; then Danly showed up to give them a taste of their dreams while helping them face the truth of life. Tired of the game, he stopped the horse in a small clearing. Sweeping his cape from his shoulders, he spread it across the fallen leaves. Lifting the girl from the saddle, he set her down on the cape and then fell across her, tasting her lips, caramel and apple. So sweet, he wanted more.

Before she could change her mind, he rolled her onto her stomach and pressed her into the ground with his full weight. Unlacing his breeches, he ripped away her annoying undergarments and held himself poised at the gate. Without preamble, he shoved deep inside her. Arching his back, he enjoyed the tightness of her body and the muffled sounds of her screams. Thinking about the night he'd spent with the Lord Raven, the prince came three times before rolling off the girl, finally sated.

Catching his breath, Danly bound up his breeches. He gave the sobbing lass a shove with his booted foot. "Collect yourself, girl, there's no need to cry. I'll leave you with a purse of golds for your trouble. And if I've planted a royal brat, you'll find me to be even more generous. A prince can always use a bastard or two." Rising, Danly grasped the end of his cloak.

Giving the green velvet a sharp tug, he dumped the half-naked girl onto the autumn leaves. Shaking the dirt from his cape, he settled it across his shoulders then threw her a generous purse of golds.

Muffled hoof beats approached. Two guards, dressed in the green-and-white livery of Lanverness, rode into the clearing and saluted the prince, their timing perfect.

The girl stared up at him, tears on her face, pain and anguish in her voice. "You can't do this! You can't take me once and just walk away!"

Danly laughed. "I took you three times, sweet, but perhaps you weren't counting." Plucking leaves from his cape, he added, "If you're hungry for more, perhaps my guards could service you...now that you're broken in."

The girl's face contorted with rage. Screaming, she lunged at the prince. Before Danly could react, she caught hold of his right hand and stuffed it in her mouth, biting hard enough to draw blood.

Pain surged through him. Pulling back, he struck her a sharp blow across the face, knocking her to the ground. A crescent of blood welled from his hand. "How dare you!"

The guards dismounted and caught the girl in a firm grip. Struggling against her captors, she squirmed and then spat in Danly's face. "You're not a prince; you're nothing but a rutting pig! My father will kill you for this!"

One guard put a meaty hand across the girl's mouth, smothering her insults. Danly wiped the spittle away, anger boiling within him. "You shouldn't have done that. You should have enjoyed my royal favor and gone quietly back to your father, thankful for the experience. But instead, you drew royal blood." Danly's voice dripped with menace, "Payment is due." He nodded toward the more senior guard. "Play with her if you like...and then kill her. Hide her body in the woods when you're done. With luck, the wolves will find her before the villagers do."

The girl's eyes widened and a muffled scream escaped from behind the guard's hand.

Mounting his stallion, the prince turned the horse toward Pellanor and rode off without ever glancing back.

# 27

# Steffan

The map was almost useless. Without a river, a lake, or a mountain range to mark the borders, it was difficult to tell one kingdom from another. The lines that men drew on maps seldom appeared on the land, and besides, the lines had a habit of changing with war and with time. Riding north on his sorrel-colored warhorse, Steffan knew exactly when he passed from Lanverness into Coronth. The landscape in the two kingdoms was the same; gently rolling hills crowned by oak trees and dotted with farms and the occasional village. He found the border not marked on the land but on the faces of the people. In Lanverness, the people were open and trusting, willing to look a stranger in the eye. The people of Lanverness smiled, waved hello and talked openly. In Coronth, eyes shied away before ever meeting other eyes. Faces were closed and stony. The people shrank back into themselves, trying to escape notice. The whole kingdom was ripe to serve the Dark Lord, full of people who would see no evil. Always looking the other way, the people of Coronth would never acknowledge the evil inflicted on their fellow man. Closing their ears, they gave evil the license to grow among them. For a couple of amateurs, the Pontifax and the Keeper of the Flame had done well, but there was so much more to accomplish. Coronth was fertile ground and Steffan had come to sow the Dark Lord's seeds.

As he rode north, he saw more signs of a land ripe for Darkness. A good harvest meant food was plentiful in the markets yet he found the prices unreasonably high, a sure sign that the people were infected with greed and paranoia. Riding between the villages, he glimpsed scores of refugees sulking in the shadows. Gaunt, disheveled, and tattered, the homeless peered out of the woods with fearful eyes. Steffan inquired about the refugees, but the villagers denied their existence. The soldiers were just as blind. Perhaps the priests had enough easy fodder for the Flames, but that was no excuse for the laxness of the guards. The apathy needed to be corrected. He made a note to himself that it was past time their commander took the Test of Faith. Steffan laughed, this was going to be fun.

Roadside shrines and temples to the Flame God began to appear with increasing frequency, proof that he neared the capital city. Preachers with shaved heads walked the roads proclaiming the love of their deity. Symbols of the Flame appeared on the sides of barns and on the lintels of shops and taverns, the religious intensity increasing with every league. Holding the stallion to a steady canter, Steffan followed the fervor straight to the capital city of Balor.

By the time he reached the city, the autumn leaves of the countryside burned red and gold, even the trees paying homage to the Flame God. Reining the stallion to a halt, he took stock of the city, pleased to see that the curtain walls were in good repair and that guards walked the battlements. Unlike other cities that had grown complacent with peace, Balor remained confined within the city walls instead of sprawling around them. The temple's gilded spire rose from the city's heart, a beacon of gold calling to the faithful.

Steffan entered the south gate and made his way toward the temple square. Near the square he found the Devout Pilgrim, reputed to be the city's best inn. A redheaded boy of twelve lounged in the shade, dirty-faced and wearing the tattered clothes of a street urchin, just the type of lad he could use. Hailing the boy, Steffan said, "I'm new to the city and I need a boy to run errands for me."

Scrambling to his feet, the boy said, "For golds, m'lord, I'm your boy. Nobody knows the city better than me."

"What's your name, lad?"

"Pip, if it please you."

"Of course it is! Pip, like the dots on a die." Steffan laughed, feeling the irony of the Dark Lord. "Well Pip, I think you were meant to serve me." He tossed a gold coin, watching as the boy leaped for it like a hungry dog. Satisfied with the lad's greed, he said, "See that you please me and there will be plenty more where that came from."

Leaving his horse with the boy, Steffan booked the inn's most expensive room, ordering a meal with a flagon of fine wine and a tub of steaming water. He tipped the innkeeper with golds to make sure the service was both prompt and good, and then spent the evening relaxing, washing away the grime from the road. The next day, he rose and dressed in nondescript clothes, the better to wander the capital without drawing unwanted attention. Breaking his fast in the inn's common room, he eavesdropped on other wealthy travelers. Most of the talk dwelt on a Test of Faith that had taken place in the temple square the day before. The devout had traveled for days to witness the religious miracle. No one seemed surprised that the heretic had burned. Steffan wondered what they'd think if someone besides the Pontifax survived a walk through the sacred flames.

After his meal, Steffan went in search of the Flame God. Using the gilded spire as a guide, he threaded his way through the side streets. He reached the square and found it nearly empty, the fire pit choked with dead ashes. His gaze was captured by the brooding temple. Squatting on a small hill, the Temple of the Flame was a massive structure made of granite. Decorated with thick columns and topped by a gilded spire that challenged the heavens, the architecture screamed of power, wealth, and dominance. It was everything Steffan hoped for.

He climbed the hill to the temple's maw. A pair of great brass doors, three times the height of a tall man dominated the entrance. A relief was worked into the brass, an image of the Pontifax bringing the sacred flame to the children of Balor. Steffan smiled in grudging admiration. The addition of the children was a nice touch, making the Pontifax appear like a benevolent father.

Crossing the threshold, Steffan felt the chill of stone-cloistered shadows. The ceiling soared overhead, but instead of being light and airy, it captured smoke and darkness. A vault of gloom pressed down, as if trying to drive him to his knees. Nothing was built to human scale. The devout knelt in small groups, their prayers hushed to a whisper, crushed to insignificance by the scale of the temple. A trick of the stonework made the cavernous place twist sounds, muting some while magnifying others.

Steffan walked the length of the central aisle, absorbing the message wrought in stone. Except for the flaming braziers, the nave was unadorned, a blank slate waiting to be filled by the faithful. Pockets of worshipers dotted the nave, each praying in their own fashion. Pairs of red-robed priests circulated among them. One carried a brazier lit by the sacred flame while the second carried an offering bowl. The first priest invited the faithful to pass their hand across the fire in order to receive a blessing, while the second extended the offering bowl soliciting coppers, silvers, and golds. The strange acoustics enabled Steffan to hear the chink of coins as they fell into the priests' bowls, the music of greed.

At the far end of the temple, steps led up to the first dais. A gilded pulpit jutted out like the prow of a ship from the right hand side while an ornate gold throne sat empty on the left. Behind the throne, a massive gold cauldron filled the second dais. Fire snapped and crackled in the cauldron, tongues of flame licking thirty feet toward the vaulted ceiling. Behind it, a giant mosaic depicted the Pontifax taking the Test of Faith. Given the scale of the mosaic, it was difficult to tell if the temple did more to glorify the Flame God or the Pontifax. Either way, the message was potent. Steffan stood before the cauldron, breathing deep the heady incense of a twisted religion. A feral smile flickered across his face; Coronth was ripe with dark possibilities.

Satisfied, he returned to the inn to prepare for the evening. He found Pip holding his black leather boots polished to a spit-shine. Pleased, he tossed the boy a coin, and gave him additional instructions before retiring to his room for a bath. It was critical that everything be perfect for this evening.

Twilight darkened the windows of the inn as Steffan's first test approached. He took care to dress in his finest clothes, knowing appearance was an important part of the illusion. Along with trousers of supple black leather, he selected a black silk shirt with the embroidered red and black badge of the raven sewn on the breast. Around his shoulders he swirled a floor length black cape lined with crimson silk. As a last touch, he wore the gold ring with the blood-red ruby the size of a pigeon's egg. A nobleman stared back at him from the mirror, the lock of white hair at his temple adding a further touch of sophistication. He was ready to start the work of the Dark Lord.

Carefully hefting his saddlebag, he left his room and found Pip at the front of the inn holding his sorrel stallion. The horse gleamed glossy red, a mount fit for a lord. He swung into the saddle and steered the stallion through the city streets to the gates of the Residence, the palace of the Pontifax. Liveried guards were stationed at the gates, but they made no move to stop him. Steffan rode through, knowing his bribes had been well placed.

Dismounting at the entrance, Steffan removed a gilded box from his saddlebag. Tossing the reins to a waiting footman, he strode through the doors of the palace.

This was his first time in the Residence, yet he knew the palace from visions in the Dark Lord's Oracle. His boot steps echoed down the long hallway, the sound of a man driven by purpose. A pair of servants scurried behind him, entreating him to wait. He reached the door to the solar and came to an abrupt stop. Turning to acknowledge an elderly servant who nearly ran into him, Steffan thrust the gilded box into the servant's hands. "Take this gift to the Enlightened One and announce me. I am the Lord Steffan Raven."

Falling back on his training, the servant moved to obey. "Yes sir." A few moments later, he returned, holding the door open wide. "The Pontifax will see you now."

Steffan entered the solar. The room was small but richly appointed with thick carpets, plush armchairs, and marble-topped tables. Exquisite tapestries covered the walls while porcelain vases crowded the mantle. Every detail screamed of opulence, the perfect setting for his offer.

Seated in plush armchairs, the two priests studied him with hooded eyes. The Pontifax had the look of a kindly patriarch. His face was time-worn with deep-set eyes and a long flowing beard of silver, yet his fingers were long and grasping, revealing the true nature of the man. His companion was less subtle. The Keeper of the Flame had the look of a muscle-bound thug despite his vestments of rich red velvet. Steffan knew the Keeper served as the enforcer, but the true power resided with the Pontifax.

Between the two men, Steffan's box sat open on a marble table, empty of its treasure. The Pontifax hefted the gold bar, slowly stroking the lustrous surface with his fingertips. "You have a strange but impressive calling card "Lord Raven". It will buy you a brief audience."

"I have come to Balor to serve as your counselor. This gold bar is but a small measure of the value of my service."

The Pontifax barked a rude laugh. "I don't recall needing a *counselor*. Is this some kind of joke?"

Steffan waited, saying nothing, a small smile on his face.

Weighing the gold bar in his hand, the Pontifax studied him. "Tell me, *counselor*, why shouldn't I keep your gold and simply order the guards to kill you?"

"The bar of gold is a gift, freely given. Five more bars are safely hidden within the city. Invite me to join you and the Keeper for dinner for the next five nights and listen to my ideas. On each night I will bring you a bar of gold. At the end of that time, if my ideas do not intrigue you, you keep the gold and I go my own way."

The Pontifax stroked the gold, a shrewd smile playing across his lips. "I doubt there is anything you could say that would truly interest me...aside, of course, from the location of your gold, but I'll make you a counter proposal. Five dinners for five bars of gold, but at the end of the five nights, if I do not see your worth you will walk the Test of Faith in the temple square. After all, the Pontifax cannot accept the service of an infidel. What say you, Lord Raven?"

Steffan schooled his face to remain expressionless, hiding the elation he felt. "I accept your proposal." Offering the two men a deep bow, he turned and left the solar. Walking back through the marble halls, he smiled. He'd passed the first test.

# 28

# Blaine

Blaine paced the common room of the inn while the other knights broke their fast on porridge and bread. Kath was normally an early riser, but there was still no sign of the girl. Concerned, he went to her room and knocked on the door. Unlatched, the door swung open. The room was empty. The bed was in disarray and her throwing axes sat on a stool in plain sight. Kath never went anywhere without her axes. Fear gripped his throat like an iron fist.

Grabbing the harness, he raced back to the common room, raising the alarm. *"The Imp's been taken!"* He brandished her throwing axes as proof.

Sir Tyrone leapt to his feet, his great sword drawn as if for battle. Captain Tellor ordered Sir Kirk to check the girl's room but the second search changed nothing. The common room erupted in arguments.

Sir Tyrone hissed to Blaine, "The god's warning!"

Blaine nodded, a sick feeling twisting his stomach.

The black knight shouted to be heard. "Arguing is a waste of breath! Spread out and search for any clues to the princess's abduction."

The men dispersed. A search of the roadhouse failed to yield any sign of forced entry, but the locks were nothing more than flimsy latches, easily breached. All of the horses, including Kath's stallion, were accounted for. Scanning the road for fresh tracks, they found none. With no trail to follow, they roused the innkeeper and a peddler, the only other guest in the roadhouse. They questioned them both, but like the knights, neither had heard anything. Without any obvious leads, the knights regrouped in the common room.

Captain Tellor banged his sword hilt on the table, silencing the arguments. "Why would anyone abduct the Imp? Most people take her for nothing more than a scruffy squire." He forked Blaine with his stare. "You know her best, can you explain this?"

Blaine locked stares with Sir Tyrone, unsure how to respond. The black knight gave a subtle nod, confirming his unspoken question. Taking a deep breath, Blaine said, "While we were on the Isle of Souls, Kath was threatened by a dwarf, but by the time we got there he'd melted into the crowd." He held the captain's stare, forcing the words out. "The Imp insisted the dwarf was up to no good. It seems we should have paid more heed to her fears."

"You were ordered to protect the girl! If there was a threat you should have reported it. Or did you forget that you guarded the king's daughter?"

The captain's words hit Blaine like a hammer blow. Bile rose in the back of his throat; he'd failed Kath and his king. "My gut tells me this is the handiwork of the Dark Lord."

A stillness claimed the room.

Sir Tyrone spoke up. "I agree with Blaine."

A horrified look crossed the captain's face. "The girl *is* a princess of Castlegard. Perhaps the Dark Lord plans to use her to weaken the king?"

The black knight turned to Sir Kirk. "Get the innkeeper back in here. We need more answers."

Sir Kirk herded the wizened old man to a chair, a circle of knights looming over him. Sir Tyrone asked the questions. "The abductors must have come out of the forest. Are there any holdfasts or farms nearby?"

The old man shrank into the chair. "T-the Kellers have a farm up the road. I buy food for the roadhouse from them. H-harmless folk they are; wouldn't be involved in this." He scratched his head. "T-the only other place is an abandoned keep in the forest to the south, but it's nothing but a jumble of old stones. No one goes there for fear of ghosts."

"Can you show us the way to this keep?"

"N-never been there myself, it's just an abandoned ruin."

The captain said, "We need hunting dogs to track the abductors. Would these farmers have dogs?"

The innkeeper bobbed his head. "Not a farmer in Wyeth that doesn't have hunting dogs. Most of us rely on venison for meat. I buy mine from the Kellers. Gunthor is a good shot with the bow."

The captain barked an order to the senior squire, Alain. "Saddle a horse and ride to the farm. Offer the man a purse of gold if he will bring his bow and his hunting dogs." He tossed the squire a small purse. "Take the princess's horse. Dancer is the fastest we have. Ride hard, there's no time to lose. May Valin speed you!"

Alain sprinted for the door. Blaine envied the squire his clear course of action. Flexing his sword hand, he tried to control his frustration. Only a fool would mount up and dash off in the wrong direction, but it was hard to wait.

Sir Tyrone organized a search of the surrounding forest; each man assigned a different direction. Desperate to find the girl, Blaine pushed through the undergrowth looking for any signs of passage. He scanned the ground as he walked but he saw no tracks of men or horses. Frustrated, he climbed an oak tree and spied the remnants of a broken tower. Wondering if it was part of the haunted ruins the innkeeper had spoken of, he scrambled down and set off at a jog. Drawing close to the ruins, he slowed to a walk, listening for voices or the chink of steel, but he heard only the song of birds. The broken tower reeked of age, moss-covered stones scattered as if thrown by a giant's hand. A wall lay in a tumbled in ruin and the single tower leaned drunkenly. Overgrown with vines and trees, the forest had almost reclaimed the keep. Blaine pushed through the tangled growth, seeking an entrance. The stone doorway gaped open, its door lost to time. A carving on the keystone caught his attention, a shield bearing an eight-pointed star. He knew most of the heraldry of Erdhe yet this device was unfamiliar. Yielding to a strange compulsion, he reached up and touched it, as if asking for leave to enter. Chiding himself for silly superstitions, he unsheathed his great blue sword and entered with steel first.

Blaine passed from sunlight into shadow. The lower hall was almost intact, rubble and leaves strewn across the uneven stone floor. Movement blurred to his left. He whirled, sword in hand. Golden cat-eyes and an angry snarl flashed from the shadows. He thought it might be a lynx but quick as a flash it fled the tower through a chink in the wall. Heart pounding, Blaine climbed the stairs to the next level and ducked as a flurry of wings beat against his face. A flock of starlings spiraled up inside of the hollow tower, exiting through the open roof like a plume of smoke. Blaine shook his head. The broken tower was nothing more than a rookery for starlings, a home for the wild things of the forest. Sheathing his sword, he stood on the topmost step, scanning the surrounding forest, but he saw no sign of movement or telltale smoke from a campfire. Disappointed, he made his way back down the stairs.

He left the tower and set out at a sprint for the roadhouse. Angry for wasting time at the keep, he forced himself to a hard run, accepting the ache in his side as punishment. Stumbling out of the forest, Blaine was the last to return. Judging from the grim faces, he knew the others had found nothing. The sun hung low in the afternoon sky and still the knights were no closer to finding the princess.

Baying hounds and the sounds of galloping horses approached from the east, sending a sliver of hope through Blaine. The squire returned with a burly blond farmer and three yapping dogs.

Sir Tyrone and Sir Blaine greeted the farmer and together they entered the inn. Holding the dogs on a leash, the farmer followed the knights to Kath's room. Before they even reached it, the hounds began to snarl, disturbed by the scent. Straining against their leashes, they traced the scent back outside.

Following an invisible lead, the hounds nosed their way deep into the old growth forest. The knights followed, keeping their horses to a slow trot, chaffing at the pace. Several times the hounds stopped to backtrack, milling with noses to the ground trying to re-acquire the scent and then they sprinted ahead, baying wildly. The sun set in a blaze of gold by the time the knights broke into a small clearing. Barking in triumph, the hounds circled the glade. Blaine swung down from his horse, his sword in his hands. The other knights drew their blades, searching the glade, hoping for a fight, but the clearing stood empty. A cold campfire looked to be at least a day old. Clumps of manure marked where horses had been tethered. On the edge of the clearing, Blaine found scuffmarks in the soil under a large oak tree. Studying the marks, his eyes suddenly widened. He called Sir Tyrone over, pointing to the ground. "See anything?"

The black knight crouched, a smile playing across his ebony face as his fingers traced a crude 'K' drawn in the earth. He clapped Blaine on the shoulder. "She's alive and leaves us a message to follow."

"Now we need to catch the bastards and send them to their graves."

The tenor of the hounds changed from excited barks to wary snarls. Blaine and Tyrone ran to join the others, a ring of drawn swords standing behind the growling dogs. "What is it?"

The farmer shook his head, struggling to keep the dogs in check. "Something in the forest."

Blaine heard it then, a low crashing sound in the underbrush. Something big and massive rushed towards them. Gripping his sword, he crouched for battle, hoping the abductors returned. The hounds strained at their leash, a snarl of frenzied teeth. A massive boar erupted from the forest. Hooves churning up fallen leaves, the razorback barreled toward them. Bristling with broken arrow shafts, it stank of rot, rushing the hounds with a mad vengeance.

*"Protect the dogs!"*

Fear pierced Blaine; lose the dogs and they lost Kath. He leaped forward, putting himself between the hounds and the boar. Dropping to one knee, he braced his sword hilt against the ground, the sapphire-blue blade angled up toward the heart of the beast. Time seemed to slow. The boar barreled forward, yellow tusks keen as sabers, red eyes rabid with pain. Blaine had a heartbeat to wish for a spear instead of a sword and then the beast was upon him. It stank of death, cloven hooves churning the ground like a plow. The strength of the charge nearly wrenched the sword from his hand, but somehow he kept the blade anchored. The beast never slowed. It barreled up the shaft, blue steel sinking deep into its chest and still it came. Blaine stared in horror as foam-flecked tusks rushed towards his face, the stink of death on its breath, but then the boar grunted to a stop, the mad light fading from its eyes. The beast fell dead, impaled to the hilt on his sword. Shaking and surprised to be alive, Blaine slumped to the ground, drenched in sweat.

The other knights gathered around. Kirk said, "A lucky strike. Your sword must have pierced its heart."

The farmer struggled to still his snarling hounds. "In all my born days, ain't ever seen nothing like it. All those arrows in its back, that boar must have been crazed with pain." He gave Blaine an awed look. "To kill a boar with a sword, that will make a fine tale."

Blaine staggered to his feet. Putting a boot on the carcass, he yanked his sword free. A stench filled the clearing, the smell of putrid rot. The boar was corrupted, its red hide scarred with festering wounds, its curved tusks glistening with froth. The massive beast looked like something spawned from the depths of hell.

Sir Tyrone met his stare. "It's as if the Dark Lord seeks to keep us from the princess."

A shiver raced down Blaine's spine. "Then by all the gods, we need to find her."

# 29

# Jordan

Jordan had small breasts and she liked it that way, otherwise it would have been difficult to wear armor. Wrapping a winding sheet around her breasts, she pulled on a quilted jacket followed by a leather jerkin and finally a coat of fine mesh chain mail, the steel links oiled and burnished to a dull shine. She buckled a worn leather scabbard holding a standard infantry sword around her waist and settled a half helm on her head, tucking her short sandy hair behind her ears. Picking up a plain round shield, she glanced in the mirror. Most people would take her for a young man-at-arms instead of a woman, unless, of course, she spoke, or they looked closely at her face. But few people ever bothered to look at the face of a man in armor; they looked at the device on his shield instead. Her plane steel shield named her a common foot soldier, someone without any title or lineage. There was no way anyone could tell she was from Navarre, let alone a princess of the seaside kingdom, and that was just the way she wanted it.

Her father had given her the task of evaluating the battle-readiness of the Rose Army. Uncle Isador had tutored her on methods of assessing an army's strength but Jordan had her own ideas; ideas that involved more challenge. From conversations in the great kitchen, she'd learned that the knights of Lanverness held sparring sessions in the Eastern Yard. She'd also learned there were no women in the Rose Army, another kingdom that believed the fairer sex should not wield a sword. The enduring prejudice angered her. She decided to join the army's sparring sessions. She'd test her skills against the Rose knights, and prove, at least to herself, that women were worthy of the sword.

Jordan hailed a page and followed the lad through a labyrinth of passageways until she heard the clanging of swords. Dismissing the page with thanks, she followed the song to the open yard. Pausing in the doorway, she took stock of the practice yard. It was a fairly large training yard with a hard packed dirt floor and sheer stonewalls on all four sides. Eight sparring groups practiced in the yard, ten warriors to each group. Judging from the swordplay, the men were participating in a form of sparring known as 'best sword', where two men fought with edged weapons until one man scored a strike to the other's chest. Once tagged, the loser left the sparring circle and a new man stepped into the ring until the 'best sword' was determined...just the type of practice session Jordan was hoping for.

Watching from the shadows, she judged the sparring circles, her gaze drawn to a spirited group at the far side. The sword work in this circle was especially fierce, perhaps because the majority carried shields bearing proud heraldic devices. If she wanted to remain unnoticed, Jordan knew she should pick a different group, but she couldn't resist the chance to dance the steel with a group of knights and noblemen.

Tightening the leather strap on her half helm, she approached the far group. Acting as if she belonged, she joined the end of the line. Five knights waited ahead of her, giving Jordan plenty of time to evaluate the competition.

The clang of swords intensified. The grizzled sergeant shouted, calling an end to the round. The victory went to the warrior bearing a shield with two white roses crossed on a field of emerald green, the standard infantry shield of Lanverness. The victor drummed his sword against his shield, inviting the next challenger. A knight bearing a chevron shield entered the circle. The two warriors saluted and then closed for the fight. The chevron knight used a stiff upright stance that Jordan recognized as an outdated style of fighting. Advancing with his shield raised in front of him, he aimed a series of slashing blows at the 'best sword'. The rose warrior deftly parried the strokes, dancing rings around the chevron knight, always attacking from different angles. Jordan recognized the rose warrior's strategy. Confronted with a stiff style of fighting, his darting dance was designed to push the chevron knight off balance. Jordan smiled as she watched her prediction become fact. Scrambling to keep up with the quickness of the rose warrior, the chevron knight over pivoted and momentarily lost his balance. Quick as a snake, the rose warrior darted in and tagged the chevron warrior, winning the bout.

Jordan watched as the rose warrior won each successive match. Tall with broad shoulders, he was light on his feet and skilled with the sword but what really impressed her was the way he adapted his fighting style to exploit his opponent's weaknesses. As the sparring rounds progressed,

Jordan watched for any sign of weakness, but it was hard to spot a pattern. The rose warrior was going to be difficult to defeat. The only strategy Jordan could think of was to try and be as unconventional as possible. If she could change her own style faster than he could adapt then she might catch him off guard.

Scuffing the hard packed dirt floor with her boot, she rubbed some lose soil in her hands. The dirt would help absorb her sweat and give her a better grip. She was going to need a good grip for her plan to work. Tightening the strap on her half-helm, she loosened her shield straps and then took her turn in the sparing ring.

Raising her sword in salute, she took a defensive stance. Staring over her shield, she waited, letting the rose warrior make the first move. Jordan was the unknown in this round and she intended to make the 'best sword' work to figure her out.

The rose warrior leaped to the attack, testing her quickness with a series of lightening strikes. Jordan stood her ground, parrying his blows with shield and sword. When he failed to find an obvious weakness, he tried to defeat her with agility. Jordan mimicked the chevron knight, remaining in place and timing her pivots to meet his sword at the last possible moment. Hoping to lull the rose warrior into complacency, she waited until the clang of swords developed a predictable rhythm. Gauging the time to be right, she danced to the side, skipping behind his shield and reaching in with her sword. Her quickness caught him off guard but he managed to twist away, blocking the blow with the chain mail on his upper arm. In a real battle, she might have dealt him a serious wound, but this was the sparring circle and only a touch to the chest counted as a 'kill'.

Jordan followed her attack with a flurry of blows, forcing the rose warrior to retreat, but she could not find an opening. Deciding that she needed to try something else, she broke off the attack, retreating to the far side of the ring. Swords raised, the two combatants circled each other, like a pair of scorpions looking for an opening.

The rose warrior tipped his sword in salute, acknowledging her prowess. Keeping her face closed, Jordan kept her sword raised. Suspecting that he might try to ram her with his shield, she carefully eased her arm out of her own shield, holding it by the straps. It was a risky move but it might give her the advantage she needed. The rose warrior continued to circle, crouched behind his shield like a bull about to charge. Watching his feet, she waited for him to break into a run. As he took the first stride, she turned her shield sideways and flicked her wrist, sending the shield spinning toward his feet. Caught in mid-stride, he stumbled over the shield. Jordan lunged forward, stabbing at his chest. Even falling, the rose warrior managed to raise his sword to meet hers, but she disengaged her blade and finished the lunge to score a hit on his breastplate. Stepping back from the fallen warrior, Jordan heard the sergeant acknowledge her as the victor.

"A victory for the plain steel shield!"

Flushed from the fight, Jordan sheathed her sword, struggling to regain her breath. The chevron knight rushed forward to help the rose warrior to his feet while the other knights surrounded her, thumping her on the back in congratulations. Surrounded by strangers, Jordan had the sudden desire to disappear.

Trying to escape the knights, she found herself confronted by the rose warrior. Tugging off his helmet, he revealed a handsome face with chiseled features and dark eyes full of laughter.

Jordan stared in shock. She felt the blood rushing to her face; the man was way too easy on the eyes. He looked even better in the simple armor of an infantryman than he did in court finery. Suddenly shy, she glanced away hoping that Stewart, the crown prince of Lanverness, would not recognize her.

"Well done!" The prince offered his hand in congratulations. "That move with your shield took me by surprise. Not a tactic I'd recommend on the battlefield, but an interesting trick for the sparring yard."

Jordan shook his hand, using a hard grip, hoping to appear 'manly'. Unable to speak lest she betray her sex, she lowered her eyes and began to back away.

The prince followed. "I don't think I know you, soldier, what's your name?"

Making vague hand gestures, she turned and ran for the nearest doorway.

Behind her, the prince called out, "Don't forget, the best sword owes us a round of ales at the Tavern of Thorns! We'll meet you there at sunset!"

Jordan raced to the safety of the nearest doorway, disappearing in a maze of hallways. With the help of a page, she eventually made her way back to the Navarren wing of the castle. Removing her helm, she shook out her sandy-blonde hair and entered the common sitting room she shared with her siblings. She found her sister, Jemma, curled up in an armchair reading a thick scroll. Even in a simple frock of blue wool, her petite sister was a vision of beauty.

Glancing up from the scroll, Jemma said, "I see you found someone to spar with. Did you win or lose?"

Dumping her half helm in a chair, Jordan unbuckled her sword and began to shrug off her coat of mail. "I managed to spar for one round and won." Free of the mail, she pulled off her boots and sat sprawled on the floor in front of the fireplace, her long legs stretched towards the crackling heat.

"And?"

Tucking her short sandy hair behind her ears, Jordan said, "What do you mean 'and'?"

"And, as in *what else*?" Jemma stared at her like a hound on a scent. "Come on Jordan, you're usually a bundle of energy after a sparring session. Instead you come in here with a glum face and just dump your gear on the floor. So I'm asking you, what else happened at the sparring round?"

Sometimes her sister was too perceptive. Shrugging, Jordan said, "I won the sparring round and ended up being 'best sword'. Apparently that means I'm supposed to stand for a round of ale at some local tavern. Only, the kingdom of Lanverness doesn't have any women in their army, so the knights think I'm a man. I left before they could learn otherwise." Jordan tore her gaze away from the fireplace to glance over at her sister. Jemma stared at her with hooded eyes. Jordan knew that look. She could never get away with anything around her sister.

Putting the scroll aside, Jemma leaned forward, a subtle smile on her face. "Since when are you bashful about showing men you're just as good as they are with a sword?" With a sly smile, she added, "If you've turned shy it means that you've met a man you're interested in. Is he the one you're supposed to meet at the tavern?"

Of her six siblings, it was tough to tell who was sharper, Jemma or Justin. With a shake of her head, Jordan gave in. "Oh, all right! Yes, but I am not going." She turned back to the fire, hoping the conversation was finished.

"What do you mean you're not going? You're fearless with a sword in your hand, but when it comes to meeting a man, all you ever do is run! You'll only be in Lanverness for a few turns of the moon, so go and meet him and see what happens. Where's the harm?"

Jordan glared at her sister. They were of the same age, both part of the royal septuplets, but sometimes Jemma acted much older than her eighteen years.

Uncurling from the armchair, Jemma went to the outer door and spoke to the guard. Returning with a smug smile, she sat cross-legged on the floor, demurely tucking her skirt around her slender legs. "I've ordered a bath for you. Get cleaned up and go and meet the man. If you want, I'll come with you."

Jordan barked a laugh. "No way, sister! You don't belong in an army tavern."

"Then take Justin, or Duncan, if you can find him." Jemma gave her a conspiring smile. "Don't you want to see the look on their faces when they realize they've been bested by a woman? It will do their prickly male pride a world of good."

Feeling a smile creep across her face, Jordan had to admit it would be fun. "All right, I'll go."

"Good, I'm glad that's settled." Gracefully rising from the floor, Jemma added, "You take care of your armor and I'll sort through your clothes."

Jordan picked up her sword and chain mail, following her sister into the bedchamber. "Just remember, Sis, it's an *army* tavern, so no dresses or anything frilly...not that you'd find much like that in *my* chest."

A turn of the hourglass later, Jordan finished her bath and pulled on a pair of black leather pants and a white silk shirt. Over the shirt, she put on her favorite red leather jerkin, the one with a white osprey eagle worked into the collar. Buckling her sword around her waist and swirling a dark blue cape around her shoulders, she returned to the sitting room to pass her sister's inspection. "What do you think, Sis, will I do?"

Jemma gave her a warm smile. "It's perfect. It's you." With a mischievous grin she added, "Have a good time and I want to hear *all* the details when you get back!"

Tossing a pillow at her sister, Jordan went out into the hallway to talk to the guard. The guard raised his eyebrows but she eventually got the directions. Along the way, she commandeered a page to lead her to the outer gates.

The bustle of the capital city started just beyond the castle walls. Jordan set out at a brisk walk enjoying the mild evening. The sun set in a blaze of colors, bathing the cobblestone streets in gold, the perfect patina for the wealthiest city in Erdhe. Merchants spilled onto the streets, using long tapers to light lanterns hanging outside their shops. A warm glow of lantern-light lined the street, another sign of outrageous wealth. Jordan shook her head, amazed to find that many of the shops stayed open after dark. People crowded the street with their comings and goings, the rich velvets of nobles mingling with the warm butternut-homespun of the common folk. It seemed the queen's city never slept.

Turning into a side lane, she heard the faint strains of a bawdy army song. The song led to a tavern, a sign overhead displaying a tangle of nasty thorns. She paused on the stairs, listening to the familiar lyrics. Vulgar and crude, the song would have embarrassed Jemma, but Jordan just took it in stride. Lewd language was something you learned to deal with if you wanted to wield a sword.

Stuffy with warmth, the tavern was overcrowded with soldiers in the green and white of Lanverness. Men argued, diced, and shouted lewd jokes, banging their empty tankards on tabletops. Serving girls navigated a gauntlet of grabbing hands, balancing huge mugs of frothing ale. A minstrel strummed a lute near the fireplace, the source of the bawdy songs. To Jordan's ear the minstrel sounded off-key, but she doubted anyone in the crowd noticed.

Unable to see an empty table, she put a hand on her sword and forced her way to the bar. Finding a place at the counter, she ordered a mug of ale. The barkeeper gave her a rude look, making it clear she did not belong. Jordan paid for the ale and then scanned the room for the prince. She found him sitting with a mixture of noblemen and infantry soldiers at a table near the bard. The prince seemed to be in high spirits, enjoying the bawdy songs as much as anyone. She liked the fact that he took his leisure with common infantrymen as well as nobles. She also liked the fact that he dressed in boiled leathers instead of the elegant finery of the court. With a rueful smile, she had to admit she liked the man no matter how he dressed. She wondered if the prince could ever like a woman who carried a sword. Putting a small stack of golds on the bar, she decided to find out. "Barkeep, a round of ales for that table over there."

The swarthy barkeep scowled at her till he saw her golds.

Covering the coins with her hand, she leaned forward. "Say that the drinks were from the *best sword*."

"As you wish." The ill-tempered barkeep palmed the coins and then filled a dozen tankards, calling to a servant girl to deliver them.

Jordan leaned on the bar, watching as the fresh tankards were passed around the prince's table. The prince inquired about the ales and the serving girl vaguely waved in Jordan's direction. He scanned the bar but his eyes slid over her without recognition. Standing with his tankard held high in salute, the prince hailed the bar, his voice cutting through the din of the tavern. "Will the 'best sword' grace us with his presence? We toast his prowess with the sword, or perhaps I should say his prowess with the shield?"

The noise of the tavern stilled, the stares of the crowd turning toward the bar. Jordan felt the blood rush to her face. This wasn't working out the way she'd planned. Steeling her nerve, she raised her own tankard and said, "I'll drink to that."

A deafening silence blanketed the tavern. The silence held an ugly edge of menace...her claim violated their male pride.

Ignoring the crowd, she focused on the prince. Surprise and disbelief warred across his face. He lowered the tankard and stood dumbstruck, staring at her with a puzzled expression on his face.

A drunken soldier broke the silence. "Come 'ere lass, I'll test your *prowess* against me stiff *sword!*"

The tavern erupted in a roar of crude laughter, all of it male.

Embarrassed beyond belief, Jordan gripped her sword hilt and shouldered her way through the crowd. Rude hands grabbed for her. Pulling away, she stepped over a leg thrust out to trip her. More hands reached for her, a gauntlet of leering men. She pushed her way to the door, escaping into the crisp clean air of the autumn night. Breathing deep to rid her lungs of the tavern's stench, she headed back toward the castle. Locked in her own anger, she did not hear the footsteps approaching from behind.

A hand grabbed her shoulder.

Unsheathing her short sword, she whirled to face the attacker.

The attacker danced back into the shadows. From the darkness a male voice said, "So it *was* you in the sparring ring."

Keeping her sword raised, Jordan waited for the stalker to make the next move.

Stepping into the light, he revealed his face. Jordan stared slack-jawed at Prince Stewart.

The prince raised his hands in surrender, "My lady, you can put your sword away...you won't need it with me...unless you are looking for another sparring match?"

For a moment she forgot the sword in her hands. Coming back to herself, she sheathed her blade. "I only wanted to pay my debt of ale. I did not mean any harm by it."

He met her stare. "And I only wanted to meet you so I could toast your prowess with the sword."

She listened closely but heard no mockery in his voice.

A sudden silence fell between them. The prince was the first to break it. "In Lanverness, women do not wield swords. I never guessed I danced the steel with a woman." Pausing he added, "You fought like a man. In fact, you fought better than most men I meet in the sparring circle." His voice trailed off and he just stood there, staring at her with a strange expression on his face.

Always the same old argument. Exasperation flooded her voice. "Lanverness is ruled by a woman. If a woman can rule a kingdom, why is it so hard to believe that a woman might also be good with a sword?"

A genuine smile lit up his face like an early morning sunrise. "Isn't mother extraordinary? Lanverness has never had a better ruler." Growing thoughtful he added, "Perhaps extraordinary women also wield swords?"

Now it was Jordan's turn to flush.

Holding out his hand, the prince said, "We've danced the steel, but I still do not know your name."

Embarrassment heated Jordan's face to a bright blush. "Actually, we've met before, but you were understandably pre-occupied by my sister. Her name is Jemma. She's the beautiful one. My name is Jordan. I'm the other princess of Navarre, the one who likes to wield a sword." She watched his face as recognition dawned.

"I remember now." With a twinkle in his eyes he said, "It seems we have much in common. We are both more comfortable in leathers than in the confining plumage of the court." Growing serious, he said, "Perhaps we could start again?"

Smiling, she replied, "I'd like that."

He answered her smile. "Let me walk you back to the castle. You can tell me where you learned that trick with the shield. I've never seen that move before."

Falling into step with the prince, Jordan thought her stay in Lanverness was going to be far too short.

# 30

# Katherine

The sun set on the third day of her captivity and still there was no sign of the knights. Their absence gnawed on Kath's mind, eroding her resolve. Despair threatened to claim her...the one emotion she couldn't afford. Bound to the saddle, a leather gag in her mouth, Kath stole another glance behind but this time the captain saw her. Reining his horse next to hers, he gave her a cruel smile. "Those shiny knights will never find us. You're mine, girlie, you'd best get used to it."

Kath bowed her head, hiding behind a tangle of dirty blonde hair. Anger warred with despair. She'd often heard the knight marshal say that 'despair was the vanguard of defeat'. Kath refused to lose this battle before the first sword was drawn. Girding her resolve, she forced herself to stop looking for the knights, swearing to find her own way to escape. Biding her time, she waited for the perfect moment.

The waiting proved hard.

Anger simmered just beneath the surface. Kath was surprised her captors never noticed the rage smoldering in her eyes, but then they expected to see a meek little girl so that's all they ever saw. It was the meek little girl who succeeded in getting her feet untied, sitting astride the horse instead of being slung over the saddle like baggage. It was the meek little girl who would get the best chance to escape...but it was *so* hard to play the role. When the strain of the charade got to be too much, Kath thought about her talks with the veteran knights and how they stressed the importance of creating advantage in battle. She knew this was one of those times when being underestimated created a huge advantage, so Kath submitted to her captors, but every day the charade grew harder.

She spent her time studying the enemy, searching for weaknesses. The days held a definite pattern. Up at dawn for a breakfast of cold dried meat and then tied to the pommel of the saddle, riding through the forest till dusk. They rode toward the northeast, always avoiding any farms or holdfasts, keeping to the shadows of the old growth forest. They stopped in the evenings for a hot dinner, spending the nights camped under the dense canopy of pine boughs. Lashed to a stout tree, Kath learned to sleep sitting up while her captors drew lots to see who stood guard. So far the pattern of days did not reveal any discernable weakness. Kath suspected her chance would come when there was a break in the pattern.

Cresting a ridge, the riders came to a small fast-flowing steam. The captain called a halt, ordering a camp for the night. The others dismounted but Kath was forced to sit on her horse until the captain had time for her. She watched as he watered and unsaddled his stallion. Finished with his mount, he flashed her a crooked smile. "The prize was good today. We covered a lot of ground." Resting his hands on either side of her saddle, he leered up at her. "Will the prize be good if I let her down from the horse?"

Bound and gagged, Kath responded with a nod.

The captain untied the rope binding her to the pommel. Grasping her waist, he eased her off the horse. Kath suppressed a shiver, hating his touch. She tried to keep her eyes averted and her body limp, hoping neither would betray her. Once her feet touched the ground, she meekly stared down.

The captain thrust the leather collar in front of her face. "The prize will be good and stretch out her neck for the collar."

Rage flooded through her, but she did her best to hide it. She knew the man enjoyed treating her like a slave but she had no choice but to comply. Raising her chin, she kept her gaze focused on the ground as the captain fitted the leather collar around her neck. He gave the leash a mild yank, reminding her that the collar was designed to choke. Putting a filthy hand under her chin, he lifted her face and peered into her eyes, his breath hot on her face. "If the prize promises to be good, then the gag can come out of her mouth. Blink if the prize promises to obey."

Kath blinked and the captain removed the hated leather gag.

Her mouth was dry and the aftertaste of the gag was terrible. In a deliberately weak voice, she croaked, "Water?"

With a laugh that sent shivers down her back, the captain held a flask to her lips. A gush of cool water flushed the awful taste from her mouth. When she finished, he tugged on her leash and led her to a spot under a tree. She sat where the captain ordered, trying to find a comfortable spot in the fallen leaves. The captain sprawled nearby, fondling the end of the leash while the other three worked to set up camp. It was always the same every night. The ogre gathered wood and built the campfire. The goblin-man spread the bedrolls and got out the bowls and the iron pot for making stew, while the other man, the archer, skinned whatever game he'd shot during the day and prepared it for dinner. Kath sat with her hands bound, a leash around her neck, using her eyes and her ears to learn whatever she could about her captors.

Tonight they were having rabbit stew cooked with a few potatoes. Kath's mouth began to water. The one thing she didn't have to worry about was being fed. Her captors seemed serious about getting her to the 'master' alive, always giving her an equal share of the food.

Bolo, the goblin-man, stirred the stew, tossing in herbs and a clump of wild carrots. The little man wore an odd patchwork of clothes, a rag-tag cloak over his stunted frame. Kath still thought of him as the goblin-man. She'd gotten use to his pointy teeth and stunted body, but what scared her about Bolo was the captain's claim that the weird little man could sniff magic. She shivered with loathing every time he came near her.

Even stranger than the dwarf was the ogre, Tiny. Standing over seven foot tall, the ogre had a strange sloping forehead and protruding ridges for eyebrows that made his face look sinister. Barrel-chested and with arms that were too long for his body, the ogre was immensely strong, snapping small logs with his bare hands. If it came to a fight, the ogre would be a formidable foe, especially if he had any skill with weapons. Turning to the captain, Kath tried to put a quaver in her voice, "Please, sir, is Tiny an ogre?"

The captain roared with laughter, "Hear that Tiny! The prize thinks you're an ogre! She probably has nightmares about you." Chuckling, the captain said, "Don't worry, girlie, as long as you're good, the captain won't let Tiny eat you." With a leer he added, "Just stay close to the captain, girlie, and you'll be safe."

Kath dropped her gaze to the ground, hating the captain's leer.

The goblin-man shuffled around the campfire, passing out bowls of steaming stew. Kath balanced the bowl in her lap, using both hands to spoon down dinner. Between spoonfuls, she dared to ask her question again. "Please, sir, is Tiny an ogre?"

This time the captain gave her an answer. "No girlie, ogres are a myth. Tiny is a Taal, a throwback. There are places in Erdhe where the land is fouled with magic from the War of Wizards. Lots of deformed babies are born in those places. Most of the grotesques die as soon as they're birthed. Those that live are always twisted. A few never grow enough, like Bolo. Some grow too much, like the Taals. All of them are twisted in some way, but the Dark Lord doesn't seem to mind the twisting." Lowering his voice, the captain said, "Some say the Dark Lord caused the land to be fouled in the first place, seeking to make better servants." With a wicked leer, the captain hissed, "Maybe when the master is done with you, he'll use you to breed more Taals for the army." His hand stole onto her thigh, giving her a squeeze. "Don't worry, girlie, perhaps I'll break you in first."

She stared at his hand as if it was a poisonous viper, fighting the urge to reach for her dagger. Time crawled. When she made no reaction, his hand withdrew. She kept her head bent, hiding the rage smoldering in her eyes.

The rest of the meal passed in silence. When everyone finished, the goblin-man collected the bowls and then set to washing them in the stream. The captain held a flask of water to Kath's mouth, giving her a chance to drink her fill. Removing the flask, the captain tugged on her leash and sneered, "Time for a walk in the forest, girlie."

Kath shuddered, dreading the walk. Pulled by the leash, she followed the captain into the shadows. Passing behind a screen of bushes, the captain stopped and commanded, "Do it here, girlie."

It was the only chance she'd have to relieve herself till morning. Gritting her teeth and looking away, she pulled down her leggings to squat.

The captain loomed over her, his voice an oily whisper. "Tell me girlie, did you lay with any of those shiny knights? Did they slip their swords inside of you while you slept?" His fetid breath was hot on her neck. "Do you miss it, girlie?"

Unsure which answer would serve her best, she kept her stare locked on the ground and remained silent.

"What did those shiny knights do with you, girlie? Did they even know how to use a skinny little girl like you?" Lowering his voice, he added, "A man could teach you, girlie. A man could teach you lots of things. You might even grow to like it."

Hastily finishing, she stood and quickly pulled up her leggings while staring at the ground. Gritting her teeth, she fought the desire to draw the six inches of good Castlegard steel from her boot...but the time wasn't right.

The captain grunted, yanking hard on the leash.

Stumbling behind, Kath struggled to regain her balance, clawing at the leash to gain a breath of air. Her frantic fingers loosened the stranglehold. Gasping, she followed him back to the campfire, like a dog on a leash. She always felt safer at the campfire, though she doubted the others would stand up to their leader.

The captain yanked on the leash, impatience on his face. He led her to a thick pine tree and pushed her to the ground. She submitted while he lashed her to the tree, pulling the rope tight enough to cut into her arms. Wincing, Kath turned her head, refusing to acknowledge his crooked smile. He gave a low chuckle as he tightened the knots.

Kath longed to wipe the smug smile from his face. In the presence of monsters like the ogre and the goblin-man, the one she most wanted to knife was the man. Obviously the Dark Lord twisted more than just the bodies of his servants.

As if he could tell what she was thinking, the captain gave the rope a final jerk but Kath refused to cry out despite the pain. He checked the bindings and then removed the collar from around her neck. Tilting her head up, he looked into her eyes. "The prize will meekly take the gag. Open wide or it will be forced into your mouth."

Closing her eyes to hide her hatred, she opened her mouth to receive the leather gag. With the gag secure, the captain groped inside her tunic to make sure the gargoyle was in place. After fondling the gargoyle, he returned to his place by the fire.

Kath sighed. She'd survived another day of threats and humiliation, but the nightmare would start all over again in the morning. Lashed tight to the tree, she thought about her gargoyle. She wondered if the little figurine was truly worth the price. Sometimes she wished her captors would just take the gargoyle and leave her behind, but then she remembered the message from the Lords of Light. If the gargoyle was so important, why had the gods given it to *her*? And why hadn't they told her how to use it? She shook her head; the gods were so cryptic they were almost useless.

Caught up in her own thoughts, Kath almost missed the signal. Instead of drawing lots for guard duty, the captain gave his crew permission to sleep through the night.

Her heart hammered in her chest.

Holding her breath, Kath watched as the four crawled into their sleeping rolls. The gods, or fate, had given her a chance. She closed her eyes, letting her head lull forward, feigning sleep. Plans formed in her mind. She'd have to be patient and bide her time. Keeping her eyes closed, she listened to the soothing sounds of cicadas, hoping the night-song would lull the captain and his men to sleep.

# 31

# Duncan

The arrow struck true. Without thinking, Duncan reached for another, aiming and releasing all in one smooth motion. Lost in the art of the bow, he was surprised to find the quiver empty. He unstrung the longbow, wiped the yew wood with a soft cloth, and then went to collect his arrows. The heart of the target bristled with arrows fletched with black swan feathers. Duncan smiled; at least the luxuries of Lanverness had not dulled his skill.

A page in the green and white livery of Lanverness tracked him across the practice yard. "The queen requests you join her for a walk along the castle walls."

Duncan spied the queen watching from the battlements, a banner of silken beauty in the afternoon light. "I would be delighted to join her majesty. Please lead the way."

He followed the page up a narrow stairwell. Castle Tandroth was a maze of passageways, impossible to navigate without a guide. Duncan wondered if the confusion was deliberate, planned as an advantage for castle defenders...but military defenses did not seem to play a role in the luxuries of Castle Tandroth...there had to be another explanation.

The queen waited on a parapet, a vision of regal splendor bedecked in pearls and purple silk. Duncan bowed low. "Thank you for the invitation. I am honored to join you."

With a wave of her hand the queen dismissed the page, leaving Duncan alone with the ruler of Lanverness. She gave him a gracious smile and then turned to stroll along the crenellated battlement. "Walk with us, Lord Duncan. Leaves fall from the trees and the sunlight fades. Afternoons like this will soon be rare."

Nodding, he fell into step beside her. Assuming she had more on her mind than the weather, he waited to see where the conversation would lead. Daring a sideways glance, he noted how the deep purple of her gown showed off her creamy skin and slender waist. Her beauty and bearing combined to create an unmistakable aura of power. Even walking on the battlements she looked every inch the sovereign. Duncan wondered if there was ever a moment when the queen took off her crown.

She gestured toward his longbow. "We watched you skewer the heart of the target. Is archery a prerequisite for ambassadors from Navarre?"

Duncan laughed. "The people of Navarre are keen almost to the point of madness for archery, but it's certainly not a requirement. No, the longbow is my weapon of choice. I practice to maintain the skill and strength needed for accuracy." Pausing, he added, "Practicing the bow is a great way to clear the mind when there are too many problems to ponder."

The queen gave him a small smile. "And what thoughts drive you to the archery yard on this sunny afternoon?"

"The Flame religion of Coronth."

Her smile turned somber. "We confess the problem weighs on our mind as well...and so far a solution has not presented itself. Religions are difficult to defeat. Fighting with swords will not work. History has proven that religions propagate when their adherents are persecuted. Fighting with logic will also fail since religions are based on beliefs not facts. Since neither swords nor words will succeed, we are at a loss to think of a potent weapon." In a thoughtful voice, the queen added, "Lanverness has a long history of tolerance towards all religions. It is a policy that has served the kingdom well, even contributing to our success at commerce. We would not change our way of life for this Flame God."

Duncan nodded. "King Ivor shares your views."

The queen paused at the rampart, gazing out across the city. "But such tolerance can also be our undoing. Religious fanatics are difficult to stop and almost as difficult to contain. A single fanatic at your archery tournament nearly claimed the life of Navarre's king. The Lords of Light be praised that King Ivor will recover." Turning aside from the view, the queen resumed walking. "A steady flow of refugees creeps across the border from Coronth. Our constables report that the refugees are terrified of the Flame priests, fleeing Coronth in fear for their very lives. Those who wish to make a new life in Lanverness are welcome, but the refugees must leave their religion at the border. With nothing but open countryside between the two kingdoms, we fear the contagion of the Flame will spread."

Duncan considered her words, remembering how King Ivor had spared the life of the rogue archer. The thought teased his mind. "Perhaps the refugees hold the key."

"How so, Lord Duncan?"

Working with half-formed thoughts, he tried to explain, "The refugees have seen a side to the Flame God that has caused them to flee their homes...fleeing in fear for their very lives. If the people of Lanverness could see the Flame religion in the same way as the refugees, then your people might be immune to conversion."

The queen stopped walking and turned her sword-keen stare towards him. "An interesting idea, Lord Duncan, but how would you get the common people to see this religion from the same perspective as the refugees?"

"Use the bards." His thoughts raced with possibilities. "King Ivor's son, Justin, is using his Wayfaring to train as a bard. There has never been a bard in the history of the Navarren royal family. Many on the king's council voted against Justin's proposal but the king overruled them, arguing that music can greatly influence the thinking of the common people. King Ivor believes that most monarchs fail to appreciate the persuasive power of a good bard."

"You're saying that music can be used as another form of image? A way to reveal the true nature of the Flame God?"

"Just so, your majesty"

"The idea appeals to us. As a woman, we understand image better than most rulers." In a calculating voice the queen added, "We begin to see where your idea might lead. The Rose crown could sponsor the local bards to interview the refugees, giving the bards the task of weaving their experiences into song. Music can bring the truth of the Flame God to every tavern and pub in the land." She gave him a shrewd smile. "Truth is a thorny ground for planting twisted beliefs. In a sense, truth will be our shield against this religion of the Flame."

Duncan gave the queen a sideways glance; the woman was shrewd as well as beautiful. "Navarre also shares a border with Coronth...the truth should be spread to more than one kingdom. With your permission, I will write to King Ivor suggesting a Navarren bard be dispatched to Pellanor to assist with the crafting of these new songs. Once the work is done, the bard can share the songs with the seaside kingdom." Pausing, Duncan added, "Prince Justin may also be of help, even though he is only a bard in training."

"We welcome the assistance of Navarre in this matter. It is in the best interests of both of our kingdoms to thwart the Flame God." She gave him a gracious smile. "We hope your suggestion will give us a peaceful means to combat this new threat."

They walked in companionable silence, surveying the city from the battlement. Duncan watched as the autumn sun began to set but his mind was fixed on the queen. He'd heard so many outrageous rumors about the

'Spider Queen' that he'd not known what to expect. In truth, she was even more formidable than the rumors implied. The woman's mind was extremely quick and she obviously cared deeply for her people, but perhaps her most impressive trait was the way she welcomed new ideas. Having met the queen, he understood why Lanverness was so prosperous.

The setting sun filled the sky with a brilliant display of purples and golds, the royal colors flung like a cloak over the grand city. The queen turned to Duncan and said, "We like the way you think, Lord Duncan. We hope to have more walks with you along the parapets."

"I welcome the opportunity, your majesty."

The queen started to walk away and then turned back. "Lord Duncan, we do not usually succumb to idle curiosity, but would you mind if we asked you a personal question?"

"As you wish, your majesty."

"How did you come to wear a patch over your left eye?"

It was the one question Duncan preferred to avoid. He hated to lie but this was one secret he needed to protect. Feeling a blush creep up his face, Duncan reached for a joking tone as he gave his standard answer. "I'm embarrassed to admit that I wear the patch as a result of a fight over a woman. I won the fight but lost the eye in the process."

Arching her eyebrows the queen asked, "And the woman?"

Shrugging, he replied, "The woman wasn't worth the eye."

"We think it was the woman who lost." She gave him a penetrating stare. "Have a good evening, Lord Duncan."

Bowing, he watched as the queen joined her guards, returning to the heart of the palace. Reluctant to leave the fresh air, Duncan lingered on the battlement, watching as the last light faded from the twilight sky. The city surrounded the castle, like a giant puzzle with pieces of every description. It was said that anything could be bought in the streets of Pellanor and Duncan did not doubt it.

As the night descended, thousands of lanterns gave the city a faint glow, beating back the darkness. Duncan shook his head. Only the capital city of Lanverness would dare to compete with the very stars. Recalling his conversation with the queen, he wondered if the light of truth could hold back the darkness of the Flame religion. For the sake of both kingdoms, he hoped the truth would prevail.

# 32

# Steffan

Five gold bars bought Steffan five nights to win the confidence of the Pontifax. If he failed, the sixth day would find him consigned to the Test of Faith...but Steffan did not fear the flames. The agony of mortal fire would be nothing compared to the Dark Lord's wrath. He had no intentions of failing.

On each of the five nights, Steffan took the time to prepare, dressing in the finery of a wealthy nobleman. The plumage of wealth added weight to his words, deepening his influence with the Pontifax.

At the appointed hour, Steffan presented himself at the Residence bearing a bar of solid gold. Servants escorted him through the marble halls to a small chamber where the Pontifax and the Keeper of the Flame waited. The two high priests sat in stuffed armchairs before a roaring fireplace. A large gilded hourglass rested on a table between them. Both men wore sumptuous robes befitting their stations, the Pontifax in spun gold and the Keeper in red velvet. The room and the men both reeked of wealth and power, the perfect setting for his performance. Stifling a smile, Steffan bowed low, presenting his bar of gold.

The Pontifax accepted the gleaming ingot, settling the heavy bar in his lap. He caressed the gold with his left hand while sipping a large glass of brandy. "Your gold has bought an hourglass of our time. Use it well."

Flashing a sinister smile, the red-robed Keeper turned the hourglass. Dark sands spilled from one glass to another.

Steffan rose to the challenge. On the first night, he played to their fears. He told them of his travels to the capital city, warning of the vast numbers of heretics fleeing toward Lanverness. "If Coronth's neighbors are flooded with refugees then the other kingdoms will have a reason to interfere in your affairs." Steffan detected a flash of fear in the dark eyes of the Pontifax; self-preservation was always a powerful motivator. "But there is a solution." Taking the role of the faithful counselor, Steffan offered his advice. "Keep the heretics within Coronth and leave the neighboring kingdoms undisturbed. Order the guards to capture those who try to flee. Once caught, the heretics can be fed to the Flames or put to work in the service of the faithful. In either case, a new general with a firm resolve to stop the exodus is required." Finished, he bowed his head and waited. A flurry of questions followed, proving Steffan had touched a nerve. The Pontifax feared interference from the surrounding kingdoms, the one threat to his theocracy. Before the sands of the hourglass ran out, the Pontifax agreed to have his general take the 'Test of Faith', replacing him with a more zealous commander. Steffan kept his smile to himself. In just one night he'd set in motion the restructuring of the army of Coronth...and he was only getting started.

On the second night, Steffan played to their vanity. "Enlightened One, the capital city of Balor is steeped in the love of the Flame God...but the people's religious intensity decreases dramatically the farther one rides from the capital. The Flame God's love should fall like a blanket across the land, from the capital city to the farthest borders." Intrigued, the Pontifax leaned forward like a fish caught on the hook. Steffan hid his smile. "The people of the countryside need to feel your presence. They need to witness the Test of Faith in order to achieve the same deep religious commitment as the capital." Seeing the gleam of interest in the eyes of the Pontifax, Steffan knew the hook was set. Despots, religious or otherwise, seldom passed up the opportunity to gain followers. "To consolidate the theocracy, I suggest you revive the age-old tradition of taking progresses through the countryside. A ceremonial journey full of pomp and circumstance will provide an opportunity to demonstrate the Test of Faith in far-flung villages. The progresses will solidify your influence across Coronth, securing the entire kingdom for the Flame God." Throwing a bone to the Keeper of the Flame, he added, "Of course, the Keeper of the Flame should rule in Balor during the absence of the Enlightened One." The sullen Keeper suddenly swung to Steffan's point of view, urging the Pontifax to undertake the journey. By the end of the evening, the Keeper and the Pontifax were both scribbling notes on a map, planning routes through the countryside. Steffan smiled as he took his leave. The puppet masters had become the puppets.

On the third night, Steffan played to their greed. Revisiting the idea of the progresses, he suggested that the towns and villages should be encouraged to offer a gift to the Enlightened One. "The gifts should reflect the love of the people for their high priest. If handled correctly, the giving of gifts will become a competition between villages. Once the tradition is established, gifts of unrivaled wealth and beauty will flow to the private coffers of the Pontifax."

The Pontifax seized the idea. "But how do we start this tradition?"

"Holy heralds should be sent across Coronth announcing the upcoming progresses. The heralds will advise the leaders of the towns and villages on the protocols of the visit. The protocols will include the giving of gifts as well as the expectation of lavish feasts and entertainment." Smiling, he added, "Each progress will serve the Flame God, but there is no reason they should not also be enjoyable." The Pontifax clapped his hands, delighted with the idea. By the end of the third night, the Pontifax was referring to Steffan by his first name. As he bowed his way out of the chamber, the Enlightened One actually thanked Steffan for his suggestions.

The fourth night was different. Having set the hook, Steffan planned to risk everything. On the fourth night, he played to their need for power. As dark sands trickled through the gilded hourglass Steffan settled his stare on the great ruby amulet worn by the Pontifax. As the symbol of the priest's high office, Steffan had never seen the Pontifax without the amulet, but it was the Dark Lord who whispered the truth of the great ruby. "Enlightened One, you've achieved undeniable greatness in Coronth...but you've barely begun to use the magic of your amulet."

"*Magic!*" The Pontifax hissed like a venomous snake, both hands covering his ruby amulet. "You risk death with such blasphemy! How dare you suggest my powers are anything but *divine favor!*" The mood in the room turned ugly.

Steffan bowed his head in a gesture of subservience, careful with his reply. "Holy One, you misunderstand me. I will proclaim to all of Erdhe that you alone hold the divine favor of the Flame God. You alone are the Pontifax of his religion. You alone wield the ruby amulet, a gift of the Flame God...but it is a gift you might wield to even greater effect." He softened his voice. "As your servant and your counselor, I only wish to *extend* your power."

The Pontifax stared at Steffan with hooded eyes. "Have a care what you say. This ruby is the sacred symbol of my office. I will hear no blasphemy. Take care lest you condemn yourself as an infidel."

Steffan nodded, daring to continue. "As you say, the ruby amulet is a divine gift. When you hold the ruby, divine protection allows you to walk safely through the raging fires." He dropped his voice to a whisper. "But there is more you might do. If you hold the ruby with one hand and concentrate, you may be able to extend the divine protection to another person, shepherding a second soul through the sacred Flames."

The Pontifax gaped, his hand clutching the amulet. The Keeper stared slack-mouthed. Recovering, the two charlatans shared sideways glances.

Steffan hid his smile.

Returning his gaze to Steffan, the Pontifax asked, "How do you know this?"

"I do not *know* it as a fact. I only *suggest* it as a possibility. If the idea works, then you will have a second miracle, a second way to magnify the people's devotion." Noting the sudden hunger in the Pontifax's eyes, Steffan continued, "I suggest you test the idea in a private prayer service. Use someone who is expendable. This new miracle may require practice."

The Pontifax took the bait. "How should this be done?"

"The trials will require secrecy and expendable 'volunteers'. Convicted criminals should serve. If the criminals pass the trial then you can spare them. If they fail then it was obviously the will of the Flame God. For your protection, the criminals should be heavily shackled. They need only be able to walk in order to be suitable for the test."

The Pontifax fondled the great ruby, his eyes glazed with visions of powers. "Yes, we can see it, a new miracle to capture the hearts of the people. I will arrange for a private prayer service to be conducted in the Residence chapel tomorrow morning. As the new counselor to the Pontifax, your first duty, Lord Raven, will be to oversee these trials. See that you return to the Residence for morning services. Now kneel, and accept our blessing."

Hiding his smile, Steffan knelt before the Pontifax, swearing his allegiance and accepting the blessing of the Flame God. In just four days he'd accomplished the Dark Lord's will. Steffan was learning to be a puppet master...and he found he liked pulling stings.

# 33

# Katherine

Night fell hard in the forest, a smothering blanket of darkness. A hint of shy moonlight hid among the treetops, a thin crescent of silver. With so little light to see by, Kath knew galloping through the forest would be dangerous, but she couldn't pass up this one chance to escape. Time crawled as she waited on the moon.

Deep within the forest, cicadas sang a soothing lullaby. Kath smiled at the unexpected ally, willing her captors to sleep. The campfire dimmed to embers, a faint red glow. Lying still, she feigned sleep, watching her captors through hooded eyes. The captain worried her the most. Tossing fitfully beneath his blanket, the oily man proved a light sleeper. He deserved a plague of nightmares, but for once she wished him a deep sleep. She'd have to be silent to avoid waking him. On the other side of the fire, the ogre snored like a wounded bull. He'd help cover any sounds of escape, but even so, she planned to be stealthy. With four against one she couldn't afford any mistakes.

Judging the pale moonlight to be at its peak, Kath decided to take her chance. Saying a quick prayer to Valin, she squirmed against her bonds, reaching for the knife hidden in her boot. Lashed tight against the tree, she brought her boot up to her hands. It took a bit of twisting but she finally gripped the hilt. Moving the boot away, she freed the dagger. It felt good to hold steel in her hand.

Careful not to drop it, she positioned the blade against the ropes. Back and forth, she sawed her bound wrists across the blade. The rope proved thick and tough but it could not contend with the sharpness of good Castlegard steel. A final stroke and the rope parted. Her hands won their freedom.

A swift glance to her captors proved they still slept. Relieved, Kath quickly cut the ropes binding her arms. Freed from the pine tree, she pulled the hated leather gag from her mouth. A hunter's smile spread across her face. The meek little captive-girl was banished, transformed into a princess of Castlegard. With steel in her hands she felt complete, a warrior once more.

But she could not afford to be brash. Knowing a single clumsy move could foil her escape, she forced herself to wait, rubbing her arms until the pins and needles went away. Feeling the pain ease, she stood and raised the knife to the heavens, saluting the Lords of Light. She'd escape or die trying. An owl hooted in the forest depths, acknowledging her vow.

Slow and wary, Kath crept toward the horses. She slunk passed the sleeping forms and stepped wide around the glowing embers.

A twig snapped.

Kath froze.

The captain rolled toward her, a thrash of blankets.

Kath held her breath, her hand clutching the dagger...but none of them woke. Her heart thundering, she made her way to the picketed mounts, careful with each step. She reached the horses and took a deep calming breath, lest her anxiety spread to the mounts. Holding her hand out in supplication, she slowly approached the stallion. If the stallion accepted her, the other horses would not fret. The stallion sniffed and snorted into her open hand. Bobbing his head, he submitted to her touch. She rubbed his silky nose, letting him breathe her scent. Accepted by the stallion, the other horses remained still. Her gaze turned to the chestnut mare. On the three-day cross-country journey, Kath had carefully evaluated each of the horses. The stallion was a proud showy animal but the chestnut mare had the best speed and stamina. She wanted the mare for her escape.

Stroking the mare to gain her confidence, Kath untied the reins from the picket stake. She cut the leads of the other horses, hoping they'd scatter. Sheathing her dagger, she glanced over at her captors one last time. The captain tossed restlessly but the others lay still. A sudden temptation gripped her, a strong desire to slit the captain's throat, but the risk was unacceptable, better to just get away.

Touching her gargoyle for good luck, she grabbed a handful of mane and vaulted lightly onto the mare's bare back. Holding the reins in her right hand and twining the fingers of her left through the mare's mane, Kath turned the horse toward the depths of the forest. She thrummed her heels, asking for a gallop. The mare leaped forward, answering her demand, hoof beats drumming loud in the night.

The other horses stamped and snorted, shying away from the picket stake. Behind her, she heard the captain shout an alarm. The race for freedom was on.

Leaning low, Kath urged the mare to speed. She brought the horse to a full gallop, plunging into the depths of the forest, a wild midnight ride. Hoof beats drummed on the forest floor. A thrill rushed through Kath, yet she needed to keep her wits. Her captors would need time to gather their horses, but she'd only have a small lead. Escape would depend on her horsemanship and the speed of the chestnut mare.

Molding herself to the flanks of the mare, Kath asked for more speed and the mare answered. Like a wild, eldritch ride, horse and rider sped through the forest. Silvery moonlight striped the forest with light and shadow. The uneven lighting made for treacherous riding. Fused to the horse, Kath strained to find the best path. She needed speed but she could not afford to risk the mare, one misplaced hoof and she'd be lost. Cresting a small ridge, she glanced behind. The captain followed on the stallion, an echo of hoof beats hunting her through the night.

Whispering encouragement, Kath urged the horse to lengthen their lead. Forgetting about pursuit, she focused on the mare and the treachery of the forest floor. Leaping over fallen logs and dodging boulders and trees, she used the pale moonlight to thread a way forward. The mare proved agile and light on her feet. Kath was pleased with her choice.

The sounds of pursuit trailed behind, yet Kath could not afford to slow. The mare blew hard, lather forming on her sides, but the valiant horse maintained the hard gallop. With each stride, they lengthened their lead but the pounding hooves always followed. Kath knew she had to do something to evade the captain and his men, but for now all she could do was ride. Time seemed to stand still. A pale crescent moon traversed the night sky giving way to the first blush of morning.

A slash of brightness cut a line across the shadows. Assuming the strip of light heralded a change in terrain, Kath slowed the mare to a walk. As the mare caught her wind, Kath listened for sounds of pursuit. Muffled hoof beats followed behind, she could not afford to tarry. Urging the mare to a trot, she approached the cut in the forest, surprised to discover a break in the canopy.

The ground dropped away to a swirling river.

Kath pulled hard on the reins, stopping the mare on the lip of a narrow gorge. Sheer rock walls plunged forty feet to an angry blue-green river. Water tumbled below, a froth of white carving a path through rock and forest. She'd risked a midnight ride only to be trapped by a gorge. Her heartbeat hammering, Kath sought a way to escape.

Upstream, the gorge got deeper but the width narrowed considerably. Downstream, the gorge widened, the height of the walls gradually diminishing. She had the choice of following the gorge downstream hoping to find a crossing, or riding upstream, looking for a place to jump.

A jump would be the riskier choice but it was a choice she believed her pursuers did not have. Without a saddle and with only her slight weight, the mare would have the best chance to make the jump, but it was still an enormous risk.

Kath turned the mare upstream. Riding along the edge of the gorge, she found a spot where the two sides narrowed to within ten feet. If she dared and if the mare was capable, this might just be the chance she needed to lose her pursuers. Judging that her side of the gorge was higher than the other, she decided to take the risk.

She let the mare catch her breath, while listening for approaching horses. Perhaps it was a trick of the forest, but it seemed to Kath that the captain and his men were drawing near. It was time to take the dare.

Kath walked the mare in a straight line away from the gorge. Pivoting the mare, she eyed the line of ground leading up to the edge. Farther down the gorge, the captain and his men emerged from the forest. With her lead gone, Kath was out of time.

She drummed her heels, asking for a gallop. The sturdy mare surged forward, responding with a burst of speed. Racing toward the lip of the gorge, Kath molded herself to the back of the horse. Approaching the edge, she felt the chestnut mare gather herself for the leap. Kath prayed the mare would not balk. Without breaking stride, the valiant mare took the leap.

Horse and rider hung suspended across the chasm.

Kath held her breath. Time slowed as the mare stretched out her forelegs. With a jarring thud, the mare's front hooves connected with the far side of the gorge. Thrown forward, Kath nearly lost her seat. She clung to the horse's mane as the mare scrabbled to for purchase, teetering on the edge. Loose stones clattered down the side of the gorge. Death nipped at the horse's hind hooves. Kath leaned forward, hugging the mare. The horse caught her balance. With a thrust of her hindquarters, the mare cleared the gorge. Coming to a stop, the mare quivered with stress, blowing hard. Kath gave the mare a mighty hug. "We did it!" Looking back across the chasm, she pumped her fist in the air, celebrating victory and freedom.

An arrow thunked into the ground in front of her.

In the flush of excitement, Kath had forgotten the archer. Her pursuers would not dare the jump but the gorge was no barrier to arrows. She needed the cover of the forest. Kath gathered the mare and urged her to a gallop.

They rode away from the gorge, plunging into the forest, passing from brightness back into shadow. Without warning the mare stumbled into a hole, throwing Kath head over heels. Pain ripped through her. Kath slammed into the tree trunk, while the mare squealed in pain. Kath tried to stand, but the world spun. Everything ached, her head most of all. The mare's squeals kept her from passing out. Kath crawled toward the injured horse.

Kicking and squealing, the mare lay on her side, struggling to rise...but she would never stand again. White bone protruded from the chestnut's front leg. Kath let out a sob. She could not bear to see the valiant mare in pain. There was only one thing to do. She knew what was required though she'd never done it before. Tears streamed down her face as she whispered words of thanks to the mare as she slipped the knife from her boot. As if the mare understood, the horse stopped struggling, staring at her with liquid eyes. Saying a prayer to the Lords of Light, Kath positioned the dagger over the mare's heart. She leaned forward, putting all her weight behind the dagger. The thrust was true. Death came quickly. Removing the dagger, Kath crawled away and slumped under a low shrub. Sick at heart, she let the darkness take her, passing out on the forest floor.

# 34

# Danly

anly was bored. As the night wore on, the dice continued to roll against him, the pile of gold in front of him dwindling. He did not mind paying for his bets, after all he had plenty to spend, but he was getting tired of the losing. He hated to lose. Ordering another glass of brandy from a passing servant, he consoled himself with the excellent liquor.

Tiring of the dice, Danly regretted accepting Lord Carrington's invitation to join the wealthy of Pellanor for a night of gaming at his manor house. The food and liquor were excellent but the evening seemed drab and colorless. He considered retiring to one of the private rooms upstairs where women of the night were available, but there was no challenge in it, no thrill of the hunt...no risk. Bored, he left the gaming table and sat in an armchair near the fireplace, quietly sipping his fourth brandy.

From the darkness behind him a deep voice whispered, "Many miss your father, the man who should have been king."

Startled by the statement as much as the voice, the prince began to turn.

A hand came from behind, resting firmly on his shoulder. "Don't turn around, my prince. Just sip your brandy and speak quietly and no one else will notice." The hand retreated back into the darkness.

Danly waited, keen with interest.

After a while, the deep voice whispered, "Do you miss your father?"

*A dangerous question,* yet Danly chose to answer. "They say my father's face looks out at me from the mirror every morning but I would not know." A long held bitterness crept into his voice. "They say that my royal mother devoured her mate once the spare heir was born. With the birth of a second son there was no more use for the father, so now the Widow Spider rules alone, the undisputed queen." With a drunken laugh, he added, "They say in the barracks that it was the prince consort who died of birthing pains not the queen." It was dangerous talk, but somehow Danly didn't care. Perhaps it was the brandy or perhaps it was the boredom, either way, the Dark Lord could take his royal mother for all he cared.

The deep voice whispered, "Many would see a king return to the Rose Throne. It is unnatural for men to be ruled by a mere woman."

"It is my royal mother who is unnatural. There's no woman in her, only queen." Danly swirled the brandy, oblivion in a glass. "She was never enough of a woman to be a mother to me." He hardened is voice. "Women are not meant to rule. The gods made women for one reason and one reason only, to pleasure men." His voice turned bitter. "My lord father failed to teach the queen that one lesson. It is a lesson that has not been lost on the son."

Fire crackled in the hearth, the scent of pine filling the room. Just when Danly began to think he was alone, the voice said, "There are many men of the kingdom who chaff under the yoke of a woman. If these men knew that a rightful king was ready to lead, they would rise up and put an end to the Spider Queen."

Snorting into his brandy, Danly said, "A rightful heir! You speak of my brother then! Crown Prince Stewart the Good! My dear brother is nothing more than an insipid lap dog for my mother, happy to trot along and play with swords. My royal *older* brother has no head for politics or the crown, perhaps that's why the queen favors him so, knowing he will never be a threat." With a cruel chuckle he added, "I'd bet all the golds in my purse that my dear royal brother has not even tupped a woman. Stewart would never dare dip his royal wick without first gaining permission from the queen. Is that the type of 'rightful heir' you seek?"

This time the voice was quick to respond. "No, my lord prince. Lanverness needs a strong ruler, a real man, a true king. Many have watched you grow and seen your worth. You have the strength to act and to take what you want. We seek to pass over the weak firstborn son in favor of the stronger second prince."

Like a spark to dry tinder, the words lit a bonfire in his soul. Danly yearned to grasp the destiny denied him. Only an insipid older brother and an unnatural mother stood in his way. But he also knew how dangerous the game could be, a tantalizing game, a game of great risks and greater consequences...a game the gambler in him could not resist. But there was no need to throw caution to the wind. In a shrewd voice, the prince said, "And who are these men who would support the rightful heir to the throne?"

Whispers from the darkness replied, "It is not yet time for us to be revealed. We are still gathering strength. Be assured, majesty, brave men will fight and die for your cause."

Danly sneered. "How brave can they be if they will not even creep out of the shadows?"

A pregnant silence filled the darkness.

Danly thought he'd scared the man away, but the voice whispered, "When our conversation is done, I will leave the room, passing in front of the fireplace. You will see my face and recognize it, but you will say nothing. You will think about how you have treated me in the past and you will make sure to continue in the same manner. Do you understand?"

A smile slid across the prince's face, the stakes of the game were getting interesting. "I understand. But if I cannot approach you, how will I contact you?"

"Are you familiar with the coat of arms of your father's house?"

A simmering anger woke in the prince. His claim to the Rose Throne, and even his surname, flowed from his royal mother's blood. In order to marry the future queen, his father had been forced to forsake his name and the noble heraldry that went with it. The coat-of-arms for house Terrel could only be found in the musty scrolls of the palace library, as if the queen had erased all traces of her dead husband. "I am well aware of my father's coat of arms, a red unicorn rampant on a field of green."

"There are others who have not forgotten. Your loyal supporters have taken the red horn of the unicorn as our symbol. If you wish to contact us, you need only draw a red horn on the rear wall near the rose bushes in the Commoners' Garden. Draw that symbol with red chalk and one of us will approach you before the day is done. But only use the symbol if you have great need. Be patient, my prince, while we build our numbers."

"And what am I to do in the meantime?"

"The queen makes enemies when she ignores the powerful men in her court. Make careful note of those enemies, for they will soon become your allies." A hand gripped his shoulder, full of assurance. "I look forward to the day when I can acknowledge you in public. Till then, remember that you must *never* approach me. Treat me the same way as you did before we had this conversation, before you took your first step towards your rightful crown."

A rustling sound came from the darkness behind him. Danly held his breath as a shadowy figure emerged from the darkness, stepping into the light of the fireplace. The prince sat stunned. With this man as his ally, there was every chance he would one day wear the Rose Crown. Playing his part, Danly remained in the chair slowly sipping his brandy, while the fires of ambition burned in his heart.

# 35

# Liandra

A mound of scrolls covered the small reading table next to the stuffed armchair. Queen Liandra sat immersed in the financial accounts of the kingdom. She could have asked her treasurer to give her a summary of the accounts but she found it beneficial to review the numbers herself. Wealth was in the details. To most people, numbers were an arcane mystery, but not to the queen. Clear as a seer's scrying bowl, she read the future in the numbers, finding new ways to multiply her golds. Wealth was the true strength of Lanverness, and the queen refused to see a single copper squandered.

A knock on the door broke the silence of her solar. Ignoring the interruption, the queen continued reading. The guards had firm orders about who to admit and who to turn away. Hearing the door open, she knew that it could only be one of a handful of people. Glancing up from the scroll, she was not surprised to see Lord Highgate, the Master Archivist. Dressed in his usual austere robes of black, her spymaster looked more like an undertaker than the chief counselor to the richest court in the land. Despite his grim appearance, the queen would have staffed her entire court with dour men provided they had half the intellect of the Master Archivist.

"Majesty, I am sorry to interrupt but I have several things to bring to your attention."

Setting aside the scroll, she offered him a nod of approval.

"The jewelers commissioned to make your necklace using the royal rubies have completed their work. They await your approval."

Intrigued, the queen replied, "Please tell us the names of the jewelers and then show them in. We are most interested to see the outcome of their work."

"The senior artisan is Master Saddler, the goldsmith, a short heavyset man with gray hair. The other is Master Geld, the gem cutter."

Liandra gave a wave of approval and the master opened the door. The two jewelers bowed their way across the floor, gawking at every detail of the royal solar.

Addressing the two men, the queen said, "Masters Saddler and Geld, we are eager to see the results of your art."

Flushed with praise, the jewelers bowed low. Master Saddler carried a pillow draped in silk. "We were honored with your royal commission. We hope you will be pleased with our work." With a flourish, he removed the silk cloth, unveiling the necklace.

The queen had a keen eye for jewelry; the piece was exquisite. Designed to cleverly capitalize on the variance of color in the dark rubies, the stones were set in a golden sunburst, with the darkest rubies close to the neck and lighter rubies radiating out towards the points of the sunburst, creating a blaze of reflected light. The queen turned her gaze to the jewelers. "What is your assessment of the royal rubies?"

Master Saddler had the look of man expecting to be rich. "As per the instructions from the palace, we let word leak to our wealthiest patrons that we were working with a new gem in a special commission for the queen. After glimpsing the work in progress, our shops were flooded with orders. There is no doubt that the royal ruby will be a great success."

The queen smiled. "We are most pleased to hear of the public's interest and we are delighted by the elegance of our new necklace." She lifted the necklace, turning it in the light. "We predict the artistry of the necklace combined with the natural beauty of the royal rubies will spark a new fashion trend in Lanverness. In recognition of your excellent work, we grant you the right to display the symbol of royal patronage above the doors to your shops for a period of one year. You may go with our thanks."

The two jewelers flushed with pleasure. The right to display the symbol of royal patronage meant their shop's business would double within a year. The queen smiled. The jewelers had been amply paid for their efforts without drawing a single gold from the royal purse. Liandra examined her new necklace, delighting in the play of light across the dark stones.

The Master Archivist hovered by her chair. "It would have been a great waste to simply close the mine."

Arching an eyebrow, the queen replied, "Yes, we cannot afford to waste the natural wealth of Lanverness." Setting the necklace aside, she studied her spymaster. "You said that you had several things to bring to our attention?"

"Yes, your majesty." Reaching into the deep pockets of his black robe, the master produced a scroll sealed with blue wax. "This arrived at the western gates of the castle."

The queen inspected the scroll, surprised to see the symbol of the Kiralynn monks in the unbroken wax seal. Her gaze snapped to her spymaster. "Do we know how this was delivered?"

"The guard has no recollection of the person who delivered it. Despite the generous use of golds, we still do not know who their agents are in the Rose Court."

The queen weighed the scroll, wondering if she held a portent of good news or bad. Either way, messages from the monks were not to be taken lightly. "The monks are too mysterious by half." Their messages often seemed irrelevant or obscure on first reading but hindsight nearly always proved them to be of great import. There was something uncanny about the monks' ability to predict the events of Erdhe, despite the fact that they lived as recluses in their remote mountain monastery...or so they would have people think. The queen suspected the monks maintained a web of spies and messengers that would put the agents of the Rose Court to shame. Her own spymaster had yet to discover the monks' agents in Pellanor. Their best hope was to trace the delivery of one of the mysterious scrolls, but once again her people had failed. Still, she would rather have the message than not. The queen was willing to consider information from any quarter, including the mysterious monks.

Breaking the seal, she unrolled the scroll. The Master Archivist waited as she read. Finished, Liandra sat back in the chair to ponder the message. Once again the monks had managed to surprise her. She studied her spymaster, knowing he burned to read the scroll yet he maintained a placid visage. The master rarely showed any emotion. It was one of the many qualities she liked about the man.

She let the scroll roll closed on her lap. "Another unusual message. We shall keep this to ourselves. Bring us the sealing wax."

A flicker of annoyance passed across the master's face but he hid it well. Playing the servant, he strode to the desk, returning with a stick of emerald green sealing wax and a lit candle. Heating the stick in the flame, he expertly dripped wax across the edge of the rolled scroll, sealing it shut. The queen used the gold signet ring on her left hand to imprint the wax, trusting the Royal Seal to ensure the confidentiality of the scroll. She handed the scroll to her spymaster. "We entrust this to your keeping. We will share its contents with you when events make the scroll relevant. Keep it safe while we will wait to see how the future unfolds."

The scroll disappeared into the pocket of the master's black robe. "As you wish."

Pondering the monk's message, the queen said, "Is there anything else you wish to discuss with us?"

"Yes, majesty, one small thing."

Her attention snapped to her spymaster. "And that would be?"

He fingered his thin gray mustache, his face thoughtful. "The prince has requested your permission to attend the council sessions. He claims a desire to learn more about the governing of Lanverness."

For the second time this afternoon the queen was surprised. Her eldest son always eschewed a seat on the council, preferring the way of the sword to politics. Still, it was never too late for her royal son to learn the finer points of ruling a kingdom. After all, the Rose Crown would one day be his to wear. Perhaps the choice of a daughter-in-law would not be as critical as she thought. "We are pleased that Crown Prince Stewart is finally taking an interest in the governance of the kingdom. We would be happy to have him contribute to our council sessions."

"Forgive me for not being clear, but it is your other son, Prince Danly, who has made the request."

She studied her councilor through hooded eyes. Coming from her younger son, the request was even more unlikely, and more suspicious. Prince Danly's interests were limited to spending golds, bedding women, and gambling. "How did this request come to your attention?"

"This morning, after the council meeting, General Helfner approached me on behalf of the prince."

"And you did not think it odd?"

"I found it to be extremely odd, that is why I am bringing it to your majesty's attention."

"Someone plays a very strange game of politics." The queen was not pleased. "We could see the general sponsoring Prince Stewart, but never Prince Danly." Suspicions ran rife in her mind, plots within plots. "We never considered the general to be a political man but perhaps we were wrong. What do you suggest, Lord Highgate?"

"The request raises too many questions. One of my shadowmen should be assigned to watch the general. We need to learn what type of relationship exists between the general and the prince. Once we understand the motive then the actions will become clear."

The queen fingered the string of pearls around her neck, considering her loyal men. "You have our permission to watch the general but it must be done with great discretion. We do not wish to sow mistrust amongst our counselors."

"And Prince Danly?"

A touch of anger rode the queen's voice. "It is past time we had a long conversation with each of our royal sons." She gave the master a sharp look. "Arrange a private dinner in my sitting room with Prince Stewart for tomorrow night and a second dinner with Prince Danly for the end of the week. In the interim, if your shadowmen learn anything from watching the general, we would hear of it immediately. Are we understood?"

"Yes, your majesty. And if the prince or the general inquire as to the status of their request?"

"Their request is under consideration by the queen." She dismissed him with a wave. "Now leave us, for we have much to ponder."

Bowing, the master slipped from the room like a dark shadow.

Alone in her solar, Liandra turned her mind to the complexities of her court. A political gauntlet had clearly been thrown down. The question was, by whom? Was the general's request a blunder or a shrewd feint within a feint? Politics was a lot like swordplay; the real danger was not the blade in front of you but the one that came out of the darkness to stab from behind. As a veteran of the game, the queen knew the hand that struck from behind was usually that of a colleague, a close friend, or even a loved one. The throne was a lonely place...but it was also a position of great power. Liandra preferred to use her power to serve the people of Lanverness, but if needs be, she would not hesitate to exert the full force of the throne to keep the crown upon her head. It was time for the 'Spider Queen' to spin a few webs of her own. She wondered who would be caught this time.

# 36

# Katherine

Rain pattered against her face, drawing Kath back to consciousness. Her head was muzzy and her throat parched. She opened her mouth, desperate to drink. A few swallows of rainwater helped to clear her mind. Cold and wet, she leaned against the tree trunk, struggling to understand. And then she saw the mare, lying dead in a pool of blood. A sob escaped her. Shivering against the damp, she wiped a tear from her eye; it was all too true. She was alone, on foot, and hunted by servants of the Dark Lord, servants she knew would never rest until they caught her. Without the mare, Kath did not give herself much of a chance but despite the odds, she refused to give up.

She reached for her boot, drawing the dagger from its sheath. Running her finger across the smith's mark, she smiled. Giving up was not the way of the Octagon. She may be the quarry in this chase, but she was also a warrior. If nothing else, she'd teach the servants of the Dark Lord a lesson about steel before she passed on to the next life.

A pale sun peered through a cloud-shrouded sky, already halfway to the noon position. Most of the morning was already lost. Kath had no way of telling how long it would take the captain and his men to find their way around the gorge, but she had no doubt that they *would* find a way. If she was going to escape, she had no time to waste.

Getting to her feet, she saluted the valiant mare, and then set off at a lope into the heart of the forest. Trees crowded close, thick trunks draped with moss, the scent of pine and cedar lingering in the morning mist. She threaded her way through the trees while her mind sought a way to elude her pursuers. The knight marshal always said the 'greatest advantage in battle was to out think the enemy.' Given the odds stacked against her, she'd need a brilliant idea in order to have any chance at all. Unfortunately, her only plan was to keep moving.

A crystal-clear stream splashed ahead. Kath dropped to the ground and drank her fill, lapping up the icy water. Her reflection stared back at her, dirty and disheveled, but then she saw herself in a different way. She was the quarry in the chase, the fox hunted by the Dark Lord's hounds. If she was going to succeed then she had to think like the fox. How would the fox use the stream? If the goblin-man could truly track the scent of her magic, then perhaps, like a true hound, he could not track the scent across flowing water.

Kath plunged knee-deep into the crystal-cold water. Keeping to the heart of the icy flow, she jogged downstream looking for a place with lots of stones littering the far bank. Finding what she sought, she firmly planted her booted foot in the muddy bank leaving a clear print exiting the stream. Five paces took her to the limits of the scattered stones. Carefully stepping onto a large rock, she hopped from one stone to another until she re-entered the stream. Surveying her handiwork, she smiled. A clear set of footprints led away from the creek, vanishing into the grass beyond. Satisfied with the illusion, she jogged back upstream, listening for any hint of hoof beats. The peace of the forest remained unbroken but Kath did not trust it.

She walked against the current, making her way upstream, scanning the banks of the creek for any advantage. A rocky ridge rose to the left and at its summit an immense oak tree stood above the autumn forest like a sentinel. That gave her an idea. She left the streambed and climbed the ridge to the tree. Old and gnarled, the oak had plenty of footholds, making an easy climb to the lower branches. Kath wriggled her way out on a thick branch, lying flat and staring south, searching for any movement. The forest spread below, a patchwork of autumn leaves, bare branches and dark fir trees. She used the stream as a marker, her gaze following it south. Basking in the sunlight, she almost fell asleep but then she saw them, a glimpse of riders crossing the stream and heading west. Relief washed through her; her ruse had worked, but the more distance she gained the better.

Kath scrambled down from the tree and returned to the streambed. Following the watercourse south, she found a break in the trees ahead. Sunlight crowned an odd-shaped hill, snaring Kath's attention.

Something caught her foot. She tripped and fell face-first toward the rushing water. Hands out, she caught herself, the tip of her nose lapped by the water.

A face stared back at her.

Pale as death, a woman's face stared up from beneath the shallow stream.

Kath gasped, scrambling backwards. Her heart hammering, she peered into the streambed. The face remained, a woman wearing a knight's helmet. Wondering if it was real or an illusion, Kath reached beneath the surface. Her hand met stone as cold as the water. She sighed in relief, nothing more than a broken statue. Glancing around the streambed, she saw other pieces of marble strewn amongst the tumbled rocks. An open hand gestured a welcome beneath the cold waters. A little farther upstream, another hand grasped a marble sword hilt, and near the bank, a moss covered shield lay half buried in the silt. The stream was a graveyard of broken statues. But what were statues doing in the heart of the forest? The mystery teased Kath.

Drawn into the riddle, she decided to investigate the glade. With luck, she might find a weapon, a sword or an axe. Leaving the stream, she climbed towards the sunlit hill. The irregular contours took shape, revealing a ruined keep, the tumbled blocks of a curtain wall and a broken tower covered with moss and vines. So overgrown, so green, the ruins looked like part of the forest. She ran her hand along the moss-encrusted wall, wondering at its history. Rounding the short curtain wall, she faced a gaping doorway to a broken tower.

The doorway beckoned.

Intrigued, Kath peered into the heart of the ruins. Sunlight streamed into the circular well of a broken drum tower. An ancient oak tree rose from the center, its roots delving deep into the jumbled stones of the tower floor. Autumn leaves shimmered gold overhead, crowning a gnarled trunk more than five hands wide. Majestic and strong, the great tree attested to the age of the ruins. A hushed stillness cloaked the broken tower, as if she'd entered a cathedral.

Kath stepped through the doorway. A woman's voice whispered in her mind, "Welcome back, Warrior of the Light."

Freezing in place, Kath listened, hearing only the faint rustling of leaves. "Who are you?"

A flock of small birds took flight from the oak tree, spiraling up into the sunshine. A shiver raced down Kath's back; the startled birds proved the woman had spoken without breaking the silence of the tower. Perhaps the tower was haunted, yet Kath felt no fear. Closing her eyes, she spoke inside of her mind, "Who are you?"

There was no answer.

Yearning for a response, Kath kept her eyes closed, listening for a reply. It seemed as if a long-hidden door opened in her mind, releasing the beat of a thousand wings. Dizzy and disoriented, she leaned against the wall. The mad rush of wings stilled and an image crystallized in her mind. She saw the tower whole and unbroken, in the grandeur of another time. Overhead, a corbelled vault of dark blue held crystals inset as stars. The ceiling was a marvel, portraying all the constellations of the night sky. The floor of the tower was almost as wondrous, a mosaic of blue and gold depicting a map of Erdhe. On the far wall, two stone knights supported a great stone shield that served as a mantle over a massive fireplace. A staircase spiraled around the walls of the tower leading to the floors above, stone swords embedded in each step forming a railing.

And then Kath realized she was not alone. A knight descended the stairs, a well-shaped man with broad shoulders and raven black hair. Kath felt a stab of longing. His face was shrouded in mist, yet she somehow knew him. A certainty swept through her. This man would stand by her side even against all the foes of the world. Longing to know his face, his name, she took a step forward. A thousand wings beat against her, holding her back. She fought against the wings but the vision faded, like sand pouring through her clenched fists. A feeling of great loss descended on her.

Opening her eyes, Kath found herself alone in the broken tower...a ruined echo of ancient glory. A sob escaped her, yearning for all that was lost. Closing her eyes, Kath willed the knight to return, for the tower to resume its ancient glory...but that other time was once again a prisoner of the distant past.

Taking a deep breath, Kath set out to explore the ruins, hoping to find clues to the vision. Walking around the great oak tree, she discovered the remains of the massive fireplace, only now the stone knights were dismembered and defaced. The great staircase was there as well, a broken spiral climbing part way around the tower, leading to nothing but open sky. Less than half of the stone swords remained, and most of those were broken.

Setting her foot on the first step, Kath heard the woman's voice again. *"Seek under the seventh step."*

A shiver raced down her spine. Ascending to the sixth step, Kath knelt to examine the seventh. Solid and firm, she tried lifting the step, but it remained fixed. It seemed immovable till she pulled the step forward. Stone grated against stone, as the step swung forward, pivoting to reveal a rectangular hollow beneath. Gold winked at her from the shallow space. Reaching into the hollow, she withdrew an ornate gold box, one foot long and five inches wide.

Sunlight glinted on gold, revealing intricate engravings. A shield emblazoned with an eight-pointed star dominated the center. The device was unknown yet achingly familiar. Reverently running her fingers across the lost heraldry, Kath searched for memories of another time.

Whispering a prayer to Valin, she opened the lid. The contents took her breath away. Nestled in blue velvet, sat a crystalline dagger.

Kath reached for the dagger, a small cross-hilt with a straight eight-inch blade honed to a keen edge. The crystal dagger felt like it belonged in her hand. Raising the dagger to the heavens in salute, the pale rose-white crystal caught and held the light, appearing luminous from within.

The dagger teased at Kath's mind, opening doors to memories she didn't even know she had. She recognized the dagger as a powerful weapon of the Light, a weapon meant for times of great need. The dagger was crafted to be the bane of a powerful servant of the Dark Lord, someone or something far more menacing than the captain and his men. Until she was free of her pursuers, the dagger should remain safely hidden in the ruins. With great reluctance, Kath nestled the dagger back into the velvet, replacing the box in its hiding place.

As the stone step slid back into place, the piercing call of a hawk split the sky.

A premonition of danger whispered through Kath. Reaching for the steel dagger hidden in her boot, she climbed the stairs, cautiously peering over the lip of the ruined tower. Despair struck as she spied the captain and his men.

They followed the course of the stream, the goblin-man leading the troop, his head swaying from side to side as if casting about for her scent. Lathered and sweat-stained, their horses followed with their heads hung low; the captain must have ridden them hard to find a way around the gorge. Watching from her perch, Kath felt a deep revulsion, the Dark Lord's servants should never befoul this place of Light. Sighing, she realized the tower must have fallen to the Dark long ago else it would not be broken. But a hidden power still lingered, something that should not be sullied by the Dark. Staring at the captain, her resolve hardened. If they left the stream for the ruins, she'd show herself and lead them into the forest.

As if sensing her vow, the goblin-man paused in mid-stream, casting his head back and forth like a hound nosing for the scent. A shiver ran down Kath spine, there was something obscene about being tracked by one's smell.

The goblin-man gave a shout, pointing up towards the ruins. The captain and his crew left the stream. Kath muttered a curse but held to her resolve. Touching her gargoyle for good luck, she sped down the tower steps and out the door. Rounding the remains of the curtain wall, she sped into plain sight. The captain shouted, "Get her!" and the last leg of the hunt was on.

Kath raced around the side of the tower, running down the hill into the depths of the forest. The slope was so steep she had to work to keep her footing. Dodging trees and leaping over small boulders, she chose a path most difficult for the horses. Brambles clawed at her skin and hair but she bulled her way through. Ignoring the curses from behind, Kath concentrated on the ground ahead. At the bottom of the hill, the forest opened up into a sun-kissed meadow. She ran hard for the golden grass, planning to make her last stand in the sunlight.

Hoof beats thundered behind. Her shoulder blades itched, half expecting an arrow, but she kept running. She wished for her throwing axes, but all she had was her Castlegard dagger. Leaping over a log, she scrambled down the steep slope, praying the dagger would be enough to take one of them into the afterlife.

Sprinting into the meadow, Kath raced toward a large boulder.

A hard stare followed her...but not from behind.

Skidding to a stop, she pivoted to look down the length of an arrow. A lone huntsman held her in the aim of his longbow.

Kath lifted her hands in entreaty. "Please help! I am being chased by servants of the Dark Lord!"

Behind her, the captain thundered into the meadow, brandishing a sword. "You'll pay for this, girlie! You'll pay with pain!"

Not knowing if the archer would help, Kath turned and ran for the boulder, needing to put an obstacle between herself and the mounted men. Just as she reached the boulder, she heard the twang of a bowstring. Her shoulder blade's twitched but no arrow came. Glancing back, she saw the captain tumble from the saddle, an arrow protruding from his chest. Hope flashed through her. Reversing course, she ran to the captain, needing to be sure.

More horses galloped into the knee-high grass.

Kath reached the captain. The arrow had struck close to his heart, his life's blood pumping bright red from of the wound. Dying but not dead, he sneered up at her, spitting in her face. "You'll pay, girlie." Kath did not hesitate. Her dagger slit his throat, taking the sword from his limp hand.

More arrows thrummed into the captain's men.

Gripping the sword in one hand and the dagger in the other, Kath raced to join the battle.

Thrown from his horse, the huge Taal advanced on the archer. Three arrows protruded from his chest but still he came, like a monster loosed from the depths of hell. Kath ran forward, putting her steel between the archer and the seven-foot Taal. She crouched in a fighting stance, the Taal looming above her, the sword a toy in his huge fist.

Howling in rage, the Taal attacked. His sword was a whistle of death. Kath dodged sideways, keeping just out of reach. The Taal's sword rent the earth, planting a deep furrow, proof of his enormous strength. Kath danced away, knowing she dare not meet his blade. He yanked the sword from the earth and slashed at her head. Kath kept moving, dodging and weaving, looking for an opening. The ogre fought like a raging bull, wild and undisciplined, but one sword swipe would cleave her in two. Feinting a strike to the giant's chest, she dodged beneath a mighty swing of his sword. Rolling to the right, she tumbled under his reach and came up behind him. Quick as summer lightning, she lashed out with her sword, slicing the tendons of his leg. The leg crumpled and the ogre crashed face-first onto the ground. Leaping on his back, she plunged her sword deep, searching for the heart. The ogre let out one last roar and then lay still.

Drenched with sweat, she wrenched the sword free and surveyed the field. The goblin-man and his compatriot lay dead, dispatched by the archer. One of the horses lay felled by an arrow, the others milled at the far edge of the meadow.

The battle was over.

She'd live to see another day.

Overcome, Kath sank to her knees in the tall grass. She clutched the hilt of the sword, offering a prayer to Valin. Staring up at the sky, she was surprised to be alive. Golden sunshine warmed her face, the drone of insects loud in her ears. The meadow was flush with a vibrancy she'd never noticed. Kath knelt in the grass, glorying in the richness of life.

The archer stood beside her.

She felt his hard stare.

Kath shook her head, trying to clear her mind. Meeting the gaze of her unexpected ally, she gasped.

The man had the eyes of a cat!

He stared at her from behind a nocked arrow...his eyes golden-yellow with black slits for pupils. *Golden cat-eyes set in a human face, just like the man chased from the inn at Ferrytown.* She shuddered, wondering if she'd escaped one evil only to fall into the hands of another. Trying to suppress her fear, she reminded herself that the archer had chosen to help. "Thank you for saving me. I owe you a debt of my life."

Cocking his head as if listening to more than her words, the archer replied, "And why is a white-eyed girl being chased by giants and dwarves? And where does a girl learn to wield a sword like that?"

The cat-eyed huntsman was tall with broad shoulders, long brown hair framing a sun-weathered face. Kath stared boldly back into his strange yellow eyes, deciding to trust her ally with her name. "My name is Kath and I am a princess of Castlegard." Gesturing toward the dead captain, she said, "Servants of the Dark Lord abducted me. I was trying to escape when you came to my aid. I owe you my life, sir. Might I hear your name, so I know who holds me in their debt?"

The archer lowered his bow. "As strange as it sounds, it seems you speak the truth...though you are a long way from Castlegard." Pausing, he added, "As to your debt, you saved my life when you stopped the ogre. The beast took three of my arrows yet refused to die." The archer shook his head as if banishing a nightmare. "If you feel you owe a debt, then pay it to those with eyes like mine who cross your path and are in need of help. My people are rarely welcome in the lands of Erdhe. The help of a white-eye could mean the difference between life and death."

Kath remembered the first time she'd seen yellow cat-eyes in the face of a man. She also remembered the way the innkeeper had threatened the man with a club. Suddenly ashamed, she nodded. "I gladly accept the debt, but I would still like to know your name...and the name of your people?"

Leaning on his bow, the man gave her a piercing stare. "My name is Jorah Silvenwood and my people are the Children of the Green." He gestured toward a dead deer on the far side of the meadow. "It's past time I returned to the depths of the forest. Baron Roanoff does not take kindly to poachers." Staring at her, he added, "Now that you're free, what will you do?"

"I was traveling with an escort of Octagon knights. I hope they're following behind. I'll take one of the horses and try to backtrack to meet up with them."

"Wyeth is a wild and dangerous place. Despite your skill with the sword, it's not the sort of place a young woman should travel alone. It's out of my way, but I'll see you at least part way back to your people."

Smiling, Kath bowed to the archer. In the depths of the forest, she'd found an unexpected ally...perhaps the gods listen to prayers after all.

# 37

# Jordan

Jordan reviewed the maneuver in her mind as she stripped off her armor. Stewart had shown her a new technique for disarming an opponent, a series of tight spirals around the opponent's sword followed by a clever binding move. The first time he did it, Jordan's sword flew a good ten feet across the sparring ring. Of course the technique only worked with straight infantry swords but Jordan believed you could never have too many tricks when it came to warfare. She'd spent the afternoon practicing until she could execute the move flawlessly. She smiled, remembering the look of surprise on Stewart's face when she'd stripped him of his sword. Of course, she'd need to practice till it became an instinctual move, she was sure Stewart wouldn't mind helping her. Perhaps together they could develop a good defense to counter the new technique. Lost in thought, Jordan did not hear her sister enter the room.

"So you are here!"

The impish grin on Jemma's face warned Jordan that her sister was up to something. "Are you looking for me?"

"There's a page in the sitting room. He has something for you." With a sly smile, Jemma whispered, "I think it's something from your prince. Come see."

Jordan felt her face flush red. She hated when that happened but she didn't have any control over it. Following her sister back out into the sitting room, she found a page in the green and white of Lanverness holding a large bundle wrapped in a checkered cloth.

"Princess Jordan?"

"Yes."

The page bowed, extending the checkered bundle. "Please accept this gift from Prince Stewart." As Jordan took the bundle, the page added,

"The prince requests you join him for dinner this evening. May I take your reply back to him?"

Feeling her face flame red, Jordan said, "It would be my pleasure."

"The prince asks that you meet him at the south gate of the castle at one turn of the hourglass after sunset."

"Please tell the prince that I will be there."

The page bowed to the two princesses and then left the sitting room. Jemma flashed her a coy smile. "So what did the prince send you?"

Setting the bundle on the floor, Jordan unwrapped it. Laughing, she uncovered a plane steel shield. Jemma's puzzled expression made Jordan laugh all the harder. "It's the shield I left behind when I won the 'best sword' competition! He's returned my shield to me!"

Jemma leaned forward, fingering the cloth wrapping. "I think the true gift is in the wrapping."

Putting the shield aside, Jordan lifted the cloth. The two sisters gasped. Free of the shield, the fabric turned out to be an exquisite cloak. The material was extraordinary, red and blue checks of crushed velvet lined with dark blue lambs wool. The checked pattern mirrored the background of the banner of Navarre.

Jemma gave her a knowing smile. "A much better present than a dented old shield. Try it on."

Settling the cloak around her shoulders, Jordan was pleased to find that it was just the right length. Soft, supple, and warm, it was the kind of cloak to hug close on a cold winter day. Jordan had never owned anything so luxurious. She beamed a smile at her sister. "What do you think?"

"Come over to the mirror and see for yourself."

Striding to the mirror, Jordan gasped. The reflection showed an elegant warrior princess draped in the colors of Navarre.

Her sister smiled. "I like this prince of yours. He found a way to give you clothes that perfectly become you. That's quite a feat for any man. I think you should hold on to this one!"

Sharing a conspiring smile, Jordan admitted, "He is something, isn't he?"

Laughing Jemma said, "We'd better get you out of your practice gear and cleaned up for this evening. It won't be long until you are supposed to meet the prince."

After much debate, Jordan selected the same clothes she'd worn on the night she'd met the prince in the army tavern. The red leather jerkin looked perfect under the checkered cape. A short time later, she found herself following a page to the southern gates of the castle. Dismissing the page with thanks, she rounded the corner surprised to find the prince pacing. He wore the simple boiled leathers of a common soldier under an elegant cape of emerald green. With his broad shoulders and dark wavy hair, the man was definitely a feast for the eyes. Trying to act casual, Jordan walked toward the prince. His eyes lit up when he saw her. Jordan could feel the blood rushing to her face. Running her hand across the soft velvet of the cape, she said, "Thank you. I love it."

Smiling, the prince replied, "It suits you."

Laughing, she added, "And thank you for returning my shield."

He grinned. "It proved such a valuable weapon in the sparring ring that I didn't want you to be without it."

For a moment, they stood still, lost in each other's eyes. Suddenly shy, Jordan broke the spell by asking, "So where are we going for dinner?"

"Come, I'll show you. I have a table reserved at the Bear's Den."

Walking in step, they threaded their way through the lantern lit streets. Small crowds wandered the cobblestone lanes, the pace of the city slowed from commerce to supper and songs. They fell into a light conversation, walking close but not quite touching. Cloaked in the warmth of Stewart's company, Jordan lost track of the twists and turns. Rounding a corner into a blind alleyway, she was surprised when they stopped in front of a jumbled hodge-podge of small buildings connected without rhyme or reason. A wooden sign over the door proclaimed the name of the establishment as the 'Bear's Den'.

Stewart laughed, "Don't worry, it looks odd on the outside but the jumbled buildings are the secret to the charm of the inside. There's no place else like it in Pellanor. Come and see."

Jordan soon found the 'Bear's Den' was not like any other pub or tavern. Instead of one large common room, the place was a rabbit warren of small chambers and mismatched passageways flooded with the savory smells of soups and stews. A servant led them through a maze of wooden hallways to a small table nestled next to a window looking out onto the streets of Pellanor. The unplanned tour gave Jordan a chance to see why the 'Bear's Den' was so unique. The strange jumble of buildings created lots of nooks and crannies, giving individual tables plenty of privacy. Most of the tables were filled with young couples enjoying that rare combination of privacy in a public place. A contented, mellow feeling flowed through the hallways. Jordan liked the place immediately.

Taking seats at the table, the prince said, "I suggest we order while we have this young lady's attention. The fare here is simple but excellent. Their specialties are stews of almost any description. I'm partial to the lamb stew myself but I'm sure that they can make any type you like."

Fish stew was one of Jordan's favorites, but she decided to try the lamb. They ordered a small cauldron of lamb's stew along with a loaf of crusty bread and mugs of mulled cider. When the servant girl left with their order, Stewart said, "I didn't mean to rush you, but part of the charm of the Bear's Den is that the guests are given their privacy. Except to deliver our meal, we won't see any of the servers for a while." Pausing he added, "So what do you think of the place?"

"It's such rabbit warren that I wouldn't be surprised if people got lost in here." Emboldened by the casual intimacy, she added, "Then again, it seems the type of place where it might be fun to get lost." Pausing, she added, "Do you come here often?"

It was Stewart's turn to blush, "No, not often. It takes the right type of company for the magic of this place to work."

Jordan tucked her short sandy hair back behind her ear, trying to hide her pleasure. To cover the sudden awkwardness, she made a comment about one of the defensive moves they'd practiced. The conversation soon turned to a debate about the different philosophies of training armies.

Caught up in the conversation, Jordan was surprised when the serving girl showed up with their supper. Setting large mugs of cider on the table, the girl served generous ladles of the thick stew into ceramic bowls. The crusty bread was warm from the oven and the stew gave off a rich salty smell that made Jordan's mouth water. The stew tasted even better than it smelled. When they were well into their second serving, Jordan said, "You seemed a bit distracted at practice today."

Stewart stared at her as if trying to decide whether to answer. With a sigh he said, "Yes. I had dinner with the queen the other night. Mother wants me to attend her weekly counsel meetings, but I prefer to spend my time in the sparring yard." He stared down into his bowl, a rueful look on his face. "I thought I had a choice but the queen made it a command."

"A seat on the council will give you more of a chance to contribute."

The prince shook his head. "Wading through ledgers of numbers and juggling politics is not for me. I prefer to hold a sword in my hand."

Jordan was puzzled. "But you're the crown prince. The queen is inviting you to train for the throne. What could be wrong with that?"

Frustration broke across Stewart's face. "You don't understand. No one could ever take the place of the queen. She finds a way to grow the wealth of Lanverness every year. I'm not just talking about the wealth of the royal treasury. New businesses flourish in Lanverness and the farms of the countryside are profitable as well. With mother on the throne, the common people have a standard of living that is the envy of Erdhe." Lowering his voice, the prince added, "I don't have the head for business that mother has. I could never serve the kingdom the way she does. My talents run to the sword not multiplying golds."

"So will you give up the throne in favor of your younger brother?"

"No!" Flushed with anger, the prince said, "Not Danly. Never Danly."

His vehemence startled her. Not knowing the younger prince, she stared at Stewart with a puzzled gaze, waiting for an explanation.

The prince parried her gaze with a shake of his head. "I've already said too much. It's enough to say that Danly is not suited to the throne." Stewart turned his attention to the remains of his stew. They finished the meal in an uncomfortable silence.

Jordan studied Stewart. The issues of succession were so different in their two kingdoms. Trying to ease the tension between them, she said, "I think I understand. Because the queen is such an excellent monarch, you believe there is only one way to rule. The queen rules by the purse so you think the future king must also rule by wealth, but that is a very narrow and destructive way of thinking." Stewart stared into his mug of cider, a stubborn look on his face, but Jordan would not give up. "In Navarre we look at the crown differently. To have rulers that are all the same is to invite stagnation. Instead, the heirs of Navarre are encouraged to pursue their own interests so that a fresh outlook is always brought to the throne, allowing the kingdom to constantly grow in different directions. One ruler develops the merchant fleet, the next builds the wealth of the treasury, and the next strengthens the army and so on." Jordan paused to study the prince. He stared back at her as if absorbing every word. "Your royal mother could sit the throne for another thirty years. Imagine what the wealth of Lanverness will be like at the end of her reign." Jordan dropped her voice to a whisper. "The queen multiplies the wealth of her kingdom each year but she neglects the army. It doesn't take a crystal ball to see that your wealth will far outstrip your swords. When that happens, Lanverness will be a tempting target for foreign powers. If you accept this seat on your mother's council, then you may be able to bring some balance back to Lanverness." Leaning forward, Jordan whispered, "Don't you see? Your talents serve the kingdom in ways that the queen never could. Gold is not the only measure of a kingdom's wealth." Reaching across the table, she put her hand on his. "Believe in yourself. Don't underestimate the value of your own talents."

He sat in thoughtful silence, his gaze turned inward. Jordan could tell that he was weighing every word. Having seen the way he adapted his thinking in the sparring ring, she hoped he was capable of making the same leap without a sword in his hand. Withdrawing her hand, she gave him the time to think.

Eventually his eyes looked outward again. With a touch of wonder in his voice he said, "You look at things so differently, yet your words make sense." In a thoughtful voice he added, "Mother is always saying that the rulers of Navarre show an uncommon wisdom. Now I understand why."

Blushing, Jordan looked away.

Stewart leaned forward, his voice earnest. "So, do you seek to wear the crown of Navarre? Would you be a warrior queen?"

Jordan caught her breath. She should have expected the question, yet it caught her off guard. In a measured voice, she replied, "If the king and the council ask me to accept the crown then I will not refuse. I wish to serve Navarre to the best of my abilities...but I would prefer the crown did not pass to me."

"What? You urge me to accept the Rose Crown yet you would pass on the throne of Navarre. Why?"

"The king and council choose the heir whose talents, skills, and temperament best fit the needs of the kingdom at the time. My talents lie with the sword. If the council chooses me then it means they foresee war. I would not have war come to the kingdom of Navarre and so I hope the crown passes to one of my siblings."

Stewart whispered, "A crown would sit well on your head."

Jordan felt her face flame red.

In a lighter voice, he asked, "So which of your siblings would you see on the throne?"

Without having to think, Jordan answered, "Jemma, or Justin...or perhaps Juliana."

Shock filled Stewart's face. "A bard? Nothing against your brother, but would you truly choose a bard to wear the crown of Navarre?"

"You're showing your narrow mindedness again! Why not a bard? Navarre has never had a bard for a ruler. It would be interesting to see what Justin could do from the throne." Noting Stewart's puzzled expression, she explained, "Justin is very insightful. He has an uncanny ability to touch people from all walks of life. Remember, in Navarre we value different ways of looking at things. Personally, I would like to see how Justin would change the kingdom. I am sure Navarre would be the richer for his rule."

"I would never have looked at it that way." Pausing he added, "It is much easier to see why Jemma would make a good queen. She reminds me of my royal mother. But what is this other sister, Juliana, like?"

"Mother always says that Juliana fell in love with the sea the first moment she spied the ocean. Juliana is a sailor, training to captain her own merchant vessel. She loves the ocean and she loves to travel, but only if she can get there by sea. We're always kidding that she must have been a dolphin in a past life."

"So why would you see her on the throne?"

"Juliana has an inquisitive mind and she's also very shrewd. Always visiting distant ports of call, she brings fresh ideas from foreign places.

She sees things that we take for granted in a different light." Looking at Stewart's puzzled face, Jordan had to laugh. "I guess it all comes back to the same thing, valuing the fresh perspective and wanting to grow the kingdom in a different way."

Easing back in his chair, Stewart gave her a deep smile. "I'm not sure what to make of your sister who is part dolphin, but I like the way you think. Lanverness could learn a lot from the kingdom of Navarre." His hand covered hers. "I'm glad you're here."

Before Jordan could do more than blush, the servant girl interrupted to see if they wanted anything else. Finished with the meal, Stewart paid the bill and they followed the girl back to the entrance of the tavern. On the walk back to the castle, Stewart asked more questions about her siblings and about her life in Navarre. He seemed to be interested in everything. He was an easy man to talk to. When they reached the castle gates, Jordan expected him to bid her a goodnight but Stewart escorted her to the wing of the castle. Their steps slowed but it did not seem to take long to reach their destination. Pausing at the start of the hallway to her quarters, Jordan asked, "So will you accept the seat on the queen's council?"

"Yes, it seems you women have won again," but despite his words, his voice was light in capitulation. "I'll do my best to learn from the queen but I'll also remember to value my own talents." Leaning close, he added, "I'll take your advice and try to remember to value the different perspective."

Jordan held his gaze till a slow heat crept across her face. Looking down, she murmured, "Thank you again for the cloak...and for this evening. The Bear's Den was perfect."

"I hope you'll join me there for many more evenings... and teach me to see the world from Navarre's perspective." He moved close, staring down at her.

Jordan met his stare, her unruly hair falling across her face. He reached out with one finger and gently brushed the wayward lock back behind her left ear. His gaze intent, he leaned forward. Jordan held her breath. Stewart closed his eyes and lightly brushed his lips against hers. She kissed him back. She kissed him more than once. Later that night, she could not remember walking back to her room...but she remembered every other detail of the evening. Brushing her hair behind her ears, Jordan wished she'd chosen Pellanor for her Wayfaring instead of the Kiralynn monks.

# 38

# Steffan

Everything was proceeding according to the Dark Lord's plan. The Pontifax and the Keeper of the Flame both benefited from Steffan's advice, benefits that took the form of enhanced power, extended influence, and increased golds. Given ample proof of the Lord Raven's value, the Enlightened One appointed Steffan to the newly created position of counselor to the Pontifax. A special ceremony of investiture was held in the temple of the Flame where the Lord Raven was presented to the people of Coronth.

Under the guise of humility, Steffan declined the gaudy robes and jewels worn by the temple rulers, preferring to keep to his elegant clothes of black trimmed with crimson; clothes conducive to working in shadows. A gold signet ring inscribed with the Flame was the sole symbol of his office.

Standing in the background, Steffan watched while the Pontifax and the Keeper basked in the adoration of the masses. Always working from the shadows, Steffan whispered advice in the ear of the Pontifax, wielding influence from behind the throne. As the third most powerful man in the theocracy of Coronth, Steffan was perfectly positioned to do the work of the Dark Lord.

The Pontifax invited his new counselor to move into the Residence, the official palace of the rulers of Coronth. Pleased by the invitation, Steffan nevertheless politely declined, explaining that he did not deserve the honor. In Steffan's humble opinion, only the Pontifax and the Keeper, both the Chosen of the Flame God, were worthy to live in the palace. His refusal stroked the ego of the Pontifax while mollifying the jealous nature of the Keeper. Neither suspected his underlying motives of maintaining distance from the two figureheads while needing privacy to carry out the Dark Lord's work.

But keeping a room at the inn was no longer appropriate. Steffan noticed a mansion three city blocks away from the Residence that seemed suited to his needs. Understated in terms of size but rich in elegance, the mansion perfectly augmented Steffan's image of the Lord Raven.

Discrete inquiries revealed that the owner was a mid-level official who collected tithes for the temple. The mansion, like the family's wealth, dated back to earlier times when a king ruled Coronth before the coming of the Flame God. It was the perfect profile for fear.

Steffan chose the dinner hour to knock on the door. A liveried servant appeared. Steffan introduced himself and asked for a tour of the house. Staring slack-mouthed, the startled servant stuttered a string of apologies before disappearing into the depths of the mansion, presumably to get the head of the household.

Steffan did not have long to wait. A short, squat man dressed in a well-tailored suit of green velvet, blustered into the marble entranceway. Bowing his way across the foyer, the man displayed a jumble of conflicting emotions, his face rigid with fear while his fawning posture signaled the desire to please. "M-my Lord Raven, you honor us with this unexpected visit. What brings you to my humble home?"

"I was out for an evening stroll and was struck by the singular beauty of your home. I hoped to meet the man with such exquisite taste and to perhaps gain a tour of the house."

Perspiration gleamed on the man's broad forehead. He stared at Steffan, indecision written across his face. Steffan remained silent, forcing him to choose between fear and fawning submission. To his amusement, the desire to please won out.

The tax collector bowed low, gesturing Steffan into the house. "It is a great honor to welcome you to my home. My name is Simeon Balrax, fourth tithe collector under master Cellant. I would be honored to give you a tour of my home." He led Steffan through the mansion, bragging about the more expensive pieces of furniture as well as his wife's fine collection of porcelain vases.

Satisfied with everything he saw, Steffan made his decision. "Master Balrax, I would be pleased to accept this home as a donation to the Flame God." Towering over the small man, he added, "But I can be generous. I give you and your family one turn of an hourglass to gather your belongings and vacate the mansion."

The small man sputtered, his face turning purple.

Before the man could do anything rash, Steffan said, "The Pontifax is well aware that your family gained this mansion through their connections to the *heretic* who styled himself as the king of Coronth."

The small man gasped, clutching his chest.

"But the Pontifax can be forgiving to true believers. You and your family are being given this *one* chance to renounce your ill-gotten gains. Purged of your sins, you will become pious members of the faithful." Steffan reached for an hourglass on the mantle. "The sands of time are flowing."

The man's protest died on his lips, fear defeating outrage. He sprang to action, marshaling his family and servants to gather as much as they could in the allotted time.

Steffan helped himself to the man's excellent brandy. Leaning on the marble mantle, he watched as the family scurried about gathering belongings into sheets used as makeshift sacks. The children cried in bewilderment and the wife sent daggered glances in Steffan's direction, but the husband understood. When the sands of the hourglass were depleted, the small man handed Steffan a ring of keys as he slunk out the front door with a last load of belongings.

Locking the door, Steffan sipped his brandy as he leisurely explored his new mansion. Fine tapestries draped the walls and thick carpets covered floors of rare pink marble. Steffan laughed, even his father the baron had never owned a home this grand. Life was good in the service of the Dark Lord.

Having claimed a home, Steffan was quick to install both himself and his servant, Pip. As a part time beggar and a part time pickpocket, Pip was turning out to be an excellent servant. Quick with both his fingers and his mind, the redheaded lad made it clear to Steffan that he considered himself fortunate to be the servant of the Lord Raven. For his part, Steffan was pleased with the boy's ability to learn and his innate attention to detail. It was easy for Steffan to mold the orphan to his needs. He even considered taking the boy with him when he finished his work in Coronth; after all, good servants were hard to come by.

Steffan instructed Pip to hire a cook and a pair of maids to service the house on a regular basis without actually living in the mansion. Steffan liked his privacy and he preferred to keep the staff to a minimum. With his domestic arrangements settled, he was free to focus on the will of the Dark Lord.

Having gained the confidence of the Pontifax, Steffan's first priority was to restructure Coronth's army. Neither the Pontifax nor the Keeper were interested in managing the details of the military so Steffan took it upon himself to shoulder the burden. During his first turn of the moon as counselor, no less than five generals perished in the Test of Faith before he found the right replacement. Promoted from the rank of captain, General Caylib displayed a harsh ruthlessness, a man who believed in discipline and training. More importantly, where other candidates insisted on confirming their orders with the Pontifax, Caylib was quick to implement Steffan's orders without delay.

With the right man wearing the gold braid of general, Steffan gave the Army of the Flame its first task: the capture of the fleeing heretics. This had the added benefit of persuading more commoners to bend the knee to the Flame God, once they realized there was no escape. Put a lid on a pot and it will come to a quicker boil. With the army sealing the borders, Coronth was set to boil.

To provide the army with added incentive, Steffan ordered the captives to be fitted with iron collars and sold as slaves in the temple square. To the Dark Lord's displeasure, slavery had been all but eradicated from the kingdoms of Erdhe. Despite the taboo, the people of Coronth quickly took to the use of slaves. Everyone benefited. The merchants and tradesmen gained cheap labor, the upper class gained another sign of wealth, and the common people gained another spectacle. Slave auctions soon became another form of public entertainment, competing with the ever-popular Test of Faith. With benefits for many, slavery became a way of life in Coronth.

Proceeds from the slave auctions were split between the soldiers involved in the capture, the general, the counselor, and the Pontifax, with the lion's share going to the Enlightened One. A steady flow of golds poured into the treasury of the Pontifax, adding further proof of the value of Lord Raven's advice. As a reward, the Pontifax gave Steffan formal control of the Army of the Flame, tightening the Lord Raven's control yet another notch.

In addition to restructuring Coronth's military, Steffan also worked with the Pontifax to extend the Enlightened One's use of the ruby amulet. Given the extreme rarity of magic in the kingdoms of Erdhe, knowledge about the use of magical focuses was almost non-existent. As a result, mastering a focus was largely a matter of trial and error. At Steffan's suggestion, the Pontifax worked to extend the "divine protection" of the ruby amulet to a second person. Trials were conducted in private prayer services held in the chapel of the Residence.

Every morning, Steffan made his way to the Residence to oversee the trials. Shackled with heavy chains, convicted criminals were poked and prodded at spear-point, herded into the Sacred Flames while the Pontifax walked beside them, his hand gripping the sinner's shoulder. Most of the criminals became human torches. Screams echoed through the small chapel, shaking the resolve of the attendants. Even the Pontifax was affected. Sharing the flames with a victim was a new experience for the holy man, but the Pontifax persevered, driven by a deep hunger to master the full power of the amulet. The prisons were nearly empty by the time he succeeded.

Elated with his success, the Pontifax was keen to demonstrate his new power to the people but Steffan urged caution. Control of the people depended on the Pontifax's ability to safely walk the flames. Failure in the public arena would be catastrophic, even if that failure involved a second person.

Further trials proved that taking a second person through the flames drained the power of the amulet. The Pontifax needed to wait at least three days between attempts in order to succeed. Although limited in the frequency of use, the success of the trials gave the Pontifax a new way to extend his power. To celebrate his new abilities, the Pontifax invited Steffan and the Keeper to a lavish dinner in the Residence.

Guards snapped to salute and servants bowed low as the Lord Raven strode through the marbled hallways of the Residence. So much had changed since his coming to Coronth. Steffan need only to make the smallest gesture and servants leaped to obey. Such power was intoxicating. Steffan struggled to bury his enjoyment under a mask of humility. The Lord Raven played the part of the valued adviser; he could not afford to be seen as a rival or a threat. Composing his face, he followed a vanguard of servants to the dining room.

Dressed in shimmering robes of gold, the Pontifax greeted him with open arms, but Steffan insisted on maintaining his carefully crafted charade. Bowing to the Keeper, he knelt to kiss the hand of the Pontifax.

Once the greetings were exchanged, the three men took seats at a small round table. A flock of servants offered platters heaped with savory delicacies. For three turns of the hourglass, the men sampled rare dishes from every corner of Erdhe. The feast was an outrageous display of wealth, far exceeded anything that Steffan had yet experienced. Clearly the Pontifax was pleased with his new counselor.

Replete with fine food and wine, the men ambled from the dining room to a cozy sitting room where three comfortable armchairs waited in a crescent before a roaring fire. On a table next to each chair was a glass and a decanter filled with expensive liquor. Servants stoked the fire and filled glasses, bowing their way out of the chamber.

The three men settled into the armchairs. As a rule, they never said anything of importance in front of the servants; the mysteries of the Flame religion were a closely guarded secret. Steffan sat quietly swirling a fine brandy, waiting for the Pontifax to start the conversation.

A fire crackled in the hearth, adding a warm glow to the effects of the liquor. Lifting his glass in salute, the Pontifax turned toward Steffan. "Lord Raven, I commend you for your brilliant advice. The convict trials were distasteful, but well worth the effort." Leaning forward, he added, "I am keen to demonstrate this new power to the people, but first I would hear your thoughts on the matter."

Trying to keep a smile from his face, Steffan used a thoughtful voice to reply, "Enlightened One, your new powers are extraordinary. The people will be stunned to witness someone other than the Pontifax survive the Test of Faith. New converts will flock to the temple and the belief of the faithful will deepen. An event with so much raw emotional power must be handled delicately."

Caught up in the vision, the Pontifax sat in a near daze, staring into the fireplace. The loud snap of a burning log brought him back to the room. "Yes, I can see how this new power will excite the people. But how do I make the most of this new miracle?"

"The question of *who* is more important than the question of *how*." Steffan sipped his brandy, watching shrewd understanding dawn across the face of the Pontifax. Hiding a smile, Steffan posed the question. "Who will be the first to prove the purity of his soul by surviving the Test of Faith?" He let his gaze settle on the burly Keeper. "The obvious choice is the Keeper of the Flame. The sight of the two most powerful clerics of Coronth taking the Test of Faith will surely solidify your stranglehold on the kingdom." Steffan stole a sideways glance at the Keeper; the ruddy man had turned ghost-pale. Having watched the convict trials, he'd seen way too many human torches to take the risk.

Clearing his throat, the Keeper said, "It would certainly be a great honor, but why take the risk when the people already accept me as second only to the Pontifax? Better to choose someone else, someone we want bound to our will."

Steffan was quick to agree. "You make a good point. But if the Keeper does not walk in the flames then we cannot chose someone with religious power. The Pontifax and the Keeper can have no rivals for the love of the Flame God." Staring at the two men, Steffan fell silent, letting them stew in their own thoughts.

Steffan sipped his brandy, watching the puzzled expressions of the two charlatans.

Stymied, the Keeper eventually asked, "So do we just choose someone at random?"

"No, this is far too important to trust to random luck."

The Keeper scowled, squirming in his chair.

Steffan sipped his brandy, appearing to contemplate the flames. He let the two priests stew, giving them a subtle reminder of their limitations. When the tension in the room was ripe, Steffan broke the silence, pretending the idea had just come to him. "The solution has been right in front of us all along!" Steffan stared at the blank faces of his comrades. "Think of the relief worked into the brass doors of the temple. It is the perfect solution. The Pontifax should walk through the Flames with a child!"

The two clerics exchanged conspiring grins.

Noting their agreement, Steffan elaborated, "There will be no rivalry from a child and the public will be taken with the idea. As an added benefit, the Pontifax will be grooming future generations to worship the Flame. We need only choose a child whose parents are dedicated to the temple. Surely the Keeper can choose a faithful family worthy of the honor."

The Pontifax nodded. "I like the idea. I like it very much. But does it matter *how* it is done? Surely there should there be a special ceremony to mark the event?"

Steffan nodded. "The people must understand that this is a blessing from the Pontifax. We will need to devise a special ceremony where the Pontifax blesses the child, perhaps something with incense to make the ceremony more dramatic. Once blessed, the child and the Enlightened One can walk safely through the Sacred Flames."

The Keeper leaned forward, his face eager. "Before the miracle with the child, we should send a sinner into the fires just to prove there is no trick." Grinning, the Keeper added, "Death and Life all in one spectacle! The new miracle will be on everyone's lips!"

Steffan nodded. "After holding a few ceremonies with children, we can start to select adults who we wish to bind closer to the temple." Addressing the Pontifax, Steffan said, "On your progresses through the countryside, you should select local priests or officials to walk with you through the Sacred Flames. Those who survive will be elevated in the eyes of the people. If handled correctly, the ceremony will bind a cadre of provincial leaders to the Pontifax. With one new miracle, you will gain an unshakable grip on all of Coronth."

The room fell silent, pregnant with possibilities. With a wolfish grin, the Pontifax said, "I like it! The plan is excellent." He turned toward the Keeper. "Select an appropriate sinner and a child from a faithful family. I want to hold the ceremony this week."

Steffan added, "May I suggest, we leak word to the people? Rumors about something special, something that should not be missed."

The Keeper nodded. "I can use the acolytes to spread the word. The temple square will be overflowing with the faithful."

Steffan smiled. "All the better. The ecstasy of the experience will be multiplied in a densely packed crowd."

The Pontifax rose, putting his back to the hearth. "Our plans are set." Raising his glass, he said, "I propose a toast, to miracles and the spread of religion!"

Drunk on power, the clerics drained their glasses, hurling them into the hearth. As the other men saluted their own cleverness, Steffan secretly praised the Dark Lord. Everything was going according to plan.

# 39

# Samson

Samson worried about his mother. Pelting rain and chilly nights only made her fever worse. It didn't help that they'd both had the runs for two days. Their last meal had been a pumpkin stolen from a farmer's field. Samson sliced it open with his sword and they both gnawed on the pulp, eager to fill their stomachs despite the bitter taste. Now he knew why no one ever ate pumpkins without cooking them first. Strange, the things you learned when you were a fugitive.

His mind was wandering again. He had to do something to help his mother or she'd never make it to Lanverness. Yesterday, they'd buried themselves in the autumn leaves, both for warmth and to try and hide during the daylight hours. Without warning, soldiers wearing the red and gold tabard of the Flame descended on the woods, brandishing swords and poking spears into bushes. They flushed a dozen heretics from the forest, marching their catch off in chains. Huddled in the leaves, Samson and his mother escaped notice. Surely the gods meant for them to survive. His mother couldn't die on him now.

They trudged south, always south, always walking at night, his mother leaning on Samson's arm. Forests gave way to tilled fields. A barn glowed silver in the pale moonlight, tempting after so many days under the cold rain. Samson decided to risk it.

Shouldering the door open, he gasped at the sudden warmth of cows and the sweet smell of hay. Except for five milk cows, the barn proved empty. Samson settled his mother on a stack of hay and covered her with their only remaining blanket, adding a second layer of hay for warmth.

Racked with hunger, he searched the barn, discovering a half eaten apple discarded near the door. He pounced on the treasure. Rejoining his mother, he settled into the straw, savoring each crisp bite. With milk cows for company, the barn was warm and the hay made an inviting bed, funny how his idea of luxury had changed. Burrowing into the hay, Samson decided to rest his eyes for just a few moments.

Feeling sunlight warm his face, he struggled to wake. A large man stood over him holding a pitchfork. Samson lay still, too stunned to react. He'd let his guard down for just one night and now they were caught. The gods were cruel.

"So you really are alive! I thought the children were playing one of their jokes, putting the old scarecrow in the barn to give me a fright. Startled me when you moved." Lowering the pitchfork, the big man pulled Samson to his feet. "Son, you must have had a tough time of it. You're all skin and bones. Are things really that bad that you have to sleep in a barn?"

Almost afraid to ask, Samson stammered, "Is t-this L-lanverness?"

Scratching his head, the farmer said, "Well of course it is! Where else but the good queen's country, may all the gods of Light bless her name!"

Samson nearly swooned in relief. Just then, the hay on the surface shifted, revealing his mother. Samson stooped to help her rise, brushing straw from her long white hair.

The farmer was visibly shocked. "A grandmother should not be sleeping in a barn."

Clutching his mother's arm, Samson stood tongue-tied, staring at the farmer.

"Come up to the house. The missus will give you a meal and we'll hear your story. From the way those clothes are hanging on you, you could both use a good feed. Maybe we can even find something better for you to wear. Looks like you've been traveling hard."

In stunned silence, they followed the farmer out of the barn and across a field to a well-kept farmhouse. The sweet smell of apples filled the morning air. The stone farmhouse was built beside an orchard. Samson smiled. His whim to buy an apple had saved their lives at the start of their journey. Now they found apples in Lanverness. Apples would forever mean life and freedom to Samson.

The burly farmer ushered them into a cozy kitchen. The smell of fresh baked bread almost made Samson swoon. A rosy-cheeked woman wearing an apron shrieked as they entered, but she quieted when saw her husband.

"Mother, I found these two sleeping in the barn. Not right that a grandmother should sleep in a barn. I brought them in for some breakfast. Why don't you serve them some of the leftovers and I'll see if we don't have some spare clothes to help them out."

Once the woman got over her fright, she took control, as wives and mothers often do. Clucking like a mother hen, she showed them to a barrel full of spring water and gave them a towel and a lump of soap and then bustled back into the kitchen. It had been so long since Samson had held a cake of soap in his hand that he stared at it, caught in a daze. A whiff of fresh baked bread was enough to prod him to action. He helped his mother wash and then tried his best to clean himself up as well. The water in the rain barrel turned black before they were done.

Returning to the kitchen, they found the table laden with thick cuts of freshly baked bread smeared with marmalade, sliced apples, and a rasher of bacon. Samson thought it a meal fit for a king. He fought the desire to pounce, taking slow bites, trying to eat like a man instead of a ravenous animal, but it was hard.

The farmer returned holding a wool dress and a clean tunic. "I think these might fit you and the woman. You're welcome to them if you like."

Tears crowded Samson's eyes. After Coronth, it was hard to believe such goodwill still existed in the world. Starved for kindness even more than for food, Samson struggled to hold the tears back, but once the dam broke, he wept uncontrollably. The farmer and his wife made him feel like a man instead of a hunted animal. They gave him the gift of humanity. He wondered if they would even understand the depth of his debt. Regaining his composure, Samson bowed his head, and said, "Thank you."

Embarrassed, the farmer and his wife joined them at the table. In silent company, they passed Samson and his mother bowls of fruit and bread until every scrap was eaten.

Replete with food, Samson began to talk. Words spilled out of him, tales of horror about the Test of Faith and their desperate flight from Balor. He told them about the soldiers in the woods and their long walk south. About being shunned by the villagers, and driven off with sticks and stones. Once he started he could not stop. The story tumbled from his lips like pus from a festering wound. He told them everything, including the fact that he'd once been a sergeant in the city guard. It was hard to meet their eyes when he admitted his position in the guards but Samson felt it needed to be said. Samson talked until he was hoarse. The sun set, plunging the kitchen into darkness but nobody thought to light a candle. Engrossed in the tale, they sat in the dark, listening to horrors of the Flame God. Finally empty of bitter memories, Samson's voice fell silent.

The farmer and his wife sat stunned. They'd heard rumors of refugees drifting south but they never understood the reasons behind the exodus. They questioned Samson into the late hours of the night. The farmer kept asking if the madness of Coronth might spill into Lanverness. After much discussion, he begged Samson to make his way to Pellanor to tell his tale to the queen.

"I'm nothing but a homeless refugee. Why would a queen listen to me?"

A smile of pride crept across the farmer's weathered face. "That's the difference a queen makes. Queen Liandra holds a commoners' audience once a fortnight. It's said she'll hear petitions from anyone in the kingdom...even a refugee." The farmer's voice grew serious. "The queen needs to hear about this madness in Coronth. Warned of the danger, she'll find a way to protect her people."

Samson protested, but the man was stubborn. He eventually gave in, seeing the trip as his only way of repaying the farmer. They stayed for a fortnight, taking real baths and becoming human again. Samson shaved his scraggly beard and the farmer's wife cut his long tangled hair. Dressed in the farmer's spare tunic, he finally looked like a man instead of a scarecrow. Clean and presentable, they began their journey to Pellanor.

The farmer took them as far as the nearest town. At the market, the farmer talked to his friends till he found them a ride to the next town. They were handed from one farmer to another until a carrot farmer drove them to the very gates of Tandroth Castle. Not a single farmer asked for payment of any kind. Samson hoped the queen was worthy of her people.

Heeding the advice of the farmers, Samson told the guard at the palace gate that he wanted to make a commoner's petition. For once, luck was with him. Having arrived on the very day of commoner's audience, Samson was shown to a small walled garden where a court official took his name. Settling his mother on a bench, he paced the manicured garden. He'd never spoken to royalty before. The prospect was daunting. Surrounded by beauty, Samson wondered how he could explain the horrors of Coronth to a queen who was used to such splendor. He stared back at his mother, a broken old woman sitting hunched on a marble bench, the battered rucksack he'd carried from Balor at her feet. The rucksack sparked a memory. He strode across the garden and knelt, searching for the roll of cloth buried at the bottom, the cloth he'd rescued from the quartermaster's stores. During the long walk south he'd bartered away many things, but never the blue tunic. Wrinkled and moth-eaten, yet the gold blazon was still bright and proud. On impulse, he pulled the tunic over his head. Wearing it felt right, a declaration of freedom from the Flame God.

As if to confirm his choice, the herald called his name. Leaving the rucksack with his mother, Samson answered the summons.

The castle proved a maze of marble passageways, each more opulent than the next. Samson wondered what he'd gotten himself into. The herald led him to a magnificent audience chamber. Samson gawked in awe, never having seen the like. A vast checkerboard floor of black and white marble stretched toward a distant throne. Ceilings soared to elegant corbelled vaults of glistening white stone. Towering walls of diamond-paned windows flooded the chamber with light, sending fractured rainbows dancing across the hall. The chamber spoke of wealth, elegance, and power. Samson stood in the shadows, wishing he could change his mind.

The herald pounded his iron-shod staff on the floor. "Presenting Samson Springwater of Coronth."

A sea of nobles clothed in velvets and silks parted to create a path across the checkerboard floor. On the far side of the chamber, a petite woman sat ensconced on a raised throne, a vision of golden glory.

Frozen like a deer before the hunter, Samson gaped at the splendor. A sharp elbow prodded him in the side and the herald hissed, "Walk to the foot of the throne and bow."

Caught by a flood of stares, Samson realized it was too late to retreat. One step and then another, he forced himself to take the long walk. Gasps rippled through the crowd as he passed. Ashamed of his scarecrow appearance, Samson lowered his head and kept walking.

An eternity later, he reached the dais. Trembling, he bowed low, waiting for the queen to speak. Darting a glance at the throne, he caught a glimpse of stunning beauty. The queen's hourglass figure and low-cut gown took his breath away. Entranced by the vision, Samson dared a fleeting glance at the queen's face...and found himself trapped by her piercing gaze. He gaped at her, a butterfly struck by a spear. Fiercely intelligent, the queen's stare bore into the depths of his soul. Samson took a half step backwards. He'd never seen eyes that keen, especially in the face of a woman. But then he'd never met a queen before, so perhaps scary eyes came with a crown. Tearing his gaze away, Samson dropped his stare to the safety of the checkerboard floor, wishing he was anywhere but the queen's court.

"We are pleased to see that the lion of Coronth is not extinct."

Samson startled at the sound of her voice.

"Who are you to wear that tabard and why do we find you in our court?"

Samson found himself sweating under the queen's scrutiny. Looking down, he realized she spoke of the gold lion emblazoned on his blue tabard. "Y-your majesty, t-to my shame I once wore the red and gold tabard of the Flame. B-but that was a lifetime ago, before my father was burnt to death in the Test of Faith." Once started, the words gushed out. "As the son of a proven heretic, I feared I'd share my father's fate. M-my mother and I fled Balor. We walked forever but eventually escaped to Lanverness. The good farmers of your land took us in. We owe them our lives and our sanity. On hearing our story they urged me to come to Pellanor to tell you my tale. They fear the horror of Flame God may spread to Lanverness but they trust in their queen to protect them."

Murmurs rippled through the chamber.

The queen studied Samson with hooded eyes. "The farmers of Lanverness have done well. But tell us, where is your mother?"

Once again, her question took him caught him off guard. "She waits for me in the garden. Something broke inside her on the day my father died. She lives in a dream world now. I take care of her as best I can."

"It is admirable for a son to care for his mother." Turning to an elderly man at the foot of the dais, the queen said, "Lord Carrington, you will see that his mother is given succor in our court. And have the Master Archivist assemble my advisors. We will meet with them in our council chambers in two turns of an hourglass." Turning back to Samson, the queen's voice held a note of compassion. "Young man, we would hear more of your story but the Audience Hall is not the place for it. In the meantime, Lord Carrington will see to your needs."

The queen gestured and a herald proclaimed, "The commoners' audience is ended. The Lords of Light save her majesty the queen."

The queen rose from her throne and the court instantly sank to a deep bow. Not knowing what to do, Samson did his best to mimic those around him. The queen swept past him, leaving a scent of roses in the air. A glittering retinue of lords, knights, and heralds followed the queen from the chamber. Stunned, Samson was left standing in their wake, floundering like shipwrecked flotsam cast on a strange beach.

A gray haired gentleman rescued Samson. "My name is Lord Carrington. Shall we find your mother and get her settled?" His glance roved up and down Samson's lean frame. "I suggest we have a meal, this afternoon's meeting could be rather lengthy."

Befuddled, Samson followed the lord to the castle's kitchen, watching as a heaping trencher of roast pork and potatoes was set before him. The sudden kindness combined with the abundant opulence of the court threatened to unman him. Samson felt as he'd been pushed into a fast flowing river and all he could do was try to keep his head above water. Since his father's murder, he'd been pushed and pulled by fate's mysterious currents, doing his best to keep from drowning. And now he was caught by a queen's command. Samson wondered if his life would ever be his own again.

# 40

# Katherine

Kath had drawn first blood and lived to tell about it. An irrepressible smile spread across her face. She'd survived her first battle, a blooded warrior! She lifted her sword to the heavens in salute, marveling at the play of light on steel. Sunlight warmed her face and insects hummed in the long grass. Life seemed marvelous and infinitely fascinating. Flushed with elation, a small corner of her mind wondered if this was the euphoria that the veterans of Castlegard often talked about, the blessing that Valin sent to victorious warriors to ease the horrors of war. Now she knew what the veterans meant when they said victory was sweet.

"Are you putting down roots?" Kath startled at he archer's gruff rebuke. "There's work to be done. Predators will be drawn to all this carrion. We need to get moving. I'll dress the deer while you round up the horses."

Yanked back to reality, Kath stared into the archer's strange yellow eyes. Golden orbs with black slits for pupils, his eyes were anything but human yet he'd saved her life. She owed him a debt. She also owed it to herself to stay sharp. She couldn't afford to drop her guard. "You're right, I'll get the horses."

With a nod of approval, the archer moved toward the dead deer while Kath took stock of the horses. The ogre's huge draft horse was dead, skewered by an arrow. The captain's stallion and the gelding milled nervously at the far end of the meadow while the pony nosed the goblin-man's corpse. Odd that the pony stayed by the goblin-man, but then she remembered how the dwarf used lumps of sugar to bribe his mount into submission. Sugar would make her task so much easier.

The pony was so preoccupied with the dwarf's pockets, that it was easy for Kath to catch his reins. As a reward, she liberated a lump of sugar and fed it to the greedy beast. Removing a stake from the saddlebags, she picketed the small horse near the edge of the forest and then returned to the goblin-man for the rest of the sugar.

Holding the sweets on her open palm, Kath approached the stallion. Skittish and proud, the stallion snorted and stamped but the sugar proved too tempting. Kath deftly gathered his reins while the stallion nibbled the treat. With the stallion settled, it was a simple matter to collect the gelding. Satisfied the horses were secure she went to check on the archer.

"We can leave whenever you're ready."

"Good. It won't take me long to finish the deer. I'll load the venison on the pony and we can be off. If there's anything you want from the dead, you best get it now."

The insult shocked her to the core. Her anger flared. "I am a warrior not a carrion scavenger! I don't rob the dead."

The archer rocked back on his heels, studying her with narrowed eyes. "You obviously know how to handle a sword but I'm guessing this was your first battle. I meant no offense." When Kath didn't reply, he continued in a kinder voice, "Think about it. You're alone in the wilds of Wyeth. An escort of knights is supposedly following, but only the gods know if you will ever find them. A few golds could be helpful. Besides, you can learn a lot from a man's belongings. Sometimes answers are worth more than golds."

Kath weighed the archer's words. The veterans of Castlegard cursed the human scavengers that followed armies into battle. Scavenging the dead was repugnant to Kath, but the archer's words made sense, especially his comments about answers. The knight marshal always said that 'the first rule of battle was to know your enemy.' She'd traveled for days with her captors and still did not know the name of their master. "Your words are wise. I do need answers and the belongings of the dead are the only clues left. Thank you for your advice."

Kath wasn't sure, but she thought that she saw a glint of approval in his golden eyes. Then again, the cat-slit eyes were hard to read. With a grunt, the archer resumed his work on the deer.

Kath returned to the dead. Thinking about it, she decided it wasn't much different from taking sugar from the goblin-man's pocket. She'd search for answers and gold, nothing more, deciding to split the gold with the archer. The decision made her feel better about the ghoulish task.

Perhaps because he seemed the least human, she decided to start with the goblin-man. Turning his pockets inside out, she found nothing but scraps of bread, partially eaten apples, and lumps of sugar. The dwarf hoarded food, or perhaps the scraps were meant for the horses. Either way, there was nothing to be learned from his pockets.

The ogre was similarly disappointing. His pockets held a strange collection of mismatched buttons and feathers, suggesting a childlike fascination for bright and shiny things. Such a small mind seemed incongruous with the ogre's body. Embarrassed, Kath put everything back and then went to search the fallen archer.

The archer carried a healthy purse of golds but there were no clues to the faceless master. That left the captain. Revulsion washed across her. She did not want to touch the captain, let alone search his pockets, but she needed answers. She nudged his corpse with her boot. A cloud of flies buzzed in anger, disturbed from their feast. With grim determination, she started with his pockets and then moved to the leather pouches strung on his belt. One pouch contained the hated collar and leash. In a flash of rage, she hurled the foul device deep into the woods. Quaking with anger, she deliberately stared at the bloody gash across the captain's throat, remembering the clean cut of Castlegard steel. It was good to know there was some justice in the world, even if it was late in coming.

Staring at the captain's throat, Kath caught a glint of silver she'd never noticed. The glint came from a silver chain around his neck. Tugging on the chain, a crude medallion emerged from beneath his tunic. Kath gasped, dropping the chain as if it burnt her fingers. The emblem on the medallion was all too familiar, a pentacle, the symbol of the Mordant. She shivered, shocked to discover that the Mordant's men had breached the defenses of the Octagon Knights. With a shudder, she realized how lucky she was to have escaped the Mordant's henchmen. Searching for more clues, Kath found a map in the captain's breast pocket, but the cloth was so blood drenched from the heart wound the map was illegible. Discarding the map, she kept the medallion, the only answer she needed.

The only other thing of value in the captain's pockets was a very large purse of golds. The Mordant paid his servants well.

A loud squawk came from the sky. A dark-eyed crow landed near the captain's head, the first of the carrion feeders. Beady eyes stared up at her.

"He's all yours." Abandoning the captain to the crow, she quickly checked the rest of the dead but the captain wore the only medallion.

More crows began to gather to death's feast.

Kath moved to an unsoiled part of the meadow. Sitting in the sweet-smelling grass, she counted the golds into two piles. The odd gold piece went into the purse for the archer. With the golds sorted, she was about to return to the archer when she realized she needed a scabbard for her sword. Kath returned to the captain. A flurry of dark wings squawked their annoyance. Waving the birds away, she unbuckled his worn leather scabbard and tugged it free from the body. The holes in the leather proved too large for her waist, so she slung the scabbard over her shoulder like a baldric. With the sword settled at her side, Kath was more than ready to leave the meadow.

The archer loaded the venison across the back of the goblin-man's pony. Golden cat-eyes flashed her way. "Any luck?"

"Evil pays well." She tossed a heavy purse to the archer. "But more importantly, I found the answer I was looking for. It seems I am even farther in your debt."

"So who's behind all of this?"

"The captain carried a token of the Mordant."

The cat-eyed man hissed in anger. "The Mordant stretches his hand too close to the Deep Green. My people must be warned."

Puzzled, Kath asked, "What is the Deep Green?"

The howl of a wolf shivered through the forest.

"Mount up and I'll tell you as we ride." He swung into the saddle of the gelding. "Where are we going? Toward Castlegard?"

Kath vaulted onto the stallion, swallowing a pain of loss for her valiant mare. "No. We head due west until we reach the lip of a deep gorge. I plan to camp at the edge. If the knights are still on the trail then I hope to find them there."

The archer shrugged. "As good a plan as any, but I can only travel for a few days. I need to return to my family. Lead the way, princess of Castlegard."

Kath urged the stallion to a trot. With the pony following on a lead, the two riders headed toward the setting sun. Fading light cloaked the forest in shifting shadows. The weary horses picked a path through the trees. As they rode, the cat-eyed archer peppered Kath with questions about the ogre and the goblin-man. She did her best to answer. "They are malformed by magic. The captain named the ogre a 'Taal'. He said the Taals are born in a place where the land is fouled with magic from the War of Wizards. The residual magic twists the newborn into giants like the Taals or stunted dwarves like the goblin-man. The twisted survivors are raised to be servants of the Dark Lord."

The archer grew strangely quite.

Thinking to reassure him, Kath added, "The Mordant's lands are far to the north. The Octagon Knights will stand firm, a bulwark to the Dark."

The archer nodded, maintaining a puzzling silence.

Kath felt as if she'd said something wrong. Hoping to bridge the silence, she asked, "So what is the Deep Green?"

A broad smile transformed his face. "The Deep Green is my home, the home of my people. It is a forest like no other. The trees grow to amazing heights." He waved toward the surrounding old growth forest. "These grandfathers look like youngsters compared to the trees of my home. The

Deep Green is so dense and wild that most white-eyes fear to enter. Like a mother to my people, the great forest protects and nurtures the clans while repelling strangers. Few of us ever venture beyond the forest." With a bitter edge to his voice, he added, "Beyond the forest, our fate is uncertain. All too often, the white-eyes hunt my people as if we were nothing more than animals. They cannot see beyond our golden eyes. Fearing anything that is different, they seek to destroy what they cannot understand." Falling into a sullen silence, the archer glared at Kath, a challenge in his stare.

She met his strange golden stare with an unflinching gaze. "I'm sorry for the plight of your people." After a while, she added, "I can only offer you my friendship and my gratitude."

He stared at her as if gauging the sincerity of her statement. She must have passed his scrutiny because he gave her a slow nod. "Some of our elders want to close the forest to outsiders. They would seal the Deep Green and leave the white-eyes to their own fate. Others, especially the young, are restless, risking much to venture into the kingdoms of Erdhe." Bitterness laced his voice, "Does it take a princess to see past the difference of our eyes?"

His bitterness struck a chord with her. "Only a princess who is forever being told she cannot be a warrior. Perhaps I understand better than you think."

His face flushed with disbelief. "They would try to keep *you* from taking up the sword? Are they blind not to see that the gods have marked you as a warrior?" Shaking his head, he added, "You white-eyes are so backwards. In the Deep Green a woman is equal to a man, free to take up any skill she fancies."

His words shocked her. "Even the sword?"

"Of course! Many of our women become rangers, although our people prefer the bow."

Kath muttered under her breath, "Why would the Children of the Green accept women as warriors yet Castlegard will not?"

She was surprised when the archer replied. "It is a simple matter of survival. Our numbers have never been great. We cannot afford to waste the talents of half our people." Pausing, he gave Kath an appraising stare. "You should have been born with golden eyes; you would have done well among us."

Kath ducked her head, embarrassed by the compliment. "Castlegard is my home but it sounds like there is much to admire about the people of the Deep Green." Filled with curiosity, she added, "My path takes me elsewhere, but I would like to visit the Deep Green some day."

"It would be good for the elders to meet a white-eye like you." He gave her a thoughtful stare. "Travel due east from here. You will eventually come to trees that will forever change your idea of a forest. Sheath your weapons and enter in peace, a ranger will find you." With a touch of pride, he added, "A white-eye would be hopelessly lost in the Deep Green without the aid of a ranger."

"I'll remember."

He winked. "See that you do."

Night settled around them, the song of the cicadas filling the forest. In the pale moonlight, Kath studied the archer. His golden eyes were the only alien feature in an otherwise human face. An old wives' tale said that the eyes are the windows of the soul. Perhaps if the difference were anything else, then Children of the Green would be better accepted. It seemed an affront to the gods that appearances mattered more than deeds. She'd only known the archer for a short time, yet he seemed noble as well as wise. She suspected the kingdoms of Erdhe were the poorer for persecuting his people. Putting a hand on the hilt of her sword, Kath silently vowed that she would offer friendship and aid to any of the Children who crossed her path. An owl hooted in the depths of the forest, accepting her vow.

The night sounds grew louder as they rode west. A pack of wolves sang to the rising moon. Instead of feeling threatened, Kath somehow felt at home. Stretching in the saddle, she tried to stay awake. The horses' hooves splashed through a shallow stream, the same stream that had led her to the broken tower. She felt a subtle tug to follow the watercourse upstream, a longing to reclaim the crystal dagger, but she suppressed the urge. She trusted the archer, but she did not know him well enough to lead him to the ruined keep.

Beyond the stream, they found the lip of the gorge. A short ride along the edge brought them to a suitable campsite. Kath unsaddled the horses and rubbed them down with handfuls of sweet grasses while the archer collected firewood and used a flint to strike a blaze. Spearing two venison steaks with a long stick, he sprinkled the steaks with spices and set them over the roaring fire. The archer's eyes glowed like lanterns in the firelight, almost like magic. Kath touched her gargoyle, knowing it was magic of a different sort.

Setting out two blanket rolls, she settled down to wait for dinner. Suddenly weary, she slumped onto the bedroll, closing her eyes for just a moment. Exhaustion struck like a hammer-blow. Without ever tasting the venison steaks, she slipped into a dreamless sleep, her hand on her sword hilt.

# 41

# Danly

D anly woke to find the scroll on his bedside table. He swore it had
not been there the night before. Suspicious, he examined the seal.
The scarlet wax portrayed a pair of entwined lovers, the seal of an
exclusive bordello hidden away in a rich section of the capital. Breaking
the seal, he found an invitation to one of the bordello's famous theme
parties. The theme for this party was the Wheel of Eros. Patrons were
asked to dress in black and to wear a black mask. It was the type of event
Danly relished, but the mark at the bottom really made his eyes widened.
Boldly drawn on the bottom was a red horn. This party would be more
interesting than most.

Throwing back the silken covers, he crossed the room and consigned
the invitation to the fireplace. He watched the parchment blacken and
burn, wondering how the Red Horns had managed to place the scroll on
his bedside table. The rebels were clearly resourceful as well as secretive,
but Danly did not like having secrecy turned in his direction. He spent the
day trying to ferret out the messenger, questioning servants and guards
but he found no clues to the culprit. Evening came and he was no closer to
solving the riddle, perhaps he'd learn more at the party.

Danly took his time dressing, choosing a wardrobe of solid black.
Deciding his appearance was too somber, he added a silk vest of emerald
green, the royal crest embroidered on the right breast. Pleased with his
reflection, Danly swirled a black velvet cape around his shoulders and
pocketed a simple black mask and a generous purse of golds.

His two guards, Hobs and Harland, stood waiting in his solar.
Physically intimidating with broad shoulders and barrel chests, the two
men were good with their swords, but even better, they knew how to
clean-up unpleasant situations. Discretion was so important when serving
a prince. With his guards trailing behind, he strode through the castle to
the eastern gates.

A black stallion and mounts for his guards were waiting as ordered. A short canter brought them to the bordello. Boys in scarlet livery rushed to hold the horses while the men dismounted.

Settling the black mask on his face, the prince entered the house. The house guards bowed as he made his way to the main sitting room. Danly stopped on the threshold, amazed by the transformation. Swaths of gold and silver fabrics draped the walls, transforming the room into an exotic tent. Braziers lined the walls providing a soft golden light while giving off the scent of cinnamon and other rare spices. Colorful cushions littered the floor, offering a comfortable place for the patrons to take their ease. The chamber resembled the inner sanctum of a harem, a gentleman's fantasy.

Nine men in black were already sampling the pleasures of the house. Young girls served glasses of fine liquors and offered exotic delicacies on silver platters. The servants were pretty things, but the crowning adornment was the costumed courtesans, the women who would be offered on the Wheel. Danly recognized many of the madam's best...along with a few fresh faces. Each courtesan expressed a different face of Eros, representing all the compass points from pleasure to pain.

Accepting a glass of brandy, Danly took his time working his way around the room. He pretended to inspect the courtesans, but it was the masked men who drew his gaze. Most were familiar, but the one face he expected was not present. Danly supposed he'd just have to play along until the Red Horn chose to reveal himself.

Cymbals crashed and the conversation came to a sudden stop. The madam of the house, a retired courtesan with shrewd eyes and a figure that had succumbed to too many delicacies, approached the prince. She dropped to a deep curtsey, showing off her ample bosom. "Lord prince, we ask you to do the honor of starting the Wheel. Choose your pleasure by selecting the First Face of Eros."

Danly's gaze was drawn to a petite blond dressed in demure robes of white. He smiled, wondering how well an accomplished courtesan could play the role of Virginal Love. He indicated his choice and the madam clapped her hands, gaining the attention of the room. "The First Face of Eros has been chosen. Tonight we start at the beginning of the Wheel, we start with Virginal Love."

A cascade of male "Hurrahs!" rippled through the chamber.

The courtesan was formally presented to the prince. The young woman bowed demurely and even managed to show a trace of blush; the girl was either an accomplished actress or else reality fit the role. Intrigued, the prince gallantly offered his arm. The couple followed the madam out of the room, the prince's two guards trailing a discrete distance behind.

Madam Stock led them up the grand staircase and back toward a suite of rooms at the rear of the house. As usual, he always got the madam's best. Stopping at the door, the madam whispered instructions to the girl and then leaned to the prince. "May you take great pleasure in the First Face of Eros. Return to the sitting room if you wish a second selection from the Wheel." With a flourish, the madam opened the door.

The young courtesan trailed her hand across the prince's chest and then flitted into the dimly lit room. Pleased with her performance, the prince followed. The girl fled the outer suite for the inner bedroom, closing the door behind her. Rising to the spirit of the game, Danly crossed the sitting room.

A firm hand gripped his shoulder.

Startled, Danly spun, his hand gripping his dagger.

"No need for that, my prince." A burly man wearing a red cape, his face hidden by a peeked hood with slits for eyes stepped from the shadows. "For the sake of the horse with the red horn, please do as I say."

Danly's eyes widened, so this was how it started. He nodded, trying to still his racing heart.

"The Red Horns wish to meet with their future king, but first tell your guards that you are not to be disturbed."

Danly complied. Returning to the sitting room, he was surprised to see a wall panel swung open to reveal a hidden staircase. He never knew the bordello had such passageways. He wondered what other surprises lay in store for the night.

The robed man offered Danly a black cape of course wool. "Please remove your vest and your cape. You'll be less conspicuous in this."

When Danly hesitated, the man said, "These arrangements are necessary for the security of us all."

Shedding his garments, the prince drew on the cape, cringing at the coarse wool. He pulled the hood up, hiding his face in shadow. The red-cloaked man picked up a candle and motioned the prince toward the staircase. "Take your time, the steps are steep."

Stone steps spiraled down into darkness, just wide enough for one man. Danly made his way down the stairs, reaching the small landing at the bottom. The masked stranger crowded close, unlocking an ironbound door. "A carriage waits just outside. When I open the door, move quickly. We dare not be seen."

Snuffing the candle, the man waited a few heartbeats and then opened the ironbound door. Danly rushed up the stairs, assaulted by the reek of a back alleyway. As he stepped into the waiting carriage, a whip cracked and the carriage lurched forward. Thrown onto a seat, the prince eyed his mysterious guide. "Is all of this really necessary?"

"We plot against the Spider Queen, pray that 'all of this' as you put it, is enough." Removing a red sash from his pocket, the man added, "I must ask you to wear this blindfold."

The man's insolence knew no bounds. "You show little trust in your future king."

"We risk our lives for the sake of your crown."

The argument quenched his anger. With a curt nod, he allowed the man to bind his eyes. Danly sat in total darkness, the sudden turns of the carriage becoming a rocking blur of motion. The carriage lurched to an abrupt halt and the man put a hand on his shoulder. "Allow me to guide you. We'll step out into the street and then descend a set of stone steps. When we reach the bottom, I'll remove your blindfold."

The door opened admitting a breeze of cool night air. The man guided Danly out of the carriage and down a steep set of steps. Wooden doors clattered overhead and then the blindfold fell away. Danly blinked in the torchlight. Alone with his guide, he stood in a stone passageway lit by torches. Cold as a cellar, the passageway sloped gently down, the cloying scent of dung hanging heavy in the air. "Where are we?"

"Somewhere safe." His red-cloaked guide gestured toward the depths of the passageway. "This way, my prince."

Danly followed, regretting the absence of his guards. He fingered the gilded dagger in his belt, but it gave him no reassurance, he was a lover not a fighter. His footsteps echoed against cold stone walls, a gradual descent into the earth. With each step the reek of dung and blood intensified, the remnants of a recent slaughter...or a sacrifice. Danly hesitated.

"Almost there, my prince."

Danly's neck prickled with warning but it was too late to stop. He reached the bottom and found the passageway opened onto the stage of an underground amphitheater.

"This way, my prince."

A hand at his back urged him forward. A ten-foot wall surrounded the central pit with tiered seats rising into shadows. Blood-soaked straw littered the stone floor, crunching beneath his boots. He'd heard rumors of such places, secret arenas used for illegal cock and bullfights. The wealthy of Pellanor always found a way to take their pleasures, regardless of the law.

A brooding silence cloaked the amphitheater...but the tiered seats were not empty. Figures cloaked in red capes and hooded masks crowded the gallery. In the dim light, it was difficult to tell how many watched from above; spectators come for a different sort of sport. Danly hesitated, feeling the weight of so many cold stares.

His guide gestured toward a throne carved of dark wood waiting in the center of the bloodstained ring. A sudden panic seized Danly, cold sweat beading his brow. Pungent smells of blood and death made him wonder if he was being led to a throne or an altar of sacrifice. Danly mastered the grim thoughts, reminding himself of how much he wanted the crown. Holding his head high, he strode like a king to the center of the arena. Refusing to sit on a throne in the coarse wool cape of a peasant, he untied the garment and let it fall to the ground. Claiming the throne, he assumed a regal pose, staring defiantly up at the gallery of watchers.

The silence built to an oppressive weight.

A clicking sound emerged from the side passageway. A tall hooded man in red strode into the arena. Bearing a gilded staff carved to resemble the long horn of a unicorn, he walked across the combat ring to stand beside the throne. Even cloaked and masked, the man had a presence about him. Pounding the iron-shod staff on the stone floor, his voice filled the arena. "We welcome our prince to the company of the Red Horns."

Recognizing the deep voice, Danly relaxed.

"Our prince has come to see for himself that the Red Horns are much more than shadows and innuendo." He gestured toward the stands. "Every man here holds considerable wealth and power. And every man has sworn an oath to restore a rightful king to the Rose Throne. In the presence of the Red Horns, I ask you, Danly of house Tandroth, will you be that king?"

Staring up into the gallery of red, Danly wondered if this stage play was for his benefit or the men seated in the stands. Either way, he was impressed. If the rest of the masked men were half as powerful as their leader, then the prince had an excellent chance of gaining the throne. Still, it was a dangerous game. Caution was advisable. Pitching his voice to fill the amphitheater, the prince replied, "In this gallery of wealth and power, only one man dares to show his face. With such an open display of bravery, why should I believe the Red Horns are capable of winning the Rose Throne?"

A rumble of anger rippled through the gallery. The leader struck the floor with butt of his staff, regaining control. "My prince, you mistake caution for cowardice." His angry tone carried a rebuke. "We risk death to challenge the Spider Queen. We cannot be too cautious."

An expectant hush filled the amphitheater.

"If you sense anger, my prince, it is because these men dare to risk everything to see you on the Rose Throne. They will not let you risk their lives needlessly. Your clumsy request for a seat on the queen's council has only served to raise the suspicions of the monarch. Instead of looking outward for threats from other kingdoms, the Spider Queen now focuses her attention on Lanverness. Even her royal son is not above suspicion. Elaborate precautions were required for this meeting." The leader lowered his voice, "My prince, you are being watched by the queen's shadowmen."

A lance of fear pierced the prince, threatening to turn his bowels to liquid. Danly's gaze darting nervously across the gallery. He'd never suspected his mother would set her shadowmen on one of her own sons...and all because he'd asked to sit on her council. Truly, the woman's ruthlessness knew no bounds. Danly had barely reached for the crown and already the game turned deadly. "I was unaware of the shadowmen." Surprised by the steadiness of his voice, he continued, "I concede that your elaborate precautions are both necessary and wise. I will do all that I can to protect the secrecy of the Red Horns...but it would help if I understood your plan."

The red-cloaked leader spoke with the voice of an orator. "One slip of the tongue can foil the best rebellion. The details of the plan must remain a closely guarded secret, but I can tell you this, we plan to seize the crown and hold it. While we gather the required swords, other plots are underway. The Spider Queen is far too popular with the common people. To keep the throne we must turn the commoners against the queen. The people must hail their new king as a savior to the queen's blatant misuse of power."

The prince stared at the leader, appalled by his regard for the common people. "The people do not matter! Power resides in gold, in the steel of swords, and in the authority of the throne. You waste your time worrying about the common people."

"Not so, my prince. Lanverness is a populous kingdom with a small army. If the people revolt there would not be enough swords to contain them." Shaking his head, the leader said, "Our way is best. We will take the throne by force and keep it by guile."

Danly was not convinced, but he was curious about their plan. "The kingdom is at peace, taxation is reasonable, and businessmen and farmers both prosper. With such plenty, how will you turn the people against the queen?"

"A shrewd question, my prince. The Spider Queen has a reputation for being tight with a copper. We will turn that reputation against her."

Puzzled, the prince replied, "I don't understand."

The leader turned to address the men in the gallery. "Our plan is a complex puzzle, with each person knowing only a single part. The whole will not be revealed until all the pieces are in place. We must each play our part, using stealth, caution and guile to avoid detection by the queen's shadowmen." Turning back to the prince, the leader said, "Will you, Prince Danly of the house of Tandroth, be our king?"

Danly considered the question. These men were shrewd and well organized, offering his best chance to win the crown. Rising, he made his voice solemn, like an oath before the gods. "The blood of the kings of Lanverness runs in my veins. I will align myself with the Red Horns. Together we will take the Rose Throne from the Spider Queen!"

Male voices took up a slow chant, "A king!...A king!...A king!" like a rumble of thunder.

The power of the chant was seductive. It thrummed through Danly's veins like the lure of destiny.

A hand rested on his shoulder, bringing him back to reality. The red-cloaked leader leaned close. "You have done well, my prince, but now it is time to go. Let me walk you to the door."

The prince acknowledged the chanting crowd with a wave and then fell into step with the leader. The two men exited the amphitheater, the rhythmic chant echoing behind. The leader turned to the prince and said, "Now you are truly one of us. For the sake of secrecy, you must not deviate in anyway from your normal routine." Lowering his voice, he added, "Remember, the queen's shadowmen are already watching you. Do you understand?"

The allure of the crown outweighed his fear...at least for the moment. "Yes, but when will I meet with you again?"

"Spend the dark of every moon at Madam Stock's bordello. Ask for the same suite of rooms and spend the evening with any girl that pleases you. When the night grows late, one of us will come to you via the secret staircase." Reaching into his robe, he handed Danly a slip of parchment. "This is the name of a discrete alchemist in the west side of the city. Valquist makes an excellent sleeping potion. Use it to drug the courtesans when you are finished. At midnight, one of us will come to you in the outer sitting room." Pausing he added, "If we need to meet for any other reason, we will contact you. Be vigilant and look for the sign of the Red Horn. Do you understand?"

"Perfectly."

"Good. Remember, when you see me at court, treat me in the same way as you did before. Is that clear?"

"Yes."

With a bow, the leader said, "I will leave you now. Be quick to enter the carriage. Hugo will see you safely back to the bordello. Stay safe, my prince. The Red Horns await the day when we will hail you as our rightful king." With a second bow, the leader turned and walked back down the passageway.

A short time later, the double doors were thrown open and the prince raced up the stairs into the waiting carriage. His original guide joined him; only this time the man wore simple boiled leathers under a dark wool cape. "Hugo, I presume?"

The burly man grinned. "At your service, majesty. Sorry for the secrecy earlier. We'll soon have you back to the bordello. The girl waits for you in the bedroom. Have your fun with her and no one will be the wiser." He handed the prince a small glass vial. "This is for the girl. Mix it with some wine. It will muddle her memory of the evening."

Palming the vial, Danly considered the events of the night. The Red Horns had exceeded his expectations, the chant from the amphitheater pounding though his mind. He grew hard just thinking about it, till his need was nearly unbearable. He wondered if this was what it felt like to be king. Truly power was the greatest aphrodisiac of all.

# 42

# Blaine

Like a beacon in the dark, the distant campfire drew the knights along the lip of the gorge. Abandoning their horses, they advanced on foot. After four frustrating days of finding nothing but cold campfires, the quarry was finally within reach. Pitch-dark with only a thin crescent moon, the night was perfect for an ambush. The knights unsheathed their steel, circling the campfire. Blaine yearned for a fight, keen to redeem himself.

The twang of a bowstring broke the silence.

An arrow thunked into a pine tree, narrowly missing Blaine's head. Startled, Blaine dove behind a boulder. He peered into the darkness, but he saw no sign of the archer. In the pitch dark, the arrow must have been a lucky shot. Regardless, the element of surprise was lost. The knights had a fight on their hands.

A stranger called from the darkness. "I respect your swords but you have no need of them. The girl is safe. Declare yourselves and come in peace."

Blaine considered rushing the archer but Captain Tellor's reply stayed him. "We are knights of the Octagon and we have you surrounded. Stand down and surrender the girl."

The voice replied, "The princess awaits her escort. She sleeps by the campfire, exhausted by her ordeal. Sheath your swords and I will join you at the camp. We are allies not enemies."

Blaine tightened his grip on his sword, refusing to be seduced by lies.

Captain Tellor's voice rang through the night. "Advance with drawn steel, we'll see for ourselves if the princess is safe."

Blaine crabbed sideways trying to get out of the archer's line of fire. Keeping low, he dashed for the campfire, risking an arrow in the back. The archer held his fire and Blaine broke through the scrub into the circle of light. At first he thought the campfire was deserted, but then he spied a tousled blonde head asleep on one of the bedrolls. Joy leapt through him but he held his silence. Aware that the camp could be nothing more than an elaborate ambush, Blaine stood guard over the princess, his gaze roaming the edge of the forest. Other knights stepped into the clearing. With military precision, they formed a defensive ring around the princess. Receiving a nod from the captain, Blaine knelt to give the girl a gentle touch.

The princess did not move. A cold pit of fear seized Blaine's stomach. He shook her hard. Sea green eyes, dazed from sleep, gazed up at him. A tentative hand reached out to grasp his mail-covered arm. "I knew you'd come."

The conviction in her words struck at Blaine's heart. There was no anger or accusation, only a steadfast belief in him. He vowed to never fail her again. Fumbling for words, he gestured to the others. "We all came for you. Forgive us for taking so long."

Kath stared at the circle of knights. "The ones who kidnapped me are dead, you can stand down now." Her voice carried a surety he'd never heard before.

Captain Tellor gestured for the knights to hold their position. "Archers hide in the forest. We stand guard against an ambush."

Kath shrugged off the blanket and rose, her hand resting on the hilt of a strange sword. "The archer is a friend. He helped me defeat the Dark Lord's men. Put your swords away. There are no enemies here."

Blaine stared as if pole-axed, ambushed by the tone of command in her voice.

Captain Tellor was slow to sheath his sword. He turned to face the princess and gaped in astonishment. Blaine understood his reaction. Her long golden hair was hopelessly tangled and her tunic was covered in dirt and grime yet she stood proud with her hand on the hilt of a captured sword. The knights had come to rescue a young girl and found a triumphant warrior-princess instead.

The captain scowled. "We failed once with our lack of vigilance. We'll not fail again."

She gave him a weary smile. "We were all caught off guard by the Dark Lord's men. What matters is that you came. Tell the men to sheathe their swords and to stand down. There are no enemies here. The archer in the forest is my friend. He has earned the gratitude of Castlegard."

With a reluctant nod, the captain ordered the men to stand down. The knights sheathed their swords and surrounded the princess. She had kind words for each of them. When the first round of greetings was done, the captain stepped in to take charge, dispatching the two squires to retrieve the horses. Sir Kirk was assigned guard duty and the big smith was asked to gather more wood for the fire. The knights began to make camp while Blaine hovered at Kath's side.

A lone figure stepped into the firelight. Dressed in simple hunting leathers, the archer deliberately unstrung his longbow. In the reflected firelight, his eyes glowed like a pair of twin lanterns.

Blaine hissed at the demon-bright eyes. Swords sprang from scabbards as the knights turned on the stranger.

The princess leaped in front of the archer. "Stop!" Her command froze the knights. "This is my friend, Jorah Silvenwood. Without his help, I would have died at the hands of the Dark Lord's men. He is welcome at our camp."

Blaine stood the closest to the cat-eyed man. As a young boy, he'd heard tales of cat-eyed demons stealing children in the dark of the night but he always assumed the stories were nothing more than old wives' tales. Now the stuff of his childhood nightmares stood at the edge of the campfire. Eyes glowing golden in the firelight, the archer seemed like a creature of evil...yet the princess stood by his side. Blaine wrestled with his nightmares but logic held sway. If the princess vouched for the cat-eyed man then that was good enough for him.

Blaine sheathed his sword and stepped forward, offering his hand in friendship. "If you've truly saved the princess then I owe you a life-debt."

The other knights hovered close, naked steel gleaming in the firelight.

When the two men clasp hands, the tension melted away. The other knights sheathed their swords and came forward to meet the stranger. Introductions were made and they soon found themselves sitting around the campfire, sharing a flagon of ale and swapping stories about the past few days.

The knights clamored for a tale of the kidnapping. The princess recounted her ordeal in a flat voice devoid of emotion. She explained about the goblin-man and the Isle of Souls. She told how the ogre carried her off in the middle of the night, deep into the forest. How her captors kept her bound and gagged. How she did her best to mark a trail, always watching for a chance to escape. She showed them the knife hidden in her boot and explained how she forced herself to wait for the right moment.

When it came to the tale of her escape, her voice dropped to a hushed whisper. The knights sat spellbound. In measured tones, she recounted the fight in the meadow and aid of the archer. When the telling was done, the princess displayed the crude medallion bearing the sign of the Mordant.

Blaine stared at the medallion, stunned by the tale.

Anger, shock, and pride warred across the faces of the other knights. Blaine shared their feelings, enraged at the treatment of the princess and shocked that the Mordant had stretched his hand so deeply into the southern kingdoms, but most of all, he was proud of Kath. She was truly a princess of Castlegard. Passing a flagon of ale, they toasted her victory. She was a blooded warrior! Their princess had killed an ogre in her first battle! This was the stuff of legends.

As the ale flowed, the knights asked the princess to repeat the tale till every detail was memorized. They hailed the cat-eyed archer as a hero, pressing him to tell his version. By the third telling, the knights were clapping the cat-eyed archer on the back, claiming him as an honorary brother-in-arms. Before the night was done, more than one oath of friendship was sworn around the blazing fire.

When the ale finally ran out and exhaustion caught up with them, the companions crawled into their bedrolls. They all slept save one.

Blaine stood guard beside the princess. In the quiet of the night, he thought about the tale of her escape. Truly, Valin had marked the girl for one of his own...but in his heart, he wondered why the gods would bestow their favor on a mere girl.

# 43

# Liandra

The queen stood at the casement window, looking down on the architectural splendors of Castle Tandroth. The view was impressive but her thoughts were turned inward. Having the lion tabard of Coronth walk into her audience chamber had been a shock, like a ghost resurrected from the past. Liandra paced a path across the carpet, searching for deeper answers. The Lions of Coronth were said to be dead, all butchered by the Pontifax and his gruesome Flame God. With the extermination of Coronth's ruling house, the emblem of the golden lion fell into disuse. The sudden re-appearance seemed like an omen. But was the return of the lion merely a ghostly reminder of the past, or did it herald the re-birth of a once proud house? Or could it be a warning to the people of Lanverness...a warning that religions seldom respect political borders. Coronth's nightmares could easily spill over into Lanverness.

The queen paused by an ivory chess set frozen in mid-game. Perhaps she was looking at it the wrong way. Instead of an omen or a dire warning, the appearance of the lion could be an opportunity...an opportunity to change the future. Fingering her emerald necklace, she considered the possibilities. A plan began to form in her mind. Much would depend on the character of the young man from Coronth. The council meeting would be the perfect setting to plumb his past as well as the depth of his character. She liked that he'd escaped with his mother, despite the fact that the feeble woman could only have been a liability on the long trek from Balor. The presence of the mother indicated he had a good heart as well as being resourceful. Both qualities would be important for what she had in mind. Perhaps there was hope for her plan.

Her musings were interrupted by a knock. The Master Archivist entered the solar and bowed. "Your majesty, the council is assembled."

"And the others?"

"Prince Stewart, Lord Duncan, Prince Justin, Princess Jemma and the court bard, Master Fallon, have all joined the council as per your instructions."

"Very well, you may escort us to the council chambers."

The Master Archivist fell in step with his queen, a black shadow beside the rustle of her silks. Never one for idle chatter, he held his silence. It was one of the many things she liked about him. As they approached the chamber, two royal guards leaped to open the doors. A herald announced. "All hail her royal majesty, the Rose Queen of Lanverness!"

As her councilors scrambled to rise, the queen swept into the chamber and took a seat upon the raised throne at the head of the large oak table. With a wave of her hand, she gave them permission to sit.

The Master Archivist took his customary seat at her right hand while her royal son, crown Prince Stewart, was seated on her left. The queen acknowledged her son and her councilors and then turned to address the contingent from Navarre. "Lord Duncan, Prince Justin, and Princess Jemma, we thank you for joining us on such short notice. No doubt you are wondering why this meeting has been called. It is our practice to hold a commoners' audience once a fortnight so that we may hear the concerns of our people. A particularly interesting petitioner approached us at this morning, a refugee from Coronth."

Prince Justin leaned forward with a gleam in his eyes. Mildly amused by the young bard's eagerness, the queen continued, "This refugee is of particular interest since he has experienced two different faces of the Flame God. The young man served in the Flame guard until the priests executed his father. Branded as the son of a heretic, he fled Coronth in fear for his life. We called this meeting so that all of you could hear his account first hand. We welcome your questions and insights in dealing with this young lion." She gestured to the guard at the door. "Have the young man join us."

Tall and gaunt, a young man wearing the tattered lion tabard of Coronth entered the council chambers. A guard announced, "Samson Springwater of Coronth."

Approaching the council table, he stood with his shoulders slouched and his hands clasped, his nervous gaze darting around the chamber like a cornered rabbit. Judging him to be in his early twenties, the queen was pleased to note he had an ordinary face, the type that would not stand out in a crowd. Thin as a scarecrow, he would need food and time to recover, but he might be the perfect candidate for what she had in mind. Much would depend on his answers. Of necessity, her questions would be harsh. She intended to find out what he was truly made of.

In a regal voice, the queen said, "Welcome to our court. We hope your insights will help us to defend Lanverness against the religion of the Flame. Will you answer our questions?"

The young man made an awkward bow. "Your majesty, the farmers of Lanverness showed me and my mother nothing but kindness. I would not wish the cruelties of the Flame God on your people. I'm only a simple man, but I'll do my best to answer your questions."

The queen gestured towards a vacant chair at the foot of the table. "We thank you for your cooperation. Please be seated so that you may tell your tale in comfort." The queen waited until the young man was seated. "You have come a long way and we would hear your story. You may start when you are ready."

All eyes turned toward the young lion of Coronth. The refugee paled, struggling to regain his composure. His voice cracked at first but then he settled into the telling. He started with the death of his father in the Test of Faith and the murder of a sergeant in the Flame guard. He spoke in a monotone, as if the grim tale had happened to someone else. The queen and her counselors sat in silence, sifting every word. Hours later, he finished, finding sanctuary in an apple farmer's barn at the edge of Lanverness. A hushed silence settled over the chamber.

The queen contemplated the tale, weighing every word. The story was simply told, but the motives beneath were missing. "We are curious as to how the Pontifax first came to power in Coronth. We have heard tales of his ascent from merchants, bards, and other travelers, but it might be insightful to hear the tale from the perspective of a citizen of Coronth."

The young man's eyes widened and his face blanched, her first question had caught him off-guard. "My memories are colored by childhood, but I will do the best I can." In a faltering voice, he explained, "I was only a young boy when the Pontifax and the Keeper came to Balor, but I remember the first time the Pontifax walked through the Sacred Flames. Everyone talked about it. The Test of Faith was a miracle! No one had ever seen a miracle before. It was proof the Flame God existed, proof that the Pontifax stood high in the god's favor. Even my parents were impressed. I remember them taking me to early gatherings of the faithful. My family was never very religious until the coming of the Flame God. The miracle of the Test of Faith was real, proof we could see with our own eyes. It changed everything." Pausing, he added, "Everyone was caught up in the new religion. It seemed only natural to join the temple and worship the Flame God."

The queen dug deeper. "And house Manfred, the rightful rulers of Coronth. What became of the king and his family?"

The young man had the grace to blush and look away. "You have to understand, everyone was caught up in the religion of the Flame. The Pontifax declared that the Flame God would not permit an infidel to sit on the throne. He challenged the king and his family to take the Test of Faith. When the king refused, the faithful attacked the royal palace. The city guard, already loyal to the Pontifax, did not interfere. The mob built a bonfire, thrusting the royals into the Flames." Samson stared at the floor, his voice a dull monotone. "Perched on the shoulders of my father, I watched as the king shook off the hands of the crowd. He walked into the Flames with dignity. Instead of moving the crowd to pity, his bravery only enraged them. The mob tore the young princes from the arms of the queen, tossing the children into the Flames like rag dolls. The queen was quick to follow." He shook his head as if trying to erase the memories. "I was only a child, but nightmares of the royal deaths plagued me for years." Pausing, Samson added. "Once it was done, Coronth needed a ruler. I suppose it was only natural for the Pontifax to take the throne." Samson stared at the queen as if begging forgiveness.

She gave him a cold, stony stare, her voice stern and unforgiving. "The Pontifax murdered a god-anointed king yet your people did not see the evil of the act." She skewered him with her gaze. "The death of the king was only a foretaste of things to come. Why did you join the city guards?"

Samson grew deathly pale but he did not flinch from her gaze. "If truth be told, I never really thought about it. My father was a baker and I hated helping him in the shop. It seemed a dull, pointless life. I wanted adventure. I wanted a flashy uniform and a sword on my hip. Joining the guards was a way to escape the life of a baker." His voice broke. "It was just a way to a better future, that's all, just a better life."

The queen twisted the verbal dagger. "So you joined the army of thugs, burning innocent citizens in the Flames."

He burst from the chair. "I never did that!" He shook his head in denial, his fists clenched. "Only volunteers work in the temple square. I never had the stomach for it. I always drew guard duty at one of the city gates. I never served in a Test of Faith."

"So why did you flee Coronth?"

His voice shook with anguish. "They burnt my father and drove my mother near out of her mind." His gaze darted around the table. "He was just a baker, an honest man who'd lived his whole life in Coronth. He paid his tithes to the temple and did devotions once a week. His only son was a sergeant in the city guards. If he had any fault, it was that he refused to attend the public gatherings for the Test of Faith...but that's not reason enough to commit *murder!*" He swayed, his voice riddled with strain. "My father was an innocent man yet they murdered him in the Flames." With a weary sigh, he added, "They murder us all in the Flames. If a family member fails the Test of Faith, then every member of that family is branded as a heretic. As heretics, the best we could hope for was to become outcasts in Coronth...or else join my father in the Flames. The only real choice was to flee." He faced them with his palms open in entreaty, as if asking for understanding if not forgiveness.

Faint smears of blood marked his palms, cut by the crescent of his nails. The queen kept her face stern. Like a surgeon cutting rotten flesh from an open wound she probed deeper. "Do you think your father was the first innocent to die in the Flames?"

Samson's face paled. "No."

The queen sat back in her throne. "Why do you wear the lost lion of Coronth?"

Again he was caught off guard, puzzlement scrawled across his face. He stared at his tabard, as if he'd forgotten what symbol he wore. "I found it tucked away in the quartermaster's stores, a bit of blue in a sea of bloody red. The blue caught my eye. Without thinking, I put it in the bottom of my rucksack. It was only later I realized what it was. When I made it to your court, it somehow seemed right to put it on." Pausing, he added, "I suppose I wore it to remind people that Coronth was once a better, kinder place." He stared at the queen. "Perhaps I hoped that the old Coronth could somehow be reborn from the ashes of the Flames, like the legends of the phoenix."

The queen kept the smile from her face. It was the answer she'd been hoping for, but she still had one more question. In a kinder voice, she asked, "Why did you come to us?"

With a small smile, he said, "At last, an easy question. I came to Lanverness seeking sanctuary." His voice deepened. "I came to your court to repay the farmers who helped us. I bring a warning, but I also pray the mighty queen of Lanverness will defeat the Flame God that has captured Coronth."

"But does Coronth want to be free of the Flame God?"

Stunned, the young man reeled backwards. "Of course they do! Every week a new life is fed to the Flame God. The forests and fields are choked with refugees running from the priests. Coronth is awash with people who have turned against the Pontifax and his cruel god!"

Anger steeled her voice, "Coronth is awash with people *running* from the Flame. Are there any willing to *stand* against the Pontifax, to challenge his rule and change the kingdom for the better?"

He had no answer.

With a deliberate sigh, the queen explained. "Whether they know it or not, the people of Coronth made a choice to be ruled by the Flame God. By your own words, the evil is obvious. An innocent is brazenly murdered once a week in the town square. The evil is there for all to see yet no one sees, hears, or speaks of the evil among you and so it is allowed to grow. You are all conveniently blind, deaf, and dumb...until the unthinkable happens and injustice visits your own home. But by then it is too late." She let her words sink in before continuing. "We will *not* risk Lanverness lives for people unwilling to help themselves. So we ask you again, do the people of Coronth truly want to be free of the Flame God?"

He stared at her, begging for pity, but she gave him none. In a weak voice, he answered, "Anyone who stands against the Flame God is marked for death in the Test of Faith. None dare speak out."

"And therein lays the problem." The queen threw down her challenge. "Change starts with one individual. Someone must make the first stand. It takes the most courage for the first to speak out, but without the first there will never be a second. People often underestimate the power of the individual. The first pebble to roll down the cliff is often the start of a landslide."

He stared at her, a drowning man begging to be saved.

Looking past his open face, the queen saw an intelligence that had never been nurtured and a good heart that ached with pain, but she wondered if he had the courage to step forward. The silence lengthened.

Eventually, he rasped in a hoarse voice, "You want me to go back?"

She nodded, waiting for him to say more.

Fear filled his eyes. "Tell me, your majesty, does the first pebble ever survive the landslide?"

The queen knew about the need for sacrifices. It was part of being a ruler. She would not lie to him but she also needed to give him hope. Without hope, he had no chance of success and even less of surviving. "The risk is great, but with careful planning, we would hope to see the first pebble live."

A desperate gratitude shown from his eyes. Bowing, he said in a hushed voice, "Though I fear it greatly, I will go back." He looked down at the blue tabard, running a hand across the golden lion. "I suppose I chose this path when I plucked the lion tabard from the quartermaster's stores." Taking a deep breath, he said, "I will be the first pebble to roll down the mountain, may all the Lords of Light help me."

The whole room began to breathe again.

In a gracious voice, the queen said, "Take heart, for you will not be alone. The best minds and the wealth of Lanverness will support you."

Smiling she added, "With your courage as an example, we are sure others will join in returning to Coronth."

She waited to let her words take root.

He looked up, giving her a small smile of hope.

Nodding, the queen continued, "You have had a long and difficult journey. Master Fallon will help you to settle in your new quarters. When you are rested, we will plot your return. Let us hope that today is the first step towards freedom for the people of Coronth." Rising, she added, "The council is dismissed. We thank you for your time."

The queen watched as Master Fallon took the battered young man in hand, shepherding him out of the chamber. She'd found a single lion brave enough to roar in the face of the storm. Liandra would do her best to help him survive the coming maelstrom. She pitied him the trials ahead, but the people of Coronth badly needed a hero. She prayed one hero would be enough to start a landslide to smother the Flames.

# 44

# Katherine

Tantalizing smells of roasting venison teased Kath to wakefulness. A loud growl from her stomach tipped the argument. Opening her eyes, she stared up at a sky crowded with clouds. The wind on her face was biting cold. The long autumn had finally succumbed to winter.

Warm within her bedroll, Kath took stock of the camp. Everyone was already up; the camp was a bustle of military efficiency. Kath sighed contentedly. It felt good to be back where she belonged.

"So you finally wake!" Tending the venison steaks, Sir Tyrone flashed her a broad smile. "Your timing is perfect, breakfast is nearly ready." Removing a steak from the spit, he added, "Everything's packed and the horses are saddled but we thought it best to let you sleep. We'll set a faster pace if you're rested." Gesturing towards the roasting venison, the black knight added, "Your archer friend kindly donated a shank of deer for breakfast, so we'll have a hearty meal before we start." Giving her a wry smile, he added "But I have some bad news for you, my Lady."

The smile on his face told Kath he was baiting her.

"On the long chase through the forest, one of the pack horses pulled up lame. We stripped the gear off the horse and left the animal to fend for itself." After a dramatic pause, he added, "We had to abandon all of your fine dresses, lost in the wilds of Wyeth."

She stared at his solemn face and then burst out laughing. She laughed so hard that tears came to her eyes, just what she needed to shake off the taint of the Dark Lord's minions. Kath flashed him a brilliant smile. Sir Tyrone was good with his great sword but he was an even better traveling companion and true friend. She silently thanked Valin that she'd gotten to know the black knight.

Tossing a saddlebag at her, Sir Tyrone added, "One of the squires salvaged a fresh tunic, leggings, and cloak for you. You might want to change before breakfast." Pointing to the end of her bedroll, he added,

"And Sir Blaine has been carrying those around since we lost you at the roadhouse. He thought that you might want them back."

Glancing down at the end of her bedroll, she saw her twin throwing axes in their tooled leather harness. With a whoop of triumph, she pounced on the axes. "Do you know how badly I've longed for these?"

The black knight smiled and waved her toward the woods. "Get yourself cleaned up. Breakfast is nearly ready. The captain will want to move out as soon as we've eaten."

Gathering up the saddlebag and a skin of water, she ducked into the woods finding privacy behind a thick shrub. Shivering in the cold, she peeled off her soiled clothes, disgusted by the smell. She washed quickly, numb with cold by the time she pulled on a fresh tunic, but it felt good to be clean again. Strapping her throwing axes on her back and a sword at her waist, she made and sure her knife was safely tucked in her right boot before returning to the warmth of the campfire.

Her companions were already gathered for breakfast. She took a seat between Jorah and Sir Blaine. Sir Tyrone handed her a mug of hot tea and a plate loaded with a thick venison steak and a hardtack biscuit. Overcome with hunger, she dove into the meal without saying a word. She was working on her second steak when the cat-eyed archer turned to her and said, "Since you're safe with your escort, I'll be leaving after breakfast. I need to get back to my family."

His words were expected but they still brought a lump to her throat. The cat-eyed archer had saved her life and in the short amount of time that she'd known him, he'd also become her friend. She would miss his company. She stared into his strange golden gaze. "Thank you for saving my life...and for the gift of your friendship. I'll miss your company."

In a quiet voice, the archer replied, "The Goddess of the Forest meant for our paths to cross. Since meeting you, I've made more white-eyed friends in one day than in my entire life. Perhaps there is hope that my people will one day be accepted by the kingdoms of Erdhe."

In a thoughtful voice, Kath said, "You'll always be welcome at Castlegard. I'll send a dispatch to my father telling him how cat-eyed archer save my life. It is an affront to the Lords of Light that your people are not welcome in the kingdoms. I will do whatever I can to help them."

Jorah stared at her as if weighing her every word. After a few moments, he bowed deeply and said, "Meeting you was truly the work of the goddess. Being welcome in Castlegard would be a great boon to my people."

"I cannot promise it, for it depends on the will of the king, but I will do my best to make it so. Meanwhile you have my thanks and my friendship." With a pause she added, "I hope some day our paths will cross again."

The archer flashed her a grin. "You should visit the Deep Green." He pressed a leather token into her hand. "Bring this with you when you come. Show it to a ranger and ask him to guide you to the Clan of the Cedars. I'd like my wife and small daughter to meet you."

Nestled in her palm, Kath found a leather token the size of a gold coin. Leaves embossed the edges, a mighty redwood tree filling the center. Closing her fist around the token, she said, "I don't know where my path will take me, but I will do my best to visit some day."

Smiling, Jorah said, "You do that." They clasped hands in friendship and then the archer bid farewell to the rest of the knights. Mounting the captured gelding, he rode into the forest, the pony trailing behind on a lead. The knights watched in silence until the archer passed from sight. The cat-eyed archer had made more than one friend around the campfire.

With the archer gone, the knights were quick to pack up camp. Captain Tellor barked orders, but Kath had other ideas. Drawing the captain aside, she said, "I know we've lost time, but I need to return to the forest before we journey to Lanverness."

The captain gave her a puzzled look. "What are you talking about? Our arrival in Pellanor is long overdue."

Kath tried her best to explain. "When I fled the servants of the Dark Lord, I stumbled across a ruined tower in the forest. I found something I must return for. It will only take a few hours at most." Staring into his skeptical face, she added, "Please, I *must* return to the ruins."

He gestured toward the leaden sky. "Winter has nearly caught us and we're long overdue in the queen's court. We don't have time to wander the woods searching for lost ruins."

Kath feared he'd be stubborn but she had no choice. Squaring her shoulders, she made her voice as hard as steel. "This is an *order* from a *princess* of Castlegard, not a request."

Resentment snapped across his face.

She met his stare without flinching.

The captain was the first to look away. "If it's truly that important, we'll follow your lead to the ruins. But be quick about it. We've wasted enough time already."

She did not like his tone, yet she held her anger. "Thank you, captain. It won't take long."

"See that it doesn't."

Kath reclaimed Dancer and led the mounted knights into the forest. Riding away from the gorge, she searched for the shallow stream. When they reached the brook, she followed the watercourse upstream to the overgrown ruins. Dismounting in the small greensward, she secured her horse, and then approached the captain, asking that Sir Blaine and Sir Tyrone accompany her while the rest of the party waited. A terse nod was the captain's only reply. Taking her saddlebag, Kath led the two knights towards the ruins.

The towers and walls were nearly swallowed by the forest, consumed by living green. Kath led the two knights up the hill and through a gap in the collapsed wall. She ran her hand along the moss-covered stone, feeling a rightness she couldn't explain. The doorway to the great drum tower gaped open, just as she remembered. Excitement claimed her and she quickened her pace. Kath felt an inexplicable longing, hoping the voice and the visions would be there to greet her. Holding her breath, she stepped into the tower. The great oak tree stood denuded of leaves, a shower of autumn gold carpeting the floor, but otherwise the broken tower remained the same...only this time there was no voice to greet her. A sigh of disappointment escaped her. The gaping silence felt like a great loss. A moment later, the two knights followed her through the doorway. A chime shimmered in the air. Inside of her head, a woman's voice whispered, *"The two knights will be true. Be welcome warriors of the Light."*

Gasping in delight, Kath stared at the knights. From the astonishment on their faces, she knew they'd both heard the unspoken words. Tears crowded her eyes; she would not be alone in the fight against the Dark Lord. "So you heard it too."

The black knight nodded and Sir Blaine whispered, "What is this place?"

Like a dam breaking, she explained everything. She showed the two knights her gargoyle hidden beneath her tunic. She did her best to explain that it was a magical focus, a powerful relic from the Age of Magic. She told them how the strange goblin-man had the ability to track magic, to follow its scent. Naming the goblin-man a 'hound of the Dark Lord', she explained how the Mordant's henchmen kidnapped her for the magical focus.

Sir Blaine nodded, understanding written on his face. "That makes more sense. None of us could figure out why anyone would steal you away. With your axes and gray tunic you look like a squire. No more and no less."

Kath said, "Master Quintus warned me that others would covet my focus, so I kept the gargoyle hidden. I never dreamed the servants of the Dark Lord would discover it merely by smell."

Sir Tyrone said, "There might be more of these goblin-men scouring the countryside for magic. We'd best be on our guard."

Kath shuddered, hating the thought of it.

The black knight put a reassuring hand on her shoulder. "It is good you told us. Now we know what to look for."

In a hesitant, voice Kath said, "Master Quintus said I should keep my gargoyle a secret. There may be others besides the goblin-man who would take it from me."

"As you wish." With a puzzled voice, he added, "But what is this place? Why did you bring us here?"

Kath smiled. "I stumbled upon these ruins by accident. I was hoping to find a weapon but I found something else. When I entered into the tower, I was greeted by the woman's voice and shown visions of the past. The voice led me to a hidden dagger...a crystal dagger. Once I held it in my hands, I knew it was meant to be the bane of a great evil. I left the dagger in its hiding place and led the captain and his men away from the tower." Dropping her voice to a hush, she said, "I did not expect to survive the fight. If not for the archer, I would have died in the meadow." She shuddered, making the hand sign against evil. "But having survived, I knew I had to return to claim the dagger." She stared at the knights, desperate to be believed.

Sir Tyrone glanced at Sir Blaine. A knowing look passed between them. Turning back to Kath, the black knight's voice was solemn. "My Lady, we both heard the voice of the tower. We have no doubt that you are marked by Valin." Dropping to his knee, he drew his sword, extending the hilt toward her. Sir Blaine did the same. In a solemn voice, Sir Tyrone said, "Our swords are yours. Accept our service in the battle against the Dark."

The air in the tower stilled as if an invisible presence waited to hear her response. Kath felt as if she had done this before, as if history repeated itself. Time shifted and for a single heartbeat she stood in the tower at the peak of its glory, the corbelled vault gleaming like a star-studded sky. A heartbeat later and she was standing in the ancient ruins. Taking a steadying breath, she reached out to lightly touch the hilts of their swords. Echoing the words her father used when making new knights, she said, "Arise Sir Knights, your oaths of fealty are accepted. Let honor, justice, and truth guide your swords in the service of the Light."

A second chime shimmered through the air, witnessing the vow.

The two knights sheathed their swords and rose to their feet, staring in awe at the ruins. The towers of the eight-pointed star were broken but an ancient power still lingered in the keep.

Kath whispered, "Truly, the Lords of Light keep watch upon this place."

The wind stirred, lifting the autumn leaves into a golden swirl. The invisible presence seemed to withdraw.

In a hushed voice, Sir Tyrone said, "My Lady, perhaps you should recover this weapon of the Light."

Kath climbed the circular stairway and knelt on the sixth step. She swung the seventh step outward, revealing the hidden place beneath. Reaching into the recess, Kath recovered the golden box. She descended the stairs and showed the box to the two knights.

Sir Blaine gasped when he saw it. "I've seen this device before! When we were searching for you, I came across some ruins in the depths of the forest. A shield bearing an eight-pointed star was carved on the keystone. I remember it clearly because the emblem puzzled me." Pausing he added, "The ruins must somehow be connected."

The thought of another ruined tower teased Kath's imagination, wondering what treasures might lie hidden among the tumbled stones. "Did you hear the woman's voice or the chime?"

Blaine shook his head. "The tower was ruined, nothing but a nest for starlings."

Kath heard the disappointment in his voice. "This place seems old, very old. I suspect the heraldry is lost to the past yet the power of the Light remains." Taking a deep breath, she opened the box and revealed the dagger.

Sir Blaine gasped, "A crystal dagger!"

She lifted the pale rose-white dagger in salute to the heavens. The hilt fit her hand as if it belonged. Smooth as silk, the crystalline blade caught and held the light till it seemed to glow from within. There was no doubt in Kath's mind that the dagger was a mighty weapon of the Light. She wondered how long it lay hidden in the ruins. She wondered if anyone remembered its true purpose.

Sir Tyrone broke the silence. "The others are waiting."

With great reluctance, she settled the dagger back into the golden box and closed the lid. Like the gargoyle, she would keep the dagger hidden until it was needed. Looking at the two knights, she saw approval in their gaze.

Hiding the golden box in her saddlebag, Kath left the broken tower. The two knights followed, guarding her back. As she stepped from the tower, the first snowflake of the year brushed against her face. Winter had come to the lands of Erdhe but the gods had not abandoned them.

# 45

# Steffan

I n just one visit, the Dark Oracle had taught Steffan many things. He'd been surprised to learn that the Dark Lord loved crowds, a fulcrum of human nature. With crowds the whole was so much less than the sum of the parts. Individuals unconsciously surrendered their intelligence and their morals to join the crowd's collective mind in exchange for false feelings of invincibility. It was almost as if a new entity was born, an entity susceptible to suggestions and ruled by the baser instincts of man. It was so much easier to twist a man's soul once he'd joined a crowd. A decent man caught up in the mentality of the crowd would do unspeakable things, things that would forever taint his soul. Once twisted to the Dark side few found their way back to the Light.

Crowds enabled moral corruption to occur on a grand scale. It was why the Dark Lord loved them so. Now it was Steffan's turn to use the power of crowds to whip the people of Coronth into a religious frenzy.

He started his work with whispers and rumors. Nothing caught the people's attention like a good rumor. The new ritual wasn't scheduled to start till noon but curiosity brought the people to the square at dawn's first light. The gathering grew as the morning advanced. To swell the crowds even further, the general ordered the city guards to attend the ritual. Red and gold tabards stood out against the everyday colors. People of every description jammed together with barely a space between. The temple square overflowed with the faithful. They'd all heard that today's Test of Faith was going to be something special, something not to be missed. Expectation charged the air. Steffan smiled. It was the perfect atmosphere for staging a miracle.

Dressed as a commoner, Steffan wove his way through the edge of the crowd. The fringe of the crowd was always the perfect vantage point to gauge the success of the pageant.

As he walked, he eavesdropped on conversations. Speculation about the new ritual was rampant. Most looked forward to a massive burning, a feast of death. Some even speculated on the names of the sinners. Opinions varied but the voices all held the same eagerness, the same morbid fascination. Steffan smiled, amused by how quickly the people of Coronth had acquired a voyeuristic taste for death. Tinker, tailor, soldier, sailor, rich man, poor man, beggar man, thief, regardless of their social station, they all flocked to see their unknown neighbor walk the flames. Death was the ultimate spectacle, the drawing card, but Steffan suspected the Test of Faith also served deeper needs. It gave the crowd tangible proof that they were special, they were chosen, they were saved. People fooled themselves into believing that the faithful watched while only the guilty burned. Laughing to himself, Steffan was sure that the Dark Lord was pleased.

Anonymous in the sea of people, Steffan elbowed his way up a set of steps overlooking the square. Satisfied with his position, he settled in to wait.

The temple drums began their thunder, marking the start of the ritual. The people turned as one to watch the massive brass doors swing open. Priests and acolytes streamed out of the temple, a stately procession of red robes and incense burners. Swaying to the rhythm of the drums, they marched toward the center of the square, taking positions surrounding the charcoal pit. The rhythm proved contagious, the drums a hypnotic heartbeat. Onlookers nearest the pit began to mimic the motion of the priests. Soon, a sea of people swayed in unison. Primed for the spectacle, a crowd was born.

The red robed Keeper emerged from the temple. Carrying a massive gold torch lit with the Sacred Flame, he made his way toward the pit. In a flourish, he touched he torch to the charcoal. The pit erupted in a ball of fire. Flames leaped and crackled, sending orange tendrils licking toward the sky. The drums quieted and the crowd stilled. The stage was set.

Into the hushed silence, the Pontifax strode from the temple. Cloaked in a cloth-of-gold, he shimmered like the dawn light. With his long flowing beard and stately bearing, the Pontifax evoked the very image of wisdom and benevolence. Women and children reached out to touch the hem of his robe, begging for his blessing.

Making the sign of the Flame, the Pontifax mounted the dais and stretched his arms in benediction. "My people! The Flame God is the very essence of love! Believe in the holy Flames and your sins will be forgiven! Follow the holy Flames and you will find salvation!" His voice fell into the cadence of a chant, seducing the people with words of love. The crowd stood spellbound, enthralled by their high priest.

The Pontifax signaled the waiting guards. A wagon surrounded by soldiers forged a path towards the fire pit. A corpulent man struggled against the wooden stocks mounted on the wagon bed. Twisting against his chains, he sobbed for mercy but his pleas fell on deaf ears.

Steffan watched from the edge of the crowd, listening as those around him strained to identify the victim. Most took delight in the fat man's fear. A few jeered while others threw rotten fruit. The wagon lurched to a stop near the flaming pit. Soldiers released the sinner from the stocks and led him in chains to the foot of the dais. His knees buckled but the soldiers held him upright. The sacrifice was ready.

The Pontifax reclaimed the attention of he crowd. "A sinner stands before the faithful, a man guilty of hoarding tithes from the temple. Yet, even now, the Flame God offers him redemption. Forgiveness waits in the embrace of the Flames!" The condemned man groveled before the Pontifax, but his desperate pleadings went unheard. The Pontifax appealed to the people. "What shall we do with this sinner? Shall we give him a chance to be cleansed of his sins? Shall we let this sinner feel the love of the Flame God?"

"Give him to the Flames!"

"Let him burn!"

"Test his Faith!"

Shouts rang from all sides of the square, but the Pontifax stood transfixed, as if waiting for something special. The people eventually understood. Like a deadly serpent uncoiling, the crowd roused its unified voice. *"The Test of Faith!"* The shout struck like thunder, a deadly verdict echoing through the square. The death of the sacrifice was now on the heads of the crowd. The crowd became a mob.

Smiling, Steffan wondered how many 'decent' people had just shouted for the death of their neighbor. It must have been legions for he could feel the Dark Lord's pleasure.

At a gesture from the Pontifax, the fat merchant was thrust deep into the heart of the flames. Screams erupted from the pit. The fat merchant danced in the grip of the flames, his face contorted in agony. His white tunic caught fire. Soldiers used spears and swords to keep the victim from escaping. Tortured screams and oily black smoke rose from the fire. The crowd strained forward, struggling to catch every grizzly detail.

Steffan watched the people around him. Their faces reflected a range of emotions, from pure cruelty to the righteous anger of true believers. Death and religion held the people of Coronth in thrall.

All too soon, the dance with death came to a close, the greasy lump succumbing to the flames.

The Pontifax raised his arms. In a voice dripping with compassion, he said, "Our dear brother died a sinner. But in the purity of the Flames, he won forgiveness for his soul. Let us rejoice in the love of the Flame God!"

The people unleashed a volley of wild cheers. A carnival-like atmosphere swept through the square. The Pontifax waited for silence to return. An expectant hush settled over the people. The high priest raised his arms in benediction. "The people of Erdhe worship many false gods, but we of Coronth know there is only one true god. Only the Flame God proves his love for the faithful by granting miracles to his high priest. Watch and see the miracles of the Flame God!" Accepting a smoking brazier of incense, the Pontifax intoned a blessing, waving the brazier over the people. The crowd stilled, sensing a change in the ritual.

Clouds of blue incense surrounded the Pontifax in a nimbus of holy smoke. Holding the brazier before him, he descended the dais and walked among the people. Like a pebble dropped in a still pond the crowd knelt in ripples. The high priest walked through a sea of bowed heads as if searching for someone. He eventually came to rest in front of a mother holding a golden haired girl of three. Blessing the child with incense, he lifted the girl into his arms and carried her back to the dais.

The Pontifax stood on the dais, the patriarch of a religion holding golden-haired child in his arms. "The Flame God shows his love for all those who believe. I have looked into this little girl's heart and found a love that is pure." He held the child aloft. "As a sign of the Flame God's love, this child will join with her Pontifax in the Test of Faith!"

A wave of shock ripped through the crowd. Men gasped in surprise and women stifled tears. Some pleaded for the child to be spared, others muttered prayers. No one believed the child would survive the Flames.

The Pontifax held the child while an acolyte knelt to remove his sandals. Descending the dais, he stood before the roaring flames.

A woman screamed, "Spare the child!"

Mutterings of protest swept through the crowd, but the Pontifax ignored them. Grasping the ruby amulet in his right hand while holding the child with his left, he walked into the flaming pit.

The crowd held its breath.

A single heartbeat pulsed through the crowd. Flames snapped and crackled around the Pontifax and the child, a roaring furnace of heat. Minutes stretched to an eternity. As if bewitched, the crowd stood spellbound, watching the flames, waiting to learn the judgment of the god.

Steffan watched with them, hoping the magic would hold.

Time crawled, the fate of a religion held in the balance.

The Pontifax emerged from the flames, whole and unharmed. Laughing in his arms, the golden-haired child reached back toward the fire as if seeking a loved one. The child's gesture broke the spell.

A woman's voice cried, "It's a miracle!"

Religious ecstasy swept through the crowd. Some fell to the ground in prostration while others chanted prayers to the Flame God. A few wept while many danced with giddy abandonment. Near the raised dais, hands reached out to touch the Pontifax. Everyone wanted to be a part of the miracle. The crowd had transformed into a frenzy of religious zealots.

Remounting the dais, the Pontifax held the child aloft. He blessed the crowd, waiting for the celebration to settle. Silence eventually returned but there was no quiet. Emotions were too raw for quiet. When the tension reached a fever pitch, the Pontifax said in a booming voice, "My people! You have witnessed the love of the Flame God! The child in the Flames is a sign that our god loves all true believers! As a token of this miracle, I have placed a special blessing on armbands bearing the symbol of the Flame. Come forward and proclaim your love of the Flame God. Wear the armband as a witness to his miracle!"

With a final blessing, the Pontifax unleashed the mob. The crowd surged forward, reaching for the armbands. Priests stationed near the fire pit handed the blessed tokens to the faithful. Small whirlpools of believers formed around each priest as the people scrambled for armbands.

Steffan turned away from the spectacle, well pleased by the performance. In a few days he'd return to the city streets to see if the armbands had the desired effect. He hoped the holy token would prolong the ritual's ecstasy. They'd also serve to distinguish believers from infidels.

Making his way into a side street, Steffan thought about the ritual. The Pontifax had worked the crowd beautifully. With one ritual, he'd turned many skeptics into believers and many believers into fanatics. Soon it would be time to unleash all of this religious zeal, to gain another victory for the Dark Lord.

# 46

# Danly

D anly's anger boiled over. He was to be their future king yet the Red Horns told him next to nothing. Tired of waiting, Danly decided take matters into his own hands. He slunk to the commoner's garden and chalked a red horn on the rear wall. The day crawled by. Danly eavesdropped on conversations and peered into the eyes of those who served him but there was never any reply. Enraged, Danly sought the solace of brandy. He considered approaching the councilor directly, but even half drunk he knew such an idea was sheer folly. He could only sit and wait. But a prince of Lanverness should *never* have to wait. Despite his frustration, his eyes grew tired; the brandy having the desired effect. He decided to turn in for the night.

He found the scroll waiting for him on his bedside table. Tearing open the wax seal, he checked the bottom right hand corner. He was not disappointed. The scroll was an invitation to an exclusive dicing party at the manor house of Lord Tweed. The party was to be held tomorrow evening. A short note scrawled in red ink advised the prince to take the landau carriage given the inclement winter weather. He usually rode his stallion but the carriage would be fine. After re-reading the scroll, he consigned the evidence to the flames.

The next afternoon, he made arrangements to attend the party. The royal landau carriage would be waiting at first dark. His two guards, Hobs and Harland, would follow on horseback. At the appointed hour, Danly tucked a generous purse of golds into his belt pouch and swirled his favorite emerald green cape around his shoulders before heading to the west gate of the castle. A footman held the door as he stepped into the privacy of the covered carriage. From the dark interior, a familiar voice said, "You asked to see me, my prince?"

Startled, the prince stared at the figure sitting in the shadows.

"Have a seat, my prince."

Danly took a seat on the opposite bench as the carriage lurched into motion. The leader of the Red Horns was dressed from head to toe in nondescript black. A simple black mask partially obscured the councilor's face. The presence of the mask surprised the prince given that he already knew the man's identity.

As if reading Danly's mind, the councilor touched the mask. "When you play against the Spider Queen, all precautions are required. I wear the mask in case an over zealous footman should happen to peer into the carriage."

Nodding, Danly said, "I'm surprised to see you here, I thought we'd meet in at the party."

"The closed carriage is a much more elegant solution. The queen's shadowmen are following the coach even as we speak. They have no idea that our meeting will be held before their very eyes."

"What about the party?"

"A sleight of hand." The counselor flashed a devilish grin. "Lord Tweed's manor is far out in the countryside so we'll have plenty of time to talk. When we reach the manor, I'll remain in the coach while you attend the party. When the queen's shadowmen transfer their attention from the coach to you, I will transfer myself to a different carriage and enjoy a leisurely return to the city" Lowering his voice, the counselor said, "To the eyes of the queen's shadowmen, I will never have been to the party and this meeting could never have taken place. I tell you this so that you appreciate the elaborate efforts the Red Horns take to ensure the security of our cause. Premature detection would be the death of us all. I mean to keep my head and to seize the crown." The councilor's voice dropped to a deadly hiss. "*Never* ask for a meeting with me...unless it is of the utmost importance."

Menace hung in the air.

Danly stared at the man, trapped between rage and fear. A bead of sweat formed on his brow.

The black-cloaked leader leaned back in his seat, his voice changing like quicksilver. "So, my prince, why did you ask to speak to me?"

Released from fear, Danly was swamped by anger. He narrowed his eyes and glared at the counselor. The man should pay for threatening his future king.

"Come, my prince, we have limited time and important matters to discuss." The man's voice was suddenly congenial.

The prince flung his words at the counselor. "Days pass and I see no evidence of change. Words whispered in secret will not win the throne. I need to know the Red Horns will take action and that the throne will soon be mine."

"For the safety of us all, we must work in the shadows until the time is right. The fact that you have not noticed our work merely means our precautions have been successful, but rest assured, the work does go on. Each day brings you one step closer to the Rose Throne."

The carriage swayed with a rocking motion, leather creaking against wood, marking the leagues. Danly stared at the Red Horn, nursing his anger.

The councilor leaned forward, his voice smooth and conciliatory. "Perhaps you would be more patient if you had a better understanding of our plans. The Red Horns are mounting a two-pronged attack on the queen. The first prong involves the army. Key army officers are being seduced to your cause. We do not yet have the numbers, but our ranks grow on a daily basis. The queen unknowingly aids our efforts by favoring the constable force. Many officers are disillusioned with her lack of leadership. Others chaff under the rule of a woman, yearning for a king. For the rest, there is always gold. All men have their price; it is simply a matter of finding it." Pausing, the councilor added, "The second prong of the plan is designed to discredit the queen in the eyes of her subjects. Only a handful of people are involved in this plot and secrecy is paramount." Spreading his hands wide in a gesture of openness, the leader said, "I hope this gives you some reassurance. Members of the Red Horns risk their lives on a daily basis to place the crown upon your head."

"But when will you strike? When will the crown be mine?"

The leader mused, "The queen is distracted by the rumblings of the Flame God. If the situation in Coronth boils over, the added chaos will present the perfect time to spring our trap. In any case, I will arrange to meet with you when the time is right. You must be prepared to take your rightful place on the Rose Throne. The people of Lanverness will need to see that they have a lawful king as a ruler instead of a corrupt queen."

Danly drank in his words, dreaming of the glorious day when he would ascend to the Rose Throne. Imagining it in his mind, he suddenly remembered an important detail. "And what fate awaits my royal mother and her first born son?"

"That will depend on the will of the king."

It was the answer Danly most wanted to hear. A satisfied smile spread across his face.

The clopping of the horses' hooves became muted as the carriage left the city's cobblestone streets for the dirt lanes of the country. The queen's councilor leaned forward, "Time grows short, yet there is one other thing that we need to discuss. The queen's shadowmen are becoming annoying. Like hounds they cast for the scent, but at times they circle too near the true plot." Pausing, he added, "When the huntsman's hounds are baying, sometimes it is best to give them a fox. The queen's men are looking for a traitor, so we shall give them one."

Intrigued, the prince asked, "Whose head will you sacrifice?"

"You may not know this, my prince, but Lord Bradshaw once competed against your father for the hand of the queen. When the king had his untimely hunting accident, whispers blamed Lord Bradshaw, claiming he'd arranged the king's death so that the queen would be free to marry another. It was never proven, but it would not take much to rekindle the fires of suspicion. When the queen's shadowmen catch the scent of a traitor, the trail will lead to Lord Bradshaw while the Red Horns are free to finish their work."

Danly could not imagine the queen ever accepting the courtship of the gray-haired, pot-bellied lord. The thought sickened him. It was yet more proof of how depraved and unnatural his royal mother was. "How will you do it?"

"By dropping hints and clues that the Lord Bradshaw intends to take by force what he could not take by marriage. It will be a pleasure to watch the queen's shadowmen chase themselves into circles."

The prince liked the imagery but he doubted that the queen's shadowmen would be fooled for long. "But surely you don't expect the ruse to work for long."

"The plot is all smoke and mirrors, but it will gain us time."

"Plots within plots." Danly smiled, knowing it was precisely the type of convoluted game required to defeat the Spider Queen.

Before more could be said, the carriage pulled to an abrupt stop. Easing back into the far corner, the councilor whispered, "Remember, the queen's shadowmen are watching. Stay late at the party and enjoy yourself. The shadowmen must be convinced you are here solely for entertainment." Pausing he added, "In the meantime, be patient my prince, you will see the Red Horns act soon enough."

As the footman opened the door, the prince stood to block the doorway. Exiting the carriage, Danly smiled, the trip to the country had been most worthwhile. He was looking forward to watching the queen's shadowmen chase false clues. In the meantime, he planned to enjoy himself. It was the least he could do to further his claim to the Rose Throne.

# 47

# Katherine

The world turned white and muted under the falling snow. More than an inch of fresh powder covered the road. Kath huddled beneath her cloak as she held her horse to a trot. How ironic that the snow waited this late to fall. If winter had started just a few weeks earlier then the knights would have had no trouble tracking the captain and she would have been spared the trials of her abduction. Then again, if the knights had rescued her, she'd never have found the crystal dagger or met the cat-eyed archer. Kath shook her head. Nothing was ever straightforward or easy, especially when the gods were involved.

She brushed the falling snow from her cloak; thankful the last week of travel had been uneventful. After leaving the wilds of Wyeth, they'd stopped at the first good inn where Kath finally had a chance to take a hot bath. Clean and warm, she took her dinner in her room and spent the night composing a long dispatch to her father while Sir Blaine stood guard outside the door. She warned the king that the Mordant had found a way to slip small bands of men through the defenses of the Octagon. She concluded the dispatch with a brief description of her escape and of the role of the cat-eyed archer. Kath asked her father to welcome the cat-eyed people to Castlegard, noting that their bows might be of value in the fight against the Mordant.

She also wrote a short note to Castlegard's master healer, explaining that the goblin-man was able to 'sniff stone' and 'track figurines from Castlegard'. She asked if the healer knew of any defenses against this type of attack, requesting that he write to her in Pellanor.

On a final sheet of parchment she wrote a long letter to her friends of the forge. In simple words she explained about her kidnapping and how their gift of the dagger hidden in her boot had been the key to her freedom. As a small token of thanks, she sent them the purse of golds she'd taken from her captors to be shared among the masters and apprentices. Gold did not come close to repaying them for their gift, but she wanted them to know how much she valued the dagger. As she finished the letter she smiled, imagining how surprised her friends would be to learn that 'the Imp' had actually killed an ogre. She longed to laugh with them and tell them about her adventures, but in her heart she knew that a difficult road lay ahead and that it would be a long time before her path took her back to Castlegard.

She sealed all three dispatches with her signet ring. The heavy gold ring bore the image of a hunting hawk, the symbol of house Anvril. There'd never been any need for her to wear the ring before, so she hadn't. How quickly everything had changed. Her father had sent her to Pellanor to turn her into a princess, but it was the journey not the destination that had changed her.

She stared at the ring's deeply etched image of a hawk attacking with talons extended. Since hearing her fortune told she'd felt like a hawk loosed from the hand of a god, but the question remained, who was her prey? Perhaps she was meant to circle on the wind till the prey broke from cover, waiting to strike for the kill. She slept that night with the ring on her finger, dreaming of hawks and gargoyles, but if there was any message in her dream she could not decipher it.

The next morning she discovered she was not the only one writing dispatches to the king. Captain Tellor had written his own missive about the events of the past fortnight. Kath wondered how the taciturn captain had described the abduction and escape, but the captain was closed-mouthed and kept his own council. Kath just hoped her father would listen to her advice despite the fact that it came from a daughter instead of one of his many sons.

After breakfast, the dispatches, the letters, and the purse of golds were placed in a special saddlebag marked with the seal of the Octagon. Sir Kirk and the junior squire, Todd, took the dispatches north, making haste for Castlegard.

Kath and the rest of the knights followed the road west to Lanverness. With each passing league, the isolated inns gave way to small villages and towns of ever increasing frequency and size. Prosperity covered Lanverness like a warm cloak, from the smiles on the faces of the people, to the stylish cut of their clothes, to the well-kept houses and towns. Markets overflowed with an abundance of goods and the people seemed cheerful and content. From snippets of conversations, Kath learned that the common people held their queen in high regard. Evidence of the prosperity deepened with every league of travel. Kath began to understand why her father had sent her to Pellanor. Queen Liandra was clearly a capable ruler with uncommon abilities for a woman.

As they neared the capital, Kath pestered Sir Tyrone for every scrap of gossip he'd ever heard about the queen. "So how did a queen come to rule alone?"

Sir Tyrone warmed to the telling, helping to ease the boredom of the long ride. "The old king had only one child, one daughter, so there was no choice. The nobles rebelled but King Leonid won the fight, insisting his only daughter take the throne. As a concession, the nobles competed for the hand of the young queen. Forsaking his own name, one of the lords married the queen and became the prince-consort but he died in a hunting accident shortly after the birth of the second prince. Rumors ran rampant after his death, but nothing was ever proven and the accident faded into the past. Since that day, the queen has ruled alone, never remarrying. The kingdom prospers and the common people flourish despite the fact that a woman sits alone on the Rose Throne."

Riding on Kath's left, Sir Blaine asked, "What did the rumors say about the prince-consort's death? Was it truly an accident?"

The black knight shrugged. "Who can say? The Rose Court is steeped in intrigue. Behind her back, the courtiers name her the Spider Queen. They say the queen uses a cadre of spies to spin tangled webs of intrigue. It's said that no one ever beats the queen at the game of politics."

"Politics!" Sir Blaine snorted in disgust. "The royal court is a game of daggers not swords. We are riding in the wrong direction."

Kath privately agreed, but instead she asked, "What else do the rumors say?"

"They say the queen has a rare gift for multiplying golds. Lanverness has never been as rich as under her stewardship. The queen's ability to multiply golds is so prodigious some whisper at the use of magic, or worse, a pact with the Dark Lord."

Shocked, Kath gaped at the black knight. "Not the Dark Lord!"

Sir Tyrone laughed. "You asked for rumors!"

"But surely you don't believe it?"

The black knight gestured toward the countryside. "Look around you. The true test of a ruler is in the prosperity and happiness of the people." With a wry smile, he added, "Remember, my Lady, there is always someone in the background eager to sling mud at those who succeed, especially if the person who succeeds is different." Pausing he added, "Look at the people and judge for yourself if the rumors are true."

Kath took the knight's advice to heart, studying the land and the people as they rode toward the queen's capital city. Signs of peace and prosperity were everywhere, from the plentiful food in the market places, to the well-ordered towns, to the people's ready smiles. The farther she rode into Lanverness, the more daunting the prospect of meeting the queen became. Kath's world was full of swords and castles, she knew next to nothing about golds and even less about politics. She wondered how she'd fare in the queen's court. Surely her sword was needed elsewhere. Lost in thought, Kath was surprised when the horses topped a hill and they gained their first look at the capital city.

'Sprawling' was the first word that came to mind. Cobblestone streets lined with buildings of brick and stone sprawled in every direction. Gazing at the stone maze, Kath realized she'd never seen a true city before. The scale was overwhelming. At the heart of the sprawl, Castle Tandroth crouched like a stone spider guarding a web of cobblestone streets. The enormous structure was a haphazard mixture of military castle, fairy tale architecture, and luxury palace. In Kath's opinion, the structure did not deserve the title of 'castle', especially since the city started at the very base of the castle walls, negating much of their defensive value. Studying the capital with military eyes, Kath was quick to conclude that neither the city nor the castle would be defensible against a large force. The queen had best hope that war never visited her capital.

Kath urged her horse to a canter, eager to explore the great city. Faces stared as they passed, most full of smiles and curiosity. Kath had hoped to enter the city unnoticed, but they soon had a following of ragtag children. Silver surcoats, maroon cloaks, and the octagon emblazoned on the knights' shields drew the children like bees to honey. Once they spied Sir Blaine's blue steel blade, there was no turning them away. Resigning herself to the escort, Kath flipped a gold coin to the oldest child and asked him to lead the way to a good inn near the castle. Captain Tellor protested, saying they should ride straight for the castle, but Kath pulled rank on him again, insisting they take rooms at the inn. The captain scowled but Kath ignored him. She needed at least a day to purchase better clothes. She couldn't appear before the mighty ruler of Lanverness dressed in her scruffy squire's clothing.

The lad led them to a well-appointed inn within the very shadow of the castle. The innkeeper, a well-groomed man with a moon-shaped face, fawned over the knights, but he barely spared a glance for Kath.

Overlooked and ignored, Kath stood in the background, shocked at how quickly she'd faded to obscurity. After the battle in the meadow, the knights had treated her differently. She'd expected others to do the same. Being invisible had never hurt so much. She gripped the hilt of her sword, trying to hide her hurt beneath anger.

Captain Tellor settled with the innkeeper, giving Kath her key. She carried her saddlebag to her room. Sir Blaine followed behind to make sure her room was secure.

The inn proved better than any they'd stayed at. Spacious and well appointed, her room reflected the wealth of the city. A thick patchwork quilt covered the four-posted bed, a washbasin stood on a table, and a small mirror hung on the wall. Kath dumped the dusty saddlebag on the floor, her eyes drawn to the mirror. Perhaps the mirror held the answer to her sudden invisibility. She approached it cautiously, as if sneaking up on an enemy. Needing to know what others saw, Kath stepped in front of the mirror, taking stock of her appearance for the first time in her life. Blonde hair cascaded down her back in a wild tangle of knots. Her gray squire's garb was dusty and tattered, the bulky tunic hiding her small breasts. Her sword rode easy on her left hip, the handles of her axes protruding over her shoulders. Sea green eyes stared back at her, forcing her to see the truth. She looked like a skinny squire, scruffy but dangerous. If the innkeeper dismissed her as inconsequential, what would the queen think? Kath's dresses were lost in the wilds of Wyeth and good riddance to them, but she needed something to wear, something that would let her be herself yet not reflect poorly on Castlegard. Besides, she refused to give up her sword and her throwing axes. She was a blooded warrior and had earned the right to wear weapons. There had to be an acceptable compromise.

Desperate for advice, Kath sought out the black knight and asked for his help. To her relief he did not laugh. Instead he just nodded and took her to the street of tailors. Kath lost count of how many tailors they visited before they found one willing to work within her requirements. The tailor was young, new to the capital, and trying to make a name for himself. When he heard her requirements, he picked up a piece of charcoal and drew a series of quick sketches. He suggested long flowing capes, tight-fitting leather bodices, silk shirts with puffed sleeves, leather pants, and knee-high boots. For every day clothes he recommended huntsman's colors of gold and green combined with supple brown leathers. For court clothes, he worked with her heraldic colors of red and white, making liberal use of the hawk in flight.

To Kath's amazement, she liked the designs. They were both practical and elegant with just a touch of femininity. With the approval of Sir Tyrone, she ordered two of every design, one to be done in court colors with the second made of durable wools and leathers in huntsman's colors. She paid triple the price in order to have one set of court clothes delivered to her by the morrow. Much as she dreaded the meeting, she dared not keep the queen waiting. Kath stared in the mirror as the tailor took her measurements. She needed to understand her friends as well as her enemies. Kath wondered which she would find in the queen.

# 48

# Samson

He'd found a safe haven in Lanverness and he never wanted to leave. Billeted with the Rose Squad, Samson shared a room with a grizzled drill sergeant named Ben Obern. The sergeant looked as tough as nails, but the twenty-year veteran had a quick wit and an amiable personality. He took Samson under his wing, showing him around the soldiers' quarters, making him feel like a one of the men.

After the terror of his long trek from Coronth, Samson wanted nothing more than to be immersed in a normal life filled with orderly routines. He took comfort in the regimented drumbeat of military life, but he couldn't stop thinking about the queen's piercing gaze. In the peaceful normalcy of Lanverness, he bitterly regretted his promise to return to Coronth...but the choice was already made.

As the days passed, Samson waited in dread for a summons from the queen, but the lords of Lanverness left him alone. He supposed they were giving him a chance to recover from his ordeal. With three hearty meals a day from the soldiers' mess, he was gaining back his normal weight, but his eyes still had a haunted look that reminded him too much of Coronth. In Lanverness, he only saw those kinds of eyes when he looked in the mirror. He did his best to avoid his own gaze when shaving.

Except for answering questions from the bards, his time was his own. Samson spent his days eating and sleeping, watching the soldiers at arms practice, and visiting with his mother. His mother was given a comfortable room in a section of the castle reserved for the cooks and servants of the Rose Court. His mother's mind was still broken but she seemed comfortable in the great kitchens, enjoying the smell of fresh baked bread and the familiar bustle of busy hands preparing meals. She took to the new life as if she had been born to it. At first, the loss of the past bothered Samson, but he eventually came to see his mother's weakness of mind as a blessing. She lived entirely in the present with no painful memories. Sometimes he envied her forgetfulness.

With time on his hands, Samson became an avid spectator of normal life. He watched soldiers practicing sword drills in the courtyard, bakers kneading the morning bread in the great kitchen, and women shopping in the city markets. Observing from the shadows, he hungered for a normal life. Sometimes he wished they would let him join the guards. He'd swear whatever oath they asked, spending his days immersed in the order of military life. Or perhaps he'd become a farmer, marry a local girl and raise apples and children. His daydreams were appealing but they could not compete with the fearsome power of his nightmares.

His nightmares always started with the relentless eyes of the queen boring into his very soul. The queen had somehow bewitched him, planting a mirror in his mind from which he could not turn away. In the depths of his dreams, the mirror showed him every detail of his father's death. He watched his father beg for mercy...but none was ever given. The crowd jeered, enjoying the spectacle of a human turned into a torch. Samson tried to look away, but the gruesome execution reflected from every corner of his mind. On other nights, he saw his own face reflected in the mirror, but in these dreams he wore the red and gold tabard of the Flame. His hands clawed at the hated wool but the tabard was like a second skin, refusing to come off. The scene shifted and Samson served as one of the guards for the Test of Faith. An innocent stranger cowered in chains, awaiting the will of the Pontifax. The Pontifax gestured and the captain ordered Samson to consign the sinner to the flames. Trapped by the order, Samson drew his sword and prodded the stranger to his death. In the searing heat, the man's face melted like molten wax, reforming into the face of Samson's father.

A scream caught in his throat. He bolted awake, his heart pounding. Slick with sweat, Samson huddled on the bed praying for morning. Somehow the dawn's light always brought peace and order, banishing the fears of the dark. In the light of day, he clung to the present, dreading both the night and the road ahead.

After more than a fortnight of nightmares, he was almost relieved when they came for him. A royal guard escorted him to a council chamber. All the queen's men were waiting: the Lord Sheriff, the master bard, Lord Duncan, and Prince Justin. A polite inquiry revealed that the queen would not be joining them. Samson sagged with relief, thankful to be sparred her penetrating gaze.

The Lord Sheriff started the meeting. "The bards are close to completing their work. The public will soon hear the new ballads designed to reveal the truth of the Flame God. On the strength of these songs, my constables will begin recruiting refugees to return to Coronth."

*Return to Coronth*, the words sounded like a doom. Samson's heart thundered.

The Lord Sheriff gestured toward him. "Led by Samson, a group of refugees will be sent back to testify that innocence is no protection against the Flame God. By returning to tell their tales, we hope the common people of Coronth will open their eyes and see the evil that has taken root in their midst. Once the veil is lifted, we hope Coronth will change from within."

Samson stared at the man in shock. The truth would condemn the refugees to the Flames...but no one asked his opinion.

Spreading a map across the table, the Lord Sheriff pointed out towns and villages along the road to Balor. "Witnesses will be seeded back into villages in a rough line between Lanverness and the capital city of Balor. The returning refugees will form a chain of contacts to relay information and assist in smuggling the wives and children of condemned heretics out of the kingdom. Knowing their families are safe, we hope the men will choose to stay, swelling the ranks of those fighting from within."

Lord Duncan pointed to the capital city. "Samson, you will lead the heart of the resistance in Balor."

Samson stared, seeing his death marked on the map.

The Lord Duncan continued, "We plan to discredit the Pontifax while giving the common people a hero to rally around. We want you to do what you can to release sinners and disrupt the Test of Faith, embarrassing the Pontifax in front of his own people. By striking in many places at once, the deeds of the hero will quickly become the stuff of legends. To improve the odds, the refugees will be prepared with sword training as well as with selective methods of the shadow. With courage, golds, careful planning, and luck, we hope to topple a false religion."

The Lord Sheriff turned to Samson. "What do you think of our plan?"

Samson felt the weight of their stares, a mouse trapped in a corner. The details were impressive, but he couldn't see himself in the role of the hero. He stared at the lords; amazed they couldn't see the nightmares crowding his eyes. Feeling like a cork swept along by a raging river, Samson realized he was too far into the current to change course. Resigned to his fate, he nodded. "I will do whatever you ask."

No one heard the fear behind his words.

Samson listened as the others talked, agreeing to everything asked of him. He hoped the bards' songs would be successful in swaying other refugees to return to Coronth. Samson suspected it would be easier to be a hero in the company of others.

When the meeting ended, he bowed to the lords and then escaped from the chamber. Walking through the cold marble corridors in a daze, he was surprised when a voice called from behind.

"Wait!"

Turning, he found Prince Justin following behind. The prince flashed a ready smile. "All this planning has made me thirsty. I know a place where the ale is dark and flavorful, the serving women are fair, and the tables are far enough apart that a man can talk without being overheard by everyone in the common room. What say you?"

If Samson had any objections, they vanished in the face of the prince's irrepressible charm. With a self-conscious smile, he nodded his assent. He liked the young bard even if he was a prince.

The prince led him out of the castle into the back streets of Pellanor. Samson was soon lost, but the prince navigated the back alleyways with confidence. They stopped at a small pub tucked into a street full of cobbler shops. A weathered sign proclaimed the name as the 'Green Stag'. Samson followed the prince inside. "How did you ever find this place?"

"Always trust a bard to know the best pubs and taverns."

The pub had a warm and easy charm that instantly appealed to Samson. A great fireplace made of river stone dominated the common room, throwing off welcome heat to dispel the winter chill. A minstrel strummed a lute in the corner, blanketing the room with soft melodies. Savory smells swirled between tables filled with as many women as men.

Samson followed the prince to one of the few empty tables near the minstrel. Taking a seat, the prince said, "The Green Stag is a neighborhood pub, favored by the common folk for its lamb pies, dark ale, and quiet music. It is a pleasant place to talk and to take the edge off of a hunger or a thirst." Nodding towards the minstrel, the prince added, "And I like that the owner is happy to give the younger bards and minstrels a chance to perform. In a place like the Stag, patrons can truly hear the music and appreciate a new composition. When we're ready to perform the new songs about Coronth, this is one of the places where I'd like to start."

Before more could be said, a large busty woman materialized, draping a beefy arm around the prince's shoulder. The prince gave the redhead a wink and a smile. "Marg! The Green Stag would not be complete without your ready smile."

"How dare you show up empty-handed! My patrons have been asking for your harp." With a proprietary wink, the woman added, "You've gained quite a following. When will you be back to play?"

"I've been working on a new composition and when it's done, I promise the Green Stag will be the first pub to hear it." He gestured towards Samson. "Meanwhile I've brought a friend to sample one of your famous lamb pies."

The buxom woman gave Samson a gap-toothed smile, playfully slapping him on the back hard enough to rattle his teeth. "Friends of the bards are always welcome, the more the merrier! Besides, this one looks like he could use some fattening up." Turning back to the prince, she asked, "So what's your pleasure?"

The prince slid a pair of silver coins across the table. "Two of your famous lamb pies and a couple of dark ales to wash them down."

Her beefy hand deftly scooped the silvers. "I'll have the girls bring your order out. And don't forget to bring your harp next time." Winking, the redhead retreated to the back room. Samson watched her go, mildly shocked by her familiarity with the prince. His face must have betrayed his feelings because the prince leaned forward and said, "Relax! Marg Staghorn is the owner. She's only being friendly and looking out for business. Marg is a good sort. She knows that a popular bard will easily double the profits, so she does her best to make us feel welcome." Winking, the prince added, "I'll wager she sends the girls out with her largest tankards, half again as big as the regular customers."

Still perplexed, Samson said, "So you actually play here? For money?"

The prince laughed. "Yes, of course! I am a bard. Bards need an audience almost as much as they need music." The prince leaned back with an easy grin on his face. "When I first came to Pellanor, I made the rounds of the pubs to hear the local minstrels and to find a place to play. I eventually found my way to the Green Stag. Good meals and honest fare attract couples as well as families, which makes a much better audience than a room full of drunken men. With quiet charm and an attentive audience, the Stag is a great place to experiment with new melodies and lyrics. In a place like this, a bard can feel the people respond to the music. Fortunately, Marg is always on the lookout for new talent. Until the Coronth commission, I was playing here twice a week."

"So you play for money?"

"No one would take me seriously if played for free."

Surprised by this other side of the prince, Samson asked, "So do they know you're a prince?"

The prince leaned forward, his voice dropping to a whisper. "No, and you'd best call me Justin outside of the castle. I want to be judged on my music not my title."

A prince masquerading as a commoner, the idea shocked Samson. Before he could respond, a serving girl arrived setting a steaming meat pie in front of each of them along with enormous tankards of dark ale. The savory aroma teased Samson's hunger.

The prince said, "Dig in while they're hot. The crust is always crisp and flaky, the lamb is always tender, and the gravy is a rare treat. You'll not find better in all of Pellanor."

Samson took his first taste. The pie melted in his mouth, flaky crust and savory gravy. All thoughts of conversation fled. Later, as Samson used the last of the crust to wipe the plate clean, the prince said in a casual voice, "So tell me, what do you really think of the plans for Coronth?"

Samson choked. Reaching for his tankard, he took a long swallow. Draining the dark ale, he set the tankard back on the table, wondering if he should tell the truth. "The plans are well thought out, but it will be very dangerous." The ale gave him courage. "The Pontifax and his priests are ruthless. If a witness is caught, they'll face a gruesome death in the Flames."

The prince leaned forward. "No one is saying it won't be dangerous, but how many more will die if Coronth does not change? And what if this evil cloaked as a religion spreads to Lanverness or Navarre? Far better to stop this evil from within than to provoke a war between the three kingdoms."

Samson nodded. "The Pontifax needs to be stopped. The death of my father haunts my every dream, but..."

"Will you go back to Coronth and lead the change from within?"

Samson studied the prince, amazed by the intensity of his passion. It seemed the young royal truly cared about the fate of Coronth. Perhaps it was the ale or perhaps it was the prince's charm, but either way, Samson needed someone to talk to. With a resigned sigh, he told the truth. "The evils of Coronth haunt me every night. I'm plagued by images of what I might have done. Sooner or later, I would have stood guard in the temple square." He shook his head, fighting back the vision of his father in the flames. "I want to make a new life in Lanverness, an ordinary life, but I know I'll never find peace unless I go back." Samson took a deep breath, trying to shake his fears. "I'll go back to Coronth and I'll do my best, but I am no *hero*." Looking searchingly at the prince, he added, "I am an *ordinary* man, just a commoner, born to follow not to lead. The lords expect too much."

"Perhaps that is the very point."

Samson stared at the prince in puzzlement.

"Evil grew in Coronth because *ordinary* men went along with it. They looked away, they closed their ears, they said nothing. We need an ordinary man to convince other ordinary men to stand up and make a difference. It is the common people we hope to reach, not the nobles."

Samson stared at the prince. The explanation made more sense than anything he'd heard before. Without thinking, Samson said, "A prince with a bard's tongue is quite a formidable combination."

Startled, the prince nudged him with an elbow. "Call me Justin. Don't ruin it for me!" He waved to a serving girl and ordered another round of ales. When the fresh tankards arrived, he leaned forward and said, "There is more inside of you than you give yourself credit for. You will do well in Coronth." In a conspiring tone, he added, "And you won't be alone. I hope to join you in Balor."

The shock must have shown on his face.

The prince smiled. "Close your mouth or you'll catch flies."

Samson snapped his mouth shut, but the question poured out. "Why would *you* go to Coronth?"

In a quiet voice, the prince answered, "I am willing to go but it remains to be seen if I am able. I cannot go to Coronth without the permission of my father, the king. I am still waiting on a reply."

"But why go?"

"In the history of Navarre there has never been an heir to the throne who was also a bard. When I proposed to study the small harp, many on the council opposed my plans, arguing that music is merely a frivolous past time, but my father understood and overruled the council." With a keen gaze, the prince said, "I became a bard for three reasons: for the love of music, for the response of the audience, and to make a difference with my songs. I can study to be a bard in Wyeth, but in Coronth I can use my music to make a real difference, to help the people of Coronth as well as Navarre and Lanverness. How can I *not* go?"

Samson just stared at the prince. The prince's idealism was infectious. The plan was undeniably mad, but it was also full of a hope, and it had been a long time since Samson truly had any hope. If Prince Justin was going to Balor, then perhaps there was a chance for this mad scheme to work. Raising his tankard in salute, Samson said, "To the noble idealist and to the ordinary man. Let nothing stand in their way!"

Clinking tankards, the prince replied, "To the power of ordinary men!"

As they finished their second ale, a strange friendship formed between the refugee who once wore the tabard of the Flame God and the prince who was also a bard. Samson did not know what the future would bring, but he suspected he would be able to sleep at nights, and for now, that was more than enough.

# 49

# Liandra

The queen fingered the scroll lying on her desk. As usual her shadowmen had been quite thorough. Told to watch for a party from Castlegard, her men had shadowed the princess from the moment she reached the outskirts of the capital city. Instead of coming straight to the castle, the party took a room at one of the better inns. Having just come from the social backwaters of Castlegard, Liandra understood the girl's desire for a better wardrobe, but instead of gowns of silk she'd sought the street of tailors. Amidst the city's dazzling markets the princess limited her purchases to the practical: a new set of clothes, a shirt of fine-linked chainmail, a studded leather hauberk, a small round shield, and a tooled leather scabbard for a short sword. Nothing but leather and steel. Even the new wardrobe was shocking, made by a gentleman's tailor instead of a lady's seamstress.

Dismayed, the queen set the report aside, another girl of royal birth unaccountably drawn to the sword, such a waste. King Ursus should have sent the girl to the Rose Court years ago while there was still a chance to salvage her. What was Ursus thinking to have waited for so long? Perhaps the man had simply been bashed in the head one too many times. Liandra had long suspected that all that bashing of swords against helmets only served to addle men's brains. Kings were no exception to the malady. With a sigh, the queen resolved to meet the girl before passing judgment. There was no use worrying about the past when it was the future that mattered.

A page knocked lightly on the door, indicating that her guest had arrived. Placing the scroll in a drawer, the queen took a seat in front of the fireplace. Privacy would give her a better chance to plumb the depths of this princess who chose to carry a sword.

A cheerful blaze crackled in the hearth with two chairs set before the fire. The queen artfully arranged the folds of her silk gown. Satisfied,

Liandra signaled the page and the Master Archivist escorted the princess into the room. With a bow, the master said, "Your majesty, may I present Princess Katherine of Castlegard."

Waving a dismissal to the men, the queen's gaze never left her guest. The door to the solar clicked shut. The queen and the princess were alone.

A believer in first impressions, the queen was always curious to see what aspect of a person's appearance or manner dominated the first meeting. For most it was their clothes, or their hair, or the expression on their face, but with the princess the dominant feature was her bearing. Her stride rang with pride and determination as she followed the master into the solar. Standing alone, exposed to a queen's scrutiny, the girl held herself upright and erect with a clear and open gaze, her hand casually resting on her empty scabbard, as if she missed the hilt of a sword. The princess projected a presence that belied her age. Clearly this was not the confused young girl that Ursus described in his letter. Instead, the queen found a young woman who understood herself and was confident in her choices. By the queen's standards, her choices were painfully misguided, but nevertheless, there was a depth to this young woman that Liandra found intriguing. Based on her first impression, the queen decided the interview would be well worth her time. "Welcome to the Rose Court."

As the queen expected, the princess made a half bow instead of a curtsey. "Thank you for the welcome. I am pleased to meet the queen who rules so well from a single throne."

The queen allowed a small smile of approval. Deciding to test the young woman's mettle, Liandra deliberately followed the greeting with silence. Knowing that few people are truly comfortable with silence, she often used it as a tool to test her guests. In Liandra's experience, the person with the least power always spoke first, the brevity of the silence defining the insecurities of the petitioner. She wondered how many minutes of quiet the princess could endure.

The silence also served another purpose, giving the queen the luxury to observe her guest. Long blond hair framed an oval face with well-defined cheekbones and a cute nose. The princess would have been merely pretty in an ordinary way were it not for her eyes. Striking sea-green eyes gave the illusion of layered depths. They were eyes other women would be jealous of and men would drown in. A pity the princess's heraldic colors of red and white did nothing to bring out her eye color. In the right gown, the young woman would be striking if not beautiful. Instead, the princess wore clothes that screamed of her choice to carry a sword. White leather pants tucked into knee-high doeskin boots and a white silk shirt set off by a red leather bodice laced tight to conform to the shape of young breasts. A white cape flowed from her shoulders and an empty red scabbard rode comfortably at her hip. The queen did not approve of the young woman's choices but at least the tailor had found a way to add a touch of style and femininity to her clothing. Perhaps all was not lost.

The logs in the fire crackled, the only sound in the room.

Finished with her inspection, the queen was mildly surprised the silence had lasted so long. It took a great deal of poise for a young person to withstand such a long stretch of quiet. Wondering how she'd gained such confidence, the queen peered into her eyes. As if acknowledging the game, the princess nodded and smiled. Amused, the queen decided to make an exception by breaking her own rule. "We are forgetting ourselves, please be seated. We have much to discuss."

The queen waited till the princess was settled. "You were late in coming to Pellanor. We trust that there were no problems on the road?"

Nodding as if she expected the question, the princess replied in a measured voice, "The journey proved longer and more difficult than expected. Henchmen of the Mordant tracked us from the Isle of Souls to a remote wayhouse in Wyeth. In the depths of the night they abducted me, taking me into the wilds of the forest." She shrugged as if the incident did not merit further discussion. "It took a few days before I was re-united with my escort."

Reading between the lines, the queen suspected that somewhere in the experience the princess had earned the right to wear a sword. Her survival did much to explain the young woman's unexpected poise. Liandra was curious to learn more but her first priority was the protection of her people. "The south has long been free of the Mordant's shadow. Are you sure these men served the Mordant?"

"The men are dead, but their leader wore a medallion inscribed with a pentacle. I've sent a dispatch to Castlegard warning the king."

A sudden chill descended on the room. The warmth of the fire did little to dispel the cold. Shadows seemed to lengthen as if reaching for the two women. "There is more you should hear." The girl's voice was grave. "There were only four in the band, but they were a strange lot. One was a twisted dwarf and the other a type of ogre. Over seven-foot tall with long dangling arms and a misshapen forehead, the captain named the ogre a Taal. He said the Mordant breeds Taals in a place fouled with magic, a place left over from the War of the Wizards."

The tale sounded like something a drunken bard might concoct to frighten small children, but coming from this strange young woman, the queen believed every word. She fingered her pearls, pondering the details. "We trust the Octagon Knights to be the sword and the shield of the southern kingdoms. Still, a warning should never be wasted. We would ask you to meet with our councilors so that they might hear your tale directly. Those who guard Lanverness must be warned."

"I will aid Lanverness in any way possible."

Pleased with the answer, the queen leaned back in her chair. The warning of the Mordant was important, but it was time to shift the conversation in a different direction. "We have behaved as princes should, speaking first of the safety of the realm, but there are other matters, private matters, that should be discussed." With a deliberate pause, the queen added, "The afternoon is young but we feel a glass of wine is in order. Would you join us in a glass of red?"

The request clearly caught the young woman off guard. Puzzled, the princess gave a slight nod of her head.

The queen rang a small bell. A servant appeared, bowing low. "We will have a glass of wine, the red claret will do nicely and the fire needs to be stoked. And see that the lamps are lit, there are too many shadows in this room."

A bustle of servants descended on the chamber. Fresh logs and a satchel of aromatic herbs were added to the hearth bringing light, heat, and the sweet scent of sage. Lamps were lit, dispelling the odd shadows. A liveried servant offered glasses of red wine served in delicate goblets. Once the wine was accepted the servants vanished and the two royal women were left to the comfort of the solar.

Despite their differences, they sat in a thoughtful silence, soaking up the heat of the fire and slowly sipping the wine. When the princess's glass was two thirds empty, the queen said, "Your father, King Ursus, has asked that you foster at our court. We are pleased to welcome you, but we wonder what your wishes are in this matter?"

The princess stared into the fireplace. The queen waited, giving her time. After a while, the princess said, "If truth be told, my father ordered me to Lanverness. I did not wish to leave Castlegard, but having left, it seems the journey was meant to be." Meeting the queen's gaze, the princess added, "I have chosen the way of the sword, yet, I am impressed that a woman rules such a rich kingdom from a single throne. Perhaps the gods sent me here for a reason. Perhaps there is something here I am meant to learn?"

Her answer rang with honesty. It was the type of honesty the queen did not often hear at court. Perhaps the princess could be nurtured into something more than a sword. "Born and raised in Castlegard, it is not surprising you chose the sword. The sword would have been the only type of power ever shown to you...but swords are the power of men. Men are born with might and so they almost always seek to rule by strength, it is their heritage and their natural advantage...but there are better ways to rule." Lowering her voice, the queen said, "Women rule by intellect, by the allure of our sex, and by the compelling power of gold. In the long run, these three will always trump the sword." Noting the stubborn skepticism on the young woman's face, the queen asked, "Who is more powerful, the king of Castlegard with all of his knights, or the queen of Lanverness with all of her gold?"

The crackling of the fireplace was her only answer. The queen let the silence lengthen and then said, "Do you have a purse of coins?"

Puzzled, the princess nodded.

"Empty your purse on the table and look for the answer among the coins."

Confused, the princess nevertheless complied. Up ending her purse, she poured a shower of coins across the tabletop. The two women peered at the coins as if studying the cards of a fortuneteller. It took the queen only a moment to read the answer but the princess examined each coin as if seeing it for the first time. Looking up from the coins, the princess said, "My father gave me this purse. There are several coins from Radagar and a few bear the many-headed hydra of the Delta, but almost all the coins bear two roses on one side and the likeness of the queen of Lanverness on the other."

The queen smiled. "Most kingdoms do not even mint coins, relying instead on the wealth and coinage of the Rose Court." Plucking a gold coin from the tabletop, she held it aloft. "Lanverness sets the pace for the creation of wealth in Erdhe. The other kingdoms do their best to follow." Offering the coin to the princess, she said, "This is power...a power far greater than any sword."

The young woman fingered the coin. "The wealth and power of Lanverness is undeniable. Your people are content and prosper under your rule. There is power in gold...but honor resides in the steel of swords, the honor of risking your life in battle in order to make a difference." She shook her head. "Few battles can be won with gold. I respect the power of gold but I *choose* the honor of swords." Staring into the blazing fire, the princess added in a quiet voice, "Somehow, I am meant to serve the Light with my sword."

The queen hated to see such honesty wasted on a sword. The young rarely heeded advice, yet Liandra gave it anyway. "You choose a dangerous path. Men will band together to crush any woman who dares to compete on their terms. To carve a place in this world, a woman must be oblique. Beauty, guile, and golds are the subtle weapons of the fair sex."

"They are your weapons, not mine. I choose the sword."

The queen was not surprised. Leaning back in her chair, she watched the play of firelight across the young woman's face. Intelligence, strength of character, and a strong streak of stubbornness shown from the girl's face, a potent mix. The princess was an open scroll, easy to read. "What gives you this conviction that you are meant to serve the Light with your sword?"

The princess sat in silence, gazing into the fireplace. As the silence lengthened, the queen had the sudden insight that the girl had never had a woman to confide in, let alone one of power. Fingering the strand of pearls at her neck, she waited, curious to see if the princess would trust enough to reply.

A loud snap of the fire brought the princess back to the solar. In a distant voice, she said, "We came to Lanverness by way of the Isle of Souls. Intrigued by the idea of seeing the future, I had my fortune told by a tarot card reader. The mystic said things she could never have known, but the really disturbing part came at the end. Instead of a woman's voice, there was a deep masculine rasp. The voice said that I was an 'old soul' and that I was meant to serve the Light with my sword. I believe it was the voice of the warrior god, Valin." Her voice held a note of defiance, as if expecting disbelief. "One of the knights heard the voice as well. His sword is now sworn to my service."

The queen stilled her face to mask her surprise. Talking with this young woman was like peeling back the layers of an onion, each layer revealing a deeper truth. Liandra had not expected the young woman to be among the god-touched. It did much to explain the depth of her convictions. It explained other things as well.

"Your majesty, do you believe in the gods?"

In an audience chamber, the queen would have given a political answer. In the privacy of her solar, Liandra felt the young woman both deserved and needed the truth. "We have never heard the voice of the gods and we have never witnessed a miracle. If the Lords of Light take a direct hand in the world, then they are careful to hide their efforts under the cloaks of nature and chance. Who is to say what is the will of the gods and what is merely happenstance? Yet evil clearly walks the world. The Dark Lord is quick to make his presence felt. If the Lords of Light do not exist, then what chance do mere mortals have? If you believe in the future of mankind then you must also believe in the Lords of Light."

"Do you believe I've heard the voice of the gods?"

"We believe that you are telling the truth. Perhaps that is enough for now." Feeling the need to bring this discussion to a close, the queen said, "You are welcome to stay in the Rose Court for as long as you like. We hope your stay with us will be worthwhile. If you find that Valin calls you elsewhere, then you have our leave to go."

Surprise and gratitude danced across the young woman's face. "Thank you for your wisdom and your understanding. There is clearly much to learn in the Rose Court."

Rising from the chair to mark the end of the audience, the queen said, "Return to the inn and gather your belongings. A place has been made for you and your escort in Castle Tandroth. Seek out the steward and he will see to it that you are settled in a wing of the palace. If you need anything, you have only to ask." Pausing, the queen added, "We have ordered the steward to put you in the same wing of the palace as the delegation from Navarre. Princess Jemma is also fostering in our court. We suggest you seek her out."

"As you wish." The princess added, "And thank you for your wisdom. You have given me much to think about."

With an answering smile, the queen said, "We will be sure to talk again soon. In the mean time, be welcome in the Rose Court."

Bowing, the princess took her leave.

The queen studied the flames dancing in the fireplace while finishing her glass of wine. There was much more to this warrior princess than met the eye. Liandra had not expected the girl to be among the god-touched. The gods played a convoluted game of chess, with little regard for the mortal pieces that littered the board. She pitied the young woman. The life of those touched by the gods tended to be one of struggle and pain. The gods played for higher stakes than the happiness of mere individuals. Catching a sudden chill, Liandra leaned forward to better feel the heat. Staring into the flames, she resolved to do her best to aid the princess of Castlegard. Dark times crowded the horizon and the queen suspected there were not nearly enough warriors of the Light for the battles that lay ahead.

# 50

# Katherine

Kath sat bolt upright in bed, her heart racing and her nightshirt
sodden with sweat. Her gaze darted warily around the strange
room. Her right hand searched the blankets for the hilt of her
sword while her left checked to make sure her gargoyle was still around
her neck. The gargoyle was where it belonged and her right hand found
the sword. Drawing the sword from the sheath, she dared the shifting
shadows to advance on the bed. With steel in her hand, her heartbeat
stilled and she remembered everything. With a weary sigh, Kath sank
back on the pillows, keeping a tight hold on the sword. The nightmares
had returned. She'd almost forgotten about them. They'd been strangely
absent on the long trip from Castlegard. Now that she was safe behind
castle walls, the nightmares plagued her again.

What amazed her most about the dreams was how real they seemed.
They always started the same way, running blindly through the stone
hallways of a castle, desperately searching for a weapon or an ally, deadly
enemies following behind. The castle was always deserted. The doors
either locked or they opened onto barren rooms that became deadly traps.
No matter how fast she ran, the race always ended with Kath trapped in a
blind hallway, her back pressed against cold hard stone, waiting for the
killing blow. But instead of death, she always found herself falling
backwards through the solid stone wall...waking abruptly in the safety of
her bed.

Kath wiped the sweat from her brow and released her grip on the
sword. The escapes from her dreams were always too close for comfort.
Thoroughly exhausted, she gave up on sleep, preferring to rise rather than
face death in her dreams again. Maybe if she understood the message
then the nightmares would stop. But whatever the message, it eluded
Kath.

Unwilling to risk further nightmares, she threw off the covers and got dressed. As the pale light of morning crept through the window, she buckled her sword belt around her waist and made sure the dagger was secure in her right boot. She reached for her twin throwing axes and shrugged the harness onto her back, knowing it was more weapons than she needed within the queen's castle but after her abduction she didn't feel safe without them. Armed for any surprise, she quietly opened the door to the common sitting room. With Lanverness soldiers stationed at the outer door, there was no need for the knights to stand guard. At least the knights were getting their sleep even if she wasn't.

Passing the closed doors to the other bedrooms, Kath crossed the sitting room and quietly opened the outer door to the main corridor. Two guards snapped to attention. Saluting the guards, she slipped into the empty corridor. At such an early hour, the castle hallways were nearly deserted.

Turning right, she headed for the parapet door. Castle Tandroth was a confusing maze of corridors, but Kath had been pleased to discover that her quarters had easy access to an outer parapet. After the nightmares, a walk in the fresh air always helped ease her mind. Opening the iron-studded door, she stepped out into the bracing cold of the winter morning.

A stiff wind carried a hint of snow. Brush strokes of pinks and golds painted the cloud-laden sky. Pulling her cloak close, Kath walked along the parapet gazing out at the city below. The view was impressive but her mind was elsewhere. Lost in the pattern of her dreams, she sought to solve the riddle of her gargoyle. If she could unlock the magic then she'd have another weapon to use against the Dark Lord. Her dreams were repetitive and frighteningly realistic, but the message was too cryptic for Kath to interpret.

Lost in the details, she was surprised by a flicker of movement. Easing her hand toward her sword, she turned to catch a glimpse of a tall dark man with broad shoulders. A shiver ran down her spine and a thousand wings beat within her mind. The world shifted as if she'd stepped through a hidden door. For a heartbeat, her mind was drawn to the broken tower lost in the forests of Wyeth. Time shifted and she found herself standing in the tower of the eight-pointed star, whole and unbroken and at the height of its power. She wore silver armor and a great sword hung at her side. A knight descended the spiral staircase of swords and came toward her. Tall and dark, she knew his face better than she knew her own. As he drew closer, her vision suddenly blurred. The wings came rushing back, beating against her. She fought to stay in the past, but she was forced back through the door of her mind. The door slammed shut and the world blurred. A sigh escaped her for all that was lost.

Staggering, Kath tried to get her bearings. Warm hands grasped her firmly around the waist, effortlessly supporting her. Through a haze, she heard a masculine voice say, "Are you all right?"

Regaining her balance, she looked up into a ruggedly handsome face framed by raven hair and marked by a black leather patch across the left eye. Without thinking, she murmured, "Is it you?"

The air stilled, and she could have sworn he whispered back, "Yes."

The moment passed and she caught her balance. The man released her, letting her stand on her own. Kath instantly missed his hands at her waist.

He stepped back giving her space, space she didn't really want. Peering into her eyes, he said, "I thought you were going to fall."

"Thank you, I'm all right now."

"Perhaps you best go back inside. A slip on the parapet could be dangerous."

"Yes, perhaps you're right." Lost in a daze, Kath turned and walked back toward the ironbound door. Confused by the encounter, it wasn't until she reached the warmth of her room that she realized she did not even know his name.

# 51

# Liandra

Servants fluttered around the small table, lighting candles and filling goblets. As was her habit, the queen limited her afternoon meal to a large bowl of clear broth. Slivers of shaved mushrooms and thinly sliced scallions floated in the savory broth. Although it looked like little more than water, the cooks of Tandroth Castle had perfected the recipe. Ever conscious of her image, the queen guarded her hourglass figure. Her petite elegance was one of the features that allowed her to easily captivate men. Liandra had no intention of relinquishing that power to age or the luxuries of the Rose Court.

Abstemious in her own eating habits, the queen indulged her guests. The richness of her table was famous throughout Erdhe, another form of image. Tempting smells of lake trout cooked in melted butter and lemon grass swirled through the chamber. As the servants presented each course, the queen studied her guest, pleased with the transformation. Princess Jemma had taken her advice, commissioning a new wardrobe. Instead of the old-fashioned, provincial gowns from Navarre, the dark-haired beauty now wore elegant styles that accentuated her petite figure and lustrous hair.

The queen could not help but smile. Underneath that petite beauty, she'd discovered a cool and calculating mind capable of keeping pace with the queen's own speed of thought. Liandra had fostered the offspring of many royal houses, but this was the first time she hosted a protégé. The queen took delight in talking with a young woman who could actually appreciate the subtleties of power and the shrewd, convoluted ways of multiplying golds. Liandra made a point of having lunch with Princess Jemma at least once a week. She justified the time by daring to assume she was grooming a future daughter-in-law. From what she had seen so far, Princess Jemma had the potential to be a worthy successor to the

Rose Court. Of course the young woman would have to prove her worth before a match could be made with her royal son. The queen had just the right set of challenges to test the young woman's abilities.

Dismissing the servants, the queen opened the conversation. "When you first came to the Rose Court, you said you wanted to learn how to grow and maintain the riches of a kingdom. Does this still interest you?"

"Now more than ever. I've already learned much by watching your court. The kingdom of Navarre would benefit from adopting some of your practices."

The words sounded like flattery, but the queen suspected the princess was sincere. Nevertheless, she set the girl a test. "If you returned to Navarre tomorrow, what one idea or practice from the Rose Court would you recommend to King Ivor?"

There was no hesitation in her reply. "I'm impressed by the way you use the commoners' audiences. The audiences let you test the pulse of the people, removing the interfering layers of courtiers that usually surround a monarch. A monarch must always keep in touch with her people, but you also use the audiences to identify new business opportunities. By encouraging merchants to open new trade routes or craftsmen to bring their skills to Lanverness, you grow the prosperity of the kingdom while also ensuring a steady stream of golds for the royal purse." Pausing to taste the trout, the princess added, "If I had to recommend one idea to the king, it would be to adopt the practice of holding regular commoners' audiences. But to gain the most benefit from the audiences, the king or one of his counselors must have an eye for business." Meeting the queen's stare, the princess said, "It is that eye for business that I hope to learn from you. The power to multiply golds is what I truly hope to bring back to Navarre."

The queen hid her pleasure by taking a sip of her soup. Many of her counselors did not understand the commoners' audience the way that this young woman did. Impressed, she said, "The best way to learn is by doing."

The princess waited, her attention focused on the queen.

"You have been in Pellanor long enough to observe the day-to-day workings of the Rose Court. If you wish to learn how to multiply golds, then we suggest you choose an established business in Pellanor, study it, and then come back and present the crown with ideas to grow the business. Does this idea appeal to you?"

"It sounds like the perfect opportunity to learn."

Pleased that the princess was so quick to accept the challenge, the queen said, "You may take your time to select a business that interests you, but once selected, we expect you to see it through to the end. Do you agree?"

Fingering the wine goblet, Princess Jemma replied, "I already know which business I would like to study."

Surprised by the certainty in the young woman's voice, the queen inquired, "What business would you choose?"

"My brother, James, is spending his Wayfaring in Tubor learning the art of the vintner. An avid farmer, James believes that Navarre has the right soil and weather to grow grapes, especially in the coastal hills around Seaside. I am sure my brother will learn everything there is to know about growing grapes and making wine, but I doubt he will learn how to turn wine into golds. If I could learn the business, then together we might bring a new prosperity to the kingdom of Navarre."

The reasoning behind the choice was interesting, revealing a rare combination of pragmatism and idealism that appealed to the queen. "We are pleased by your choice. The wineries of Lanverness are modest compared to those of Tubor or even Radagar, but perhaps they could be improved. We will follow your work with great interest. How will you begin?"

A slight blush crept across the princess's cheeks. "To be honest, I do not know." Pausing, she added, "I've never done anything like this before."

Amused by the young woman's refreshing candor, the queen allowed herself a polite laugh. Seeing a puzzled look on the princess's face, the queen explained, "A monarch is ever surrounded by counselors, courtiers, advisors, and generals. If you ever wear a crown you'll soon discover that the royal court is much like the rutting of stags; the great beasts competing with their antlers to obtain dominance and influence. In such an arena, you will never hear the words 'I do not know' spoken within proximity of your throne. Allow us the small pleasure of talking with someone who is not afraid to say the words. After all, it is these simple words that allow a person to learn." The queen paused to take a small sip of wine. She could tell that her young protégé did not quite know what to make of her last statements. Relieving her of the need to reply, the queen said, "As to how to begin, we suggest you talk to those who already work in the business: from the farmers, to the vintners, to owners of the pubs, and even to the nobles who consider themselves experts in matters of wine. As you learn about the business, patterns will emerge. These patterns are the key to multiplying golds."

The princess looked doubtful. "Forgive me your majesty, but I don't understand what you mean by a pattern."

"*That* is precisely why you must learn by doing. It sounds simple, but few have the gift to see the patterns. Talk to the people involved in the making and selling of wine and we'll discuss your findings. Together we will see if the gods have graced you with gift of multiplying golds."

The princess turned back to her meal, a thoughtful expression on her face. The queen let her protégé eat as she finished her own bowl of broth. A companionable silence settled between the two women. Liandra was surprised by how much she enjoyed her meals with the young princess. In her mind, she considered the princess a worthy daughter-in-law, in her heart, she felt as if the daughter who hadn't lived had been given back to her.

# 52

# Steffan

Like flies to carrion, petitioners and supplicants began arriving in ones and twos at the gates of the Residence. Drawn by the absolute power of Coronth's religious dictator, they sought to offer their services in exchange for crumbs of wealth. At first, the Pontifax granted them an audience, but the Enlightened One soon tired of the game. Hearing the Pontifax complain, the Lord Raven offered to shoulder the burden. Steffan knew there was always a chance of finding a skill or talent that could deepen his stranglehold on the cult of the Flame.

Sitting on a gilded chair at the left hand of an empty throne, Steffan received petitioners in the small but opulent audience chamber of the Residence. With vaulted ceilings and an abundance of gold leaf, the architecture served to intimidate the petitioners, separating the meek from the bold. Bowing their way across the marble floor, the bravos, alchemists, scholars, mercenaries, fortunetellers and hedge witches came forward one at a time to profess their skills. Steffan listened to their arguments and watched their demonstrations, bored by the endless stream of charlatans, mummers, and frauds. The procession of wastrels proved the old adage; like truly attracted like. He thought of the supplicants as 'flocks of parasites'. The arrival of the parasites proved that the power of the Flame God was waxing, even beyond the borders of Coronth.

Most of the supplicants were frauds, but there was still a chance he could make use of their talents, after all, the business of growing a religion was all about seducing the emotions and fears of the common people and who better to do that than a troupe of mummers and con men. Sifting through the supplicants, he managed to find a few that could be of use.

One that stood out was the giant, Olaff. Seven-foot tall with a bald head and a bushy black beard, the giant presented Steffan with a small scroll. The scroll explained that his name was Olaff and that he sought service as a bodyguard. Olaff started his demonstration by opening his mouth to show off the stump of an amputated tongue. Steffan had heard rumors that noblemen of Ur excised the tongues of their guards but he'd never seen proof of the practice. Intrigued, he gestured for the giant to continue.

Taking up an inch-thick iron bar, the giant easily bent it into a v-shape. He next drew a scimitar and proceeded to cleave imaginary opponents with vicious strokes of the curved sword. Impressed, Steffan offered Olaff a position as his personal guard and doorman for his manor house, tossing a purse to the giant to seal the bargain. From the widening of the man's eyes, it was clear the offer far exceeded the giant's hopes. Deliberately generous with his golds, Steffan put his trust in the avarice of his servants, providing wages that far exceeded potential bribes from other masters. As a dedicate of the Dark Lord, he valued obedience over loyalty. Loyalty, after all, was really only a matter of price. He'd never been disappointed by overpaying and he expected the results to be the same with his new guard.

The other find was the pyromancer, Alan Jellikan. A tall, skinny, rat-faced man dressed in outlandish robes of purple, Jellikan claimed to be a failed alchemist who'd unlocked the mysteries of fire. Carrying a small brazier to the foot of the dais, he used a flint to strike a modest blaze in the stacked charcoals. "Fire is a magical element, controlled by the arcane." Muttering incantations and waving his arms, he flung handfuls of powders and splashes of liquids into the brazier. "A flame becomes a bonfire!" Flames belched toward the ceiling, expelling a fierce heat. "Heat becomes color!" Another handful of powder and the fire spat sparks in a rainbow of colors. "Color becomes scent!" Jellikan flung more ingredients into the flames. A pillar of smoke evoked the pine scent of a mountain forest followed by the noxious brimstone of hell.

Servants at the far end of the hall muttered exclamations of awe.

Steffan smiled at the intrusion, more proof the pyromancer had possibilities. His outlandish dress and clumsy arm waving screamed of fraud, but the man had a true gift for manipulating fire. His gift could be of great value, but only if his nature proved compatible with the religion of the Flame. A test of character was in order. The Lord Raven invited the pyromancer to join him for breakfast the following morning. Clearly overawed by the invitation, the pyromancer almost tripped and spilled the brazier in the process of bowing his way out of the chamber.

The next morning, at the appointed hour, Olaff, resplendent in his new uniform, showed the pyromancer into the dining room of Steffan's manor house. The Lord Raven sat at the head of the table while Pip stood waiting to serve the morning meal. Exotic delicacies crowded the long table, a sumptuous feast fit for the wealthiest men of Balor. With a negligent wave Steffan invited Jellikan to join him.

The pyromancer's jaw dropped as he surveyed the feast.

Steffan stifled a smile.

Once the pyromancer was seated, Pip presented a host of dishes. His guest accepted a serving of each, but it was the outrageously expensive caviar that caught and held the pyromancer's attention. Despite a plate loaded with food, the man took three servings of caviar.

Pleased by the man's gluttony, Steffan asked, "So how did you come to be a master of fire?"

Between bites of food, Jellikan answered, "I started as an apprentice to an alchemist. The idea of converting ordinary metals into gold seemed like the easiest way to wealth. For three years I slaved under the old fool grinding powders and collecting rare elements yet in all that time I never once saw the sweet gleam of gold in the bottom of the crucible." Leaning across the table, the pyromancer helped himself to more caviar. For a skinny man he had the appetite of a starving wolf. "I never transmuted iron to gold, but along the way I noticed that certain powders caused the flames to give off beautiful colors or strong scents. Disillusioned with alchemy, I perfected my mastery of the flame. When the terms of my apprenticeship ended, I took my hoard of powders and began visiting the homes of wealthy nobles, reading their fortunes in the colors of the flames."

Steffan signaled Pip to refill the pyromancer's wine glass. "Could you do the same sort of thing in a large fire pit?"

Using a crust of bread, Jellikan scrape the last of the caviar from the bottom of the serving bowl. "I would need a lot more powder but the results should be even more spectacular."

"Could you time the effects, so the color changes were delayed for a set amount of time?"

"It could be done." Warming to the subject, he finished his goblet of wine. "The easiest way is to throw powder into the flame when you want the effect to occur. The second, more subtle way, is to construct the fire pit with layers of fuel and powder so the fire would have to burn through each layer before the flames reached the powder. It would take some experimenting to get it right, but it could be done."

Steffan came to his final question. "So what brought you to court of the Flame God?"

A cloud of fear passed across the man's eyes.

Steffan waited, slowly sipping his tea. His actions gave the man the chance to see the gold ring with the blood red ruby the size of a pigeon's egg. Jellikan's stare followed the ruby ring. The display of wealth proved enough to conquer his fear. "My talents were wasted on the nobles of Radagar. I thought my skills would have more value to the rulers of Coronth."

Leaning back in his chair, Steffan considered his guest. The pyromancer had expensive tastes and a gluttonous nature. These were traits Steffan could work with, but it remained to be seen if the man could accept the true nature of the Flame God. "After such a filling breakfast, I often find the need to take a walk. Join me in a stroll and we can continue our conversation."

The pyromancer gaped, his plate half full, but Steffan did not wait. He rose from the table and swept into the foyer, the skinny man rushing to catch up. Pip handed Steffan his black wool cape, the blood red raven badge prominently displayed on the right breast. Settling the cape around his shoulders, he accepted a silver-tipped walking stick. Steffan rarely walked the streets of Balor as the Lord Raven, but today it suited his purpose. With a nod to Pip, he led the pyromancer out into the cobblestone streets.

A light fall of snow gave the capital city a pristine appearance. A short walk brought them to the temple square. Despite the snow, a crowd swarmed the square waiting for this morning's Test of Faith.

The blood-red badge of the Raven was enough to part the crowd. Commoners cringed away, opening a path to the fire pit. Steffan watched the pyromancer out of the corner of his eye. The man was visibly impressed by the subservience of the crowd. Hiding his smile, Steffan led his guest to the very edge of the pit. "Have you ever witnessed a Test of Faith?"

Stuttering, the pyromancer replied, "I-I've only been in Balor for a week. Out of curiosity, I attended one ritual...but it was difficult to see from the edge of the crowd."

Steffan smiled. It was one thing to stand on the edge of the crowd, it was quite another to experience the ritual at the edge of the pit, to see the agony of the sinner, to feel the full force of the crowd's emotions. This was going to be interesting. In a smooth voice, Steffan explained, "The Test of Faith is central to the worship of the Flame God. If you are going to serve the Pontifax, then you need to understand the nature of our religion."

The pyromancer gave a grim nod.

As it always did, the Test of Faith started with the booming of the temple drums and the procession of the Flame. Steffan positioned himself to study the pyromancer's reactions as the rite progressed.

The slow chanting of the crowd thundered around them, rising to a fever pitch. Raw emotion pulsed through the faithful becoming a palpable force. They stood in the heart of a human maelstrom. Steffan watched as the pyromancer succumbed to the ecstasy of the massed believers. Jellikan swayed to the seductive rhythm of the drums, becoming one with the crowd. When it came time for the soldiers to prod the sinner into the Flames, Jellikan leaned forward with the rest of the throng, eager to witness the gruesome death. His face twisted into a mask of ecstasy when the sinner's clothes burst into flames. It was only when a whiff of charred flesh came their way that the man turned away, his face turning pale. Steffan was impressed; the pyromancer managed to hold down his meal despite the stench. The man must have a cast-iron stomach. When the ritual was over, Steffan led his dazed guest back through the dispersing crowds.

Steffan walked in deliberate silence, letting Jellikan reflect on the Test of Faith. Ritualized death was a powerful spectacle, especially for the uninitiated. Instead of returning to his home, Steffan led Jellikan to the Residence, the palace of the Pontifax. Guards snapped salutes and servants bowed low as the Lord Raven and his guest walked through the marbled halls. Jellikan gaped at the grandeur of the Residence. Steffan took the long way, letting the luxury further seduce the pyromancer. Eventually, he led Jellikan to the private chapel in the rear of the Residence.

Crowned by a domed ceiling ornate with gold leaf, the small round chapel reeked of wealth. A pair of red-robed acolytes tended a central fire pit. Light from the flames danced within the golden dome. Dismissing the acolytes, Steffan turned to study the pyromancer. "Master Jellikan, with my patronage, I believe you could be of value to the Pontifax, but first you must pass a final test." Gesturing toward the fire pit, Steffan said, "I want you to arrange a demonstration for the Pontifax using the chapel's fire pit. I want the color, odor, and other changes to occur at predicted intervals without the obvious addition of any powders or fluids. I leave the choice of effects to you, but before the fire is lit, you must predict in advance exactly what effects will occur and in what sequence. Do you accept the challenge?"

The man was clearly tempted yet he hesitated. "I will need to experiment in order to get the sequencing down."

"You will have access to the chapel for your experiments and acolytes will serve as your assistants. I give you two weeks to prepare the demonstration." He handed the pyromancer a bulging purse of golds. "This is merely a token of my goodwill. You will find the Lord Raven is very generous to those who serve him well."

Greed gleamed in the pyromancer's eyes. "It will be an honor to serve you."

"One more thing, your work must be done in total secrecy." Steffan gave the pyromancer a menacing smile. "It would be a *sin* if word of your work leaked to the people...and in Coronth sinners walk the Test of Faith."

Clutching the purse of golds, the pyromancer turned slightly green. "I understand, my lord. I will work in confidence to serve the Pontifax...and the Lord Raven."

"See that you do." Steffan left the pyromancer alone in the chapel. Walking back through the snow-dusted streets, he considered the value of his new servant. Assuming the demonstration proved successful, his ability to manipulate the Flames offered almost limitless possibilities for new miracles to further twist the beliefs of the people. He'd soon have the people dancing like puppets on a string. Religion was such a joy. Steffan felt the Dark Lord's pleasure. After all, one lifetime was not enough.

# 53

# Katherine

Holding the whetstone at the proper angle, Kath scraped long sure strokes along the edge of her sword. Stretched out on the rug in front of the fireplace, she inspected the blade. The sword didn't need sharpening, but there was something comforting about the simple motion of using a whetstone against good Castlegard steel.

Feeling lost in the grandeur of the Rose Court, she'd decided to spend the afternoon sharpening her weapons and burnishing her armor; something familiar for her hands to do while her mind wondered what she was doing in Pellanor. If truth be told, she was really hiding. The queen's court was all about political intrigue and the power of gold, no place for a princess dedicated to the sword. The problem was Kath really didn't know where she belonged. Essentially banished from Castlegard by her father, she couldn't return home and Pellanor was turning out to be nearly as bad as she'd expected. Staring at the glint of firelight reflected on the keen edge of steel, an image of the broken tower sprang unbidden into her mind. Kath felt an intense sense of longing for that other time. The irony was she'd felt more at home in that brief vision of the past than she'd ever felt in the present. And then there was that strange incident on the parapet. The dark-haired man had invaded her dreams yet she did not even know his name. Perhaps she was losing her mind. She shook her head in defiance. Better not to think about a past that was nothing but dust. She needed to focus on finding her way in the present. Stroking the whetstone across her sword, she stared into the flames of the fireplace searching for answers that weren't there.

An abrupt knock intruded on her thoughts. The outer door opened and a tall leggy woman with short-cropped sandy hair stepped into the sitting room. Dressed in simple leathers, the young woman wore a short sword belted to her waist. *A sword!* Kath blinked, wondering if she was imagining things.

The mysterious woman smiled. "I assume you're Princess Katherine. The guard said I'd find you here."

Kath stared, too stunned to say anything. She'd never seen another woman with a sword.

Undeterred, the woman offered her hand in friendship, the way a man would greet another man of equal status. "I'm sorry, I should introduce myself. My name is Jordan and I'm the official welcoming committee from Navarre."

Rising, Kath shook the woman's hand. The grip was firm and sure, the palm lined with calluses. "Thank you for the kind welcome, but who are you?"

"I'm a princess of Navarre. I'm here in Pellanor with two of my siblings, Justin and Jemma. Jemma is spending her Wayfaring, a kind of fostering, in Pellanor with the queen. The queen mentioned to my sister that a princess from Castlegard had arrived and I volunteered to greet you."

Confused, Kath just stared.

Jordan laughed. "The Rose Court can be overwhelming. I'll do my best to explain."

Kath gestured for the young woman to be welcome and then sat cross-legged on the carpet, the naked sword cradled in her lap. Jordan stretched her long legs toward the roaring fire. "I have to admit I'm surprised to see you with a sword."

"Not half as surprised as I am to see *you*! I've never met another woman who carried sword. I thought I was the only one."

Jordan gave her a conspirator's smile. "I know what you mean. But I thought Castlegard didn't train women?"

"They don't, that's why I'm stuck in Pellanor."

"But...you're a princess of Castlegard?"

"It doesn't matter. I've always wanted to wield a sword, but my father forbade it. A year ago, I convinced one of the knights to secretly give me weapons training; only we were discovered. My father was furious. He sent me to the Rose Court for fostering, hoping that the queen would 'turn me into a lady', but the journey only deepened my dedication to the sword. I will not give it up." Kath saw understanding in the other woman's eyes.

"Then I'm the lucky one." Jordan tucked her wayward hair behind her ear. "My father always supported my choice. I wanted to go to Castlegard for my Wayfaring, but the council turned down my request. They said the knights would never train a woman." She gave Kath a solemn nod. "It's disappointing to hear they won't even train one of their own." Her voice carried a hint of anger. "The reluctance to train women with the sword runs deep in the men of Erdhe. It is almost a primal fear."

Kath stared, amazed to find a kindred spirit. "So where will you foster?"

Disappointment flickered across Jordan's face. "Instead of Castlegard, I'm bound for the Southern Mountains to train with the Kiralynn monks. The monks are not known for their sword work, but they're supposed to be wise in the art of war. So you see, I am also trying to find my way with the sword." She extended her hand in friendship. "We should be friends. After all, we're sisters of the sword."

The two women grasped forearms in the way of warriors. Looking into Jordan's eyes, Kath felt she'd finally found a kindred spirit. "I like the idea of having a sword sister."

Jordan smiled. "Then it's settled. We're true sword sisters. Of course, we'll have to dance the steel to celebrate." A competitive gleam filled her eyes. "I've never crossed swords with someone trained by the Octagon. I warn you, I intend to win!"

It was the perfect thing to say. Kath laughed. "I expect nothing less from my sword sister!"

Sharing a laugh, the two women fell into an easy conversation, talking first about their experiences with the sword and then trading stories from their childhoods. Kath talked about growing up in the legendary castle built by the ancient mages and about the prowess of the Octagon Knights. She showed off her throwing axes with the red hawk tooled on the leather harness. Feeling comfortable with Jordan, she described her kidnapping and the sword fight in the meadow. The tale was simply told, minus any reference to her gargoyle or to the broken tower. Finishing the story, she studied her friend's eyes for any sign of disbelief but all she found was respect. Kath was surprised at how much it meant to her.

"So you're a blooded warrior."

Kath nodded, and then smiled. "Tell me about Navarre."

Jordan explained the Navarren custom of Wayfaring and about her six siblings, each with an equal chance at the throne. She explained how Jemma wanted to foster with the queen in order to learn the power of multiplying golds and how Justin hoped to go to Coronth to change hearts his music. The conversation deepened to a heated discussion about Coronth when Jordan suddenly glanced over at the casement window. Astonishment washed across her face. "The sun has nearly set and I almost botched my mission."

Kath gave Jordan a confused look. "Your *mission?*"

"I was supposed to invite you to soup night. My siblings want to meet the mysterious princess from Castlegard. So can you come?"

"What, now?"

"Yes, now. Dinner was supposed to be at sunset, but I got caught up in our conversation and I forgot to ask you. So can you come?"

Intrigued by the idea of meeting Jordan's siblings, Kath replied, "Why not. But shouldn't I change first?"

"No need. Soup nights are always casual, Duncan wouldn't have them any other way." Gesturing toward the weapons and armor strewn across the floor, she added, "I'll help you put these away and then I'll show you to our quarters. Castle Tandroth is a labyrinth, but we're just one floor below you." The two women gathered up the weapons and then left the suite. The floor below turned out to be identical to the one above.

Entering the Navarren suite, Kath caught the savory scent of fish chowder. A round table set for six waited in front of a roaring fireplace. Three people were already seated. Rising from his seat and executing a courtly bow, a young man with mousy brown hair and an irrepressible smile said, "Welcome to soup night! We've banished the servants and we're about to serve supper. Come join us."

Kath assumed he had to be Justin.

Jordan led the way to the table. "Sorry we're late. We got to talking and found we had a lot in common, but introductions first." Gesturing around the table, Jordan said, "My brother, Justin the bard. My sister, Jemma." Resting her hand on the shoulder of a handsome man in the green and white of Lanverness, Jordan flashed a brilliant smile. "And this is Stewart, captain of the Rose Squad and the crown prince of Lanverness, but we don't bother with titles on soup night." Turning toward Kath, Jordan added, "And this is Princess Katherine of Castlegard. She likes to be called Kath, and she's a fellow dedicate of the sword. She's here to foster with the queen."

Greetings exchanged, the two women took seats at the table. Jordan slid into the seat next to Stewart. Kath took a seat next to Jordan.

Jordan asked, "Where's Duncan? It's not like him to miss soup night."

Shrugging, Justin answered, "Something came up. He said not to wait for him." Reaching for the tureen, he added, "I suggest we start before the soup gets cold." Justin served Kath a large ladle of steaming chowder rich with chunks of potatoes and river trout. Stewart poured the wine. Fresh bread and spicemelon were passed around the table. A light banter flowed between the siblings. Kath found the conversation even more welcoming than the food. The meal was like nothing Kath had ever experienced, awash in friendship and sibling banter, but her chance to sit back and listen was short-lived. Justin peppered her with endless questions about the legends of the blue steel blades and the great castle raised by forgotten magic. Kath did her best to answer, but the bard's interest was insatiable. The candles melted to stubs and still their questions did not tire.

Jemma rescued Kath. "You've told us so much about Castlegard I feel I know the great castle even though I've never been there. There must be something you'd like to know about Navarre. Jordan couldn't have told you everything in one afternoon."

Accepting the invitation, Kath said, "There is one thing I'm curious about. Seven siblings and you all have names that begin with the letter 'J'? Did your parents just like the letter or is there more to it than that?"

Jemma smiled, a gleam of amusement in her dark eyes. "It's tradition. In Navarre, each successive generation to the throne advances one step down the alphabet. We are the Royal $J$s just as our father, the king, is a member of the Royal $I$s." Winking, Jemma added, "As Royal Js we are always on the lookout for first names that begin with $K$."

Justin said, "We're always joking about future generations stuck with some of the uglier letters like $U$ or $X$ or $Y$. Can you imagine some poor future queen having to name her children $U$na, $U$ta, $U$rsula, $U$rsus, $U$ther, $U$lysses and $U$mtilla? But she'd better limit her brood to seven. Collecting names is a family hobby, but no one has ever discovered more than seven first names that begin with the letter U and even then there's some debate about whether Uta is for a boy or a girl."

Jordan added in a hushed voice, "And then there is the curse."

"That's right!" With a mischievous grin Justin added, "We mustn't forget the family curse, the dreaded Curse of the Vowels."

At this point, Kath thought the siblings were pulling her leg.

Her disbelief must have shown on her face because Jemma looked at her and said, "No, it's true! There really is a Curse of the Vowels. And it is nothing to laugh about. If we seem to joke about the curse, it's only a sign of relief, knowing that we won't be tested again for many generations."

Kath was surprised to see solemn agreement on the faces of both Jordan and Justin. Still doubtful, she asked, "But that would mean that your parents' generation was somehow cursed?"

Jemma said, "That's correct. According to the curse, there is a bad seed sown in every royal generation where the first names begin with a vowel. Our father's generation was no exception."

With the voice of a seasoned story teller, Justin jumped in to tell the tale. "There were eight children born in the generation of the $I$s, Igraine, Ivy, Iris, Ingrid, Isador, Irwin, Ian, and our father, Ivor. The curse did not rear its ugly head until the siblings had completed their Wayfarings and were being judged as possible candidates for the throne. Rumors said

Irwin was always our grandfather's favorite. Irwin was a natural born diplomat, able to resolve any argument, but his talent also gave Uncle Irwin a way with the lasses. One day, he did not return from his tryst on the beach. They found the young lovers dead, their lips and mouths stained a dark purple from the summer wine. The royal healer was suspicious and kept the remnants of the summer wine for study but his findings came too late to make a difference. The treachery of the curse had already passed to another."

Taking a deliberate sip of wine, Justin continued in a hushed voice. "The second candidate for the throne was said to be Ingrid. Much like our Juliana, Ingrid was a sailor of uncommon ability. A nimble climber, she was at home in the rigging and the crows nests but she fell to her death on a routine training cruise just outside of Seaside harbor. They say the sea that day was as smooth as glass. Ingrid's death shocked the royal family but there was no explanation. The mystery deepened and the curse moved on."

The logs snapped and crackled, giving the listeners a start. With a nervous laugh, everyone focused back on Justin and the telling of the tale. "The next to fall victim was Uncle Isador. Isador was captain of the royal guards. He'd never been sick a day in his life, but he suddenly came down with a severe burning in his stomach and an intense thirst. Suspecting poison, he abstained from all foods except for apples picked fresh from the trees and tea boiled over his own fire. As he began to recover, he convinced his brother Ivor to help him search the castle for telltale poisons. Ever conscious of the curse, Isador suspected his sister Iris. Iris was ever the ambitious one yet the crown never seemed within her grasp. Isador's suspicions were compounded by Iris's Wayfaring. She'd gone to Radagar to study healing with a master, but the nobility of Radagar is famous for their artistic use of poisons, killing each other for a chance at the royal succession. As it turned out, Isador's suspicions were well founded. In the false bottom of a locked chest, the brothers discovered Iris's secret hoard of herbs and poisons. Among the collection of dried plants and roots, they found a stoppered flask of the deadly nightshade berry, with its distinctive dark purple color. There was also a pouch of small black seeds from the hemlock plant, known to cause vertigo and death. Sorting through the powders and vials, the apothecary found the last piece of evidence, a vial containing the colorless powder of the bloodroot plant, a deadly poison said to cause an intense burning in the stomach and an unquenchable thirst. Hidden within Iris's locked chest were poisons that could account for the dire symptoms of all three siblings."

The bard paused, staring at his audience. "The brothers confronted their sister with this evidence, but Iris only laughed, saying she was weeding out the weak so only the strong survived. Furious, Isador demanded his sister's death, but their grandfather could not give the orders to have his beautiful daughter killed. Instead, he exiled his dark daughter to a small rock in the harsh chain of islands known as the Orcnoths. Given a fisherman's cottage and surrounded only by goats and the rough ocean waters, Iris was expected to live out her days in isolation. She had no visitors except for the guards who delivered her food once a week. But rumors said that Aunt Iris had more skills than just the craft of herbs and poisons. Whispers said that the true purpose of her Wayfaring was to study art of seduction."

The fire cracked, sending a shower of sparks onto the hearth. The friends laughed, reaching for more wine, as the bard continued his tale. "Iris stayed on the island for exactly six turns of the moon, long enough for the guards to grow complacent. One day, the guards did not return. A search party found them naked in the bed of the cottage. One had his throat cut and the other had a knife in his belly. They also found a note written in Iris's spidery hand. She vowed to return to Navarre when she was ready to claim the throne. No one knows where she went and none have seen her since."

The room fell quiet except for the crackling of the logs. No one wanted to break the spell of the dark tale. Kath shivered, making the hand sign against evil. "So the curse is real?"

Justin nodded, his face solemn. "It's real. Some believe the curse is an evil seed planted by the Dark Lord himself, an attempt to gain the throne of Navarre." Lowering his voice, the bard added, "No one knows the reason why, but there is always one dark seed in each generation named by a vowel; one seed that holds the promise of death, destruction, and treachery."

"Then why not skip the vowels altogether?"

Justin flashed Kath a broad grin. "A logical suggestion, except for the other part of the curse. If the royals ever skip a letter, a vowel or otherwise, then the kingdom of Navarre will fall." Justin shrugged. "No one is willing to take the risk, so we stick to the alphabet, vowels and all."

"At least you're forewarned."

Jemma shook her head. "You'd think knowing would be a blessing but sometimes evil is most cruel when it is predictable. Imagine the torment of the queen who knows she is about to give birth to a cursed generation. The Dark Lord's cruelty knows no bounds."

Justin uncorked the last bottle of wine, topping all the goblets. "Enough talk of curses and the Dark Lord, I have some good news to share. Bring your glasses and let's get comfortable by the fire."

The table was quickly deserted. Everyone found a comfortable spot in front of the warming fire. Jemma curled her slender legs under her long wool skirt and reclined like an elegant princess while Jordan and Stewart snuggled comfortably against the back of a chair. Kath sat cross-legged in front of the fire, sipping her wine and waiting to hear Justin's announcement.

Taking a seat in front of the fire, Justin raised his glass in the manner of a toast. "This morning I had the honor of joining Master Fallon in a private performance for the queen. Her majesty graciously approved the new ballads related to Coronth." Stewart and the siblings cheered the news. Bowing to his audience, Justin said, "So you are all formally invited to attend the first public performance. I've booked a front row table at the Green Stag for three nights from now." Looking specifically at Kath, Justin said, "I hope you'll be able to attend."

Kath nodded, pleased to be included.

Jordan said, "Give us a song!"

Justin cradled his small harp and began tuning the strings. His fingers rippled across the harp, releasing melodies that teased the heart and rhythms that soothed the soul.

Basking in the heat of the fire, Kath felt a warm glow inside. She wasn't sure if it was the wine, the fire, or the music. Looking at her newfound friends, she felt an acceptance and strength she'd never known. Kath smiled. Perhaps there were good reasons to be in Pellanor after all.

# 54

# Blaine

The great blue sword whistled as it sliced through the cold morning air. In the dawn light Blaine practiced the classical forms. Raising the sapphire blue blade high above his right shoulder for a powerful diagonal attack, he executed *slash of the eagle*. The diagonal slash flowed directly into *strike of the snake*, followed by a sweeping undercut named *claws of the mountain lion*. Each form flowed seamlessly into the next, carving graceful arcs through imaginary foes.

Stepping through the forms, Blaine's boots beat a soft rhythm into the hard-packed dirt floor of the training yard. His strength was such that he could execute some of the forms with a single hand on the sword. Cut, parry, and thrust, Blaine picked up the pace until the sword blurred into a shimmering slash of blue, creating the illusion of many blades instead of one.

In the solitude of the early morning, he lost himself in the dance of steel, exalting in the feel of the great blue blade. The sword became an extension of his arm, an extension of his will. As the pale winter sun rose over the castle walls, he made a final lunge to end the dance with the deadly *strike of the dragon*.

Breathing hard, he wiped the sweat from his brow. Too deadly for sparring matches, he could only use the great sword in solitary practices. By rising early he avoided the hero-worshiping crowds that gathered whenever he unsheathed the blade. He'd learned to ignore their stares, but he had a harder time avoiding warriors who sought to challenge him. Looking for bragging rights, they yearned to defeat a knight who carried a hero's sword. Remembering the words of the knight marshal, Blaine had to agree that the blue steel blade had a way of constantly testing him, as if it was the man who was being shaped on the forge to meet the needs of the blade. He laughed at his own thoughts, awfully deep for such an early morning.

Finished with his practice, he wiped the sword clean with a soft cloth and sheathed the great blade in his shoulder harness. He paused to watch the sun's golden rays edge over the castle ramparts. Now that they were safe behind castle walls, there was little to do besides train. The princess put her whole heart into the practice sessions but outside of the sparring ring it was obvious she chaffed at the Rose Court. He had to admit a queen's court was no place for a princess dedicated to the sword, but he looked at their time in Pellanor differently. To Blaine, it was the calm before the storm, a time to prepare. With the intervention of the gods at the Isle of Souls and later at the broken tower, Blaine had no doubt that a dark storm was looming on the horizon. Each day in Pellanor gave them more time to sharpen their fighting skills before the storm struck.

Retrieving his maroon cloak, he left the sparring yard to make his way back to his quarters. Lost in thought, he must have taken a wrong turn, suddenly finding himself in an unfamiliar part of the castle. Roaming the stone corridors looking for a landmark, he almost slipped on a slick puddle. A heavy metallic tang hung in the hallway. Recognizing the coppery smell, he unsheathed his sword. A pool of fresh spilled blood stained the castle floor.

Bloody footprints led to a door standing slightly ajar. Blaine heard a faint moan from within. Kicking the door open, he entered with steel first. Two bodies lay in an otherwise deserted room, both soldiers of Lanverness. One man twitched, clutching at his abdomen. Kneeling, Blaine tried to comfort the injured soldier, but the wound was clearly fatal. Wadding his cloak into a ball, Blaine eased it under the soldier's head to cushion him from the cold stone floor. "Who did this?"

The soldier's eyes told Blaine he knew his wound was fatal. "Tricked us into coming here. Traitors...traitors in the army. We refused ...staying loyal to the prince." Staring up at Blaine with urgent eyes, the man struggled to say, "W-warn the queen...traitors from within."

The man's eyes began to glaze. Desperate to learn more, Blaine shook the dying man. "Who are the traitors? Who did this to you?"

The man's eyes fluttered, refocusing on Blaine's face. With a last effort he gasped, "The red...horns." A look of peace settled over his face and then he was gone.

Muttering a prayer to Valin, Blaine eased the dead man's eyes shut and gently reclaimed his cloak. Stepping around the body, he knelt to check the second man. The second soldier had died quickly, a stab direct to the heart. Blaine searched for clues to the violence, finding a crumpled note clutched in the second man's hand. He freed the note and smoothed the parchment to better read the spidery handwriting.

"*Politics!*" Blaine made the word a curse. Staring at the note, he considered his options. His only recourse was to take the information directly to the queen. Anyone else could be in league with the traitors.

Leaving the room much as he'd found it, Blaine tucked the note into a pouch on his belt. He retraced his steps, looking for a way out of the maze of corridors, eventually finding a page who led him to the queen's section of the castle. A pair of stern faced guards blocked his way, refusing entry. Undaunted, Blaine insisted he had an urgent message for the queen. The guards showed him to a small sitting room where he was told to wait.

A succession of sleepy-eyed officials grilled Blaine about the nature of his message. Not knowing whom to trust, he refused to talk to anyone save the queen. His stubbornness eventually won out. A herald and a pair of guards escorted him through the tower. At the door of the solar, he was asked to relinquish his sword and other weapons. Feeling naked, Blaine entered queen's sanctum.

The queen sat on a throne in front of a roaring fire. Despite the early hour, she was already bedecked in finery. Strands of pearls bound her raven-black hair away from a heart-shaped face. A green silk gown accented her hourglass figure, a gleam of rings on her fingers. Blaine steps faltered, the woman was a vision of beauty and power, the perfect image of a queen. Without thinking, he dropped to his knee and waited for permission to speak.

"You may rise." Her voice carried the sultry tones of a woman in command. "Why does a knight serving the princess of Castlegard suddenly seek an urgent audience?"

Standing, Blaine dared to look the queen full in the face. A fierce intelligent met his stare. He took a step backward, retreating from the queen's scrutiny. The woman's gaze cut like a sword. Realizing he was way out of his depth, he took a deep breath and carefully recounted the events of this morning. He explained about his habit of practicing in the dawn hours and about getting lost in the lower levels of the castle. He told the queen about the pool of blood in the hallway and about the dying soldier's last words. Finished, he handed the queen the crumpled note.

The queen read the note in stony silence.

Blaine waited, watching for any reaction, but her face remained devoid of emotion. He supposed her mask of calm was all part of being a queen.

"Tell us again. What did the soldier say when you asked who was responsible for the attack?"

"With his dying breath the soldier said, *the red horns.*"

"Yet the note invites the soldiers to join the *griffins* in putting a king on the throne. It seems the soldiers were never meant to have a voice beyond the note placed in their hand. By finding one alive, you have allowed the truth to prevail." Pausing, the queen added, "The truth can be a powerful weapon if wielded wisely."

Blaine waited while the queen studied the crumpled note.

"It seems to us that we gain the greatest advantage if the traitors assume the truth died with the soldiers. We will ask you to recount your tale to our closest advisor, the Master Archivist, but no one else. Our shadowmaster will see to it that one of his most trusted men raises the alarm when the two *dead* soldiers are discovered *later* this morning. The man will also discover the crumpled note." The queen's stare drilled into him. "Your conversation with the dying man never happened. If you are questioned about your meeting with the queen, you will say you were simply delivering a private message from Princess Katherine. Are we understood?"

"Perfectly."

In a solemn voice, the queen said, "You have done the Rose Crown a great service, Sir Blaine. We are in your debt."

"Thank you, your majesty."

The queen rang a golden hand bell. The outer door immediately opened and two guards entered the room. Turning toward Blaine, the queen said, "The guards will show you to my private meeting room. The Master Archivist will join you there shortly. Thank you again for your service." Nodding, the queen added, "Please give our regards to Princess Katherine. We will give careful consideration to her request."

Bowing low, Blaine left the solar and reclaimed his blue sword. While waiting for the queen's counselors, he considered the events of the morning. Lanverness was not as peaceful as everyone thought. Storm clouds were gathering within the queen's own castle. Blaine suspected it would take more than swords to defeat the gathering dark.

# 55

# Katherine

U nable to sleep, Kath roamed the cold marble corridors of Castle Tandroth trying to unravel the riddle of her dreams. The dawn light cast subtle shadows in the deserted hallways, a good time to be alone, a good time to think. Kath turned a corner, surprised to glimpse a dark figure ahead. The man stalked the corridor with a confident stride yet the hallway was empty of footsteps. Intrigued, she followed, her doeskin boots whispering down the marble corridor.

The figure stepped into a circle of torchlight. Kath's breath caught, recognizing the man from the parapet. Clad in black leathers, he moved with a feral grace. Tall, with the broad shoulders of an archer, he prowled the corridor like a hungry black panther. A shiver ran down her back igniting a heat in her loins. Something about this man awakened deep feelings within her. Struggling to understand, she gave in to the need to follow.

He pivoted without warning, piercing her with his one-eyed gaze.

Kath froze, a deer trapped by a lion.

"What do you want?" His voice was rich and deep, riddled with undertones.

Stepping out of the shadows, her heart thundering, Kath closed the distance between them. Memories of the unbroken tower beat like wings against her mind. She stared up into his face, seeking a match with the distant past. Tanned by the sun, his face was ruggedly handsome, the black leather eye patch adding mystery to his good looks. His sapphire blue eye held her in a steady gaze. The blue eye was a relief. In her visions from that other time, Kath was sure the knight had soft brown eyes, the kind of brown eyes you could drown your soul in. This could not be the same man. A strange mixture of relief and disappointment flooded her. A small sigh escaped her lips.

The man reached out a hand as if to steady her.

His touch sent sparks through her, making her doubt her earlier conclusions. Confused, she peered into his face.

"Are you all right?"

Finding her voice, she asked, "Who are you?"

"My name is Duncan Treloch. Do I know you?"

"Yes...I mean no." Shaking her head, she tied to untie her tongue. "It's just that it seems like I've met you somewhere before, but it couldn't be, could it?" As her mind cleared, his name fell into place. She stared up at him, relieved to know that he truly belonged to this time. Recovering her composure, she flashed him an impish smile and said, "So you're the Duncan who missed soup night."

Now it was his turn to look puzzled. "Yes, but what would you know of soup night?"

Seeing his confusion, Kath said, "Perhaps I should introduce myself. I am Princess Katherine of Castlegard, recently arrived to foster with the queen. As a welcome to the court, Jordan invited me to soup night. There was an empty chair at the table for you. You missed a fun evening."

"Ah, the princess with the sword. Jordan mentioned you at breakfast the next morning." With a courtly bow, he added, "I am pleased to meet you. Welcome to the Rose Court. The Royal J's enjoyed your company the other night...so perhaps we will be seeing you at future soup nights."

With a warm smile, Kath said, "I would like that."

A slightly awkward silence settled between them. Staring up at his face, it seemed as if they shared a conversation without any words being spoken. She'd never experienced anything quite like it.

He gave her an intense stare. "I've seen you before, haven't I? Out on the parapet, in the cold morning wind?"

She nodded, wondering how to explain. "Nightmares. Sometimes the fresh air helps."

His one-eyed stare raked across her, pausing at the sword at her hip. "You don't look like the type to be bothered by nightmares. Coming from Castlegard, I'll wager your good with that sword."

She expected irony or derision in his voice but heard only sincerity. The compliment was so outrageous for a man of Erdhe that Kath stood slack-jawed, staring up at Duncan in disbelief. Perhaps he did come from another time.

He chuckled but it was full of warmth.

Kath felt her face flush red. Struggling to hide her embarrassment, she reached for something to say. "Do you often walk the parapets at dawn?" She instantly regretted the stupid question.

He flashed her a roguish smile. "I've a restless spirit." He shrugged. "I'm not one to be contained behind stone walls."

She stood rooted to the ground, trying to see past the blue gaze of this mysterious man. She had a thousand questions she wanted to ask, a thousand things she wanted to say, but she found herself suddenly speechless. All she could do was stare.

He nodded. "I'm sure we'll meet again, perhaps at another soup night." He gave her a half bow. "In the meantime, I wish you good dreams, Katherine of Castlegard." He turned and left her standing in the hallway.

She didn't want him to go but she couldn't think of a reason for him to stay. She watched as he prowled down the corridor, his black leathers highlighting his muscular frame. A spark burned within her. She knew his name but she did not understand why he intrigued her so...or why he reminded her so much of that other time. She would have to talk to her sword sister about Duncan. Smiling, she whispered his name, "Duncan Treloch," liking the sound of it. Kath did not know why the gods had brought her to Pellanor, but one thing was certain, she was looking forward to unraveling this enigma wrapped in black leathers.

# 56

# Liandra

Traitors from within. It was a grim thought but one any monarch, especially a sovereign queen, had to constantly consider. Plots within plots. Evidence indicated that this threat from the Red Horns was better planned and better organized than any plot Liandra had yet faced. All the more reason to out scheme this current crop of traitors, but to weave her tangled web she'd need the aid of two of her men, her shadowmaster and her soldier-son. Liandra narrowed her gaze, considering her two men. The soldier-prince stood next to the spymaster, bright armor contrasting with dark shadows, a pair of opposites. Her shadowmaster was tempered steel, tested with many a secret, while her son was a novice at court intrigue. Liandra knew every secret shared was a risk, but in this case, she judged it acceptable. In measured tones she explained the ruse of the Red Horns. "We would have your advice on this matter."

Prince Stewart was quick to respond. "The first priority is to protect the queen. The sergeant's dying words prove the traitors have not corrupted the Rose Squad. The Rose Squad should be assigned to guard the queen's tower."

Liandra appreciated her son's concerns, but his blunt, straightforward suggestion proved the young soldier-prince saw the world in black and white. Perhaps this threat would teach him to manipulate the countless shades of gray that defined the political world. Before the queen could rebuke the prince, the Master Archivist intervened.

"My prince, you raise a good suggestion however it is far too obvious. Replacing the royal guards with a squad from the army would send a clear signal to the traitors that the crown is suspicious. The traitors would merely go to ground, regrouping to surface at another time. As it stands, we have the advantage of being forewarned. We must use the advantage to flush out the traitors and apply a lethal end to their schemes. We must pull the traitors out by the root, not merely trim the branches. To do that, we need names, especially the names of the leaders."

Frustration filled the prince's face yet he held his silence. The queen approved of her royal son's control. Perhaps it was not too late to teach him the subtleties of intrigue. "Our shadowmaster is correct. We need to tease out the traitors. Our actions must be subtle, flowing beneath the normal patterns of the court. We must weave our own webs and wait to see who is ensnared by their actions." Turning her gaze to the master, the queen said, "Your shadowmen must be vigilant. We suspect there will be more clues pointing toward this fictitious plot. Perhaps the clues can be traced backwards to discover these Red Horns."

"It shall be as you command."

Seething with anger, the prince glared at the spymaster. "I wish you good hunting, but the safety of the queen should *never* be a matter of luck. If your webs of intrigue do not catch the traitors then this revolt may very well become a matter of swords. Political intrigue and shadowmen will not protect the queen once swords are drawn. I say again, we need to surround the queen with loyal steel."

Her royal son raised a good point. "Now you have hit closer to the mark. The Rose Squad is too obvious but protection will be needed." The queen eased back in her chair, considering the problem. "The question is whom do we trust?" She considered her two advisors. "One of you deals with the sword and the other with shadow. We would ask each of you to compile separate lists of those swords that you believe to be loyal. We will trust only those names that appear on both lists, appointing them to guard the Queen's Tower."

Shaking his head, the master said, "The Queen's Tower is the domain of the royal guards. The plan will only work if there are sufficient guards on the list. Anything else will alert the traitors."

"Then it must be done in secret. We must find a way to surround ourselves with loyal swords that appear to be something else entirely. Shadow and subterfuge must be used to our advantage."

The prince and the master nodded but neither offered a suggestion.

After a while, the queen smiled seeing the solution. "Who is always present but seldom seen?" Seeing puzzlement on the men's faces, the queen explained. "Servants. The Queen's Tower is full of servants yet few ever bother to look closely at their faces. We will replace our servants with loyal swords. Perhaps some of our veterans retired from the army could be recruited to the task. Gray hair is a common trait among the servants senior enough to attend the Queen's Tower. The sooner this is accomplished the better."

Both men bowed their heads to the queen's commands.

"Prince Stewart, will this plan satisfy your concerns?"

"Yes, your majesty, but I have another issue to discuss."

The queen gestured for the prince to continue.

"If this revolt becomes a battle, then it will be difficult to tell friend from foe since all will wear the green and white of Lanverness." Lowering his voice, the prince added, "We will need a way to identify those loyal to the crown."

It was an excellent point. Perhaps, there were advantages to having an advisor with a military mind. "What do you suggest?"

"Armbands. Easily hidden in belt pouches or pockets, the armbands will only be used if fighting breaks out."

The master asked, "What type of armbands?"

"Black armbands. When soldiers of Lanverness fight against each other it will be a black day."

Nodding, queen said, "Armbands are an excellent idea, but we should also have a password." Seeing agreement at the table, the queen added, "We play a complicated game of chess with the leader of the Red Horns. Our password will be *white's gambit*."

The two men signaled their agreement.

"There is one other aspect to consider." The queen lowered her voice. "To have a chance at success, this Red Horn's plot must be, by its very nature, broad reaching. Such reach would require a powerbroker in the Rose Court, someone with a seat at our council table."

The prince looked shocked but the master nodded, his face grave. "Unmasking this traitor must be our highest priority."

In a quiet voice, the prince asked, "Whom do you suspect?"

The queen considered her loyal lords. "The plot implies there are traitors within the army. That alone would point toward General Helfner but the man is too blunt and straightforward. No, we are looking for someone who is devious and careful."

Clearing his throat, the master said, "Unfortunately, your majesty has a penchant for choosing shrewd men to sit on the royal council. There are several who would make excellent candidates for the leader of the Red Horns."

The prince stared at the black-robed master. "And those candidates are?"

With a rare smile, the master replied, "Aside from myself, the suspects would include the Lords Sheldon, Turner, and Hunter. Lord Sheldon controls the constable force. The constables are not as overtly threatening as the army but they are a force to be reckoned with. Then there is the Knight Protector, Lord Turner, who controls the royal guard, a key position for capturing the queen. Given the small size of the guards, Lord Turner would need the help of the army in order to secure the throne. The other candidate is Lord Hunter. As a diplomat, Lord Hunter has a very devious mind and he may have allies outside the kingdom." After a pause the master added, "We must also consider the men who have resigned from the royal council. Many men have left the court harboring a grudge against their queen. Lord Nealy left the council in disgrace over a matter of incompetence and Duke Anders under suspicion of corruption. Lord Nealy is too much of a bungler to be the leader of the Red Horns, but Duke Anders could be a serious threat."

The queen nodded. "We concur with your analysis. It makes for a grim but accurate assessment. We trust your shadowmen will keep a close but discrete watch on Lords Sheldon, Turner, Hunter, and Anders."

"It is already being done."

"Then the stage is set. We will spin our webs and watch to see who is entangled by their own words and actions." In a thoughtful voice, the queen added, "We suspect the traitor will tip his hand by being over zealous in his professed loyalty. With a smile on his face, the traitor will seek to distract us from the knife hidden in his hand. We must learn the traitor's identity before he gets close enough to strike." Sitting back in her chair, the queen fingered the strand of pearls at her neck. "The murder of the two soldiers will be 'discovered' later today by a member of the Rose Squad. A full council will be convened to discuss the threat. The three of us will wear masks of shock at the council table." She stared pointedly at Prince Stewart. "Play your parts well. We must out-charade the traitor in order to see behind his mask." Waving her hand in dismissal, the queen added, "There is much to be done. We thank you for your advice and we release you to your duties."

At the queen's words, both men came forward to kiss her emerald ring of office before taking their leave.

Sitting alone in the counsel chambers, the queen considered the threat posed by the Red Horns. She had no doubt that her opponent was both devious and brilliant, but the queen had practice in dealing with both. Few men could appreciate how difficult it was for a woman to gain and then hold a throne. The days ahead would be dangerous but Liandra had no intention of losing to the Red Horns. When it came to plots within plots, she had yet to find her equal.

# 57

# Jordan

Word that the bard from Seaside was playing spread through the south side of the city like wildfire. Jordan knew her brother was good, but the size of the crowd amazed her. The Green Stag was crowded with families, the low hum of conversation filling the pub's common room. Jordan was glad they'd decided to have an early supper, laying claim to a table near the front.

At Justin's request, they tried their best not to stand out, but it simply wasn't possible. Stewart wore the boiled leathers of a common soldier but there was no hiding the handsome crown prince. Having two Octagon knights at their table did not help. The mere sight of surcoats emblazoned with maroon octagons stirred interest, but Sir Blaine also carried a hero's blue sword and Sir Tyrone was fascinating with his dark ebony skin. Whispers and stares swirled around the tavern, drawing the owner to their table. Marg Staghorn made a loud show of greeting the prince and the two knights, insisting the first round of drinks was on the house. Shirking attention, Justin fled to a back room with the excuse that he needed to practice. Jordan, Jemma and Kath smothered smiles, enjoying the men's embarrassment, while Duncan seemed oblivious to it all, an island of calm in his black leathers.

The friends tucked into a hearty meal of savory meat pies and tankards of rich dark ale. The fare was simple but tasty. Jordan enjoyed her lamb pie, but she could not help noticing the suggestive looks the other women kept throwing Stewart's way. Annoyed, she possessively rubbed her thigh against his leg. He flashed her a smile that took all her doubts away.

Sir Blaine also garnered the interest of more than a few fair-haired lasses. The tall lanky knight was handsome in his own way, yet Jordan thought it curious that Kath showed no interest in him. She studied her sword sister, sitting next to Duncan, a pensive look on her face, paying more attention to her meat pie than the conversation. Surprised to see Kath so withdrawn, Jordan leaned forward to try and draw her into the conversation, but then Justin emerged from the back room, his small harp cradled against his chest.

Applause rippled through the common room, leaving an undercurrent of expectation. Justin took his place on a tall stool by the roaring fireplace. Bending over his small harp, he tuned and tested the strings. Jordan smiled. She'd once asked her brother if his harp really needed tuning before every performance. Justin had winked and replied that whether the harp needed it or not, the tuning of the instrument was a bard's trick to gather the attention of the audience without saying a word. The trick seemed to be working. The low murmur of conversation stilled and the faces of the crowd turned toward the bard like flowers toward the sun.

Justin did not keep them waiting. Finished with his adjustments, he set his fingers to the strings and began to rip through a series of rousing chords. Jordan smiled as Justin launched into a lively sea chantey popular with the sailors of Seaside. The rhythm proved contagious, sweeping through the Stag. Smiling, the audience swayed and clapped to the chantey. Jordan was surprised to find the seaman's ditty so popular with a bunch of land-lovers. Her brother must have spent more time in the Stag than anyone realized.

The tempo of the chantey increased and the Stag's patrons clapped faster, chanting the sailor's refrain to the captain's orders. With just one song, Justin had captured his audience, almost like magic.

Finished with the sea chantey, Justin moved to other songs beloved across all Erdhe. Well-known classics like the *Milkmaid's Dilemma*, the *Dog and the Pussy Cat*, and the *Lover's Knot* kept the audience involved. More people streamed into the Stag, crowding the tables. As the latecomers crammed into the Stag, the intensity of the music somehow increased till it seemed like the small harp was strung with raw emotions instead of ordinary strings.

Jordan glanced around the tavern, watching the faces of the patrons. Bright eyes, hearty smiles, and clapping hands proved the crowd hung on every chord. Her brother had the gift.

Justin launched into a new set of songs, rousing the audience to laughter with the *Farmer and the Donkey*, and then he brought them to tears with the *Ballad of the Forgotten Princess*. Playing for the better part of an hourglass, he led the crowd through a gamut of emotions before the music stilled to silence.

Released from the spell, the crowd broke into a deafening round of applause, demanding more. As Justin bowed to his audience, a serving girl brought the bard a large tankard of ale. He raised the tankard in salute, and then took a long swallow, signaling the start of the break.

A bevy of serving girls poured from the backroom. Balancing trays above their heads, they circulated the Stag, offering fresh tankards of ale, cider, and spiced wine. A cheerful tide of conversation flooded back into the great room as the patrons took their ease.

Stewart ordered a round of drinks for their table. Leaning toward Jordan, he said, "I've heard your brother play before, but I had no idea he was this good."

Flushed with a sister's pride, she smiled. "It is only when you hear him play to an audience that you understand the true power of his music." Glancing around the crowded tavern, she added, "Justin truly has the bard's gift. The people of Pellanor seem to love him almost as much as the people of Seaside."

Jordan noticed that Justin's guest, Samson, was staring at the bard with something akin to awe on his face. The shy young man from Coronth was a stranger, but any friend of Justin's was more than welcome at their table. Reaching across, she tapped the young man on the shoulder. "What do you think of Justin's music?"

The skinny young man blushed and stammered. "I didn't know the Princ...I mean, Justin, was so good. It's been a long time since I've heard such music."

Before Jordan could reply, a hush settled back across the common room. The bard returned to his stool, nestling his small harp on his lap. A flurry of chords ripped through the tavern, drawing a gasp from the crowd. Justin launched into complex melody that stretched the range of the harp, his fingers flying in a blur of notes. When he finished, the great room hushed to a solemn stillness. Into this quiet, Justin said, "Now I'd like to play something new for you, something I've just finished writing. It's called *The Ballad of the Flame*."

Justin tightened the strings of the small harp, heightening the tension in the common room. Carefully setting his fingers to the strings, he began to play. The first notes evoked a haunting melody, his clear tenor voice weaving words to the music.

> *With open eyes we did not see.*
> *The horror came we let it be.*
> *And when he failed to pass the test,*
> *We thought him guilty like the rest*
> *Who knew that I'd be next?*

*We did not hear their sobs and tears.*
*We offered only cruelest jeers.*
*To those they chained upon the rack,*
*We closed our minds and turned our back.*
*Who knew that I'd be next?*

*Beware to claim what priests' desire,*
*Daughter, home, or wealth acquired.*
*Whispers started by a liar,*
*Innocent condemned to fire.*
*Who knew that I'd be next?*

*Darkness spreads across our souls,*
*We turned our neighbors in for gold.*
*We hid amidst a chanting mob,*
*Devotion to a craven god.*
*Who knew that I'd be next?*

*No god of love could be so cruel,*
*Loved ones used as living fuel.*
*Join now brothers and make a stand,*
*And drive this evil from our land,*
*Who knew that I'd be next?*

*We must act now or live in shame,*
*To see good folk die in the flame.*
*No longer to this con we kneel.*
*Arise and fight this flame with steel,*
*Fight now or you'll be next!*

The melody hung in the air long after the bard had finished. Looking up from his small harp, Justin's face was full of trepidation. He sat on the edge of his stool, waiting for the crowd's reaction.

Jordan held her breath, knowing how much the crowd's approval meant to him.

The mood in the room was complex and hard to read, almost as if each person silently weighed the message of the music. One person applauded. Soon one turned to many. An avalanche of clapping swept through the great room. *"Again! Again!"* The room fairly shook with the chant, the people paying the bard the highest compliment.

Jordan clapped with the others, happy for her brother.

Justin flashed a dazzling smile. Bending his head toward the small harp, he began to repeat the opening chords.

Watching from the front table, Jordan wiped a tear from her eye. Her brother was amazing. Listening to the ballad a second time, she prayed the gods would keep Justin safe. Their father had granted Justin's request to take his music to Coronth. Jordan understood her brother's desire to make a difference, but she also feared for his safety. Coronth was a dangerous place. As the haunting melody washed through the tavern, a chill ran down her back. She prayed to the gods to keep her favorite brother safe.

# 58

# Danly

With a final thrust Danly finished with the girl. Freeing himself, he rolled sideways, sprawling naked and sweaty on the sheets. Danly slapped the harlot across her upturned rump, signaling he was through. He would have liked another romp but he didn't want the leader of the Red Horns to catch him with his pants down.

Shielding the bedside table, he flicked open the secret catch of the poison ring and sprinkled the alchemist's white powder into an empty goblet. Filling the goblet with rich red wine, he swirled the mixture with his finger and then turned back to the girl. Holding the goblet to her lips, he forced her to drink. A trickle of dark red wine escaped, running down the side of her chin. Against her fair white skin it looked like blood. Tipping the goblet, he forced the rest of the mixture into the girl's ample mouth, igniting a touch of fear in her eyes. Her fear excited him. Pity he didn't have the time to indulge himself. Perhaps next time he would do more than simply ride her.

It wasn't long before the girl's eyes glazed and her breathing slowed. To be sure, he pinched her right nipple. The girl did not even flinch. Satisfied, he rose from the bed to dress. Fastening the gold buttons on his emerald green vest, he left the bedroom for the outer sitting room.

A warm blaze crackled in the fireplace. Danly filled a fresh goblet with brandy and took a seat in a plush armchair by the fire. Sipping the brandy, he kept watch on the wooden wall panel that hid the secret staircase. He did not have long to wait. With a soft click, the panel swung open and the leader of the Red Horns joined him in the small sitting room.

Bowing to the prince, the counselor crossed the room and poured himself a generous portion of brandy. Swirling the fine liquor, he raised the glass in a toast. "To the future king of Lanverness."

Danly raised his glass. "I'll drink to that."

The counselor settled into the opposite armchair, firelight flickering across his face. "I trust you enjoyed yourself this evening."

The man was baiting him again. Danly knew the counselor held his sexual adventures in contempt. Brushing the remark aside, the prince parried with a touch of anger. "I trust you came here to report on the cause rather than to simply drink the madam's excellent brandy?"

The counselor's gaze narrowed. "Progress has indeed been made. The first seeds of deception have been planted. Two soldiers were murdered as props for our little charade. An infantryman from the Rose Squad discovered the bodies. One of the dead held a note indicating a plot by the so-called *Griffins* to put a king on the Rose Throne. The shock of the murders was enough to catapult the news directly to the queen. The queen convened a meeting of her most trusted advisors. I did my best to look shocked." The counselor grinned as he stared into his goblet, swirling his brandy. "And now the queen's vaunted shadowmen chase their tails, searching for the imaginary Griffins. We've bought ourselves some breathing room." Staring into the fire, the leader added in a musing voice, "I thought it was most interesting that the queen asked for extra guards to protect her royal person, but no one suggested additional guards for her second son." He stared at the prince, a sneer on his face. "The queen is such a loving mother, don't you think?"

Danly bristled at the insult. He knew his royal mother was a bitch but he did not like hearing it from others, especially the counselor.

"And why is it that your brother, Prince Stewart, gets a seat on the council and *you* do not? Could it be that your royal mother does not trust you?"

The counselor was full of nasty barbs. Danly took a long drink of brandy, trying to quench his anger. He glared at the counselor and threw a barb of his own. "So when will the Red Horns make their move? It's past time I took my rightful place on the Rose Throne."

"Patience, my prince, all in good time. There are still obstacles to be surmounted before we can tip our hand."

"Obstacles or excuses?"

"*Obstacles* of course. We will only get one chance to grasp the Rose Throne. We cannot afford any mistakes."

"So what are these obstacles and when will we be ready?"

"One of them is the crown prince and his loyal band of men." The counselor sipped his brandy, his gaze locked on Danly. "Since we could not turn your brother's men to our cause, we must find a way to get the Rose Squad out of the palace, or better yet, out of the city. I am working on a plan to do just that." He gave the prince a piercing stare. "You understand of course, that in order to ascend to the throne your older brother must first be dead. I trust you have no qualms about eliminating this particular obstacle?"

Danly smiled. So this was the reason the counselor goaded him. It was almost amusing how little the counselor understood him. "I assure you, I have no love for my insipid older brother. Stewart is nothing more than a lap dog for the queen. You have my royal permission to execute him." Putting steel in his voice, Danly added, "But *not* the queen. The royal bitch will kneel before me and I *alone* will decide her fate. If her tears amuse me, I may spare her life, confining her to the deepest dungeons of Castle Tandroth, or I may let the royal executioner take her head. Only a king should make a decision regarding the life of a queen."

The counselor bowed his head in acceptance. "It will be as you have ordered, my prince. The queen is a mere woman not a leader of men. Once the swords come out, she will not be a factor in the uprising."

Danly smiled, looking forward to the day. He poured himself a second brandy. "How long will it take to get everything in order?"

"We will strike once Prince Stewart and the Rose Squad are out of the way. Once we have confirmation that the crown prince is dead, then the revolt can begin." The counselor rose and bowed to the prince. "And now, with your leave, I should go. It is not wise for the two of us to spend too much time together, even in secret."

The prince waved approval for the Red Horn to take his leave.

The counselor opened the secret panel. "Remember my prince, we must remain vigilant against the queen's shadowmen. It would not do to make a mistake when our plans are so close to fruition." The counselor stared at the prince as if to reinforce his point. "I look forward to the day when you will take your rightful place on the Rose Throne. Lanverness deserves to be ruled by a strong king." With a last bow, the leader of the Red Horns disappeared down the hidden staircase. The wooden panel clicked shut, hiding the secret entrance.

The prince sat alone in front of the fire, finishing his brandy. The counselor was infuriating, but he had his uses. Danly would repay every insult and settle every score once he sat on the Rose Throne, even scores that stretched back to childhood. Dealing with his royal mother would be especially sweet, but first he needed to claim the throne. He felt his manhood stiffen with anticipation. All of his dreams were full of crowns.

# 59

# Jordan

Jordan had always loved the Feast of Midwinter, the celebration of the solstice, when the Lords of Light conquered darkness and the days became progressively longer. Lanverness celebrated Midwinter in much the same way as Navarre, with evergreen trees, yulecakes, presents, and feasts. Jordan cajoled her siblings into setting up a small pine tree in their common sitting room. Decorated with strings of popped corn, ribbons, and ornamental pinecones, the evergreen tree was a delight to the senses. A few well-wrapped presents glittered beneath the lower branches. An odd shaped package wrapped in gold looked particularly tantalizing but Jordan refused to investigate. She suspected that Justin put his presents out early to tease his sisters. The temptation was hard to resist but Jordan refused to give her brother the satisfaction. Despite her burning curiosity, she resolved to wait till Midwinter morning, besides she had other things on her mind. Her presents for Jemma, Justin, and Duncan were already wrapped and hidden in the trunk in her bedroom, but the most important present, her gift for Stewart, was not yet finished. The jeweler had promised to have it done today and Jordan was anxious to pick it up.

The snow-dusted streets were busy with merchants hauling their wares and shoppers carrying baskets laden with packages. The city of Pellanor never slept and the variety of goods available in the markets and craft shops was astounding. Jordan had enjoyed exploring the city searching for the perfect Midwinter gifts. In a musty shop off of a side alleyway, she found an old scroll with the works of Xel, a master harpist from the Age of Magic. She was sure Justin would be delighted with the rare find. For Jemma, the fashion maven, the choices in Pellanor were limitless. Jordan finally decided on a bolt of blue damask silk worked with a rich pattern of silver thread. She purchased the whole bolt, avoiding the thorny question of what was 'in' or 'out' of style.

As to Duncan, the man was always hard to shop for, but the markets of Pellanor proved equal to the challenge. Since Duncan was the companion for her Wayfaring, Jordan wanted to get him something special to mark the start of her traveling years. The taciturn archer liked things that were practical, but he also had a weakness for excellent craftsmanship. His taste for excellence held the key to Duncan's present. Knowing it was a waste of time to shop for anything having to do with archery in Pellanor, she'd settled on the idea of a new pair of boots. She'd overheard the infantrymen in the Rose Squad talking about a cobbler who made boots using the hide of an exotic lizard found only in the great southern swamps of Radagar. Boots made of this rare hide were said to be water tight, light of weight, comfortable, and durable enough to last a lifetime. From the soldiers' description, they almost sounded like the fabled 'boots of walking' supposedly worn by the wizards of old. Curiosity alone was enough to get Jordan to search out the shop. The wizen old cobbler wanted a small fortune to make the boots, claiming the exotic lizard was a man-eater, making the hide doubly rare. The price was prohibitive but Jordan was hooked once she fingered the supple smoke-gray hide. The boots would be perfect for Duncan.

With her shopping for Duncan finished, that left Stewart. She'd put a lot of thought into Stewart's present, wanting her gift to reflect Navarre. Making the rounds of the shops on Gold Street, she finally found a jeweler who would accept her unusual commission. Jordan hurried though the back streets, eager to see the finished product.

The bell on the shop door rang as she entered. Looking up from his work bench, the hunchbacked goldsmith flashed a smile. "The piece is finally finished and I think you will be pleased." He opened a locked cabinet and removed a small handful of cloth. "I've never worked with this combination of materials before. Your commission was challenging and the piece is quite unique. I hope you are happy with it."

Jordan held Stewart's present to the light, carefully examining the design. The piece was beautiful, the workmanship exquisite, but the proof would be in the listening. Holding her breath, she held it to her ear. A smile spread across her face. It was perfect. She paid the man his price while the jeweler wrapped the piece in a checkered red and blue silk handkerchief, the colors of Navarre. She tucked Stewart's present in her pocket and headed for her last stop.

Jordan loved the tradition of yulecakes. Individual gingerbread cakes, no larger than the palm of the hand conveyed a heartfelt wish for the new year. Yulecakes came in four shapes, a diamond for wealth and prosperity, a circle for peace and harmony, a star for fame and success, and a heart for love and happiness. The cake's shape expressed the wish and the coin baked inside expressed the nature of the relationship. Copper coins were used for new friends and acquaintances while silver coins were meant for good friends, light lovers, and distant relatives. Gold coins were reserved for close family members and life-long friends. Gold coins also symbolized true love. A nervous flutter ran through her. This year she needed her cakes to be perfect.

Having sampled the different bakeries across the city, she'd found a shop that made the most delicious gingerbread and then wrapped them in bright shiny foil. Her last errand was to pick up her order before returning to the castle.

The bakery was mobbed. When her turn finally came, Jordan inspected the cakes, quizzing the baker to be sure the hidden coins were just as she'd ordered. Satisfied, she paid for the cakes and threaded a path out of the crowd. The cheerful smell of fresh baked gingerbread clung to her cloak as she made her way back to the castle.

By tradition Midwinter day was spent with close family members but the eve of the solstice was reserved for good friends and lovers. Jordan was especially looking forward to the evening. Stewart had invited her out for a private solstice eve dinner. He'd offered to take her anywhere, but the only place she wanted to go was the Bear's Den. The cozy, casual intimacy of the Den suited Jordan perfectly. She couldn't imagine a better place to spend her first solstice eve with Stewart.

Returning to her bedroom, Jordan was surprised to find a steaming tub of hot water waiting for her. On a table next to the tub was a small package with a note. The note was in her sister's handwriting. 'Dear Jordan. An alchemist in the old part of town swears by this secret concoction of herbs and spices. Sprinkle it in your bath and you're guaranteed to find true love! I suspect the old alchemist is a bit of a fraud but the mixture smells wonderful. Enjoy your solstice eve with Stewart. I won't be waiting up for you. Love, Jemma.'

Half embarrassed and half amused, Jordan picked up the package and sniffed its contents. Rich aromas of sandalwood and cinnamon evoked a hint of the mysterious. Jordan didn't believe in love potions but the powder smelled delightful. She dumped the contents into the tub and slipped into the heated water. Fragrant swirls of steam danced across the water. Succumbing to the heat, Jordan considered her plans for Midwinter. Her solstice eve with Stewart would be special. Outside of her parents, she'd never given anyone a heart-shaped yulecake with a gold coin inside. Jordan wondered if she was being rash, but her heart was sure. For once she would let her heart lead.

Climbing out of the tub, she toweled off in front of a blazing fire. She'd given a lot of thought to her choice of clothes, determined to be herself. In the end, she settled on a combination of new and old. For the old, she pulled on her favorite pair of black leather pants and knee-high boots. For something different, she put on a cream-colored silk shirt with puffed pirate sleeves and ruffles around a low-cut v-neck. Over the silk shirt, she wore a dark blue suede jerkin that conformed to her slender waist and small breasts. Pleased with her reflection, she swirled her checkered cape around her shoulders. Placing her Midwinter gift and yulecake for Stewart in a small leather pouch on her belt, she gave herself a final check and then headed out to meet her prince.

She found him waiting at the castle's southern gates. Their embrace was full of unspoken emotions. With arms linked and heads nearly touching, they walked through the streets of Pellanor, taking a familiar path to the Bear's Den. Under a light frosting of snow, the city looked magical. The night held the promise of a perfect solstice eve.

At the Bear's Den, they were shown to their favorite table, tucked away in a private nook next to a roaring fireplace. Jordan ordered a creamy clam chowder while Stewart ordered his favorite lamb stew. The mere thought of the simple but savory fare made her mouth water. When the serving girl left with their order, they both leaned forward across the table, holding hands and talking about memories of favorite Midwinter Feasts from childhood days.

They were both surprised when the girl returned. After serving large bowls of soups and pouring mugs of mulled wine, the girl ceremoniously placed a platter of fresh-ocean mussels cooked in a garlic butter sauce in the center of the table. Jordan stared in amazement. The dish was unheard of for land-locked Lanverness. It was also Jordan's favorite. "I can't believe you did this!"

"I wanted to make this evening special."

Blushing, she replied, "You've certainly done that."

Their eyes locked and the food was momentarily forgotten. Giving her a soft smile, Stewart said, "Try them and tell me if they are as good as the ones you get from home."

Anticipating the taste, she pried a succulent morsel from a black shell. Swirling it in the buttery sauce, she popped it into her mouth. Closing her eyes, she savored the taste. The tender mussel gushed with juices full of garlic and butter, a small bite of heaven. Opening her eyes, she laughed to see the way Stewart was staring at her.

With a shy grin, he explained, "It's amazing the way that you get so much pleasure out of such simple things."

Blushing again, she laughed, "My mother always told me that the secret to a happy life is to savor the small things. The small things in life often bring the greatest joy."

"Your mother is a wise woman." After a short pause, Stewart added, "I would like to meet her some day."

"Mother will love you." Realizing what she'd said, Jordan added, "You'll have to come with me to Navarre sometime. There is so much I want to show you." Selecting another mussel, she leaned across the table and offered it to Stewart. "Have a taste of the seaside kingdom."

Stewart seemed to enjoy the delicacy almost as much as Jordan did. They shared the mussels, wiping the last bit of garlic sauce from the platter with torn pieces of crusty bread. Between morsels they traded stories from their childhoods. With six siblings, Jordan had plenty of tales to tell. They were laughing over one of Justin's pranks when the serving girl came to clear their table. After removing the dishes, the girl placed a traditional bayberry candle and flint striker in the center of the table.

When it was just the two of them again, Stewart handed Jordan the striker, indicating she should do the honors. The gesture touched her heart. By tradition, the oldest male at the table lit the candle. By handing her the striker, Stewart proved he considered Jordan his equal. Perhaps all men should have strong queens for mothers. She lit the candle, saying the traditional prayer. "We are only mortals, but we do what we can to aid the Light. May this candle join with all the other candles of Midwinter to light a blaze that pushes back the Darkness. May the peace of the Light reign across the land."

The mood changed between them, both reminded of the heavy responsibilities of future crowns.

Stewart reached across the table to take her hand. "So which shall it be, my lady? Will you have your Midwinter present first or will you start with your yulecake?"

By tradition, the yulecakes were exchanged first, but tonight the small gingerbread cakes were more important than the presents. Suddenly hesitant, Jordan said, "The presents first, I think."

Smiling, Stewart reached for a large sack. She'd eyed the sack on their walk from the castle but the contours of the bag gave nothing away. The sack yielded a long rectangular box wrapped in gold paper. "I hope you like it."

Overcome by curiosity, she tore the paper from the box. Inside, she found a straight infantry sword in a scabbard. The scabbard was magnificent. Made of tooled red leather, it was embossed with soaring osprey eagles, each clutching a bouquet of roses. Running her hand across the details, her fingers lingered on the combined heraldry of their two houses. Her heart beat faster at the meaning behind the design. Before she could say anything, Stewart said, "Draw the blade."

She drew the blade, noticing the maker's mark, an anvil within an octagon. Jordan gasped, the smiths of Castlegard were renowned for their blades. With the exception of blue steel blades, there were none better in all of Erdhe. She did not know how to thank him.

"I want you to have the best sword at your side." Dropping his voice, he whispered, "May it protect you when I cannot."

Her heart melted. Leaning across the table, she kissed him. He deepened the kiss, sending a searing heat through her. Cradling her face, he whispered, "Now that was the perfect Midwinter gift."

Jordan flamed red. They broke apart, pausing to catch their breath.

Still recovering from the kiss, Jordan produced a small package wrapped in checkered silk. "I hope you like it."

He took his time opening it, nearly driving her to distraction. Finally the silk fell away, revealing the broach. Circular in design, the top half was a golden sun setting on a sea of turquoise. A speckled cone shell was mounted midway between the sea and the sunset. Leaning across the table, Jordan explained, "I wanted to give you something of Navarre. This little cone shell is one of the few things I brought from home. If you press the shell to your ear you can hear the sound of the ocean waves." Pausing, she added, "I had to find a jeweler who could make it without ruining the magic of the shell. Press it to your ear and listen." She knew Stewart had never experienced the wonders of the ocean. By giving him the broach, she hoped to give him something of her home. She held her breath as he pressed the broach to his ear.

"So this is what the ocean sounds like!" Puzzlement transformed to wonder. "How amazing! So much sound from such a little thing." He pinned the broach to his cape. "My Lady of the Seashell."

Suddenly shy, Jordan knew it was time to exchange the yulecakes. Her heart pounded with trepidation. She'd be crushed if her yulecake from Stewart did not contain a gold coin. Swallowing her fear, she shyly handed Stewart a foil wrapped cake in the shape of a heart.

Stewart accepted the cake and gave her one of the same.

Jordan held the fragile cake with shaking hands. She carefully removed the wrapping not wanting to incur bad luck by pre-maturely breaking the heart-shape. As tradition dictated, she nibbled a small bite of the gingerbread but she couldn't taste a thing. Taking a deep breath, she broke the cake open. A gold coin winked from the center. Jordan rubbed her eyes, trying to hold back tears of joy. Stealing a glance at Stewart, she saw that he'd discovered his own gold coin. Their hands met across the table. A hungry intensity filled their touch.

In a throaty voice, Stewart said, "I don't want this night to end." He voice dropped to a whisper. "Will you come with me to a nearby inn...or should I walk you back to the castle?"

They were both acutely aware that Jordan's time in Pellanor was coming to an end. A deep hunger grew within her. She'd never done this before, but she wanted it more than anything. "Let's find a room..."

He squeezed her hand and then fumbled with his purse to pay the bill. Wrapping an arm around her waist, he guided her out of the Bear's Den and into the snow-covered streets. She couldn't remember the walk through the streets, only the urgency to get there.

They took a room at one of the capital's better inns. Stewart fumbled with the key at the door. The furnishings were rich and a blaze roared in the fireplace. There was a large four-poster bed but Jordan spied the lush fur of a snowcat's skin spread before the fire. Stewart swept her into his arms to carry her to the bed but Jordan gestured toward the snowcat. Laughing, he gently laid her on the lush white fur. Resting his full weight on top of her, he kissed her deeply. His fingertips caressed her face, running through her sandy hair. His touch was slow and gentle as he gazed into her eyes. Without speaking, he asked if this was what she truly wanted. His look alone woke an ache deep within her...an ache she'd never known before. Closing her eyes, she met his lips, answering him with a kiss. Their kisses deepened and a blaze of heat swept through them. Their clothes became too much to bear. With a mixture of tenderness and laughter they stripped away the encumbering garments. When she finally saw him naked she gasped. Stewart was hard and beautiful. Her hands reached out to trace the contours of his body. With hands and lips they explored all the differences between them. Tenderness gradually gave way to urgency. Jordan could tell that Stewart was trying to wait, but she urged him on. The ache within grew unbearable. She arched her back with need. In a blaze of love and urgency, Stewart succumbed, joining with her in the shared ecstasy of two becoming one.

In a small corner of her mind, Jordan knew the first time was supposed to hurt, but it didn't. Stewart was wonderful. He filled the ache within her...until it came back with an even more powerful surge. Letting their bodies follow their instincts, they rode each wave of passion until they collapsed spent on the soft white fur. Jordan twined her fingers in Stewart's dark hair, wishing the night would never end.

# 60

# Liandra

The queen contemplated the chessboard. The game had reached that critical stage when major pieces on both sides would be sacrificed for the sake of strategy. The game was about to get bloody. Staring at the board, Liandra discovered a clumsy trap and a clever feint, both designed to screen red's attack on her white knight. Mentally playing both sides of the game, she anticipated the future moves of the Master Archivist. A smile played across her face as the master's strategy became clear. Having learned the game of princes at her father's knee, the queen was well versed in the two keys to victory: using layered strategies and always seeing more moves ahead than your opponent. It was a philosophy the queen applied to many things besides chess.

Fondling a defeated pawn, the queen considered her next move. She decided to take the red castle with her monk in order to protect her knight. As the trickiest piece on the board, Liandra had an innate fondness for her knights. Moving the ivory monk diagonally across the board, she took the red castle, rescuing the beleaguered knight. Satisfied with her decision, she considered future moves. Chess held so many similarities with life, but the designers of the ancient game had gotten some of the pieces wrong. The tricky moves assigned to the knights should belong to the monks. In real life, the knights were a straightforward lot, solving every problem with the edge of a sword, while the monks, cloaked in the guise of serving a higher power, were ever the devious ones. In the queen's opinion, the movements of the monks warranted closer scrutiny. She longed to decipher the convoluted strategies of the elusive Grand Master of the Kiralynn Order. Staring at the board, the queen wondered how the game would play out.

A knock interrupted her thoughts. The queen did not bother to reply. The guards had instructions to admit her guest as soon as she arrived. The outer door opened and closed. From the corner of her eye, the queen watched Princess Katherine bow as she entered the room.

Keeping her face turned to the board, the queen said, "Do you play?"

The princess crossed the room with a warrior's lithe grace and stared down at the chessboard. "Yes, of course." She fingered a defeated pawn. "My father insisted that my brothers learn to play, saying they needed to learn the art of strategy just as much as the art of the sword." Shrugging, the princess added, "No one taught me, but I watched anyway. It wasn't until the master healer came to Castlegard that I had someone to play against."

The queen gestured for the princess to take the opposite chair. "You did well to study the game of princes despite the lack of encouragement. Chess keeps the mind sharp, always looking for plots within plots, a skill that is much needed for those who sit a throne." Setting the captured red castle with the other defeated pieces, the queen added, "There are not many in the Rose Court who can offer us a game worthy of our time. We play a running game with the Master Archivist, although we seldom sit across from each other." Pausing to study the princess, the queen added, "We are always looking for a new challenge. It is a pity we have not had a chance to test our wits with you across the chessboard. It would be interesting to see how Castlegard plays the game of princes."

The princess returned the queen's stare, a guarded expression on her face.

The queen let the silence settle across the board. Pine logs snapped and crackled, releasing the scent of a summer forest. The queen studied her guest. "In terms of the chess pieces, how would you describe yourself?"

The young woman picked up a defeated white pawn. Rubbing her thumb across the carved ivory, she answered, "My father, the king, clearly considers me a pawn, but I see myself as a knight, serving the Light with my sword...but perhaps it is too early in the game to tell where I belong or what the gods intend for me." In a fervent voice, she whispered, "Do you know where I belong?"

The question hung in the air, a bridge connecting the two women.

Once again, the young woman had surprised her. "It is true you started the game as a pawn but it is clear you have a different destiny. Under the guise of a pawn, you march across the board, slipping past the major pieces. First Castlegard, then the Mordant's men in the wilds of Wyeth...and now you have the attention of the Kiralynn monks."

Shock claimed the young woman's face.

The queen read between the lines. "So this is not the first you've heard of the Kiralynn monks."

The princess took a deep breath. "Just yesterday, in my bedchambers, I found a scroll bearing the monks' seal."

More proof that the monks had spies within her castle. She'd long suspected it yet the truth hit hard. Liandra resolved to ferret them out. "Do you have any idea why the monks are so interested in you?"

"No. Castlegard has never had any dealings with the monks. I know very little about them."

Hearing truth in the young woman's words, the queen allowed herself a small laugh. "The monks would have us believe there is very little to know, yet they keep their fingers on the pulse of power in the southern kingdoms. Quite an amazing feat for monks who supposedly lead a cloistered life behind the distant walls of their mountain monastery."

Seeing the look of puzzlement on the princess's face, the queen explained, "From time to time, the Rose Crown receives messages from the Grand Master of the Kiralynn Order. The messages often seem irrelevant or obscure on first reading but experience has shown that they are always of great import." Picking up a defeated white pawn, the queen said, "For the first time in recent history, we received two scrolls from the monks bearing identical messages." Studying the princess, the queen said, "Both scrolls request that a Princess Katherine of Castlegard be sent to the Southern Mountains for fostering. So I will ask you again, why are the monks so interested in you?"

"Their scroll offered a compelling argument for fostering at their monastery...though I confess I am confused by the depth of their knowledge. The scroll implies there are some things only the monks can teach...so perhaps I should go to their monastery and see what they have to offer."

"So will you go?"

"I know very little about them. What do you advise?"

Pleased with the question, Liandra replied, "The monks are too mysterious for our liking. Their objectives are not obvious, yet it seems they serve the Light." Pausing, the queen added, "You are of royal birth, but duty has not yet claimed you. Perhaps you are meant to travel this road. You have our leave to go or to stay as you see fit. The choice is yours. But remember, the monks' words are not to be taken lightly." Gesturing toward the board, the queen added, "Like the game of chess, we suggest you make the move which will ultimately bring you the greatest advantage."

"Thank you for giving me the choice."

Curiosity plagued the queen, but she held her silence, waiting to see what the princess would reveal. When nothing more was offered, she said, "Princess Jordan of Navarre is also meant to foster with the monks. Perhaps you should join her and Lord Duncan on the trek to the Southern Mountains."

The princess's face brightened. "I'd like that...perhaps this journey is meant to be."

Seeing the decision was made, the queen said, "Given the winter conditions in the mountains, we expect you will have a turn of the moon before starting your journey. Perhaps you will consent to a game of chess before you go?" Wanting to learn more about this intriguing young woman, the queen gestured toward the chessboard. "If you were red, what would your next move be?"

The princess bent her head to the board, her gaze darting across the pieces. The queen waited, interested to test the depth of the young woman's thinking.

The princess pointed to the red king's side of the board. "I'd advance the castle's pawn to threaten the white monk."

The queen studied the board. At first glance, the move appeared to be nothing more than an annoying nuisance, causing a slight delay to white's inevitable victory. Disappointed, Liandra looked at the princess. Seeing a small smile play across the young woman's face, the queen took a closer look at the board. Mentally working through the moves, Liandra was surprised to discover that the move could evolve into an unorthodox attack on the white king. It was a risky gambit, requiring the sacrifice of the red queen, but it had the possibility of leading to a swift checkmate, reversing the outcome of the game.

Liandra smiled. "Very shrewd. You use a minor piece to snatch victory from defeat."

The princess returned the queen's smile. "I don't like to lose. Besides, minor pieces can sometimes offer the greatest surprise."

Nodding in approval, the queen studied the young woman who had started the game of princes as a pawn. Ursus might overlook his own daughter but Liandra intended to keep an eye on the young woman. Of all the chess pieces, only the pawn had the potential to be transformed into a powerful queen.

# 61

# Jordan

Their swords met with a clash. Jordan pivoted away, catching a second blow on her shield. Feinting to the left and then pivoting right, she slipped her sword inside of her opponent's guard to tag Kath on the breastplate. The move won the sparring match, but it was all too easy.

Shaking her head in disbelief, Jordan stepped out of the ring. She was taller and had the advantage of reach, but the younger woman was by far the superior sword. Except for the Octagon knights, Jordan doubted any man in the training yard could best Kath in the sword ring. Something troubled her sword sister...enough to make her lose. Worried, Jordan removed her half helm. "You've worn me out. Let's take a short walk on the parapet before we get back to the ring."

Kath sheathed her sword and nodded, a distracted look on her face. Leaving their helmets and shields on the bench, they twirled cloaks around their shoulders and climbed the narrow stairs to the battlement. A crisp wind tugged at Jordan's sandy hair, pulling it from behind her ear. Walking along the snow-dusted parapet, she watched Kath from the corner of her eye. The younger woman stared off in the distance with a troubled gaze. Concerned, Jordan said, "You weren't yourself in the sparring ring. What bothers you?"

Kath startled, as if she'd been discovered doing something she shouldn't. Jordan held her breath hoping the younger woman would trust enough to confide in her. In a hesitant voice, Kath said, "I've got a lot on my mind...and I do need someone to talk to."

Jordan walked in silence, giving her time.

The words came slow at first, like a trickle from a leaking dam. "I had a meeting with the queen yesterday. A scroll arrived from the Southern

Mountains. I don't really know much about the Kiralynn monks...but it seems that they want me to come to their monastery for fostering."

Jordan let out a whoop of joy. Flashing Kath a smile, she said, "I've been dreading the thought of leaving Pellanor...but if you're coming I won't be leaving so much behind." Glancing at the knights practicing below in the yard, she asked, "So will the knights be going with you?" She still regretted not going to Castlegard for her Wayfaring. Finding the knights in Pellanor had proved an unexpected boon.

"Sir Blaine and Sir Tyrone are pledged to me but the others will return to Castlegard. The smith has all the measurements he needs to complete the queen's commission, so their work here is done." Kath murmured, "I'll need to send another dispatch to my father. The queen gave me her blessing. Hopefully that will mollify father." Shrugging, she added, "Either way, I'll be too distant to feel his wrath."

"I'll be glad to have your company, but why are you suddenly going to the monks?"

Kath walked in silence, absently knocking snow from the notched battlement. "I have a secret."

Jordan stilled. The younger woman always seemed to carry a hidden burden far beyond her years. She hoped Kath would share whatever troubled her. "I have your back, sword sister, on or off the battlefield."

"This secret stays between us?"

"I swear."

Kath gave her a solemn nod. Reaching beneath her tunic, she tugged on a leather cord, revealing a small figurine. Carved of stone, the squat gargoyle had amazing details, a mythical mix of a hawk's beak, a lion's body, and bat wings. "I found this in Castlegard. It's made of mage-stone, the same as the inner castle. It's supposed to be magical but I don't know how to use it. The monks claim they can teach me the secret of my gargoyle." Falling silent, Kath looked warily at Jordan as if she expected to be scorned.

Her wariness was understandable. Most of Erdhe considered magic to be evil, something tainted by the Dark Lord, but the royal house of Navarre was no stranger to magic. "I do not fear magic. Magic enables the queens of Navarre to give birth to the tuplets that are so necessary to the royal succession. Without magic, my siblings and I would never have been born." Putting a reassuring hand on her friend's arm, she said, "Magic is like a sword, used for good or evil depending on the hand that wields it. The gods have seen fit to entrust you with magic. I know you'll find a way to use it for good. Your secret is safe with me."

"Then you understand why I must go to the monks?"

"Magic is a great responsibility. If the monks can teach to use it then of course you must go."

A weight seemed to lift from the young woman's shoulders. Tucking the little figurine beneath her tunic, Kath said, "Only a few people know about my gargoyle. The two knights, Sir Blaine and Sir Tyrone...and there is one other." With a puzzled look on her face, she added, "It's a mystery to me how the monks learned of it."

Jordan shrugged. "Perhaps it is a blessing they know. Otherwise you might never learn to master it."

Kath nodded. "Just so."

The two friends walked along the snow-dusted parapet, occasionally pausing to lean on the battlements, watching the knights cross swords in the training yard below. After a while, Kath said in a serious voice, "Can I ask you something else?"

"Of course."

"Tell me about Duncan."

Jordan tried to keep the shock from her face. So this was the reason Kath became strangely silent whenever the leather-clad archer was around. Jordan studied her sword sister. The princess of Castlegard carried a weight of responsibility that was far beyond her years, but when it came to love it was clear she was inexperienced. Duncan, on the other hand, was a good man but he was also very...worldly. On the face of it, Jordan could not see the match working. "What do you want to know?"

With a wry smile, Kath replied, "Anything...everything."

So it was as bad as that. Knowing that love was rarely logical, Jordan decided to keep her doubts to herself, after all, who could say where Eros would send his lightening bolts. Perhaps there was more to this match than met the eye. Shrugging, she gave in to the simple sisterly pleasure of gossiping about an interesting man. "I hardly know where to begin."

Kath grinned, an eager gleam in her eyes. "The beginning is always a good place. Have you always known Duncan?"

"Almost always. My father met Duncan on a boar hunt in the Delta. He was hired as a scout to track a wild boar. The boar was dangerous, said to be a ferocious killer. My father's party cornered the beast in its lair. The boar charged. My father set the butt of his spear to take the weight of the charge, but the spear shattered without slowing the boar. The others watched in horror as the beast bore down on the king. Somehow Duncan loosed an arrow over the king's shoulder, straight into the beast's eye. The shot struck true, piercing the boar's brain. The beast dropped dead at my father's feet. They said that it was an amazing shot, for it's almost impossible to fell a wild razorback with an arrow. The king was safe, the killer boar was dead, and Duncan was hailed as a hero. When my father returned to Navarre, he brought Duncan with him. In time, Duncan became a trusted advisor and a true friend to the king."

"So Duncan is originally from the Delta?"

"No, Duncan was an adventurer looking for a home. I guess he found what he was looking for in Navarre."

"So where's he from?"

"If you ask him, I'm sure he'll say what he always does, 'from everywhere and nowhere'."

Kath walked in silence, her face thoughtful. "So how did he come to wear a patch on his eye?"

Jordan hesitated but Kath deserved the truth. "He always says he lost the eye in a fight over a woman. He never says more than that. Just that he won the fight, lost the eye, and that the woman was not worth it."

A frown passed across Kath's face. In a quiet voice she asked, "So does he have a woman back in Navarre?"

Now they'd come to the heart of the matter. Jordan said gently, "You have to understand that Duncan is a very private, very discrete man...but he also has a way with women." Pausing to choose her words carefully, Jordan added, "I've always felt Duncan never lacked for female companionship...yet he never brought any woman to the Midwinter Feast or talked of anyone special. Somehow I always felt none of the women of Navarre ever captured his heart."

A smile spread across Kath's face.

Jordan hesitated; worrying her friend would be hurt. Breaking off an icicle, she watched the icy spear plummet to the yard, shattering into a thousand shards. "Be careful Kath. If your heart is somehow set on Duncan, be warned you're sailing into deep, uncharted seas."

Kath whispered, "I know." She shook her head. "This makes no sense. My way is the sword. There's no room for anything else, especially not a man. But somehow I cannot help myself. Duncan tugs at both my heart and my mind."

Jordan was not surprised. In hindsight, it was clear from the way Kath acted around the leather clad archer that she was smitten. Hoping to lighten the mood, she said, "Then let's hope one of Eros can penetrate the thick leather hide he wears around his heart like armor."

Flashing a smile, Kath said, "We'd best get back to the training yard or the knights will begin to worry." The two friends returned to the yard, challenging the knights to a round in the sparring ring. Jordan watched her friend, relieved to see that she moved with a lighter step, as if talking had somehow lessened her burdens. She was glad Kath had shared her concerns but she worried about her friend's happiness. Love could cut deeper than swords.

# 62

# Liandra

The queen was never one to miss an opportunity. The monks' interest in the princess of Castlegard might prove the opening she'd long looked for. Something stirred in Erdhe. Liandra sensed a deeper game, something beyond the politics of mere kingdoms. Darkness claimed Coronth and Lanverness could be next. The monks knew something and the queen refused to enter the game blind.

Pulling her ermine cloak close, she stepped out onto the frosted balustrade, a cold morning for such dire thoughts. At a gesture her guards fell back and she continued on alone. She found him leaning against the battlement, staring down into the sparring yard, the sound of swords drifting upwards. She took a moment to admire the view. Sir Cardemir was a man built for power, tall and imposing with a knight's broad shoulders and a tapered waist, yet Liandra knew a shrewd mind lurked beneath the chain mailed exterior. Born the fifth son of a powerful duke, he openly chaffed at his lesser position, using his sword to win acclaim. But victory in the tournament field was hollow compared to a duke's seat. His burning ambition had not gone unnoticed. The queen had plans for Sir Cardemir, but only if he passed her test.

She continued toward him and he turned as if sensing her presence. Always the gallant, he gave her a courtly bow, the wind tugging at his powder blue cloak. "My queen." He flashed a deep smile, his auburn hair framing a ruggedly handsome face. "Your summons was a pleasant surprise, but why the battlements?"

"Walk with us."

He offered his arm and she accepted, the clang of swords forming a counterpoint to her thoughts. "There are many paths to power."

His gaze turned her way, snared with interest.

"Your desire for a seat on our royal council has not gone unnoticed, but we need to be sure that your mind and your tongue are as sharp as your sword, and that your loyalty is unswerving."

He leaned toward her, a bear baited by the scent of honey.

"We have decided to send an emissary to the Kiralynn monks, to their bastion of secrets set deep in the Southern Mountains."

"But I thought the monks a myth?"

"Exactly what they would have you believe. The monks work hard to hide behind their myths but those who wear a crown know otherwise."

"A royal secret," a hungry smile crossed his face but it soon turned to shrewdness. "What you really want is a spy."

"No need to be rude. Emissary is a much more polite term, though it serves the same purpose."

"But why me? I'm no diplomat."

"There's a chance the monks may overlook a shrewd mind hidden beneath chainmail. And your skill with a sword will endear you to the others."

"Others?"

The queen paused to stare down into the sparring yard, watching as two women danced the steel amongst a dozen knights. "You are to accompany the princesses of Castlegard and Navarre to the mountain monastery."

"Hence our meeting on the battlement."

The queen watched as the princess of Castlegard dodged a blow and then ducked inside the reach of the knight, her sword striking his breastplate. "Are they as good as reports indicate?"

"They are amazing," a hint of admiration crept into his voice, "especially the shorter one, the princess of Castlegard. Despite her lack of reach and strength she has a sixth sense for the sword, displaying a skill I'd never thought to see in a woman."

The queen raised an eyebrow. "Then we've chosen wisely."

His grin evaporated. "But the Southern Mountains are far from the Rose Court."

She resumed walking. "Don't think of it as an exile, think of it as an opportunity."

"For how long?"

"Three months if you are very shrewd. Bring us the secrets of the monks and you shall have a seat on our council. But it must be done delicately. We wish to forge an alliance not make an enemy. Invite them to send an emissary to our court. We would put a face to the monks instead of having them lurk in the shadows."

"But if the monks are so secretive will they welcome an emissary, especially one that is not invited?"

It was a shrewd question, just the type she expected from him. "Let your mission become known throughout the court. The monks have spies everywhere. They will make their wishes known before your party ever leaves the Rose Court."

"And once there?"

"Gain their trust and win their secrets. We would know the source of their power, and their interest in the southern kingdoms. We wish to learn the nature of their game. Do this and you will win our royal favor."

Ambition kindled his gaze. "It shall be as you command."

Kissing her emerald ring, he lingered over her hand. It was not unpleasant. "Will you need an introduction?"

"To the princesses?" He gave her a rogue's smile. "Charm is the best introduction to any woman."

For a moment she wondered at the depth of his ambition. "Careful, lest you overreach."

He had the intelligence to look chagrined. "Majesty, I am ever your servant, for none can outshine the Rose Queen. I'll merely offer the wild hawk a velvet glove instead of a mailed fist."

"See that you remember your mission."

"Always." He gave her a sweeping bow and then sauntered from the battlement.

The queen lingered, gazing down at the sparring ground. Her decision was made and the die cast. She'd send her emissary to the monks, seizing the chance to learn their secrets, but she wondered if she'd loosed a fox among the royal hens. Only time would tell.

# 63

# Steffan

The Dark Lord gave Steffan three gifts when he surrendered his soul at the Oracle. The first gift was the luck of the dice. Unable to lose without concentrating, Steffan amassed a small fortune in golds at the dicing tables. His wealth bought him a lavish lifestyle with plenty of golds to advance the Dark Lord's plans. Life was good in the service of the Dark Lord.

The Dark Lord's second gift was a lesson on human nature. By understanding human nature, the Dark Lord gave Steffan the means to twist and corrupt the souls of men. By unlocking the secret motives of those around him, Steffan manipulated lords and commoners alike, puppets dancing to the strings of their desires. With bribes of gold, power, sex, and religion, he created the Lord Raven and then schemed his way into controlling the kingdom of Coronth.

The third gift from the Dark Lord was the most powerful of all. The third gift would enable him to reach beyond Coronth, unleashing a terrible chaos among the kingdoms of Erdhe, the chaos the Dark Lord so craved. The third gift was the vision of prophecy.

The Dark Oracle showed Steffan visions of many possible futures. In the waters of the Oracle, he'd learned how the Dark Lord tended the threads of different possibilities, herding the kingdoms of Erdhe toward terrible futures where all of mankind bowed to the Dark Lord's will. The futures were wildly divergent, but a handful of common events were inevitable. These common events held the key to duping others into believing he had a true gift of prophecy. Seduced by prophecy, the people would eagerly follow any leader who could foresee the future.

Steffan used the first two gifts to secure his influence on the Pontifax. Now it was time to use the third gift to reach beyond Coronth. He started by arranging a dinner with the Pontifax when the Keeper was absent. As the two men dined on expensive delicacies and extravagant wines, Steffan drew on all of his skill to weave a vision of the future, a future where the Pontifax ruled over all of Erdhe. In this future, the Pontifax was revered as a demigod, the Beloved of the Flame God. Befitting his exalted status, he lived in unbelievable luxury, his many palaces making the Residence look like a hovel. His treasury overflowed with gems and bars of gold. Fathers willingly brought their virginal daughters to the temple begging for special blessings. Steffan painted a vision lavish with luxury, each detail designed to ensnare the imagination.

Sipping a glass of Urian brandy, the Pontifax gave his counselor an indulgent grin. "My dear Lord Raven, this all sounds marvelous but it is only a dream, nothing more."

Knowing that the hook had been set, Steffan infused his voice with humility. "Enlightened One, despite all you have achieved in Coronth, you still underestimate the power of religion. The people will do anything for the promise of heaven...even throw their lives away in a religious war." Steffan leaned forward, his voice intense. "Do not underestimate the power of a single fanatical warrior, let alone an army of them. A fanatic does not care about common sense or logic, he does not care about the odds in battle, he does not even care about his own life...he cares only about his reward in heaven. Where other warriors surrender or flee in panic, the fanatic is unstoppable, fighting to the death. Fanatical warriors of the Flame are the true untapped power of Coronth." Dropping his voice to a whisper he added, "You are the beloved of the Flame God, you are the religious leader of the people...only the Enlightened One can awaken the awesome power that slumbers just below the surface of Coronth."

The Pontifax had a hungry look on his face yet he kept his silence. The man was tempted but not convinced. Having prepared the field, Steffan planted the seed. "Enlightened One, I have a confession to make... a secret to tell." Putting anguish in his voice, he said, "I feel compelled to reveal this secret to you so that you can achieve your true destiny...though I fear what you might think of me." He hid his gaze from the Pontifax, his face composed in a mask of fear.

The Pontifax took the bait. "There is nothing you cannot tell me. Surely you can share this secret with me."

Maintaining his mask, Steffan took a tortured breath. "There is a blessing, or perhaps a curse, that runs through my family, through the house of Raven." Dropping his voice to a reluctant whisper, he said, "Males of my line who are born with a white lock of hair, inevitably develop dreams of true seeing."

Shock caused the Pontifax to drop his own mask. Naked greed flashed from his eyes.

Steffan hid his smile; the glimpse of greed proved the old charlatan was smart enough to grasp the limitless value of prophecy.

The Pontifax leaned forward, his voice rich with paternal undertones. "And have you experienced these dreams of true seeing?"

"Yes, Enlightened One, it is how I knew to come to Coronth. My dreams told me to seek out the master of the Flames. Together I knew we would do great things."

"And what do your dreams tell you now?"

Adding a touch of fear to his voice, Steffan asked, "You won't reject me because of the taint in my blood?"

The Pontifax gave Steffan a benevolent smile. "Perhaps this *taint*, as you call it, is actually a *gift*. Now tell me of your dreams and together we'll make sense of the future."

"You must understand that I cannot control these dreams. They come of their own accord...but lately I have risen each morning with the same vision seared into my mind. A dream so real, so vivid, that I am compelled to share it with you. I swear on my soul, it is a dream that could change the world!" Steffan stared into the eyes of the Pontifax, his voice dropping to a hushed whisper. "Holy One, in two turns of the moon, there will be a great sign in the night sky. The heavens themselves will foretell your victory, for the Flame God will brand the sky with his mark. A red star will blaze a path across the heavens etching a wound in the dark of night. This red star signals your ascent to greatness."

The Pontifax studied Steffan, his face skeptical.

"Now is the time! Rouse the people! Call them to arms! Build an army of fanatics and tell them that the Flame God will grant them a celestial sign for all to see, proof of a righteous Holy War." Exerting his full powers of persuasion, Steffan whispered, "I have seen it, Holy One. Under the light of the red star, your armies will advance across Erdhe. Nothing can stand in their way. The religion of the Flame God will spread across Erdhe and you, the Pontifax, the Beloved of the Flame...will be the demigod that rules over all." In a hushed voice, Steffan added, "It can happen, Holy One, but only if you dare to use my visions the same way you use your ruby amulet." His stare drilled into the Pontifax. "Dare to unleash the Holy War and take all of Erdhe into your hands."

The Pontifax had a glazed look of an addict. Steffan waited, letting the temptations work their own form of magic.

A shrewd look filled the high priest's face. He studied his counselor through hooded eyes, his voice dropping to a deadly rasp. "How much faith do you put in your visions?"

"I'd stake my life, my very soul, upon their truth!"

The Pontifax whispered, "So be it! I will take your advice and call the people to arms. I will build an army and foretell the coming of the red star. I will do all this, *but*...if the star does not appear as foretold, then the army will stay home and my ambitions will remain within Coronth." Staring at Steffan with hooded eyes, the Pontifax added, "If the red star does not appear, then, as the price of failure, the Lord Raven will walk the Test of Faith."

The logs snapped and crackled in the fireplace, the only sound in the small room. Steffan kept his face still as stone, struggling to hide his elation.

"Is this acceptable...or will you recant your visions?"

Bowing his head in surrender, Steffan replied, "I know my dreams are true. I know it is your destiny to start a Holy War and claim all the kingdoms of Erdhe for the Flame God. If you agree that the Lord Raven will remain by your side as your trusted advisor through all the victories to come, then I will agree to your price. If the red star does not appear as foretold then I will walk into the Flames of my own accord."

The Pontifax gave him a predatory smile. "So be it."

Steffan hid his smile. In the privacy of his mind, he saluted the Dark Lord. The seed of war had found fertile ground in Coronth. The three gifts of the Dark Lord would bear their bitter fruit and Steffan would have his chance at immortality. He could feel the Darkness gathering, ready to feast on all of Erdhe.

# 64

# Jordan

Jordan loved a good mystery. After giving the Octagon knights the slip, she and Kath followed the clues through the twists and turns of Castle Tandroth like a game of seek and find. "This has to be it." She checked the clue. "Seek protection in the hall of martial prowess." They stood in the doorway of a lofty dining hall. Sunlight flooded through stained glass windows embellished with jousting knights, sending rainbows of color across the wood floor. Battle banners hung from the rafters, emblems of so many proud houses. Jordan spied the red wyvern of Kardiff, the iron fist of Lingard, and the silver seahorse of Graymaris amongst the lesser houses. "This must be the place, but why here?"

Kath approached the long table. "Jordan, look."

She joined her sword sister and gaped at her find. Arrayed on the table were a shield and a helm. Rimmed in sparkling silver, the shield was small and round but cunningly wrought, the crest of Navarre enameled in the center, a winged osprey upon a checkered field of red and blue. Beside the shield sat a helm. The shield was a thing of beauty but the half helm was magnificent. Studded with garnets, the helm gleamed red in the sunlight, a golden hawk perched upon the top, a maroon octagon inscribed above the nose guard. Kath picked it up and tried it on, sparkling links of silvered chainmail protecting the back of her neck. It seemed a perfect fit.

"I'm glad you like my gifts." A knight stepped from the far shadows, his pale blue surcoat embroidered with a silver seahorse.

"The seahorse knight," the words whispered from Kath.

The knight inclined his head. "So you've noticed my blade work upon the sparring grounds, though we've yet to cross swords." He came towards them, a handsome man with auburn hair framing a noble face. "I never thought to meet two princesses so good with the sword." Jordan expected to hear sarcasm but his voice held only admiration. He made a courtly bow. "Allow me to introduce myself, Sir Cardemir of Graymaris."

Jordan's gaze narrowed. "But why the gifts and the string of clues?"

"I sought a better way to meet, something more memorable than a cold introduction by the queen. Please accept the gifts from one who hopes to be your traveling companion."

The seahorse knight was full of riddles. "Companion? What are you talking about?"

"The queen has appointed me as her emissary to the Kiralynn monks." His gaze turned serious. "I seek to join you in your travels to the monastery, if you'll have me?"

His question seemed sincere, as if they truly had a choice. Jordan turned towards Kath, a knowing look passing between them. "He *is* good with a sword." Kath nodded, a mischievous smile breaking across her face, "and he knows enough to ask instead of commanding." A look of agreement flashed between them. Kath turned towards the seahorse knight and gave their answer. "Your sword is welcome among us. We leave within a fortnight."

The knight grinned. "Then we are well met. Perhaps you'll join me for dinner before we depart?"

Jordan said, "Come to Soup night."

"Soup night?"

Kath answered. "It's Duncan's idea. A night of good hearty soup, warm conversations, and no titles."

Sir Cardemir frowned. "Duncan?"

Kath flashed a dazzling smile. "You'll meet him at Soup night."

"Then I will strive to be intrigued," he gave them a courtly bow, "until Soup night." He turned and left, his pale blue cloak swaying from his shoulders, a jaunty swagger in his step, as if he was accustomed to conquest.

Kath and Jordan shared a look. "That was something." Jordan was the first to laugh. "At least he's easy on the eyes."

Kath lifted the helm, admiring the workmanship. "And his gifts are amazing. I've never seen a finer helm."

Jordan sobered. "A gift of arms instead of lace or silk, it shows a rare insight, especially for a knight."

Kath's gaze narrowed. "Insight or shrewdness? He does come from the queen."

Jordan shrugged. "Either way, I think I like him. He'll make for an interesting traveling companion." A thought occurred to her. "And he might make Duncan jealous."

Kath rolled her eyes. "Jealous! I'd settle for interested."

"Duncan is more interested than you know. I've seen the way he looks at you."

Kath's gaze turned hungry. "How?"

"Like something rare, something he never expected to find, something he can't quite believe." Kath's eyes misted over. Jordan gathered up her shield, pleased with the way it fit her arm. "Come on, we have a Soup night to plan." Kath fell into step beside her. They'd gained a traveling companion, and perhaps a riddle wrapped in chainmail, but either way, Jordan expected the journey to be interesting.

# 65

## Samson

Like wildfire in a bone-dry meadow, the songs of the bards swept through the inns where the refugees stayed. Most of the ballads stirred the people's courage, rousing them to take up swords against the Flame God, but other songs touched at the heartstrings, reminding the refugees of loved ones lost. Samson walked through the inn, listening to songs and hummed bits of melody. The music of the bards lodged deep in the hearts of the refugees, giving them a way to express their anger and their grief, becoming both a soothing balm and a rallying cry.

Before the songs, Samson would have bet golds that none of the refugees would ever return to Coronth. Yet the songs worked like magic, proving a pebble truly could start an avalanche. In the wake of the bards' performance, the queen's constables received a mob of volunteers. Samson shook his head in amazement, relieved and humbled to know he would not be alone.

He joined the other volunteers in the inn's common room, waiting for the first day of instruction from the queen's men. Having worked with the recruiters, Samson knew most by face if not by name. They were good people, filled with a conviction forged of great loss. Sixty-two men and seven women, including one silver-haired grandmother agreed to return. The constables objected when wives and mothers first began to volunteer but the women's unbridled fury caused the constables to back down. The recruiters begrudgingly agreed to let the women attend the first meeting, leaving their fate to be decided by a senior lord. Knowing the stubbornness of the women, Samson expected the first meeting to be interesting.

He took a seat at a front table, joining two men and the silver-haired grandmother. He knew the men but the old woman remained a mystery.

Grandmother Magda kept to herself, a tattered shawl wrapped tight around her shoulders, her head bent over a pair of knitting needles. Samson wondered if she truly intended to return to Coronth, but despite his curiosity, he did not pry. By common agreement, refugees never asked a fellow survivor for their story; the recent past was still too raw and painful. Samson nodded to the old woman, finding a homey comfort in the rhythmic clacking of her knitting needles.

A wave of excitement rippled through the tavern. Samson peered through the crowd, searching for the source. Dressed in commoners' clothes, Prince Justin slipped through the back door, taking a seat among the refugees. Rumors had circulated for weeks that the bard who was also a prince would be joining the volunteers in returning to Coronth. Radiating an aura of optimism, the royal bard had become a sort of talisman of luck for the refugees. His presence confirmed the rumors, stirring hope and excitement in the crowd. Samson wondered if Justin understood how much his presence meant to the refugees. He felt honored to call the bard his friend.

A pair of guards tramped into the tavern followed by Lord Kitteridge, a deputy minister to the queen. The lord trailed a pair of scribes and two constables. Clad in bright velvets, his face round with soft living, Lord Kitteridge strode to the front of the room. Samson stared at the aging dandy, wondering if he was the best choice to lead the meeting.

Clearing his throat, the lord said, "Welcome to the first meeting of the free people of Coronth. My name is Lord Kitteridge and I am here on behalf of her majesty, Queen Liandra."

The crowd responded with a stony silence.

Undaunted, the lord said, "Before we start, take a moment and look around the room. The person sitting next to you could be a hero."

The lord's words caused a rustle of surprise and amazement. Samson wondered if he'd been too quick to judge the velvet-clad dandy. When quiet returned, Lord Kitteridge said, "You have all seen the true face of the Flame God and having seen that evil you volunteered to return. In daring to return, you are all true heroes. Her gracious majesty, Queen Liandra, salutes you."

An avid stillness settled over the room.

"The people of Coronth have been duped by a false religion. They follow their religious leaders down a path to oppression, slavery, and death. You refugees know this better than anyone. You have seen the underlying evil that is the Flame God. As living witnesses to the truth, it is hoped you will return to Coronth and open the ears and the eyes of your fellow citizens. By revealing the truth, you will change Coronth from within."

From the back of the room someone shouted, "Free Coronth!" The chant spread till the room shook with conviction.

The lord smiled, raising his hand for silence. "Coronth is your home. It is up to you, the survivors of this evil, to start the change, but you will not be alone. The resources of Lanverness will stand behind you. For those of you who have families, the Rose Throne will care for them in your absence."

A weak smattering of applause broke out. Samson knew the clapping would have been louder but most volunteers had lost their entire families to the Flame God.

Raising his hands, the lord continued, "For those who return to Coronth, we will give you training with the sword and with the knife. We will teach you methods of the shadow so you can identify and communicate with your fellow witnesses by means of hand signs and passwords. We will work with you to seed you back into the villages and cities of Coronth where you can best make a difference." Lord Kitteridge paused, surveying the room. "Before we go any farther, I need to ask if any of you wish to change your minds and remain in Lanverness. Returning will be dangerous. Each of you must make your own decision. All we ask is that you make this decision before the training program starts. I will give you a moment to consider."

A quiet murmur filled the room. Samson's gaze flicked across the crowd, finding his own fear reflected in too many faces. Everyone knew the dangers of Coronth. He watched the others wrestle with the choice. The moment passed and not one volunteer left the room. A quiet pride flowed through the refugees.

Lord Kitteridge focused his gaze on Grandmother Magda. "What about you madam? Surely it would be better if you remained in Lanverness?"

For the first time since the lord's arrival, the silver-haired grandmother raised her head from her knitting, but the rhythmic clacking of her needles never stopped. "Young man, I know what I'm doing. I will return to my home and use my final days to defeat the Pontifax." As if the discussion was over, the old lady turned her attention back to her knitting.

The lord tried again. "This is important and dangerous work. We do not wish to send women, especially grandmothers, into harm's way."

The clacking of the knitting needles stopped.

Everyone in the room caught their breath.

The old woman glared at the lord, her voice full of steel. "Let me tell you about *harm's way*. My husband and I had many children but only one lived past childhood. Our son, Martin, followed in my husband's footsteps and became a butcher. Savings his golds, Martin opened his own shop on the north side of Balor where he met a woman of extraordinary beauty. Jumping the Flame, they married and had a child, our beautiful granddaughter, Lily. My son made a decent living and he was happy with his family. They were good law abiding citizens who prayed at the temple and paid tithes to the priests. They even attended the Tests of Faith in the temple square, but none of that mattered." The old woman lowered her voice. "You see, in Coronth, *beauty* has become a *curse*. The Keeper of the Flame spotted my daughter-in-law in the temple square. He invited her to the Residence but she refused. Acolytes of the Flame followed her home with invitations but again she refused. At first we feared for her safety but nothing happened. Just when we thought she was safe, the soldiers came knocking on their door. They dragged my son from his house and chained him to the sinner's wagon to await the Test of Faith. They took my daughter-in-law to be sold in the slave market. By the time the rumors reached us, my son was already dead on the pyre, nothing but ashes. We rushed to their home only to find it ransacked by neighbors. Our three-year-old granddaughter, abandoned as worthless, was found huddled in a basket of dirty clothes. Shocked from the ordeal, she'd lost all ability to speak. While I cared for Lily, my husband rushed off to the slave market to try and save her mother but the Keeper was already there. He toyed with my husband, letting the bidding climb till the price reached an outrageous sum. My husband bid every gold we had but it was not enough. In the end, our daughter-in-law was led off in chains to service the Keeper. The cruelty and the strain of it were too much for my husband. The dear man returned to me, but then crumpled to the floor clutching his chest in agony. He died later that day. Numbed by it all, my only thought was to get my granddaughter away from the curse of the Flame God. I gathered what I could and we left that day. It took most of my golds just to get a ride in a wagon leaving Balor. Traveling was hard, the weather was bad, and there was no help along the way. My granddaughter came down with a terrible fever but no one would give us shelter. She died in my arms just a stones throw from Lanverness." Taking a deep breath, the old woman said, "The Keeper and the Pontifax have taken *everything* from me. I *will* return and spend my last breath fighting against this evil. So do not preach to me about *harm's way*, young man, for I know it all too well."

A shocked silence settled over the room. The old woman resumed her knitting. The sharp staccato clacking punctuated the silence, as if to drive home her point.

In a quiet voice, Lord Kitteridge said, "My condolences for your losses, but we do not want your life to be added to those claimed by the Flame God. A grandmother cannot be trained in the way of the sword or even the knife. We cannot, in good conscious, send you back. It would be suicide. Surely you understand our position?"

The knitting needles stopped. The old woman reached down, fumbling with a bag of yarn by her feet. The crowd stilled, watching. The old lady sat up and flicked her hand forward. A loud thunk echoed in the room. A vicious meat cleaver quivered in the tabletop, inches away from the lord's hand. Grandmother Magda's voice cut through the silence, "My husband was a butcher. I know meat cleavers very well."

Lord Kitteridge took a step backwards, staring at the cleaver.

The knitting needles returned to their rhythmic clacking. The old woman said, "I trust the issue is settled."

The lord nodded, his face pale.

From the back of the room, a male voice said, "Never argue with a woman holding a meat cleaver."

A wave of laughter swept the room. Even Grandmother Magda allowed a smile to cross her face.

Struggling to recover his dignity, Lord Kitteridge tugged on his doublet. "Your training will start tomorrow. In the mornings you will learn to use swords and knives. In the afternoon, you will receive training from the queen's shadowmen, learning how to disappear into a crowd and how to communicate with simple hand signals. We will do the best we can to prepare you." Nodding towards Grandmother Magda, his voice turned conciliatory. "Madam, given your skills with the um...butcher knife, we will, of course, not expect to see you until the afternoon session."

Grandmother Magda glanced from her knitting, giving the lord a nod of approval.

Samson could have sworn he saw a look of relief on Lord Kitteridge's face.

Clearing his throat, the lord said, "That concludes the business of the day. Give your name and home village to the scribes before you leave. Good luck with your training." Turning, he strode from the common room, his guards trailing behind.

A hum of conversation seeped back into the room. Lines began to form in front of the two scribes while a small crowd gathered around the silver-haired grandmother. The worth of the training remained to be seen, but everyone agreed that Grandmother Magda was a force to be reckoned with.

# 66

# Jordan

The sands of time had run out. Jordan spent her last night with Stewart. They talked almost as much as they touched; promising they'd find a way to be together once her Wayfaring was done. Neither wanted the night to end but they both had responsibilities. The tenderness of the night blurred into day.

In the small hours of the morning, Stewart finally fell into an exhausted sleep. Ignoring her own tired eyes, Jordan gently smoothed the hair from his face and watched her lover dream. She etched his image deep in her mind, refusing to yield a single moment to the greedy demands of sleep. As the dawn's first light crept through the window, she softly kissed Stewart and reluctantly left his bed.

Pulling on her clothes, she gathered up her saddlebag and met her companions in the courtyard of the castle. The others were ready to ride. In addition to Kath and the two knights and Sir Cardemir, Duncan had decided to bring two Navarren guards. Besides providing extra swords, the guards would act as couriers carrying messages back to Navarre once they reached the Kiralynn monastery. Jordan was pleased by the addition of the guards, knowing she'd have a chance to write Stewart before being locked behind monastery walls.

Tightening the girth on her saddle, Jordan thought about her last night with Stewart, committing every moment to memory. Given the terms of her Wayfaring, it'd be two long years before she'd see him again. She'd have to survive on memories for a long time to come. Listening to her own thoughts, Jordan chided herself for being so gloomy. Her Wayfaring was supposed to be an adventure. Across the courtyard, she heard Kath's laughter. Her sword sister was in high spirits, eager to be on the road, hoping to find her own place in the world. Watching Kath,

Jordan knew she should feel the same. Perhaps the excitement would come once Tandroth Castle was behind them.

Satisfied with her mount's tack, Jordan secured the horse's reins to the hitching post and went to say goodbye to her siblings. Jemma gave her a fierce hug and whispered in her ear, "Don't worry sister, I'll look after Stewart. We'll both be waiting when you get back."

Jordan could only nod a wordless reply. Releasing Jemma, she turned to Justin. Her musical brother had always been her favorite. Hugging Justin close, she whispered, "Promise you'll stay safe in Coronth."

Justin returned her hug. "I promise." Stepping back, he gave her one of his irrepressible grins. "I expect to hear about all the monks you defeat in the sparring ring. I'd love to see their faces when they lose to a woman!" Justin gave her one last hug, whispering encouragement in her ear. "You're going on a grand adventure, Sis, riding into mystery. Bring back some stories for my songs. And make sure you remember to enjoy yourself!"

Releasing him, Jordan turned toward her horse, hoping her brother didn't see the tears crowding her eyes. Glancing around the courtyard, she looked for one more face but he wasn't there. Perhaps it was better this way.

"*Jordan!*" Stewart raced across the courtyard, his long black hair in disarray, his shirttail hanging out the back of his hose. He scooped her into his arms, pressing his lips to her ear. "You left without waking me! I almost slept through the morning!"

Not knowing what to say, she answered him with a kiss. Feeling the stares of everyone in the yard, they finally broke apart. She stared at Stewart, memorizing his face. It was time to leave.

Stewart pushed a thick bedroll bound in oiled leathers into her arms. "This is for you."

She hugged the bedroll to fill the void in her arms. "What is it?"

"It'll keep you warm at night." Leaning close, he whispered, "Remember the inn where we spent our first night? I went back and bought the snowcat skin spread before the fireplace. You'll find it sewn into the lining of the bedroll." Reaching out to brush her wayward hair back behind her ear, he whispered, "Think of me when you sleep in it at night."

A sob escaped her. She had to leave or she'd start crying. Biting her lip, Jordan tied the bedroll to the back of her saddle. Turning back to Stewart, she gave him one last fierce kiss before mounting her horse.

The others were already mounted. The horses pawed at the thin covering of snow, impatient to be off. Duncan nodded toward Jordan.

"Time to ride." The leather-clad archer took the lead, nudging his horse to a trot. The others formed a line behind.

Jordan gazed down at Stewart, drinking in the lines of his face.

Stewart smiled, touching the cloak pin at his shoulder, her Midwinter gift to him. "Promise to come back to me, my Lady of the Seashell."

Unable to hold back the tears, she said, "I promise." Spurring her horse, she followed the others out of the castle and into the streets of Pellanor.

# 67

# Blaine

They were traveling to a place that could not be found on any map of Erdhe. It was almost as if all reference to the monks and their mountain monastery had been carefully erased from written records. Blaine knew this because he'd searched through the racks of maps in Queen Liandra's library of scrolls, all to no avail. The library held stacks of maps both old and new and even some of foreign lands, but none of the maps contained a single reference to the Kiralynn monastery.

Blaine knew enough to look for the monastery beyond the end of the great southern road, but the maps only showed a track wandering off the edge of the parchment, lost in the depths of the mountains. As he unrolled each map, Blaine half expected to see the age-old words *"There be dragons here"*. Everyone knew dragons were the stuff of legends, but it seemed as if the monks were nearly as mysterious. He found it passing strange that no one ever bothered to record the monastery's location. It made him wonder what type of monastery the monks were running, but then the mystery only added spice to the adventure. Either way, he was sworn to follow the princess to whatever destiny the gods had in store, even if that destiny led to the very edge of the known world. Perhaps blue steel swords were meant for adventures that ran off the edge of maps. Blaine was keen to finally earn a name for himself and his sword.

Keeping their horses to a steady trot, the eight companions followed the scant directions provided by the monks' message scroll. To save time, they rode cross-country cutting through the forests of Wyeth, heading for the tail end of the great southern road. A note scrawled on the bottom of the scroll urged them to haste, warning that they needed to cross the mountains before the spring thaw.

Six weeks of traveling saw the snow give way to the first green of spring. Buds appeared on the trees and an earthy smell pervaded the air. Fresh green sprouted beneath the last of the snow. For the travelers, spring came as a warning, quickening their pace. Rising with the first light of dawn, the companions pushed on well into the dark. The passes of the great southern mountains were said to be brutal in winter but it was the spring when they were at their most treacherous. Spring was the season of avalanches. They found themselves racing to beat the spring warmth to the high passes.

As the unspoken leader, Duncan set a blistering pace with Sir Cardemir riding close behind. Blaine was reluctant to risk the horses after sunset but Duncan urged them on. The leather-clad archer took the lead. Riding in a single line, they followed the archer well into twilight, adding extra leagues to each day of travel. So far there'd been no accidents.

Each day the great southern mountains loomed larger against the sky like jagged snow-capped teeth. Blaine had never seen such mountains. He was beginning to understand why there were no maps of the region; he couldn't imagine anyone exploring the forbidding wall of rock and snow.

As they pressed south, the companions fell into a routine with Duncan in the lead, riding with his small bow in hand, searching for game. Blaine rode in the center, with Sir Tyrone and Jordan, while Kath kept pace with Duncan and Sir Cardemir. The two Navarren guards rode in the rear with the pack horses.

At the start of the journey, Jordan had been miserable, red-eyed and sad. Kath tried to cheer her but nothing seemed to work. It was Sir Tyrone who found a way to lift her spirits, spinning tales of his travels. On most days, she sought out the two knights, riding between them, asking for tales of Castlegard and the Octagon Knights.

Kath started out riding with the princess from Navarre, but as the journey progressed, she spent more time riding at the front with Duncan and Sir Cardemir. Whenever Blaine rode forward to join them, he found them deep in conversation about the history of Erdhe or the philosophy of the gods. He was surprised to find the princess interested in such scrollish subjects, but then he remembered the intervention of the gods at the Isle of Souls. It made sense that she'd turn to philosophy looking for answers. In a flash of insight, Blaine realized this trip to the mountains was all about finding answers, answers to the crystal dagger and the riddle of the tarot cards. He understood Kath's need for answers, but it bothered him the way she was always casting mooncalf eyes at Duncan, as if the leather-clad archer was the first man worthy of her notice. Blaine watched the two of them, annoyed at how much time they spent together, always finding ways to interrupt.

Days passed and they eventually left the forest for a meadow-clad valley where the great southern road dwindled to an end. This far south, the road was little more than a rutted cart track, but at least they had a path to follow.

Spring weather dogged their heels like a relentless hound. The companions pushed their horses hard, following the track into the mountains. Steep and treacherous, the trail wound upward, shrinking to little more than a goat path. They met no travelers but came across deep ruts carved by wagon wheels, proof that others had once braved the road. On the steeper sections, they found wagons abandoned with broken axles. Judging from the bleached wood, the wagons had weathered more than one winter on the mountainside. Farther up the trail they found crude grave markers, more evidence the mountains exacted their own deadly toll. The signs of passage were grim but Blaine was encouraged. The passage of other implied there really was something beyond the edge of the queen's maps besides dragons.

Four days into the foothills, they came across a stone marker in the middle of the trail, a three-foot tall column of gray basalt capped by a weathered bronze sundial. The sundial looked ordinary until Blaine noticed the shadow. "Do you see the shadow?"

Duncan answered, "Every sundial casts a shadow."

"Not like this." A dark mark was permanently fused into the bronze dial. Seeing the strange shadow, more than one companion made the hand sign against evil. "It's as if time stopped."

Sir Cardemir placed his hand on his sword hit. "An ill-omen."

Duncan shrugged. "At least it proves we're on the right track." He reached into his saddlebag and retrieved the monks' scroll. "The sundial marks the start of Drumheller pass."

As one, the companions turned to stare up into the mountains. Since turning south, the mountains had loomed like a fortress guarding the sky, but the perspective of the marker revealed a deep notch etched in the snow-capped range. That notch was the key to crossing the southern ranges. Drumheller pass really did exist. Blaine grinned, feeling relief dispel his tension.

Duncan studied the scroll. "We should keep riding. We'll make camp in the top of the treeline and then tomorrow we'll make a push across the pass. Once across, we should have a view of the village of Haven." Rolling up the scroll, he added, "If nothing else, we should be able to purchase more supplies from the villagers."

Sir Tyrone brightened, "A night in a feathered bed would not be a bad thing."

Jordan added, "While you're making a list, don't forget a hot bath."

The two got nothing but agreement from their fellow travelers. Eager to be finished with the journey, they mounted their horses and urged the beasts up the steep path. The trail soon gave way to a series of switchbacks. The horses plodded upwards, blowing hard against the thin air. Alpine forests thinned to scrub and then there was nothing but rocks and scree and snow. Exposed to the chill winds, the companions slowed to a halt, watching as the sunset ignited the frozen peaks in a blaze of red and gold.

"We'll make camp here." Duncan swung down from the saddle. Having left any semblance of flat land long behind, the trail was the only decent place to camp. They tethered the horses in a line and gave them the last ration of oats. From now on they'd have to forage for their own food. Duncan cleaned a brace of rabbits, while Blaine and the others scavenged through the edge of the forest for wood. Most of the wood was wet, but there was just enough dry tinder to coax a smoky blaze. Sir Tyrone set up the cast iron pot and began to melt snow for a stew. Huddled beneath blankets, the companions sat around the fire, watching as the black knight added winter-thin rabbits and diced potatoes to the pot. Sir Cardemir retrieved his lute from the packhorse and began to strum a love song much to Blaine's annoyance. He glared at the knight, seeing through his shallow attempts to curry favor with princesses.

Once the stew was served, the seahorse knight put his lute away. Talk around the campfire turned to speculation about the mysterious monastery. Over the course of their travels they'd developed a game where each person spun an outrageous tale about the monks and their monastery. Any leftovers from dinner were awarded to the spinner of the best tale. Each companion had a favorite theory. Blaine liked to imagine that the monastery was the last bastion of dragons and any knight that found their lair could claim their mythical treasure. Jordan spun a tale of magical weapons once wielded by ancient heroes while Sir Tyrone spoke of dark-skinned beauties serving a feast fit for a king. Kath suggested that the monastery was really the home of the gods and that each adventurer would be granted their heart's desire upon reaching the golden gates. Intrigued by her suggestion, the companions spent a good part of the evening composing their one wish and debating the wisdom of their choices. Sir Cardemir wished for a lute that would win the hearts of fair maidens, drawing blushes from the Jordan and Kath and a chorus of jeers from the men. Getting back to the game, Duncan said, "Do you want to know what I think?" The companions leaned forward, keen to hear. "I think the monks are really a coven of beautiful women eager to give their love to any adventurers daring enough to find their mountain sanctuary." Male laughter rippled around the campfire. Kath and Jordan both scowled but Blaine and the other men voted for Duncan. Hefting the ladle in victory, the archer scraped the cook pot dry, taking the last of the rabbit stew.

A gust of wind rattled down the mountains, as cold as an ill omen. Everyone shuffled closer to the fire, trying to ignore the bitter chill. Farther up the pass a lone wolf began to howl at the rising moon. The eerie song startled Blaine. It was the first wolf he'd heard since entering the mountains. By unspoken agreement, the companions crawled into their bedrolls, fully clothed, their weapons at their sides. They didn't expect trouble but they refused to be caught unprepared. Blaine took the first watch, with Kath agreeing to the second. Throwing an extra log on the fire, Blaine drew his great sword and set it across his knees. The crackle of the fire and the whistle of the mountain wind were the only sounds in the night.

Clear of clouds, the night sky blazed with stars, more than he'd ever seen before. A thrill of expectation coursed through Blaine. He stood in unexplored mountains, on the very edge of the world, with a blue sword in his hand. Surely adventure and glory lay just beyond the ice-carved mountains. He wasn't sure what they'd find when they reached the mysterious monastery, but standing under the stars, so close to the heavens, Blaine knew he'd get his chance for glory.

# 68

# Liandra

The Spider Queen strung her court with webs of intrigue. She tended each strand of rumor hoping to catch a traitor. Two of her counselors struggled in the traps, caught in the sticky strands of politics. One was a player, the other was not, both asked for a private audience. The queen forced her counselors to wait, letting them stew in their own thoughts, but now the waiting was over. It was time to see if her webs held predators or prey.

Liandra arranged the deep burgundy velvet of her gown, a perfect color for her petite figure. Satisfied, she rang the hand bell on the side table. A page responded, bowing low.

"You may admit the general."

A moment later, General Helfner strode into the solar, a large beefy man gone to seed. A long gray mustache drooped over his mouth and his stomach sagged over his sword belt, a warrior defeated by age and fine living. Liandra doubted he'd fit into his armor. Peace had not been kind to the general. She extended her hand with her emerald ring of office.

He bowed, kissing the ring. "Your majesty, thank you for seeing me."

The queen gestured for him to rise. "We always have time for our loyal men." She watched his face but there was no sign of dissemblance. "But we wonder what needs to be said in a private audience that cannot be said in the counsel chambers?"

The general fidgeted under her gaze, one hand on his sword belt, the other pulling on his long mustache. "It's the damn high constable! The Lord Sheriff recruits more men, swelling the constable force to twice that of the army!" He shook his head like a wounded bear. "Majesty, you must give more funds to the army. The constables are mere peacekeepers while the army is the sword and shield of Lanverness!" His voice turned grim with warning. "Do not neglect your soldiers."

She watched him through hooded eyes. "But peace reigns within the southern kingdoms. What need is there for a large army?"

"Peace now, but what about the trouble brewing in Coronth? Majesty, you cannot count on peace!" His face turned red with bluster.

"We have seen the bills your quartermaster sends to the royal treasury. Even a small army eats like a plague of locusts. Why pay good golds for an army that does nothing but train?"

The general shook his head, his voice gruff. "The old king understood. Your royal father used to say that the cost of war is less if one is prepared. He ordered me to keep Lanverness prepared, but you neglect the army." Exasperation crept into his voice, "Majesty, you have made the kingdom rich, the envy of others. We must not appear to be a ripe fruit waiting to be plucked." He shook his head like an angry lion. "You must allow me to recruit more men."

"*Must* is not a word used with princes."

The general had the grace to blanch but he stood his ground. The old soldier had gone to seed yet he'd not lost his courage. She studied him, letting him feel her displeasure. "Whom do you serve?"

His face bleached bone-white. Dropping to his knee, he said, "My queen! I live to serve you and the Rose Throne."

"See that you remember." She waved him to his feet. His knees creaked as he straightened. She pretended not to notice. "We do not believe in war, it is a waste of men and golds. We put our trust in golds and guile to circumvent war...but we will consider your request. Perhaps there is merit in being prepared."

The general bowed. "Thank you, your majesty."

She extended her ringed hand. "You have our leave to go."

He leaned forward to kiss her ring and then turned to leave.

She waited till he was almost at the door. "General, why did you request that we give our son, Prince Danly, a seat on the royal council?"

He turned, his eyes wide in surprise. "Because the prince asked me to." His face turned to puzzlement. "He is your royal son, I only obeyed the wishes of my prince."

The queen saw no guile in the man, only a straightforward old soldier. "You have our leave to go. We will consider your request."

General Helfner bowed, exiting the solar.

The queen sat in thought, the crackle of the logs loud in the fireplace. She rang the hand bell. When the page responded, she said, "Admit the Knight Protector."

The Lord Turner was cut from a different cloth than the general. He strode into the chamber, dapper and daring, and sure of his charm. Tall and elegant, he kept a trim figure and a neat blond mustache, one of the more handsome men of her court.

Liandra extended her ringed hand, a coy smile on her face.

The Lord Turner bowed low, kissing her ring and lingering over her hand. "My queen." His voice was full of suggestion. He straightened and studied her with intelligent blue eyes. "I wish to thank you for the gift of the sword."

Liandra kept her face still, studying her Knight Protector, the man charged with her royal safety.

His eyes made a quick survey of the chamber, his gaze lingering on an ornate screen set in the corner. "Of course I've heard the rumors but I don't believe them." He smoothed his mustache, returning his gaze to the queen. "I told the gossipers that the queen would not waste a blue steel blade on an old man, a diplomat, or a fop. A blue steel blade belongs in the hands of the lord uniquely positioned to protect the sovereign."

"So you've come about the rumors."

"I've come about the truth."

She gave him a piercing stare. "What blade would you choose?"

"The blade of a gentleman, a rapier of course."

"A court sword." She smiled. "Some would say a rapier is a waste of blue steel."

He rose to the challenge. "Only those who miss the subtlety."

"How so?"

"Made of blue steel, the rapier will have the strength of a claymore. Strength hidden beneath grace, the perfect sword to protect the beauty who sits on the Rose Throne."

The queen gave him a silken smile. Leaning back in the throne, her fingers traced the strand of pearls at her neck, following them down into the vee of her neckline, lingering between the cleavage. Lord Turner's stare followed the pearls. She lowered her voice to a purr. "And you, of course, would be the perfect man to wield that sword."

"With the skill only a queen could appreciate." He leered down at her.

Her voice was silk over steel. "It is something to consider." Tiring of the game, she held her ringed hand out in dismissal.

Disappointment flickered behind his eyes, quickly buried beneath a court mask of obedience. But just before the mask fell, Liandra thought she caught a glimmer of something else, something sinister, but she wasn't sure. The Knight Protector was an artful player.

He went to his knee, kissing her ring, but also her hand. Capturing her hand within his, he gazed up into her face. "And the sword, my queen?"

Reclaiming her hand, she said, "We have not yet decided on the third sword." She softened her words with a smile. "But we admit the sword would suit our Knight Protector."

Ever the gallant, he flashed a smile full of charm. "Then I look forward to wearing blue steel in your service." He rose and gave her an elegant bow before leaving the chamber.

She watched him go. Handsome, charming, and intelligent but the Lord Turner had far too much ambition. Ambition was a common fault within her court. Liandra stared into the blazing fireplace, considering her royal councilors.

A black-robed figure glided from behind the ornate screen. Moving to stand in the firelight, the Master Archivist bowed to the queen.

Liandra acknowledged her spymaster. "You heard them both. What did we catch in our web? Predators or prey?"

"Both men were predictable. The general was blunt and straightforward, always arguing for a larger army. The man is too honest to be sinister."

The queen nodded. "We agree, an old soldier as straight and honest as his sword. But the man is well past his prime, perhaps it is time to find a new general." The queen paused. "And the other?"

The master's gaze narrowed. "The Lord Turner would charm his way into the queen's bedchamber, a back route to the throne."

The queen thought she detected a hint of anger in his voice, a rare slip for her spymaster. "Is he the one we seek? Is the Lord Turner the leader of the Red Horns?"

The master hesitated. "He has the intelligence, but his ambition is too naked. I would not expect the lure of a blue steel sword to so easily catch the leader of the Red Horns."

"Then our webs have not yet caught their intended prey." Disappointed, she moved to the desk on the far side of the chamber. Taking a seat, she chose a sheet of parchment, dipping a quill in an inkwell. The scratch of quill on parchment was loud in the small chamber. Finished, she held a stick of green wax in the flame of a candle. Sealing the scroll, she imprinted the hot wax with the royal seal of Lanverness and then handed it to the Master Archivist. "See that this is sent by courier to Castlegard."

The master accepted the scroll. "The decision about the third sword?"

"Yes." The queen studied her spymaster. "The lure of a blue sword has proved a valuable distraction. We kept Castlegard's master smith quite busy. In addition to our two royal sons, the smith measured the general, the Lord Sheriff, the Knight Protector, the Lord Hunter...and one other"

"Five men but only one blue steel blade among them." Hefting the scroll, the master asked, "Which of the five will not be disappointed?"

"A queen is allowed some secrets."

The master bowed, a small smile on his face.

"Lord Highgate, we wonder why you have never petitioned us for the third blade?"

"A spymaster uses daggers not swords."

"Clever daggers wielded in shadow."

"Always in the service of my queen." The master bowed, slipping the scroll into the deep pockets of his robe. "Is there anything else, majesty?"

"No, that is all."

She watched him go, the best of her counselors. Fingering her pearls, she considered her royal men. The game was getting complicated. The queen wondered whom she could trust.

# 69

# Blaine

"Whooo!" The single word echoed off of the walls of the mountain pass. "Whooooo!" The word hung in the morning like a mystical challenge. "Whoooooo!"

The call roused Blaine from a restless sleep. His hand found his sword hilt. Through narrowed eyes he cautiously peered at the dawn. Snow-capped peaks loomed overhead, cold and forbidding, crowding out the morning sky. Rising, he took stock of the camp. The others still slept; lying huddled in a row along the length of the trail. The horses stood picketed farther downhill. The campfire had gone cold and the Navarren guard, Jacob, was sound asleep at his post. Anger blistered through Blaine, the guard should never have fallen asleep, yet the camp seemed in order. Looking around, Blaine wondered if he'd imagined the ghostly challenge.

"Whooooooooo!"

Drawing his sword, Blaine pivoted to face the challenge. Perched on a nearby boulder, an immense white frost owl stared back at him. Strange golden eyes studied him, as if the owl questioned his right to cross the pass. Blaine froze, caught spellbound by the owl's stare. The world stilled to a cold hush, a breath of wind on the back of his neck.

The owl blinked and Blaine was released.

Spreading enormous white wings, the owl took flight. Beating against the thin air, it soared up toward the mountain pass. Blaine watched transfixed as the bird flew overhead, a whisper of feathers against the wind. As the ghost-white owl crested the pass, he yelled, "TELL THEM WE COME IN PEACE!"

"PEACE...Peace...peace." echoed back down from the mountains.

Sir Tyrone sprang from his bedroll, snatching up his sword. Duncan and Kath both rolled to their feet, reaching for weapons while Sir Cardemir stood over Jordan in a protective stance, his sword drawn.

With a sheepish grin, Blaine sheathed his sword. "There's no threat, I'm sorry I woke you."

Sir Tyrone lowered his sword. "What was it?"

Blaine shrugged. "The biggest damn owl I've ever seen! It seemed like some kind of mountain guardian or something..."

The black knight sheathed his sword and began to chuckle. "An owl?"

Realizing there was no danger, the companions had a laugh at Blaine's expense, but it was all good-natured. As they roused the rest of the party, he tried to explain his encounter with the giant frost owl, but it didn't make a lot of sense, another story for the campfire.

They broke camp with quiet efficiency, loading their meager supplies onto the packhorses. Anxious to be away from the exposed trail, they ate strips of dried venison in silence and then mounted their horses for the last push to the top.

The air was thin and the horses struggled up the last switchbacks, a crust of snow crunching beneath their hooves. Blaine clung to his saddle, startled by the sheer steepness of the trail. His horse stumbled and his heart skipped a beat. A stone skittered off the trail, falling to oblivion. Blaine watched the rock fall, deciding he did not like the steep-sided cliff. Hunched in the saddle, he urged his horse forward, eager to be done with the mountains. Behind him, Sir Cardemir raised his deep baritone in song, belting a ballad to the mountains, *"I knew a village maid fair of face and blonde of hair..."*

His words echoed back in a twisted melody. Blaine swiveled in the saddle, "Keep quiet!"

The seahorse knight gave him a slanted look. "Why? Afraid I'll wake the dragons?"

Blaine growled, "Only the gods know what these mountains hold. Better to come in silence."

Sir Cardemir threw him a scathing look. "But they already know we come in peace!"

Chagrined, Blaine turned his back on the knight, but at least the singing stopped. Huddled in the saddle, Blaine wondered why he was the only one to see through the wiles of the troubadour-knight.

A cold wind blew down out of the ice-bound peaks, a breath of snow buffeting his face. The horses struggled up the switchbacks, blowing plumes of frost into the thin mountain air. By mid-day they reached the crest. What they found at the top proved more daunting than anything they'd yet faced.

Blaine clung to his saddle. "We're going to cross that?"

It seemed like suicide. The trail dwindled to a rocky strip just wide enough for a single wagon. On either side, the sheer rock plunged to bottomless depths, a balancing act with death on two sides. As if the knife-edge was not threat enough, a great fist of sapphire blue ice hung suspended from the nearby mountaintop. The ice shimmered with unearthly beauty, casting a shadow over the pass, death waiting in frozen form. The pass was the anvil and the frozen glacier the hammer. This was the reason they'd raced the spring thaw to the mountains. Blaine prayed they weren't too late.

Kath muttered, "It seems the monastery is protected by more than just mystery."

Sunlight glinted on blue ice, awaking the beauty of the glacier, a thousand frozen diamonds crowning the mountaintop. The companions stared in silent awe, mesmerized by the wind-sculpted ice. It was Duncan who finally got them moving. "Waiting won't make the pass any safer. Best we just cross it and see what challenges lie on the other side."

The archer dismounted and the others joined him. "We'll blindfold the horses and walk them across one at a time. If your horse shies or bucks along the way, release the reins and get yourself across. Better to lose a horse than to risk your life." Nodding toward the Navarren guard, he added, "Jacob, stay here with the packhorses, and we'll come back to help once everyone else is across." Duncan tore a strip from his blanket to blindfold his gelding, and led the horse out onto the narrow pass.

Kath whispered. "Keep safe!"

Duncan turned and gave her a reassuring smile, tugging the reins of his horse.

Blaine stood with the others, half holding his breath, wishing there was another way.

The archer and the horse seemed to crawl across the pass, smothered by the shadow of the glacier. A cold wind whistled across the ice like a warning. The gelding whinnied. Distorted by the mountains, the sound echoed back as a high-pitched wail. Tugging on the reins, Duncan kept moving. The archer and his horse passed beneath the glacier, safely reaching the far side. A wave of relief flooded through Blaine, perhaps this would not be as daunting as it seemed.

# 70

# Jordan

Jordan stepped forward. "I'll go next." Spooked by the icy heights, she decided it was better to cross than to wait. Blindfolding her horse, she led him out onto the narrow pass. Step by step she coaxed her warhorse across the spine of the trail, like threading a needle across a chasm of death. Refusing to look down, Jordan kept her gaze fixed on Duncan, his reassuring smile pulling her forward. Nervous, she wrapped the reins around her wrist, keeping a close hold on the blindfolded horse. She was doing fine till she entered the glacier's shadow. Sapphire blue ice loomed overhead, blocking out the sun. Crystalline forms jutted from the glacier like great swords, as if awaiting the hand of a god. It was like nothing she'd ever seen, a frozen ocean hanging suspended from a mountain. Sparkling in the sun, the glacier creaked and groaned like a live beast. A loud crack echoed through the pass. A massive shard of blue ice broke off the main face, arrowing down into the void. Caught off guard, her warhorse shied and crabbed sideways, his rear hooves skittering on the edge. The reins tightened on her wrist, yanking her forward. Jordan struggled to keep her footing. She hauled on the reins but the horse panicked, lunging toward the chasm. Dragged forward, Jordan's boots slid across rock, unable to find purchase. Loose rocks clattered off the side, dropping into deadly silence. The glacier groaned, releasing a volley of ice darts. Sharp as glass, the shards sliced Jordan's face and hands. Her horse reared in terror, dragging Jordan closer to the chasm. The reins tightened around her wrist like a noose. Jordan fought to get loose, one boot skittering over the edge. Death hung in the balance.

*"Hang on!"* From the corner of her eye, she spied a glimpse of pale blue. Sir Cardemir raced to her side, his shield raised against the ice darts. His sword slashed the reins binding her wrist. One quick cut and she was

loose. Jordan scrambled to her feet, crouched beneath the shelter of his shield.

Her horse reared, iron-shod hooves lashing towards them. Fearing for her mount, Jordan yelled, *"My horse!"* Sir Cardemir urged her forward, "No time to save the beast." They sprinted across the pass, shards of ice pelting down, beating a pattern on Cardemir's shield. Behind them, her horse bugled in terror. Jordan turned in time to see her mount lose the war of balance. Hooves flailing, the gelding slowly toppled, falling sideways into the chasm. Terrified squeals seemed to echo forever.

Jordan realized she was shaking.

Sir Cardemir wrapped her in his arms. "Are you well?" The knight's strength seeped into her, easing her trembling. Jordan took a steadying breath and then stepped away. "I'm fine. Thank you." Regaining her composure, she met his gaze. "You saved my life." He gave her a soft smile. "The duty of any knight."

And then Duncan was there, wrapping a blanket around her shoulders. "You scared the hell out of me." Jordan hugged the blanket. "I scared myself. I should never have wrapped the reins around my wrist. I'm a better horsewoman than that. And now we've lost my mount." Her voice trailed to a whisper, remembering the awful squeals.

"You can ride one of the packhorses, there's not much left of our supplies." Duncan shepherded her away from the pass. Steering her towards a boulder, he pressed a flask of brandy into her hand. "Drink this, it will help."

Jordan gulped the brandy, a blaze of heat running down her throat. Her gaze sought the seahorse knight, thankful the gods had brought him on their journey. Without his help, she might have died, pulled to her death by her horse.

The others made it across without incident. Kath came straight to Jordan, giving her a ferocious hug. "Don't you dare leave me! You're the only sword sister I've got." Blaine stood behind Kath, looking as pale as Jordan felt. The others gathered around. They passed a flask of brandy and a pouch of dried venison strips, talking about anything but the crossing. The meager meal helped to lessen the terror of the pass. Taking a last sip of brandy, Jordan said. "I'm ready."

Duncan gave her a measuring look and then nodded. "Let's mount up. We've a long way to go and little supplies to get there."

Jacob cut the straps from the packhorse, throwing a spare saddle blanket across the mare's back. He offered her a leg up and Jordan wasn't too proud to take it. She gripped the reins, nudging the mare into line between Kath and Sir Cardemir.

Duncan led them down out of the pass, into a series of steep switchbacks. The narrow trail meandered around a bend. The view was both breathtaking and fearsome, a jumble of snow-capped mountains stretching for as far as the eye could see. Jordan began to wonder if they would ever find the monastery, but then a cry came from ahead. Rounding the bend, she saw the reason for the yell. Spread out below was a valley of tilled farm fields with a cluster of stone houses nestled at the far end. They'd found the village of Haven at the very edge of the map. Jordan urged her mount forward, wondering if the monastery was worth the terror of the mountain pass.

# 71

# Duncan

On the surface, Haven seemed like any other town but the details kept screaming of differences. For a man who relied on all of his senses, including his intuition, the differences were unsettling enough for Duncan to keep his bow strung and a full quiver close at hand.

A hard packed dirt road served as the main street of the village. The companions rode past predictable storefronts interspersed with well-kept stone and clapboard houses. People smiled and the town seemed prosperous but the differences gnawed at Duncan's mind, creating a sense of unease. It took him a while to realize what was missing. The main street was clear of the usual refuse that tended to accumulate in cities and towns and the air smelled clean like a well-kept stable instead of reeking like a forgotten chamber pot. And no beggars plied the street looking for handouts, and no one skulked in side alleyways looking for unwary travelers. Once he realized the differences, he felt more comfortable but his curiosity deepened. He kept his gaze sharp, looking for the reasons behind the differences.

The sun set on the mountains in a blaze of reds and golds as the companions reached the village stable. They took careful care of the horses, ordering an extra ration of oats for the weary animals, and then they booked rooms at Haven's only inn, appropriately named the Mountain's Rest.

Eager for the bliss of a hot bath and good food, the companions dispersed to their rooms, reassembling in the inn's common room for dinner. The inn did not disappoint. Roast lamb served with a mint sauce and garlic roast potatoes was good enough to grace the queen's table. While the others indulged, reaching for seconds, the excellence of the meal bothered Duncan, another subtle difference that kept gnawing at him like an irritating itch. When he commented about the meal, the others shrugged off his remarks. Sir Tyrone argued that mountain altitudes made for hearty appetites. Duncan had to admit that it could be the thin mountain air, but he decided to keep his bow within reach just in case.

Sated by their meal, the companions turned in for the night, exhaustion lining their faces. Duncan tried to sleep, but his mind was too restless. Giving up, he pulled on his boots and decided to explore the town. He slipped down the stairs, surprised to find the portly innkeeper still tending the bar. Knowing that innkeepers kept their fingers on the pulse of gossip, Duncan approached him with a smile. "Not much business for such a well-run inn."

The fat man nodded, a jovial smile on his ruddy face. "True but a town needs an inn. We get by." Wiping his hands on his apron, he selected a bottle of brandy. "Join me in a glass of amber delight? Takes the chill off the mountain nights."

Duncan slipped a silver coin onto the bar top, enough to encourage more than one glass. "A glass of brandy would go well after such a fine meal."

The innkeeper poured two glasses, passing one to Duncan.

Smooth as a summer night, the amber liquor left a welcome trail of warmth down his throat. Setting his empty glass on the bar top, Duncan studied the portly innkeeper. "We've crossed the mountains looking for something, I'm wondering if you can help? We were told to get directions to the Kiralynn monastery in the town of Haven."

Pouring another round of drinks, the innkeeper gave Duncan a shrewd wink. "Thought you might be looking for the monastery. Strangers in Haven usually are. Do the monks expect you or do you have reasons of your own for seeking them out?"

"We've been invited but I'm not sure we're expected. Why? Does it matter?"

The innkeeper offered a good-natured smile. "Not to me, just curious. Either way, the monks will decide for themselves if you're welcome." Reaching under the counter, he produced a scroll. "I'm supposed to give one of these to anyone who asks. The scroll provides directions for the next leg of the journey. You'll need to talk to Martin at the stables in order to arrange reindeer."

Wondering if he'd heard right, Duncan said, "Reindeer?"

The innkeeper chuckled. "First time visitors always say the same things. Yes, reindeer. We raise them in the valley, good for meat, hides, and even milk, makes a tasty cheese with a tang to it. The reindeer are easier to raise in the highlands than cattle and they also serve as dependable pack animals for the steep mountain trails. Horses would never make it up to the monastery. You'll have to arrange to board your mounts at the stables. And you'll have to think about what to pack, for the reindeer can't carry as much as a horse. Might explain why the monks aren't keen on possessions. Anyway, there's plenty of storage space in the attic. For a small fee, I can store whatever you don't want to take up the mountain."

"How long of a journey is it?"

"Rumors say the journey is different for everyone. Some strangers come back never having found the monastery." Leaning forward, the man whispered, "The mountains have a way of protecting their own." Nodding sagely the man added, "If you're supposed to find the monastery, then the monks will see that you get there."

Curious, Duncan asked, "Do the monks have a temple or a chapel in town?"

The innkeeper laughed. "No. The monks aren't like that, but you'll find that out for yourself."

Duncan mulled over the innkeeper's answers. The man seemed as full of riddles as information. "What do the townspeople think about the monks and their monastery?"

A glint of amusement filled the innkeeper's eyes. "The town wouldn't be here without the monastery. Monks sit on the town council and their advice is always sound. Between the mountains and the monks we have a better life here than you flatlanders. You'll be hard pressed to find a highlander who has ill to say about the Kiralynn Order." Grinning, the man added, "Read the scroll and then see the stable master tomorrow. You might also want to purchase fur-lined jackets; the mountain weather can be tricky." With a final nod, the innkeeper added, "I'll bid you good night. S'pect I'll be seeing you in the morning."

Duncan stood at the bar, finishing his brandy, his mind churning with questions. Too restless for bed, he left the inn to roam the streets of Haven. The shops were closed but candlelight flickered from the windows of some of the houses. Walking down the dark street, his gaze was drawn to the night sky. Maybe it was a trick of the mountains, but it almost seemed as if a man could stretch his hand out and touch the very fabric of the heavens. Staring up into the night sky, Duncan wondered if he'd ever find what he was looking for. He'd spent enough of his life wandering. He reached up and touched the black patch covering his left eye, bitter memories flooding his mind. On impulse, he flipped the eye patch up and stared at the stars in silent challenge, wondering why the gods had seen fit to make him the way he was. The heavens looked the same, cold and indifferent. Tugging the patch back over his eye, he turned away.

Thoughts of Kath intruded, though he had no right to think of her. She'd be better off with someone like Cardemir. Strange how the thought hurt like an arrow to the chest. He laughed but the sound was bitter. Turning his back on the stars, he returned to the inn. He'd wait to see what insights the mysterious monks had to offer...if any.

# 72

# Liandra

Bloody and battered the royal courier bowed low before the queen. The messenger's tabard was soiled, a hasty bandage on his left arm. Swaying on his feet, his face showed signs of strain. The mere sight of the bloody courier would ignite a blaze of rumors in her court. Despite the early hour, the Master Archivist had done well to bring him directly to her solar.

Liandra waved the courier toward the nearest chair. "You have our permission to sit."

With a grateful look, the young man slumped into the armchair.

Behind the courier, the door opened to admit Prince Stewart. The prince bowed to the queen and then stood with the Master Archivist in the shadows. With her two advisors present, the queen was ready to unravel the bloody riddle. "You have served well but questions must be asked and answered. We will start with your name and your assigned post."

The courier straightened. "My name is Donal Cleary, I'm assigned to carry messages between Pellanor and Kardiff." He clutched a leather pouch embossed with the twin roses of Lanverness. "I was carrying the monthly dispatches from the Duke when it happened. I did my duty and rode on...though it was hard to leave the others behind, but the dispatches are safe." He gave her a pleading look. "As a courier my first duty is to get the messages through."

His answers raised alarm bells within the queen's mind. Kardiff was the second largest city in Lanverness, which meant that the bloody incident occurred within the borders of her own kingdom. "Conveying the dispatches to safety is indeed the first duty of a royal courier. You have done well, but tell us, who would dare attack a royal messenger of the Rose Court?"

A look of horror washed across the young man's face. "T-they wore red. They killed them all! It made no sense!"

The queen raised a hand, forestalling his panic. "Take a deep breath and start at the beginning. Tell us what happened."

The young soldier nodded, struggling to gain control. "I took the main road between Kardiff and the capital, just as I always do. I was riding through Glenn Gorge when I caught up with a merchant and his family traveling to Pellanor." Flushing, he stammered, "His two d-daughters were b-beautiful. I enjoyed their company, perhaps too much. I rode with them for a while, but I didn't see the harm in it." His voice broke and he paused for a moment to collect himself.

The queen waited in silence.

Taking a shaky breath, the courier continued, "We were almost through the gorge when it happened. They swarmed down from the forest brandishing swords and flaming torches. They attacked without warning...without reason! I reached for my sword to defend the women...but then I remembered my duty. Knowing that I had to get the dispatches to Pellanor, I disengaged from the fight. I took a sword cut to the arm, but somehow I got free. I urged my horse to a gallop and rode for the far end of the gorge. When I realized no one was following, I paused to look back." The courier's voice faltered, his eyes haunted. "I still can't believe what I saw. They killed the whole family, even the women! And then they set fire to the wagon! If they were thieves, you'd think they'd have wanted the wagon, or at least the goods in it, but they didn't seem to care! It was pure slaughter! It was madness. Part of me wanted to turn back, to fight the bastards, but my message pouch was full. I rode straight for Pellanor, not stopping for anything." Staring at the queen with pain filled eyes, the young man said in a wavering voice, "I hope I did the right thing?"

In a regal voice, the queen replied, "Donal Cleary, you have honored your oath by faithfully fulfilling your duty as a courier. Do not doubt that you did the right thing. You have the thanks of the Rose Crown."

Relief and gratitude passed in waves across the young man's face. "Thank you, your majesty."

"There is still the matter of justice. We need to determine the parties responsible for this vile act. Tell us what you remember about the attackers."

"There were at least a dozen of them, some with flaming torches, others with swords. They were a rough lot, some in chain mail others in leathers, but now that I think about it, some of them wore red tabards but I don't remember any device or emblem, just red, bloody red."

From the side of the room, the Master Archivist asked, "Do you remember if they said or yelled anything when they attacked?"

Nodding thoughtfully, the courier replied, "Yes, now I remember. When they first came at us, they were yelling something about the Flame God." The courier's eyes flared wide. He stared at the Master Archivist. "I've heard the bards singing ballads about the evils of the Flame God...but I thought it was just a tavern songs. Is the evil real? Could the attackers have come from Coronth?"

Regaining control of the conversation, the queen said, "The bards' songs are indeed true, the evil of Coronth is very real, but this matter of Glenn Gorge must be carefully investigated before we reach any conclusions." Pausing, the queen added, "Is there anything else you remember?"

"No, your majesty."

"Then we charge you to not speak of this incident until we call on you to give testimony before our full council. It would not do to have rumors spread through the court. Are we understood?"

Bowing, the courier said, "Yes, your majesty. It shall be as you command."

Nodding, the queen said, "You will be given lodging in the castle until you are called on to speak before the council. In the meantime, make sure your wounds are seen to." Extending her hand, the queen said, "You are dismissed with our thanks."

Bowing low, the awe struck courier came forward and reverently kissed the queen's ring. With a second bow, he left the chamber.

When the door closed, the Master Archivist was about to speak but the queen forestalled him with a wave of her hand. Turning instead to her royal son, Liandra said, "Prince Stewart, you are our military advisor, tell us what you think of the courier's report."

The prince stepped from of the shadows, anger in his voice. "The description sounds more like brigands than soldiers, but perhaps the army of Coronth is nothing more than rabble in surcoats. Either way, we cannot ignore the threat. You should send the Rose Squad to search the area and root out these brigands before they can cause more harm."

It was a simple straightforward answer, the type of answer she was likely to get from her council, but the thinking behind it ignored the layers of politics and plots that were an integral part of the Rose Court. And worse yet, the answer did not consider the threat of the Red Horns. With a glance, she forestalled the Master Archivist from speaking. In a quiet voice, the queen asked, "Tell us, why should we send the Rose Squad?"

Without hesitating the prince replied, "This is a task for the army, not the constable force, and the best squad in the army is the Rose Squad. I humbly ask your permission to lead the Rose Squad to the Glenn Gorge to put an end to these brigands."

The queen sighed inwardly; her royal son had much to learn. Turning to her shadowmaster, the queen said, "Please give us your advice on this matter."

"Assuming the merchant was not much of a threat, the incident involved twelve swords against one. With such odds, I am surprised the attackers let the courier escape. One wonders if perhaps the courier was meant to survive."

The queen nodded.

The master continued, "We are assuming that the leader of the Red Horns is a member of the royal council, therefore the man will be familiar with your royal concern with Coronth. A few red tabards and a scripted war cry could easily misdirect the court's attention toward Coronth."

The queen finished the analysis. "And thus we are duped into sending our most loyal squad of the army to the far corner of our kingdom, giving the Red Horns a free hand in the capital."

The master said, "Just so."

"What have your shadowmen learned about the plot of the Red Horns?"

"All too little. We've intercepted messages pertaining to the supposed plot of the *Griffins*. It is implied that since the Lord Bradshaw could not gain the throne by marriage, he instead seeks to gain it by stealth and treachery. Unfortunately my shadowmen have not been able to trace any of these messages back to their source."

Prince Stewart erupted in anger. "Arrest Lord Bradshaw and put him to the question! Once we have the leader the others will quickly fall."

In a pointed voice, the queen said, "That is precisely the problem. We do not know the identity of the Red Horns. The evidence pointing toward Lord Bradshaw is nothing more than a clumsy feint. We know Lord Bradshaw well. It is true he once sought our hand, but these days the old dear is more interested in his vineyards than in the Rose Throne. Nevertheless, we must play our part in this charade if we hope to catch the culprit who pulls the puppet strings of the Red Horns."

Nodding, the master said, "Shall I have my men arrest Lord Bradshaw?"

"Yes, but make it a house arrest. The old dear would have a heart attack if you dragged him off to the dungeons." In a musing voice, the queen added, "Yes, make it a house arrest, and do it discretely. Of course, you will be sure to let word leak that Lord Bradshaw is being questioned regarding a possible plot against the throne."

"It shall be done just as your majesty commands."

"But what about the attack at Glenn Gorge?" The prince reeked of frustration.

Annoyance crept into the queen's voice, "We are coming to that." Turning back to the master, the queen said, "We have noticed that our servants in the Queen's Tower are looking particularly fit these days. What is the status of our plan to replace the servants with loyal swords?"

"The head steward has been taken into our confidence and veterans have been seeded into the Queen's Tower as well as the Throne Room. We've also hidden caches of weapons in strategic areas. Your majesty should be safe in those two sections of the castle, but we cannot do more without risking the attention of the Red Horns."

"Then our defenses are set and we must play this charade to its end." Turning toward the prince, the queen said, "News of the bloody courier will sweep through the castle despite our precautions. We must call a full meeting of the council to decide on a response. We expect the council to insist on sending the Rose Squad to investigate the incident. If our thinking is correct, this will play into the hands of the Red Horns. Nevertheless, if the council suggests it, we must agree, playing our part in the charade. We expect the Red Horns to show their hand once the Rose Squad is out of the way."

Understanding finally dawned on the prince's face.

The queen gaze drilled into her royal son. "You have a roll to play in this charade. As the leader of the Rose Squad, you must play your part well. Lead your men to Glenn Gorge and look for these brigands, but be swift about it, and return with all possible speed. We may need your swords to thwart this threat."

"But, I cannot leave..."

"You cannot stay." The queen forestalled her son with a raised hand. "This charade is our best hope to unmask the traitors. Since we know of the intended trap, we will evade it. Meanwhile the game must be played till checkmate."

"I like it not." The prince glared with argument, but he bowed his head. "But it will be as you command."

Nodding, the queen turned toward her shadowmaster. "Then the stage is set. Assemble the full council to deal with this attack on our royal courier. And let the final act of this dark game begin."

# 73

# Katherine

The clanging of the bell on the lead reindeer marked each step up the steep trail. Behind them, the town of Haven dwindled to a speck on the valley floor. Mountain peaks loomed overhead, shrouded in thick white mist. It seemed to Kath that the monks had built their monastery on the very edge of the world. She wondered if the remote exile was driven by fear or a deep desire for seclusion. Either way, the extreme remoteness only served to deepen the mystery. Gazing up at the mountains, she wondered what lay hidden behind the swirling mists. She hoped the final destination proved worthy of the journey. After Jordan's close call in the pass, she was beginning to think the price might be too high, but they were too close to turn back now.

The eight companions hiked and sometimes climbed single file up the steep trail. The lead reindeer, burdened by an immense rack of antlers, followed behind on a rope, a bell marking each step. The two Navarren guards, Jacob and Thomas, had taken change of the reindeer, tugging on the reins. The other pack deer ranged freely at the back, trained to follow the clang of the leader's bell.

Except for the tolling of the bell, they climbed in silence, struggling for each breath. Kath scrambled up a rocky outcrop, certain the horses would never have managed the trail. Looking back, she watched as the nimble reindeer scampered up the slope without breaking stride. She'd never imagined that reindeer could be trained as pack animals; she wondered what else she'd learn before this trip was over.

Duncan took the lead, setting a steady pace. Sir Cardemir shadowed the archer as if the two were in some type of competition. Kath liked the seahorse knight. He was good with a sword and a lute and she owed him a deep debt for saving her sword sister, but her gaze was always drawn to

Duncan. The leather-clad archer seemed impervious to the challenges of the mountain, tackling the steep path with a confident stride. For the thousandth time she admired the breath of his shoulders and his lithe grace, the man was certainly easy on the eyes.

"Daydreaming again?" Her sword sister caught up, giving Kath a knowing grin.

Caught staring, Kath felt her face flame red. She shared a knowing look with Jordan and then they scrambled up the path. The others followed behind, doing their best to keep pace. They'd left Haven before first light, reaching the three-way fork in the trail by mid-morning. There were no markers at the fork, but the stable master had warned them to take the right hand trail. After the fork, the trail grew more difficult, the distances between the companions gradually increasing. Sir Tyrone lagged the farthest behind, struggling against the thin air. Kath kept an eye on him, asking for a rest whenever the black knight fell too far behind.

It was late afternoon by the time they crested the tree line. The trail leveled off into an alpine meadow, the first green shoots of spring pushing through the snow crust. Relieved to walk on flat land, the companions took the time to stretch their aching muscles, pausing to sip from the icy-cold stream before following the trail across the meadow.

Relying on the scroll for directions, Duncan led them across a mountain stream rimed by ice and around a rocky outcrop to a second meadow. At the far end of the meadow, the trail ended absurdly at a bright red pavilion. With a tiled roof and latticed walls, the hexagonal wooden structure seemed like an illusion. Kath gazed at the pavilion almost expecting it to shimmer and disappear.

Breaking the spell, Duncan said, "I think we've arrived. We're supposed to wait at the pavilion until a guide comes to take us the rest of the way." Surveying the companions, he added, "Kath and Sir Tyrone, why don't the two of you investigate the pavilion while the rest of us get the packs off of the reindeer. According to the stable master, there's supposed to be a stash of dried wood and a stone fireplace for cooking. We might as well make ourselves comfortable while we wait." As an afterthought, Duncan added, "Kath see if there is some sort of a gong in the pavilion. We're supposed to sound it to let the monks know we've arrived."

While the others worked to free the reindeers of their packs, Kath followed the black knight up the stairs, keen to explore to the pavilion. The hexagonal structure proved a strange building for a mountain wilderness. Made of wood, the pavilion had an ornate wooden lattice that ran around the six sides but otherwise the building had no solid walls. The tiled roof provided protection from snow and rain, but Kath couldn't understand why anyone would build a structure without walls. To Kath's eyes it didn't seem very defensible; still, it would be far better than sleeping on the frozen ground.

A large stone hearth dominated the center of the pavilion, a chimney poking up through the tiled roof. Kath discovered a tarp protecting a cache of dried firewood; at least they'd have plenty of wood and a place to cook. While the black knight kindled a fire, Kath explored the rest of the pavilion. Rounding the fireplace, she stopped and stared. A huge golden gong, some six feet across, hung suspended from the rafters. Engravings covered the golden disc, strange runes spiraling toward the center. She studied the etchings but the runes made no sense. Then her gaze spiraled to the heart of the gong. Her heartbeat quickened. Perhaps answers lurked near. Reaching out with a tentative hand, she traced the central engraving, half expecting to find herself in another place...or another time...but nothing happened. Kath remained fixed in the present, her fingertips touching the chilly metal of the golden gong. Lost in thought, she was startled by the sounds of the others bringing the packs up the steps. Turning, she called to Duncan. "I've found the gong. It's covered in strange engravings. Come tell me if you recognize anything."

The archer crossed the pavilion with his typical lithe grace, more like a leather-clad panther than a man. She held her breath, watching his face as he studied the gong. For a moment, Kath thought she saw a flash of recognition in his eye but the moment was fleeting. Shaking his head, Duncan said, "The writing makes no sense...but there is something about the star." Shrugging, he said, "It means nothing to me."

Disappointed, she reached out to caress the engravings. Etched in the center was the outline of a human hand with an open eye engraved in the palm. The seeing hand reached toward an eight-pointed star; the same star engraved in the broken tower where she'd discovered the crystal dagger. She'd hoped the sight would awaken memories in Duncan, memories of a distant past. Perhaps the monks held the answers she sought.

Behind her, Duncan said, "You might as well sound the gong. The sooner we reach this monastery the sooner we'll have some answers."

Kath hefted the striker, aiming a blow at the heart of the gong. Her blow struck true, waking the voice of the gong.

BOOOOOOOMmmm.

The deep-throated sound reverberated through the pavilion, punishing Kath's ears. Her companions cringed. Metal plates on the hearth rattled and shook. The sound escaped through the open walls. Bouncing against the snowcapped mountaintops, the boom echoed back through the meadow.

Booooommm. boooomm. boom.

Her companions stood stunned. Cringing, Kath half expected a dragon to appear in answer to the summons.

From across the pavilion, the black knight flashed Kath a grin. "If that doesn't get their attention, nothing will."

The others laughed and then continued setting up camp in the pavilion.

Kath stood frozen, staring at the gong. She had a lot of questions. She hoped the monks were good with answers.

# 74

# Jordan

B y the light of the dying embers, Jordan read the scroll from Stewart. She'd found it hidden inside the fur-lined bedroll, his parting gift at the castle gates. The words of the scroll were etched in her heart but her eyes feasted on his handwriting. Wiping away a tear, Jordan burrowed into the luxurious fur of the snowcat lining. So soft and warm, the fur brought memories of another sort.

The ordeal of the mountain pass haunted her mind. Without Sir Cardemir's help she might have plummeted to the depths like her horse. She shuddered at the thought, forcing her mind to the adventure ahead. She stared at the rafters painted red by the glow of the embers. So strange to find a pavilion in the middle of the mountains, but it was better than being exposed to the bitter winds. She stared up at the red tiled roof, thinking about the monks and her Wayfaring. She was eager to learn the way of the general but she also missed Stewart; two years was a long time to wait. It was all too much to think about. Tired beyond exhaustion, Jordan welcomed sleep knowing that Stewart would be waiting in her dreams.

She slept straight through the night, waking to find the morning sun already up and her companions attending to the camp. Stretching, she crawled out of her bedroll and strapped on her sword before heading off to find some privacy for her morning toilet.

When she returned, the black knight was serving bowls of porridge. Jordan joined her companions in a circle around the hearth. The meal was grim, lukewarm tea and lumpy porridge, hardly the repast of heroes. Jordan forced down a swallow of sticky gruel, wondering what she was doing in the middle of mountains when she could be in Pellanor with Stewart. Jemma was definitely the smart one in the family.

Finished with the meal, they had nothing to do but wait. Sir Cardemir brought out his lute, his baritone voice providing a pleasant distraction. Jordan liked the seahorse knight, forever thankful that he'd joined their party. He'd proved a boon companion, skilled with a lute and a sword and a quick wit. Kath seemed to like him as well, but Blaine and Duncan both bristled around the knight. The subtle competition might have been amusing if not for the ordeal of the pass.

They lounged around the fire, speculating on the monks. When the sun was a quarter way across the sky, Duncan spied a lone figure striding across the meadow. Dressed in robes of midnight blue, the man carried a quarterstaff as a walking stick. The stranger climbed the steps of the pavilion and threw back the cowl of his robe, revealing a tanned face with smoke-gray eyes. Smiling, he held his right arm straight out. A seeing eye tattooed in dark blue ink stared from his open palm. "Seek knowledge." He closed his hand into a fist and placed it over his heart. "Protect knowledge." He extended his arm and opened his hand. "Share knowledge."

Not knowing the proper response, the companions held their silence waiting to see what would come next.

The stranger joined them by the hearth. "I greet you. My name is Tomay, and I am a monk of the Kiralynn Order. I am a Gatekeeper for the monastery, summoned by the sound of the gong." Nodding toward Sir Blaine, the monk added, "I hear that you come in peace."

Blaine blanched but held his silence. Jordan wondered at the knight's reaction but now was not the time to ask.

The monk turned his gaze to the seahorse knight. "You come to the monastery unbidden."

Sir Cardemir said, "I come as an emissary of the queen of Lanverness. Queen Liandra wishes an alliance with the Kiralynn monks"

Kath said, "Sir Cardemir is a friend and a loyal companion."

The monk nodded. "Your words have been noted."

Duncan slipped a scroll from his saddlebag. "The rest of us have come at the invitation of your Grand Master. We carry his scroll as proof. We request you guide us to your monastery."

The monk nodded. "All in good time." He gestured towards the hearth. "Please, be seated. It is a tradition of the mountains for strangers to share tea." Seeing the companions' hesitation, the monk added, "There is much to discuss. I would like to learn more about each of you before we travel farther." Without waiting for a response, the monk reached into a leather rucksack, removing a battered metal teakettle and a set of small porcelain cups.

Puzzled, the companions sat on the floor in a circle around the hearth.

The monk spooned tea and herbs into the kettle and set it to boil over the flames. Sitting cross-legged on the floor, he stared at the teakettle as if willing it to boil. Jordan sent a pointed look to her sword sister but Kath just shrugged. When the water boiled, the monk filled the teacups, handing one to each of the companions. "Tea is a very old tradition of the mountains. It is said that peace and harmony hold sway while strangers share a brew from a common kettle." He lifted his cup in salute. "Join me in drinking to peace and harmony among strangers."

Hesitant, the companions watched as the monk sipped his tea. When they saw his cup was empty, they began to drink. Jordan took a small sip. The tea had a pleasant flavor but there was an underlying taste she could not recognize. As if the monk read her mind, he said, "The herbs in the tea will help with the altitude. Teas have many curative qualities." Reaching for the kettle, the monk refilled each cup. "But you have not come all this way just to sample a mountain brew."

Duncan cut to the heart of the matter. "Will you take us to the monastery?"

"Perhaps." The monk sat cross-legged with his open palms turned up on his knees. "You have traveled far, but tests must be passed before you can go further. The Kiralynn Order walks in the Light. If you cannot accept this then you should turn back now."

The monk waited but no one objected. Raising his right hand, he revealed the tattoo of the Seeing Eye. "The Kiralynn Order remembers what the rest of the world has long forgotten. Great evils called harlequins walk among you. Hidden under the guise of men, they work the Dark Lord's will, seeding chaos among the kingdoms of Erdhe. The Order is the nemesis of these evil ones. The Dark Lord and his minions have long sought to destroy the monastery and crush the Order, to eliminate mankind's best hope against the harlequins. To protect the monastery, I must ask each of you to pass a test." His hand closed into a fist. "This test is neither dangerous nor harmful...but it is revealing. Do you agree?"

A shiver ran down Jordan's back. There was more to this monastery than any of them suspected.

Duncan spoke for them all. "And there is no other way of gaining the monastery?"

"None."

"Then I would see this test before we agree to take it."

The monk nodded. "That is only fair." He reached into his rucksack and withdrew a pair of iron tongs and a rectangular wooden box. Opening the box, he removed a blue silk pouch. He loosened the drawstrings and tilted the pouch. A crystalline shard tumbled into his palm.

Jordan heard Kath gasp, but her reaction made no sense.

The monk held the five-inch crystal up to the light of the fire. Pleasing to the eye, the crystalline shard had a pure geometric shape that begged to be touched, a rose-white tooth plucked from the mouth of a deep cavern. "This is a Dahlmar crystal." He turned the shard as if to catch the light. "Crystals combine the elements of earth, air, and water. Born in the depths of the earth, crystals defy their dark heritage by transmitting light with the ease of air while their shape mimics the appearance of frozen water. But Dahlmar crystals are special, for they are the only crystals also attuned to the element of fire. By drawing on all four elements, Dahlmar crystals have a rare and valuable power." The monk rotated the crystal, the facets of the shard winking in the firelight. "They give mere mortals the ability to detect a harlequin, the ancient evil that walks in the guise of a man. This crystal is the test."

Jordan stared at the shard, wondering what magic hid within the crystalline form.

Without warning, the monk tossed the crystal into the fire.

Jordan lunged forward, trying to catch it, but she was too slow. The shard landed among the flame-licked embers.

The monk smiled. "The crystal will not be harmed. Fire is necessary to prove this is a true Dahlmar crystal and not just a common shard of quartz." Flames licked at the crystal, turning it cherry-red. The monk used the tongs to extract the crystal. Free of the fire, the crystalline shard glowed with a brightness of a lantern, as if fire burned within the heart of the crystal.

Taking it in his hand, the monk held the crystal aloft. Bathed in the eerie red light, the monk said, "An ordinary quartz crystal would shatter in the heat of the flames. Fire, like the ancient evil, will wake the magic of a Dahlmar crystal, releasing the red light locked within the crystal's heart. In the absence of evil, the light will slowly fade."

As the monk spoke, the red light began to fade like an ember losing heat. In a few minutes, the crystal dulled, looking once more like an ordinary shard of rose-white quartz. "And now the test begins." The monk placed the crystal in his fist so that only half of the shard was visible. He held the crystal so each companion could see it. "My name is Tomay and I am a monk of the Kiralynn Order. I walk in the Light."

Jordan held her breath, expecting some reaction, but the crystal lay dormant in the monk's fist.

"As the Gatekeeper of the monastery, I ask each of you to take the same test. Hold the crystal as I have done and state your name and your reason for seeking the monastery. If the ancient evil is awake within you then the crystal will reveal your true heart by glowing red." Pausing, the monk asked, "Will you take the test?"

Duncan held out his hand. "Let me be the first."

"As you wish."

Accepting the crystal, the archer examined the shard. Satisfied, he mimicked the monk by holding the crystal so that half of it protruded from his fist. "My name is Duncan Treloch and I come to the monastery as the companion of Princess Jordan's Wayfaring. We come at the invitation of the Grand Master."

The Dahlmar crystal remained unchanged.

The monk held his open palm toward Duncan, displaying the Seeing Eye. "Be welcome, Duncan Treloch, for you have passed the test. May you always walk in the Light."

Duncan passed the crystal to Sir Cardemir. The knight held the crystal aloft. "I am Sir Cardemir, a knight of Lanverness, an emissary of the queen, and the son of the Duke of Graymaris. I walk in the Light." The crystal showed no change.

One by one, the companions took the crystal. Jordan watched the monk, noting how his face eased with relief as each companion passed the test...almost as if he expected, or feared, a different outcome. The Navarren guards were the last to take the test.

The monk reclaimed the crystal, a smile brightening his face. "You have all passed the test of Light. We should celebrate with a brew of tea." He returned the crystal to its box and then began spooning tea from different tins into the kettle.

"We've had enough tea." Duncan speared the monk with his one-eyed gaze.

"You'll find this brew is exceptional," the monk continued adding crushed leaves to the kettle, "befitting a celebration."

Quick as an arrow, Duncan grabbed the monk's arm. "No more tea."

Tension flared between the two men. The monk met Duncan's stare, but this time his mask of congeniality was gone. "You all need a cup of this brew."

"Need?"

Kath gasped, her hand going to her sword. "What did you put in the tea?"

"Nothing the second cup won't cure."

Duncan snarled, "Why should we trust you?"

"Because you need answers."

"But we came in peace! At the invitation of your own Grand Master."

"Not all of you were invited." The monk's gaze slid to Sir Cardemir. "It would be best if I made the tea."

Duncan released the monk, watching as he set the tea to boil. "So you hide menace beneath courtesy?"

"The Kiralynn monks prefer courtesy and persuasion to violence." His voice held a deadly edge, "You cannot fathom the evil of our enemy. The monastery must be protected."

"So you poison your guests?"

"Not poison, never that!" The monk was quick to protest. "Merely something to help subdue a harlequin. The tea is a precaution, nothing more. None of you will be harmed by it." The monk lifted the kettle, filling each cup to the brim. Reaching for his own cup, he drank the tea in one long draught.

Jordan looked at Kath. Her sword sister shrugged. "He's right, we need answers." Kath reached for her cup, but Duncan stayed her hand. "No, let me test the truth of his words." The archer stared at the monk. He took a small sip, considered the brew and then finished the cup.

The monk smiled. "It will only do you good."

Jordan took a hesitant sip. The tea carried a hint of cinnamon and apple, and something she could not name, but it had a pleasant taste. She finished the cup, searching herself for any ill affects.

"Thank you for your trust." The monk bowed toward them. "And now I must speak of another precaution. You have passed the test of the crystal, but you must also agree to a rule of the monastery. There are two important colors within the monastery. A yellow-gold color is meant for guests, fosterlings, and initiates of the Order. A dark blue color, like my robe, is restricted for monks and masters. Within the monastery every floor and doorway is painted either yellow-gold or midnight-blue. As a guest, you may *only* walk on floors or pass through doorways that are golden-yellow in color. Everything else is forbidden to you. If you violate this rule for any reason, then your very *life* is forfeit to the will of the Grand Master." Pausing, the monk said, "It may sound like a simple thing, but the Rule of Color is crucial to the Order. If you cannot swear to abide by this rule then you should leave the mountain now and never return." Pausing, the monk asked, "Will each of you swear to honor this rule?" When Duncan hesitated, the monk added, "The rule will not be confining. The monastery is large and you will not feel constricted by staying within the yellow-gold, but it is necessary that you swear to obey our law. The rule gives the monks and masters their privacy, but it also protects visitors from things that should remain hidden."

Duncan replied, "And if we obey your rules, will you swear that none of us will be harmed within the walls of your monastery?"

The monk nodded, his face solemn. "I so swear."

Duncan said, "Then I swear by the Light to obey your rule and remain within the yellow-gold."

Each companion swore the oath in turn.

The monk bowed his head in acknowledgement. "I thank you for your patience. You have passed the tests of the Gatekeeper and you are all welcome to enter the Kiralynn monastery. A Guide will lead you on the last leg of your journey."

Rising with a fluid grace, he walked to the doorway of the pavilion and reached into the pocket of his robe, producing a flute carved of wood. He put the flute to his lips and played a complex trill of notes. The melody pierced the peace of the mountain meadow like the call of a rare bird. Returning the flute to his pocket, the monk rejoined the companions and took a seat on the floor. "Your guide will be here shortly. You'll enter the monastery before the sun sets this day." With a slow smile, the monk added, "I know you have many questions but it is not for me to provide the answers. Once you reach the monastery, each of you will be given a private audience with a master. Take this time to think about the questions you most want answered." Almost as an afterthought, he added, "Remember, the Kiralynn Order serves the Light by seeking, protecting, and sharing knowledge. I hope each of you will find the knowledge you seek."

The companions sat in silence considering the words of the monk. Questions tumbled through Jordan's mind but she kept them to herself. All this talk of the Dark Lord and an ancient evil hidden in the guise of men came as a surprise to her. Rumors about the Order were murky at best, but now that she'd finally met a monk, the mystery only deepened. She did not know what to believe or whom to trust, especially given the duplicity of the tea ceremony. She studied the blue-robed monk, more confused than ever about the monastery, wondering what they'd learn before the day was done.

# 75

# Samson

Promises had a way of coming due, whether you wanted them to or not. Samson's time of safety in Lanverness had come to end. The training was finished and the volunteers were being secreted back into Coronth. Samson shuddered, steeling his courage for the journey ahead. At least he would not have to face the nightmare alone.

The wagon was packed and the draft horses hitched, but Samson kept checking everything, hoping for a reason to delay. Ben sat mounted on a nag of a horse, wearing a patched jacket, slouching like a poor tradesman instead of a drill sergeant. Grandmother Magda sat perched on the wagon's front bench, bent over her knitting needles. Samson had grown fond of the old woman. She looked like a harmless old lady, but the steely-eyed grandmother had won over the hearts of the refugees, becoming a symbol of hope and determination. Even the Master Archivist treated the old woman with deference. Frugal with her words, no one doubted a keen mind resided behind her gray eyes. The old lady seemed to watch everything while never missing a stitch of her knitting.

His second companion, Ben, was a retired drill sergeant from the army of Lanverness. The gray-haired veteran volunteered to go to Coronth, eager for a chance to make a difference. Ben's task was to train new recruits to the sword, no one expected the Pontifax to relinquish control of Coronth without a fight.

It was the drill sergeant who suggested they return to Coronth posing as failed cobblers. As the son of a cobbler, the sergeant could actually make a decent boot but Samson found the trade difficult. With a lot of effort, he could produce something that resembled a boot, but it flooded in the rain and was anything but comfortable. His poor skills would add credibility to their story. From all appearances, the threesome looked like tradesmen down on their luck, returning to Coronth in a desperate bid to make a living.

Samson checked the harness of the two draft horses and then walked to the rear of the wagon to make sure the tailgate was secure. Skins of tanned shoe leather and boxes of cobbler tools covered the wagon's false bottom, hiding access to a cache of swords and gold. Just thinking about the secret cache made Samson nervous.

"Seems you've checked the tailgate a hundred times." Looking down from the saddle of the nag, Ben gave Samson a half-smile. "Time to go."

Resigned to his fate, Samson climbed up on the wagon bench and took a seat next to Grandmother Magda.

"Delaying only makes things worse. Time to go, dear." She gave him a smile while keeping her knitting needles in constant motion, never missing a beat.

He took a last look around the courtyard, but there was no one to bid farewell. Prince Justin and some of his other friends had already left for Balor. Samson had no excuse to delay; yet he sat drinking in the peace of the castle courtyard like a condemned man grasping at a dream of safety. Grandmother Magda paused in her knitting and laid a warm hand on his arm, her voice as soothing as honey in tea. "It will be all right, dear."

Shamed by the old woman's courage, Samson picked up the reins and clucked to the draft horses, taking comfort from the steady clacking of Grandmother Magda's knitting needles. Just by her presence, the old woman gave him the courage to quell his own fears. After all, how could a man fear to tread where a grandmother dared to go. The horses lurched forward and they left Pellanor without fanfare.

# 76

# Jordan

Summoned by the flute, a second blue-robed figure approached from across the meadow. Like the first, this monk also walked with a determined stride and carried a stout quarterstaff, but his face remained hidden within the shadows of a deep cowl. The monk climbed the steps and then reached up to let the cowl fall back. Jordan gasped; the second monk was a woman, chestnut hair framing a heart-shaped face. Somehow, she hadn't expected the monks to be women.

The monk held her right hand palm-out, revealing a Seeing Eye tattooed in blue. "Seek knowledge...Protect knowledge...Share knowledge. My name is Lavidia and I am a monk of the Kiralynn Order. I am your guide. Having passed the tests of the Gatekeeper, you are welcome to enter the monastery. Assemble your belongings and I will lead you to the home of the Kiralynn Order."

Kath stepped forward, Jordan's astonishment mirrored on her face. "Women can be monks?"

With a light laugh, Lavidia replied, "You are thinking like a flatlander. You should have abandoned that narrow way of life at the mountain pass. In the Kiralynn Order we are judged on our abilities, our efforts, and our deeds, nothing more and nothing less. So yes, a woman can become a monk, a master, or even the Grand Master."

Jordan watched as a slow smile spread across her sword sister's face. Kath flashed Jordan a conspiring smile; perhaps they'd both find much to like about the monks and their monastery.

Lavidia clapped her hands. "Gather up your belongings. Time is wasted here. After your long journey I would think you'd be eager to reach the monastery."

The monk's words sent a ripple of excitement through the companions. The fabled monastery was finally within reach. The companions broke camp and loaded their gear onto the reindeer. When everything was in order, the guide said, "Before we set out, I need to ask that you do not walk in a line behind me. Instead, choose your own path. Follow in my direction but walk apart. The alpine plants are fragile and fare better if they are not overly trampled."

Duncan muttered, "And that way we won't leave a trail for others to follow."

The guide gave Duncan a shrewd smile. "Exactly, but it is also true that the alpine plants are fragile. If you are ready, please follow me."

Without looking back, she set off across the meadow at a brisk pace. Jordan and the others hurried to keep pace, the reindeer bringing up the rear. Like a gaggle of chicks they followed the guide on a convoluted path. Jordan found it took a conscious effort *not* to walk in line. She glanced over at Kath and the two shared a laugh, eager to discover the wonders of the monastery.

Beyond the alpine meadow, they scampered over rocky outcrops and scrambled up steep moraines of tumbled rock. Jordan thought they doubled back at one point, but she couldn't be sure. A boulder shaped like a rearing bear seemed familiar, but then again, maybe not. Still, she wouldn't put it past the monks to walk them in circles before finally leading them to the monastery.

The sun passed the zenith and still they walked. Scrambling up onto rocky ledge, Jordan was shocked to find a massive statue blocking their way. A giant stone hand confronted them, the palm held outward like a warning, a seeing eye inscribed in the center. Jordan found the statue forbidding, even menacing. A wall of white fog swirled behind the hand, so dense it seemed as if the world came to a sudden stop. Jordan stared at the mist. The sharp division between clarity and cloud was anything but natural.

The guide stood next to the statue, dwarfed by the stone-wrought hand. "Now we have come to the last part of the journey." She gestured to the solid wall of white. "This is the Guardian Mist. The Guardian is an ancient magic, wrought before the War of Wizards. Some believe the Mist is sentient, while others see it as nothing but a magical construct. Regardless of its true nature, the Guardian has one purpose, to defend the monastery. In order to reach the monastery we must pass through the Mist. There is no other way." The monk stared at each of them, her face solemn. "The Mist is a protection, it is not a test, but for some, the Mist will be a terrible trial. This is by far the most dangerous part of the journey. In defending the monastery, the Mist will peer into your minds seeking images it can use to frighten, trick, or entice you into turning away from the monastery. Some of you will see loved ones begging for help, while others will see monsters attacking from all directions. Or the Mist may simply part to show you a bottomless chasm gaping at your feet. Everything you see in the Mist is an illusion. *Everything.*"

Sir Cardemir strode forward, daring to touch the mist. "So this is magic."

Jordan held her breath, half expecting the mist to react, but nothing happened.

The seahorse knight turned toward the guide. "Why do you hide behind walls of magic?"

"If you knew our enemy you would not ask." The guide removed a long coil of gray silken rope. "You need not fear the Mist. As a guide, I have an amulet which enables me to see the true path to the monastery. Only guides are immune to the illusions of the Guardian Mist. To pass safely through the Mist, all you need do is keep hold of this rope and keep walking. No matter what you see, no matter how real it seems, ignore the illusions and keep a firm grip on the rope. If you follow my directions you will pass safely through the Mist." Her stare circled the companions. "Any questions?"

Duncan asked, "What if we let go of the rope?"

"At best, you will find yourself back on the outside of the Mist. At worst, the Mist will lead you to your death, enticing you to walk over a cliff. More than one visitor has died trying to pass through the Mist. The danger is very real. Do not release the rope."

A grim silence settled over the companions.

Without warning, Duncan picked up a stone and hurled it at the Mist. The stone disappeared into the white fog but there was no reaction, not even the sound of a stone clattering against rock, as if the Mist swallowed it whole.

Jordan shivered, making the hand sign against evil.

Duncan faced the monk. "There's no other way?"

"No. But if you keep hold of the rope, you *will* reach the monastery. If any of you do not wish to attempt the Guardian Mist, then you must wait here and I'll escort you back to the pavilion after the others make the crossing. It is your choice."

Duncan said, "After the tea ceremony, we have little cause to trust you, yet I sense no lies in your words." He turned face the other companions. "Will you take the risk?"

Sir Cardemir was quick to answer. "I've come on behalf of my queen. I'll not be turned away."

Sir Tyrone said, "Sir Blaine and I have pledged our swords to Princess Katherine. We'll follow her lead into the Mist or back to Haven. It is her choice to make."

Kath nodded, acknowledging the two knights. "From what I've seen so far, the monks have answers I need in order to serve the Light. For me, there is no question of turning back."

Duncan turned to Jordan. "It is your Wayfaring, Jordan, therefore it is your choice. In truth we know little about these monks, but I will accompany you either way. It is up to you to decide if the monastery is worth the risk."

Jordan thought about Stewart. If she refused to attempt the Mist, then she could return to Pellanor and her love. The thought was tempting...but only for a moment. If she turned away from the Mist, she'd be forever forfeiting the chance to learn the art of the general. It was too much to give up...and besides, Stewart loved a woman who knew how to wield a sword. Jordan realized she intended to find a way to have both the man and the sword. "It's too much of a challenge to pass up. I say we go through the Mist and find out what these mysterious monks have to offer."

A slow smile spread across Duncan's face. "Your father would be proud."

Jordan blushed, grateful for his approval. She could not imagine a better companion for her Wayfaring.

With five of the companions decided that left the two Navarren guards. Duncan turned towards them. "There is no need for you to take the risk. You will return to the pavilion and await my dispatches. Once you receive the dispatches, return to Navarre with all haste. The king will be want word of his daughter."

Jordan quickly added, "I would ask you to return by way of Pellanor in order to deliver a letter to Prince Stewart."

Jacob, the senior guard bowed. "It will be as you command."

With the arrangements made, the companions quickly sorted the packs on the reindeer and then bid farewell to the two guards. The six companions stood ready to brave the Mist. The guide played out the length of rope giving each companion a knot to hold, with a good five feet of rope between each knot. Duncan took the first position behind the guide with Sir Cardemir second. Jordan took the third. Kath moved to follow Jordan but Sir Tyrone interceded. "Our swords are sworn to protect you. If there's any danger in the Mist, I'll meet it first. Sir Blaine will protect from the rear."

Kath acquiesced, taking a place between the two knights. When everyone was in position, the guide said, "Remember, *never* let go of the rope. To ward against visions of the Guardian, I suggest you repeat a simple phrase like *I walk in the Light*. Keep your mind focused and the

Mist may not tempt you." Pausing, the guide said, "If you are ready, I will lead you through the Mist."

From the back of the line, Sir Blaine asked, "What about the reindeer? Will they follow through the Mist?"

"The Mist only defends against humans. To animals it is just ordinary fog. The reindeer will not hesitate to follow the bell of the leader."

Sir Blaine muttered, "Lucky reindeer."

Seeing that there were no more questions, the guide said, "Then let us begin." She took one step into the Mist and vanished. The gray rope stretched from the Mist, a taut line leading into nothingness.

A slight tug pulled the companions toward the wall of white. Jordan shuffled forward, watching as the swirling white swallowed Duncan and then Sir Cardemir. In just one step, the seahorse knight disappeared. Shivering, Jordan peered into the Mist but could find no trace of him.

The rope pulled her forward.

With her free hand, she reached out to touch the Mist. There was no substance to it, just a cold, damp sensation, like touching a cloud, yet this was no ordinary fog. A shiver raced down her back. Step by step, the rope drew her forward. Her hand disappeared, swallowed by white. Cold dampness lapped at her face. Taking a deep breath, she plunged in the strange fog. In the blink of an eye, the world became white and muted. Her own heartbeat sounded loud in her ears. She strained to peer through the Mist but she could not even see the hand in front of her face. Clutching the rope, she shuffled blindly forward, trusting the guide to lead her to safety.

She probably should have kept her eyes closed but she couldn't resist peering into the Mist, looking for an anchor of reality in the sea of endless white. All around her, the cold dampness pressed close, like a smothering blanket, but it was more than just physical, something white slithered across her mind.

"*Jordan!*" From the depths of the whiteness she heard her name called. She thought at first that it was one of the knights but then the voice drew near and she recognized her brother.

The Mist parted and she saw Justin, his small harp on his hip. He waved for her to follow but Jordan knew it was a trick. She held tight to the rope but her eyes refused to look away.

The image of her brother solidified, becoming more real. Soldiers dressed in red sprang from the fog, arresting her brother. The Mist vanished and Jordan found herself walking the cobblestone streets of a city. She watched in horror as soldiers forced her brother toward a burning pyre. Chaining his hands, they prodded him towards the flames.

*"Jordan help me! Don't let them burn me!"* He stared at her, his face begging for help.

Jordan shook her head. "It's just a trick.

The soldiers forced Justin into the flames. Screams of agony rang through the streets, raking across her nerves. Jordan could not watch her brother burn. Her right hand reached for her sword. Grasping the hilt, *she realized she'd released the rope!*

The streets of Coronth vanished, replaced by white fog.

Jordan whirled, groping for the rope but her hands found only damp fog. She strained to see through the swirling cloud. The Mist accommodated her. The cloud parted and Jordan gasped, standing on the edge of a bottomless chasm.

She jerked backwards, scrambling away from the edge. Her foot slipped, sending a shower of rocks tumbling into oblivion. She watched the stones fall but never heard them hit bottom. Her heart raced out of control. She clung to the ground, struggling to think. *The Mist is trying to trick me, but why a chasm?* And then the answer came, to keep her from finding the rope. She stared at the chasm, trying to defy the illusion, imagining solid ground instead of a bottomless abyss...but the gaping chasm remained. Death taunted her, but she had to take the chance. Sending a quick prayer to the Lords of Light, she gathered herself and then leaped out into the abyss. For a heartbeat she hung over emptiness. Her arms strained forward; reaching for a rope she could not see. Her fingers brushed against a taut line. She grabbed the rope and held on with both hands. Her feet found purchase on solid ground. Below her, the rocky abyss disappeared, consumed in an angry swirl of white. Jordan clutched the rope, drenched in fear.

Slick with sweat, she ran her hands along the silken rope until she found a knot. A wave of relief washed through her, she was safe. White mist surrounded her like a malevolent fist. She saw no more illusions...yet a nagging fear clawed at the back of her mind. She began to wonder if the rope was real. If the Mist could convince her that the streets of Coronth were real then surely the Guardian could project the image of a simple rope. If the rope was an illusion, she could be walking to her death. She tightened her grip, refusing to consider the possibility. To counter her fear, she began to chant, *"I walk in the Light. I walk in the Light."* She closed her traitorous eyes, blindly walking forward. The walk seemed never ending.

The cold disappeared, banished by a gentle warmth. A hand grasped her arm. Unsure if the sensations were real or illusion, Jordan cautiously opened her eyes.

Sir Cardemir gripped her arm. "You're through Jordan. You're safe."

Not wanting to be tricked twice, Jordan looked for the guide. The monk was standing next to Duncan, coiling the rope while keeping a steady tension on the line. Seeing Jordan's hesitation, the guide said, "It's true. You have passed safely through the Guardian Mist. You can let go of the rope now."

Jordan forced her hand to unclench from the rope. Shaking from the ordeal, she hugged the knight, needing proof he was real. Sir Cardemir gave a throaty chuckle, "So the Mist holds the secrets to a woman's heart, and all this time I thought it was the lute."

Blushing, Jordan stepped away. She turned to watch the rest of her companions emerge from the Mist.

The black knight stumbled out of the wall of white. Kath followed five steps later. Jordan let out a whoop of joy, relieved to see her sword sister, but her joy quickly twisted to a shout of despair. Behind Kath, the silken rope dragged on the ground. Blaine was lost to the Mist.

Kath screamed, "*Nooooo!*" She drew her sword and stepped toward the Mist.

Duncan raced passed Jordan, grabbing Kath from behind. "*You can't go in there!*"

The guide stepped between Kath and the Mist. "It is death to enter the Mist without a guide. If you enter, we'll lose two instead of one."

Kath struggled in Duncan's arms but the archer held her firm. She glared at the guide. "Then help me find him!"

Sorrow filled the guide's brown eyes. "The Mist is vast. Even with the aid of an amulet, the knight will not be found unless it is the will of the Guardian."

Duncan said, "Is there no hope?"

Jordan held her breath, fearful of the answer.

"No one has ever made it through the Mist without a guide. The knight's fate is in the hands of the Guardian."

"You can't just give up! We have to search for him." Kath struggled against Duncan.

The guide nodded. "I will retrace my steps, but only if you agree to remain in the safety of the sunlight."

Kath nodded, a stubborn set to her face. "I'll wait here till you find him."

Jordan moved to stand next to Kath, offering support. The companions watched as the guide stepped back into the Mist, vanishing in a swirl of white. Standing close together, they kept vigil on the edge of the fog. Jordan shuddered, thinking about her own trials in the Mist. Swords were nothing against the magic of the Guardian. Jordan wondered if they'd ever see the knight again.

# 77

# **Steffan**

Flaming torches lined the stone walls, casting flickers of pale light into the yard of the fortress. The moonless night formed a dark vault, sucking on the feeble torchlight, a perfect evening for the new ritual.

At the heart of the yard, a freshly raised mound of earth rose to the height of a man. Hidden within the earthen mound was a special fire pit, designed by the pyromancer to burn with the fearsome heat of a forge. Jellikan added the last batch of powders and oils to the complex layers of fuel and reagents. Finished with his preparations, he bowed toward Steffan and then climbed the stairs to the parapet.

Torchlight guttered in the chill wind, sending shadows writhing along the fortress walls. As was his usual practice, Steffan took a position at the rear of the yard, allowing him to watch the ritual from the perspective of the audience. Cloaked in his black cape, he stood with his back to the wall, the only substantial shadow in a courtyard of darkness.

Light flashed from the parapet above. Steffan heard the army's drummers and horn blowers take positions along the battlement. An unearthly wail flooded the courtyard, raising the hairs on the back of his neck. The curved aurochs horns were the general's idea. Twisted and eerie, the low moaning tugged on the soul as if summoning the very dead to serve the Flame God.

Steffan smiled, religion was all about sleight of hand.

The unearthly wail slowly faded, leaving an expectant hush. A pair of ironbound doors crashed open. Soldiers marched into the yard, their boots beating a military tattoo on the rough cobblestones. General Caylib, a mountainous man in black leathers, led the elite squad to the heart of the yard.

Taking his place at the base of the earthen mound, the general pivoted to watch as the guards formed into neat ranks. Bare-chested, the soldiers' oiled torsos gleamed in the torchlight. Wearing only leather boots and black pants, they stood rigid at attention despite the biting cold. Steffan smiled at their discipline. The culling process had been deliberately brutal. For every soldier who passed, two more died or were seriously injured. The men that survived were obedient, tough, and skilled with weapons. More importantly, they were ruthless warriors, hardened to the rape of women and the slaying of children, trained to form the brutal heart of his army. Steffan smiled, knowing the Dark Lord was pleased.

A bright light appeared on the battlement. Searing white, the light was so intense it looked like no flame ever lit by the hand of man. A murmur of amazement swept through the soldiers despite their discipline. Against the dark of the sky, the blinding light was mesmerizing, like a star flung to earth.

Steffan smiled. The pyromancer had developed a new fuel for the ceremonial torch. The man was proving well worth his weight in golds.

The drums began a slow heartbeat. The Keeper descended the stairs bearing the star-bright torch aloft. Ascending the earthen mound, he touched the torch to the fire pit. Flames roared to life, belching to a height of sixty feet. The bonfire pierced the night sky, putting the stars to shame. Heat pulsed through the yard, fierce as any forge, strong enough to make Steffan flinch into the shadows.

The drums fell silent. The Pontifax appeared at the top of the battlement, his golden robes shimmering in the light of the flames. The patriarch made his way down the steps and then climbed the mound, standing at the very edge of the fire pit. An acolyte knelt to unlace the Enlightened One's sandals. A second acolyte handed him a long spear with a broad crossbeam affixed to the end.

Gasps of disbelief rippled through the soldiers. They'd all witnessed the Test of Faith, but this fire was unearthly hot. Steffan reveled in the soldiers' fears. Some murmured, "No! Don't do it!" But the Pontifax did not listen. Holding the spear aloft while grasping his ruby amulet, the holy man walked into the raging inferno.

It was a miracle of rare intensity. Even Steffan had to applaud the courage of the Pontifax. Soldiers fell to the cobblestones in prostration, awed by the spectacle.

Flames roared and licked at the Pontifax, yet the patriarch stood unharmed in the melting heart of the blaze. He gazed at the soldiers, his voice ringing through the courtyard. "Our god is a god of love! The Flame God gives us light to beat back the darkness. The Flame God gives us heat to beat back the chill of winter. Through his gifts of light and heat, the Flame God gives us life. He nourishes and sustains the faithful." Raising the spear, he made the sign of blessing. "The Flame God looks after our spiritual needs as well as the physical. He gifts us with the Test of Faith so that our sins may be redeemed. Yes, our god is a god of love." The Pontifax lowered his voice. "But our god has another face. It is a face he turns toward all unbelievers, a face that burns and destroys all those of impure hearts. In his wrath, the Flame God consumes the infidel, reducing them to nothing more than ash." Raising the spear high into the air, the Pontifax pounded the iron-shod butt straight down into the fire pit. "To the infidels the Flame God shows the face of war!"

A shower of sparks erupted from deep within the fire pit. Crimson veins of color shot through the golden flames. Gas belched from the pit like the breath of an angry god. A noxious cloud of brimstone rolled down the earthen mound swirling around the soldiers as if the gates of hell had opened. One soldier crumpled in a dead faint. The line of soldiers wavered, but discipline held. No one dared move.

The voice of the Pontifax thundered from the flames. "Fear not, for you are the chosen, the elite warriors of the Flame God. The sins of your past are forgiven. You are pure warriors of the Flame. You strike with the might of the Flame God. If you fall in battle, a place will be made for you in heaven. The warriors of the Flame will prevail!"

A rousing cheer rose from the soldiers. When the cheer subsided, the Pontifax continued, "As holy warriors, you will fight under a new standard, the standard of the Black Flame!" He shook the spear, unfurling the cloth attached to the crossbeam. The standard snapped in the flames, blood red with a black flame boldly emblazoned on the center. "Blessed by the Flame God, I give you the standard of victory!" The standard snapped in the burning maelstrom but it did not burn. Seeing the invincibility of their new battle banner, the men roared their approval. "Carry it before you into battle. Carry it to victory!"

When the soldiers quieted, the Pontifax continued, "Tonight you are reborn from ordinary soldiers to elite warriors of the Flame. A new weapon, consecrated in the Sacred Flames, has been forged for you. A weapon designed to drink the very souls of the infidels. In the hands of true believers, the black halberds will be invincible." A dozen acolytes hurried forward to remove coverings from the base of the earthen mound, revealing bundles of weapons gleaming in the firelight.

"Soldiers of the Flame! Take up your holy halberds and dip them in the Flames of War! Let each warrior pledge his life and his soul to the Flame God! Come forward and be consecrated in the Sacred Flames!"

General Caylib was the first to answer the call. Selecting a halberd, he whirled it above his head, demonstrating the fearsome reach of the seven-foot weapon. A halberd was three weapons in one, a foot-long steel spike at one end, a vicious half-moon axe below the spike, and a long blackened shaft of polished ash that served as a quarterstaff. Moving like a demon possessed, the general twirled the weapon with a savage grace. He finished the exhibition with a thundering war cry. *"Death to the infidels!"*

The soldiers echoed his cry, fists pumping the air.

Saluting the Pontifax, the general climbed the mound of earth to stand before the Flames. Bowing low in homage, he thrust the blackened axe-head into the fire. Crimson sparks erupted from the halberd, like a sign from the god. The general twirled the halberd, blazing a trail of sparks like a comet.

Gasps of amazement rippled through the soldiers, overwhelmed by the miracle.

Steffan smiled knowing it was merely a coating on the steel, another trick of the pyromancer.

The Pontifax made the sign of blessing. "Bless this weapon of the Flames. May it drink the souls of the infidels and prove invincible in the hands of the faithful."

The soldiers roared their approval.

The general removed the sanctified weapon. Waving the halberd over his head in triumph, he let out a blood-curdling war cry. The raw savagery of the man was visible to all. Steffan smiled, he'd chosen his general well.

The general strode back down the mound and stood at attention while the ranks of troops came forward to select their halberds and receive their blessing. A line of bare-chested warriors coiled at the base of the mound like a serpent mesmerized by the Flames.

Steffan watched as the Pontifax blessed the halberds. Gleaming in his gold vestments, the old showman did a masterful job. The projection of his voice and the timing of his delivery perfectly matched the pyromancer's effects, making the flames appear alive with the presence of the god. The illusion was powerful, as if the god himself called the soldiers to war. Raw religious fervor thrummed through the courtyard like unchained lightning. Steffan reveled in the power. With just one ceremony, he converted ordinary soldiers into fanatical warriors. The Black Flames would form the core of a ruthless army. Soon it would be time to loose them on the kingdoms of Erdhe. Steffan smiled from the shadows, pleased with the layers of illusions. The soldiers thought they worshiped the Flame God, but in truth, it was the Dark Lord they served.

# 78

# Blaine

Blaine watched the Mist swallow each companion whole. Step by step, they disappeared, consumed by the swirling white, till he was the last one standing in the clear light of day. Shuddering, he made the hand sign against evil. He didn't trust the Mist. It reeked of magic. Knights preferred sharp steel to the murkiness of magic, but he'd sworn to follow the princess. Tightening his grip on the knotted rope, he took a deep breath and followed the others into the Mist.

Fog clamped around him like a suffocating fist. The world went white, nothing but damp fog in every direction. Straining his senses, he tried to see, he tried to listen, but the only sound was the drumbeat of his heart. Blaine had never seen fog so thick, or so smothering. He knew Kath walked five feet ahead yet he couldn't catch a glimpse of the girl, not even a silhouette. Blinded by white, he stumbled forward, keeping a tight grip on the rope.

The rope pulled him forward, a lifeline in a sea of Mist. He lost count of the number of steps, nothing to do but follow. Yet the brooding white preyed on his mind.

Something dark skittered ahead. Blaine stared, not trusting the fog. Catching movement from the corner of his eye, he whirled but the Mist was empty. The white cloud mocked him. Suspicious, he scanned the Mist, his unease growing with every step.

A sword slashed through the fog.

Blaine dodged backwards, keeping a hold of the rope. A second blade hissed past his face. *Ambush!* His heart racing, he reached for his sword. Wielding it with one hand, he struck at the fog in a blind slash. His blue blade whistled though white. *Nothing!* He shook his head, unsure if the attack was real or illusion. Peering into the fog, he held his sword at the ready.

Time crawled.

A sound cut through the Mist, the harsh clang of steel. Dark silhouettes danced ahead. Blaine suspected an illusion, but he couldn't stop staring. The Mist parted. Three men in scarred leather armor attacked a single foe. Swords clanged with a furious tempo. Someone waged a fierce defense. The attackers shifted and Blaine glimpsed the lone figure at the heart of the fight. *Kath!* She dodged and parried, one sword against three. The girl was good but not against those odds. Blaine told himself it was an illusion but he couldn't look away. Fear clawed at the back of his mind. What if the attack was real? He'd sworn to protect her. Honor pulled him toward the fight. He made his choice, deliberately dropping the rope and grasped his sword with two hands.

He half expected the brigands to disappear but the clang of swords continued.

A cry rent the air. One of the brigands lunged inside Kath's guard, his sword piecing her side. Bright blood bloomed on her leather jerkin as she crumpled to the ground, her sword dropping from her hand.

"*No!*" Blaine covered the distance in two leaps. His great blue sword slashed a deadly arc toward the attackers. The sword sliced clean through the brigand's neck without resistance! The attacker disappeared in a swirl of angry white. Blaine staggered with surprise, but refused to leave anything to chance. He whirled a backhanded cut toward the second brigand, a whisper of death in the fog. The second man raised his sword for the parry. Instead of meeting steel with steel, his sword found only mist. The second attacker vanished. The third met the same fate, nothing but a gang of phantoms. His heart hammering, Blaine stood guard, peering into the malevolent Mist. The attackers were gone but the princess remained, bright blood leaching her side. Blaine knelt, afraid to find the blood was real.

Kath gazed up at him with pain-filled eyes. "I knew you'd come."

Her trust cut him to the core. He should have been quicker. "But I came too late." His words were a whisper. He reached out to tend her wound. His hand passed through her side, finding only white. The princess disappeared. Relief washed through him. He hadn't failed after all. But then anger struck. His honor remained intact, but he'd been tricked by the Mist.

"*Show yourself!*" Anger burned through him.

He pivoted, searching for a landmark but every direction was white. A drop of fear trickled down his back. He was lost, caught in the deadly grip of magic. He tried to retrace his steps, reaching out for the rope, but found only damp air.

Lost in a sea of fog, fear gripped his stomach. Not trusting the cursed Mist, Blaine slid his right foot forward, testing the ground, searching for reality. He refused to die, lost in this wizard's nightmare. He forged his way forward, muttering, "I walk in the Light. I walk in the Light."

The Mist swirled, white riddled with gray. Figures danced ahead, silhouettes against the white. A breeze stirred, carrying the mingled scents of blood, sweat, and gore. If valor had a smell, this was it. Blaine followed the scent of battle. Steel clanged on steel. Men shouted and the wounded moaned. Death surrounded him. Blaine's mind warned of illusion but his senses screamed otherwise. He tightened his grip on his sword. The Mist thinned and details became distinct. Shattered shields, trampled banners, and broken men littered the ground. Blaine stood at the center of grim battlefield. Disciplined lines were gone, dissolved into the chaos of individual conflict. Pockets of knights battled hordes of soldiers in black and gold. The last defenders of the eight-pointed star wavered against the relentless onslaught of the pentacle. Blaine watched as the gold and blue banner fell, the eight-pointed star tramped in the bloody mud. The battle was lost but the knights fought on, refusing the odds.

A black warhorse reared out of the Mist. The rider's armor was fearsome, his helmet forged in the shape of a skull crowned by a spiked circlet of gold, his breastplate etched like the ribs of a skeleton. Death rode a horse. The rider gestured with an iron staff and a second horde in black and gold swept across the field. The battle ebbed and flowed around Blaine as if he did not exist. A path opened to the Skeleton King. Blaine saw his chance. Raising his great blue sword in a two-handed grip, Blaine charged. "*For the Octagon!*"

The warhorse reared, striking out with iron-shod hooves. Blaine ducked, lunging for the heart of the stallion. His blade struck true. The stallion dissolved in an angry swirl of white but the Skeleton King remained. Mocking laughter cut through the sounds of battle. The king raised his iron staff, the tip glowing red with a baleful light. He pointed his staff toward Blaine. Menace and magic hung in the air, binding Blaine in place. The Skelton King strode toward him. His dark armor rippled with magic, radiating fear. "Kneel to me!" The voice struck like a sword full of malice.

"*No!*" Blaine fought the shackles of fear and charged. A wave of pain ripped into him, a clawed hand tearing his guts. He stared down but there was no blood, no wound. The invisible hand twisted and Blaine sank to his knees, a scream on his lips.

The Skeleton King towered above, his staff raised to strike. Blaine's stare fell to the blue sword still clutched in his hand. King Ursus had given him a hero's blade yet he knelt crumpled before evil without ever striking a single blow. Anger pulsed through him; he refused to fail. Fighting the pain, he thrust upwards. His great blue sword sliced deep into the armor of the Skeleton King. Blue lightening crackled around the hilt. Dark blood dripped down the blade. The world shattered. The white returned.

Shaking, Blaine stood, planting his feet wide in defiance. The pain was gone, the wound only a memory. He wiped the sweat from his brow and held his ground, scanning the Mist. All signs of the battle were gone, wiped clean by the infernal white. Cold fog pressed close around him, watching, judging, but Blaine was done with games. "What do you want?"

Silence was the only answer.

*"What do you want?"* His shout challenged the Mist.

A single figure beckoned in the distance.

Blaine gripped his sword and moved closer. Details solidified from the white. A knight stood alone in the Mist, his silver plate burnished bright, an eight pointed-star embossed on the breastplate. Gauntleted hands gripped a great sword, a winged helmet studded with stars upon his head. His face was lined with hard decisions, a black beard tinged with streaks of gray. Dark fathomless eyes heavy with the weight of too many memories pierced Blaine to the core.

Blaine whispered, "Who are you?"

The knight's voice filled the Mist, coming from all directions. "You walk through the Mist without a guide. Your life is forfeit."

A bead of sweat trickled down Blaine's face.

The knight stared into his soul. "Whom do you serve?"

"The Octagon and the princess of Castlegard."

"Can a sword serve two masters?"

Blaine stared at the knight, caught off-guard by the question.

"A day will come when you will have to choose."

Blaine shook his head, angry at the question. "What games are you playing? Who are you?"

"One of your party carries a crystal dagger. Long have we waited for its return. We give you warning. Dark times are coming." The knight's voice deepened. "Your life is forfeit but you fought for the sake of honor and the Light. Every blade will be needed for the trials ahead." The knight lifted his great sword, pointing the tip at Blaine's heart. "The Guardians charge you to keep your vow to the one who wields the crystal dagger. She is the pivot of this time." The tip of the great sword rested against Blaine's chest. It felt like steel not illusion.

"Knight of the Octagon, will you be true?"

The question rang through the Mist, as if challenging Blaine's very soul. He met the knight's penetrating stare. "By Valin and the Lords of Light, I do swear."

A ripple passed through the knight and his face began to fade. The knight grimaced as if struggling to hold his form. For a moment, Blaine thought a different face peering out from the Mist, a dark-haired woman, but then the knight's eyes blazed and the sharpness returned. "Be warned. The battlefield was a memory of the Mist, an echo from an age long gone. You must learn from the past to win the future. For a thousand years, the Enemy has grown in power and cunning. Swords must fight, but tt will take more than steel to defeat this evil." The knight gave a Blaine a crooked smile. "We release you from the Mist, Sir Blaine, go forth to fight another day." The knight dissolved into the white.

Blaine stepped forward. "No, wait! Who are you? How do you know so much?"

The Mist swirled. Blaine thought the knight returned, but then a blue-robed figure stepped through the white, chestnut hair framing a heart-shaped face. The guide's face blanched white. "You live!" She gripped his hand, flesh against flesh, wonder on her face. "No one ever survives alone in the Mist." She studied his face, as if seeking an answer to a riddle. "Come, your friends await."

Shaken by his experience, he followed the guide, but this time the Mist was empty of illusions, nothing but damp cloud. Blaine took a single step and the world changed. Sunlight and the clear mountain air returned in a rush. Breathing deep, he purged his lungs of the taint of magic.

A cry of joy echoed against the mountains. Kath raced across the distance, wrapping Blaine in a fierce embrace. "I knew you'd find a way!" Tears hung in her sea green eyes.

He stared down at her, touched by her tears, realizing he felt more for her than just duty. His voice was rough with meaning. "I'll always be there for you." For a moment, they stood alone, and Blaine hoped she understood. She gazed up at him, her voice a soft whisper. "I never doubted you," but then she stepped away and her smile held nothing but friendship.

Blaine struggled to hide his feelings. He felt the Mist watching at his back, bearing witness. "I swore before but this time I mean it. My sword is yours." He dropped to his knee, extending the sapphire hilt. She touched his hand and the bond of loyalty tightened between them. The moment passed and the other companions crowded around, pounding his back in celebration.

The voice of the guide cut through the gathering. "What did you see in the Mist?"

The others fell silent.

"I met the Guardian. He warned that dark times are coming."

The guide blanched. "You saw one of the Guardians?" The monk shook her head. "There is more here than meets the eye. Truly, this is a riddle for the Grand Master." She added in a quiet voice, "Come, I'll take you to the monastery now."

The companions turned as one to look at the goal of their long journey. Rising to three times the height of a tall man, the gray stone wall stretched across the meadow, seamless except for a pair of iron bound doors. Inlayed with gold, the massive doors each bore a stylized Seeing Eye, like the tattoos on the hands of the monks. Perhaps it was a lingering effect of the Mist, but to Blaine the monastery seemed like a huge stone beast crouched at the very edge of the world, watching through golden eyes. Blaine sheathed his sword, prepared to follow his princess into the very belly of the beast.

# 79

# Katherine

**M**age-stone! Kath stood rooted to the ground, staring up at the monastery walls. So seamless they looked poured and molded from molten granite, the same as her beloved Castlegard. But mage-stone was rare, very rare. She never expected the monastery and the castle to share a common heritage; another question to add to her growing list. Kath hoped the monks were good with answers.

A bell clanged and the lead reindeer emerged from the Mist. The sound startled Kath, she'd forgotten the pack deer. She turned to watch as the other deer emerged from the white. Once all the reindeer were accounted for, Blaine reclaimed the rope of the lead reindeer and they followed the guide to the massive gates. Golden eyes engraved on the doors watched their approach. Kath couldn't decide if the eyes were welcoming or forbidding.

A small gong hung suspended from a wooded frame. The guide used the striker to announce their arrival. Kath covered her ears, but the smaller gong had a sweet voice.

The massive doors swung open.

Kath held her breath, not sure what to expect. After the Mist, anything seemed possible...but the gates swung open without spectacle or sign of magic, pushed by a pair of golden robed monks. But even something so ordinary could not dim her curiosity. She followed the guide through the gates, eager for answers.

*Color.* Intense color was Kath's first impression. The monastery gates opened onto a rectangular courtyard awash with a rich yellow-gold color. Painted on the mage-stone floor, and the nine doors opening onto the yard, the courtyard glowed like a captured sunlight. But gold was not the only color. Bold brushstrokes of ruby red, emerald green and sapphire blue enlivened the mage-stone walls. Each wall was a canvas of illuminated texts painted in rich jewel tones. Swirls of calligraphy adorned with birds and vines and castles and knights, covered the walls with stunning detail. Everywhere she looked, vibrant texts seemed to leap from the walls, ensnaring the eye and begging to be read. Taken as a whole, the courtyard might have appeared garish or gaudy but instead it somehow seemed tasteful and infinitely intriguing. Colors and complexity teased the eye, engaging Kath's imagination. She felt as if she'd lived in a black and white world all of her life.

Summer was her second impression. An unexpected warmth cloaked the monastery, as if summer hid behind the stout mage-stone walls. A dry heat radiated up through her boots, warm and welcoming. It seemed an impossible illusion till Kath noticed the raised flowerbeds. Outside the gates, the alpine plants struggled to show the first green of spring but inside the courtyard the same plants were in full bloom. The monastery was full of surprises, the boon of summer an unexpected gift.

A rhythmic clacking filled the courtyard. Curious, Kath drifted towards the sound, discovering a second sunken courtyard four times the size of the first. Rows of monks in robes of gold and midnight blue practiced below. Quarterstaffs whirled and stuck with blinding speed, marking the rhythm of war.

Kath leaned on the balcony, watching the martial display. The practice was truly impressive. So this was the reason the gatekeeper and the guide both carried wooden staffs. Kath smiled, relieved to discover the monks had a martial side. She would have been deeply disappointed if the monastery turned out to be nothing more than a bunch of musty old hermits studying ancient tomes.

Duncan joined her on the balcony, a hint of surprise in his voice. "I always thought the quarterstaff was a peasants' weapon, yet the monks make it look formidable." He gave her a wry smile. "Perhaps there's something here for each of us to learn." But then his face sobered. "Be wary of the monks, Kath. They speak the truth yet their words carry layers of hidden meaning." His voice dropped to a hush, "Kingdoms could flounder in those meanings."

Kath knew what he meant, but before she could reply, the guide called them back to the courtyard.

"My duty ends at the gates." The blue-robed guide gestured toward the reindeer. "Please remove your packs and I'll lead the reindeer back to your guardsmen waiting on the far side of the Mist."

The companions quickly sorted through the packs. With thanks to the guide, they watched as the monk led the reindeer back out through the gates, disappearing into the Mist. Kath shivered as the Mist swallowed the last of the reindeer. Magic was hard to get used to.

Beside her, Duncan echoed her thoughts. "The Mist is a formidable barrier, but is it meant to keep intruders out...or to lock us in?"

She gave him a wary nod, another question needing an answer.

Turning back to the courtyard, they found five golden-robed monks waiting. A tall monk with close cropped blond hair and a ready smile approached Kath. "Greetings. My name is Bryce. I am an initiate of the Kiralynn Order and I'll be your guide for your first few weeks at the monastery." Giving Kath a welcoming smile, he added, "Might I know your name?"

"Princess Katherine of Castlegard, but call me Kath."

"Kath it is then." With an answering smile, he waved toward the mound of packs. "Let me help you with your things and I'll show you to your quarters."

"What about my companions?"

"They each have their own guides. The monastery is a labyrinth of passageways. First time visitors often find it confusing, and besides, guests usually have a never-ending stream of questions. The masters always assign one senior initiate to each guest to make sure your needs are cared for." Shrugging, Bryce added, "It is our custom, a way to help guests become acquainted with our ways."

Kath decided she liked the custom, it sounded both polite and civilized. She joined the others in sorting through the mound of packs. Her belongings made a small pile, a bedroll, a saddlebag stuffed full of clothes from Pellanor, a small round shield, a chainmail shirt, her garnet helm, a gift from Sir Cardemir, and a leather rucksack with her few valuables.

"Is this all of it?"

Now that she looked at it, it seemed a meager pile, but she'd never cared much for clothes. With her rucksack slung over her shoulder, she picked up the shield and the heavy sack with her chainmail, leaving her guide to grab her saddlebag and the bedroll. Burdened with gear, Bryce led her to one of the golden doors at the far end of the courtyard. The others followed, bedrolls and saddlebags slung over their shoulders.

The door opened onto a maze of corridors, revealing a blaze of colors. All the floors glowed a warm golden-yellow color while every wall was adorned with illuminated text. Elegant calligraphy filled every corridor, giving the impression that the monks did not waste a single surface that could be used for writing or illustration, a true testament to their love of knowledge. Each wall seemed more beautiful and fascinating than the last. Intrigued by everything she saw, Kath rushed to keep pace with her guide.

Bryce set a fast pace, offering a running commentary as they made their way through the corridors. "You probably noticed the warmth of the monastery. It's the first thing most visitors comment on. There's a simple explanation and it's *not* magic." He glanced back over his shoulder, as if checking to see she was listening. Satisfied, he continued without breaking stride, "Built over a natural hot springs, the monastery was designed with hot water pipes running through the floors and even some of the walls. We also have the most marvelous bathes for soaking. After a hard practice session with quarterstaffs, there's nothing better."

They came to an intersection of four corridors. Without hesitating, he chose the corridor on the right, pointing out a bronze bell suspended in the corner. "You'll find bells like these in all the intersections. First-year initiates ring the bells at the beginning and the end of each meal. We have three meals a day, at sunrise, noon, and sunset. Each meal service lasts for exactly one turn of the hourglass. If you don't make it to one of the common rooms in time then the cooks assume you've decided to fast, so heed the bell if you don't want to go hungry." As an afterthought, he added, "The bells are also rung if there's a fire, but there's never been one for as long as I've lived here, so you needn't worry."

He turned into a side corridor and stopped at the fourth door in the hallway. Opening the golden door, he gestured for Kath to enter. "This will be your room for the duration of your stay."

She entered the small spare room, not sure what to expect. Ten feet in length and six feet wide, the cell was empty except for a narrow bed and a small table with a lantern. A row of hooks ran along one wall. A small square window at the far end let in the afternoon light. Except for the yellow-gold floor, the room was plain and unadorned, almost peaceful in its simplicity. It was the first room she'd seen that looked like it belonged in a monastery.

"It's not much but it's home." Bryce stacked her belongings in the corner. "I know it's small, but everyone in the monastery has the same size room. It's even said the Grand Master's room is no bigger than an ordinary cell."

Kath started to say it was fine, but then she noticed there was no chamber pot. Flushing red, she had to ask. "What do I do for a chamber pot?"

"The privy is just down the end of the corridor." Pausing, he added, "Best I show you. Most visitors find it unusual."

"*Unusual?*" Puzzled, Kath followed him back down the corridor. Near the end of the hall they came to a golden door with a dark blue half moon painted in the center.

"Doors marked with a half moon are privies. Don't ask me why a half moon is used to denote a privy. No one seems to know the reason but it's the same all over the monastery, some sort of tradition that's lost to the ages." Pausing, he added, "Best to knock before entering." When there was no response, he opened the moon-marked door, revealing a small room with a stone bench along one wall and an enclosed basin on the other. The round hole cut in the bench was self-explanatory but the clean smell amazed Kath. Even the best-kept privies were haunted with a foul odor. Sniffing, she approached the bench.

Bryce must have seen the puzzlement on her face. "Separate pipes run under the bench for wastes. If you look through the hole you'll find a stream of running water below. Everything gets swept away so there's no mess or smell."

Kath peered through the hole, shocked by the flowing stream. Truly, the monks were amazing.

"You can wash here." Bryce pointed to the steady stream of water flowing into the washbasin. "The water is always warm. For bathing, we have the hot springs. I'll show you the baths tomorrow." Seeing Kath's wide-eyed amazement, he chuckled. "I know. Most visitors can't get over the privies. Sometimes I think they're more impressed with the privies than all the magic of the monastery."

Not sure what to say, Kath just nodded. The wonders of the monastery were truly marvelous.

Bryce led her back out into the corridor, but Kath's gaze was drawn toward the far end of the hallway, to a midnight blue door. *The forbidden color!* Her first glimpse of a midnight-blue door tugged on her imagination. "What lies beyond that door?"

Bryce shrugged. "I can't say."

"You can't say or you don't know?"

His face reddened. "I don't know. I'm only an initiate. Like you, I'm bound by the rule of color. Midnight blue doors are only for monks and masters. I'll find out once I take my oath and am bound to the Order."

"But aren't you curious?"

"Of course, but I respect the rules."

Hearing the honesty in his words, she asked no more questions, but the midnight door haunted her mind. Pre-occupied with the mystery, Kath followed her guide back to her room. Along the way, Bryce said, "Take a close look at each of the doors."

Kath studied the doors, surprised to notice a pattern of cut crystals embedded in the wood.

"The crystals are arranged in the shape of star constellations, with a different constellation marking each door. Your door bears the constellation for the big ladle. Just remember to look for the big ladle and you'll find your room."

Kath hadn't noticed the star patterns before. Running her fingers across the raised crystals, she wondered what else she'd missed.

Bryce opened the door to her room. "You're to have a private audience with a master in a turn of an hourglass. I can leave you here to rest in peace or I can try and talk the cook into parting with a pot of tea and some biscuits from lunch." He flashed a friendly smile. "Which will it be, privacy or company?"

She was tempted to have some time to herself, but she needed to learn as much about the monastery as possible. "Tea and biscuits sounds great. Breakfast was a long time ago and there was no time for the noon meal. Besides, I am truly enjoying your company."

Bryce flashed a broad smile, reminding Kath of Jordan's brother, Justin. "Your wish is my command. I'll see to the tea at once, while you make yourself comfortable."

Kath could not help but laugh. She liked the young monk-initiate and was glad to have him as her guide.

With a parting smile, Bryce closed the door behind him. Kath used the time to visit the amazing privy and then to organize her meager belongings. She wondered how her friends were faring. Sir Tyrone and Duncan would both be eager to explore but she wondered what Jordan and Sir Blaine thought about it all. Kath was looking forward to sharing her discoveries with her friends.

A polite knock sounded on the door. She opened it to find Bryce juggling a teapot, two cups, a plate of biscuits, and small jar. Giving her an impish grin that Kath was growing to like, he shrugged. "The cook likes me."

They sat cross-legged on the warm floor with the teapot between them. The idea of sharing a meal of smuggled food appealed to Kath's sense of fun. She was glad she'd ask the young monk to return...yet she hesitated over the tea. "Is this safe?"

"Yes, of course!" Understanding sobered is face. "Oh, the tea ceremony. That was only a precaution, but now you're safe inside our walls." He shrugged, giving her a disarming smile. "It's just tea." He took a sip and then held up a small jam jar like a rare prize. "You have to try the raspberry jam. The berries grow all over the mountain. The cooks have a way of turning them into a heavenly jam, a rare taste of summer."

Kath spread the thick red jam on one of the biscuits and took a bite. Her mouth flooded with the tart taste of summer. "It's good!" They shared the biscuits, slathering them with jam and sipping tea while Kath plied Bryce with questions. "So how did you come to be an initiate of the Order?"

"My father is a monk. I've always wanted to join the Order."

Kath choked on her biscuit. "You're *father?*" The idea that monks could marry and have children shocked her. "So is your mother is a monk as well?"

"Oh no. Mother is an expert candle maker. She owns the chandler shop in Haven. I have five siblings and they've each chosen to make their way in Haven or down in the flatlands. I'm the only one who followed father into the Order." With a touch of pride in his voice, he added, "I was accepted at the age of twelve. I've been an initiate for a little more than ten years now. To me, the monastery is home."

"So why do you want to be a monk?"

"What I really want is to be a healer. There's nothing like the gratitude in a stranger's eyes when you ease their pain. If you haven't seen it for yourself, then it's hard to explain, but once you experience the rewards of healing, fills your soul till it's all you want to do." The young man looked away, as if lost in thought. "I was lucky to be born in Haven, at the very doorstep of the monastery. There's no better place to learn any craft than with the monks, and it's especially true for the art of healing." Pausing he added, "In Haven, we have a saying. *The monks remember more than the rest of the world has forgotten.*" Shrugging, he said, "Once I take my vows, I'll not only be a healer but I'll also have access to the libraries. Master Garth, my mentor, believes there are many methods of healing lost to the memories of man. He believes these remedies reside in the libraries of the monastery. Just a few turns of the moon ago, he rediscovered the recipe for a forgotten herbal solution effective in treating the bending disease of old age. It's not a cure but it eases the pain and it allows the joints to move with more flexibility." Suddenly turning shy, the young man looked down at the floor and said, "I'm sorry if I babbled on, but I have a passion for healing." He shrugged. "There's nothing else I'd rather do."

The timber of his voice and the sparkle in his eyes proved the young man had found his true calling. Bryce reminded her a bit of Quintus, Castlegard's master healer. Before Kath could ask any more questions, he glanced at the small window, a startled look on his face. "The afternoon grows late. I should take you to the garden for your audience with the master. Mustn't be late for that."

Gracefully rising from the floor, he ushered Kath toward the door. She was about to leave when she remembered her rucksack. She darted back to grab it from the bed.

"No need to take that. It will be safe in your room."

Kath slung the rucksack over her shoulder. "No, I want it with me, especially for this meeting."

Shrugging, he hurried her out of the room, leading her back into the maze of yellow-gold corridors. Kath tried to memorize the twists and turns but all the corridors looked alike. They eventually came to a set of steps that led down to another golden corridor. The temperature grew warmer. Kath guessed they must be close to the source of the hot springs. And then she noticed the doors. Instead of cut crystals; each door had a small glass-paned window, each one fashioned in a different geometric shape. Bryce stopped in front of a door with a diamond shaped window. "This is one of our gardens of contemplation. Enjoy the garden while you wait. A master will meet you here shortly. I'll come back for you when the evening bell rings for dinner." He made a formal bow, his voice turning solemn. "Seek knowledge. Protect knowledge. Share knowledge. May you find wisdom in your conversation with the master."

Kath stepped through the door into a room full of green. Plants of every description crowded the walkway. Warm, moist heat wrapped around her like a comforting blanket. She breathed deep, enjoying the lush scent of moss and leaves mingled with the smell of rich, moist soil. Beams of sunlight streamed through a vaulted ceiling, adding spears of warmth to the garden. She stared up in wonder, surprised to find a ceiling made of glass. Amazed, she turned to take in the whole of it. Like a glass jewel filled with summer, the garden proved a wonder.

Tearing her gaze from the ceiling, she explored the depths of the garden. A narrow walkway led down and around a raised reflecting pool. Stone benches stood at strategic spots along the quiet pool, lush plants crowding the raised beds on either side. Statues peered out from among the green, faces frozen in marble. Kath strolled toward the back, her fingers caressing the leaves. Overhead, the clouds shifted, sending a single shaft of sunlight to illuminate a stone statue at the far end of the garden. Intrigued, Kath moved closer, peering through the leaves.

Carved out of white marble, the statue portrayed three creatures sitting in a row. The odd little creatures had rounded ears and long tails of animals, but they also had human-like hands and feet. Their flattened faces looked vaguely human, like mythical caricatures of man. But the oddest aspect was the way the artist had given each creature a different human gesture. The first covered his ears with his hands, the second covered his eyes, and the last covered his mouth. Kath stared at the statue, trying to understand the riddle cast in stone.

A deep masculine voice said, "So I see you've found our statue of the three monk-keys."

Startled, Kath pivoted to meet the gaze of a tall athletic man in his late fifties. Dressed in robes of midnight blue, the monk had short gray hair peppered with black. His face was weathered by the sun and creased with deep laugh lines, the kind of face leavened with wisdom and experience and a touch of humor.

"I'm sorry if I startled you." The monk studied her with jewel-blue eyes that sparkled with amusement but also spoke of hidden depths. "My name is Master Rizel and I am pleased to meet Princess Katherine of Castlegard. The Grand Master extends his welcome. He is pleased that you choose to accept his invitation."

Caught off guard, Kath didn't know what to say.

Gesturing toward the statue, the master said, "The gardens are full of many things that catch the eye and tease the mind. It is always insightful to see what speaks to a guest."

Kath didn't know if the statue had 'spoken to her', but it certainly was curious. She waited in silence to see where the conversation was going.

He gestured to a bench directly across from the statue. "Shall I tell you the story behind the statue?"

Intrigued, Kath joined him on the bench. Without waiting for a reply, the monk took up the cadence of a storyteller. "This statue is one of the oldest pieces of art in the Order's collection. It is also one of my favorites. A traveling monk discovered it in a distant empire and was so impressed with the lessons behind the carving that he had it transported at great expense back to the monastery. According to the records of that time, the god-emperor Diabolus came down from the heavens to give his people a new law, the Law of Virtue. Diabolus promised the people that if they followed his Law then peace and prosperity would reign for a thousand years. The Law of Virtue was simple, it said that if the people refused to hear evil, refused to see evil, and refused to speak evil, then evil itself would be banished from the land and peace would reign. Seeing wisdom in the Law, the people of the empire set out to live by the new code, but what they did not know was that the god Diabolus was really another guise for the Dark Lord, and above all else, the Dark Lord is always the Great Deceiver. Mistaking Diabolus for a Lord of Light, the good people of the empire adopted the Law of Virtue. In the years to come, the people looked away and closed their ears, giving the true minions of Diabolus free reign to perpetrate every dark desire. Innocents were killed and tortured in the streets of the cities but the public closed their ears to the cries for help. Children were enslaved and put on the auction block for sale but the good citizens closed their eyes and refused to see. Property was stolen to support the minions of Diabolus but the public refused to speak of the crimes. In the end, the streets of the empire ran with blood and chaos. Riddled with decay and evil, the empire crumbled from within. The survivors of the catastrophe commissioned this statue to remind their people that it is the *duty* of every citizen to hear evil, to see evil, and to speak of evil. For ignoring evil is the surest way to aid the Dark Lord. Only by confronting evil directly can it be destroyed." Gesturing toward the statue, the master added, "The ancient empire is long gone, but the lesson of the statue remains."

Listening to the tale, Kath could not help but think of Coronth. "Like the Pontifax and Coronth."

He gave her a solemn nod. "Just so."

Remembering Justin's ballads about the Flame God, Kath realized his songs were meant to be a musical version of the statue. She hoped Justin fared better than the monk-keys and their failed empire. "So the past has a way of being reborn?"

"Unless we learn from the past, evil has a way of returning."

Thinking of the endless corridors covered in illuminated text, Kath realized the monastery was all about remembering. "So why do you want me here?"

He gave her a sideways glance. "I think you already know...but perhaps you need to hear it anyway."

Kath nodded, almost afraid to hear the answer.

"The Kiralynn Order is ancient, as old as the Age of Magic. The War of Wizards caused the world to forget many things...but the Kiralynn monks remember." His jewel-blue eyes pierced her to the core. "One of the most important things the world has forgotten...is magic."

Kath gasped, reaching for the gargoyle hidden beneath her tunic.

"Very little magic remains in the world below the mountains. And even more dangerous, there is little understanding of magic in the minds and the hearts of men. In such a world, a single focus can be very powerful, a mighty force for good or ill." She heard the threat in his voice. "The Kiralynn monks keep watch over the kingdoms of Erdhe. When magic appears, we invite the person keyed to the focus to come to the monastery. We help these people to understand and control their focus. For some, we also offer refuge from the world below. Some magics are too powerful to remain in the kingdoms of Erdhe. Many choose to live in the monastery where they are accepted and can use their magic in peace." Pausing, the master added, "We know of your gargoyle. We offer to teach you how to use it, and, if you wish, we offer you sanctuary."

Kath tugged on the leather cord revealing the small mage-stone figurine. "But how did you know?"

The master smiled. "Not all monks serve in the monastery."

Kath's eyes widened. "So do you know what it does?"

"The key is in your dreams."

"But my dreams make no sense!"

He gave her an amused smile. "That is because you refuse to accept the possibility of magic. In the dreams induced by a focus, the bearer always performs some type of magic. The magic you do in your dreams is the magic of your focus."

Kath gaped. "But that's not possible!"

He chuckled. "You underestimate the power of magic."

Kath's mind reeled. She tightened her fist around her gargoyle, determined to unlock its secrets. "I want to learn."

He gave her a satisfied smile. "Then it will be arranged."

Remembering the crystal dagger, Kath reached for the rucksack. "There's something else I need to show you." She watched his face, noting how his eyes widened as she removed the golden box. His response told her that the monks did not know everything. "I found this in a ruined tower in the wilds of Wyeth." She opened the box and revealed the crystal dagger. "Can you tell me what it is?"

The breath hissed out of him. "Something rare and unlooked for." He gave her a complex stare that was hard to read. "Who else knows about this?"

"Only Sir Tyrone and Sir Blaine."

"Good, best if you keep it that way."

"But why? What is it for?"

"The crystal dagger is a herald of dark times. Daggers like this one were created during the Age of Magic. A powerful weapon of the Light, it is a bane to an ancient evil. The daggers only reappear when the ancient evil is reborn." Lowering his voice, he added, "The burden to use the dagger falls to the one chosen to find it."

Kath shivered, staring at the dagger. "Can you tell me about this evil?"

"To understand this evil, you must know something about the Lords of Light and the Dark Lord. The Lords of Light reward their followers in heaven, in the after-life, but the Dark Lord offers something different. To those who serve him well, the Dark Lord offers more than one life."

"It's not possible." Kath shook her head in disbelief, but the master continued, his voice laden with conviction. "A select few who serve the Dark Lord are given twice the lifespan of a normal man and when that life is over, if they have pleased their Dark master, instead of crossing the gray veil of death, they are reincarnated back into this world." The master paused, lowering his voice. "What makes these creatures so potent is that when the reincarnated reach the age of twenty or so, they are Awakened with the full memories of all of their past lives. Imagine a man with the memories and experiences of hundreds or even thousands of years. The reincarnated are an unfathomable evil. These monsters that walk in the guise of men are called Harlequins. A dagger made from a Dahlmar crystal is the only weapon that can break the cycle of rebirth. If a Harlequin is killed with a Dahlmar dagger then its evil soul is consigned to hell, never to be reborn again."

Kath sat statue-still, chilled by the tale. It seemed impossible, yet the conviction of his voice held sway. "Why have I never heard this before?"

"So much has been forgotten, lost since the War of Wizards, but the Kiralynn Order remembers. Knowledge is our purpose." The master's voice softened, his voice touched with sadness. "You are young to have such a burden placed on your shoulders. If you do not wish to accept this task, then I advise you to seek out the tower where you found the dagger and return it to its hiding place. Another champion will be called to take up the weapon of Light."

The choice surprised her. "I have a choice?"

"There is always a choice. Free will is the greatest gift of the Lords of Light. But choose carefully, for the gods work in mysterious ways."

Choice was something she'd rarely had in her life. She looked away, catching a glimpse of her reflection in the still waters of the pool. Beside her, the master rose from the bench and moved toward the statue, as if giving her room to decide. Kath stared at her reflection, remembering her fortune at the Isle of Souls and her visions in the broken tower. She'd left Castlegard yearning for a destiny, but she'd never expected this. To herself, as much as to the master, she whispered, "No. I am meant to wield the dagger. I will not give the dagger up, though I barely understand it."

A hushed silence settled over the garden.

"Why me? Why did I find the dagger?"

From behind her, the master replied in a gentle voice, "Perhaps if you look inside yourself, you will find the answer."

She gazed at her reflection, considering his words. Shifting on the bench, she noticed the gleam of gold on the bottom of the pool. Brushing a floating leaf aside, she waited for the ripples to disappear. When the ripples stilled, she gazed through the water to find four lines of a poem inscribed on the bottom of the pool.

*"An autumn leaf floats,*
*Casting a starfish shadow on the ocean floor,*
*A wave gives the starfish life,*
*Reincarnation?"*

Kath gasped. Perhaps the answer lay hidden in another time...when the tower of the eight-sided star was whole and unbroken. Questions flooded her mind. There was so much she didn't understand. She turned to ask the master...but he was gone, almost as if he'd disappeared. Kath shivered despite the warmth.

Left to the solitude of the garden, she sat by the reflecting pool, contemplating the riddle of her life, but every answer opened the door to another question. She'd come to the monastery for answers but so far they'd only shown her more questions. She reached into the golden box and removed the crystal dagger. The dagger fit perfectly to her hand. She held the crystalline blade up to the light, wondering how a single dagger could defeat a thousand years of evil.

# 80

# Danly

Danly's anger built to a rage as he rode through the streets of Pellanor. Instead of spending the evening with friends at an exclusive dicing party, he found himself rushing to the bordello. By the time he'd received the Red Horns' message he was already hours late. He whipped his horse to a lather, seething at the thought of the future king of Lanverness rushing like a lackey to answer the summons of a mere politician. The man was going to pay for his insolence. Danly looked forward to the day.

Arriving at the bordello, he threw the reins of his stallion to a waiting boy and then went straight to the selection parlor. What he found in the parlor further soured his mood. Due to the lateness of the hour only the tired dregs remained. He needed a woman to justify his visit but he couldn't bring himself to select one of the nags on display.

Madam Stock rushed into the room, effusive with apologies. "My Lord, we will find something suitable. I've been saving, a rare flower waiting to be plucked." She offered the prince a new girl, a country maid fresh arrived from a remote village. The old harlot even offered to wave the extra maidenhead price usually charged for a virgin.

Suspicious, Danly insisted on seeing the girl.

"You will not be disappointed." The madam forced a large glass of brandy into his hand and ushered him to a seat.

Danly sipped the brandy, drumming his fingers on the armrest. He finished the glass and poured a second, irritated by the wait. He was about to storm out of the room when the madam returned leading a young woman. Perfumed and swathed in layers of sheer silk, the girl pirouetted for his inspection. Backlit by the fire, she appeared slender and shapely but Danly insisted on seeing her face. With a flourish, the madam removed the girl's veil. A lush mane of chestnut hair framed an oval face, but it was her mouth that stirred his manhood. Moist and full, her pouting lips begged to be bruised. Perhaps he could salvage some pleasure from the evening after all. He signaled his acceptance, but Madam Stock intervened. "As it is her first time, lord, give me a chance to prepare the girl for your pleasure." The madam bowed as she led her charge out of the parlor.

Impatient, Danly paced the parlor. After his first meeting with the Red Horns, Danly had reserved the suite with the secret staircase for his exclusive use, paying the madam a monthly stipend for the privilege. It proved to be a wise decision given the unpredictability of his meetings with the rebel leader.

Madam Stock returned and escorted him to his usual suite. He entered the outer room and found the girl's silk veils strewn in a perfumed path across the floor. The trail of enticement led to the bedroom. The game was getting interesting. Throwing open the inner doors, he found the girl naked in bed. A silken sheet clutched to her breasts, she stared at him with wide frightened eyes. Danly wondered if the girl would be passive or feisty. She remained mute, quivering beneath the sheets, shrinking from his touch. Her fear pleased him. Pity he couldn't take the time to properly enjoy the girl.

Pressed for time, he decided to not even bother undressing. He eased the ties binding his codpiece, watching the girl's eyes. Taking her face in his hands, he bruised her lips with a kiss. She shrank from his touch, a scream struggling to escape her lips. Her eyes went wide and wild. Danly smiled, the little vixen knew what was coming. Her hopeless struggle only excited him. Fully clothed, he crawled on top, eager for the mount, but something broke inside the girl. Snarling beneath him, she unleashed a fury of nails and teeth. She fought like a she-lion. Clawed nails racked across his face gouging five bloody tracks into his cheek, just missing his left eye. Danly recoiled. His face stung. Blood dripped onto the sheets. His blood!

Danly exploded in rage. He lashed out with his fists, pummeling the girl into submission. When his anger subsided, she was nothing more than a mewing mass of welts and bruises. Danly rolled off of her and paced in front of the fireplace, his fists clenched in anger. The girl deserved a slow death, but he dare not do it here, not with the leader of the Red Horns coming. The least he could do was to break her maidenhead. He strode back to the bed to get what he'd paid for. Bruised and battered, the girl submitted with barely a whimper. Lacing up his codpiece, Danly had the satisfaction of seeing her blood on the sheets. At least the madam hadn't lied about the girl's virginity.

Sated for the moment, he left the girl spread senseless on the bed.

Pouring a goblet of red wine, he was going to add the alchemist's powder but the hidden compartment on his poison ring was empty. Seething, Danly hurled the goblet across the room. The glass shattered, leaving a red stain dripping down the wall.

Looking down at the girl, he studied her. She hadn't moved, despite the sound of the shattering goblet. He prodded her but she didn't respond. Perhaps he wouldn't need the drug after all, the girl was obviously too broken to cause any more trouble.

Danly fingered the cuts on his face, wincing at the pain. Madam Stock owed him for breaking in her wildcat. The old harlot should know better than to disappoint a prince of the realm.

Straightening his shirt and adjusting his codpiece, Danly opened the doors to the sitting room. He was surprised to find the leader of the Red Horns already waiting. The counselor looked up, sneering at the sight of Danly's face. "So the vixen had claws tonight?"

Danly sent the counselor a daggered glance. Crossing the parlor, he poured himself a large brandy, downing the glass in one long swallow. Wiping his mouth, he poured a second.

"You might want to save some brandy for your face, my prince. We wouldn't want those five telltale cuts to become scars. People might get the wrong impression. Too many battles in the bedroom, makes you look like a rapist instead of a lover."

Danly scowled, refusing to engage.

Ever the politician, the counselor's voice changed from mocking to solicitous. "Such scars would not be dignified for the next king of Lanverness."

Danly snapped, "More words!" He flung the glass into the fireplace, the brandy adding sparks to the flame. "I'm tired of your words, counselor, just as I'm tired of waiting for the Red Horns to defeat the queen. When your future king goes out of his way to meet with you, he expects to hear something of substance. Now, tell me news of the revolt."

The politician bowed low.

The gesture of submission helped mollify Danly's anger.

"My prince, you will sit on the Rose Throne before the end of the next fortnight."

Danly stilled, absorbing the counselor's words. A thrill that was almost sexual coursed through him. Not trusting his voice, he stared at the counselor, waiting for an explanation.

"The last time we met, I told you of a plan to eliminate the crown prince and his loyal men. I am pleased to report that the first stage of the plan has been successful. It is only a matter of time before your brother's head graces the portcullis of Tandroth Castle."

Danly filled a second goblet. "Tell me more."

"Given the queen's preoccupation with Coronth, I arranged for mercenaries wearing the Flame God's colors to attack a royal courier. The mercenaries made bloody work of a merchant family but they let the royal courier escape." The counselor smiled, smoothing his mustache. "The queen took the bait, and is sending the crown prince and the Rose Squad to find the soldiers of the Flame and drive them out of Lanverness." The counselor moved to the sideboard and poured himself a glass of brandy. "Mercenaries will of course be waiting to ambush the prince and his men." The counselor flashed a wolf's smile. "With an advantage of three to one, the outcome is assured. The mercenaries will send the prince's head back to Pellanor in a sack. Once the head graces the gates of the castle, the good people of Pellanor will know that you, Prince Danly, are the one and only rightful heir to the Rose Throne. Then we can move on the queen." The counselor's smile deepened. "With the Rose Squad out of the way, there should be little resistance." He raised his glass in salute. "So you see, my prince, it is only a matter of time before Lanverness once again has a rightful king."

"Where did you find the mercenaries?"

"Radagar of course." His voice deepened, "I trust you approve, my prince?"

A slow smile spread across the Danly's face. He swelled with thoughts of the throne, thoughts of power. "You've done well." His earlier anger forgotten, Danly added, "What should I do to prepare for the great day?"

"Stay close to the castle for the next fortnight. Avoid any dicing parties and of course, the bordello. The Red Horns will rise as soon we have the prince's head. Once the queen is taken, our soldiers will need to see their rightful king on the throne." Pausing, he added, "Stay in your chambers till a guard identifying himself as a Red Horn comes for you." Flashing a wolf's smile, he raised his glass in salute. "To the victory of the Red Horns and the triumph of the king!"

Danly raised his glass to the toast. He drank the brandy in a single long swallow and then dashed the goblet into the fireplace. The glass shattered like a broken kingdom.

"It is best if I leave. We must still contend with the queen's shadowmen." The counselor triggered the mechanism, opening the secret staircase. "Next time we meet, I will bow to you as my king instead of just my prince. Fair well, my lord."

The Red Horn slipped into the staircase. The concealing wall slid back into place with a soft click.

Danly stood in front of the fireplace, a sense of destiny flooding through him. Soon, he would wear the crown of the greatest kingdom in all of Erdhe. A thrill that he could only described as sexual flooded through him. So this is what power truly felt like. He was going to enjoy being the king of Lanverness...but first he would satisfy the needs of a prince. With his codpiece straining at the bindings, he left the suite to find the madam. He wanted fresh women for his bed and a room with clean linens. It was time to celebrate his coming ascension.

He strode from the suite, failing to notice that the door to the bedroom was slightly ajar.

# 81

# Katherine

A knock sounded on the door to her sleeping cell. Kath leaped to open it, expecting Duncan, surprised to find a blue-robed master instead. Swallowing her disappointment, she offered a cautious smile. "Master Rizel?"

His sun-weathered face gave little away. "You came for answers."

"Yes."

"Then answers you shall have. Come with me." He turned without waiting for a reply and Kath found herself rushing to match his stride. "Where are we going?"

"To the Grand Master."

Her footsteps faltered, her hand reaching for her good luck charm. She wanted answers but she hadn't expected an audience with the mysterious Grand Master. "Now?"

"Yes."

She rushed to catch up. "But why am I summoned?"

"You bear something of great importance to the Order."

Her breath caught, so this was about the crystal dagger. She remembered the look on his face when she'd first shown him the golden box from the ruined tower. He'd tried to hide it, but she'd caught the glint of surprise in his eyes, perhaps even shock, proving the monks did not know everything. They'd invited her to the monastery for her gargoyle, never expecting the crystal dagger. His surprise only deepened her curiosity.

Morning sunlight streamed across the golden floor. Kath followed the master, losing track of the twists and turns, realizing he led her to a part of the monastery she'd never seen. The mage-stone hallways narrowed and the calligraphy became more elaborate, swirls of gold decorating each letter. Torches replaced windows, sending a mix of light and shadows skittering across the written walls. Something about the narrowing hallways evoked a feeling of great age, as if she walked towards an ancient secret. And then the color of the doors began to change from golden to midnight-blue. So many dark blue doors, the forbidden color snared Kath's imagination, making her wonder what secrets they guarded. The monastery was full of mysteries and now she was going to meet the elusive Grand Master. She shivered, feeling the pull of destiny, as if she walked toward an audience with the gods.

The hallway widened abruptly, sunlight streaming through panes of glass inset in the vaulted ceiling. Kath blinked at the sudden brightness, stunned by the unexpected grandeur. Soaring walls filled with calligraphy flanked steps leading to a pair of massive double doors clad in shimmering beaten gold. Dark blue lapis inset in the gold formed a pair of Seeing Eyes, a great guardian keeping watch...or passing judgment. The effect was both stunning and humbling. Struck by the weight of the moment, Kath clutched her stone gargoyle, sending a silent prayer to Valin.

A pair of blue-robed monks with quarterstaffs flanked either side of the doors. Nodding to Master Rizel, they tugged the massive doors open. Kath felt the master's stare. "This way," he gestured for her to go first. Taking a deep breath, she passed between the Seeing Eyes, entering a large square room. Sunlight flooded the chamber, illuminating the floor. The near half was golden, warm and welcoming, but the far half was a raised dais of deep midnight blue. The implications of the divided floor were chilling. So this was the room where the outside world met the inner mysteries. Drawn like iron to a lodestone, Kath crossed the golden floor to stand on the border between gold and blue. A short ornate railing bumped against her shins, a reminder not to step onto the forbidden blue.

Behind her, Master Rizel said, "So you are drawn to our mysteries."

Kath could only nod, taking in the wonders of the chamber.

Beyond the railing, a great folding screen dominated the dais. Made of dark blue lapis, the screen was inlaid with faceted crystals and fine strands of gold. Clear crystals set in the patterns of the stars glowed like diamonds in the midnight sky, the fine gold wire outlining each constellation. Over seven-feet tall and more than twice as wide, the screen formed a map of the heavens, a treasure like none Kath had ever seen.

"The Star Screen is one of the master works of the monastery. Come and see the other."

Turning from the screen, Kath discovered an immense pane of glass dominating the opposite wall, but this was no mere window. Impossibly large and flawless in its clarity, the glass pane formed a seamless part of the mage-stone wall. Kath join the master at the window. His voice carried a hint of pride. "Made of rare mage-glass, the window is transparent rock, one of the few of its kind." Kath glimpsed the town of Haven nestled in the valley below, looking small and insignificant, like a child's toys set amongst the fallow fields. "The Window of the Gods reminds us of how the Lords of Light view us mortals." Pausing, he added, "The gods have a very different view of the mortal world."

Kath shivered, gripped by a sudden insight, "Nothing more than pieces on a chessboard."

The master smiled, the light dancing in his blue eyes. "Perhaps, but each piece that serves the Light is given the freedom to choose their own moves. Never underestimate the power of choice."

The great golden doors swung silently open and Kath heard familiar voices. A pair of blue-robed monks escorted Sir Blaine and Sir Tyrone into the chamber. The sight of the knights in their octagon surcoats sent waves of gratitude through Kath. She rushed to greet them, glad to have them by her side.

"We thought the knights should know the enemy they face."

The master's words held an ominous chill. Kath turned towards him. "What enemy?"

"You'll know soon enough."

His face told her she'd get no more from him. "What of my other companions?"

"They have come to the monastery for different reasons, different fates."

Kath did not like being separated from Jordan and Duncan and the seahorse knight, but now was not the time to argue.

The deep note of a gong shivered through the chamber.

Master Rizel gestured toward a pile of embroidered pillows strewn across the floor in front of the star screen. "Please be seated. The Grand Master will be with you shortly." Bowing, he followed the other monks towards the golden doors.

Kath said, "You're leaving us?" She'd only known the master for a few days but she valued his wisdom and his advice.

An enigmatic smile played across the master's sun-weathered face. "You'll be fine." Gesturing toward the dais, he added, "The words of the Grand Master are for you and your companions alone. May you find wisdom in his words." He bowed towards her and then left the chamber, closing the golden doors behind him.

The chamber seemed suddenly empty. Kath and the two knights settled on the cushions strewn at the foot of the dais. They sat close like allies expecting an ambush. Sir Tyrone leaned toward her, his voice a low whisper. "Why are we summoned to audience?"

She shared her guess. "The crystal dagger."

His eyes widened. "So you told them?"

Kath nodded. "We need to know what it does, what it's for." She thought she saw approval in his dark brown eyes.

They settled down to wait. Like a temple to knowledge, the chamber discouraged idle talk. The silent waiting wore on Kath's nerves. She stared at the star screen, her mind full of questions, her stomach clenched tight as a fist. Hopes and doubts assailed her, wondering what answers the monks might hold.

The gong rang a second time, startling her.

A silver-haired monk emerged from behind the screen, age marking his face with a map of wrinkles. Bowing to Kath and her companions, he settled on a cushion to the right of the screen. Removing a flint striker from the folds of his robe, he lit a silver brazier set into the dais. Flames leaped up, giving off the sweet scent of incense.

The gong rang a third time.

The silver-haired monk began to speak, his rich-timbered voice full of solemnity. "The Grand Master of the Kiralynn Order is present. Be aware that he sees you, he hears you. I am the Voice; in my tongue will you hear the words of the Grand Master." He raised his hand to reveal the tattoo of the Seeing Eye. "Seek knowledge...Protect knowledge...Share knowledge. Let the audience begin."

A presence seemed to fill the chamber.

Kath held her breath, waiting to see the face of the Grand Master. When no one appeared, she understood the function of the magnificent star screen. She stared at the screen, trying to sense the man hidden behind the stars.

The silver-haired monk reached behind the screen, accepting a scroll of parchment. Unrolling the scroll, the Voice began to read, "The crystal dagger has chosen a bearer." Kath felt the hand of destiny reach towards her. "The Blade that Slays Souls has returned, heralding a time of prophecy. A future long foretold unfolds. Know that your presence here is not an accident, but by grand design. The Lords of Light assemble those who will stand against the gathering Dark."

The sound of the gong shimmered through the room. Kath leaned forward, hearing the summons of the gods.

"To understand the future, one must first look to the past. Centuries before the War of Wizards, the Kiralynn Order was founded by scholars possessing a rare and powerful magic known as the Orb of Seeing. The Orb cast visions of possible futures. Many of those futures were dark and dire, where mankind fell under the eternal lash of the Dark Lord. Appalled by the horrors, the monks dedicated their lives to studying the Orb. The masters came to understand that because the gods gifted man with free will, the future is not set. The choices we make today can change what is to come. For a few individuals, the choices are pivotal."

The Voice looked up from the scroll, staring straight at Kath. His gaze stabbed into her, issuing a silent challenge. She met his stare, refusing to look away.

The Voice continued reading, "The Orb showed the monks a myriad of futures, a spectrum of possibilities, but the masters discovered that there are key events common to many futures. A change in these events signals a major divergence in the fate of the world. Some of these divergences bring peace while others bring great victories for the Dark Lord. The masters used the Orb to search out the events that led to the grimmest futures, discovering ways to oppose the Dark Lord's plans. The result of this great work is the Book of Prophecy. Like most of the great magics, the Orb was destroyed in the War of Wizards, but the Book remains as one of the Order's greatest treasures. Using the Book as a guide, the Order has worked through the centuries to thwart the will of the Dark Lord."

The Voice paused to survey his audience. When no one spoke he continued, "The discovery of the crystal dagger is heralded within one of the quatrains of the Book of Prophecy, one of the darkest futures foretold by the Orb. Listen and learn." Taking a deep breath, the Voice read in a sonorous voice,

> *The Lost Dagger claims an ill-refuted heir,*
> *The Liar King awakes behind safest walls,*
> *Fire burns the sky yet kingdoms remain unaware,*
> *Darkness arises yet steel alone cannot prevail.*

The words thundered in Kath's soul. She'd left Castlegard hoping to make a difference with her sword and now destiny leaped to embrace her.

The Voice stared at each of the companions, his gaze coming to rest on Kath. "If choices are not made, if events are not changed, then the kingdoms of Erdhe will succumb to the rule of the Dark Lord. A tidal wave of Darkness will sweep down from the north. The first to fall will be the Octagon Knights."

*"No!"* Kath leaped to her feet, raising her voice to a clarion shout. "This cannot be! The Knights will never fail." Her unbridled defiance echoed through the chamber, as if challenging the gods. But the echo soon faded and she blanched, realizing she'd interrupted the words of the

Grand Master. Embarrassed but undaunted, Kath stood her ground. Crossing her arms, she sent a stubborn glare at the star screen issuing a silent challenge. If the monks knew so much, let them steer a course past this terrible future.

A deep stillness descended on the chamber, the sound of a quill scratching against parchment the only sound. Self-conscious, Kath resumed her seat but her stare never wavered from the screen.

The scratch of the quill stopped.

The Voice received a second scroll. Unrolling the scroll, he read, "We are not the pivots of this future. You are. Others have significant roles to play, but the wielder of the crystal dagger must avert the gathering Dark. *Your* choices, and the choices of your companions, will make the greatest difference."

Kath sat stunned. The words brought meaning to the strange riddle of her life. "What must I do?"

Returning to the scroll, the Voice read, "The Book of Prophecy provides guidance to avert the darkest futures. Listen to the wisdom of the Book;

> *Faith follows lies and multitudes march,*
> *Rose and Harp must find the foil,*
> *Flames burn bright and carrion birds soar,*
> *The Elder leaps forward lest ashes till the soil.*

We believe this quatrain refers to the rise of the Flame God in Coronth. The queen of Lanverness will stand against this cruelty of the Flames but without the advice and aid of the Elder, the Kiralynn Order, there will be little hope for victory. For this quatrain, the burden of choice rests with the queen and the Order, but the second quatrain is the true crux of the future. The outcome of this quatrain depends on *your* choices.

> *The Reborn rides north to the dark fist of stone,*
> *The Blade must strike true ere the comet fades,*
> *North becomes south as castles fall,*
> *Victory balances on the unforeseen blade.*

The Voice let the parchment curl, holding it above the flames of the brazier. Knowledge flared bright and then faded to nothing. "Taken together, the three quatrains predict a war in the heart of the southern kingdoms and a second, more terrible war loosed from the North. The North is the domain of the Mordant, the oldest of the Harlequins."

Beside her, Sir Tyrone muttered, "The dark fist of stone...the citadel of the Mordant!"

*The Mordant, the ancient enemy of Castlegard,* Kath felt the call to battle echo within her very blood.

The scratch of a quill filled the chamber. The Voice reached behind the screen to accept a third scroll. "A thousand years of evil must come to an end. Will the Wielder of the Crystal Dagger see the Blade to the finish? Will the princess of Castlegard seek out the Mordant and forever end his life?"

Kath sat frozen, stunned by the words. Destiny had come for her but it seemed an impossible task.

"Will you send her to her death?" Blaine's outburst surprised Kath, a look of anger riding his face. "The Mordant rules from the Dark Citadel, an impenetrable stronghold set deep in the north. All the knights of the Octagon could not breach that foul fortress."

An angry quill scratched across parchment. The Voice read, "Such doubt does not become a champion of the Octagon."

Blaine began to rise, but Kath gripped his arm. "Let it go."

He gave her an incredulous stare, his words an angry whisper. "These monks cower in their monastery. They don't understand the danger of the North."

"Let's hear them out."

Their stares locked, but then he gave her a terse nod, sinking back to the cushions.

The Voice continued. "You misunderstand the task. According to all the signs, the Mordant is not yet Reborn. A red comet tearing the sky will herald his return. Prophecy predicts that the oldest harlequin will arise within the Southern Kingdoms, sowing Darkness beneath a new face, a new guise."

The answer took Kath by surprise. "So how do we find him? I don't even know what he looks like."

"The prophecies are unclear. Some believe that he will find you."

*He will find me,* a bolt of fear spiked through Kath. The Mordant had long been the bane of Castlegard, a powerful enemy, yet she was expected to slay him with a mere dagger? Only the gods could ask for such an impossible feat. She fingered the hilt of her sword, the sword she'd fought so hard to gain, and her thoughts turned in a different direction. In her mind's eye she saw Castlegard proud and undefeated. She saw the captain putting the hated leash around her throat, treating her like a slave. She saw wisdom and unexpected friendship in the face of the queen of Lanverness. She saw wonder and forgotten knowledge in every corner of the monastery. They were images worth fighting for, worth fighting against. She'd asked the gods for a chance to make a difference and it seemed they'd heard her prayers. Kath took a deep breath and rose to her feet.

Behind her, the two Octagon Knights rose as one, their swords whispering from their scabbards.

Their strength gave her strength, she would not fight alone. Kath reached for her own sword, a simple infantry sword made of good Castlegard steel, and unsheathed the blade. The magnitude of the task beat against her like a battering ram, yet she forced the words out. "I will end this evil, so help me, Valin!"

A chime sounded.

A rush of power flooded Kath's veins like an elixir.

"The vow is made before the gods. May the Lords of Light guide your hand and the crystal dagger strike true." The Voice bowed toward her and then disappeared behind the star screen.

Kath lowered her sword and stood waiting, but nothing more was said. The abrupt dismissal staggered her. The power of the vow thrummed through her like a current. Kath felt the need to rush into battle and slay demons, but she was left standing before an empty dais, her sword in her hand. "Come," Sir Tyrone touched her arm, "it's oft like this after battle."

Such a strange comment, yet it rang of truth.

"Come." Sheathing her sword, Kath followed the two knights from the chamber. A pair of blue-robed monks waited beyond the golden doors, escorts to guide them back through the maze of corridors. The rush of power bled from Kath like a receding tide, leaving her exhausted, a thousand questions raging through her mind. Haunted by the Grand Master's words, Kath walked in a daze, stunned by the revelations. So the bane of Castlegard was a harlequin, a thousand-year-old evil, an endless enemy, yet she'd always thought the Mordant was an inherited title, like a king or an emperor. Now she learned he was a nightmare, reborn again and again from the depths of hell. A single soul steeped in so much evil and she was tasked to kill it. An impossible task, an impossible tale, yet it rang with heart-binding truth. Shivering, Kath stared at the writing-filled walls, wondering what else the monks knew, what else they kept hidden. Surrounded by knowledge, she should have drawn comfort from the writings, but instead she felt lost. Something nagged at her soul, a premonition, a hint of dread. Unease rode her shoulders, making every shadow look sinister. Despite the remoteness of the mountain monastery, Kath gripped her sword hilt. Evil suddenly seemed very near.

# 82

# The Mordant

In the beginning there was only darkness. The darkness of an infinite black void, the darkness of a night without stars, the all-pervasive Darkness of his Lord. Summoned from the depths, the ancient darkness poured into a fresh mind, a fresh body. Like a smothering avalanche, the original soul was buried under centuries of evil.

Closed eyelids became twin canvases for dreams...for visions...for memories. The Mordant remembered his last death, the chamber at the heart of the dark monolith where stones dripped like blood from the ceiling, the chamber where it all started, where he'd first pledged his soul to the Dark Lord so many centuries ago. Images of the past blended with visions of the future. He saw his armies in black and gold marching south, spreading chaos, fear, and death. Mortals trembled at the mere sight of his black battle banner. Across the centuries, he tasted victories...and learned from defeats. His mind was flooded with the rich details of many lives and many deaths. He remembered the flash of silver as the executioner's axe descended. He remembered laughter and the face of the trembling guard as he peered through the eyes of his severed head. Images swamped his mind, images of other places...other times...other lives.

He opened his eyes and the room was bathed in a baleful blood-red light. He did not need a mirror to know that if he closed his eyes, the darkness of the room would return. It was the Awakening. The Mordant was reborn.

He stretched on the narrow bed, exploring his new, young body. What he found pleased him. Young and male, tall and strong...and virile. It had been more than fifty years since he'd last enjoyed the pleasures of sex. The sudden virility of this young body spiked through him, threatening to swamp his mind. It was always this way at the start. Succumbing to the long un-tasted pleasure, he let his hand tease his rod to attention. Shorter than in other lives, but what it lacked in length it made up for in rock hardness. He gloried in his sudden youth. With expert hands he let the waves of pleasure build. Arching his back, he spewed his seed in a triumphant arc. It was good to be young again. There was nothing better than an old mind coupled with a young body. He had so much to look forward to.

Temporarily sated, his mind was free to examine his host. In a small corner of his being, a tortured soul screamed in agony. He played with the soul, a cat toying with a mouse, teasing thoughts from his victim's mind. *"So, you're name is Bryce, an acolyte of the Kiralynn Order."* Laughter bubbled from his throat. Truly the Dark Lord had a twisted sense of humor. He'd been reborn in the hidden sanctuary of his bitterest enemies, wearing the face of one of their own. He could not stop laughing. A pity the boy was only an initiate and not a full-sworn monk, but his mind was excited by the possibilities. Perhaps he'd finally have the opportunity to destroy the enemy that relentlessly plagued him through all the centuries of his lives.

Keen to learn more, he focused his will on the small soul trapped within his mind. His prey fell suddenly silent, like a mouse overshadowed by an eagle, but there was nowhere to hide. "I see you mortal, you cannot hide. I know your name was Bryce, but I shall call you 'monk'. It amuses me to have one of my enemies trapped within my mind. I give you leave to speak."

*Get out of my mind, foul demon! Be gone! Leave me alone!*

"Silly mortal, you cannot banish me. My soul carries the memories of more than a thousand years of life. Your pitifully short span of years is nothing compared to the weight of my pasts. Submit of your own free will or to be crushed and subsumed into my greater mind. What is your answer?"

*You 're a monster! An evil spawn of the Dark Lord! I will never join with you!*

"You amuse me monk. You think you can keep your meager secrets from me, but your thoughts are mine to do with as I will. I can take them gently like a tender lover or I can make it a brutal rape. You will soon learn to please me. Now tell me what you know of the crystal dagger."

*A crystal dagger? I'm only a healer, only an initiate. I know little of weapons.*

"Liar! Tell me what you know or I will wrest it from you."

He felt the monk's mind scurry like a rat in a maze. *There's something written on one of the walls. It speaks of a crystal dagger but I never paid it much mind. I study healing not weapons.*

"You must know more than that. It is futile to refuse. This first time shall be rape, so that you understand me." The Mordant battered the captured soul with the strength of his will, like a relentless weight crushing down. The monk twisted and shrieked, like a maid trying to escape, but the Mordant smashed his way in, violating the monk's most secret thoughts. He took what he wanted, leaving the soul howling in torment. It was a good beginning.

"So you don't know." The Mordant brooded on the discovery. Perhaps the higher magics were kept secret, known only to a select few. He cursed the fact he wasn't reborn as a fully sworn master, yet he'd gained much from a mere initiate. He need only kill a guide to gain an amulet, the key to the Guardian Mist and the enemy's stronghold would be laid bare before his armies. He focused his will on the captured monk. "There is nothing you can keep from me. From your mind I know it would be death to pass through the doors of forbidden blue. Fresh in this new body, I am vulnerable, so that pleasure must wait for another time. With your knowledge of the mountains and the monastery, I will make my escape...but first I will read this wall that tells of the crystal dagger. Once I've reclaimed by power, my armies shall return. Then we shall see what lies beyond the blue doors and all the secrets of the monastery shall be mine."

He reached out with his mind to caress the shattered soul. "Speak to me. Now that you know me, what do you choose?"

*I walk in the Light. I walk in the Light.*

Laughter bubbled from the Mordant. "Monk, you amuse me. Pray all you want to the Lords of Light, for it will do you no good. I assure you, the Lords of Light do exist, and the gods may even hear your pitiful prayers...but the plight of a mere individual is of no concern to them. They will never answer. If you want answers, if you want action, then you are praying to the wrong god. The Dark Lord knows the number of every soul in his keeping. Serve him well and you will bask in his favors." His voice deepened. "Look at me, monk. The Dark Lord's favors are real. His rewards are enjoyed in *this* lifetime, not some vague promise of a mythical heaven. My rebirth is proof of the Dark Lord's bounty." He studied the soul huddled within the prison of his mind. "Watch through my eyes, monk, and learn what it is to have the favor of the Dark Lord. In the end, you will willingly offer your soul up to Darkness. Pray all you want, but sooner or later you will see that only one god is worthy of your prayers."

He withdrew from the monk, leaving the lost soul to scream his useless prayers.

The Mordant opened his eyes. Baleful red light flooded the small cell. From experience he knew the telltale light would soon fade, but until then he was vulnerable to detection. He must hide until it receded. He'd wait within the monk's cell, using the time to master his new body. There was no reason not to continue with his own enjoyment. His hand moved down to his stiffening rod. May the Dark Lord's pleasure reign over all the lands of Erdhe.

# 83

# Cardemir

Sir Cardemir paced his sleeping cell, frustrated by his lack of progress. In many ways, the monastery remained a riddle but the queen was right to fear the Kiralynn Order. The passage through the Mist had more than alarmed him. Shaking like a virgin at the marriage bed, he'd stumbled from the cold Mist into the sunshine, grateful to be alive. He didn't like what he'd seen in the Mist, he didn't like it at all. The Mist was a fearsome magic and he shuddered to think what else might lay hidden behind their midnight blue doors. He shook his head, remembering the old adage, *never trust a man in a robe.* And then there was that tea ceremony, very devious. It seemed the monks had much to hide. Mindful of the queen's charge, he'd probed his guide with questions, but he'd yet to loosen the young man's lips. A pity he hadn't stashed a bottle of Urian brandy in his saddlebags. Brandy might go a long way towards befriending the pasty-faced scholar, but then he had another thought. The monks didn't say much but they scribbled all over their walls. Grabbing a lighted candle, he went in search of answers.

Night cloaked the monastery, the perfect time to explore. Holding his candle aloft, he prowled the halls. Every wall was crowded with calligraphy, proving the monks were obsessed with their own writing. Some walls spoke of legends from the distant past while others prattled on about some obscure prophecy. Most of it seemed like a fable, a tale of Light against Dark, nothing the queen would be interested in. Frustrated, Cardemir lengthened his stride. Ignoring the writing, he focused on the painted images instead, scanning the walls for castles and knights and swords entwined amongst the letters, looking for the teeth of meaning behind the flourish of words. And then he found it...the image of a knight in a winged helm holding aloft a dagger. Light streamed from the dagger, like a blade forged from legend. *Magical weapons*, just the sort of power the queen would be interest in. He stepped closer for a better look.

A voice came from behind. "So you seek the crystal dagger?"

Cardemir whirled, his hand on his sword, but it was only an acolyte, another pasty-faced scholar in golden robes. "So they let you out of bed at night?" Dropping his hand from his sword, Cardemir turned his gaze back to the illuminated blade. "I couldn't sleep, so I decided to read your walls. This one looks interesting, the tale of an enchanted dagger. Is it real?"

"Oh yes."

"What does it do?"

"A blade of great power, a slayer of souls. Would you know more?"

The hairs prickled at the back of his neck, but the words seduced him. "Power you say." He turned towards the acolyte, keen for answers. "Tell me more."

"I'll do better. I'll show you." The acolyte stepped close, lowering his hooded cowl.

Cardemir gasped, the acolyte's eyes glowed red! He lurched backward, reaching for his sword, but something slammed into him. Darkness reached through his eyes, invading his mind, probing his very soul. Pain spiked through him yet he was held motionless. *Why do you seek the crystal dagger?* The unspoken words boomed through his mind. *No need to speak. Think the thought and I will hear it.*

Cardemir struggled to reply, but his mouth did not respond. His will had been severed from his body. Trapped within his own mind, the knight screamed in panic. *What are you?*

*Tell me what you know of the dagger? Are you the champion summoned to wield the crystal blade?*

The knight howled, fighting the bonds of magic. *I'll tell you nothing!*

*Then I'll take it from you. Ambition is the pathway to your soul.*

Pain exploded in the knight, as if a thousand daggers hacked at his mind, yet he could do nothing to stop it. Held by a Dark power, he stood mute as a statue, enduring the torture, not even a whimper escaping his lips.

*You know nothing, just an emissary of a petty queen, but why serve a mere woman when a greater power beckons?*

*What power? Who are you?*

*I could use a knight of your prowess. Ambition sheaths your soul, the endless hunger of a fifth son. Serve me and you'll have power undreamt. The power of gold, the power of a legendary sword in your hands, the power of legions at your back."

Visions flooded his mind, so real they seemed like a certainty. Armored in gold, he led an army south, a jeweled crown upon his helm. The wind stirred and his personal banner snapped overhead, while a bevy of lords rode close, vying for his favor. Pride and power swelled through him, all the things he'd dreamt of, all the things denied him, finally his for the taking. Entranced by the visions, a virulent hunger rushed through him. *I want it! I want it all!*

Footsteps whispered down the corridor. "Who's there?"

*Swear it!*

He did not have time to think. *I so swear!*

"Who's there?"

The demon-acolyte retreated to the shadows, releasing the knight just enough to turn his head, but Cardemir already knew the voice, willing the princess to turn away.

Jordan came closer, her blonde hair tussled, her face open and trusting. "Sir Cardemir? So you couldn't sleep either. I swear I spend half my nights wandering the corridors, admiring the scripts."

*Kill her.* The command spiked his mind.

*No, there's no need! She's only a girl, a friend, she'll listen to me.* Outrage thundered through him, he'd saved the girl's life and now this demon demanded her murder. *Let me talk to her, I'll send her away.* A vast gaping silence was the only reply. He found himself turning, his hand reaching for his dagger. She came to him, all open and trusting. He struggled to warn her, but all he managed was a weak groan.

"Are you ill?" She closed the distance. "Your face is ashen." She took his arm, her voice full of worry. "What's wrong?"

The concern on her face tugged at his heart.

*Do it now*

His hand closed on the dagger. Controlled by the demon, he watched in horror as he lunged towards her. The girl didn't have a chance. A quick thrust and the dagger slid deep into her abdomen. *Twist the blade* His hand obeyed, ensuring a mortal wound. A scream burbled out of her, a look of shocked disbelief on her face. "Why?" Jordan slumped to the floor, clutching her stomach, a pool of blood forming around her.

Furious, he turned on the demon, but Darkness still gripped him.

*Take her sword.*

*Why?*

*Take her sword.*

He found himself bending to draw the sword from her scabbard, avoiding the shattered look in her dying eyes. The naked blade gleamed cold in the moonlight, a blade of good Castlegard steel. Gripping the sword, he stared at the acolyte, desperate for answers. A memory scratched at the back of his mind. *I know you, you're the acolyte-guide to the other princess. But you're supposed to be a healer. How does a healer deal such death?*

The acolyte gave him a lazy grin. And then Cardemir heard another voice in his head, *Run!* Muffled and distant, the voice carried a slight echo, as if from the bottom of a well, or a deep dungeon. *Run! Or if you can't run, kill it! KILL ME!* Terror clawed at Cardemir's mind, the terror of a prisoner buried alive. And then a door slammed shut, silencing the scream. Staggered by the other voice, Cardemir stared at the fiend, a beast with glowing red eyes, a demon that walked in the guise of a man, and then he remembered the sword in his hands.

*Yes, the sword,* the fiend grinned. *Use it to kill yourself.*

Rage erupted in the knight. He fought against his bonds, fought to slay the beast, but his body would not obey. Desperate, he tried another ploy. *You promised me power! I could still serve you.*

The demon sneered. *You'd trade lies with the King of Deceivers?*

Pain roared through him. Cardemir struggled to control his own body, but the blade turned in his hands, the point positioned beneath his breast, poised for a killing stroke.

The demon turned and began to walk away, not even bothering to watch.

Horror-struck, Cardemir stared at the sword, sweat trickling down the side of his face. *You can't do this to me!*

*Do it now.* Both hands jerked the sword upwards, striking for the heart. Pain ripped through him, his heart spitted on the blade. With a last gasp his eyes flew wide, struck by the bitter truth: he'd betrayed himself, his queen, and the princess. *Forgive me!* The agony seemed to last forever and then he fell forward, into eternal night.

# 84

# Steffan

A mighty fist of molten metal gripped Steffan's heart. He clutched his chest, waves of agony pouring through him. The great hand slowly squeezed, branding him with searing pain. Steffan arched his back, his mouth stretched in a wordless scream. Pain consumed him, pushing him to the edge of madness.

Just when he thought he could no longer bear it, the Hand of Darkness withdrew bringing the agony to a sudden halt. His heart beat wildly; thankful the pain was only a memory. Drenched in sweat, he lay naked on silken sheets, trying to still his racing heart. It took time to recover from his first taste of hell.

His mind raced faster than his heart. In the midst of the searing agony of the Dark Lord's touch, the message had been clear...a rival for the favor of the Dark Lord was reborn. Somewhere in Erdhe, in the dark of the night, a Harlequin had Awakened. Tonight's visit was a warning, or perhaps a challenge, to let Steffan know he had serious competition for the Dark Lord's favor. His service to the Dark Lord brought many benefits and privileges, but the greatest reward was longer life...more life. Only a few attained the ultimate prize of being reborn as a Harlequin. Those who failed were consigned to the tortures of hell for all eternity. Having experienced his first searing taste, Steffan did not plan on failing. Whatever this unknown rival could do, he would do better.

Since coming to Coronth, he'd felt the Dark Lord's pleasure grow, reveling in the false religion of the Flame. Given his accomplishments, Steffan had no doubt that he was a Harlequin-candidate, yet nothing was promised. He needed to be relentless in pursuing the Dark Lord's plans if he hoped to win the ultimate prize.

Thinking of the Dark Lord's plans, a thread of fear ran through Steffan. *What if the Dark Lord deserted him?* Rising from the bed, he pulled on a cloak and rushed to the balcony door. Stepping out into the cool spring night, he scanned the sky. It was there, just as the Dark Lord promised, a blood-red comet blazing a scar across the night sky. Steffan sank to his knees, weak with relief. The comet was proof he still stood high in the Dark Lord's favor.

Steffan smiled. The appearance of the comet fulfilled the prophecy he'd given to the Pontifax, a sign to rouse the faithful of Coronth and unleash the holy war. In the name of religion, tidal waves of fanatics would roll across Erdhe. Death and destruction would be Steffan's gift to the Dark Lord, his way to earn another lifetime.

Staring up at the comet, Steffan began to laugh. Perhaps the newly reborn Harlequin was the one who should fear a rival. After all, one lifetime was not enough.

# 85

# Katherine

Kath woke with a shudder, her bedding damp with sweat. Reaching for her sword, she sat up and listened, searching for the cause of her unease, but she heard nothing. Night darkened the window panes of her sleeping cell, and the monastery seemed at peace, yet a grim feeling hounded her dreams. Something was wrong. Giving up on sleep, she hastily dressed, strapping on her sword and her twin throwing axes. Opening the door, Kath stepped into the golden hallway. Tranquility sat like a blanket on the monastery, not a sound to be heard. Her fears seemed unfounded yet a sixth sense told her to explore. Heeding the warning, she unsheathed her sword and slipped down the hallway.

The monastery was a maze. She let intuition guide her. All the hallways were empty, striped by shadow and moonlight. Sleep claimed the monastery, yet she could not shake the feeling of doom. A night breeze stirred carrying a faint metallic tang, *the coppery smell of blood.* Her heart racing, she followed the scent of battle.

Something dark lay crumpled at the far end of the corridor.

Moonlight spilled through the hallway. Kath gasped, recognizing the checkered cape. Fear sliced through her. *"Jordan!"*

She raced to her sword sister, shocked at the horror of finding two friends instead of one. *"Sir Cardemir!"* Spitted upon a sword, the knight lay felled by Jordan's side. *"No!"* Desperate to save him, Kath grabbed the sword and yanked it from his body. The sword slid loose with a gush of dark blood but the knight made no sound, his body as still as death. A sob escaped her realizing he was gone. She closed his eyes and then turned to attend her sword sister. Jordan lay crumpled in a pool of blood, too much blood. Fear stabbed Kath, "Not you too!" Whispering a prayer to Valin, she gently turned her sword sister, searching for a wound. Her breath hissed at the sight. A deep gash cut Jordan's abdomen, a mortal wound, a soldier's worst fear. Tears crowded Kath's eyes. "Don't die on me!" She held her friend close, desperate to rouse her but she got no response. And then she spied the bloody dagger on the floor. A dagger and a sword, making it look as if the two friends had fought. The wrongness of it thundered through Kath, "A lie! *A foul lie!*" The monastery was supposed to be a safe haven, yet treachery stalked the hallways. Grief warred with anger. And then she realized that Jordan was still warm. A thread of hope shivered through her. Laying her friend on the golden floor, Kath whispered a fervent prayer, "By Valin, let her live." And then another thought pierced her like an arrow, *a warm body means the enemy is still near.*

Kath leaped to her feet, her sword in her hand. She scanned the hall but found no movement. "*Help!*" Her cry echoed through the empty corridor, but no one came. An icy fear gripped her heart. Jordan needed a healer but Kath needed to find the enemy. She raced to the far end of the corridor. Moonlight glimmered on a bronze bell. She yanked the rope, frantic for help, sending an urgent peal through the monastery.

Doors opened. Pounding footsteps raced toward the tolling bell. A pair of blue-robed monks reached her first.

"My friends have been attacked, you have to help!" She pointed toward the crumpled bodies. "Which way to the outer gates?"

The first monk ran to attend the fallen but the second answered. The words were barely spoken and Kath was speeding through the corridors, racing an unseen enemy to the outer gates. The hallways seemed to stretch to forever, but then she burst through a golden door and into the outer courtyard. The gates gaped open. The enemy had fled. Kath refused to give up. She ran through the gates and spied a golden-robed initiate descending the hill.

"Stop and fight me!" Her words rang against the mountains. "Stand and fight!"

He turned and she knew his face.

"*Bryce!*" Shock brought her to a gaping standstill, her mind rebelling at the revelation. She'd liked him, yet he'd attacked her friends.

He gave her a scathing glance, contempt twisting his face, and then he laughed, a cruel mocking sound that ate at her soul.

She'd been mocked before, ever since she'd first picked up a sword, but somehow this was worse, like a sword flaying the very core of her being. Rage thundered through her. "*No!*" Kath refused to be diminished. And she refused to let her friends go unavenged. Gripping her sword, she hurled a challenge at the murderer, "By Valin, I'll slay you for this!" But

Bryce paid her no heed. With a cruel mocking smile, he settled the golden chain of an amulet around his neck and stepped into the Mist.

Without thinking, Kath followed. She raced down the hill, intent on closing the distance. From the monastery gates, someone yelled, *"You dare not enter!"* but Kath paid no heed. Steel first, she entered the Mist.

# 86

# Katherine

White surrounded her, nothing but white. Kath kept to a run, her sword in her hand, refusing to let him escape. With every stride the fog thickened, pressing close like a smothering fist. So thick, so unnaturally thick, she slashed at the fog with her sword, but it made no difference. Cold and clammy, the mist seeped close, deadening her senses. Needing to hear her own voice, she shouted a challenge, "Stand and fight!" but her words were swallowed by the white. Frustrated, Kath pressed ahead, desperate for a glimpse of the enemy.

The mist hid everything, even the ground, but Kath refused to be daunted. Her first time through she'd expected illusions or conjurings of some sort, but none came her way. Despite the monk's warnings, the mist was boring, nothing but cold, damp white...yet she'd felt something then and she felt it again now. She felt *watched*. Like ants crawling down her spine, the eerie feeling returned with a vengeance. The mist taunted her, nothing but silence and white. But then she heard something, faint at first, a whisper at the edge of hearing, but then it grew stronger.

*"She enters the Mist without a guide."*

A woman's voice came from the right, *"Without an amulet."*

A man's voice came from the left, *"Without the crystal dagger."*

From behind, *"Her life is forfeit."*

Kath whirled, her sword held at the ready. "Who are you? Where are you? Show yourselves." Shadowy figures swirled through the mist, vague and insubstantial, staying just beyond reach of her sword.

*"Naught but a raw girl."*

*"Untested."*

*"Untried."*

*"Untempered."*

*"Unworthy."*

Whispers taunted Kath from every direction. She strained to see through the fog. "Who are you? What do you want?"

*"Not enough...not nearly enough."*

*"And this time she comes without the dagger..."*

*"More proof she is not the one..."*

Kath struggled to make sense of the phantoms. "Are you ghosts or illusions? At the very least you're cowards, afraid to show yourselves." As if in answer, a horrid smell speared the mist, so strong she almost gagged. Blood and offal, the rotten stench assailed her, the reek of a slaughterhouse...or a battlefield. Details solidified from the mist. She stood in the heart of a great killing field. Corpses stretched in every direction, not a breath of movement among them. Even the battle banners hung limp, as if Death was the sole victor. Kath tried to dispel the vision, but the stench gave proof to the dead. Perhaps if she touched a corpse then they'd all disappear in a swirl of white but a sixth sense told her to wait, to unravel the mystery set before her. She wandered among the slain, soaking up the details. Some were ancient beyond telling, bleached bones picked clean, their armor rusted, their cloaks rotted to dust, while others were fresh killed, their wounds bright as flowers. The oldest bore the emblem of the Star Knights, while all the fresh-dead carried the maroon octagon. Her breath caught, afraid to find familiar faces. Kath tightened her grip on her sword. "What is this? A vision of the past or the future?"

*"Both."*

The single word sent a shock through her mind. Such a slaughter would decimate the Octagon Knights. *"No, this cannot be."*

sixth sense drew her forward, compelling her towards a rounded hill, a thicket of battle banners hanging limp at the top. Slain knights covered the hillside, thick as autumn leaves. Most bore multiple wounds. The fighting must have been fierce, yet where was the enemy? Kath picked a path amongst them. Her boot slipped on something slimy. Real or imagined, she refused to look. And then she reached the top. Gold gleamed amongst the fallen, a crowned helm upon his head. *"No!"* She rushed forward, a veil of tears in her eyes. King Ursus lay on his back, a great sword impaling his chest. *"Father!"* Grief dropped Kath to her knees. She stared at his face, refusing to believe. Always stern and sometimes forbidding, yet Kath worshipped her father as an invincible hero, tough as steel, as permanent and enduring as Castlegard. His loss was unimaginable. Shaking, she stretched a tentative hand towards his face, praying for him to disappear. Cold flesh met her fingertips. *"No!"* She tried to rouse him but death had already laid its claim. Stiff and cold, his eyes gaped open, his face frozen in disbelief. She howled her grief to the gods, *"No, this cannot be!"* Leaping to her feet, Kath raised her sword in defiance. "Take this back and I swear to serve you!"

Thunder clapped overhead and the mist returned like a suffocating tide. The battlefield was gone, wiped clean by the ocean of fog. White surrounded her, nothing but white. Kath glared at the malevolent mist. "Come forward! Show yourselves!"

Figures began to appear, shadowy forms taking shape just beyond reach. Some wore elaborate helms and breastplates, while others wore long, flowing robes, yet they all seemed insubstantial, specters condensing from the mist. Despite their ghostly raiment, their words jabbed her like spears. *"What makes you think you'll succeed when so many others have failed...failed...failed?"*

Kath whirled to face them. "Is this a true vision? Will it happen? Why did you show me the king's death?"

*"The Octagon Knights have forgotten."*

A shiver raced down her spine. "What do you mean?"

*"The oldest evil will not succumb to mere swords. Darkness is not so easily slayed. Yet you, a mere girl, think you can do better?"* Their words struck from all directions. *"Why did you come?"*

*"Why did you enter the Mist?"*

*"Your life is forfeit!"*

Kath struggled to quell her fear. Parrying their words with logic, she fastened her mind on the reason she'd entered the Mist. "The Mist serves the monastery, so you must serve the Light. Help me, for I seek a murderer."

"Murder is the least of his sins."

The words punched through the mist with a surprising solidness. Kath turned towards the sound, a real voice, a man's voice, laden with the surety of command. "Who are you? Where are you?"

The others faded away, bowing into the white. Beyond them, a figure emerged. A tall knight in silver armor burnished bright, and upon his head a winged helm emblazoned with stars. He strode towards her, drawing within a sword's length. Seemingly real enough to touch, his face was graven with the deep lines of hard decisions, his black beard tinged with streaks of gray, his eyes full of wisdom. "A better question is when, child."

Dignity rode his shoulders like a cloak. Kath felt as if she stood before one of the kings of legend. "My lord." Bowing, she kept her gaze fixed upon him, lest he disappear.

"You've dared much to enter the Mist alone."

"I chase a murderer. I ask your help."

"Did you even think before daring the Mist?"

Kath felt her face blaze red but she refused to shirk his gaze.

"He bears an amulet while you do not."

"He murdered my friends. I've sworn to slay him."

"A worthy vow," he stared at her, his eyes like chips of flint. "But do you know the truth of the one you chase?"

"Bryce, his name is Bryce."

Disappointment flooded his gaze, "An answer as shallow as the shape of your face. In your heart you know better. Listen to your heart. Seek the truth within the lineage of your own blood. Put a name to the implacable foe, the oldest evil."

*The lineage of my blood...the kings of Castlegard...*the answer stole her breath. "The Mordant!"

The king nodded. "The Mordant reborn."

A vision of the battlefield assailed her mind. "My father! Castlegard must be warned."

"Their fates are entangled."

Urgency thrummed through her. "Then the Mordant must be stopped. We dare not waste a moment."

"So you'd face a thousand-year-old evil, alone, with merely a sword? Are you so eager to join the dead?"

Kath forced herself to hold his gaze while swallowing her own fear. "Someone has to try."

"In a thousand years, many have tried, yet none have succeeded."

An image of Jordan and Sir Cardemir haunted her mind, their blood staining the monastery floor.

"It takes many to defeat the Dark. When one falls another rises to take up the burden, yet you come alone."

Kath tightened her grip on her sword. "Lend me your aid. Perhaps together we can put a stop to this evil."

His gaze pierced her soul. "Courage comes in the form of girl, yet you are nothing but unforged steel."

"Let me try."

"Stubbornness mixed with folly, have you learned nothing? You come armed with only steel. Even if you somehow succeed you will utterly fail. To kill the Mordant with cold steel is to plunge the kingdoms of Erdhe into an even worse future. Kill him now and he will merely assume a different shape, a different time. Only the crystal dagger can truly slay a harlequin."

She'd left the dagger behind, unaccustomed to carrying it. Despair crushed her shoulders. "Then you won't help? You'll let the evil escape?"

"I did not say that. I've done what I can. The burden to defeat the Dark falls on the living." He gave her a piercing stare. "The straight path has bought time but never success. Seek to do the unexpected, for therein lies the greatest chance." The king began to fade. "Many have sacrificed all to fight the Dark. How much will you risk? How much will you dare?" With a swirl of white, he disappeared into the Mist.

"No, wait!" She sprinted forward but he was gone. The others were gone as well, leaving her alone in the white. Suddenly cold, Kath stared at the mist, so quiet, so eerie, so...empty. They'd abandoned her and she'd lost all sense of direction. "Come back!" but there was no reply. The damp white pressed close, so thick she could barely see the ground. Kath gripped her sword and edged forward, fearful of plummeting from a cliff. Anger thrummed through her, but then she realized the mist was a trial, requiring wariness and an iron resolve. "By Valin, I will not fail." Blinded by the white, she shuffled forward, plagued by her own imagination. Sweat beaded her brow, what if she walked towards a chasm? A hundred paces of uncertainty, a hundred chances to die, but her resolve never wavered. With a single step she escaped the mist, emerging into the dawn's first light. The world returned in a rush of light and sound and smells. Kath breathed deep the fresh, clean mountain air, but it did nothing to lighten her burden, the weight of destiny riding her shoulders. She stared towards the hilltop. Like an all-knowing beast, the monastery crouched upon the rocky outcrop, the golden eyes of the great gate peering down at her. Monks stationed by the gate gave a shout but Kath was beyond caring. She staggered to a halt, weariness dropping her to her knees.

Everything had changed. Prophecies rushed to be born and the world seemed to know it. The signs were writ large across the sky. A terrible gash scarred the heavens, a red comet, the mark of the Mordant, and in the east a bloody sun staggered aloft. Kath shivered at the sight, a red dawn, a bloody dawn, an omen of death and war. Bathed in the bloody light, Kath felt like a pawn loosed upon a chessboard she barely understood, yet she'd sworn to make a difference. Gripping her sword, Kath stared at the heavens, praying for the strength to prevail.

# Appendix

# CASTLEGARD

Three hundred years after the War of Wizards decimated the kingdoms of Erdhe, a group of knights banded together to protect the southern kingdoms from the ravages of the north. They claimed Castlegard, the great mage-stone castle left empty after the War of Wizards, as the seat of their power. Adopting the shape of the great castle as their symbol, they became known as the Octagon Knights.

To bolster their cause, the knights were ceded land running along the length of the Dragon Spine Mountains. Stretching from Castlegard all the way to the Western Ocean, this land became known as the Domain. A series of castles, keeps, and walls were built along the Dragon Spines, allowing the knights to control the mountain passes and deny access to the southern kingdoms. The Domain also includes the only iron ore mine in all of Erdhe to yield blue ore, the rare ore required to forge the knights' fabled blue steel swords.

As a sworn brotherhood of elite knights, the candidates forsake their lineage and their past when they win their maroon cloaks. Their symbol is a maroon octagon emblazoned on a silver shield.

KING URSUS ANVRIL, King of Castlegard and the Knights of the Octagon, Lord of the Domain, hero of the Battle of Raven Pass, bearer of a great blue sword named *Honor's Edge*.
❖ his wife, QUEEN PHYLA, died giving birth to their only daughter-their children:
- PRINCE ULRICH, First-born son of the king, a sworn knight of the maroon, commander of the wall at Raven Pass, bearer of a great blue sword named *Mordbane*
- PRINCE GRIFFIN, Second-born son of the king, a sworn knight of the maroon, commander of Dymtower
- PRINCE GODFREY, Third-born son of the king, a sworn knight of the maroon, commander of Shieldhold
- PRINCE TRISTAN, Fourth-born son of the king, a sworn knight of the maroon, slain while leading a patrol into the steppes
- PRINCE LIONEL, Fifth-born son of the king, a sworn knight of the maroon, commander of Cragnoth Keep
- PRINCESS KATHERINE, Sixth child of the king, a girl of fifteen, also known as the Imp or Little Sister or Kath. As a female, the

Octagon symbol of Castlegard is forbidden to her. Instead she uses the Anvril's ancient heraldic symbol of a red hawk attacking with talons outstretched on a field of white.

❖ his sworn knights and retainers:

- SIR OSBOURNE, The Knight Marshal of the Octagon, right hand of the King, a hero of Raven Pass, a one-eyed man, he wields a saber as his weapon of first choice.
- SIR BLAINE, fresh-sworn knight of the maroon, bears a newly made great sword of blue steel
- SIR TRASK, knight of the maroon, leader of a dissident faction, champion of the battleaxe
- SIR TYRONE, knight of the maroon with skin the color of ebony, often referred to as the 'black knight', he wields a great sword
- SIR LEWIS, knight of the maroon, follower of Sir Trask, he wields a saber
- SIR RAYMOND, knight of the maroon, follower of Sir Trask, he wields a saber
- SIR TELLOR, a knight-captain of the maroon, he wields a mace
- SIR CLEMENT, knight of the maroon, Sergeant of Arms
- SIR BREDON, knight of the maroon, sits on the council of candidates
- SIR PENFORTH, knight of the maroon, he wields a battleaxe
- SIR MALLORY, knight of the maroon, he wields a great sword
- SIR GUILFORD, knight of the maroon, he wields a mace
- SIR THORLIN, knight of the maroon, he wields a great sword
- SIR BRENT, knight of the maroon, he wields a battleaxe
- SIR BEARHART, knight of the maroon, he wields a morningstar
- SIR KIRK, a fresh-made knight who takes his vows with Blaine, he wields a claymore
- SIR JOHN, a fresh-made knight who takes his vows with Blaine, he wields a battleaxe
- DEVLAN, a squire of the maroon assigned to the armory
- ALAIN, a squire of the maroon
- TODD, a squire of the maroon
- OTTO, the Master Swordsmith of Castlegard's forge, responsible for forging all blue steel weapons
- CARL, a Master Smith of Castlegard's forge
- TEEG, an apprentice of the forge
- QUINTUS, the Master Healer of Castlegard

# NAVARRE

The youngest kingdom of Erdhe, Navarre was founded less than four hundred years ago by a daring adventurer, Alaric Navarre, who rescued the youngest daughter of the king of Coronth from a band of sea pirates infesting the Orcnoth Islands. Gaining the king's confidence, and his daughter's hand in marriage, Alaric earned a freehold of land running along the Western Ocean where he later established his kingdom. His domain includes the Orcnoth Islands.

While defeating the nest of pirates, Alaric discovered a long-forgotten focus. The magic of the focus renders the royal house very fecund, enabling the queens to bear six to ten children in a single pregnancy. After using the magic, both the king and the queen become sterile. The focus is the secret strength of the royal house of Navarre, the bedrock for the succession to the throne. Alaric abandoned the convention of primogeniture, declaring that all of the tuplets have an equal chance to the throne. He instituted the practice of Wayfaring, a type of fostering where the heirs develop their greatest interests, striving to become excellent at a skill, a knowledge, or a trade, so that they can bring this knowledge back to Navarre and thus enrich the kingdom. After the Wayfaring, the King, together with the royal council, chooses the successor to the throne based on the talents, skills, and temperament that best fit the needs of the kingdom at the time. Navarre is well known for its uncommonly wise rulers...but with every great boon there is also a cost, the hidden focus brings with it the Curse of the Vowels.

The symbol of Navarre is a white osprey soaring on a checkered field of red and blue. The seat of their power is Castle Seamount, perched on a rocky outcrop on the edge of the Western Ocean. Navarre has always had close ties to the sea.

KING IVOR NAVARRE, the eighth ruler of the kingdom of Navarre
❖ his siblings:
- PRINCE IRWIN, died of poison, believed to be a victim of the Curse of the Vowels
- PRINCESS INGRID, fell from the rigging of a ship and died, believed to be a victim of the Curse of the Vowels
- PRINCESS IRIS, accused of murdering her two siblings, exiled to the Orcnoth Islands she murdered her guards and fled

- PRINCE ISADOR, Commander of the Army of Navarre, advisor to the king, nearly fell victim to the Curse of the Vowels
- PRINCESS IGRAINE, Counselor to the king, court historian, tutor to the Royal Js
- PRINCE IAN, Royal Bowyer, advisor to the king
- PRINCESS IVY, Captain of a royal merchant vessel of Navarre
- his wife, QUEEN MEGAN, a princess of Tubor their children known as the Royal Js:
- PRINCESS JEMMA, Wayfaring with the Queen of Lanverness to learn the way of multiply coins
- PRINCE JUSTIN, Wayfaring in the Rose Court in route to Wyeth to apprentice with a master bard
- PRINCESS JORDAN, Wayfaring with the Kiralynn monks to learn the art of war
- PRINCE JARED, Wayfaring with the Octagon Knights to learn the way of the sword
- PRINCESS JULIANA, Wayfaring with Navarre's merchant fleet to learn the way of the sea
- PRINCE JAMES, Wayfaring in Tubor to learn to become a master vintner
- PRINCE JAYSON, Wayfaring in the Delta to learn the secrets of a new water wheel
- his retainers:
- DUNCAN TRELOCH, advisor to the king, master archer
- MASTER SIMMONS, the royal healer

# LANVERNESS

Carved from the ashes of the War of Wizards, Lanverness is an old kingdom, steeped in tradition, often relying on its wealth of natural resources and the shrewdness of its rulers to grow in prosperity and influence. Never fecund, the royal line of Lanverness has been forced to branch out several times over the centuries. The Rose Throne is currently held by the Tandroths. The Tandroths nearly lost the throne when the last king of Lanverness, King Leonid, failed to produce a male heir. The king survived a revolt and forced his noblemen to accept his only daughter, Liandra, as the heir to the Rose Throne on the condition that she marry a peer of the realm. Liandra is the only queen to rule a kingdom of Erdhe. Under Queen Liandra's stewardship, Lanverness has become the wealthiest kingdom in all of Erdhe.

The symbol of Lanverness is two white roses crossed on a field of emerald green. The seat of their power is Castle Tandroth, rising from the heart of Pellanor, the capitol city.

QUEEN LIANDRA TANDROTH, ruler of the Rose Throne, also known as the White Rose of Lanverness, also known as the Spider Queen, also known as the Black Widow Spider
❖ -her husband, PRINCE-CONSORT DONALD TERREL, chosen from among the noble families of Lanverness, Lord Terrel was raised up to be the Prince-Consort to the Queen on condition that he forsake his name and his lineage. He died in a hunting accident shortly after the birth of his second son. The heraldry of house Terrel is a red unicorn rearing on a field of green.
❖ their children:
  • PRINCE STEWART, heir to the Rose Throne, Commander of the Rose Squad
  • PRINCE DANLY, spare heir to the Rose Throne
  • PRINCESS ASELYNN, died at birth
❖ her councilors:
  • LORD HIGHGATE, the Master Archivist, the queen's shadowmaster, right hand to the Queen
  • LORD WESLEY, Lord of the Treasury
  • LORD TURNER, Lord of the Royal Guard, also known as the Knight Protector, responsible for the queen's safety

- LORD SHELDON, the Lord Sheriff, leader of the constable force of Lanverness
- LORD HELFNER, General of the Army of Lanverness
- LORD HUNTER, a skilled diplomat, used as a roving ambassador to the other kingdoms of Erdhe
- LORD BRADSHAW, the Lord Steward, responsible for crops and farms,
- LORD RICKMAN, the Lord of Mines, responsible for the ruby, emerald and iron ore mines of Lanverness
- LORD QUINCE, Lord of the Hunt, Warden of the Royal Forests
- LORD CADWELL, Master of Letters, the secretary to the Royal Council

❖ other members of the court:
- LORD NEALY, forced to resign in disgrace from the Royal Council over a matter of incompetence
- DUKE ANDERS, resigned from the Royal Council after vehement arguments with the Queen
- LORD KITTERIDGE, a deputy of the Master Archivist assigned to work with the refugees of Coronth
- LORD PENROD, a royal historian
- MASTER FALLON, the Queen's Royal Bard
- CAPTAIN DURNHEART, a captain of the Rose Guards assigned to protect the Queen
- SIR CARDEMIR- fifth son of the Duke of Graymaris, a knight who wins acclaim on the tournament field, the seahorse knight
- LORD CARRINGTON, a wealthy lord retired from court
- JON HOBS, Prince Danly's personal guard
- BRUCE HARLAND, Prince Danly's personal guard
- DONAL CLEARY, a courier of the Rose Army

❖ the people of Pellanor:
- MASTER SADDLER, a royal jeweler
- MADAM STOCK, the madam of an exclusive bordello
- MARG STAGHORN, owner of the Green Stag tavern
- BEN OBERN, a drill sergeant in the Rose Army
- GRANDMOTHER MAGDA, a refugee from Coronth

# CORONTH

The kingdom of Coronth was long ruled by one of the oldest royal families in Erdhe. Tracing their lineage back to before the War of Wizards, the Manfreds struggled to maintain their kingdom despite the aftermath of chaos and famine caused by the magical war. Their descendents ruled in an unbroken line for over a thousand years until a preacher of the Flame god brought a new religion to the capitol city of Balor. Enthralling the crowds with the miracle of the Test of Faith, the Pontifax gained a rabid following. In less than a year, the new religion consumed the kingdom, making the Pontifax more powerful than the king. Ruling from the pulpit, the Pontifax declared that only a true believer of the Flame god could wear the crown of Coronth, forcing the king, his wife, and all of his children to submit to the Test of Faith. When the searing flames consumed the royal house, the Pontifax became the spiritual and secular ruler of Coronth.

The symbol of house Manfred was a golden lion rearing on a field of blue. The new symbol of Coronth is a golden flame on field of red, the symbol of the Flame god. The seat of power is the capitol city of Balor.

THE PONTIFAX, the supreme spiritual and secular ruler of Coronth, also known as the Enlightened One, beloved of the Flame god
❖ his priests and counselors:
  • THE KEEPER OF THE FLAME, Senior priest of the Flame
  • LORD STEFFAN RAVEN, Counselor to the Pontifax
  • GENERAL CAYLIB, General of the Army of the Flame
  • ALAN JELLIKAN, Pyromancer of the Flame
❖ the people of Balor:
  • SAM SPRINGWATER, a baker accused of sinning against the Flame
  • SAMSON SPRINGWATER, son of Sam the baker, a sergeant in the Balor guard
  • SERGEANT VILLARS, a sergeant in the Balor guard
  • SERGEANT ELDER, a sergeant in the Balor guard
  • JON CHAMMERS, a turnip farmer
  • CAPTAIN PENDER, a captain in the Balor guard
  • OLAFF, a mute giant, a guard serving Lord Raven
  • PIP, an orphan lad who serves Lord Raven

# THE KIRALYNN MONKS

Founded over two thousand year ago by a group of scholars, knights, and wizards, the Kiralynn Order has always presented an enigmatic face to the world, a face that is open yet closed. One hundred years before the start of the War of Wizards the monks withdrew from the southern kingdoms, retreating to their monastery hidden deep in the Southern Mountains. As if erased from the minds of men, the location of the monastery disappeared from the maps of Erdhe. The memory of the Kiralynn monks has slowly faded, becoming little more than legend and myth. Yet select rulers of the southern kingdoms still receive scrolls sealed with the symbol of the Order. History has proven that these scrolls contain an uncanny prescience. Kings ignore the advice of the Order at their own peril.

The symbol of the Kiralynn monks is a Seeing Eye in the palm of an Open Hand. Their seat of power is their mountain monastery. The motto of the Order is "Seek Knowledge, Protect Knowledge, Share Knowledge".

THE GRAND MASTER, the leader of the Kiralynn Order, his/her identity is a closely guarded secret
❖ monks and initiates of the Order:
  • TOMAY, a sworn monk of the Order, one of the Gatekeepers of the monastery
  • LAVIDIA, a sworn monk of the Order, one of the Guides of the monastery
  • MASTER RIZEL, a Master of the Order
  • MASTER GARTH, a Master Healer of the Order
  • BRYCE, an initiate of the Order, studying to take his vows and become a healer

# ABOUT THE AUTHOR

KAREN L. AZINGER has always loved fantasy fiction, and always hoped that someday she could give back to the genre a little of the joy that reading has always given her. Eight years ago on a hike in the Colombia River Gorge she realized she had enough original ideas to finally write an epic fantasy. She started writing and never stopped. *The Steel Queen* is her first book, born from that hike in the gorge. Before writing, Karen spent over twenty years as an international business strategist, eventually becoming a vice-president for one of the world's largest natural resource companies. She's worked on developing the first gem-quality diamond mine in Canada's arctic, on coal seam gas power projects in Australia, and on petroleum projects around the world. Having lived in Australia for eight years she considers it to be her second home. She's also lived in Canada and spent a lot of time in the Canadian arctic. She lives with her husband in Portland Oregon, in a house perched on the edge of the forest. The first four books of *The Silk & Steel Saga* have already been written and she is hard at work on the fifth and final book. You can learn more at her website, www.karenlazinger.com or at her Facebook page for The Steel Queen.

**The Front Cover** artwork was done by the Australian artist, Greg Bridges. Greg's artwork has appeared on the book covers of many well-known fantasy authors. His cover perfectly captures Kath and the feel of the saga. To see more of his art or to contact Greg, visit his website at http://www.gregbridges.com/

**The Map and the Back Cover** artwork was done by a graphic artist from Oregon, Peggy Lowe. Her illustration of the map helps to bring the kingdoms of Erdhe to life. Peggy can be contacted at her e-mail address, peggy@portfoliooregon.com

Look for **The Flame Priest,** the second book in *The Silk & Steel Saga* to be published by December 2011.

CPSIA information can be obtained at www.ICGtesting.com
Printed in the USA
LVOW061425140112

263886LV00001B/237/P